Harry Bowling was born in Bermondsey, London, and left school at fourteen to supplement the family income as an office boy in a riverside provisions' merchant. He was called up for National Service in the 1950s. Before becoming a writer, he was variously employed as a lorry driver, milkman, meat cutter, carpenter and decorator, and community worker. He lived with his wife and family, dividing his time between Lancashire and Deptford. We at Headline are sorry to say that THE WHISPERING YEARS was Harry Bowling's last novel, as he very sadly died in February 1999. We worked with him for over ten years, ever since the publication of his first novel, CONNER STREET'S WAR, and we miss him enormously, as do his many, many fans around the world.

The Harry Bowling Prize was set up in memory of Harry to encourage new, unpublished fiction and is sponsored by Headline. Click on www.harrybowlingprize.net for more information.

Gaslight in Page Street

Harry Bowling

headline

First published in 1991
by HEADLINE BOOK PUBLISHING

This edition published in paperback in 2009
by HEADLINE PUBLISHING GROUP

5

Cataloguing in Publication Data is available from the British Library

ISBN 978 0 7553 4038 5

Typeset in Times by Avon DataSet Ltd,
Bidford-on-Avon, Warwickshire

Printed and bound in Great Britain by
Clays Ltd, St Ives plc

Headline's policy is to use papers that are natural, renewable and recyclable
products and made from wood grown in sustainable forests. The logging and
manufacturing processes are expected to conform to the environmental
regulations of the country of origin.

HEADLINE PUBLISHING GROUP
An Hachette UK Company
338 Euston Road
London NW1 3BH

www.headline.co.uk
www.hachette.co.uk

To Shirley, in loving memory

Prologue

All day long the November fog had swirled through the Bermondsey backstreets, but now that the factories and wharves had closed the fog thickened, spreading its dampness over the quiet cobbled lanes and alleyways. Only the occasional clatter of iron wheels and the sharp clip of horses' hooves interrupted the quietness as hansom cabs moved slowly along the main thoroughfares. The drivers huddled down in the high seats, heavily wrapped in stiff blankets against the biting cold, gripping the clammy leather reins with gloved hands as they plied for hire. The tired horses held their heads low, their nostrils flaring and puffing out clouds of white breath into the poisonous fumes.

Behind the main thoroughfares a warren of backstreets, lanes and alleyways spread out around gloomy factories and railway arches and stretched down to the riverside, where wharves and warehouses towered above the ramshackle houses and dilapidated hovels. Smoke from coke fires belched out from cracked and leaning chimneys and the fog became laden with soot dust and heavy with sulphur gases. Hardly ever was the sound of hansom cabs heard in the maze of Bermondsey backstreets during the cold winter months, and whenever a cabbie brought a fare to one of the riverside pubs he always sought the quickest way back to the lighted main roads. There was no trade to be had in these menacing streets on such nights, and rarely did folk venture from their homes except to visit the nearest pub or inn, especially when the fog was lying heavy.

Straddling the backstreets were the railway arches of the London to Brighton Railway and beneath the lofty archways a gathering of vagrants, waifs and strays spent their nights, huddled around low burning fires for warmth. Sometimes there was food to eat, when someone produced a loaf of bread which had been begged for or stolen, and it was sliced and toasted over the crackling flames, sometimes there were a few root vegetables and bacon bones which were boiled in a tin can and made into a thin broth; but often there was nothing to be had and the ragged groups slept fitfully, their bellies rumbling with hunger and their malnourished bodies shivering and twitching beneath filthy-smelling sacks which had been begged from the tanneries or the Borough Market.

One bitterly cold November night, William Tanner sat over a low fire, wiping a rusty-bladed knife on his ragged coat sleeve. Facing him George Galloway watched with amusement as his young friend struggled to halve the turnip. The railway arch that they occupied faced a fellmonger's yard and the putrid smell of animal skins filled the cavern and made it undesirable as a place to shelter, even to the many desperate characters who roamed the area. For that very reason the two lads picked the spot to bed down for the night when their finances did not stretch to paying for a bed at one of the doss-houses. Usually there was enough wood to keep a fire in all night and no one would intrude on their privacy and attempt to steal the boots from their feet while they slept. At first the stench from the fellmonger's yard made the two lads feel sick but after a time they hardly noticed it, and they became used to the sound of rats scratching and the constant drip as rain-water leaked down from the roof and dropped from the fungus-covered walls.

William passed one half of the turnip to George and grinned widely as his friend bit on the hard vegetable and spat a mouthful into the fire.

'It's bloody 'ard as iron, Will, an' it tastes 'orrible,' the elder lad said, throwing his half against the wall.

William shrugged his shoulders and bit on his half. 'I couldn't get anyfing else,' he said. 'That copper in the market was on ter me soon as I showed me face.'

George threw a piece of wood on to the fire and held his hands out to the flames. He was a tall lad, with a round face and large dark eyes, and a mop of matted, dark curly hair which hung over his ears and down to his shabby coat collar. At fourteen, George was becoming restless. He had attended a ragged school and learned to read and write before his street trader father dragged him away from his lessons and put him to work in a tannery. At first George had been happy but his father's increasingly heavy drinking and brutality made the lad determined to leave home and fend for himself. Now, after two years of living on the streets, he felt it was time he started to make something of himself. George had experienced factory life and had seen how bowed and subservient the older workers had become. He had walked out of his job at the tannery and did not return home, vowing there and then that he would not end up like the others.

William Tanner sat staring into the fire, his tired eyes watering from the wood-smoke. He was twelve years old, a slightly built lad of fair complexion. His eyes were pale blue, almost grey, and his blond hair hung about his thin face. Like

George he had never known his mother. She had died when he was a baby. Of his infancy he could only vaguely remember stern faces and the smell of starched linen when he was tended to. His more vivid memories were of being put to bed while it was still daylight and of having to clean and scrub out his attic room with carbolic soap and cold water. He had other memories which were frightening. There was a thin reed cane which his father had kept behind a picture in the parlour. Although it had never been used on him, the sight of that device for inflicting pain had been enough to frighten him into obedience.

When his father lay dying of typhoid in a riverside hovel, William had been taken to live with an aunt and there taught to read and write. The woman made sure he was properly dressed and fed but the home lacked love, and when his aunt took up with a local publican William became an unwanted liability. Like his friend George he began to feel the weight of a leather belt, and after one particularly severe beating William ran away from home. He had stumbled into a railway arch, half-frozen and with hunger pains gnawing at his stomach, and had been allowed to share a warm fire and a hunk of dry and mouldy bread with a group of young lads. Their leader was George Galloway and from that night William and George became firm friends. Now, as the fire burned bright, George was setting out his plans. The younger lad sat tight-lipped, fearful of what might happen should things go wrong.

'Listen to me, Will,' George was saying, 'yer gotta be 'ard. Nobody's gonna come up an' give yer money fer nuffink. It's dog eat dog when yer up against it. All yer 'ave ter do is foller me. We'll roll the ole geezer an' be orf before 'e knows what's 'appened. I've cased the place an' 'e comes out the same time every night. If all goes well, we'll 'ave a nice few bob. Yer gotta 'ave the shekels ter get started, Will. One day I'm gonna 'ave me own business. I'm gonna wear smart clothes an' 'ave people lookin' up ter me. "There goes George Galloway. 'E's one o' the nobs," they'll say.'

William nodded, disturbed by the wild look in the large dark eyes that stared out at him from across the fire.

The fog had lifted a little during the morning, but now it threatened to return as night closed in. From their vantage post in a shuttered shop's doorway the two lads watched the comings and goings at the little pub in the Old Kent Road. William made sure there was no more pork crackling left in his piece of greasy newspaper then he screwed it up and threw it into the gutter, wiping his hands down his filthy, holed jumper. He shivered from the cold and glanced at George, who was breathing on his cupped hands. 'P'raps 'e ain't there,' he said, trying to inject a note of disappointment into his voice.

''E's in there,' George scowled. ''E's always there.'

A hansom cab rattled by and then George's hand closed around his friend's arm. 'There 'e is!' he whispered.

Joshua Wainwright burped loudly as he fished into his waistcoat pocket and took out his timepiece. The hands seemed to be spinning and he put it away with a frown, hunching his shoulders as he walked off rather unsteadily in the direction of Surrey Square where he had his London residence. It had been a good week, he thought. The case was progressing nicely and the judge had been more than usually receptive when points of order had been raised. There would be a substantial settlement, of that he was sure, and the fee would be a good one too. 'Damn this gout,' he grumbled to himself. It had been playing him up all day.

A sudden tug on the tails of Joshua's frock-coat made him lose his balance and as he tried to fend off his attackers he tumbled heavily into the entrance of a dark alley. His stovepipe hat was knocked from his head and a sand-filled sock crashed down on his exposed pate, sending him into oblivion.

The attack had been well timed and George and William made good their escape along the dark, reeking alleyway. The older lad had pocketed the barrister's gold watch-and-chain together with his wallet. When they had put some distance between themselves and their victim, George stopped to catch his breath and motioned William into a doorway.

'I'm goin' straight ter see Stymie wiv this,' he gasped, opening the palm of his hand and letting William catch a glimpse of the watch. ''Ere, there's some tanners in the wallet. You go an' get us both some faggots an' pease puddin', Will,' he went on, passing over a silver sixpence. 'Make yer way back ter the arch an' keep the fire in. I shouldn't be too long, then we can 'ave a share out.'

A wind had got up and it swirled into the evil-smelling railway arch as William tended the fire. The lad was still shaking from his first experience of foot-padding and occasionally he glanced over his shoulder as though expecting to be apprehended at any minute. As he sat before the flaring wood-fire, William saw again the face of the groaning man who had struggled to get to his feet. He shivered violently. He knew he should not have gone back but he was fearful that they had killed the old man. When George left him in the alley, William had taken a circular route into the Old Kent Road and ambled along as casually as he could towards the alley entrance. He had nothing on his person to link him with the robbery except for the silver sixpence, and he was sure that the victim had not caught sight of him as he tugged on his coat from behind. As William reached the entrance to the alley he had heard a groaning sound, and out of the corner of his eye had caught sight of a congested face as their victim staggered to his feet, cursing loudly. William had breathed easier as he hurried away to the butcher's shop to buy supper.

When George finally reached the railway arch, he sat down with a scowl and ate the faggot and pease pudding ravenously. 'The ole bastard tried ter do us up, Will,' he spluttered between mouthfuls of food. 'Two quid, that's all we got. That watch must 'ave bin werf a small fortune. I tel yer straight, I'm gonna do fer Stymie one day, see if I don't.'

William watched while George wiped his greasy lips on the back of his coat sleeve and then counted out the money from their victim's wallet before handing over three one-pound notes and four sixpences. William realised that he had never in all his life had more than sixpence in his pocket. He carefully folded the notes and tucked them down the side of his boot before stretching out in front of the dying fire.

George had covered himself with a large sack and was staring up at the sodden brickwork of the arch. It was only right after all, he thought. It was he who had masterminded the job and done all the work. It was he who had had to bargain and argue with Stymie over the money for the gold watch. Then there was the time he had spent eyeing the pub and half freezing in the process. He was the leader and if it wasn't for him they wouldn't have had any supper that night. Yes, it was only right he should have the larger share of the proceeds.

William was still too excited to sleep. He turned on his side to face his friend. 'We can kip in Arfur's doss-'ouse termorrer night, George, now we've got money,' he said cheerfully.

George grunted. 'Yeah, an' we can pay tuppence an' get proper blankets. Those bleedin' penny beds ain't too clean. Last time we was there I got bitten all over.' He yawned and turned on to his side. 'One day I'm gonna get meself an 'orse an' cart an' do deliveries. There's a good livin' ter be made cartin' skins about. I'm gonna make me pile an' 'ave me own cartage business, Will, you see if I don't.'

William sighed contentedly. His belly was full and the warmth from the fire had penetrated his cold, aching limbs. The thought of owning his own business did not excite him, but driving a horse and cart was another thing. William often hung around the stables in Long Lane and earned pennies for running errands. The carmen were a good lot, and sometimes they paid him to muck out the stalls and fill the nosebags with fresh chaff. He loved being around horses and often picked up a few carrots from the Borough Market or from under the market stalls in Tower Bridge Road for the nags.

'I just wanna drive a pair o' dapple-greys, George,' he said, staring into the grey embers of the fire. 'I'd plait their tails an' polish the 'arnesses – I'd 'ave the smartest pair of 'orses in the ole o' Bermon'sey.'

But George was already fast asleep, and dreaming of bigger things.

1900

1900.

Chapter One

On Sunday, 20th May 1900 church bells rang out in Bermondsey. People were out on the streets to celebrate, and along the Old Kent Road horse buses and the new electric trams rattled by, garlanded with Union Jacks and bunting. The cheering crowds exchanged newspapers and waved excitedly as an open-topped tram came into view with local councillors aboard. The mayor, wearing his chain of office, stood at the front of the upper deck holding a portrait of Queen Victoria aloft. Loud cheers rang out as spectators caught sight of the large framed picture, and then the waiting crowds hoisted the children on to their shoulders as the procession came into sight.

At the head of the parade a team of horses was drawing a brewery dray which contained an effigy of a Boer soldier with his hands held over his head being prodded by a British Tommy. Along the side of the cart a white sheet was tied, with the words 'Mafeking Relieved' painted in red along its length. Behind the leading dray there were smaller carts, pulled by well-groomed horses. 'Broomhead' Smith the totter came by sitting proudly on his creaking cart, tufts of ginger hair sticking out from under his battered trilby. His horse looked unusually spruce despite the dirty, moth-eaten Union Jack that

11

had been laid over its withers. On the back of the cart there was a rusty wringer which Broomhead had meant to remove before the parade started. He had covered it over instead and now the blanket had slipped off. The crowds laughed as he waved his whip in their direction and doffed his cap.

Carrie Tanner stood beside her father on the kerbside, holding his hand and shifting from one foot to the other. Her new button-up boots were pinching slightly but Carrie was too excited to care as the parade moved by. She was waiting for the Galloway cart with its team of two greys. She had helped her father to brush the horses and tie on their coloured ribbons; she had used the curry-comb and the large, heavy brush until their coats glistened and her arms ached. Her father had laughed as she reached up to the nags' manes and carefully plaited the coarse strands of hair as she had been shown. At last the horses had been fed and given their tit-bits of carrot and Carrie hurried from the stables to get cleaned up. She felt proud of helping her father, and as she spotted the Galloway team jumped up and down excitedly. 'Look, Dad, look!' she cried out. 'Don't they look luvverly?'

William Tanner smiled at his eldest child and moved to one side so that she could get a better view. 'You did a good job, Carrie,' he said, his hands resting on her shoulders. 'I should reckon we stand a good chance o' gettin' the prize.'

As the cart drew level William cast a critical eye over the cart. He had spent much time scrubbing the paintwork and the name 'George Galloway, Carter' now stood out clearly on the side. Galloway's longest serving carman Sharkey Morris was up in the dicky seat and waved to Carrie and William as he rode by. Sharkey had a bowler hat on, and for the first time in his life was wearing a white starched collar and black tie. The brown tweed suit which he wore was not his. It had been loaned to him by the owner of the cartage firm, who was anxious to snatch the first prize for the best turned-out entrant in the parade. William smiled to himself as he recalled what Galloway had said when he saw Sharkey march into the yard early that morning: 'Gawd 'elp us, Will. 'E looks a bleedin' scruff. I can't 'ave 'im sittin' up on that cart lookin' like that. Bring 'im in the office an' I'll send young Geoff 'ome fer one o' me old suits.'

The parade had passed by. William took his daughter's hand as they followed on to New Kent Road where the judging was to take place. Carrie felt the excitement growing inside her as she hurried along beside her father. Her tight boots were making her hobble but she ignored the pain. She wanted desperately for Galloway's horse and cart to win the prize, for her father's sake. He had worked hard on the wagon and team and she knew how much winning would mean to him.

At nine years old Carrie was more like her father than her three younger brothers. She was slim, with long fair hair and blue eyes a shade or two darker than his. She was a pretty girl with a saucy smile which seemed to start at the corners of her mouth and light up her whole face. Carrie loved her father dearly and spent as much time as she could in the stables, helping him with the horses and polishing the brasses and harnesses. She loved the warm sweet smell of the stalls and the sound of steel horseshoes over the cobbles as the animals set out each morning pulling the empty carts. On occasions she would feign sickness or a sore throat to escape having to go to school, but then she would make a miraculous recovery during the day and slip out from the house to the adjoining yard.

Her father laughed at his wife Nellie's concern over their daughter. 'She's a bright child an' she's gonna do all right,' he had told her.

Nellie had shaken her head in dismay. 'It's not right, 'er bein' away from school so much, Will,' she replied. 'The child needs ter learn 'er lessons. Besides, it's not proper fer a young gel ter 'ang around in that yard. She could get injured wiv those carts in an' out.'

William had pulled a face. 'Look, Nell, the child's 'appy wiv what she's doin'.' he retorted. 'She's gonna grow up soon enough, an' what's in store fer 'er? I'll tell yer – she's gonna slog away in a tannery or in one o' the factories. Then she's gonna get married an' be saddled wiv kids. Let 'er be 'appy while she can.'

The day was bright with a warm sun shining down on the entrants as they lined up in New Kent Road. All the carmen stood beside their horses, waiting for the mayor to arrive. Broomhead Smith scowled as he looked at the rusty wringer on the back of his cart. He was upset by some of the comments made to him by the waiting crowd.

'Oi, Broom'ead! Are yer gonna mangle the mayor if yer don't win?' one wag called out.

''Ere, is it all right fer me ter bring a pissy mattress round an' sling it on the cart, Broom'ead?' shouted someone else.

The totter tried to ignore their remarks but he could barely contain his anger after one of the councillors strolled by and then had a whispered conversation with a policeman standing nearby. The PC strolled up to Broomhead with a wide grin on his ruddy face. ''E asked me ter get yer ter move the cart, Broomy,' he said, trying to look serious. ''E didn't know yer was in the parade.'

'Silly ole sod,' Broomhead spluttered. 'Where'd they dig 'im up from?'

The policeman's face broke into a grin again. 'I reckon the wringer ain't too bad. Could do wiv a rub down an' a coat o' paint though,' he said as he walked off.

The mayor was walking slowly along the line, stopping at each cart and consulting with his colleagues. Notes were scribbled down into a notebook by one of the judges and heads nodded vigorously. When they reached the totter's cart the judges shook their heads and walked on quickly, much to Broomhead Smith's chagrin, but when they arrived at Galloway's horse and team the mayor looked pleased with what he saw. Carrie looked up into William's face, her hand tightening on his. Crowds were milling around the dais which had been set up by the park gates, and when the mayor climbed up on to the stand and held his hands up for silence everyone started jostling.

'Quiet! Quiet!' one of the councillors called out. 'Be quiet for the mayor.'

Broomhead recognised the man as the one who had earlier had words about him with the policeman. 'Shut yer gob, Ugly,' he called out. ''Ow d'yer like ter get mangled?'

The laughter died away as the mayor began his speech, in which he praised the hard work undertaken by everyone involved. He then went on at length about the gallant soldiers who had held out at Mafeking for so long and the equally valiant action which had finally relieved them. Loud cheers went up at his words, but when the mayor started to itemise the good work being done by the local council the crowds became restless.

'Knock it on the 'ead, mate,' someone called out.

'Tell us who's won, fer Gawd's sake,' the cry went up.

The dignitary held up his hands and as the crowd quietened he put on his pince-nez and stared at the slip of paper in his hands for a few moments.

'The first prize goes to George Galloway,' he said in a loud voice. 'Second prize goes to . . .'

Carrie's squeal of delight almost drowned out the name of

the runner-up as she hugged her father. 'We won! We won!' she cried out, looking up into his smiling face.

William looked over to the park railings and saw the bulky figure of George Galloway being patted on the back and having his hand pumped by his supporters.

Carrie turned to her father as she saw the firm's owner starting to walk towards the mayor. 'It should be you goin' up ter get the prize, Dad,' she said with a small frown. 'It was you what won it.'

William smiled briefly. 'It's all right, Carrie. Mr Galloway knows that.'

After a few words had been exchanged between Galloway and the mayor, the trophy, a large silver tankard, was held up in the air and clapping broke out. The winner was surrounded by his friends and well-wishers as most of the spectators moved off home. William took his daughter's hand and they left too, walking back to Page Street in the spring sunlight.

The Tanners' home was a two-up, two-down house which adjoined the Galloway cartage firm in Page Street. It was the end house in a row of terraced houses that led from Jamaica Road towards the River Thames. From the main thoroughfare the narrow turning looked like most of the working-class streets in Bermondsey. It was cobbled and gaslit, with a small pub situated on the left-hand corner and a tiny tobacconist and sweet shop on the right. Two rows of identical houses stretched down towards the Galloway yard which stood on the bend, where the street turned to the right. The cartage contractor's headquarters was a brick-built construction with a weather-board frontage and wooden gates which swung back into the cobbled stable yard. The gates faced the Jamaica Road end of the turning and the right-hand part of the premises, which were used to store the wagons, stretched along past the bend

16

to where another two rows of houses faced each other across the narrow turning as it led along to Bacon Street.

The street looked very much the same as many other Bermondsey backstreets. Lace curtains hung in the windows of the ramshackle houses and the doorsteps were whitened. Most of the chimney-pots leaned askew and the grey slated roofs dipped and curved in an uneven, untidy fashion. Bacon Street had its own particular blight, however, in the shape of a tall four-storey tenement block. Even the tenants of the damp, draughty and overcrowded houses surrounding the building dreaded the thought of having to live in such a terrible place.

Inside the Tanners' house, the family was gathered around a low fire. The evening had turned chilly and the parlour door was closed against the draught which blew along the passage from the ill-fitting street door. Nellie Tanner was sitting in her usual armchair beside the fire, a partially finished piece of embroidery lying in her lap. Nellie was a slim, attractive woman with a fair complexion and deep blue eyes. At thirty, her face was unlined and smooth. Her rather shapely figure was accentuated by a close-fitting long dark skirt which reached down over her ankles and a high-buttoned linen blouse with ruffled sleeves which hugged her full breasts and narrow waist. Her fair hair, which was a shade lighter than her husband's, was swept up from her neck and piled on top of her head, secured with a wide mother-of-pearl fan comb.

Nellie liked to dress up on Sundays. When the main meal of the day was over she would go to her room and wash down in the tin bath before putting on her clean, freshly ironed Sunday best. She knew it pleased William to see her looking nice when they sat together in the long evening after the children had gone to bed, and she was aware that it roused him when she wore her tight-fitting clothes. Her long neck and high round forehead were exposed by her swept-up hair, which

Nellie occasionally touched as she talked with her husband.

William Tanner was of medium height and powerfully built. His wide shoulders and muscular arms bore witness to eighteen years of hard manual work for George Galloway. Now, having seen his efforts with the parade wagon rewarded after a long hard week in the stables, William was feeling relaxed and contented. He eased back in the armchair facing Nellie's and stretched out his legs. His pale blue eyes stared into hers as she spoke and he could sense irritation in her voice.

'I know yer was pleased, Will, an' yer've a right ter be, but yer'd fink Galloway would 'ave at least come over an' fanked yer,' she was saying.

William raised his eyes in resignation. 'It was awkward, really, Nell,' he replied. 'There was people millin' around 'im an' I don't s'pose 'e got the chance. 'E'll see me termorrer. There'll be time then.'

Nellie felt angry that her husband had been ignored by George Galloway at the parade. Every weekday morning William opened the yard and issued Galloway's work orders to the carmen. Then there was the managing of the stables and the locking up after the last van was in, sometimes late in the evening. It was the same when one of the horses was lame or a horse sale was going on. Her husband was on call from dawn till dusk. True, William was paid two pounds a week, but he earned every penny of it, she told herself. It would cost George Galloway much more to call the vet in every time. Ever since they had married ten years ago, and Galloway rented them the house the carter had taken advantage of William – and her – one way or another, Nellie thought with bitterness. She knew she could never talk to her complaisant, easy-going husband of her own hatred for Galloway, and it tormented her cruelly.

William leaned forward in his armchair and Nellie was brought back to the present.

'I'll need ter slip into the yard before it gets too late,' he said, yawning. 'There's the cob ter check. It might be the strangles.'

Nellie sighed and shook her head. 'Yer'd better get in there then, Will. Yer promised me we was goin' ter the pub ternight.'

William grunted as he eased himself out of the chair. 'I'd better call up ter Carrie. She wanted ter come wiv me.'

Nellie was about to object but then thought better of it. Carrie was so like her father. She loved the horses and was worried about her favourite, the small Welsh cob that had been running a fever and had been taken out of the main stable.

Nellie heard her husband call Carrie and then the sound of the front door opening and closing. With a sigh, she leaned back in her chair and closed her eyes.

William undid the padlock and pushed open the wicket-gate. The yard was shadowy and quiet as he led the way to the left-hand side of the cobbled area where the horses were stabled. The building had two levels, and the upper floor was reached by a long straw-covered ramp. A loophole looked out from the higher level, near the noisy chaff-cutting machine and the harness room. The lighter, younger horses were stalled on this floor, and below in the larger stable were kept the heavier shire horses.

Carrie stayed close to her father as he passed the main stable and stopped outside a weather-board shed at the end of the yard. It was in this shed that the sick horses were kept in isolation from the rest. William had transferred the cob here as soon as it started coughing, aware that the sickness could easily spread and put the firm out of business.

William picked up the kerosene lamp which was hanging

outside the stable door. When he had lit it, he went in with his daughter at his side. The horse was standing in its stall, munching on the last of the chaff. As the yard foreman eased in beside it, the animal turned its head then went back to its munching.

'That's a good sign,' William said, easing down the side of the cob and taking hold of its halter. 'Well, I fink he's over it, but 'e'd better 'ave one more day in 'ere.' He rubbed his hand over the horse's nose and felt its neck just below the ear. 'The swelling's gone down too.'

Carrie had eased herself into the stall and stood beside her father, stroking the cob's neck. 'Can I exercise Titch in the yard termorrer, Dad?' she asked excitedly. ''E's gotta get strong before 'e can pull that cart.'

William laughed aloud. 'It's school fer you termorrer, me lass,' he said quickly. 'Yer muvver's bin on ter me about the time yer missin'.'

Carrie sighed. 'Can I do it after school? Please, Dad?'

Her father put his arm around her shoulders as they stepped out into the dark yard. 'We'll see. Maybe after tea.'

William and Nellie had left for the corner pub and the fire in the grate had burned down to white-hot ash. The eldest of the boys, eight-year-old James, had gone to bed with no fuss, having complained of a sore throat, but Charlie and Danny were reluctant to follow him. They wanted to stay up longer while their parents were out, but Carrie would have none of it.

'Muvver said yer gotta be in bed by nine, Charlie,' she scolded him. 'Besides, Danny won't go up on 'is own. Yer know 'e's scared o' the dark.'

Charlie stared down at his stockinged feet for a moment or two then his wide grey eyes came up to meet Carrie's. 'Can't we stay down 'ere wiv you, Carrie? There might be ghosts upstairs,' he said in a whisper, his eyes rolling around in exaggerated terror.

Five-year-old Danny was already half-asleep. He huddled closer to his elder brother for comfort. 'I see a big ghost on the landin' once, Carrie. I wanna stay down 'ere,' he said in a hushed voice.

She chuckled as she lit a candle and set it into a metal holder. 'Come on, I'll see yer up the stairs. There's no ghosts in this 'ouse. Only 'orrible children get 'aunted. Come on now, follow me.'

The candlelight flickered up the dark stairs and across the narrow landing, casting eerie shadows on the grimy wallpaper and brownish-stained ceiling and glimmering back dully from the brown paint of the back bedroom door. The boys huddled together, having frightened themselves with their stories of lurking ghosts, and when Carrie led the way into their room they jumped into bed and pulled the clothes up around their ears.

'Stay up 'ere, Carrie,' Danny pleaded. 'I'm scared.'

She glanced over at James, sleeping soundly in the single bed by the window, and then set the candleholder down on the rickety washstand. 'All right,' she sighed. 'But just till yer both asleep.'

Charlie turned on to his back. 'I'm not tired,' he moaned.

Within ten minutes both the boys were sleeping soundly and Carrie tip-toed down to the parlour. She rekindled the fire so that the room would be warm when her parents returned from the pub, then sat back in her father's chair. It was past her own bedtime but Carrie was still wide awake. It had been an exciting day but she felt sad that her father had not been allowed to collect the prize. As she stared into the flickering flames she felt suddenly deflated. She had been happy for her father that day and wanted him to be happy too, but she had seen something in his eyes. They had a sad look in them at times. Was her father happy? she wondered. Would he always be there to care for the horses and let her help him in the yard?

The wind rattled the front door and Carrie shivered as she made her way upstairs to her front bedroom.

The usual early morning bustle had died down at Galloway's yard, and as soon as the last horse and cart had left the cobbles were swept clean of droppings. The sound of the chaff-cutting machine carried down into the stable yard and in through the open window of the small office as the two men sat facing each other. George Galloway was sitting on a thin-framed oak chair beside his open roll-top desk, his elbow resting on a jumble of invoices and work orders which were strewn over its surface. He wore his usual single-breasted, black serge suit and a bowler hat pushed back from his forehead, and there was a satisfied look on his broad face as he fingered a small medallion that hung from his silver watchchain.

'The milit'ry are comin' down in a couple o' weeks, Will,' he was saying, 'an' the 'orses are comin' in this Friday, so there's a lot ter do. I want them nags lookin' well groomed an' sprightly. If Sharkey an' Soapy ain't out on the road, they can give yer a bit of 'elp: I expect we'll 'ave those silly cows Aggie Temple and Maisie Dougall groanin' again but they'll just 'ave ter put up wiv it.'

William Tanner leaned forward in his chair and nodded. It seemed a whole lifetime since they had both run the Bermondsey streets as waifs. It was almost thirty years since the two of them had robbed the toff in the Old Kent Road and shared the proceeds, he recalled, yet only recently had George told him how he removed the medallion he was now fingering from their victim's watch-and-chain to keep as a memento before he went to Stymie the fence. George was beginning to look old now, William thought. His heavy, powerful shoulders had started to droop and his face appeared to have a bluish colour about it. His hair was greying too, but it was the eyes that seemed to age the man most. They were puffy and heavy-lidded, and their whites had acquired a yellowy tinge. Nellie was convinced the man was killing himself with whisky, and William decided his wife was most probably right. George had been knocking it back ever since his own wife died three years ago after giving birth to Josephine.

'If those two awkward mares come in 'ere moanin', tell 'em ter piss orf,' George was going on. 'Better still, tell Oxford ter see 'em orf. 'E frightens the life out of 'em.'

William smiled wryly as he thought of Jack Oxford, but he had no intention of inflicting the firm's simpleton on the two women. They had a genuine grievance anyway, he thought. Running the horses along the street was not only exhausting for him, it could be very dangerous too. It meant that the turning had to be kept clear of people, especially children.

'Where are the 'orses comin' from?' he asked.

'They're three-year-old Irish Draughts,' George replied, leaning back in his chair and tucking his thumbs through the armholes of his tight waistcoat.

The yard foreman could not help wincing at the news although he had guessed the answer. He knew that Irish Draughts were popular with the army, who used them for pulling gun carriages and for riding. He also knew that horses of this particular breed often had Arabian or Spanish blood in them, and that they were inclined to be temperamental until they were used to the harness and saddle. Running three-year-old stallions on a short halter along the cobbled street was often a tricky business, but the army buyers required it to be done so that they could be satisfied there was no lameness in the animals. William realised that this time he alone would be expected to exercise the animals. George Galloway would not let any of his carmen run the horses, not after the last débâcle.

It had been Sharkey Morris who slipped on the cobble-stones and let the rope go at the end of the turning, and by the time he had regained his feet his horse was galloping away along the Jamaica Road. The terrified animal had kept running. After scattering pedestrians in its path and kicking in the side of a tram, the sweating stallion had been captured by a young lad who calmly walked up to it and fed it a carrot before claiming the trailing rope and holding on to it until a fuming George Galloway drove up in his pony and trap.

The yard owner interrupted William's thoughts as he stood up and slipped his fingers into his waistcoat pocket.

'By the way, Will, 'ere's a little somefink fer the good job yer done on the wagon,' he said, pressing a gold sovereign into William's hand. 'There's 'alf a sovereign fer young Carrie too. She worked 'ard.'

The foreman's thanks were brushed aside with a sweep of the hand but as William made to leave George waved him back into the chair.

'Sit down a minute, Will,' he said, going to a wall cupboard and removing a bottle of Scotch whisky and two small glasses.

William did as he was bid, noticing the unsteady way in which his employer filled the glasses. Some of the spirit spilled over the top of the glass as he took it from George's shaking hand.

'Me an' you go back a long way, Will. 'Ow long 'ave yer bin workin' fer me now?'

'It's comin' up eighteen years,' William replied, taking a swig from the glass.

Galloway stared down into his whisky for a time, a thoughtful look in his heavy-lidded eyes, and the younger man cast his eyes around the small dusty office, feeling suddenly uncomfortable. He remembered well the day when, as a young man in his early twenties, he had been persuaded by Galloway to give up his carman's job with McSweeny's the grain merchant's and come to work for him as a yard foreman. The two had kept in contact over the years and William was flattered by the offer, but he had been worried about his old friend's growing reputation for being a bad employer. There was much talk in the coffee shops and cafés then about the Galloway firm. Other employers paid more and were less likely to sack their carmen for minor things, so the talk went. William had been well aware of George Galloway's hard nature and determination to get on as a businessman. Although they had grown up together, he knew he would not have an easy time as George's employee. In fact, George might well take advantage of their friendship and leech off his good will.

William had considered the job offer carefully. He was earning eighteen shillings a week and George was offering him twenty-five. He remembered what George had said when the subject of Will's having to issue orders to older, experienced Galloway employees was raised. 'Look, Will, I didn't build this business up by bein' soft, an' I know a good man when I see one. Yer know more about 'orses than all my drunken sods put tergevver. They'll take orders, or they'll soon find themselves out o' work. Besides, yer a good carman. Yer 'andle a team of 'orses as good as anybody I've got workin' fer me. Better, in fact.'

George was staring at him now, his tired eyes unblinking as though he were reading Will's thoughts. 'Yer know, I've never got over my missus dyin' the way she did,' he said suddenly. 'It was only this business o' mine that stopped me from doin' away wiv meself.'

William remained silent, waiting for the older man to go on.

'It's bin 'ard at times, tryin' ter keep this business on its feet,' George said finally. 'A couple o' years before Martha died, I thought I was goin' under. Yer remember when I was scratchin' fer work an' the 'orses got that fever? Well, that was the worst time. Luck was wiv me though, Will. After I got that contract ter deliver the 'ops an' then that contract wiv the skindressers, I didn't look back. Mind you, I've 'ad ter put the fear up some o' those carmen o' mine. Sackin' one or two of 'em brought the rest in ter line. I know yer didn't approve o' those sackin's, but I fink yer knew I was right.

'Yer see, that's the difference between me an' you, Will. Yer a gentle man. Outside yer 'ard, but inside yer just soft. Yer always was, even as a kid. Remember the time we knocked that ole toff over? Yer could 'ave got yerself nicked goin' back ter see 'ow 'e was. Softness is weakness in business, Will. It's why I've succeeded. I'm 'ard where me business is concerned. I swore I'd do well one day, never 'ad any doubts abaht it. When yer sleepin' wiv yer arse restin' on the cobbles an' yer belly cryin' out fer food, yer know yer can't get no lower, 'cept under the ground, so there's only one way ter go, an' that's upwards. Yer done well too, Will, in yer own way. Yer got a nice wife, an' four respectful kids. Yer gotta job fer life wiv me, an' yer've earned the men's respect. Yes, yer done well.'

William had let George go on without interrupting him, surprised to find him in one of his rare talkative moods. There was a lot of truth in what he had said. There was a difference between the two of them. It was something they had both always been aware of and something that had tended to put a distance between them as kids, even though they were good friends then.

'Yeah, I'm satisfied wiv the way fings turned out, George,' he replied. 'They're all good kids, an' Nellie's a diamond.'

Galloway finished his whisky and then reached for the

bottle. ''Ave anuvver drop, Will,' he said, filling his own glass.

William shook his head. 'Better not. I gotta check on the feed, an' there's the end stable ter clean out.'

''Ow's the cob?' George asked, the whisky bottle still held in his hand.

'Carrie's asked me if she can walk 'im in the yard this evenin',' William replied. ''E should be ready ter go back in the cart termorrer.'

George swallowed the contents of his glass and pulled a face. 'She's a good gel is your Carrie,' he went on. 'I only wish my two lads would take as much interest in the business. I've spent a small fortune payin' fer 'em both ter get an education at that private school. Admittedly it's knocked the rough edges orf 'em an' they both speak like a couple o' toffs, but I want the lads ter give the firm a bit o' consideration, Will. After all, I'm not gonna be around ferever. If those two lads o' mine put their minds to it, this business could grow. There's quite a few new firms springin' up in Bermon'sey, an' there's a lot o' trade ter be done cartin' stuff back an' forth from the wharves an' docks.'

The conversation was interrupted as the firm's elderly accountant walked into the office mumbling a 'good morning' as he hung up his rolled umbrella and Homburg before sitting himself at the far desk.

Horace Gallagher had been with the firm since the very beginning and he had managed to stay aloof from the day-to-day problems of the business, applying himself singlemindedly to his job of keeping the books up to date and dealing with the men's wages. As he prepared himself for the day's work he removed his thick-rimmed spectacles and polished them with his pocket handkerchief, a habit he constantly resorted to. Galloway watched the man's pallid, expressionless face for a few moments with amusement, comforted by the knowledge that whatever secrets or peculiarities he might have, Horace Gallagher was a conscientious accountant.

William tried to find a reason to leave. He was aware that Jack Oxford had been working the chaff-cutter and knew that once the man had run out of hay he would most probably find himself a warm corner in the loft and drop off to sleep, instead of getting another bale from the shed.

The sound of iron wheels and the clip of hooves over the cobbles gave the yard foreman an excuse to get up and go to the door of the office. Soapy Symonds had driven his horse and cart into the yard. As he jumped down from his seat, he pointed to the horse's front leg. ''E's gorn lame.'

William thanked his boss for the drink and walked over to Soapy's cart. He reached down and ran his hand along the horse's leg, feeling the soft swelling. ''E's got a bucked shin,' he said, straightening up. 'We'd better get a poultice on it. Take 'im out o' the sharves, Soapy.'

The carman mumbled to himself as he undid the harness straps and led the limping animal across the yard. The prospect of spending the rest of the day in the yard did not please Soapy. He had been on contract to the rum merchants in Tooley Street, and most afternoons after he picked up a load of barrels from the Rum Quay at the London Dock he would get a tot of the strong dark spirit. Today he would have to forgo his drink, and instead would most likely end up helping out on the chaff-cutting with that idiot Jack Oxford.

He had guessed right, for as soon as the horse was settled in the stall William pointed to the loft. 'Take anuvver bale of 'ay up ter Jack, will yer, Soapy. An' tell 'im no dozin' on the job. Galloway's in the office.'

Chapter Two

On Tuesday morning at number 10 Page Street, Florrie 'Hairpin' Axford was entertaining her longtime friends Maisie Dougall and Aggie Temple. The trio sat in Florrie's tidy front parlour sipping tea, and Maisie was holding forth.

'Well, accordin' ter Mrs Tanner there's anuvver load of 'orses comin' in soon,' she was saying. 'She don't know exactly when but yer can bet yer life it won't be long. I reckon we ought ter put a stop ter that Galloway runnin' 'em up the street.'

Maisie's friends nodded in agreement and Aggie put down her teacup. 'Somebody's gonna get killed before long, mark my words,' she declared with a severe expression on her face. 'If it ain't Will Tanner it's gonna be one o' the kids. It's bloody disgustin'.'

Maisie put her hands into her apron pockets. She was a short, plump woman in her mid-thirties. When she was ten years old she had been orphaned and sent to a home for waifs and strays, and at fourteen she went into service. Her outspokenness and forthright manner had not endeared her to her employer, however, and after a few weeks she found herself back on the streets with just a few coppers in her pocket. Maisie was determined not to be beaten by circumstances and she walked the whole distance from the grand house in Chislehurst to the little backstreet in Bermondsey where she had grown up. Hungry and blue with cold she arrived at the house that had once been her family home and stood staring at the door, feeling suddenly lost and alone.

When Bridie Phelan had seen the pitiful figure standing outside the house next door she immediately recognised her and felt that she had been given a sign from heaven. Bridie had never forgiven herself for allowing Maisie to be taken away when her mother died, and now there was a chance to make amends. She quickly ushered the young girl into her parlour to warm her and feed her, and on that cold night Maisie was given a new home. Maisie had grown to love and cherish Bridie and she repaid her kindness in full, caring for her until the day the old lady died. Maisie and her docker husband Fred still lived in Bridie Phelan's house.

Maisie leaned forward in her chair, her large eyes dark with anger. 'I was sayin' only the ovver night ter my Fred – why don't they run them 'orses while the kids are at school? It's always in the late afternoon. Yer can't expect the kids ter stay indoors. My Ronnie an' Albert won't stop in.'

Aggie recrossed her tightly laced leather boots, and nodded. 'Well, if I 'ad any kids I'd be terrified. The sound o' those 'orses clatterin' up the turnin' scares the bleedin' life out o' me. Some o' them beasts are wild, an' I can just picture that Tanner feller goin' under the 'ooves.'

Florrie brushed some imaginary crumbs from her spotless apron and fished into her pocket for her snuff box. A good-hearted woman in her early forties, Florrie had been widowed when she was twenty-five. She had married again five years later but her husband ran off after less than a year of married life. Most of Florrie's neighbours did not blame her for the break-up, only for her choice in men. She was a tall, lean woman with grey hair and sharp features. Like Aggie, Florrie had never had children, although she was the street's midwife, confidante, and a good friend to any of her neighbours who were in difficulties.

Florrie loved snuff and was never without her 'pinch', which she kept in a tiny silver box. Rumour had it that she had trained as a nurse but left to marry her first husband who had knocked her about before taking ill and dying of peritonitis. After he died, Florrie had taken to drink for a time and was always to be seen in the Kings Arms. One evening a fight broke out in the public bar between some dockers and carmen. The carmen were getting the worst of the exchanges and one of them smashed a bottle on the counter and advanced on a docker, holding the jagged bottle's neck in a threatening manner. Florrie stood up from her chair and calmly told the man to put down the weapon, but he brushed her to one side. When she had regained her composure she slowly walked up to him, removed a long steel hatpin from her hair, and without hesitating stuck the sharp end into the enraged man's rump. The bottle fell to the floor as the carman screamed out and reached for his rear end, and both the drunken workers were ejected from the pub in short order. Florrie still wore the hatpin through her bun, but now she only took it out in public when she used it on Sunday afternoons to ease winkles out of their shells.

Aggie watched as her hostess delicately took out a pinch of snuff between her thumb and forefinger and laid it gently on the back of her long, thin hand. Aggie was the eldest of the trio. Her husband was a lamplighter and she took in washing and ironing. She also knew everyone's business and always had a sorrowful look about her face, even when she was feeling quite happy. Her other idiosyncrasy was cleanliness.

Aggie cleaned her windows at least twice every week, and her doorstep was always spotlessly white. Her aprons were invariably starched and her brown hair always neatly in place on the top of her head. When her husband Harold set off to light the streetlamps he made sure not to mark the doorstep with his boots, and when he came home late at night he left them on a piece of newspaper which had been put down in the passage for that specific purpose.

Florrie sniffed up the snuff and her friends waited until she had finished twitching her nostrils.

'I was talkin' ter some o' the women last week an' they said they'd be wiv us,' Maisie went on.

'Why don't we do a bit o' doorknockerin'? The more the merrier,' Aggie suggested.

'Good idea,' said Florrie. 'I should fink a crowd of us outside the gates might make Galloway fink twice.'

'Last time we went ter see 'im, 'e sent that Jack Oxford out. Ooh, 'e gives me the creeps, really 'e does,' Maisie said, shuddering.

Florrie laughed. ''E's 'armless enough. My ole man told me it was an 'orse what done it.'

'Done what?' Maisie asked.

'Sent 'im dopey,' Florrie replied, wiping her nose on a clean handkerchief. ''E got kicked in the 'ead when 'e was a carman. Apparently 'e was a smart man once. 'E 'ad a lady friend as well. You remember that ginger woman wiv all those kids? The one who used ter live in Bacon Street Buildin's? You know 'er – Dingle I fink 'er name was. She used ter fight 'er ole man in the street when they came out o' the Kings Arms on Saturday nights. Pissed as 'andcarts the pair of 'em was every Saturday night. They didn't 'alf used ter 'ave a punch-up, though.'

'Jack Oxford didn't take 'er out, did 'e?' asked Aggie.

'No, not 'er – 'er sister Clara. She was ginger too. Nice-lookin' woman. She ended up marryin' a copper an' they moved away. Somewhere in the country, I fink it was. Bromley, if I remember rightly.'

'Pity it wasn't ole Galloway who got kicked in the 'ead instead o' Jack Oxford,' Maisie remarked. 'We wouldn't 'ave ter go roun' doorknockerin' then.'

Aggie folded her hands on her lap. ''Ere, I know what I meant ter tell yer,' she began. 'The police went in the Eagle last night. It's bin closed down accordin' ter my bloke. 'E said they was usin' the place fer fightin' . . .'

'That don't surprise me,' Florrie cut in. 'That Eagle was always a rough 'ole.'

'My 'Arold gets ter know all the news,' Aggie went on eagerly. ''E said there was a bloke fightin' at the Eagle last week called Gypsy Williams an' 'e nearly killed the ovver poor bleeder. 'Arold said there was blood everywhere an' 'e said George Galloway was watchin' the fight.'

''E would be,' Florrie said contemptuously. 'Well I tell yer somefink. There'll be blood on Page Street if we don't stop ole Galloway runnin' them 'orses.'

'Yer right there, Florrie,' Maisie said, nodding her head vigorously.

Florrie gathered up the empty teacups. 'Let's 'ave anuvver cup, gels, an' then we'll work out what we're gonna do.'

Carrie lay back, feeling the sun warm on her face. The creaking of the laden cart and the scrunch of the iron-rimmed wheels over the cobbles were music in her ears as she stretched out in the hay. From above, the shadow of the high walkway across Tower Bridge blotted out the sun for a moment or two and she opened her eyes. She could see the high sweep of the massive girders and the clear blue sky above. She eased her position in the well amongst the stacked hay that her father had made for her and looked down from the top of the bales. Below, the River Thames was at high tide and she could see the line of steamships moored in the Pool. In midstream a brace of flat, tarpaulin-covered barges lay at anchor, moored to a huge iron buoy. In the distance she saw the grimy, square stone London Bridge, and beyond the grey dome of St Paul's, its giltwork glistening in the sun. The hay smelled sweet and the gentle rocking and swaying of the cart made her feel drowsy. Carrie lay back and closed her eyes once more.

It was Carrie's favourite treat to be allowed to accompany her father on his journey to Wanstead to bring back a supply of hay. He usually made the trip on Saturday mornings, but on this occasion he had had to go Tuesday, since the stock of bales at Galloway's was running low. The previous evening, as they were exercising the cob in the quiet yard, Carrie had pleaded with her father to let her go along the following morning. He had pulled a face but she knew he would take her. He always did.

On the outward trip she had stood in the well of the cart, holding on to the base of the dicky seat. They were using Titch the Welsh cob, who seemed to have fully recovered. They had stopped on the way at a small country pub where her father had bought her a lemonade and they had eaten their brawn sandwiches, sitting at a wooden table in the back yard. Now, as she leaned back on top of the hay bales, Carrie sighed contentedly. Most of the children in her class would have given anything to go on the trip, of that she was sure. There were Billy and Tommy Gordon who were very poor and had to share a pair of boots. Then there was Sara Knight – her clothes were almost hanging in shreds and she was often ill. Wouldn't it be nice if they all could have gone on the trip?

thought Carrie. Sara had probably never tasted lemonade. Tommy and Billy would have been really excited and it wouldn't have mattered if they hadn't had a pair of boots each. The hay was soft and they would have loved to feed Titch with pieces of carrot and turnip.

Carrie sighed as she snuggled down in the hay and felt the cart sway as it turned into Tooley Street. She would be home soon and tomorrow she could tell her school friends all about the day out. Sara would listen wide-eyed and the Gordon brothers would say how they wished they could have fed the horse and sat on top of the hay. Suddenly Carrie could picture their envious expressions. She bit on her bottom lip. Why were her best friends so poor? she wondered sadly. It was then that she made up her mind to tell them she had been in bed with a sore throat.

On Friday morning a dozen Irish Draughts arrived from the horse repository in Walworth. They were led in teams of four by walkers, young lads who knew the backstreets very well and who had managed to keep the animals quiet by avoiding most of the noisy traffic in the main roads. William and some of the carmen had already moved the carts out of the large shed and hung up the stall-boards. The food trays were filled and there was clean straw bedding in place. George Galloway was on hand to take delivery. He gave every horse a quick inspection, running his hand over the withers and down the flanks. He was watched by his elder son, Geoffrey, who stood to one side looking slightly bored with the whole process. Geoffrey was a tall, dark lad in his sixteenth year, his last at school. Lately he had been having differences with his father over his future plans. Geoffrey wanted to be an engineer but his father was adamant that he should come into the business. The boy decided he would have to bide his time for the present and try to show some interest in the cartage business, while he waited for the right moment to confront his father.

The women of the street had been keeping themselves alert to developments at Galloway's yard, and when the heavily shod animals clattered into the cobbled turning the leaders of the protest group started to gather at number 10. One or two women who lived in the stretch of the turning leading out into Bacon Street turned up, as well as the women from the Jamaica Road side of Page Street. They had realised that if Florrie and her friends managed to stop the horses being run along their end of the turning then Galloway might simply decide to run them along to Bacon Street and back. The women understood that they would have to stick together, and if the horse trader wanted to show off his nags to the military then he would have to do it inside his own yard.

Eight women in all sat in Florrie Axford's parlour, chatting together.

'We'll 'ave ter be ready, an' that means we gotta know exactly when the army's comin',' Maisie Dougall said in a loud voice, her large eyes glaring.

'Why don't we jus' go an' tell that whoreson we ain't gonna put up wiv it?' Dot Argent said with venom.

Sadie Sullivan leaned forward in her chair. 'What's the use o' that?' she growled. 'The ole bastard'll say, "All right, ladies," then when the army arrives 'e'll jus' go on an' do it. I reckon we ought ter tell 'im if 'e don't listen ter what we're sayin', we'll chuck a lighted lamp in the stable. That should make 'im sit up an' take notice.'

Florrie shook her head. 'We can't do that, Sadie, much as we'd like to. We don't wanna end up in 'Olloway, do we? If we get done fer arson they'll lock us up an' chuck the key away.'

Maudie Mycroft nodded her head vigorously. 'Yer right, Florrie,' she said, her eyes widening with concern. 'Ole Bridie

Kelly burnt 'er 'ouse down over in Abbey Street a few years ago. They stuck 'er in Colney 'Atch.'

'I should fink so too,' Aggie Temple cut in, frowning crossly. 'Bridie Kelly was as mad as a March 'are. She'd already tried ter burn the Post Office down in the Old Kent Road, then she set the Relief Office alight when they refused ter give 'er a few bob. A few weeks later she laid 'erself down across the tramlines in Tower Bridge Road sayin' she was fed up wiv it all. The trams was lined up as far back as the Elephant an' Castle. It took two burly great coppers ter shift 'er. Nearly bit one o' the coppers' ears orf, she did. The woman was a bloody lunatic!'

When the laughing had died down, Florrie held up her hands. 'Look, gels,' she said quietly, 'we gotta do this right. We don't want no violence or 'ollerin' an' 'ootin'. First of all, we gotta get the day right. If we know exactly when the army's comin', we can be ready. What we gotta do is all march out at both sides o' the turnin' near the gates. We'll take the kids wiv us and we'll all sit ourselves comfortable. If any of yer 'ave got knittin' or socks ter mend, bring 'em wiv yer. Let 'em see yer ain't in no 'urry ter leave. I tell yer, gels, there's no way they're gonna run them 'orses while we're sittin' there.'

Maudie pulled at her chin with her thumb and forefinger 'S'posin' they bring the coppers down? We could all get locked up,' she said fearfully.

Florrie smiled at the worried-looking woman. 'Look, luv, what we're gonna do ain't breakin' the law. Well, not very much anyway. We can block our street up if we like. We're the ones who live 'ere. Jus' come out an' act like yer mean it. Jus' say ter yerself, sod 'em all. Are we all agreed?'

Determined, excited voices rang out and then Aggie stood up, waving her hands for the women to quieten down. 'The question is, 'ow we gonna find out fer sure when the army's comin'?' she asked Florrie.

Florrie grinned slyly. 'Now listen ter me. Yer all know Nellie Tanner's ole man is the yard foreman? Well, she's gonna find out from 'im when they're comin'. She's got kids like a lot o' you women an' she ain't none too 'appy about 'avin' ter keep 'em off the street. Besides, it's 'er ole man who's gonna 'ave ter run the bleedin' nags. She told me only the ovver day she worries over 'er Will gettin' trampled on if one o' them 'orses falls over. She told me 'e's fair copped out by the time 'e's finished.'

Sadie put up her hand for attention. She was a large, middle-aged woman with dark hair and deep blue eyes. Her flat, friendly face belied a volcanic temper and she was renowned for her ability to stand up in the street and fight like a man. One or two bullying women had come to grief in the past when they had had the temerity to challenge Sadie to a fight, and on one occasion she had been taken to court and fined ten shillings for a street affray in which her opponent, a drunken docker who had questioned her birthright, was laid out cold by a swinging right-hand punch from Sadie's massive fist. She had seven children by her devoted docker husband, Daniel, who idolised her. Sadie's brood were often involved in scraps, and more often than not the fights were between themselves. The family had become known as 'the fighting Sullivans', although when Sadie and her Irish husband Daniel marched their tribe to Mass on Sunday mornings, they all looked positively angelic.

At the moment Sadie looked far from angelic. She glanced around at the other women. 'I reckon if we stick tergevver we're gonna beat ole Galloway, but we've all gotta see it out,' she said resolutely. 'That connivin' ole bastard might see us all sittin' in the turnin' an' e' might well phone up fer the coppers.

What we gotta do is refuse ter move. All right we might get nicked an' put in the Black Maria, but at least we can tell our side of it ter the beak. If we get a decent magistrate we might get a restraint put on Galloway. Some o' them magistrates ain't so bad.'

The mention of the Black Maria and possibly going before a magistrate sent shivers through Maudie Mycroft. She went to the women's meeting every Monday afternoon at St James's Church, and already had visions of the other ladies there whispering together and giving her dark looks. She could hear them now: 'Ten shillings fine and bound over to keep the peace. Isn't it disgusting? Wouldn't you think the woman would have better sense than to throw herself in front of the horses? Disgusting behaviour! I should think the Reverend Preedy will ask her to stay away. It's such a bad example to the other women . . .'

Maudie fidgeted uncomfortably in her seat. She wanted desperately to speak about her misgivings but she bit on her tongue. If she opted out of joining the rest of the women, they would all think her a coward and pass her by in the street. Maybe she could feign illness, or perhaps go to see her sister in Deptford when the women took to the street? She could say that her sister was suddenly taken ill.

The women were getting ready to leave and as Sadie stood up she grinned widely at Florrie and said, 'I'm bringin' me rollin'-pin wiv me, Flo. If one o' them coppers touches me, I'll crown 'im wiv it.'

Maudie dabbed at her hot forehead and decided there and then that she just had to find a very good excuse.

It was early evening and Carrie and her younger brothers were playing outside the house. Inside in the small parlour William sat beside the empty grate, watching Nellie's deft fingers working away as she darned one of his socks. She had been quiet for some time but suddenly she looked up and said casually, 'I s'pose they'll 'ave you runnin' those stallions again, Will?'

He nodded and leant his head back against the chair, letting his eyes close. He knew Nellie was always worried when he worked the sale horses, and had to admit it got no easier as time went by.

'I saw the 'orses comin' down the turnin',' she went on. 'I s'pose the army'll be 'ere next week, won't they, Will?'

'Next Friday,' he replied. 'About four, so George Galloway said.'

Nellie felt a little guilty about the way she had gleaned the information, but she knew that William would have kept it from her if she had told him of the women's plans. She had voiced her fears of someone getting hurt before, but he had only shrugged and changed the subject. She knew that her husband did not like having to run the horses along the turning, yet he kept his dissatisfaction to himself to save vexing her. William was a loyal and conscientious man, and it angered her to see that lately he was being taken advantage of more and more. She understood too well how difficult it was for him not to accept the added responsibilities. They were living in one of Galloway's houses, and if her husband lost his job they would soon be forced to leave. How hard that would be on Carrie! The girl was devoted to the horses and would be heartbroken if they had to move away. Maybe William should not have encouraged her so much when she was younger. He had introduced her to the stables when she was quite small. She had ridden on the backs of those nags almost before she could walk. Her schooling was probably suffering too, Nellie worried. Carrie would make any excuse to miss a day if something was on at the yard. The child was happy and not often given to moodiness though, she had to concede. Maybe William was right. She would be working in a factory or behind a shop counter in a few years' time, unless her schooling improved dramatically. Perhaps it was best to let the girl carry on as she was doing. It would not be long before she found out how hard life really was.

William's regular snoring sounded loudly and Nellie reached out with her foot and touched the toe of his boot. He grunted and then moved his head to one side and the snoring ceased. Nellie felt a sudden tenderness as she looked at him sleeping. His fair hair was dishevelled and a tuft lay over his forehead. Maybe he won't have to run those horses after all, she thought with a wry smile, although he wouldn't thank her for giving their neighbours the information she had just coaxed out of him. She would have to be careful. If George Galloway found out it was she who had given the news to the women he would make things very difficult for her husband. William was a quiet, easy-going man but he could be pushed only so far, and as for Galloway – he would not allow his childhood friendship with William to influence a business decision, of that she was sure. It had nearly come to that eight years ago, she recalled with a shudder. Thankfully, William had never found out what had taken place. It had been a bad time for everyone then, a time which Nellie tried not to think about, but although she had managed to be a good wife and mother to the children over the years, she knew she would never be allowed to forget what had happened.

Chapter Three

George Galloway lived in Tyburn Square, a tidy place where the large Victorian houses looked out on to tall plane trees enclosed in a small garden area in the centre of the square. The garden was surrounded with iron railings and had an arched entrance. Inside there were wooden benches set out under the trees and around the circumference of the garden, and flowers grew from square beds set amongst the paving-stones. The houses were fronted by ornamental iron railings and the place was quiet, although it stood just behind the noisy Jamaica Road.

Tyburn Square had originally been built to accommodate the shippers and businessmen who owned the Bermondsey wharves and warehouses, men who had earned their fortunes trading along from Greenwich Reach to the Pool of London. As industry moved into the area, many of the original occupants of the houses moved away to escape the ever-increasing danger of contracting illnesses spread by the yellow, sulphurous fogs or the fevers which were constantly breaking out in the riverside hovels. Now Tyburn Square had a second wave of prosperous tenants, like George Galloway who had built his business up from trading with one horse and cart. The square now boasted solicitors and ship-chandlers, cordwainers and wheelwrights among its community, as well as a few retired businessmen who were loath to leave Bermondsey despite the growing dangers and the constant noise and bustle.

George Galloway lived at number 22. His two-storeyed house was tastefully furnished. Thick draperies covered the windows, and the furniture was of rosewood and oak. Heavy carpets covered the floors, and the downstairs and first-floor rooms were kept warm with open fires.

Galloway employed a housekeeper who lived in a room on the top floor of the house. Mrs Flynn had come to work for the cartage contractor soon after his wife Martha died. She was herself a widow who had lost her two children while they were still babies. Mrs Flynn's husband had been the first carman to work for Galloway. He had died under the hooves of a team of horses which had bolted when they were frightened by the exploding boiler of a steam tram in the Old Kent Road. Nora Flynn was still only thirty-five, although her thin frame and gaunt face made her seem much older. She looked stern with her tightly swept-up black hair and her piercing dark eyes, but beneath the surface she was a kindhearted woman who had borne the tragedy in her life with fortitude. She had taken care of George Galloway's young daughter Josephine from birth, and had been a restraining and calming influence on her employer's two lively sons who had taken their mother's death very badly. The Galloway children all loved her, although the boys were very careful not to anger her. As far as Josephine was concerned, Nora was her mother, although she had always been taught to call her by name. It was something George Galloway had insisted upon.

Most of the top floor of the house was used for storage. Nora occupied only the front room which looked down on to the square. It was simply furnished, containing a wardrobe and dressing table, a bed in one corner and a table beneath the wide window. The floor was carpeted, and the small open fire provided enough warmth for Nora's needs. The housekeeper lived a spartan life, rising early and washing in cold water from the washstand bowl. She prepared the food in the large ground-floor kitchen at the back of the house and spent a considerable time each day keeping the whole house in spotless condition. Her only relaxation was to take long, leisurely walks in the early evening after her day's work was done. Sometimes she called on old friends and often visited nearby St James's Church to hear the evening services, but when it was very cold or when she was feeling too tired to take her walk, she would sit in her room and take up her embroidery, although the poor light afforded by the flickering gas-mantle made it rather difficult for her. Nora lived her life the way she wanted to and had grown used to her employer's ways and increasingly black moods. She could understand and sympathise with him over the sad loss of his wife but would confront and remonstrate with him when he came down too heavily on his children, for which they were grateful.

George Galloway owned a pony-and-trap which he entrusted to a livery stable just behind the square, where the ostler kept both animal and contraption in good condition and ready for use. Often Galloway would knock the stable-owner up late in the evening or early in the morning as the mood took him and ride out in his gig. It was a source of great pleasure to him to sit in the upholstered seat and flick on the reins to send the animal at a fast trot through the streets of Bermondsey. He sometimes took the conveyance down to his yard in Page Street although more often than not he walked the short distance. On occasions when the loss of Martha weighed heavily upon him and a black mood descended,

Galloway would sit in his large front room with the curtains drawn and consume a bottle of Scotch whisky. Mrs Flynn recognised the signs of an approaching drinking bout and left him alone in his grief, making sure that the boys and Josephine were kept out of the way.

One night in late autumn as Nora stood in the kitchen cleaning a pan with a scouring pad, she knew that the confrontation she had been expecting for some time now was about to happen. Geoffrey was sixteen and beginning to find his feet. He no longer seemed to have any fear of his father. He was due to leave school soon, and had recently spoken to her of his desire to go into engineering. When the boy had come in earlier that evening and said he wanted to speak with his father, Nora had tried to put him off. She had warned him that his father had shut himself in his room with a bottle of whisky but Geoffrey would not heed her.

'I've decided on engineering, Nora. It's what I want to do,' he had said forcefully. 'I don't want to follow Father into the business. He runs it the way *he* wants to, and there'd be no changing things. Maybe if he was older it'd be different. Maybe then I'd be allowed a free rein. As it is now, I'd be little more than his clerk.'

Nora shrugged her shoulders and gave a resigned sigh. There would have been no use in saying any more. The boy was like his father in his determination, and a trial of wills was inevitable.

In the darkened room George and his son faced each other. The gaslamp had been turned down and its pale yellow light played on the iron figures along the high mantelshelf. The fire had been left to burn low although there was a filled coal-scuttle beside the grate, and the room smelled of stale tobacco smoke. The older man sat a little slumped in his wide leather chair with an open bottle standing on the companion table at his elbow. Geoffrey could see two patches of hectic colour on his father's broad face, standing out against the dark stubble around his chin. He felt very conscious of the heavy-lidded eyes as they stared out at him.

George held a tumbler of undiluted spirit in his thick, calloused hand and his legs were splayed out against the brass fender. 'I can't understand yer sudden change o' plans,' he said in a husky voice. 'Only last week yer told me yer was gonna give it a chance. Yer promised me yer was gonna try. It's a good respectable business, not one ter be ashamed of.'

Geoffrey sighed in frustration. 'Look, Dad, I'm not ashamed of working in the business, it's just that I'm set on taking up engineering. It's what I want to do.'

'I was countin' on yer comin' in wiv me,' George said, a note of bitterness in his voice. 'I 'ad ter struggle an' go wivout ter get where I am now. It took a lot of 'ard work an' deviousness ter build up the firm. I ran the streets, slept under arches, an' went 'ungry most o' the time. I've felt the pain in me guts when there was no food ter be 'ad. Yer've never known the pain of an empty belly, of livin' on turnips, bacon-bone soup an' crusts o' mouldy bread. I don't want yer ter know. That's what I sent yer ter that school for. I want yer ter come in wiv me an' use yer education. There's a lot of opportunity in the cartage business. Firms are springin' up all over Bermondsey an' there's a lot o' tonnage that's gotta be moved.'

Geoffrey met his father's hard stare. 'I know I told you I'd give it a try, and I've been all through the books like you suggested. I've studied the contracts, invoices and order forms. I spent all last Monday afternoon with Mr Gallagher going over the accounts. I spent the whole of the weekend thinking about the business, Dad, and I know I wouldn't be happy managing that side of it. I know I wouldn't.'

George swallowed the contents of the tumbler he held in his hand and winced as the spirit burned his throat. He filled the glass with an unsteady hand and placed it on the table beside him.

'So yer don't wanna manage that side of it?' he said, a note of sarcasm in his hoarse voice. 'Tell me, what *do* yer wanna do? D'yer wanna go out an' get the contracts? D'yer wanna tout fer business? Well, I'll tell yer what yer gotta do – yer gotta learn the business from the bottom. Yer gotta learn ter balance the books an' order the supplies. Yer gotta know 'ow ter give the work out an' sort out the problems wiv the carmen. And that's jus' ter begin wiv. Then yer gotta know 'ow ter size up a good 'orse an' buy well. If I'd 'ave made too many bad buys, there'd be no business now. When yer know all there is ter know o' that side of it, yer'll need a spell wiv Will Tanner. 'E knows almost as much as I do about 'orses. 'E's got respect, an' the carmen know they can't take 'im on. After a go in the office an' then six months wiv Tanner, maybe yer'll be ready ter go out an' tout fer work. As it stands, I get the contracts 'cos I can trade on me name. Yer've gotta earn a name, earn a reputation. It don't come easy, boy.'

Geoffrey ran his fingers through his thick dark hair and leaned back in his chair. 'I know what you're saying, Father,' he said slowly. 'I'd be quite willing to start the way you said. I wouldn't want it any other way if I wanted to come into the business, but I don't. I want to learn engineering, and that's the way it is.'

George shook his head sadly. The boy was so like his mother. She had had the same look when she was angry. She had always been dogged and determined when she made her mind up about anything. Geoff had inherited his tenacity from both of them. He was going to be hard to sway. George decided that he should play along for a while. Let the boy see

48

that his father was recognising and understanding his position. After all, he was not seventeen yet. He might change his mind in six months, thought George, without believing it.

'All right, Geoff,' he said quietly. 'I can see yer not 'appy about comin' in wiv me. There's no rush ter go inter this engineerin', is there? The problem is, I'm desperate fer a bit of 'elp wiv the business at the moment so I'd appreciate it if yer could give me a bit o' yer time ter straighten fings up down at the office. Give it six months, eh? Then, if yer still feel yer should make engineerin' yer career, I won't stand in yer way. 'Ow's that sound?'

Geoff swallowed a sharp reply. As much as he wanted to tell his father there and then that he would not change his mind, he held back. He had gained some measure of acceptance for his plans, and his father had ended up being less hard and aggressive than he might have expected. He seemed a little sad, thought the boy. He was going through one of his bad periods, as Nora had noticed. There would be other times for Geoffrey to assert his will. In the meantime he would try to settle into the business for six months but at the end of that time would make a final decision, he resolved, even if it meant breaking with his father.

Geoffrey looked up from the flickering coals and met his father's questioning gaze. 'All right, Dad, I'll try for six months,' he said with a deep sigh.

Jack Oxford was employed to do the dirty jobs around Galloway's stables. He'd been a simpleton since a run-in with a horse in his previous job and was considered harmless by the other workers. He was tall and thin, with stopping shoulders and jet-black hair which hung down to his collar, and his large dark eyes stared out from an angular white face. He seemed to bend from the knees as he walked, and had large hands and feet that looked enormous in the pair of heavy, studded boots he always wore.

Today Jack had swept the yard clean and refilled the sacks of chaff; he had been in amongst the newly arrived horses and mucked out the stalls; he had topped up the drinking trough at the end of the yard with fresh water, and now he felt he had done just about enough for one day. It was time to relax.

Jack idled up to the office and looked in at the window. He had noticed that Galloway's trap was not in the yard but he knew that the boss often walked to the stables. He could not see Galloway, only Mr Gallagher the accountant, bending over the desk in the far corner. Jack growled to himself. He had taken a dislike to Gallagher ever since he had accidentally sprayed the elderly man with water while hosing down the yard. Gallagher had walked in unexpectedly and been soaked. It was an accident and no lasting harm had been done, but the accountant had tattled to George Galloway who came out of the office and yelled at Jack in front of the carmen. The yard man's sluggish brain had caught most of the tirade of abuse and he took umbrage at being called a lazy, incompetent bastard. He wasn't sure what incompetent meant, it was the other word that Jack objected to. There was no need for the boss to fly off the handle. Jack had always done what he was told. It was only when he was chaff-cutting that he took a nap, and then only when the bale was finished.

It made no difference how hard he worked, the boss always shouted at him and made him look silly in front of the men. He was doing it more lately, and usually for no reason. Well, not for much of a reason anyway. Jack decided it was about time he started looking after himself for a change. A little nap was nothing to be ashamed of. Not when all the work was finished. He could do with one right now, in fact.

Jack sauntered away from the office window. The mid-afternoon sun was shining down from a clear sky and felt hot on his head. Too much sun gave Jack a nasty headache, and that was another good reason for him to take a nap. Will Tanner was at the farrier's, and the carmen would not be back for a good two hours he reasoned as he rubbed his hands together and grinned to himself. He crossed the yard and walked up the long steep ramp to the upper stable. The door to his left led into the chaff-cutting room and Jack strolled through, relishing the thought of settling down in the hay.

Carrie left school in Dockhead late in the afternoon. She was walking home with her friend Sara when she spotted the two Galloway wagons. Soapy Symonds was in the leading cart, his head slumped down on to his chest as he nodded off. Soapy knew that he could rely on the horse to take him home without prompting and had let the reins hang loose. Sharkey's cart was following behind, his horse nuzzling the tailboard in front as they plodded home to Page Street. Carrie shouted out to Soapy but he did not hear her. Sharkey spotted her as she ran to the kerbside.

'I s'pose yer wanna lift, do yer?' he grinned as he jumped down from his seat and lowered the tailboard on its chains.

'I didn't 'spect ter see yer,' Carrie said as Sharkey hoisted the two girls up on to the tailboard.

'Me an' Soapy got finished early. There's a stoppage at the docks,' he said with a chuckle as he climbed back into the driving seat.

Carrie and Sara sat giggling on the back of the cart as Sharkey slapped the reins and sent the horse into a slow trot in an effort to catch up with Soapy.

'I wish my dad worked in the stables or was on the 'orse-an'-carts,' Sara said, grinning happily at Carrie.

The Tanner girl looked at the pale drawn face of her friend

and smiled kindly. 'Next time my dad takes me ter get the bales of 'ay, I'm gonna ask 'im if yer can come wiv us,' she said.

'Would 'e really take me as well?' Sara asked, her dark-circled eyes lighting up.

'I 'spect 'e will,' Carrie said confidently. 'We can 'ave a lemonade an' ride up on top o' the load. It's really luvverly.'

Sara squeezed her friend's arm. 'You're my bestest friend, Carrie,' she said, her face beaming.

Carrie suddenly felt a sadness which seemed to clutch at her insides and tighten her throat as she looked into her friend's pallid face. Sara lived in Bacon Street Buildings and her father, who had been crippled in an accident at the docks, was reduced to selling bits and pieces from a suitcase at the markets. Her mother took in washing and scrubbed floors in an effort to provide for her five children, and as Sara was the eldest she had unavoidably become the household drudge. Life was not very nice for her, Carrie thought, squeezing her friend's arm in a spontaneous show of sympathy. Well, she was going to make sure Sara accompanied her on the next trip to Wanstead. She would speak to her father about it as soon as she got home.

The carts swung into Page Street and as they slowed at the firm's gates Carrie and Sara jumped down. The Tanner girl stood beside her front door until her friend reached the end of the turning, then after exchanging waves she went into the house.

Once inside the yard the two carmen unhitched their horses and led them to the watering trough to let them drink their fill before settling them into the stalls. When the empty carts had been manhandled out of the way back up against the end wall, and the harness hung in the shed, Soapy and Sharkey walked up to the office and peered in.

'Seen Will Tanner?' Soapy asked, scratching the back of his head.

Horace Gallagher looked up from the ledger and peered over his thick-lensed spectacles at Soapy. 'He's at the farrier's. I don't know when he'll be back,' he said irritably.

Soapy looked at Sharkey and pulled a face. 'Let's sort dopey Jack out, Sharkey. 'E might 'ave some tea brewin',' he said, grinning.

The two sauntered from the office over to the rickety shed at the end of the yard and looked in. The place was a mess, with brooms and buckets scattered around everywhere. On the bench beneath the dust-covered window was an assortment of well-worn harness straps that the yard man was in the process of repairing. Of Jack Oxford there was no sign.

'P'raps the lazy ole sod's takin' a nap, Soapy,' Sharkey said, aiming a kick at the nearest bucket.

'Let's go up the loft. That's where 'e'll be, it's a dead cert,' Soapy replied.

The two carmen walked up the ramp and entered the chaff store. The belt-driven chaff cutting contraption had been installed by George Galloway after he had seen a month's bills for feedstuffs. It was driven by a leather belt which ran from the flywheel of a steam engine housed in the shed below. The cutter was a large, square contraption with revolving blades. From its funnel chopped hay was spewed out into sacks. Around the machine there were a few bales of uncut hay and in one corner loose stalks had been piled into a heap. Bedded down in them was Jack Oxford. He was lying on his back, snoring loudly, his cap pulled over his face and his hands clasped together on his chest.

'Look at the lazy, dopey ole git,' Soapy said, picking up a piece of wood that was resting against the cutter.

Sharkey grabbed Soapy's arm and put a finger to his lips. ''Ere, let's 'ave a lark. C'mon.'

Soapy followed his friend back down the ramp, puzzlement

showing on his hawklike features. 'Where we goin'?' he asked.

Sharkey hunched up his broad shoulders and grinned evilly as he pushed his cap on to the back of his head. 'We're gonna give Oxford a spruce-up.'

The scheming carman led the way back to the shed and rummaged around Jack Oxford's bits and pieces until he found what he was looking for. Then, with the giggling Soapy hard on his heels, he marched back to the stable and walked quietly up the ramp.

Jack Oxford was still snoring loudly in the hay. When a coating of leather preservative was brushed across his forehead, he merely grunted. The second stroke was applied along his stubbled cheek. He waved an imagined insect away with a sweep of his hand. A few more strokes were deemed enough to finish the job on the by now uncomfortable yard man, who turned over on to his side and began scratching his painted ear.

The sound of horses being led into the yard sent the two carmen hurrying from the loft. As they came down the ramp, they saw William Tanner.

'What are you two doin' 'ere?' he asked, frowning.

'We couldn't get in the docks fer the second load. There's a stoppage or somefink,' Soapy replied, standing in front of Sharkey who had the tin of preservative hidden behind his back.

'Well, take these two an' bed 'em down, then yer can go,' William said, walking away to the office. As he reached the door, he turned towards the two grinning carmen. ''Ave yer seen Jack Oxford?' he called out.

The two shook their heads and walked off with the newly shod horses, grinning at each other like a couple of children.

*

Nellie Tanner was in the scullery doing the washing up while Carrie stood beside her drying the plates, a miserable expression on her pretty face.

'But Sara's my best friend, an' she's never even bin on an 'orse-an'-cart,' she said plaintively.

Nellie sighed irritably. 'Look, Carrie, yer farvver shouldn't really take you wiv 'im, let alone 'alf the street. S'posin' somefing 'appened? I mean, there could be an accident or somefink.'

'But it's not 'alf the street, Mum,' Carrie persisted. 'It's only Sara, an' nuffink bad would 'appen. She'd be no trouble. She's so poor, an' she stays away from school lots o' times ter look after 'er bruvvers an' sisters. I'm only askin' fer Sara, nobody else.'

Nellie put down the last of the plates and undid her apronstrings, leaning back against the copper. 'Yer say Sara's poor? We're *all* poor. All right, yer farvver's got a regular job, but there's no spare money comin' in this 'ouse, let me tell yer. It's a job ter manage, what wiv food an' clothes, an' we still 'ave ter pay rent, even though Mr Galloway owns this 'ouse. *Everybody* round 'ere's poor. It's 'and ter mouth fer all of us, luv, so don't go gettin' the idea that we're better off than everybody else. Some's jus' poorer than ovvers.'

'Well, I fink Sara's family are poorest of all,' Carrie said, gathering up the dried plates and placing them in the cupboard. 'She 'ad no coat on yesterday when it was chilly an' she 'ardly brings anyfink ter school. I don't fink she's ever tasted lemonade, an' when she come 'ome wiv me on the back o' Mr Morris's van she was so excited. She's nice.'

Nellie bit back an angry reply and said quietly, 'Yer know yer shouldn't go ridin' on the back o' those carts, Carrie. I've told yer before, yer could fall off. An' what would Sara's muvver say if she knew she was ridin' on them wiv yer?'

Carrie shrugged her shoulders. 'I don't fink she would say anything. She don't treat Sara very nice, what wiv makin' 'er do all that work indoors.'

Nellie sighed deeply, not really knowing how to reply to her young daughter. Carrie was a caring, thoughtful girl who was saddened and upset by the poverty around her, and Nellie knew there was nothing she could do to protect her from it. She was going to learn a lot more about heartache and sadness as she grew up.

'Yer gotta understand, Carrie, Mrs Knight 'as ter work 'ard, what wiv Mr Knight being the way 'e is,' she said slowly. 'Sara's gotta 'elp out in the 'ome. After all, she is the eldest, an' don't ferget the youngest is only a few months old.'

Carrie sighed. 'Well, I'm still gonna ask Dad if she can come wiv us next time,' she said firmly.

Nellie shook her head in resignation as Carrie walked out of the scullery. Just like her father, she told herself with a smile. Once she made up her mind, there was no shifting her.

As Nellie started to fill the copper with fresh water, she suddenly began to wonder what sort of a reception the army would get the following day.

Chapter Four

The Kings Arms stood on the corner of Page Street and was managed by Alec Crossley and his wife Grace. Alec was a tubby character with a bald head, a ruddy face, and a liking for brandy which made his face flush up like a beacon. Grace, on the other hand, remained sober and took charge of the pub on the frequent occasions when Alec had had too much of his favourite beverage. She was a large, jolly woman with an infectious laugh. Her blonde hair was worn piled up on top of her head. The Crossleys kept a happy pub and had installed a snug bar where the local women congregated for a drink and a chat in comfort, safe in the knowledge that they were not seen as tarts because they dared enter a man's domain. The snug bar was the women's own little haven where men did not intrude. It was Grace's idea and she served the women herself. There was a saloon bar too at the Kings Arms which was carpeted and tastefully furnished, but almost all of the local folk used the public where a piano and round iron tables stood on well-scrubbed floorboards.

Soapy and Sharkey sat together in the public bar chuckling at the little joke they had played on the unfortunate yard man.

'Wait till 'e looks in a mirrer,' Sharkey laughed. "E'll fink 'e's got yeller fever.'

Soapy almost choked on his beer at the thought. 'Jack Oxford wouldn't look in a mirrer,' he spluttered. "E couldn't stand the sight of 'imself. Anyway, I don't fink they 'ave mirrers in the doss-'ouse where Jack stays. If they did 'e wouldn't cut 'imself so much when 'e shaves. Ain't yer ever noticed 'ow many bits o' fag paper the silly bleeder 'as stuck round 'is clock in the mornin's?'

Sharkey grinned as he picked up his pint of ale. 'Jack Oxford gets those cuts from the blunt carvin' knife 'e uses,' he replied. 'One o' these days 'e's gonna cut 'is froat, that's fer certain.'

Soapy wiped the froth away from his mouth with the back of his hand. "Ere, Sharkey, d'yer reckon we should've used that dye stuff?' he wondered aloud. 'The poor sod might be stained fer life.'

Sharkey shook his head emphatically. 'Nah. It'll wear orf in a few weeks. Anyway, it won't 'urt 'im. That stuff don't do the 'arness any 'arm, an' it'll certainly be an improvement on ole Jack. Bloody 'ell, Soapy, 'e's enough ter frighten the daylights out o' the kids when 'e's normal. Yer should 'ave 'eard ole Fanny Johnson go orf at 'im. 'E made 'er baby cry when she come by the yard the ovver day, an' she told 'im ter piss orf out of it. Mind yer, 'e was only tryin' ter make the little mite laugh. Trouble was Jack was dribblin' all over the pram.'

Soapy finished his beer and pushed the empty glass away from him. 'Well I'm orf 'ome,' he announced.

As the two made to leave Alec Crossley leaned across the counter. 'You lads look pleased wiv yerselves,' he remarked.

'Yeah, we bin doin' a bit o' sprucin' up in the yard,' Sharkey told him straight-faced. 'Turned out a treat it did.'

Alec pointed to the leather dye on Soapy's hands. 'Yer

wanna be careful o' that stuff,' he said. 'I knew a bloke who got dye splashed all over 'is face once. Terrible face 'e 'ad.'

'Did 'e?' Sharkey replied, giving Soapy a worried glance as they left the pub.

When Jack Oxford roused himself he felt a tightness in his face and he scratched at his chin. 'Bloody gnats,' he grumbled aloud as he stood up and brushed himself down. He could hear his name being called and peered out of the window down into the yard.

'Jus' tidyin' up,' he called down, looking to make sure there were no telltale pieces of straw stuck to his clothes.

'Get orf 'ome, Jack, I wanna lock up,' the voice called out.

Jack Oxford hurried down the ramp, still scratching at his irritated face. As he walked past the office, the accountant came out.

'Good Lord!' Gallagher gasped, adjusting his spectacles in disbelief.

Jack shrugged his shoulders and walked out into Page Street, intending to go straight to the fish shop in Jamaica Road. Florrie Axford was standing at her front door pondering over just where she would place the women for the demonstration when the yard man walked by.

'Oh my Gawd!' she gasped, following the retreating man with her bulging eyes.

Jack frowned in puzzlement. 'What's the matter wiv everybody?' he said aloud as he hurried across the busy main thoroughfare.

The smell of frying fish and chips made him lick his lips. As he walked through the door of the shop an old lady gave him a stare and hurried out. The shopkeeper was shovelling hot chips from the fryer into a container and did not look up as Jack approached the counter.

'Give us a pen'orth o' cod an' a 'a'porth o' chips,' he said, slapping down the coins on the high counter.

The proprietor served up Jack's order into a sheet of newspaper. As he wrapped it and put the bundle down on the counter, he looked up. His mouth dropped open and his eyes stared out at his customer in shocked surprise. 'Christ Almighty!' he gasped, snatching up the coins and backing away a pace.

Jack picked up his parcel of fish and chips and was about to give his food a liberal sprinkling of vinegar when the shopowner snatched the bottle away.

'Yer better get out o' me shop,' he said quickly, his voice rising. 'Go on, 'oppit!'

The yard man walked to the door and turned back, wondering what he could have done to upset the shopkeeper.

'Go on, I told yer ter 'oppit!' the man said, holding the wire scoop up in a threatening manner.

'Sod yer then,' Jack called out as he turned on his heel and walked off towards the lodging-house in Tower Bridge Road, picking at the fish and chips as he went. Faces turned as he walked by and one old lady crossed herself as she passed him.

Jack sat down on a low wall to finish his meal. Passers-by stared at him and gave him a wide berth. Only a mangy dog warily came near him and sat down, hoping for a scrap of food to come its way. Jack threw the animal a piece of crackling but the dog merely sniffed at it and trotted off.

By the time he had reached his lodging-house, Jack was totally perplexed. As he walked through the open door his way was barred by a frightened-looking man holding up his hands.

'Yer can't come in 'ere!' he cried, backing away.

'Why not?' Jack said, scratching his itching face.

''Cos I'm full up,' the lodging-house keeper said quickly, shutting the door in his face.

*

At seven-thirty sharp on Friday morning George Galloway drove up in his pony-and-trap. William had already opened up the yard and some of the carts were leaving. George was wearing his brown tweed suit and brown derby hat, as was his custom on selling days. When he had parked the trap he walked into the office and seated himself at his desk.

His yard foreman was giving instructions to one of the carmen. 'Mornin' Guv'nor,' he said, looking over.

'Mornin', Will. Can yer get Oxford ter swill the yard down an' put the broom over it? I want the place clean an' tidy when the army arrive.'

William walked to the office door and looked away up the street before replying. ''E's not in yet, George,' he said. 'It's unusual fer 'im. Usually he's waitin' at the gate fer me ter open up.'

Sharkey and Soapy were making heavy work of harnessing their horses in the hope that the victim of their jape would soon appear. Their dalliance had not gone unnoticed by the firm's owner.

'What's them two 'angin' about for, Will? They should 'ave bin out o' the yard ten minutes ago,' he growled.

As he went to the door, William caught sight of Jack Oxford just coming into the yard. 'Gawd 'elp us!' he gasped, staring at the yard man's bright yellow face. 'What yer done ter yerself?'

Sharkey and Soapy sat up in their seats, laughing loudly. 'It's the dreaded fever!' Soapy shouted.

'Bring out yer dead! Keep 'im away from the 'orses!' Sharkey called out.

William gave the two carmen a blinding look and waved them out of the yard. He recalled the twosome's strange behaviour the previous evening and suspected that they were behind Jack's strange appearance. 'Come in the office,' he said, taking the yard man's arm and leading him to a cracked mirror propped up on the desk top.

When Jack saw his reflection he backed away from the mirror in disbelief. 'What is it?' he cried, staring at William in shock.

'I'd say yer got a dose o' black swine fever,' George said, winking at William. 'D'yer feel sick or sweaty?'

The yard man shook his head vigorously. 'I wondered why everybody was lookin' at me last night,' he sounded off. 'I got chucked out o' the fish shop, an' they wouldn't let me sleep at the lodgin'-'ouse. When I went ter the 'orseshoe fer a drink they wouldn't let me in so I 'ad ter get ole Blind Bill ter go in an' get me a quart bottle o' stout. I 'ad ter kip down in the park, that's why I'm late.'

George glanced at William, a smirk on his face. 'I bet it was them two whoresons,' he whispered, nodding his head in the direction of the yard.

William shrugged his shoulders. 'Your guess is as good as mine,' he answered, trying not to laugh at Jack's predicament.

'Is it painful?' George asked, beginning to enjoy himself.

'It's bloody itchy,' Jack replied, scratching at his face again.

'Um. That's always the trouble wiv black swine fever. I tell yer, it can be pretty nasty,' George pronounced, looking suitably serious.

William was beginning to feel sorry for the unfortunate man who had slumped down in a chair, dismayed. 'It's all right, it ain't deadly. It'll soon go,' he said kindly.

George was not feeling so sympathetic towards his retarded employee. 'I don't know so much,' he said, stroking his chin. 'Normally it only attacks 'orses. It's carried by the black mosquito. They bite pigs an' suck their blood, then they pass it on ter the 'orses. I remember when ole Charlie Brown lost 'alf 'is stable over black swine fever. 'Ad ter shoot the lot of 'em in the end. Suffered terrible, they did.'

Jack was now in a panic. He looked up at them with a pitiful expression. 'What am I gonna do?' he groaned.

'D'yer feel ill?' George asked, turning away from the man to hide his amusement.

'I feel all right, apart from this bloody itchin',' Jack said hopefully.

'Um. May not be swine fever, then. P'raps it's straw blight,' George said, thoughtfully stroking his chin.

'What's that?' Jack asked quickly, fearing some more frightening information.

'It's caught from straw flies. Sometimes when yer sleep in 'aystacks, yer get bitten. Yer ain't bin sleepin' up in the loft lately, 'ave yer, Jack?' George asked, hardly able to contain himself.

The yard man did not know what he should say and merely shook his head.

'Well, it must be the black swine fever then,' George declared, shaking his head sadly at William.

'I, er, I did sort o' take a nap yesterday afternoon, Guv'nor,' Jack said in a crushed voice. 'All the work was done though. I jus' come over tired.'

George sat down in his desk chair and looked hard at the pathetic character facing him. 'It serves yer right fer sleepin' on the job,' he said sternly. 'I'm gonna overlook it this time but I don't want no more slackin', understand?'

Jack nodded his head vigorously. 'All right, Guv'nor, I won't let it 'appen again. Will this get better?' he asked, touching his face.

'It should wear off in a year or two, I reckon,' George replied, glancing at his foreman.

'A year or two?' Jack groaned.

William felt that the joke had gone on long enough. 'P'raps we could try the turpentine treatment, Guv'nor,' he suggested.

George nodded and held his hand up to his face. 'Let 'im clean that yard up first, Will,' he spluttered.

'Right. Out yer go, then,' William said. 'An' make a good job of it. We've got the army comin' down terday. After yer finished, I'll get my Nellie ter try the treatment on yer face.'

As soon as the yard man had left the office, George and William burst out laughing. George wiped his streaming eyes with a handkerchief and William sat holding his middle.

'What did they use on 'im, fer Chrissake?' George asked, still grinning widely.

'It must 'ave bin that preservative we keep fer the 'arness,' William answered through chuckles. 'My Nellie's gonna need ter take the scrubbin' brush ter the poor sod.'

There was an atmosphere of excitement in Page Street as the women hurried back and forth with their shopping. As she did the dishes and tidied up her scullery, Maudie Mycroft could not stop thinking about the conversation she had had with her husband Ernest the previous evening. It had left her feeling piqued by his lack of understanding.

'I'm worried about what the women are gonna say, Ern,' she had told him. 'If it gets in the papers, I won't be able ter 'old me 'ead up at the church women's meetin'.'

'Sod 'em,' was his short answer.

'It's all right fer you,' Maudie complained. 'I'm the one who's gotta take the dirty looks an' the nasty remarks. Put yerself in my place. 'Ow would you like it?'

Ernest put down the boot he was polishing. 'Look, Maudie,' he said quietly, 'I fink what yer doin' is very brave. Yer all goin' out there an' facin' up ter that ole bastard Galloway. Yer doin' it fer the kids. It's a wonder one of 'em ain't bin killed already. Yer like our army goin' out ter face the Boers. Come ter fink of it, it wouldn't be a bad fing if yer all started singin' when yer facin' 'im.'

'Singin'?'

'Yeah, singin'. Yer could start up wiv "Onward Christian Soldiers". If that got in the papers, yer'd be looked up to at the muvvers' meetin'.'

Maudie's face brightened up considerably. 'What a good idea,' she cried. Then her enthusiasm suddenly faded. 'S'posin' they bring the Black Maria down, Ern?'

'Don't worry,' he laughed. 'I'll come an' bail yer out.'

Now as Maudie unpacked her shopping and adjusted her clean curtains, she was feeling very nervous. She had already seen Sadie Sullivan who said she had sorted out a rolling-pin for the occasion. What must those suffragettes feel like? she agonised. Chaining themselves to railings and being sent off to prison then being force-fed when they went on their hunger strikes. They must be very brave, what with having to endure the jeers and bad stories about them in the newspapers. Would she be as brave if things got out of hand? As she dusted her mantelshelf and adjusted the ornaments, Maudie had visions of being led away by two burly policemen and after a trial at the Old Bailey having a cell door slammed on her. 'Oh dear, oh dear. What have you got me into, Florrie?' she moaned aloud.

The redoubtable leader of the forthcoming protest was becoming impatient. Florence Axford looked around, her bottom lip pouting. The house was tidy and the washing was hanging out in the backyard. The front doorstep was clean and the scrag of mutton was cooking slowly in the kitchen range oven. She looked at herself in the overmantel mirror and pushed the hairpin further into her tightly gathered bun.

Florrie liked to keep herself busy during the day. She always finished her cleaning job at the Tooley Street offices by nine o'clock in the morning, and her evening job serving behind the counter at the faggot and pease pudding shop did not start until seven. She needed little sleep, and today of all days she felt too excited to take a nap. The kettle was singing in the grate. As she set about making yet another cup of tea, Florrie heard the loud clip-clop on the cobbles.

George Galloway was standing in the yard, his thumbs hooked into his waistcoat as the two riders trotted into the yard and dismounted. Jack Oxford had hosed down the yard and busied himself about the stables. He was anxious to get something done about his itching, bright yellow face but was ushered quickly out of the way into his store shed as soon as the soldiers appeared, earlier than expected.

'Get in there quick or you'll scare the 'orses,' William said, grinning. 'I'll get yer sorted out later.'

The tall figure of a Royal Artillery major was wearing breeches and highly polished boots. His black peaked cap reflected the sun as he stepped up to the firm's owner and shook his hand warmly.

'Nice to see you again, Mr Galloway,' he said in his clipped voice. 'I'd like you to meet Lieutenant Robinson. He's our new adjutant. Knows a thing or two about horses too, I might add.'

The second officer stepped forward to shake hands with Galloway, and after the pleasantries were over the three men walked into the office. George took a bottle from the drawer of his desk and poured three measures of Scotch.

'We've got a good selection,' he said, passing over the drinks. 'Good Irish Draughts. First-rate condition an' they're all seventeen 'ands. Ideal fer pullin' gun carriages, I would say.'

'Well, that sounds fine, Mr Galloway,' the major said, glancing at the adjutant. 'We've the authority to purchase and you've got the bid price from the War Office, I understand.'

George nodded and reached for the bottle once more. 'I fink you'll like what yer see, Major,' he said, refilling the glasses.

Along the street outside, the women were ready. Front doors were open and folk stood around waiting for Florrie Axford to give the word. They did not have long to wait. When the first horse was led up to the gates, Florrie marched down the middle of the turning. 'Righto, out yer come!' she cried.

'Good Lord! What the devil's going on?' the adjutant asked, glancing at his fellow officer.

George joined the soldiers at the gate. His face flushed with anger. The women had formed themselves into two lines, blocking both ends of the street, and were now making themselves comfortable. Sadie Sullivan had a rolling-pin resting in her lap and Maisie Dougall had brought out a colander and was proceeding to shell peas. Aggie Temple was starting on her knitting. Only Maudie Mycroft pinched her jaw nervously as she stared at the group by the gate.

'C'mon now, ladies, don't be silly,' Galloway called out. 'We've gotta run these 'orses up the street.'

'Not in our bleedin' turnin' yer don't,' Florrie called back defiantly.

Galloway walked quickly up to the women's leader and stood facing her, his features dark with anger. 'What's all this about?' he demanded.

'I'll tell yer what it's about,' Florrie replied, glaring back at him. 'We're just about fed up wiv' avin' ter keep our kids off the street while you run those 'orses. One o' these days a kid's gonna get killed, so we're stoppin' yer little game.'

'Game! Game!' George spluttered. 'I'm sellin' those 'orses

ter the army an' they've a right ter see what they're buyin'. I've gotta run 'em.'

'Not in our street yer don't. Not any more,' Florrie said firmly.

'Walk 'em up an' down in yer poxy yard,' Sadie called out.

'Piss orf out of it,' shouted Maisie.

'Tell the army ter piss orf back where they come from,' someone else called out.

Galloway held up his hands. 'Now look, ladies. The kids are at school. We can be finished before they come 'ome.'

'It ain't jus' the kids,' Florrie said, looking around at the nodding faces. 'We're all likely ter get trampled on. It ain't right ter gallop them bloody 'orses up an' down outside our 'ouses. Now I'm tellin' yer straight – yer ain't gonna do it so yer might as well get used ter the idea.'

Galloway glared at the determined woman and tried to decide what to do. 'I'll get the police,' he threatened.

'You do that,' Florrie goaded him. 'We'll tell 'em the same as we're tellin' you. Besides, if yer bring in the rozzers it'll get in the papers, an' ovver streets might back us up. Nah, I don't fink that's a very good idea, do you, gels?'

Loud voices shouted their support along the turning and the cartage contractor winced. 'Right,' he said, his eyes narrowing with menace. 'I'm givin' yer five minutes ter clear the street, an' if yer ain't gorn by then I'll turn the 'ose on yer.'

Florrie watched as Galloway strode quickly back to the gates. 'Stay put, ladies,' she called out. ''E wouldn't dare.'

The two officers had retreated back into the office and were looking perplexed. Galloway stormed back into the yard, cursing loudly. 'Oxford! Get yerself out 'ere,' he bawled out.

The soldiers peered out of the office window and saw the tall, shuffling figure of the yard man emerge from the shed. They looked at each other in disbelief. 'Good God! Who's that?' the adjutant gasped, wide-eyed. 'It looks like a blasted banshee.'

Galloway took Jack Oxford roughly by the arm. 'I've got a job fer yer,' he bellowed. 'Get that 'osepipe out an' connect it up.'

Jack scratched his head in puzzlement. He had only just rolled it up and now they wanted him to do the yard again. 'It's clean, Guv'nor. I done it first fing,' he said in a pained voice.

'Jus' do as yer told an' connect it up,' Galloway growled.

The yard man shuffled back to his store shed and came back carrying the heavy rubber hosepipe. When he had secured the connection to the stand pipe, Galloway handed him the nozzle. 'Right. Get outside an' 'ose those silly mares down,' he said gruffly. 'If yer make a good job of it, I'll buy yer a pint.'

Jack did not understand what the boss was talking about but his face broke into a crooked grin. He had worked at the yard for a number of years and had never known the boss offer to buy him a pint before. He shuffled out through the gate, pulling the heavy hose behind him. When he saw the two lines of women sitting across the street, he chuckled loudly.

When they caught sight of Jack Oxford brandishing the hosepipe, they gasped and stared open-mouthed.

'What the bloody 'ell's 'e done ter 'is face?' Maisie asked Aggie.

'Get back in that yard, yer syphilitic ole sod,' Sadie shouted at him.

'Where yer takin' that 'osepipe – down the chinkie laundry?' someone called out.

Jack Oxford leered at the women. There were one or two of them he was going to take pleasure in dousing. That Sullivan woman had clipped him around the ear when he chased her son away from the yard, and that Axford woman was always giving him funny looks when he passed her in the street. He stood with his feet apart and the hose pointing at the women and waited while Galloway addressed them.

'Right then. Yer've 'ad yer five minutes,' the firm owner said in a loud voice. 'Now yer gonna get wet.'

Jack's leering grin widened and he jerked the nozzle in the direction of the women in a threatening manner. Galloway stormed back into the yard. As he was about to turn the water on William confronted him.

'Look, George, there's no need ter go this far. We can exercise the 'orses in the yard. There's room ter trot 'em,' he said quietly.

Galloway glared at his yard foreman. 'I want those 'orses run up the street,' he declared. 'I ain't bowin' ter a load o' scatty women. I've give 'em fair warnin' an' they won't move, so I'm gonna make 'em.'

William stood in front of the stand pipe, his face set hard. 'I still reckon yer makin' a mistake, George,' he said.

The two stared at each other. There were times in their boyhood when there had been a clash of wills and in the past Galloway had always got his way. On this occasion, however, he was not so sure.

'Get out o' the way, Will,' he said in a low voice.

Outside in the street the women had become quiet and Jack Oxford stood with a maniacal expression on his bright yellow face.

The curtains in the house adjoining the yard moved back into position as Nellie Tanner hurried out to the backyard. She had been watching the developing situation with mounting concern. Florrie had not invited her to take part in the women's demonstration. 'I won't ask yer, Nell,' she had said. 'We all know your Will works fer the ole bastard an' it's likely ter cost 'im 'is job if Galloway sees yer in the street alongside us. Yer done yer bit tellin' us when the army's comin' so don't worry about it. We all know yer position.'

Nellie had agonised over what Florrie said. They were demonstrating for the kids, after all, and she felt deep down that it was her duty to join them, regardless of what Galloway might do in reprisal. Will would not have forbidden her to join the women if he had known, she felt sure. He would take his chances and face Galloway. Now, as she saw Jack Oxford pulling out the hosepipe, Nellie knew what she had to do.

Maudie was shaking from head to foot as she waited. Suddenly she remembered her Ernest's advice. Slowly, she stood up.

'"Onward Christian soldiers, marching as to war,"' she began to sing in a shrill voice.

'Sit down, yer silly mare,' Maisie said, pulling at her coat sleeve.

Maudie slumped down in her seat, suddenly feeling very silly, but she was heartened to see Sadie Sullivan jump up.

'Good fer you, Maudie,' she cried out, waving her rolling-pin over her head. 'That's what I say too. Onward Christian soldiers! I'm gonna crown that yellow-faced, stupid-lookin' bastard right now.'

Florrie caught her arm and Sadie rounded on her. A violent confrontation between the two seemed inevitable, but at that moment a murmur passed through the assembled crowd. The figure of Nellie Tanner suddenly appeared in the street. Without saying a word she marched up to the gate, took out a chopper from beneath her shawl, raised it high above her head and brought it down heavily on the hosepipe.

A loud cheer rang out as Nellie straightened up and stood looking at the women for a moment or two, then without further ado she turned on her heel and walked back into her house, closing the door.

Jack Oxford realised he was not now going to use the hosepipe. He shuffled back into the yard, trailing a length of rubber tubing behind him, with the obscene remarks of the victorious women ringing in his ears.

'Shut them gates,' Galloway shouted, his face a dark mask. 'We'll parade the 'orses in the yard.'

William could hardly believe his eyes when Nellie came on to the scene. Now, as he went to fetch the first horse from the stable, the gravity of her act of defiance began to sink in. Galloway was not the sort of person to forget what had happened and he would certainly remember that it was Nellie who had humiliated him in front of all the women. As he led the first horse out into the yard, William was feeling more than a little worried.

Chapter Five

Carrie felt miserable as she walked home from school with Sara. It was two weeks since the trouble at the yard and there had been a big row between her parents. It had created a strained atmosphere in the house which even the boys had noticed. Carrie was especially unhappy because she knew that her father was going to Wanstead for fresh bales of hay on Saturday and she had not been able to bring herself to ask if Sara could go with her on the trip. In fact, the way things were her father might decide not to take her either, she thought. He had become grumpy and short-tempered, and when she had asked him to let her help him in the yard the previous evening he had said no.

That Friday evening everyone had been talking excitedly about the protest. Carrie had sat in her back bedroom and heard harsh words between her parents. From what she had gathered, it seemed her father blamed her mother for making things difficult for him. But Mr Galloway was wrong to attempt to use the hosepipe on the women, and it was brave of her mother to stop it happening, she reasoned. It was also Mr Galloway's fault that her mother and father were rowing and that her father might not take her and Sara on the next trip. It wasn't fair, she told herself. She had been on the trip many times, but poor Sara had never been once and had been hoping to go next time. Why did she have to tell her friend all about how nice it was and how she would speak to her father about taking her next time? She should have asked him first before saying anything to Sara. Well, she wasn't going to give up, Carrie decided. She would ask him anyway.

Sara had been quiet on the walk home and when they neared Page Street she suddenly broke her silence. 'I don't fink I'll be in school termorrer, Carrie,' she said. 'Me mum's not well an' I might 'ave ter mind the little ones.'

Carrie smiled sympathetically. 'I 'ope she gets better soon.'

Sara fell silent again until they reached Carrie's front door, then she fixed her friend with her pale blue eyes. 'If the trip is this week, don't ask fer me ter go, Carrie. I won't be able ter come.'

The Tanner girl nodded sadly and watched her friend walk away along the turning.

That night after tea her father said that he had to go and clean out the boiler, ready for the chaff-cutting. Carrie asked if she could help him. William was surprised. Whenever he went into the yard to tend the horses Carrie was at his heels, but she had never offered to help him with the messy job of boiler-cleaning. 'All right, but change that school dress,' he told her.

While William cleaned out the fire pan and then set about unbolting the inspection plate on the side of the boiler, Carrie made herself busy sweeping out the shed. Then she sat on an upturned crate by her father's side while he reached inside the boiler to remove the loose scale. Suddenly he cursed and withdrew his hand quickly. Blood dripped from his finger. He sucked on the deep cut, spitting a mouthful of blood on the clean floor. Carrie quickly reached down to the hem of her petticoat and tore off a strip of linen. William watched the serious expression on his daughter's face as she deftly bound up his finger, and a smile formed on his lips. 'Proper little nurse, ain't yer?' he said quietly.

Carrie grinned back at him and suddenly he melted. She was certainly a grown-up nine year old, he thought. Maybe he had been a little hard on the children lately, but it had been difficult at the yard since the trouble with the women. George had been like a bear with a sore head, even though he had managed to sell all twelve of the horses to the army. He had not mentioned Nellie's part in the protest but there had been a strained atmosphere whenever the boss walked into the office. No doubt he blamed Will for Nellie's actions, but George had known her long enough himself to realise she was a very determined woman. Once she made her mind up there was no putting her off.

William set about refitting the inspection plate with Carrie handing him the bolts. When the last one had been screwed down tight, she fixed him with her eyes.

'Dad, I was gonna ask yer if me an' my best friend Sara could come wiv yer on Saturday but it doesn't matter now,' she said quietly.

William could see the sadness in his daughter's eyes. 'Don't yer wanna come then?' he asked.

'Of course I do, Dad, but I've bin lots o' times an' I thought it'd be nice if Sara could come this time. She's never bin anywhere, an' I've bin tellin' 'er all about the trip. I said I was gonna ask yer if she could come wiv us, but she can't now.'

'Oh, an' why's that then?' William asked.

''Er muvver's took ill an' Sara's gotta look after 'er,' Carrie replied.

William sat down on the brick base of the boiler and studied his bandaged finger for a few moments. 'Is Sara that gel yer walk 'ome from school wiv? 'Er wiv the raggety clothes?'

Carrie nodded. 'It's ever so sad, Dad. Sara 'as ter look after all 'er bruvvers an' sisters while 'er muvver goes out ter work, an' 'er farvver's a cripple. Sara gets ill a lot. I don't fink they 'ave much food.'

'Fings are bad fer most people,' he said quietly. 'It's lucky fer us I'm in regular work. Mind yer, after what yer mum done ter Galloway's 'osepipe, it's a wonder I ain't got sacked.'

Carrie caught the humorous look in his eyes and suddenly they both burst out laughing.

'Serves the ole goat right,' he spluttered, wiping his eyes on the back of his hand.

'Can Sara come wiv us one time, Dad?' she asked suddenly.

William nodded. 'I should fink so. If she wants to.'

'She'll be so pleased when I tell 'er,' Carrie said, suddenly hugging her father.

William was embarrassed by her spontaneous show of affection and he looked down at his feet. 'Well, we'd better get these tools tergevver an' lock up,' he said, 'or yer mum'll nag me fer keepin' yer up.'

The hour was late and Nellie was making cocoa. She felt happy that the tension between her and William had vanished, and hummed softly as she stirred the hot liquid. William had slipped up on her and put his arms around her waist as she was drawing the blinds. His lingering kiss on the back of her neck had made her shiver with pleasure. She had turned to face him and returned his kiss. Now, as she handed him a large mug of steaming cocoa and sat down facing him, Nellie could see William had become thoughtful. For a while they were both silent as they sipped their hot drinks, then suddenly he put his mug down on the edge of the fender and looked at her.

'Carrie was tellin' me about that friend of 'ers.'

Nellie shook her head sadly. 'It's a shame about that family,' she answered. 'They live in Bacon Street Buildin's. Florrie Axford knows them well. She said the gel's farvver is on relief an' 'e sells bits an' pieces from a suitcase in the markets. 'E 'as ter go over the water ter do 'is sellin'. Poplar an' Whitechapel, I fink Florrie said. 'E can't do any sellin' around 'ere, somebody's bound ter give 'im away. Bloody shame really.'

'Can't 'e do anyfink else?' William asked.

Nellie shook her head. ''E 'ad a bad accident in the docks a few years ago. Got smashed up bad, by all accounts. Florrie said 'e broke 'is back an' both legs. One's inches shorter than the ovver. 'E can't do any 'eavy work at all now.'

'Carrie told me she was goin' ter ask if I'd let Sara come wiv us on Saturday but the kid can't come now. 'Er muvver's ill apparently an' she's gotta look after 'er.'

Nellie finished her cocoa and put the mug down on the table. 'It mus' be bloody 'ard fer the kid. She looks a poor little mite. 'Er clothes look like they're fallin' off 'er. I fink I'll 'ave a word wiv Florrie termorrer. P'raps we can sort a few bits an' pieces out fer the kid ter wear.'

William nodded. 'I don't s'pose Florrie's got anyfink though,' he said. 'She never 'ad any kids.'

'Florrie knows a lot o' people round 'ere,' Nellie replied. 'I bet she'll scrounge somefink.'

William stood up and yawned, then he reached out for Nellie's hand. 'C'mon, luv,' he said. 'Let's go ter bed.'

She stood up and felt the strong grip as his hand closed around hers. 'I mus' remember ter talk ter Florrie termorrer,' she said, yawning.

*

It was late when Nora Flynn heard the front door shut. She had looked in at the room directly below hers once or twice and satisfied herself that Josephine was sleeping soundly, then she had settled down to read. The book fell from her lap as she stretched her arms above her head and yawned widely. The sound of a deep chuckle followed by a high-pitched giggle carried up to her room and she sighed irritably as she glanced up at the clock on the mantelshelf. It was past twelve. They'll wake Josie up if they're not careful, she thought, walking over to her door and pressing her ear against its panel.

There was a clattering noise and then the sound of a door closing. Nora waited a few minutes and then quietly went down the carpeted stairs and peered into the child's room once more. Josephine was sleeping soundly and Nora breathed a sigh of relief. As she turned and made her way back up to her own room she heard mumbled voices and then giggling. It was always the same with George, she thought. He would spend a week or more sitting in his darkened room in the evenings, drinking heavily, then as though feeling he had done his penance he would suddenly change and become almost friendly. It was then that he brought back those women. Nora knew where George spent his evenings when he went out. He had told her about the music hall in Abbey Street where saucily dressed girls danced around the tables. It was at the music hall that pleasure could be bought for a drink or two, but of course George had not told her that. Nora had known for some time of the dubious reputation of that particular hall and guessed that George's latest woman friend had been solicited there.

She sighed as she got undressed. There was a time when she would have welcomed George Galloway into her own bed, she admitted to herself. He was still an attractive man, although coarse and very often ill-mannered, and fate had made them akin. Both had lost their partners in tragic circumstances, and through the children Nora had steadily grown to know George. When the pain of her loss had eased and nights became more bearable, Nora had begun to think about her employer in a physical way. She had taken pains to make herself as presentable as possible and tried to please him with the meals she knew he was fond of. There had been little if any response from him, although occasionally he sat with her and talked at length about his problems. Nora had tried to open up to him about her own feelings but natural reserve inhibited her. In his own way George was still grieving, and her discreet attempts to let him know the way she felt were lost on him.

Nora had finally realised that she was not going to lure him into her bed and resigned herself to doing the job she was paid to do. Lately, George had become more morose, and a hard, unfeeling father to his two sons. As far as Josephine was concerned, his attitude seemed to be one of thinly veiled dislike. He spoke to the child only when he had to. It was left to Nora Flynn to provide the love and care lacking in the child's natural parent.

It was patently obvious to his housekeeper that George blamed the child for Martha's death. What he would not admit to himself, Nora reflected, was the fact that Martha was thirty-six and not very strong when he had made her pregnant. There had been a gap of eleven years since young Frank's birth and Martha had paid a tragic price for her third pregnancy. Maybe George did blame himself, she thought. Maybe in his inner thoughts he knew that he had been unfeeling and clumsy. Perhaps that was why he punished himself with the bottle, and with the hard-faced, painted tarts he brought home. He would do better to stay sober long enough to take stock. Maybe then he would see what was there for him under his own roof.

*

The following evening the two women walked purposefully along Page Street and turned left into Bacon Street. Each of them carried a brown paper carrier bag. As they reached the tenement block, Nellie Tanner pulled a face. 'Gawd 'elp us!' she breathed.

Florrie Axford nodded at Nellie's reaction on seeing the buildings close to. 'What a bloody dump,' she remarked, her eyes flitting over the front exterior of the dwellings and catching sight of a mangy cat sniffing at a kipper bone in a block doorway. 'Fancy 'avin' ter live in a place like this.'

Nellie nodded, screwing her face up as she stepped over an old newspaper that contained the remains of some fish and chips. 'I thought our ole 'ouses were bad enough, Flo,' she muttered incredulously.

Bacon Street Buildings was a four-storey tenement block which had been built in 1840 and had long since fallen into disrepair. There were four entrances which led up flights of stone stairs to small, unconnected landings on each level. On every landing there were four flats, and each storey contained sixteen flats. At the back of the building was a foul-smelling tannery. It was one of the larger rear flats on the top floor overlooking the factory that Florrie and Nellie were making for.

As they climbed the well-worn stairs, puffing at their exertions, the two women saw naked gas-jets spluttering out dim light on landings where the front doors had long since shed their coats of varnish. Sounds came drifting out from the flats. They heard babies crying and voices raised in anger as young, miserable children were scolded by despairing, miserable mothers.

When they reached the top landing Florrie stopped outside

number 32 and gave Nellie an anxious glance before knocking. After a few moments the door opened and they were confronted by the young Sara Knight, clad in a long dress with an apron tied around her middle. The child stood wide-eyed, her pallid face full of surprise as she looked up at the two visitors.

'We've got a few fings fer yer mum, Sara,' Florrie said, holding up her carrier bag.

The child stood back for the women to enter. As they walked into the disordered flat, they saw two young children sitting at the kitchen table. Both children's faces were smeared red as they ate slices of bread and jam. There was a low fire burning in the grate which was enclosed by a metal fire-guard. Freshly washed napkins had been placed across the guard and were steaming dry. The windows were covered with holed and grubby curtains, and equally grubby wallpaper hung down from the walls.

Sara led the way to the bedroom and Florrie and Nellie followed her in. The child's mother was propped up in bed with a blanket wrapped around her shoulders and a towel around her neck. On top of the bedclothes there was an old overcoat, and beside the bed medicine bottles and an empty soup bowl were sitting on a chair. A baby slept fitfully in a cot beneath the window and in the far corner a battered metal trunk stood against the water-stained wall.

Annie Knight pulled the blanket closer about her and forced a smile. 'Sara luv, bring the ladies a chair, there's a dear,' she croaked.

Sara left the room and returned with only one chair, looking at her mother for guidance. Florrie smiled at the child. 'It's all right, Sara, I'll sit on the bed,' she said.

When the child left the room, Florrie turned to Annie. 'I'm Florrie Axford and this is Nellie Tanner, Carrie's mum,' she

81

told her. 'We've got a few fings 'ere fer yer. 'Ope yer not offended?'

Annie smiled at Nellie. 'She's a nice gel, your Carrie. 'Er an' Sara seem ter git on very well.'

Nellie smiled back at the sick woman. 'Yeah, they do. My Carrie's always talkin' about your Sara.'

Annie's eyes suddenly clouded and she reached up the sleeve of her nightdress and pulled down a handkerchief with which she dabbed at her eyes for a moment. 'I'm sorry,' she said quietly. 'The place is a mess an' the doctor told me I can't get up yet. It's a lot fer Sara, but she's a good gel. She does the best she can.'

'What's wrong wiv yer, Annie?' Florrie asked.

'Doctor Preston said it's quinsy. It's burst, but it's left me so weak. I've gotta keep this towel roun' me neck. Sara does me bread poultices an' it's eased the pain. She's a good gel.'

Florrie fished down into her carrier bag and took out a bundle of clothes. 'Yer might be able ter make use o' these. There's a coat might do Sara a turn, Annie,' she said. 'They're all clean an' I know where they come from, gel.'

Annie smiled her thanks and watched as Nellie unpacked the contents of her bag and laid the articles on the end of the bed. The sick woman's eyes opened in surprise and gratitude as she saw tins of soup, a pat of butter wrapped in waxed paper, a large bag of biscuits and a block of strong red cheese. There was also a packet of tea and a tin of condensed goat's milk. When Nellie brought out the last item from the bag, a packet of dolly mixtures, Annie broke down and cried. She knew only too well how hard it must have been for people to provide her with such gifts from their own impoverished larders. The gift of sweets for the children had touched her heart and she shook her head as she struggled to find words to express her thanks.

'There's no need ter fank us, Annie,' Florrie said quietly. 'Yer'd be the first ter give if yer was able. We all look after our own round 'ere. It's the only way we can survive, an' bloody survive we will.'

Nellie had been choking back her own emotions as she saw the look of gratitude and wonderment on the white face of Annie Knight. Now she swallowed hard. 'Look, Mrs Knight, I was finkin',' she said. 'I don't know if Sara mentioned it ter yer, but my Will 'as ter collect bales of 'ay from the country now an' again an' 'e usually takes my Carrie wiv 'im. 'E was gonna take your Sara too but she told my gel she wouldn't be able ter go, what wiv yer bein' poorly. I was wonderin' if yer'd let 'er go? I could come in an' keep an eye on the little ones till she gets back in the evenin'.'

Annie was still trying to comprehend her good fortune and her eyes were bright with surprise as she nodded. 'It'd make a luvverly change fer her. She 'as worked 'ard an' she never complains. That's if yer really don't mind?'

Florrie reached out and touched Annie's arm. 'I'll come wiv Nellie too,' she said, smiling. 'It'll be no trouble, will it, Nell?'

Annie leaned back on her pillow and sighed deeply. 'I was feelin' very low when I woke up this mornin',' she said in a husky voice. 'The kids was bawlin' an' young Sara was strugglin' ter keep 'em quiet an' get me breakfast. I didn't care if I lived or died right then, but now I'm feelin' much better. Yer mus' fank all those people fer me, gels. An' fank yer both fer all yer kindness. I'll never ferget it.'

The women sat chatting for some time, then, as they said their goodbyes and made their way out into the kitchen, Nellie and Florrie exchanged glances. The two young children were sitting cross-legged in front of the fire-guard as Sara shared out the dolly mixtures between them.

The two women walked out of the flat and made their way back down into the dark street. It was not until they had turned into Page Street that they broke silence.

'Did yer see the look on those kids' faces when we came out?' Nellie said to her friend.

Florrie nodded. 'It was somefink ter see, wasn't it?' she said quietly.

Chapter Six

Sharkey Morris and his friend Soapy Symonds were sitting together in Charlie's coffee shop in Tooley Street. When the café owner's wife Beattie slapped down two thick toasted teacakes on the grey marble table, Sharkey opened his and looked at the cheese filling before taking a bite.

'I tell yer, Soapy, I reckon we should 'ave a word wiv Will Tanner first,' he said through a mouthful of food. 'Yer know what the ole man's bin like lately. P'raps if Tanner talks to 'im, 'e might cough up.'

Soapy pulled a face and wiped the hot butter from his full moustache with the back of one dirty hand. 'I dunno,' he said thoughtfully. 'Since that turn-out wiv Will's missus, 'e ain't bin the best o' pals wiv Galloway. Still, it might be the right way ter go about it at that. One fing's fer sure, the ole man's gotta know 'ow we feel. Tommy 'Atcher pays 'is men better wages than Galloway, an' even Charlie Morgan's carmen get bonuses.'

Sharkey snorted. 'I should reckon so too! The stench o' those skins is enough ter make a bloke ill. They 'ave ter swill their carts out every night before they go 'ome.'

'Well, that's as may be,' Soapy argued. 'What I'm sayin' is, we should put in fer a rise now. We should go in fer 'alf a crown a week.'

Sharkey took a large bite of his teacake and washed it down with a gulp of tea. 'Ten years I've worked fer Galloway,' he said, burping loudly, 'I'm the oldest servin' carman 'e's got since ole Bill Wimbush retired, and I ain't never known ole Galloway ter cough up wiv a rise unless we asked fer it. Tommy 'Atcher's carmen get a rise wivout askin'. If I could get a job there, I'd go termorrer. They wouldn't 'ave me there, though. Not since I clouted ole Spanner at the docks.'

Soapy had often heard the story about Sammy Spanner, Hatcher's shop steward, and queue-jumping at the docks, and each time it was different. 'Well, we gotta do somefink. It's a bloody pittance Galloway pays us,' he moaned. 'We should get one of us ter be a shop steward an' then we'd get fings sorted out.'

Sharkey grunted. 'An' who we gonna get? There's only eight regular carmen an' I ain't gonna do it fer one.'

'Me neivver,' Soapy replied. 'Yer can't expect those two new blokes ter do it. What about Sid Bristow? 'E seems ter get on wiv Galloway all right.'

Sharkey Morris shook his head. 'Sid's got a nice little job wiv the sack people, an' I fink 'e earns a bit on the side. I don't reckon fer one minute 'e's gonna be interested.'

'What about Lofty Russell?' Soapy persisted. ''E seems a sensible sort o' bloke. I 'eard 'im goin' on about the Boer War the ovver day. 'E seemed ter know what 'e was talkin' about.'

Once again Sharkey shook his head. ''E's got eight kids. Yer can't expect somebody wiv eight Gawd-ferbids ter stick 'is neck out.'

'Well, that only leaves the Blackwell bruvvers. I wonder if they'd be interested,' Soapy Symonds said hopefully.

This time Sharkey was silent for a few moments. 'Fred

won't, 'e's too quiet. Scratcher might though,' he said,
thoughtfully stroking his chin. ''E don't seem ter let fings get
on top of 'im. Remember when that 'orse bit 'is bruvver Fred
an' 'e punched it in the chops? I was sure that nag was gonna
drop when I saw its front legs splay out an' its eyes go all
funny.'

Soapy looked pleased. 'Right then,' he said cheerfully,
'when I get back ternight I'm gonna see if I can catch
Scratcher. I'll put it to 'im an' see what 'appens.'

Jack Oxford was busy cutting chaff. Occasionally he stroked
his still tender stubbled face. It was now two weeks since he
had been led into Will Tanner's house and subjected to the
turpentine cure. It had been a painful experience but it had
worked. The first application had stung his face but hard
rubbing with a house flannel produced results. When he
looked into the mirror which Nellie held up to his face, he saw
that the bright yellow colour had become dull and there were
patches of his own natural colour showing through. Jack had
subjected himself to another course of treatment before he was
satisfied that the yellow colouring was gone. The problem was
that the skin of his face had become very tender and he had
had to stop shaving for the past week. Now, as he pressed
down the hay into the cutting machine, the yard man was
feeling the need to take a nap, but the thought of being
attacked by insects and catching straw blight again deterred
him from settling down in the hay.

As he finished the remaining bale and turned off the
machine, Jack heard his name being called. He peered out of
the round loft window.

'Get yerself down 'ere, Jack,' William called up to him.
'I've gotta go out an' there's nobody in the office.'

When William left the firm the yard man made himself

comfortable in the office chair and stared at the phone. He had been instructed in what to do should the contraption ring but he felt a little nervous. He had never used a telephone and never learned to read and write. He would have to memorise any messages that came through and that was the main reason he was nervous. He knew that his memory wasn't too good, and if the message was a long one he would be in trouble.

The place was quiet, bright sunlight was shining down into the yard, and Jack started to relax a little. Maybe the phone wouldn't ring, he hoped. Maybe he could settle down for a little nap before Tanner got back. He eased himself back in the comfortable chair and placed his feet up on the open roll-top desk.

The loud ringing in the yard man's ears made him jump and his feet slipped from the desk top. For a few moments he sat rigid in his chair, staring at the telephone, then he stood up and backed away. The thing he had dreaded was happening. Jack bit on his bottom lip. Should he let it ring? No, he would have to answer it, he decided. It might be the boss ringing in with a message, and if he did not answer the phone he would be in trouble. He approached the instrument as though the thing might bite him, and with a shaking hand reached out and picked up the earpiece.

The voice at the other end spoke in a cultured tone. 'Johnson's Tanneries here. I'd like to speak to George Galloway, please.'

Jack looked around him in panic. ''E, er, I'm er, Oxford,' he stuttered.

'He's in Oxford, you say?'

'No. I'm Oxford. I'm, er, I'm mindin' the phone 'case it rings, yer see. Who are yer?'

'Well, now the phone has rung, will you kindly go and get

Mr Galloway, if you please?' the voice requested in a sarcastic tone.

Jack scratched his head and put his mouth closer to the mouthpiece. 'Mr Tanner's 'ere but 'e's 'ad ter go out an' 'e asked me ter mind the telephone,' he shouted.

There was a crackling sound as the caller puffed in exasperation then the measured tone sounded loudly in Jack's ear. 'Look, whoever you are, I don't want to speak to Mr Tanner, and I can't very well if he's had to go out, now can I? I would like to speak to Mr George Galloway. Will you go away and get him please, if that is all right with you?'

Jack was gaining in confidence now that he realised the telephone was not going to bite him. 'I jus' told yer, mate, 'e's gorn out,' he said boldly.

'No you did not,' the voice said, sounding angry. 'You said Mr Tanner went out. Now is Galloway there or isn't he?'

'Mr Galloway's not 'ere, but I can take a message,' Jack said helpfully.

'Ah. Now we're getting somewhere,' the voice continued more calmly. 'This is Mr Forbes of Johnson's Tanneries. Now have you a pencil handy?'

'What d'yer wanna pencil for?' Jack asked, frowning.

'Oh my God!' the voice exclaimed. '*I* don't need a pencil, *you* do! Now listen, the message is this: Mr Galloway is to ring me. I need to get his signature on the contract before next Thursday. Is that understood?'

Jack Oxford nodded.

'Well, is it?' the caller demanded in a loud voice.

'I'll tell 'im soon as 'e comes in,' Jack said, thankful that the message was not too difficult.

There was a loud click as the phone was slammed down, and for a while Jack stood listening to the burring noise.

'You gorn?' he shouted into the mouthpiece, and hearing no reply carefully replaced the earpiece on its hook.

The carts were beginning to return to the yard and William still had not returned. In the meantime, Jack had been reciting the message to himself over and over again. By the time the yard foreman walked into the office, he was sure that he had got it right.

'Any phone calls?' William asked.

'Yeah,' Jack replied, going over the message once more in his head.

'Well?'

'Mr Forbes rung the phone from Johnson's Tanneries,' Jack began. ''E said fer Mr Galloway ter give 'im a ring on Thursday. It's about the contract what's gotta be signed.'

William scribbled the message down on a slip of paper and placed it on Galloway's desk, then he marched out to confront the carmen who were standing in a group looking very serious about something.

On Saturday morning Sara Knight arrived at the Tanners' front door at eight o'clock sharp. She was wearing a long grey dress that had a patch in the bodice and hung loosely over her narrow shoulders. Her lace-up boots were polished and she carried a small parcel under her arm. Her long brown hair had been painstakingly brushed. It shone in the early morning light as she waited for her knock to be answered. Sara had been up since dawn. Already that morning she had cleaned the house and heated the porridge for her two younger brothers. The baby's rusk had been powdered into a small dish and when she heard the sound of the milkman's cart on the cobbles, Sara had hurried down to him carrying a jug. She had also cut some cheese sandwiches and wrapped them up in brown paper. The last thing she did before leaving was gently to take the baby from her cot and place her beside her sleeping mother. The tot had stirred then settled down. Sara had picked up the parcel and hurried down into the empty street, her stomach churning with excitement. When she reached the Tanners' house, she had to take a deep breath before she reached for the knocker.

When Carrie answered the door, she smiled happily at her friend. 'Cor, don't you look nice?' she said kindly. 'Me mum said she'll be leavin' in a few minutes. Mrs Axford is gonna sit wiv yer mum too, so it'll be all right.'

When the two children hurried into the yard, they saw William backing Titch between the shafts. They stood to one side, watching as he hooked up the cob's harness chains, and when he was satisfied all was ready William strode up and took Sara's hand.

'Wanna give Titch 'is titbit?' he smiled, handing her a knob of sugar.

As she timidly complied the horse bent its head and sucked up the sugar lump into its mouth, leaving Sara's hand wet. She wiped it down her dress and giggled happily.

'C'mon then up we go,' William said, hoisting the two girls into the back of the open cart and then leading the horse out into the street. The two friends stood at the front of the cart and waited while he relocked the front gates, then he took the reins in his hand and flicked them over the horse's back. As the cart picked up speed, William sprang up on to the shafts and into the high dicky seat. The girls held on tightly, smiling excitedly at each other as the cart rattled over the cobblestones and turned into the quiet Jamaica Road. Soon they were passing over Tower Bridge and could see the ships and barges moored beneath them. Above, the blue sky was streaked with cloud and a light breeze carried the smell of the river mud up on to the bridge. Sara's eyes were wide with excitement and

Carrie felt so happy that her friend had been able to come after all. At the far side of the bridge William pulled the cart up beside a water trough and let the horse drink its fill.

As they continued their journey along through the wide Mile End Road towards Bow, he chatted to the girls and pointed out the places of interest they passed. When they drew level with Bow Church, the two friends settled down in the well of the cart on the two sacks of chaff William had put there for them, and chatted together happily.

The day had remained fine and warm. Now, with the sun dipping below the high wharves, the tired horse pulled a full load of hay bales past the white stone Tower of London and on to the bridge. William sat slumped in the seat, his hands loose on the slack reins, allowing Titch to travel at his own pace. Above him the two girls lay in the well between the bales, staring up at the evening sky.

Sara sighed happily and thought of all the things she would be able to talk about when she got back home. It had been a very long journey. It must have been miles and miles, she recalled. They had left the houses and factories behind them and then taken a road that had trees and open fields on either side. They had stopped at a little pub with flowers growing around the door and sat at a table in a lovely garden, and then Carrie's dad had brought them out glasses of fizzy lemonade. Carrie had opened the brown paper parcel and shared her cheese sandwiches, and then they had left for the farm. It had cows and pigs and geese, whose feathers were all muddy.

They had held hands as the nice lady at the farm took them to the barn to see the calves. The lady had given them each a glass of milk and biscuits, and before they left Carrie's dad had climbed on top of the load and made a space for them to lie in. They had climbed up the rickety ladder, each clasping a little bunch of wild flowers they had picked, and then nestled down in the hay to share the last cheese sandwich as the cart pulled out of the farm and drove down the bumpy lane to the main road. There was so much to tell, so much to remember, she thought. As the hay wagon passed the brewery and turned into Tooley Street, Sara felt it had been the happiest day of her life.

On Monday morning, after the last of the vans had left the yard, George Galloway put his head out of the office door and called out to his yard foreman. William walked into the office knowing a row was brewing. George had driven his trap in early that morning and had stood in the office doorway to watch the carts leaving with a stern look on his face.

'Close the door an' sit down, Will,' he said, sitting himself at his desk and swivelling round in the chair to face the younger man. 'Now what's all this about the carmen 'avin' a grouse?'

William had noticed George talking to Sid Bristow earlier and was sure the carman had informed him of the grievance. He took a deep breath. 'The men wanna see yer about a rise,' he began. 'They've got themselves a spokesman an' they wanna join the union.'

'Oh, they do, do they?' George replied. 'An' whose union do they wanna join then? Not that Ben Tillett's mob, I'ope. 'E's bin causin' ructions in the docks.'

'I dunno,' William answered, looking hard at the firm owner. 'They reckon they've got a genuine reason ter complain. Tommy 'Atcher's put 'is carmen's wages up an' word's got around. The men thought they should've got a rise last year an' now they reckon they're fallin' be'ind ovver firms' carmen.'

George slipped his thumbs into the pockets of his waistcoat

and leaned back in his chair. 'Who's their spokesman?' he asked.

'Scratcher Blackwell,' William replied. ''E asked me ter let yer know the way the men feel, an' 'e wants ter see yer ternight when 'e gets finished.'

'Oh, 'e does, does 'e? Well, you can tell Scratcher I'm not 'avin' a union in 'ere. What's more, I'm not gonna be bullied inter givin' rises, jus' because Tommy 'Atcher's decided ter give in ter 'is men.'

William stood up quickly. 'Maybe it'd be better if yer told 'im yerself, George,' he said, a note of anger in his voice. 'I'm paid ter look after the 'orses an' keep the carts on the road. I give out the work an' do a lot of ovver jobs around 'ere. I'm not paid ter be runnin' from pillar ter post wiv messages an' threats.'

George stared at his foreman for a moment or two, then his face broke into a smile. 'Sit down, Will,' he said with a wave of his hand. 'All right, I'll see Scratcher ternight, but I'm not gonna be intimidated. I ain't 'avin' the union people comin' in 'ere tryin' ter tell me 'ow ter run my business. Yer know me of old, I don't bow ter threats. Tell me somefink, Will, d'yer fink I should give 'em a rise?'

William shrugged his shoulders. 'That's fer you ter decide, George,' he replied, looking up quickly. 'One fing yer gotta remember though – those carmen of ours could get better wages workin' fer 'Atcher or Morgan. If yer wanna keep yer men, yer'll 'ave ter fink about that.'

Galloway nodded. 'All right, I'll give it some thought. By the way, 'ow's your Nellie? Does she still bear me a grudge?'

William was taken aback by the sudden enquiry. It was the first time George had said anything concerning Nellie's involvement with the women's protest. 'Nellie thought she was right ter do what she did,' he said quickly. 'She reckoned it was wrong ter send that idiot Oxford out there wiv an 'osepipe. An' I tell yer somefink else, George – *I* fink yer was in the wrong too. If she 'adn't cut that pipe, those women would 'ave got soaked. But as for bearin' yer a grudge, my Nellie ain't one for that. I should reckon she's fergot all about it.'

George nodded his head slowly. 'Well, that's nice ter know,' he said, a smile playing around his lips. 'Me an' you are old friends, Will. Yer do a good job 'ere an' I wouldn't wanna lose yer. Now, what about those two lame 'orses? 'Ow are they?'

William had sensed a veiled threat in his employer's remark. He knew that their old friendship would not count for much if George wanted to get rid of him.

'I've got 'em in the small stable,' he answered. 'They've both bin sweatin'. It may jus' be a cold fever. I won't know fer a day or two.'

'Yer don't fink it's the colic, do yer?'

William shook his head. 'I don't fink so. They're not rollin' in the stalls an' there's no sign o' blood in the dung. I'm keepin' me eye on 'em an' I'm gonna look in ternight. If there's any turn fer the worse, I'll get the vet in.'

Galloway nodded, content to leave the animals' welfare to his capable foreman. The trouble brewing with the carmen worried him though, and as soon as William had left the office he made a phone call.

When Sharkey drove back into the yard that evening, he saw that the trap was still there and took his time unhitching his horse. Soon Soapy drove in, closely followed by Scratcher Blackwell, who looked a little anxious as he led his pair of horses to the stable.

'Yer gonna see the ole man ain't yer, Scratch?' Soapy asked.

'I'm waitin' 'til everybody's in,' Scratcher replied quickly.

'Don't take any ole lip, mate. We're all be'ind yer,' Sharkey called out loudly as he led his horse to the water trough.

Scratcher winced, hoping that Sharkey's comment had not reached the office. He had had second thoughts about volunteering to be the spokesman and Sharkey's words worried him. It was a small firm by comparison with Tommy Hatcher's business and Scratcher knew only too well Galloway's reputation for dealing briskly with troublemakers. The information he had gathered from the union office in Tooley Street did not encourage him very much either. Picketing the yard and stopping Galloway trading would not do him any good if he was out of work, he thought. There was Betty and the two kids to think of. How was she going to manage if he put himself out of work?

The anxious carman suddenly found that he had no more time for worrying when William walked up to him. 'The ole man wants ter see yer in the office,' the yard foreman said, taking him by the arm. 'Mind 'ow yer go, Scratcher. Take a tip an' don't get too stroppy. Yer know 'ow cantankerous 'e can be.'

Scratcher nodded and hurried across the yard, William's warning adding to his feeling of dread.

'C'mon in, Blackwell. Sit down,' Galloway said without looking up.

Scratcher sat down and clasped his hands together, eyeing the firm owner warily. He had gone over in his mind the argument he was going to use, but now as he sat uncomfortably he felt more than a little worried.

Suddenly George Galloway swivelled his chair round and leaned back, his fingers playing with the silver watch chain hanging across his chest. 'Yer wanna see me?' he said.

'Well, Guv'nor, the men asked me ter come an' see yer,' he began quickly. 'It's about a rise. They reckon . . .'

'What about you? What der you reckon?' Galloway cut in.

'Well, I, er, I reckon we're entitled ter get a few bob extra a week. Most o' the ovver cartage firms 'ave give their carmen a rise,' Scratcher said spiritedly.

'An' yer've put yerself up as the spokesman?' Galloway said, still fingering his watch chain.

The worried carman looked down at his hands, then his eyes went up to meet Galloway's. 'The men asked me ter do the talkin'. They wanna get unionised. They reckon we should go the way most o' the ovver cartage firms 'ave gone.'

Galloway took his cue from the man's obvious discomfiture and leaned forward, his eyes boring into Scratcher's. 'Yer keep on about what *they* want an' what *they* said – I fink yer've bin primin' 'em up. I reckon yer've bin listenin' ter those troublemakers at the union an' yer fink yer can put a bit o' pressure on.'

Scratcher shook his head. 'I'm jus' a spokesman,' he answered.

Galloway took out his watch and glanced at it. The phonecall he had made to the union office had reassured him. 'Let me tell yer what I'm prepared ter do, Blackwell,' he said quietly. 'I'm puttin' the men's wages up by 'alf a crown a week. As fer joinin' the union . . . there's gonna be no union in this yard, yer can tell the men that from me. Oh, an' anuvver fing. I don't care fer troublemakers. Yer can finish the week out. Yer leave Friday.'

Scratcher stood up, his face flushed with shock. 'Yer mean I'm sacked?' he gasped.

'That's right. That's exactly what I mean,' Galloway said derisively, swivelling round to face his desk.

The shocked carman walked out of the office and crossed the yard to his waiting workmates. 'Yer've got 'alf a crown a week,' he said in a flat voice. 'An' I'm out the door.'

''E can't do that!' Sharkey shouted.

'Well, 'e 'as,' Scratcher replied.

'What we gonna do about it?' Soapy asked, looking around for support.

The rest of the men were silent. Lofty Russell looked down at his feet. 'What can we do? If we try anyfing the ole bastard'll sack the lot of us,' he moaned.

The men shuffled about uncomfortably, shaking their heads. Scratcher's brother Fred suddenly rounded on Soapy. 'You was the one who wanted 'im ter go an' see Galloway,' he said, glaring. 'You was the one who said the men was gonna back 'im. Well, c'mon then. Let's see yer back 'im now.'

Soapy averted his eyes. 'I'll back 'im if the rest will,' he said unconvincingly.

'Well, what about the rest of yer?' Fred cried, his face dark with anger.

'I didn't want any part o' this,' Sid Bristow said, waving his hand as he walked away from the group.

'I can't afford ter be out o' collar,' Lofty Russell said. 'I've got eight kids ter fink about.'

'What about you, Sharkey?' Fred called out, glaring at the tall carman.

Sharkey shrugged his shoulders. 'It's no good unless we all stick tergevver. They won't back yer, Scratch,' he said, nodding in the direction of Lofty and Sid who were walking away from the group.

Fred Blackwell suddenly turned on his heel and stormed over to the office. 'Oi! What's your game?' he barked as he stepped through the open door.

Galloway stood up, his bulk dwarfing the slightly built carman who faced him angrily. 'I've jus' sacked a troublemaker, that's my game,' he growled.

Fred Blackwell glared up at the firm's owner, trembling

with temper. 'I've worked fer some nasty bastards in my time,' he sneered, 'but you take the prize. Yer fink yer can ride roughshod over yer workers, an' if they as much as walk in yer light yer sack 'em. Well, let me tell yer, Galloway, yer gonna come ter grief before long. Somebody's gonna stand up ter yer one day, an' I 'ope I'm around ter see it. Yer can stick yer job up yer arse! There's ovver jobs around. I won't starve.'

He turned on his heel and stormed out of the office.

1905

1905

Chapter Seven

Carrie Tanner pulled the collar of her coat up around her ears as she walked quickly along Spa Road on her way to work. A cold early morning wind whipped up the brittle brown leaves from the gutter and sent them swirling along the street as she passed the council depot. Roadsweepers were pushing their barrows out of the yard and she saw the water cart drive out, with the carman clicking his tongue at the horse to hurry it on. The sight of the horse-and-cart awoke memories, and Carrie's face became serious as she turned into Neckinger and walked along past the leather factories to her job at Wilson's.

It seemed only yesterday that Sara Knight had given her a present of a small, fan-shaped marcasite brooch and she had handed her friend a box containing three lace handkerchiefs as they left school for the last time. It was nearly nine months ago now, she recalled, and in that time she had seen Sara only on odd occasions. They had vowed to stay friends and go out together in the evenings and at weekends but it had been difficult. Sara seemed to be a prisoner in her own home since her father had gone into the sanatorium and she had had to take on the mantle of breadwinner. Her mother still did early morning cleaning when she was able, although from what

Sara said she seemed to be getting weaker and was often confined to bed with a bad chest.

It was not very easy in her own home either, Carrie allowed. Her father seemed to be working harder than ever at the yard since the young Geoffrey Galloway had come into the business. He returned home exhausted and fell asleep every evening after he had finished his tea. George Galloway was spending less time at the yard now and more time on his other ventures, and the young man was learning the business. Carrie's father was having to make decisions for him and take the blame if things went wrong, which had happened on more than one occasion recently. There had been the fever which struck down the horses and all but paralysed the business. Then there was the trouble over Jack Oxford – Carrie had heard her parents talking about how he'd once bungled a telephone message and almost lost Galloway a lucrative contract. It appeared that Mr Galloway had wanted to sack the yard man a long while ago but her father had managed to talk him out of it. There was also the terrible time when her favourite horse Titch had become ill and died. Carrie remembered how she had cried when the box van drew up and she watched from the upstairs window while poor Titch was winched up and into the van by ropes that were tied to his legs. And just after that young Danny took ill with pneumonia and pleurisy and almost died. James had been ill too with scarlet fever, and had been taken to the fever hospital. Of the three boys only the quiet and studious Charlie seemed to stay well, she thought, hoping uneasily that the future would not bring more worries and troubles.

As she reached the factory where she worked, Carrie remembered fondly the times when she had gone on those trips with her father. Now the hay was delivered to the yard and things would never be the same. She sighed to herself as she entered the factory and slipped her time-card into the clock.

Wilson's was a busy firm of leather-dressers. Hides and skins were cured and dyed at the factory and Carrie worked on the top floor. Her job was to hang the heavy hides over stout wooden poles and to stretch the skins on frames. It was heavy, tiring work for which she was paid fifteen shillings a week, much better than the money Sara earned as a sackmaker, Carrie had to admit. At least the factory was airy and conditions there not as bad as in some of the other firms in the area. Her parents had been apprehensive when she told them about the job, but they realised that the alternative was for her to work in one of the food factories or go into service, where the money was very poor and she would have to live in as well.

At the factory Carrie worked alongside Mary Caldwell, a short, plump girl of seventeen who had dark frizzy hair and peered shortsightedly through thick spectacles. Mary was strong and agile for her size, and she had an infectious laugh that helped to brighten the day for Carrie. Mary spent most of her free time reading and it was she who explained to Carrie about the growing suffragette movement. She often went to their meetings and had been reprimanded on more than one occasion for sticking up posters and leaflets in the factory. Although she had a pleasant nature, Mary got angry at the disparaging remarks made about the movement by some of the other factory girls.

'They don't understand, Carrie,' she said as the two threw a large wet hide over a high pole. 'Those women are fightin' fer all of us. We should 'ave the vote. I wanna be able ter vote when my time comes. We gotta make those stupid people in Parliament listen. Until we do we're gonna be exploited, that's fer certain.'

Carrie wiped her hands down her rubber apron and took

hold of another hide. 'My mum said she don't worry about votin',' she remarked. 'She said she leaves it ter me dad. 'E knows best, she reckons.'

Mary peered at her workmate through her steamy spectacles. 'That's where yer mum's wrong, Carrie,' she replied. 'Men vote fer what suits them, an' a lot of 'em don't bovver ter find out what they're votin' for anyway. When women get the vote they'll change fings, you wait an' see. 'Ere, I'll give yer some leaflets if yer like. Yer can read all about what the movement stands for, an' maybe yer can come wiv me ter one o' the meetin's.'

Carrie nodded as she helped Mary pull another wet hide from the trolley; her workmate made it all sound sensible to Carrie. Until now all the stories she had heard about those smart women who chained themselves to railings or threw themselves down on the steps of government buildings made her feel that it was a futile and silly campaign, but Mary's argument began to make her think. After all, it was the women in Page Street who had stopped Galloway running his horses along the street and putting the children in danger of being trampled. Her own mother had taken part, although she did not seem to have time for the suffragettes. Maybe she should find out more about the movement and go along with Mary to one of the meetings? It would be exciting to see those well-dressed women chaining themselves up and addressing large gatherings.

'I'll bring the leaflets in termorrer,' Mary said as they leaned against the trolley to catch their breath. 'I've got loads of 'em. 'Ere, by the way, Carrie, fancy comin' wiv me this dinner time? I've promised ter put a poster up outside the council depot.'

Carrie grinned. 'All right. We won't get arrested though, will we?'

Mary laughed. 'Not if we're quick!'

The morning seemed to pass slowly. When the factory whistle sounded at noon, the girls all trooped down to the ground floor where they sat in the yard to eat their lunch. Mary ate her thick brawn sandwich quickly and drank cold tea from a bottle. Carrie finished her cheese sandwich and gulped down the fresh, creamy milk she had bought on her way to work.

'C'mon, Carrie, we'll 'ave ter be quick,' said her friend, getting up and pushing her glasses up on to the bridge of her nose.

The two slipped out of the factory and walked quickly towards the council depot. Outside the gates a few men were standing around, leaning against the railings and talking together. A few yards further on there was a large notice board fixed to the railings. When they reached it, Mary took a large poster from beneath her long coat. Without hesitating she tore down a notice of coming elections and spread out her notice in its place.

'Hold yer 'and on the bottom of it, Carrie,' she said, licking a strip of brown sticking-paper.

Carrie reached up to the high notice board and pressed her hand against the poster which read 'Votes for Women' in large black letters.

Mary was just fixing the last of the corners when they heard the loud voice behind them: "Ello. Bit young fer this sort o' fing, ain't yer?"

The two girls turned to see a large policeman standing there with his hands tucked into his belt.

'D'yer know this is council property?' he said, looking at them quizzically.

Mary peered at him through her thick glasses. 'We ain't doin' any 'arm,' she said spiritedly.

'Oh, is that so?' the constable replied mockingly, rocking back on his heels. 'D'yer know yer defacin' a private notice board, apart from destroyin' council property?'

'We ain't destroyed nuffink,' Mary said, glancing quickly at Carrie.

'What's that then?' the policeman said, pointing down at the torn poster at the girls' feet.

'That's only an old poster. It ain't nuffing important,' Mary replied.

The constable raised his eyebrows. 'That 'appens ter be an election notice. What 'ave yer got ter say about that, young lady?'

Mary's face was flushed. She adjusted her spectacles and bravely replied, 'Women should 'ave the vote. Shouldn't they, Carrie?'

The Tanner girl nodded, wishing she had never agreed to go with Mary.

'We was only puttin' one little poster up,' she said in a quiet voice, glancing coyly at the large guardian of the law.

The policeman took out his notebook and licked on the stub of a pencil. 'Right then, let's 'ave yer names an' addresses.'

'Freda 'opkins, an' I live at number seventeen Salisbury Buildin's, Salisbury Street,' Mary answered without batting an eyelid.

The policeman looked at Carrie who was desperately trying to think of a name and address. ''Ave you got a name?' he asked.

'I'm, er, Agatha Brown,' she said quickly, suddenly remembering the girl she most disliked at school.

'D'yer live anywhere?'

''Undred an' two Bacon Street Buildings,' Carrie blurted out.

'Right. Now I don't wanna see you two under-aged suffragettes tearin' down any more council posters, is that quite clear?' the policeman said, giving the two a stern look. 'An' don't go chainin' yerselves ter the council railin's in future, 'cos I might jus' leave yer there all night.'

Mary nodded. Carrie merely stared up fixedly at the towering policeman.

'All right then, on yer way,' he said, holding back a grin.

The two young protesters left the scene of their misdemeanour and hurried back to the factory. Mary had a satisfied smile on her face. 'That's what yer gotta do when yer get caught puttin' posters up, Carrie,' she said firmly. 'They don't check up – 'ardly, anyway.'

Carrie's heart was still beating fast. She glanced at Mary. 'I 'ope they don't! We could go ter prison fer givin' the wrong names.'

'That's what we gotta be prepared ter do in the movement,' Mary said proudly. 'Lots o' suffragettes go ter prison, an' they carry on when they come out. I might 'ave ter go ter prison meself.'

Carrie felt worried as she listened to her workmate. The incident at the council depot had been a frightening experience and she felt she was still a bit young to get herself arrested for the cause. Mary did not seem a bit concerned, and was smiling with satisfaction as they walked back into the factory.

The men at the depot gates had dispersed but the policeman remained standing in a doorway opposite. He had watched the two young girls depart with a smile on his face. They would no doubt end up chaining themselves to railings, he thought. The one with the glasses seemed very determined. Maybe they had a genuine argument. His wife was always on about women having the right to vote. The policeman sighed and took out his notebook. Smiling wryly to himself, he tore out a page, screwed it up in his fist and dropped it into the gutter. He had had reason to visit Bacon Street Buildings many times and knew that the numbers only went up to sixty-four.

Geoffrey Galloway was busy sorting through the pile of papers on his desk. He felt depressed. He had bowed to his father's wishes and gone into the business but it seemed a far cry from what he really wanted to do in life. The five years he had spent at the yard had taught him a lot, although he still had to rely on Will Tanner where practical matters were concerned. True, he had had a good education and the clerical side of the job posed no problems. The accounts too were easy to understand and Horace Gallagher handled that side of it competently enough, although the man seemed to be cracking up physically.

What troubled Geoffrey was handling problems with the carmen. He knew only too well that he lacked his father's ruthlessness, and were it not for his yard foreman would have found himself hopelessly lost. William seemed able to keep the men's grouses to a minimum and sort out the work without much trouble. The horses were always well groomed and fit for work, and the carts were maintained to a good standard. He had spoken to his father about getting in a couple of motor vans but the old man had been against it. He seemed to think horses would always have pride of place in the cartage business, and maybe he was right. Most of the firm's business was done with local concerns and the journeys were of a short distance. A horse cart was more manoeuvrable in the tight lanes and on the wharf jetties, and with a pair of horses and one of the larger carts a considerable amount of tonnage could be transported.

Geoffrey tidied up the papers and leaned back in his chair. It was early afternoon and the yard was quiet before the hustle and bustle around five o'clock when the carts rolled back. He could see Jack Oxford crossing the cobbles with a bucket in his hand, and Will Tanner winching up a bale of hay into the loft. The sun was shining brightly and its long rays penetrated the gloom of the office and lit up the dust motes floating in the air. Geoffrey felt trapped in the job, and not a little irritated by his younger brother's attitude. Frank was nineteen and after he left school had been allowed to go on to college with the old man's blessing. He had sat for a diploma in accountancy and was now working in the City for a firm of business accountants. Frank was leading an active social life, often visiting the West End with young women on his arm to see the best shows and revues. He had said he was not interested in going into the family business and his father had not shown any anger or disappointment. How different it had been in his case, Geoffrey thought resentfully. He had been pressured into taking over at the yard, with no consideration for what he wanted. Even now, when he had agreed to submit to what was required of him and had proved himself capable, his life was still strictly monitored by the old man. Even Geoffrey's choice of women had been deemed a subject for discussion with his father, and the two girls he had taken home so far had been met at best with criticism, at worst with outright hostility. Maybe he should have stood out and refused to submit to his father's wishes, and taken home the sort of girls Frank seemed to socialise with.

Geoffrey leaned back and sighed. Well, as far as business went, if he was going to stay he would expect to have a bigger say in its running and development, he told himself. He had served his apprenticeship and now he had some ideas of his own to put forward.

*

Jack Oxford had finished his chores and was taking a rest in his store shed. He was never disturbed there, summoned usually by a shout from the yard. Inside the shed he had an old armchair with broken springs and horsehair protruding from both arms, and had made himself a cushion from a sack stuffed with straw. The only problem with resting in the shed, Jack rued, was that there was no room to stretch out. As he reclined in the chair with his feet propped up on a littered bench, he was thinking about the yard's cat. It had crawled away the previous day without eating the supply of fresh catmeat laid out for it and Jack was sure it had gone somewhere to have its kittens. He would take a few more minutes' rest and then make a search. It would most probably have crawled into the small stable where the sick horses were kept in isolation. There had been no horses in there for the past week and cats were clever, he reasoned.

When the yard man finally made a search he found the cat nestling in the far corner of the small stable beneath a pile of loose straw. It had had a large litter of kittens which all looked healthy. Jack scratched his head and pondered on what he should do. The boss would not permit a family of cats in the yard, and if he found out about the litter would order Jack to drown the kittens. Maybe he could give them away when they were ready to leave their mother. There would be no shortage of takers in the street for a cat that was a good mouser. Their mother was the best mouser he had seen and the kittens would most probably take after her, he reasoned.

As the tall, gangling man left the stable, he thought about knocking on Florrie Axford's door to make enquiries. He had never liked the woman very much but had to admit that she knew everyone in the turning and could put the word around. Having to knock on 'Hairpin' Axford's door was preferable to putting the kittens in a bucket of water, he assured himself.

On his way home that evening the yard man timidly knocked at the door of number 10. When Florrie Axford opened it she looked surprised. 'What d'yer want?' she asked, eyeing her visitor warily.

'Sorry ter trouble yer, missus,' he said, scratching the back of his head. 'I've got kittens, yer see.'

'That's nice fer yer,' Florrie said sarcastically. 'What d'yer want me ter do, feed 'em?'

'I was finkin' yer might want a cat, or else one o' the ovver women might. They'll be good mousers. Their muvver's the best I've seen.'

Florrie shook her head, wanting to get rid of the man as quickly as possible. 'They've all got cats,' she said curtly.

Jack pulled a face. 'If ole Galloway finds out she's 'ad kittens, 'e'll get me ter drown 'em. Bloody shame really.'

Florrie stroked her chin thoughtfully. 'I s'pose I could ask around,' she said. 'When can they be took away from the muvver?'

'A couple o' weeks should be all right,' Jack said, his face brightening up considerably.

'When yer ready, give us a knock an' I'll see what I can do,' said Florrie, stepping back inside the house.

Jack was feeling better as he walked off along the street, blissfully unaware of what was in store for him.

On a Thursday evening four of George Galloway's carmen sat around an iron table in the Kings Arms, engaged in a serious discussion.

'I don't fink the bloke's a nark,' Sharkey said, putting down his drink and wiping the back of his hand across his moustache. 'I've known the silly bleeder fer a few years now, an' as far as I know 'e's always minded 'is own business.'

Soapy Symonds nodded his agreement. 'Yeah, that's right. Jack Oxford might look stupid but 'e knows what day o' the week it is. 'E knows when it's pay day,' he chuckled.

The two carmen sitting facing Sharkey glanced at each other. 'Well, I dunno about that, but somebody seems to keep the ole man informed,' one of them said. 'That soppy git always seems ter be 'angin' around. 'E talks ter Will Tanner a lot as well.'

Soapy took another swig from his glass and wiped his lips with the back of his hand. 'If yer ask me, I'd say it was more likely ter be that Sid Bristow,' he cut in. ''E's always talkin' ter Galloway. I reckon it was 'im what put the word in about ole Scratcher Blackwell when we tried to get the union in years back. Bristow wouldn't back us fer a strike neivver. Yer gotta watch that cowson.'

Sammy Jackson hunched his broad shoulders and leaned forward over the table, his large, calloused hands clasped around his glass. 'That was before my time but the old man knew what we was plannin' an' 'e warned me about gettin' involved wiv the union. Somebody must 'ave told 'im,' he growled.

'Well, my money's on Sid Bristow,' Soapy said firmly.

'P'raps it was Will Tanner,' Sammy's friend suggested.

Sharkey shook his head. 'It wasn't 'im, Darbo. Will's as straight as a die. 'E's always standin' up fer the blokes, an' what 'e knows 'e keeps ter 'imself. All right, 'e's the yard foreman an' sometimes 'e gets a bit shirty wiv us, but that's 'is job. We all know that.'

Ted Derbyshire shrugged his shoulders. 'Sammy might be right about Jack Oxford. That bloke gives me the creeps. 'E's always slouchin' around the yard wiv that funny look in 'is eyes. I 'eard 'e sleeps in the doss-'ouse in Tower Bridge Road. Somebody told me they seen 'im standin' outside that school in Fair Street watchin' the gels doin' their exercises. Yer gotta watch people like that. Them dirty ole gits are dangerous where kids are concerned.'

Sharkey finished his drink and made to leave. He did not like the way the conversation was going and it seemed to him that the two new carmen had it in for the yard man. He had known Jack Oxford for many years and felt sure the man was just a harmless simpleton.

Chapter Eight

Florrie Axford had been making herself busy during the past two weeks and felt happy with the response she had got from her neighbours and friends. It looked as though she had now found enough homes for the whole litter and she felt she had better go and see Jack Oxford instead of waiting for him to call. 'That silly bastard's prob'ly fergot 'e's s'posed ter come round. 'E'll drown the poor little mites if I don't go an' tell 'im I've found 'em 'omes,' she groaned to her friend Maisie Dougall.

Maisie had said she would take one of the litter and her next-door neighbour had found a home for another with a friend. Aggie Temple had been approached but had declined. It was bad enough as it was keeping the place clean without cats messing everywhere, she told Florrie. Sadie Sullivan had said she was willing to take one, and there were a few more offers of a home for the remainder of the litter.

When Florrie called at the yard, Jack was busy with the broom. She beckoned him to the gate. 'I've got people ter take them all,' she said.

He grinned lopsidedly. 'Righto. I'll bring 'em round ternight,' he replied.

'I ain't 'avin' 'em all in my place, an' I certainly ain't runnin' aroun' deliverin' 'em,' Florrie said pointedly. 'I'll tell 'em ter come an' pick 'em up themselves.'

Jack nodded and got on with his sweeping, happy in the knowledge that now he would not have to drown the kittens. His only fear was that George Galloway would find out about them, despite the precautions he had taken, and stop him giving the litter away.

The next morning, as soon as the last cart had left the yard, Maisie Dougall called in and Jack Oxford took her into the small stable. She soon selected her kitten and went away, happily cuddling it to her ample bosom. During the day two more callers went away with their chosen kittens. Maggie Jones had intended to go to the yard that morning but her youngest daughter Iris wanted to select the kitten herself and so she decided that the child should call in at the yard on her way home from school.

It was a quiet afternoon when ten-year-old Iris Jones called in and was shown to the stable by the grinning Jack Oxford. He stood back while the child bent over the litter and made a fuss of each small bundle of fur. At last she made her choice and slipped the kitten under her coat. She walked out into the bright sunshine, smiling happily at Jack Oxford.

At the same time as the young girl arrived at the gate that afternoon, Darbo was driving his cart down the turning. He saw Iris cross the yard with Jack. As he drove into the yard and jumped down from his seat, Darbo looked around him, frowning. They were nowhere to be seen now. The curious carman walked quickly into the office and saw Horace Gallagher bent over his desk.

'I've jus' seen Oxford bring a young gel in the yard,' he exclaimed loudly.

The elderly accountant peered over his glasses. The figures

did not seem to be making sense that afternoon and he was feeling irritable. 'It's nothing to do with me,' he replied. 'Go and tell Mr Tanner.'

Darbo hurried from the yard and looked around. The foreman was most probably up in the large stable, he thought. There was no time to waste. Anything could be happening to that child.

He hurried to the store shed and peered in. It was all quiet. As he turned to leave he saw the girl and the yard man walking to the gate. The gangling figure stared after her and gave her a wave as she disappeared along the turning. Darbo's immediate reaction was to confront Jack Oxford, but as he watched the yard man loping up the long ramp he thought better of it. Best wait until Sammy gets in, he decided. People like Oxford could be violent at times. Sammy would be able to handle the situation if it got dangerous.

When Sammy Jackson drove into the yard fifteen minutes later he was confronted by the excited Darbo, and while their animated conversation was taking place George Galloway drove his trap into the yard with Geoffrey sitting at his side. Immediately the two carmen hurried up to the trap and Sammy leaned on its brass side-rail.

'Yer've got a dirty ole git workin' fer yer, Guv',' he said quickly. 'Go on, Darbo, tell the guv'nor what yer jus' told me.'

When Darbo finished his account, George Galloway, turned to Sammy Jackson. 'What d'yer wanna do about it?' he asked.

Sammy clenched his fists and nodded in the direction of the upper stable. 'I've got young kids meself, Guv'. I reckon we ought ter teach 'im a lesson 'e won't ferget.'

George nodded. 'It's up ter you what yer do. I 'ad no part in this, understand? If yer do dust 'im up, don't go too mad. I don't want a bloody murder on me 'ands.'

As Sammy and Darbo hurried towards the ramp, Geoffrey

turned to his father in disbelief. 'Are you going to let those two loose on Oxford without finding out exactly what *did* happen?' he asked incredulously.

George smiled crookedly at his son. 'What would you do in the circumstances?' he asked.

'Well, I'd at least call the man into the office and confront him,' Geoffrey replied, staring hard at his father.

'An' what's 'e gonna say? "Yes, Guv', I've jus' molested a child." Grow up, Geoff. Those two 'ave got more chance o' gettin' the truth out o' the man than me an' you.'

Geoffrey bit on his bottom lip and glanced anxiously towards the stable. 'They could kill him. I'm going to stop them.'

George put out a restraining hand. 'I said leave 'em,' he growled. 'That bloody idiot's bin a burden ter me fer years now. I dunno why I listened ter Tanner in the first place. I should 'ave done what I intended ter do an' sacked the dopey whoreson long ago.'

Geoffrey got down from the trap and made his way to the office. 'Where's Tanner?' he asked the accountant, who by this time had finally sorted out the figures and was leaning back in his chair looking exhausted.

Horace Gallagher shook his head. 'He had to go out. One of the carts broke an axle. What's going on?' he asked, noticing the young man's worried expression.

Geoffrey ignored the question and stood by the door, gazing across the yard. Horace Gallagher had worked for the Galloway company for a number of years and he had witnessed some strange goings-on but on this occasion he had a strong feeling that he should make himself scarce. He quickly gathered up his ledgers and stuffed them into his tatty briefcase, then putting on his trilby he squeezed past Geoffrey and hurried out of the yard as fast as he could.

When Sammy and his friend Darbo reached the upper level they saw the yard man raking over the bedding at the end stall.

'Oxford, we wanna word wiv yer,' Sammy growled, his face contorted with anger.

'Yer'll 'ave ter wait. Can't yer see I'm busy?' Jack called out.

The two carmen walked along the stable and Darbo put his foot on the end of the rake as Sammy walked up to Jack and took him roughly by the collar of his shirt.

'What's goin' on? Leave me alone,' Jack croaked.

Sammy forced the yard man against the wall, his large fists pressed up under Jack's chin. 'Leave yer alone? Why yer dirty ole bastard! Why d'yer bring 'er in the yard? What yer bin doin' ter that little gel? Darbo saw yer bring 'er in.'

Jack felt he was going to choke and he gulped for breath. 'I didn't do nuffink. She wanted ter come in. I didn't make 'er,' he gasped.

'Well, I'm gonna show yer what we do ter the likes o' you,' Sammy spat out, releasing his hands from the unfortunate's throat and giving him a heavy back-handed slap across the face.

Jack slid down the wall, blood starting from his nose and lips. 'I ain't done nuffink. Leave me alone,' he whined.

Sammy stood over the bloody figure with his legs astride and he turned to Darbo. 'Go down ter the shed an' get the 'orse-shears. 'Urry up.'

Darbo was beginning to feel anxious. 'What yer gonna do, Sammy?' he asked.

'When I've finished wiv 'im, 'e won't be able ter molest anyone any more. Now go an' get them shears.'

Darbo hurried down the ramp to the yard, wondering whether Sammy would really go as far as mutilating the man. As he returned from the shed holding a sharp pair of shears he saw the bulky figure of George Galloway in the office door-way. The man made no attempt to stop him and Darbo noticed the broad grin on his face as he turned to hurry back up the ramp.

'What's he got those clippers for?' Geoffrey asked his father anxiously.

'It looks like Jack Oxford's gonna get a short 'aircut, if I'm not mistaken,' the elder Galloway remarked.

'Go and stop 'em,' Geoffrey pleaded. 'They'll kill the man.'

George chuckled and leaned back against the doorjamb. 'They won't kill 'im. They've got more sense. They jus' wanna put the fear o' Christ inter the bloke.'

When Darbo walked back into the stable, he saw Sammy bending over the huddled figure of Oxford. The yard man's face was streaked with blood and his eyes were wide with fear. 'No, don't! Please don't 'urt me! I didn't do nuffink. Honest ter Gawd I never,' he wailed.

Sammy's face was contorted with rage and there was a white smear of foam on his lips. 'Grab 'im,' he snarled, taking Jack's arm and pulling him to his feet. 'Lean 'im up against the stall.'

Darbo did as he was told and Sammy nodded over to a length of rope that was hanging from a wall ring. 'Bring me that,' he growled.

Jack closed his eyes and prayed hard as he felt the rope slip over his head and tighten around his neck. He winced with pain as his arms were yanked backwards and pulled down behind the board and he felt the rope tighten over his wrists. He tried to kick out at his tormentors with his feet but Sammy had slipped the end of the rope around his ankles and pulled the knot tight. Jack groaned in anguish. He was trussed up like a chicken and they were going to mutilate him for nothing. Why didn't they believe him? He had done no harm to the child. 'She only wanted a kitten,' he cried out, tears beginning to run down his ashen face.

Sammy did not hear, consumed with blind hatred and disgust. He could still hear them all calling him a monster for chastising his own daughter. They had all shunned him and called him evil when he took the whip to her, but she had deserved it and needed to be punished. The weals on her body had healed in time and she had learned her lesson. He was right to do what he had to do; he was no monster. Not like this perverted wreck, who had molested an innocent child.

'The shears. Give us the shears,' he snarled at Darbo as he quickly unbuckled his victim's belt and yanked down his trousers.

Darbo was holding the sharp animal-shears limply in his hands. He took a step backwards. He had never seen Sammy like this. The man's mad, he thought. He's really going to do it. 'No, Sammy!' he shouted. 'Yer've scared the life out of 'im. That's enough.'

The maniacal carman stepped forward and grabbed the shears from Darbo's grasp. ''E won't trouble no ovver little gel in future,' he said in a voice that made Darbo shudder.

'Don't, Sammy. Leave 'im alone.'

Sammy's wild eyes fixed on Darbo who was backing away towards the ramp. 'I told yer I'm gonna fix 'im, Darbo. I don't need yer anymore. I can manage wivout yer. 'Oppit!'

Down in the yard the rest of the carmen were standing together in a bewildered group. They had been ordered to stay out of the upper stable by George Galloway. As they stood beside the tired horses, talking in low voices, they saw young Geoffrey come out of the office. He looked agitated, saying something to his father then pulling away from his restraining arm and hurrying across the yard towards Will Tanner's approaching figure. The men saw the two speak together for a few moments and then the yard foreman broke away and ran towards the stable. At that moment Darbo came running down the ramp, his eyes wide and his mouth hanging open. 'Quick, Will!' he screamed. 'Sammy's gorn roun' the twist. 'E's gonna cut 'im up!'

Before William could move, a loud piercing scream carried down into the yard.

'Oh my Gawd! 'E's done it!' Darbo cried.

William pushed the horrified carman to one side and ran up the ramp. As he dashed into the stable he blinked to accustom his eyes to the dim light, then saw the tethered Jack Oxford with his head sunk forward on his chest. Sammy was standing in front of him, his face twisted in an evil grin. 'Stay away, Tanner,' he called out.

William took a deep breath and slowly advanced on him. 'Leave 'im,' he said quietly. 'Step away from 'im.'

Sammy leered and hunched his shoulders as he turned and looked down on his victim. William strode across to Sammy's side and what he saw made his blood go cold. Jack Oxford was bloodied and sprawled out in the straw and Sammy was about to close the blades together. With a gasp William grabbed at Sammy's wrists and held them apart with all his strength. He knew that if he let go now, Jack would be instantly mutilated. Sammy was growling, white flecks of saliva showing on his lips as he struggled to close the blades. William gritted his teeth as he fought to hold the man's wrists apart. The yard foreman could feel his strength fading.

With a last mighty effort, he pulled his shoulders back and sucked in air as he took up the pressure. Sammy was gasping too. He leaned forward over the shears to exert more pressure. Suddenly William threw his head upwards and sideways and caught Sammy on the bridge of his nose. The man staggered back, losing his hold on the clippers. William stepped forward a pace and swayed from the hips as he threw a looping punch that hit Sammy on the side of his head. With a grunt he dropped down on his knees and glanced up at his opponent, his eyes glassy. The yard foreman was about to aim a kick when Sammy fell forward, his face buried in the straw bedding of the stall.

Carrie had left the factory with her mind full of Mary's tales about the campaigning women and their long marches through the streets of London. She had heard about the smartly dressed females who had been taken away by the police and sentenced to imprisonment for inciting riots and causing a public disorder, and she felt a little apprehensive. The recent incident at the council depot was still fresh in her mind and she bit on her lip as she turned into Page Street. If that policeman spotted her again he might arrest her for giving a false name. Mary had said there was nothing to worry about but Carrie did not feel so confident.

As she walked down the street Carrie saw Iris Jones sitting on her front doorstep, peering into a cardboard box.

'Wanna see my little kitten, Carrie?' the girl said with a grin.

Carrie looked into the box and saw two bright eyes peering out from what looked like a bundle of fluff. 'Oh, isn't she luvverly?' she said, taking the kitten from the box and gently stroking it. 'Where did yer get it?'

'That nice man in yer dad's yard give it me,' Iris said, taking the kitten from Carrie and putting it back into the box. ''E let me pick it fer meself. There was lots there. Must 'ave bin twenty or firty but I liked this one best of all. I'm callin' it Sparky. Do kittens 'ave ter get christened, Carrie?'

The Tanner girl laughed aloud. 'No, I don't fink so,' she said as she walked on.

As she neared her house, Carrie saw her mother standing by the yard gates. Men were milling around and she saw her father and Sharkey holding on to Jack Oxford as they walked him towards the office.

'What's 'appened ter Mr Oxford?' she asked as she reached her mother.

Nellie had heard the full story from Darbo who had been at pains to tell anyone, including her, that he had done his best to prevent the yard man from getting harmed and it was only his timely warning that had saved the poor man from a terrible fate. Nellie shook her head. 'They said Jack Oxford's bin messin' aroun' wiv a young gel, Carrie, an' one o' the men set about 'im,' she said, slipping her hands beneath her apron. 'I don't believe it. Jack Oxford wouldn't 'arm a fly.'

Carrie folded her arms across her chest. 'Who did they say the little gel was, Mum?' she asked.

'I dunno. Nobody seems ter know. Apparently Jack Oxford's s'posed ter 'ave took a little gel in the stable. One of the men see 'er come out later wiv Mr Oxford, an' 'e waved to 'er at the gate.'

'Well, she wasn't 'armed then, Mum,' Carrie remarked.

'We don't know fer sure yet,' Nellie said quietly. 'The men fink 'e interfered wiv 'er. You know what I mean.'

'Iris Jones went in the yard terday, Mum,' Carrie said suddenly.

'What! 'Ow d'yer know?' Nellie exclaimed.

'She told me just a minute ago. Showed me the little kitten that Jack Oxford gave 'er.'

Nellie beckoned to Soapy who hurried over. 'Tell my bloke I wanna see 'im, soon as yer can. Tell 'im it's important,' she said in a firm voice.

The early evening street was quiet, but behind the closed gates of Galloway's yard a heated discussion was taking place. George Galloway leaned back in his chair as he listened to his yard foreman. Things had not turned out the way he expected and he felt very relieved that he had not been a party to murder. Duffing up the idiot yard man and then terrifying him with the threat of mutilation was one thing, George thought, but actually attempting to carry out the act was another thing entirely. He felt grateful to William for his timely intervention but he was now becoming irritable at the turn the discussion was taking. Geoffrey seemed to be in agreement with Tanner's argument, and remained quiet when the foreman demanded that Sammy Jackson and Darbo be sacked.

When William finished talking George stayed silent for a few moments, fingers toying with the gold medallion on his silver watch chain, then he looked at his foreman. 'I can't sack 'em, Will,' he said quietly. 'I was party ter what 'appened, although I didn't fink for a minute Jackson was gonna go that far. What I'm sayin' is, it's Oxford who'll 'ave ter go. There's no ovver way.'

Geoffrey looked quickly at William before catching his father's eye. 'But the man's done nothing wrong,' he said incredulously. 'You heard what Will just said. Those two carmen didn't give Oxford a chance to explain. They beat him up, then subjected him to a terrifying ordeal, and now you want to sack the poor so and so!'

George gave his son a hard look and sighed testily. Taking on Jack Oxford had been a mistake in the first place. It had been Martha's idea. She had felt sorry for the man and suggested he could be found a sweeping-up job in the yard. George never could say no to Martha, although he had told her at the time the man was going to cause him trouble. Jack Oxford had almost lost him a contract a few years ago, and now he had caused a big upset in the yard. Sweepers and odd-job men were two a penny, George reasoned, but good reliable carmen were harder to find.

George clasped his hands over his large middle and switched his gaze to William. 'Put yerself in my place, Will,' he began. 'On one side I've got two carmen who can 'andle a pair of 'orses an' who both know the 'op trade, an' on the ovver side I've got a stupid odd-job man who 'as ter be supervised even when 'e's sweepin' the yard up. So what do I do? Sack the carmen an' maybe lose the contract wiv the brewery, or give Oxford the elbow? You tell me.'

Geoffrey was about to cut in but Will caught his eye. 'Yer missin' the point, George,' he said forcibly. 'In the first place it's a question of what's right an' what's wrong. As I said before, the Jones kid told my Nellie that Oxford didn't even go near 'er. The girl's muvver confirmed that she knew about 'er kid comin' in ter get the kitten, so that rules out the idea that Jack Oxford enticed 'er inter the yard. Yer've already said that Jackson an' Darbo took too much on 'emselves, an' now yer sayin' yer gonna sack Oxford an' keep the ovver two on, jus' because of yer brewery contract. I don't fink yer too worried about the contract. Yer know yerself there's plenty o' carmen on the dole who can 'andle 'ops an' drive a team. No, George, yer see Jack Oxford as a pain in the arse an' yer want 'im out yer way. It don't seem ter concern yer that the man's worked 'ere fer the past fifteen years.'

George's face darkened with anger. 'All right, I've listened ter yer argument, but I run this business,' he said quickly. 'I make the decisions, even though they don't always tally wiv your views. I'm gettin' Gallagher ter make Oxford's money up. I'll give 'im an extra week's pay an' that'll be the end of it.'

William took a deep breath and got up from his chair. 'Well, yer better get Gallagher ter make my money up too, George. I can't be a party ter what yer doin',' he said, his face white with anger as he got up and made for the door.

Geoffrey quickly called William back and then rounded on

his father. 'I don't want to have a family quarrel here, Father, but Will's right. I feel the way he does,' he said with determination. 'If he goes, then so do I.'

George looked at the angry faces of the two men for a few seconds, then he slumped back in his chair with a mirthless smile on his face. 'All right, Oxford stays,' he sighed. Then he looked hard at Geoffrey. 'As you feel so strongly about the rights an' wrongs of it, I'll let you sack Jackson – but Darbo stays, an' that's me final word. If yer don't like it, then yer can both please yerselves what yer do about it.'

The yard was in darkness with only the light from the street-corner gaslamp casting eerie shadows along the stable walls. In the solitude of the small stable Jack Oxford sat in the hay, sharing the last of his fish-and-chip supper with the mangy yard cat and her remaining kittens. His face hurt and the salty food stung his sore lips but the hot tea had made him feel a little better.

Jack eased his position on the bed of hay and propped his back against the whitewashed wall of the stable. It all seemed unreal. One minute he was cleaning out the stall and the next he had been attacked and nearly killed by the two carmen. He shivered as he recalled the terrible ordeal. What was going to happen to him now? he fretted. Will Tanner had said he would be all right and Nellie had told him not to worry too much as she bathed his face with hot water. They had been good to him and it was nice of Nellie to send him that large can of tea. Will had told him he could stay in the yard that night but not to let on to anyone. It wouldn't be hard, he thought. He could just slip out of the stable with his broom next morning and no one would know he had been there all night. It was better than going to the doss-house. He would only be the laughing stock of all the other men when they saw his face. Well, he would have to face them soon, he told himself. George Galloway would sack him in the morning, despite what Will Tanner had said. The boss had it in for him and was always moaning at him. Where could he go and what could he do? He couldn't drive horses after his accident. He got giddy and sick when he climbed up into a cart. He had tried it often enough but it was always the same, and his head hurt a lot as well and he couldn't concentrate. He wouldn't be able to make deliveries and collections. It was unlikely he could get another job sweeping and doing odd-jobs.

The two kittens were clambering over his legs and Jack clutched them to him, stroking their soft bodies. Maybe he should have told Galloway about the cat having kittens, he reflected. The boss would most probably have told him to drown them but it would have saved him getting into all that trouble. They wouldn't have known anything. It would have been over in seconds. Maybe that was the answer to his problems, Jack thought suddenly. He could go along to the river on a dark night and let the water close over him. There would be no more worrying about where to sleep and earning enough money for food. There would be no more shouting and swearing at him for not cleaning the yard properly and no more headaches. Well, he would think about it, he told himself with a dignified nod of his head, and if he did get the sack next morning he just might well go down to the river.

The pain of his bruised face had eased a little, and he sighed as he lay back down in the soft hay. The quietness of the stable was pleasant, he thought to himself, not like the loud snoring at the doss-house. He closed his eyes and with only the animals for company drifted off to sleep, aware of a gentle purring in his ear.

Chapter Nine

Carrie had settled down into factory life at Wilson's and the work did not seem so hard now, especially since she was partnered with such a lively girl as Mary. Her friend had been on a suffragette march at the weekend and on Monday morning was eager to tell Carrie all about it. There was little time to talk as they hurried to hang up the ever-mounting pile of skins and hides, but when the factory whistle sounded for lunch and the two joined the rest of the girls in the large room on the ground floor, Mary could no longer contain her excitement. As the rain fell heavily and thunder rolled outside Carrie became aware of the occasional glances their way and the stifled giggles as Mary waved her arms enthusiastically.

'Cor, yer should 'ave seen it, Carrie,' she was saying. 'There was fousands of us. The policemen was marchin' along beside us an' when we got ter Parliament Square there was a bit of a scuffle. These 'orrible men was laughin' an' jeerin' and one o' the ladies crowned one o' the blokes wiv 'er banner, then this policeman grabbed the lady an' marched 'er off. The men were still jeerin' an' singin' dirty songs so we all rushed over an' started ter clout 'em. I was carryin' this banner on a long pole an' I got trampled on. It was really frightenin'. Quite a lot o' the ladies on the march got took away but I was lucky. It was really excitin'. There's anuvver march planned next Saturday. Why don't yer come? There's lot's o' young gels go, it's not only old women.'

Carrie shook her head. 'Me mum won't 'ear of it. She said I'm too young ter worry about them sort o' fings.'

'That's the trouble,' Mary scoffed. 'If more an' more women took ter the streets an' went on the marches, those stupid men would 'ave ter listen. They're all the same. I can't stand 'em!'

'They're not all the same,' Carrie asserted, surprised by Mary's outburst.

Mary put her hand on Carrie's arm. 'I don't go out wiv boys,' she said in a low voice. 'I know the ovver gels take it out o' me an' call me funny names, but I don't care. I only go out wiv gel friends.'

Carrie had been puzzling over the other girls' attitude to Mary and thought it was due to her political views, but this awakened a new train of thought. She had heard of those women who dressed and acted like men and went out with pretty girls but had not likened Mary to that sort. Now, she felt confused and a little frightened. They had worked together for some time. Once or twice Mary had put her arm around Carrie's shoulders, and had even kissed her on the cheek on one occasion, but she had not thought anything of it.

She suddenly felt awkward and pulled her arm quickly away. 'Well, I like boys,' she said, easing her position on the wooden bench very slightly.

Mary laughed and seemed not to have noticed her reaction. 'Well, don't let 'em take liberties, that's all,' she said firmly.

In the Tanner household, Nellie was sitting at the fireside with a worried look on her face. 'I know I should be pleased now there's gonna be a few more coppers a week comin' in, Will, but it still worries me,' she said with a frown. 'There's Carrie working at that factory, an' now Jimmy's startin' work termorrer in the sawmills, and they're still only kids. Next year Charlie leaves school. What sort of a job is 'e likely ter get?'

William sighed and leaned back in his chair. 'There's not much choice fer the likes o' the kids around 'ere, Nell,' he said sadly. 'There's plenty o' factory jobs but yer need a good education ter get a decent job wiv some future in it. All right, I s'pose we could 'ave insisted Jimmy got an apprenticeship but it costs money. He wouldn't 'ear of it when I spoke ter 'im about it. It's the same wiv Carrie. What's the alternative fer 'er? A job in service at twelve quid a year. She'd 'ave ter live in too. Yer wouldn't like that, would yer?'

Nellie shook her head. 'I s'pose I worry too much. If our kids are gonna get on in life they will, despite startin' off in factories.'

William nodded. 'You take George Galloway. 'E didn't get an education, well not the sort we're talking about. 'E learned 'is trade runnin' the streets an' sleepin' rough, the same as I did. Now look at 'im. 'E's got a business, an' 'e owns this row of 'ouses. I've 'eard talk about 'im buyin' a few more in the turnin'. Gawd knows what else 'e's involved in. If 'e fell in shit 'e'd get up smellin' o' lavender. Look at that time 'e lost the army contract fer the 'orses. A few weeks later 'e landed the brewery contract. I wouldn't worry too much, Nell. If our kids are destined ter get on in life, they will.'

She reached down and picked up the poker. The mention of George Galloway had made her feel bitter and she tried not to show it in front of her husband. 'I wouldn't like my kids ter turn out like Galloway,' she said quickly. 'Look what 'e would've done ter poor ole Jack Oxford if it wasn't fer you standin' up to 'im.'

'It was young Geoff what made 'im change 'is mind,' William replied. 'If it'd jus' bin me, I'd 'ave bin out the gate. 'E's a nice lad that Geoffrey. 'E's a bit soft an' 'e don't like makin' decisions but 'e's a good lad fer all that. It's a pity the ovver boy wasn't made ter do 'is share. Come ter fink of it, p'raps it's just as well. Two Galloways ter deal wiv is enough wivout anuvver one in the office!'

Nellie laughed briefly and then prodded at the fire, a feeling of apprehension mounting inside her. She had been aware for some time now of the strain beginning to show in Will's face. As she stole a glance across at him, she could see how the years and the toil were beginning to mark him. William was still robust and healthy, but there was a certain sad look in his pale blue eyes. His face had started to show lines too. His fair hair was thinner and he looked tired. She was beginning to feel the burden of the years herself. When she looked in the mirror that morning, Nellie had seen the signs around her eyes. Her figure was still slim and rounded, but she had gazed wistfully at her sagging breasts and the looseness of the skin on the backs of her hands.

The passing of the years was apparent too in the way her children seemed to be hurrying towards adulthood. Carrie's body was developing quickly, and she was growing up into a pretty young woman. James, too, had seemed to grow up suddenly. He was tall and gangling, and his abrupt manner and tendency to anger quickly reflected his passage into manhood, she thought. Then there was Charlie. He was fair-haired like the others, but his eyes were grey and he had a quiet manner.

Nellie sighed deeply as she recalled the feelings she had kept from William and the secret agony she suffered during the time when she carried Charlie inside her. There had been no one she could turn to and the memory of those anxious days and nights of pregnancy had stayed fresh in her mind. She could see the narrow alley as though it were only yesterday, with the smell of rotting vegetables, and the black-painted door with the large iron knocker. She remembered looking at the address on the small piece of paper and then raising her hand to the knocker. It was the faint cry of a baby that had checked her. She had turned abruptly and hurried from the alley, suddenly determined to give her unborn child its chance in life, come what may.

William's repeated question interrupted Nellie's troubled thoughts. 'I said, young Danny looks like 'e's picking up.'

'Sorry, I was miles away right then.' She smiled dismissively, loath to meet his eyes at that moment. 'Yeah, 'e looks like 'e's puttin' on a bit o' weight. I worry about Danny. There's always one weak 'un in the family.'

William smiled. 'Danny's gonna grow up the toughest o' the bunch, mark my words.'

Nellie leaned back in her chair and let her stockinged feet rest on the edge of the brass fender. 'Our Carrie seems ter be gettin' 'erself involved wiv those suffragettes,' she said. ''Er mate at work 'as bin tellin' 'er all about 'em. The gel goes on the marches, by all accounts.'

William looked at Nellie with concern. 'She's a bit too young fer that sort o' fing. The kid's only jus' turned fifteen. I wouldn't wanna see our Carrie get involved wiv that lot. I was readin' in the paper the ovver day 'ow they go on 'unger strikes in prison an' 'ave ter be force-fed.'

Nellie shrugged her shoulders. 'Yer know 'ow 'eadstrong Carrie is, Will,' she said. 'Nuffink we can say will make any difference. Look 'ow she used ter get on ter yer about 'elpin' out in the yard an' goin' on those journeys wiv yer.'

'Well, I 'ope she don't go gettin' any fancy ideas,' he said quickly. 'I'm not against votes fer women but I fink they're goin' the wrong way about it. Chainin' 'emselves ter railin's ain't gonna do any good.'

Nellie got up and moved the iron kettle over the fire. 'Well, sometimes yer gotta take drastic measures,' she replied. 'Look at that time the women blocked the turnin'. It worked, didn't it?'

William's face relaxed into a smile. 'I don't fink it did. What stopped ole Galloway was a certain little troublemaker who marched out o' the 'ouse wavin' a chopper.'

Nellie glared at him. 'Well, it stopped the women gettin' a soakin', didn't it? Now what about gettin' up out o' that chair an' callin' the kids in before it gets dark?'

Nora Flynn had finished washing the dishes and scouring the pots and pans after the late tea, and was preparing to take an evening stroll. The two lads had been subdued at teatime, she thought; and Josephine seemed to lack her usual sparkle. There had been an atmosphere. At such times Nora wished she could eat alone, but it was her employer's wish that she should join the family for meals. She had seen the fleeting glances which flashed between the boys and noticed George's reluctance to make conversation. He had answered Josephine's questions in monosyllables and had left the table as soon as he could. As Nora reached for her coat Josephine walked into the room, a sad look on her pretty young face.

'Why does Father shut himself up in that miserable room, Nora?' she asked, sitting down in a chair beside the large table.

Nora gave the child a brief smile. 'Yer farvver needs ter be alone, child,' she replied. ''E's got a lot on 'is mind.'

Josephine ran her finger along the raised grain of the wood. 'Geoffrey took me to the stable today to see the horses. They're lovely, but Father said I shouldn't go near there any more. He told Geoff so. Why, Nora?'

'Yer farvver's worried in case yer get knocked down by one o' them carts, luv, or in case one o' them 'orses kicks out at yer,' Nora told her kindly. 'A transport yard can be a dangerous place for a little gel.'

Josephine clasped her hands on the table and looked wide-eyed at the housekeeper. 'When I was at the stable I saw the children playing out in the street. Isn't it dangerous for them?' she asked.

'They've got no choice, they live beside the stable,' Nora said, smiling. 'Yer lucky. Yer live in a nice 'ouse in a nice square, an' there's no 'orse-an'-carts ter worry about, 'cept the traders who call.'

Josephine pouted. 'I think it's much nicer in Page Street, and the children there seem very nice too,' she remarked. 'Geoffrey told me that the boy who waved to me was Mr Tanner's son, Charlie. I think he was very nice.'

Nora glanced up at the large clock on the mantelshelf. 'I've got ter go out, Josephine, an' you'd better get off ter bed, it's gettin' late,' she told the child.

Josephine stood up obediently and presented her cheek to receive Nora's goodnight kiss, then as she was going out she stopped suddenly and turned in the doorway. 'You'd never leave us, would you, Nora?' she asked, her violet eyes gazing appealingly at the housekeeper.

Nora shook her head firmly. 'I'll always be 'ere, child, an' yer can always come an' talk ter me if yer need to. Now off ter bed wiv yer this minute.'

Josephine was about to say something, but instead she just smiled quickly as she turned and hurried up to her room.

Nora put on her coat and walked down the stairs, hoping to catch Geoffrey before he left. He had said he was going out to meet someone and Nora wanted to find out just what was wrong. Geoffrey was always ready to confide in her, although lately he appeared to have something on his mind and she felt he had become evasive.

The house was quiet, however, and as Nora let herself out of the front door she heard George Galloway's throaty cough coming from his room. It was cold and damp and not an evening for taking a stroll, but she wanted time to think. Things had changed in the house of late and she did not understand why George was so morose this evening. Recently he had become very talkative and often, after Josephine had gone to bed and the two young men had gone out, had called her into his room. They had chatted about the early days and of trivial things which Nora found amusing. George had laughed with her, and on one or two occasions had tempted her with a glass of port. Nora had found herself becoming excited in his presence and her long suppressed physical feeling for him had been rekindled. George had not made any advances, other than to remark on what the lads might think should they return unexpectedly, and she had not felt able to give him any hint of her secret desire.

At first she had felt pity for George, pity for a distraught man left alone to care for three young children, but her pity had soon changed to something deeper. She soon realised that he hardly ever noticed her. He was a hard man, with a streak of arrogance and meanness in his nature, but there was something difficult to define about him which she found very attractive. Maybe it was the single-mindedness that had brought him comparative wealth. Such strength of purpose might change to devotion and release the goodness in his character, Nora thought to herself, if he would only start to be aware of her as a woman. He had never seen her as anything other than hired help and she had suppressed her feelings for him and gone about her tasks, wishing secretly that one night he might visit her, if only out of loneliness. He never had, and the solitariness of her own existence weighed heavily on her.

I've been alone too long, she thought as she crossed the square and walked out into the empty Jamaica Road. Why can't I show him how I feel about him? Maybe he is only waiting for a sign or a hint.

George had not been drinking so heavily of late and seemed to have come to terms with his bereavement, but tonight there was something on his mind. Maybe she should confront him in his room and let him see she was concerned for his happiness.

The muffled sound of a tug whistle carried from the river lanes as the fog drifted down. Nora pulled the collar of her coat around her neck and buried her hands deeper into her fur muff. Her high-heeled shoes echoed on the deserted pavements and when she reached the park gates she stopped and turned round. Normally she would have carried on a little further but the fog seemed to be getting thicker. She hurried back towards the quiet square, her thoughts centred on a warm fire and a hot drink before retiring for the night.

It was then that she saw the couple standing in a dark doorway. The man had his back to her and was pressing against the woman whose face was resting on his shoulder. Her eyes were closed and she was groaning as the man's rhythmic movements became faster. Nora turned her head as she walked quickly past, but the couple seemed oblivious to her presence. She hurried on and turned into the quiet square feeling strangely roused. The woman was probably one of those tarts who frequented the music hall, she thought, and he might be a merchant seaman. Maybe she was wrong. Perhaps they were two young lovers who for their own reasons had to resort to a dark doorway on a cold miserable night to express their love for each other.

Nora let herself in the house and closed the door behind

her. She stood in the hall for a few moments, then taking a deep breath tapped gently on the front room door. She heard George's gruff voice and as she stepped into the room Nora saw her employer sitting slumped in his armchair before the fire. He had a glass of whisky in his hand and his face was flushed.

Nora's heart sank as she sat down facing him. He looked at her enquiringly. She hesitated before speaking.

'I wanted to 'ave a chat, George,' she said at last. 'I noticed you were quiet ternight. Is anyfing wrong?'

He shook his head and stared down into the fire. 'I've 'ad a few words wiv young Geoffrey. It's nuffink really,' he said quietly.

Nora paused for a moment then sat forward in her chair. 'I've bin enjoyin' our little chats, George,' she began. 'I 'ope yer feel the same way. I jus' want yer ter know I'm always 'ere, in case yer need me.'

George looked up and noticed that his housekeeper was eyeing him intently. 'Yer look a bit edgy, Nora. Anyfing wrong?' he asked.

She smiled. 'I came in 'ere wiv the same question. I don't like ter see yer miserable, George. It grieves me ter see yer drinkin' alone.'

'I don't 'ave to,' he replied. 'Yer could always join me.'

'I didn't mean it like that,' she said quickly, her face flushing slightly. 'It used ter upset me when yer spent all that time shut away in 'ere wiv the bottle. I wanted ter 'elp yer, but I didn't know 'ow. I know yer was grievin' over Martha but it's bin a while now an' I was pleased when yer let me share the evenin's wiv yer. I thought it was 'elpin' yer, an' me too. I don't like ter see yer go back ter drinkin' 'eavily again, George. Don't shut the children out o' yer life, an' me too fer that matter.'

He was watching her closely while she spoke, aware of her embarrassment. Nora was strange, he thought. She had always seemed so prim and proper, never giving way to her feelings. Now she was making him feel uncomfortable. She was a fine woman, he had to admit. Her face was well shaped and her eyes warm and friendly. The high-necked blouse seemed to accentuate her sloping shoulders and small breasts, and her hands were those of a younger woman, long and slender. George noticed how she sat upright in the chair, with her long black cotton dress almost touching the floor. Her still raven hair was pulled high on top of her head and secured with a fan-comb, giving her a matronly appearance that was more suited to an older woman. He realised he had never seen it any other way and wondered if she wore it like that when she went to bed.

Suddenly he got up, averting his eyes from hers. 'Let me get yer a drink,' he said, walking over to the sideboard.

Nora felt she should decline his offer but the strange excitement she had felt on seeing the lovers still persisted. She made no effort to stop George pouring out a large port, telling herself she was going to need it if she were finally to unburden herself to him. The time was ripe, she tried to convince herself.

George was standing beside her with the glass of port held out to her. He smiled, and she noticed how his eyes appraised her.

'Yer know, I've never seen yer wiv yer 'air let down,' he said suddenly.

Nora took the glass from his hand and sipped the port, hoping it would ease her fluttering stomach. 'That's a strange fing fer yer ter say,' she replied, attempting to stay calm.

'Let it down,' he told her.

'I beg yer pardon.'

'Let it down. Let me see yer wiv it down on yer shoulders,' he said.

Nora's face felt hot and her cheeks flushed a bright red. 'Mr Galloway,' she said indignantly, 'I'm forty years old. You're making me feel like a flighty young woman.'

George put his hand on her shoulder and squeezed gently. 'Martha used ter wear 'er 'air like that an' she would never let it 'ang loose. Take it down, Nora, please.'

Slowly she placed her glass on the small table at her elbow and reached up to her hair with both hands. George sat down on the edge of his armchair, transfixed, as she removed the fan-comb and the two long hairpins. Her hair dropped down and she slipped her fingers through the raven locks until they were spread evenly and resting on her shoulders. Her face had paled and her eyes dropped as Galloway reached out his hand to hers.

'Yer've got beautiful 'air,' he said in a low voice that made her tremble inside. 'Will yer stay wiv me ternight?'

Nora picked up her glass and sipped the drink, purposely evading his gaze. 'Are yer sure, George?' she whispered, hardly recognising her own voice. 'Is it me yer desire? Me, Nora Flynn?'

He held her trembling hands in his and fixed her with his dark eyes. 'I've wanted ter make love ter yer fer a long time, Nora,' he said softly. 'Yer've always fended me off wiv yer reserve, but I knew that there'd come a time. I could sense it when we talked. Until now I couldn't make a move wivout yer givin' me a sign. Yer never did, though.'

'Is ternight so different?' she asked.

He looked down at her hands for a moment. 'Young Geoff an' me got at it again,' he said with a sigh. 'It was nuffink really, only about Jack Oxford. I was gonna put the idiot off an' Geoff was against it. 'E sided in wiv that yard foreman o' mine. I gave way in the end but Geoff wasn't satisfied. 'E felt I should give 'im more sway in the runnin' o' the business. That's what the argument was over ternight. When Geoff finally stormed out I got ter drinkin' an' I realised 'ow empty me life's become. Ternight I need yer, Nora. Yes. Ternight I need yer, an' ternight I could see the change in yer eyes the minute yer walked in that door.'

Nora felt her breath coming fast as he stood up and reached down to her. She got up from her chair to face him and he pulled her to him, kissing her hard. 'No, George!' she gasped as his hands moved down her body. 'Give me a few minutes, then come to my bed. Please?'

Before he could say anything she turned and hurried from the room, her whole body shaking as she made her way quickly up the stairs.

When she reached her room Nora stripped and climbed into her old bed, eagerly listening for his footsteps on the stairs. She stroked her hands along her hot body as she waited for what seemed an eternity, then at last the creaking of the stairs sounded loudly and she heard the door opening. He stood silhouetted there by her bed, his bulk rising above her, then he was beside her, his hands roughly caressing her nude body, his wet lips moving along her neck. Her whole body shook and she let out a faint sob as he joined with her in a fierce embrace.

Chapter Ten

Carrie made her way to the factory, her coat collar turned up against the bitter cold. She was now just seventeen and it seemed to her as though she had worked at Wilson's for ever. It was really only three short years since she started, but in that time she had been moved from the top floor to the floor below, where she learned to trim the hides and chamois leather pieces, and then to the ground floor to learn grading and sorting. Each move had been a step up the ladder for her but she felt a little sorry for her friend Mary, who seemed to have been overlooked for promotion and was still sweating away on the top floor. Carrie knew that her friend had not helped herself by her frequent absences from work and her reputation for being actively involved with the suffragette movement. Mary seemed happy enough though, especially since she had got herself a new workmate.

Carrie normally took little notice of the stories abounding throughout the factory, but this time she knew it was true that Mary had found herself a lover. Her new companion was a girl of her own age who would sit enthralled as Mary went on about her campaigning. The two were inseparable and sat holding hands during their lunch breaks, leaving the factory in the evenings arm in arm. Nevertheless, although Mary's private life was the talk of the factory, she had earned the girls' respect for her dedication to campaigning on behalf of women. Some of the other girls were becoming interested in the suffragette movement, and one or two had gone along to watch the marches. There had also been a lot of publicity in the newspapers recently and only a week ago it was reported that two of the leading figures in the movement had been arrested and sent to prison for interrupting a court hearing in Manchester.

As she walked into the factory on Thursday morning Carrie was thinking about the coming weekend. She and two of her workmates had agreed to join Mary on a big march to Trafalgar Square where they would be addressed by prominent figures involved in the movement. Carrie's decision to join the marchers had caused some tension at home and her brother James had been forthright in his condemnation. 'Bloody stupid if yer ask me,' he had growled. 'They should lock the lot o' yer up.'

Charlie had merely grinned and got on with his tea, but the youngest member of the Tanner family was curious. 'Why are you goin'?' Danny had enquired. 'If yer get locked up, they'll stick a tube down yer froat an' force-feed yer. Our teacher told us that's what they do.'

Silence was restored around the meal table by her father, who glared at Danny and threatened to force-feed *him* if he didn't finish his meal.

The day seemed to drag on and Carrie's two workmates, Jessica Conway and Freda Lawton, chatted away incessantly about the big day. Carrie was thinking of other things as she sat at the wide bench, sorting and grading the leathers. She had met Sara Knight in the street a few days ago and persuaded her to go along with her to the church club in

Dockhead that evening. Carrie had a special reason for going, for that evening the club was putting on a boxing tournament and Billy Sullivan was fighting in one of the bouts. Billy was eighteen and the eldest of the Sullivan boys. He had asked her to come along to see him box. Carrie had grown up with the Sullivan boys and was looking forward to the evening. Of all the brothers Billy was her favourite. When they were children he had always been quick to single her out from her friends and often gave her little gifts as a token of his friendship. Once he had offered her a whole set of cigarette cards, though she had not taken them, knowing how he treasured them. On another occasion he had removed a bandage from his finger, purposely to show her his painful whitlow, and when she screwed her face up he stole a kiss, only to receive a sharp kick on the shin as Carrie wiped her cheek with the back of her hand. They had remained friends, however, and one time Billy had taken her brothers' part against the boys from Bacon Street Buildings.

'Mary reckons we'll be asked ter carry a banner,' Jessica was saying. 'I'm gonna feel silly. Will yer carry one if they ask yer, Carrie?'

'Sorry. What d'yer say?'

The two girls exchanged glances and Freda nudged her friend. 'Carrie's got ovver fings on 'er mind,' she giggled.

''Ave yer got a young man then, Carrie?' Jessica asked.

She blushed and tried to ignore the giggling. 'It's just a boxin' match,' she answered quickly. 'Billy Sullivan's fightin' an' 'e asked me ter go an' see 'im, that's all.'

Jessica turned to Freda. 'I know Billy Sullivan. 'E's nice. Fancy our Carrie goin' out wiv a boxer.'

She smiled and got on with her work. Billy *was* nice, she thought. He was the oldest of the seven Sullivan boys and had often been involved in scraps to defend his brothers or to defend himself when his younger brothers turned on him. The Sullivans were always fighting, but most people in the street realised that the family were more often than not the victims of their own reputation. Carrie was aware that her youngest brother Danny idolised Billy Sullivan and had been taking boxing lessons from him. Billy had told her that young Danny was a natural and should join the boxing club. Her mother had forbidden it but her father felt it would do the lad good. Danny was forever pestering his mother to let him join and in the meantime continued to take lessons.

At the end of the working day Carrie left the factory and hurried home with excitement building up inside her. Her workmates' taunts had set her thinking. Billy Sullivan was just one of the lads in the street but he had taken an unusual interest in her lately and she was flattered. All the local girls liked him and she felt it would be nice if she could boast that Billy was her real beau.

As she hurried into the house and helped her mother set the table for tea, Carrie hummed happily, and when the family gathered for the meal she became the object of a certain amount of banter from her brothers.

'So yer gonna see Billy Sullivan fight, are yer, Carrie?' James said, looking at Charlie for support.

'Billy's gonna win easy,' Danny butted in.

'I dunno so much,' James said through a mouthful of sausage. 'I 'eard that bloke 'e's fightin' is pretty good. 'E's the East End champion.'

'That's nuffink,' Danny countered. 'Billy's the best boxer in Bermondsey.'

'Shut yer traps an' get on wiv yer food,' Nellie grumbled.

James folded a thick slice of bread and dipped it into his gravy. He had grown into a hefty young man since starting work at the sawmills. The heavy work had developed his arms, and his thick neck was set on wide shoulders. His fair hair was full and tended to curl, and his dark blue eyes were deep-set and wide-spaced. James had begun to feel grown-up and tended to ape his father's mannerisms. Charlie, on the other hand, was a quiet, studious lad who had just started work in an office. He had had to take a certain amount of good-natured teasing about the sort of job he did – his older brother was always reminding him that office work was for cissies. Charlie took it all in good part and rarely lost his temper, to the chagrin of his two brothers and particularly James.

'One day yer might be comin' ter see me fight at the club,' Danny remarked after a while.

'Oh no she won't,' Nellie said firmly. 'I'm not 'avin' any o' my kids growin' up ter be boxers, so shut up an' get on wiv yer tea.'

Danny pulled a face and bent his head over his plate. William looked up at Nellie. 'I dunno, Nell. It's a good club an' it teaches the kids ter look after 'emselves,' he said, pushing his empty plate away from him. 'Billy Sullivan ain't turned out such a bad lad. Look 'ow 'e used ter fight in the street. Those Sullivans were always gettin' inter scrapes. Ole Sadie used ter pack a punch too, although she seems ter be quieter lately. I remember the time when . . .'

'All right, Will, let 'em finish their tea,' Nellie chided him. 'I wanna get cleared away early. I've got Flo an' Maisie comin' roun' later. We got some fings ter talk about.'

William did not want to ask just what schemes the women were planning and decided it would be better if he departed to the Kings Arms as soon as they turned up.

At seven o'clock Sara Knight arrived and the two girls left for the club at Dockhead. Carrie was pleased to see Sara looking well. She seemed to have put on weight and her long brown hair was well brushed and tied neatly at the nape of her neck with a ribbon. Her eyes were bright, and as they made their way through the drifting fog she giggled happily and took Carrie's arm, falling into step beside her.

'I'm startin' work at the tea factory in Tooley Street next week, Carrie,' she said. 'It's much better than sackmakin'. The girls earn good money there an' yer get packets o' tea cheap. Me mum's ever so pleased. She didn't like me doin' that sackmakin'. Yer 'ad ter supply yer own string an' the money was terrible. Some weeks I only took 'ome ten shillin's. I'm gettin' fifteen at this job.'

'Is yer dad all right?' Carrie asked.

Sara nodded. ''E's found a real job. It don't pay very much but it's better than sellin' shoelaces an' collar studs. We don't 'ave the relief man callin' on us any more an' me muvver can put 'er china plates on the dresser now. The lady next door used ter mind 'em fer 'er. If the relief man 'ad seen 'em, 'e'd 'ave made 'er sell 'em.'

'What's yer dad doin', Sara?'

''E's workin' fer the council on the gate. 'E 'as ter book the carts an' fings in an' out. 'E 'as ter do nightwork as well, but Mum don't mind.'

When the two girls reached the club they saw Sadie Sullivan standing at the entrance with her boys. Eight-year-old Shaun stood between the ten-year-old twins, Patrick and Terry, and Joe, a thick-set eleven year old, was talking to some of his friends. The two older teenage boys, Michael and John, were standing with Billy and all looked serious-faced. Their father Daniel, a docker at the Surrey Docks, stood beside them proudly, looking dignified in his brown suit and knotted red scarf.

When Billy caught sight of Carrie and Sara, he came over. He had grown tall and his powerful shoulders were hunched as he faced the girls. Carrie could see the excitement written on his wide, handsome features, and she gazed at his dark, curly hair and his wide-spaced blue eyes which seemed to sparkle in the evening light.

''Ello, glad yer could come,' he said breezily. 'I've gotta go in an' get ready. Can I walk yer 'ome afterwards, Carrie?'

'If yer like,' she replied, flushing slightly.

Sadie Sullivan walked up to Billy with her youngsters in tow and kissed him on the cheek. 'Good luck, boy,' she said heartily. 'Yer better not lose, d'yer 'ear me?'

Billy winced at the kiss and hurried off into the club, with his family following along into the hall. Carrie and Sara found seats near the front a row behind Billy's family. It was noisy in the hall, with people milling around and talking in loud voices, and Carrie was enthralled by the air of excitement and anticipation.

Suddenly the lights went out, leaving the boxing-ring illuminated by a large gaslamp set high in the ceiling. The announcer climbed into the ring and welcomed everyone, including the supporters of the visiting team from Stepney. Soon the first two contestants climbed into the ring and the bout commenced. Sara held Carrie's arm as the two thin, pale lads belted each other around the ring, and when one lad's nose started to bleed she put her head down on Carrie's shoulder. The lad went after his opponent with both fists flying.

When the three rounds were over and the referee raised the Bermondsey lad's hand, a loud cheer went up. Sadie Sullivan had been getting more excited as the bout went on. She stood up at the decision and clapped loudly, only to be pulled down by her embarrassed husband.

'Wait till my Billy gets in there. 'E'll show yer,' she shouted loudly to the Stepney contingent.

'Shut up, luv, fer Gawd's sake. Everybody's lookin' at yer,' Daniel growled.

'Sod 'em,' Sadie said in a loud voice.

As the bouts progressed, the Stepney club were proving themselves to be worthy opponents. They won two contests in succession and after nine bouts had won a total of four. Sadie had been vociferous throughout and when the last two contestants left the ring, turned to Daniel.

'When's my Billy gonna come on?' she shouted above the din.

''E's on next. It's the last bout,' Daniel replied. 'If 'e loses, the match is a draw. It'll be five all.'

'What d'yer mean, if 'e loses?' Sadie screamed. 'Billy's gonna slaughter 'im.'

'All right, Muvver, keep yer voice down,' Daniel muttered, his eyes rolling with embarrassment.

During the fights Carrie had been on the edge of her seat with excitement and the sight of blood did nothing to lessen her enthusiasm. Sara, on the other hand, was constantly turning away when the exchange of blows became furious.

'It's a wonder they don't kill each ovver,' she remarked, averting her eyes again as one lad's lip started to spurt blood.

'They don't really 'urt each ovver, well not much anyway,' Carrie laughed. 'Look at the size o' those gloves.'

Sara was not convinced and gritted her teeth as the blows sounded.

When the last two contestants climbed into the ring, Carrie leapt to her feet trying to catch a glimpse of Billy over the shoulder of Sadie Sullivan who was shouting instructions to her eldest son. 'Don't let 'im get inside, Billy,' she screamed out. 'Use yer jab.'

'Shut up, Sadie, they ain't started yet,' Daniel groaned, hearing the laughter from the other side of the hall.

'You can laugh,' the excited Sadie shouted out. 'Wait till my Billy clonks 'im. 'E'll go down like a sack o' spuds.'

The boxers were being introduced and when Billy's name was announced the local fans' cheers rang out. All the Sullivan boys were on their feet as the fight got under way and Carrie stood on tiptoe to get a glimpse of the ring. Sara pulled at her coatsleeve. 'Is Billy winnin'?' she asked above the roar.

'I dunno,' Carrie replied. 'I can't see a fing.'

Suddenly a shout went up and Sadie jumped up and down in anguish. 'Get up, Billy!' she screamed.

'It's all right, luv, 'e's only slipped,' Daniel reassured her.

Carrie was feeling a little apprehensive as she peered through the crush in front of her. Billy's opponent looked much bigger than him and he was moving around the ring confidently. As the bell went for the end of the first round, Sadie looked as though she had just stepped out of the ring herself. Her face was a bright red and her piled-up hair had slipped down on to her shoulders. ''Ow's 'e doin', Dan?' she asked anxiously.

'I make it about even,' her husband replied, aware that Billy's opponent packed a good punch.

Carrie could see blood on Billy's lip and he looked tired as he slumped down on to the stool.

As the bell went Sadie was on her feet once more and screaming louder than ever. 'Do 'im, Billy! Knock 'im out, fer Gawd's sake!' she cried.

'Why don't yer sit down, lady? I can't see a bloody fing,' someone shouted.

Sadie did not hear the remark. She was punching the air and leaping up and down, with Daniel holding on to her coatsleeve in an attempt to restrain her.

'That's better! Go on, yer got 'im now! Use yer jab. Jab 'im!'

Billy's father seemed more confident at the end of the

second round. 'If 'e keeps out o' trouble, 'e's won it,' he told Sadie.

The bell sounded for the last round and the hall erupted as the local hero went all out to finish his opponent. The East Ender was plucky and fought back gamely, but as the bell sounded for the end of the contest everyone realised that Billy Sullivan had won. The two lads stood side by side with the referee holding on to their wrists, and when he raised Billy's hand the hall erupted in loud cheering. ''E's won! 'E's done it!' Sadie cried out, her face scarlet and tears running down her cheeks. 'What did I tell yer?' she said proudly to Daniel. 'Didn't I tell yer 'e'd win?'

Carrie stood beside Sara, who was glad the tournament was at last over, and when the boxers left the ring and walked past her along the aisle, she called out to him. 'Well done, Billy.'

He gave her a smile through battered lips and left the arena to back-slaps and compliments as the lights came up. Sadie had just about managed to compose herself and sat down in her seat exhausted after her feats of vocal support for her son.

The crowd was leaving and as one party walked along the aisle, a man among them turned to his friend. 'Bloody disgrace if yer ask me,' he said. 'Our boy won two o' the rounds. I reckon the ref must 'ave bin blind, or else 'e couldn't count the score.'

Sadie was on her feet in a flash. 'Oi! I 'eard what yer said That's my Billy yer talkin' about. 'E won easy. If it 'ad gone on anuvver round, 'e'd 'ave knocked your bloke spark out.'

The man laughed at her. 'What der you know about boxin', yer silly ole mare?'

'She can shout a good fight,' his companion said loudly.

Sadie turned and glared at the smartly dressed woman by the man's side. 'Who you talkin' to, yer ponced-up prat?' she sneered.

'Who you callin' a ponced-up prat?' the woman screamed back.

'You, that's who,' Sadie said menacingly.

The woman tried to get to Sadie but was held back by her companion who glared at Daniel. 'Take 'er 'ome, mate. She should be kept locked up,' he remarked. 'She's a bloody nuisance.'

'Who d'yer fink you're talkin' to?' Daniel retorted, trying to put himself between the two irate women.

Carrie took Sara's arm and steered her out of the hall as quickly as she could. 'I 'ope that woman don't start a fight,' she said quickly. 'It was Mrs Sullivan who taught Billy 'ow ter box!'

The hall was emptying and when the East End party spilled into the foggy night the angry woman pulled away from her companion. 'I don't care. She ain't gonna talk ter me like that an' get away wiv it,' she shouted.

Sadie was trying to calm down as she left the hall. Daniel was holding on to her and talking in a soothing manner. 'It don't matter, luv. Our Billy won fair an' square an' that's all that there is to it. Don't let 'em get yer dander up. They're only sorry their bloke didn't win. Now, if they're outside, just ignore 'em an' walk away. Are yer 'earin' what I'm sayin'?'

'All right, Dan, I'm listenin' ter yer. I'll just ignore 'em,' she said, trying to convince herself.

As they reached the street Sadie was immediately confronted by the woman who stood with her feet apart and her hands on her hips. 'Oi, Bigmouth, I wanna word wiv yer,' she shouted.

Daniel held Sadie's arm in a tight grip. 'Remember what I said, luv,' he muttered out of the corner of his mouth. 'Let it be an' jus' walk on by.'

Sadie gave her husband a quick smile and suddenly tore

her arm free. Before Daniel could do anything, his fighting wife was squaring up to the angry woman.

'C'mon then, yer scruffy-lookin' cow,' she jeered. 'We won five-four. 'Ow about makin' it six-four?'

The East Ender suddenly made a grab for her hair but Sadie dodged sideways and then threw a punch in the woman's face which sent her staggering backwards into the gutter.

Sadie was shaping up with her fists and snarling as she watched the woman closely. 'C'mon then,' she sneered. 'Want some more? There's plenty where that come from.'

Daniel was a slightly built man and no match for his large wife. As he tried to restrain her, she swept him to one side.

The woman who had confronted Sadie was now holding a handkerchief to her bloody nose and crying hysterically. 'She attacked me!' she cried. 'The woman's a ravin' lunatic. She should be locked up.'

The large crowd who had enjoyed the tournament stood around hoping for an extra bout, but they were disappointed. The bloody and bowed woman was led away by her companion muttering into her handkerchief. Sadie turned away, feeling quite pleased with the way the evening had turned out, when she was suddenly halted in her tracks.

'Now what's bin goin' on 'ere then?'

Sadie looked at the uniformed figure in front of her and gave him a weak smile. 'It's nuffink, mate. We was jus' 'avin' a little disagreement, that's all,' she said meekly.

The bloodied woman's companion had seen the policeman approach and hurried over, still holding on to the casualty. 'That woman attacked my lady friend,' he said, jerking his thumb at Sadie. 'She's mad, I'm sure of it. Look what she's done.'

PC Harkness had been patrolling the local streets for many years and he knew all about the fighting Sullivans. ''Ave yer bin up ter yer tricks again, Sadie?' he said in a tired voice.

156

Daniel tried to speak but the constable held up his hand. 'I'm askin' Sadie,' he said.

'She started on me,' Sadie replied, trying to look suitably aggrieved. 'She pulled me 'air out. I 'ad ter defend meself, officer, didn't I?'

The policeman took out his notebook and sucked on a pencil stub. 'D'yer wanna make a complaint?' he asked the woman's companion.

'Yer bet yer life I do,' the man replied. 'People like 'er should be locked up. My Clara wouldn't 'arm a fly, would yer, luv?'

'Right, I'll 'ave yer names an' addresses. An' don't walk away, Sadie. I want your particulars as well,' the constable sighed.

Carrie had been watching the affray along with Sara, and when Billy emerged from the hall they ran up to him. 'Yer mum's whacked this 'orrible woman, Billy,' Carrie said quickly. 'She's got nicked. There was a copper an' 'e took 'er name.' Billy winced. Carrie could see his swollen lips and the graze under his right eye. 'It's all right though. Yer mum an' dad's gone 'ome wiv yer bruvvers. Are yer feelin' all right?'

Billy laughed painfully. 'Yeah, it ain't so bad. I bet the ovver bloke's a bit sore too.'

The Sullivan boy carried his boxing-trunks and vest rolled up under his arm as the three of them made their way home through the swirling fog. A tug whistle sounded as they turned into Page Street and when they neared Carrie's front door, Sara turned to her friend.

'I've enjoyed ternight, Carrie – except fer the blood,' she said with a big grin. 'It was nice comin' out wiv yer. It's bin a long time since we did it. I'm so pleased yer won, Billy. Me an' Carrie was cheerin' fer yer.'

Carrie looked at the young man. 'We'll see Sara 'ome, won't we, Billy?'

He nodded. 'It's a bad night ter be out alone. Take me arm.'

The two friends walked the length of the dimly lit turning, each holding on to one of Billy's arms. They were laughing happily as they turned into Bacon Street and strolled along to the ugly tenement block. The two girls hugged each other good night, and when Sara's footsteps had faded on the stone stairs Carrie and Billy retraced their steps back into Page Street. Billy was chatting away about his bout and Carrie held on to his arm feeling very grown-up. She liked the young lad and hoped he would ask her out in the near future, but Billy was feeling hazy after his exertions and was still carried away by the excitement of beating the East End champion. When they reached Carrie's front door he kissed her on the cheek shyly and quickly made off to his house at the end of the turning, leaving her feeling a little disappointed.

Chapter Eleven

On a cold damp Saturday Carrie left the Wilson factory at noon with Jessica and Freda and hurried along to the pie shop in Dockhead. The three girls joined the line of customers. When they were eventually served with plates of hot pie, mashed potatoes and steaming hot parsley liquor, they slipped into a bench seat and quickly devoured their meal.

Jessica swamped her plate with sour vinegar and garnished the pie with a liberal amount of salt and pepper. She was a big girl with chubby features and untidy, mousy hair cut in a straight line above her neck. As she ate the food quickly, her deep-set eyes blinked constantly and the liquor dripped down her chin. Freda, by contrast, was a tallish, slightly built girl with a flat chest and long arms that seemed to sprout from the sleeves of her tight-fitting coat. She was just twenty-one but her thin face and long neck made her look older. Her dark hair was brushed into a tight bun on top of her head and secured with a large comb, and she was wearing a fur muff which was secured to one of the large buttons of her shabby grey coat. Freda had been made pregnant when she was sixteen by a local lad who had then run off to sea. She had had the baby adopted. She had since become bitter and resentful of men and saw the women's suffrage movement as a cause she could identify with. Unlike Jessica, who had a more casual approach to it, Freda was becoming a dedicated follower and had already been on quite a few marches during the past year.

Carrie finished her meal and glanced at her two friends as a poorly dressed young woman came along the aisle with her two children following her. The youngsters' clothes were in rags and they looked tired and cold. Each of the children carried a plate of mashed potato and liquor. When they had slipped into the bench seat behind the three girls, Carrie glanced around and saw the woman cut her pie in half and put the portions on her children's plates. They all ate ravenously, unaware of her eyes on them.

Freda and Jessica had seen the destitute family too and exchanged sad glances.

'They've got one pie between 'em,' Carrie whispered to her two friends.

Freda looked at Jessica who glanced quickly at Carrie. Without a word she dipped down into her large handbag and put three pennies down on the table. Her spontaneous gesture was immediately matched by her friends, and between them they collected nine pennies. Jessica quickly scooped up the coins and walked up to the counter. 'Three pie an' mash, an' plenty o' liquor,' she said saucily.

The young man behind the counter served up the portions and slapped the plates down on the marble counter.

'More liquor,' Jessica said, giving him a hard stare.

The man ladled more of the parsley gravy on to the plates without comment and when Jessica was satisfied she walked back and put the brimming portions down in front of the mother and her two children. ''Ere, get that down yer,' she said, smiling widely.

The woman looked up at her benefactor. 'Gawd bless yer, luv,' she said quietly.

The three girls hurried from the pie shop, smiling with satisfaction, and hurried to the tram stop.

'When women get the vote there's gonna be a few changes made, mark my words,' Freda said in a firm voice. 'People round 'ere are starvin' while up West those bloody dandies in top 'ats an' fur coats are stuffin' themselves full o' the best food an' drink. It ain't fair.'

Jessica nodded. 'Yer right, it ain't fair, but there's a lot o' well-ter-do ladies in the suffragettes, Freda,' she remarked. 'They ain't all turnin' a blind eye.'

Carrie remained quiet, thinking of what her mother had said about getting herself into trouble. She wondered just what the march was going to be like. Lately everyone seemed to be talking about the suffragettes and some of the stories she had heard made her feel a little apprehensive. Apart from the leaders who regularly got themselves arrested and imprisoned, there were those who came before the courts and were fined for disorderly conduct. Mary had been arrested and fined on two or three occasions and Freda had told her how groups of young men gathered at the meetings to heckle and jeer the speakers, and that fights often broke out during which the police ignored the young men but arrested the women at every opportunity.

When the tram shuddered to a halt and the three climbed aboard, they saw Mary sitting on the lower deck and joined her. Mary was bubbling with excitement and carried a roll of posters which she opened to show her friends. Carrie was aware of whispered remarks from some of the passengers, and the conductor gave them a suspicious look as he walked up and down the aisle to collect the fares.

'I 'ope yer not finkin' o' stickin' them there posters on my tram, are yer?' he said in a gruff voice as they swung round into Tower Bridge Road.

Mary gave him a blinding look and nudged Carrie. 'Silly ole goat! Who wants ter stick posters on 'is rotten old tram?'

When they pulled up at the Tower Bridge Road market, the conductor jumped down and hurried into a café. As soon as his back was turned, Mary got up from her seat and threw the posters into Carrie's lap. 'Won't be a minute,' she said, giving the girls a saucy wink as she dashed back along the aisle.

The conductor soon emerged from the café carrying a can of tea and the tram moved off. At the Elephant and Castle the girls alighted and Mary gave the conductor a wide grin. 'Fanks fer yer 'elp,' she called out to him as the tram pulled away from the stop with a 'Votes for Women' poster clearly visible on the rear end.

The marchers were congregating in Lambeth Road. When the girls reached the old Bedlam Asylum, Mary was greeted warmly by a smartly dressed woman who handed her a white, green and purple-coloured banner with the letters 'WSPU' boldly emblazoned on it. 'We're waiting for the East End contingent and then we're starting,' she said, taking the posters from Mary.

Carrie looked around her and saw young women standing in groups, each with their own distinctive banner. They had come from all over London. Some of them wore factory aprons and white linen caps.

'They're from the chocolate factory in Walworth Road,' Mary said, and pointed to another group. 'That lot comes from Waterloo.'

Soon the East End women arrived, riding in two open horse carts driven by bored-looking carmen. A cheer went up as the women jumped down and hurried to take their places. One of them carried a banner which proclaimed, 'Poplar Women

Want The Vote', and to the rear of the group another two women shared a large wide banner which said in bold letters, 'Stepney Women Unite'.

Organisers hurried up and down along the lines as the long column started off along Lambeth Road and into Westminster Bridge Road. Up ahead, Carrie could see the tall tower of Big Ben. Folk stared at them as they passed, some of them bemused but others openly mocking. Some children ran alongside the column for a time, and then with their curiosity satisfied darted off down side streets.

As the column reached the wide bridge and started to cross, a group of young men gathered at the kerbside and began to shout out obscene comments. Carrie's heart beat wildly as she glanced across at the men, fearing that violence would erupt at any second. Some of them were joking and jeering, but it frightened her to see how some faces were twisted with malice and hatred. She turned her head away and looked straight ahead, breathing a deep sigh of relief when the column had passed by without incident.

She was beginning to feel more relaxed by the time the women reached Victoria Street and neared the railway station. Policemen were flanking the procession and some way in front two mounted officers were clearing the way. Mary was shouting slogans and walking proudly, her banner flapping in the slight breeze, Freda and Jessica were walking beside Carrie with serious expressions on their faces, and for the first time she felt a little thrill of exhilaration at taking part in the march.

Soon the head of the column veered to the right and as the line straightened the women were leered and jeered at by a large group of young men who had gathered at a corner of the street clutching dirty sacks of overripe fruit.

'They're a local gang of nasty young troublemakers.

They did that last time,' a well-dressed woman shouted to Carrie and her friends above the din. 'Keep your heads down, ladies.'

A heavy shower of rotten fruit and cabbages fell among the women, and scuffles broke out as some men managed to get at the marchers, kicking out and yanking at their hair. The escorting policemen rushed up and chased them off, but by now some of the women who had been hit were in extreme distress. One young girl was led away with a handkerchief held up to her face and others were crying and screaming out in anger. Carrie and her two friends felt shocked and stunned, hardly able to believe they had escaped unharmed, but Mary had been hit on the back of the head by a soft orange and her hair was a soggy mess.

The column finally halted outside Hyde Park in some disarray. The organisers moved quickly among the ranks of women, taking stock of the situation and trying to restore order. When the injured and distressed had been consoled and spirits were restored the marchers set off again, walking stalwartly through the gates singing and laughing defiantly.

Carrie felt a surge of elation and pride as she strode into the park alongside the other women. After the attack on the march everything happening around her seemed suddenly different, and she began to feel a sense of belonging that was new to her. At first she had gone along with reservations, feeling unsure of herself, but when she watched the distressed women being led away and saw how the rest of them closed ranks and took over the banners, she felt an anger and determination she had never known before. Her curiosity had been fired by listening to Mary's outbursts and hearing a lot spoken about the protests, but she had attended the march with a childish sense of adventure, not really thinking that the campaign had any bearing on her own life. Only now was the real meaning of the movement and what the march represented slowly dawning on her. Women from all over London and from different backgrounds were marching together and facing ridicule and violence to win a say in the way the country should be governed.

Mary had told her about it often enough and she had thought about it vaguely, but until now she had not envisaged the depth of feeling shared by the campaigners. Their zeal was inspiring, and Carrie understood why they believed so passionately that with the vote women could change things and stand up against the poverty and slavery that ruled their lives. She realised that in a few years' time she could be old enough to vote, and thought of the hungry woman and her two children in the pie shop who had looked as though they were starving. She thought of her friend Sara and her ailing mother, and of Sara's father who had once sold matches in the gutter to feed his children. Maybe women could dispel the squalor and deprivation if they got the vote. Their anger at being denied a say in their own lives was now her anger, and Carrie felt a sudden determination to find out what needed to be done so that she too could help to make things better.

When the marchers reached their destination inside Hyde Park, Carrie could see a high platform around which people were gathering. The long column had now changed into a milling crowd, and people were closing in on the dais and pushed forward to get near to the speakers. Dampness rose from the sodden grass and the sky above their heads remained leaden as the meeting got under way. Speaker after speaker rose to demand the vote for women and to expound on what could be achieved if they were allowed into Parliament.

Mary seemed to know all about the speakers. 'That's Christobel Pankhurst,' she pointed out. 'See that man sitting next to 'er? That's H.G. Wells, an' that's George Bernard Shaw sittin' next to 'im. That lady wiv the black bonnet is Mrs Shaw.'

Carrie had been listening intently to the speakers and suddenly Mary nudged her. 'Keir 'Ardie's gonna speak now,' she said in a reverent tone. ''E's the Labour leader, an' 'e's really good.'

When the bearded man in the ragged suit got up and raised his hands there was complete silence. Then his reedy voice rang out over the gathering and Carrie was spellbound, forgetting the coldness that assailed her body and her tired, aching limbs. Keir Hardie was eloquent and impassioned as he talked of the poverty and squalor prevailing everywhere. He angrily decried the evils of starvation wages and the exploitation of workers, and reminded the gathering of the power of ordinary people to force changes and demand a better standard of living and quality of life. When he ended by lifting his hands high above his head and demanding the vote for women, the meeting erupted into deafening applause and wild cheering. Carrie felt drained as she joined in the clapping.

The meeting finally ended and the women started to disperse. Mary had disappeared into the crowd and Carrie left the park holding on to her friends' arms.

For a while the three were quiet, each wrapped up in their own thoughts, then Freda broke the silence.

'Wasn't that 'Ardie fella good?' she said with awe. 'When 'e was goin' on about the squalor an' starvation wages, I got so worked up I wanted ter scream.'

Carrie nodded slowly. 'I know what yer mean, Freda. I reckon 'e was the best speaker o' the lot. I'm glad I came terday. When yer listen ter those speakers, it makes yer fink.'

Jessica smiled. 'I reckon 'e was right about starvation wages. That's what we get at Wilson's. I reckon we should 'ave a strike, don't you?'

Freda snorted. 'A fat lot o' good that'd do. I 'eard they're finkin' o' puttin' us on short-time. I couldn't manage on short-time money. I'm the bread-winner in our 'ouse.'

The thought of being laid off and losing their wages weighed heavily on the three girls as they walked along Victoria Street and down to the Embankment. An elderly lamplighter was busy turning on the tall gaslamps by the river and at the Embankment steps a chestnut-seller was stoking up a glowing brazier. The three girls stood shivering at the tram stop, and by the time they clambered aboard the tram home they were feeling exhausted. Along the river a mist was rising, blotting out the far bridge, and through the gathering darkness rain started to fall.

Fog had been threatening for most of the day and now, as night fell and mists rose from the river, it thickened and swirled into the narrow Bermondsey backstreets. Page Street was fog-bound. The yellow light from the corner gaslamp barely pierced the gloom as William Tanner set his lighted paraffin lamp down outside Galloway's stables. He unlocked the small wicket gate and let himself into the yard, his footsteps echoing eerily as he walked across the cobbled area and entered the small stable at the far end of the premises.

The black Clydesdale was standing quietly in its stall, coat glistening with sweat. It looked balefully at the intruder. William could see that the horse's food had not been touched. He patted the horse to reassure it before running his hand down its withers and under its belly. 'C'mon, boy, we'll give yer a rub down,' he said, taking hold of the horse's bridle and backing it out of the stall. William hummed tunelessly to himself as he rubbed the large horse down with handfuls of straw. When he was satisfied that the coat was dry and shining, he led the Clydesdale around in a circle once or twice before putting it back into its stall.

The previous evening when Sharkey Morris had driven his pair of horses into the yard and jumped down from his cart he had been confronted by an irate George Galloway.

''Ave yer bin makin' 'em trot?' the owner enquired angrily, glaring at the distressed horse. ''E's sweatin'.'

Sharkey looked aggrieved as he ducked under the horse's head to face the owner. 'I never run my 'orses, Guv', yer know I don't,' he said quickly. 'The black's bin a bit ropy all day. 'E ain't touched 'is nosebag an' 'e wouldn't drink when I stopped at the trough at Dockhead.'

Galloway slid his hand under the horse's belly. ''Is stomach don't feel swollen, but yer never can tell.'

William had walked across the yard and taken hold of the horse's bridle, looking the animal over with a critical eye.

'It could be colic,' he remarked to Galloway.

'It might be, Will,' Sharkey cut in. ''E's bin lookin' at 'is flanks.'

George Galloway pulled a face. He had acquired the big Clydesdales and a large cart for the renewed contract with the rum firm in Tooley Street. This required transporting casks from the docks to the firm's arches in Tooley Street where the rum was bottled, and the Clydesdales were the only horses in the stable capable of pulling the heavy loads.

'We'll 'ave ter let the vet take a look at 'im, Will,' he said. 'It could be colic.'

'It might be the bloat or the twist,' Sharkey volunteered, only to be rewarded by a murderous look from his boss who knew only too well that the twist was a knotting of the intestine and nearly always fatal in horses.

'Get that 'arness off 'im and put 'im in the small stable,' George told his carman. 'Watch 'im ternight,' he said, turning to William, 'an' if 'e starts rollin' get the vet in straight away. I'll 'ave ter get anuvver firm ter do the run termorrer.'

William stood in the dark stable for a while, watching the horse nuzzling at the hay and blowing hard through its nostrils. He felt sure that there was nothing seriously wrong with the animal and before he left he patted its neck fondly.

As he walked back through the cobbled yard the sound of a horse moving in its stall made him look up instinctively to the stable on the upper level. His eyes widened in surprise. He was sure he had seen a flicker of light. He stood still. For a fleeting moment he saw it again and clenched his teeth, realising there was someone in the stable.

With an uneasy feeling William crept quietly over to the ramp and turned up the burner of his lamp before going on tip-toe up the steep incline. At the top of the ramp he turned right and walked quietly into the long stable, holding his lamp above his head. Most of the horses were lying in their stalls but one or two were standing, nuzzling at their hay nets and stamping. It all looked normal enough and William walked back out to the ramp with a puzzled frown. He crossed the level and looked into the chaff-cutting loft, immediately catching a whiff of paraffin. The hairs on his neck rose as he realised that someone was in the loft. He held the lamp high and saw the straw in one corner move.

'Who's there?' he called out, moving forward cautiously.

'It's only me, Will,' a low voice answered.

William moved his lamp a little and saw the face of Jack Oxford. The man's eyes were wide open and he wore a silly grin as he emerged from his hiding-place.

'What the bloody 'ell yer doin' 'ere?' William asked him.

The yard man shuffled uncomfortably from foot to foot. 'I'm sorry, but I lost me digs, yer see,' he said awkwardly.

'What d'yer mean, yer lost yer digs?' William asked.

Jack Oxford lowered his eyes and studied his boots. 'I got chucked out fer causin' trouble, but I didn't really. Well, I did, but I didn't start it, it was Fatty Arbuckle's fault, an' . . .'

''Old up, 'old up,' William interrupted. 'Yer sayin' yer got chucked out o' the doss-'ouse fer fightin'? You, fightin'?'

Jack nodded slowly. 'It was over me boots, yer see,' he began. 'Every night when I get inter bed I put the posts o' the bed in me boots. That way nobody can nick 'em wivout movin' the bed. Well, last night I 'ad me fish an' chips an' me pint o' porter an' I was just about ter leave the pub when ole Tommy Carberry walked in. You remember Tommy Carberry, 'im who used ter be a carman 'ere a few years back? Well, me an' Tommy gets talkin' an' 'e asked 'ow yer was gettin' on, so I told 'im 'ow yer was an' 'ow yer kids was all growin' up, an' . . .'

'What's all this got ter do wiv yer gettin' chucked out o' the doss-'ouse?' William asked, sighing with impatience.

'Well, yer see, Tommy bought me anuvver pint o' porter an' then I gets 'im one back an' . . .'

'So yer ended up gettin' pissed?'

'That's right, Will.'

'Let me guess the rest,' William said, grinning. 'Yer fergot ter put yer boots under the bedposts an' this Fatty what's-'is-name nicked 'em?'

Jack Oxford grinned back at the yard foreman. 'Next mornin' I got up early an' caught Fatty Arbuckle walkin' out wiv me boots on. Fatty Arbuckle ain't 'is real name but everybody calls 'im that. Anyway, I ses, "Oi, them's my boots," an' 'e calls me a stupid so-an'-so, so I ses, "I know them's my boots 'cos they've got 'orse shit on 'em." Well, 'e tries ter leave an' I grabs 'old of 'im, an' next fing yer know I'm on the floor. The noise woke everybody up an' the bloke in the next bed ter me grabs Arbuckle an' makes 'im give me me boots back. Funny fing was, who d'yer fink the bloke in the next bed was, Will?'

William shook his head slowly. 'Gawd knows.'

'It was me ole mate Tommy Carberry,' Jack said, chuckling. ''E was so pissed 'e kipped in the doss-'ouse. Mind yer, though, Fatty Arbuckle didn't argue wiv ole Tommy. "Give the man 'is boots back, yer fievin' git," 'e ses. By that time everybody's shoutin' out fer Arbuckle ter give me me boots back so they can go back ter sleep. That's when ole Chopper Chislett who owns the doss-'ouse told me ter piss orf an' don't come back. That's why I'm kippin' 'ere ternight. Yer don't mind, do yer, Will?'

William puffed hard. 'It's not a case of do I mind,' he said wearily. 'If Galloway knows yer kippin' in the stable, 'e'll sack yer fer sure. Anuvver fing, it's Saturday night. 'Ow was yer gonna get out termorrer mornin' wiv the place all locked up?'

'That's easy,' Jack replied, 'I was gonna get over the back wall an' drop down in the alley.'

'Well, yer'll 'ave ter go, Jack. Yer can't stop 'ere all night,' William said firmly.

'But I ain't doin' any 'arm,' he pleaded.

William raised his eyes to the ceiling. 'Look, Jack, the ole man only wants the slightest excuse ter put yer off, so don't go givin' 'im one.'

The yard man nodded slowly and bent down to gather up his few possessions. 'All right, Will. Yer right, I shouldn't be 'ere,' he said. 'I'll try the kip 'ouse in Bermondsey Street. They might 'ave a bed fer the night.'

William looked at Jack Oxford for a few moments then sighed in resignation and took the yard man by the arm. 'Look, yer won't get a bed this time o' night an' the fog's gettin' worse. Yer'd better stay 'ere, but fer Gawd's sake don't let anybody know I said that, an' don't let anybody catch yer dossin' down up 'ere, all right?'

Jack's face lit up. 'Will, yer a brick. Don't worry, I'll be careful.'

William walked off down the ramp and as he reached the gate he heard Jack whistling after him. He turned and saw the yard man's head poking out from the loft. 'I won't get me boots nicked 'ere, Will!' he shouted.

Chapter Twelve

1909 started cold and damp, and the new year brought fresh worries for the folk who lived in the Bermondsey backstreets. Wilson's leather factory went on to short-time working, and the river men found themselves struggling for work as trade slumped and the dockside berths stayed empty. The Surrey Docks were almost idle and local dockers stood around at the gates every morning hoping for a call-on. At the Galloway yard there was talk of at least two carmen being put off in the next few weeks, and added misery was heaped upon the hard-pressed tenants of Page Street when they heard that George Galloway had bought more houses in the turning and was going to raise the rents.

The latest rumour was the main topic of discussion for Nellie Tanner and her friends when they had one of their get-togethers in Nellie's neat and tidy parlour.

'I'm lucky I don't 'ave ter pay any rent,' she said, sipping her tea. 'I've got 'em all workin', now young Danny's got a job as an errand boy, but I'm worried in case Will loses 'is job. If that 'appens we'll be out on the street. I can't see Galloway lettin' us stop 'ere.'

'Yeah, it mus' be a worry fer yer,' Florrie Axford remarked.

'Yer kids don't bring in much, an' yer still gotta feed 'em all.'

Maisie Dougall nodded in agreement. 'Yer right there, Flo. My two boys are workin' now, but they don't bring 'ome much. They're only factory 'ands. Mind yer, the money comes in 'andy now me ole man ain't doin' much at the Surrey.'

''Ow much d'yer fink 'e's gonna put the rent up by, Nellie?' Aggie Temple asked, straightening the front of her flowered pinafore.

Nellie shrugged her shoulders. 'I 'eard 'e's puttin' it up ter ten shillin's a week. Mind yer, it's only a rumour. My Will don't get ter 'ear much. Galloway don't let 'im know anyfink.'

'I reckon it's bloody scand'lous,' Maisie said. ''Ow we gonna be able ter pay it? An' what's 'e gonna do if not? Chuck the lot of us out in the street?'

Florrie put down her teacup and leaned back in the chair. 'I fink it's best ter wait an' see,' she said. 'It's no good upsettin' ourselves before it 'appens.'

Aggie nodded. 'I s'pose yer right, Flo. At least I ain't got no kids ter worry about an' me ole man's job is pretty secure. Lamplighters don't bring in much money but they're always in work. Mind you, it's the bloody hours what get ter me. It's not so bad in the winter but in the summer 'e don't go out lightin' up till nine or ten.'

Florrie folded her arms inside her loose apron. 'Well, I ain't got no ole man ter worry about,' she said cheerily. 'I can come an' go when I like an' me time's me own.'

'Don't yer sometimes wish yer was married again, Flo?' Aggie asked. 'I mean, it mus' get lonely in that place all by yerself.'

Florrie shook her head vigorously. 'I've 'ad two ole men an' that's two too many.'

Maisie turned to Nellie. ''Ow's your Carrie gettin' on wiv

them suffragette people?' she asked. 'She goes on the marches, don't she?'

Nellie pulled a face. 'Don't ask me,' she said, gesturing with her hand. 'She nearly got 'erself locked up on the last march. Apparently all the women sat down in the middle o' Parliament Square, an' it was only when the mounted police galloped up that they moved. I told 'er she could 'ave got 'erself trampled on but she just laughed. Trouble is, if they do get arrested their names go in the papers an' everybody knows yer business.'

'Well, I wouldn't worry too much about that,' Florrie said. 'I fink it's a good cause. All right yer worried over Carrie goin' on them marches but at least it shows the kid's got pluck, and sense. I mean ter say, it's diabolical we can't vote. I fink we've got more idea than 'alf the men. They all seem ter get pissed on pollin' day, an' if yer ask 'em who they voted for they can't remember.'

'It must be a worry though, Nell,' Aggie said. 'It might be better when yer gel gets 'erself a chap. Ain't she got one yet?'

Nellie picked up the big iron teapot and started to refill the cups. 'Carrie's sweet on that Billy Sullivan,' she said, putting the teapot back down on the hob. 'She's always talkin' to 'im but they ain't walkin' out tergevver. The boy's boxin' mad, an' accordin' to Sadie 'e's gonna start fightin' fer money. She said 'e wants ter get a fight at the Blackfriars Ring.'

Aggie pulled a face. 'I 'eard that's a right rough place. I wouldn't like a son o' mine ter be a boxer. Look at ole Solly Green who's got the paper stall in Jamaica Road. 'E was a boxer when 'e was a young man, now look at 'im. 'E's got a nose spread all over 'is face an' yer can't get more than a mumble out of 'im. My 'Arold said Solly used ter fight at the Blackfriars Ring. Bloody shame really.'

The women lapsed into silence while they sipped their tea. After a while Nellie put down her cup and turned to Florrie. 'I bin finkin',' she said, 'why don't we get a beano up like the men do?'

'That's a good idea,' Florrie enthused. 'We could go ter Eppin' Forest an' stop at a pub.'

Maisie stroked her chin. 'They don't like women goin' in pubs, Flo. Will they let us in?'

Florrie waved Maisie's reservations aside with a sweep of her arm. 'It's different when yer go on beanos. There's a pub on the way ter Eppin' where the trippers pull up, an' they let yer buy drinks an' sit out on the grass. There's a special bar fer women. I've bin there so I know.'

Aggie looked thoughtful. 'I've never bin in a pub before, 'cept the snug bar at the Kings Arms,' she said. 'P'raps we could 'ire one o' them new-fangled motor charabangs if we save up enough money.'

Florrie looked doubtful. 'I don't fink we could get enough money fer that, Aggie. We might be able ter get an' 'orse-an'-cart. Galloway'll let us 'ave one, won't 'e, Nell?'

'I should fink so,' Nellie replied. ''E won't let us 'ave it fer nuffink though, knowin' 'im. Still, I could see Will. Long as they don't let ole Sharkey drive it. That bloke's always pissed. My Will reckons 'e'll be one o' the first ter go if any o' the men do get put orf.'

Florrie put down her empty cup. 'Right then, I'll put the word round the street an' see 'ow many names we get.'

'I'll talk ter Will soon as 'e's finished work,' Nellie promised.

The tea party finally broke up, and while Nellie turned her attention to the empty teacups, Maisie left to do the huge pile of washing and ironing she had taken in and Aggie hurried

176

home to put the duster over her spotless front parlour. Florrie meanwhile went away eagerly looking forward to starting on her list for the beano.

Carrie Tanner was looking forward to her eighteenth birthday, aware of the feelings stirring inside her. Often when she met Billy Sullivan on the street her stomach churned and she felt her breath coming fast as he stopped to talk, but there were times when she felt uncomfortable and miserable and was uneasy about seeing him. From listening to the other girls at the factory talking about the monthly curse she knew that they had similar feelings. She had also heard from listening to the older women that babies were made at certain times of the month and there were times when it was more likely to happen than not. The information she gleaned had left Carrie feeling confused. She had been experiencing her menses for some years now and knew what to do about them, but she had not been able to bring herself to ask her mother about how to avoid becoming pregnant.

It was lunch time and Wilson's workers were sitting in the ground-floor room eating their sandwiches when the subject of babies came up again. Freda Lawton was talking about the time she got pregnant.

'I went ter see this ole woman,' she was saying. 'The bloke what got me pregnant told me about 'er an' 'e reckoned she could get rid of it. I was only about two months gorn when I went ter see 'er an' I tell yer, the 'ouse stunk ter 'igh 'eaven. She was a scruffy ole cow wiv long straggly 'air. She looked like an ole witch. Anyway she give me this stuff ter drink. It tasted so 'orrible I was nearly sick right there an' then. She told me ter go 'ome an' 'ave a good soak in the tub. Trouble was, when I got 'ome me muvver was boilin' the clothes in the copper so I 'ad ter put the stew-pot on the fire. It took bloody ages an' before I 'ad enough water fer the tin barf I was sick. Me stomach was burnin' an' me muvver called the doctor in. 'E reckoned I'd bin poisoned. Anyway it never stopped me 'avin' me baby.'

Jessica shook her head. 'Some o' those people who get rid o' babies ought ter be locked up,' she scowled. 'There was this gel in Bacon Street Buildin's who got 'erself pregnant an' she went ter this place in Bermondsey Lane. This woman give 'er somefink ter drink, then she put this long knittin'-needle inside 'er. Nearly killed the poor cow she did. They couldn't stop the bleedin' an' she was carted orf ter Guy's. If I ever got pregnant wivout bein' married, Gawd ferbid, I'd sooner bear the shame than get rid of it.'

Freda nodded in agreement. 'Us workin' gels ain't got much of a life when yer come ter fink of it. We go ter work till we find a bloke an' get married, an' then we're pregnant in no time. Some are lucky an' don't 'ave many kids but ovvers 'ave one every year. The woman what delivered my baby was tellin' me about this young gel what kept gettin' pregnant. Ten kids she 'ad by the time she was twenty-seven. The woman told me she delivered every one, an' she told me that when she went ter the first confinement the gel didn't know a fing about 'ow babies get born. She even asked 'er 'ow the baby was gonna get out.'

Carrie had been listening intently to the conversation and she remembered some of the things she had heard said about birth control and limiting the amount of children in families. One of the women speakers at the suffragette meetings had mentioned setting up clinics for pregnant women and giving women more information about how to prevent unwanted babies. Carrie found herself becoming more and more confused as she listened to her friends. For some time now she had been thinking about what would happen if she walked out with Billy Sullivan and he tried to make love to her. What would he do if she said no?

'Would you let a boy 'ave 'is way wiv yer before yer got married, Carrie?' Jessica asked suddenly, interrupting her troubled thoughts.

Carrie shook her head. 'I couldn't. I'd be too frightened in case I fell fer a baby. What about you, Jess, would yer let a boy make love wiv you?'

'No fear,' Jessica replied quickly. 'If I got meself pregnant me farvver would chuck me out, I know 'e would.'

Freda smiled cynically. 'I remember sayin' that once, but I still got put in the pudden club. We're all the same. We say one fing an' mean anuvver. Take me. I was sure I wouldn't let a bloke take advantage o' me but I was wrong. I went out wiv this good-lookin' bloke an' I was feelin' good at the time an' 'e was very gentle. I remember it well. We was in the park an' 'e was gettin' 'andy. I told 'im ter stop it but 'e knew I didn't really want 'im to. Funny fing was, when we got around ter doin' it, I remember feelin' disappointed. It wasn't as good as I expected. I never went out wiv 'im after that one night, and as soon as 'e 'eard I was fallen 'e was off ter sea!'

'S'posin' yer liked a feller,' Carrie said to Freda, 'really liked 'im a lot an' 'e asked yer ter walk out wiv im? Would yer let 'im 'ave 'is way in case 'e never asked yer out again?'

Freda shook her head. 'I don't know, Carrie,' she answered. 'It all depends on 'ow yer feel at the time. Sometimes yer can say no an' mean it, an' ovver times yer tingle all over an' yer feel like yer on fire. All I know is, if yer do manage ter say no an' the bloke don't ask yer out anymore, yer ain't missin' much. Any bloke who finks that way ain't werf 'avin' in the first place.'

The whistle sounded and as they all trooped back to their

work benches, Carrie found herself feeling more confused than ever.

Jack Oxford was feeling very pleased with himself as he trudged through the foggy February evening to Abbey Street. Ever since his accident he had moved from place to place, sleeping in doss-houses and on park benches during the summer, but now he had found himself a regular place to stay. He had always thought himself fortunate in having a steady job which at least allowed him to have a full belly, but how much nicer it was now to go into a warm house and sit down to a hot meal beside a roaring fire. Now there was no more worrying about getting his boots stolen or his pockets picked while he slept. Now he could go to bed between clean sheets and get a wash and shave without having to wait his turn to use the grimy stone sinks in the doss-house.

Jack had been very lucky to find Mrs Cuthbertson. She was a big, motherly woman with red hair and a wide smile whose wayward husband had suddenly left her for a younger and prettier woman. After a few weeks of dejection and loneliness Amy Cuthbertson had quickly pulled herself together. She had a large house in Abbey Street which she had inherited, and a little money put aside. She also had a shrewd mind and realised that there was money to be made by taking in working men as lodgers. Amy's one failing was her weakness for stout, and when she was suitably fortified with a few bottles of the dark brew she became very passionate. More than one lodger had left her house due to her excessive demands upon him, and after each rejection she grew more determined than ever to find someone who would give her a little loving as well as the weekly rent. Amy had a strong streak of compassion in her make-up, and when Jack Oxford appeared on the scene it served him just a little too well.

There were three other lodgers in the house before Jack arrived but they were younger men who had come over from Ireland to work on building the railways and they usually kept themselves aloof from Amy. She liked older men, and when she spotted the yard man sitting mournfully on a park bench in Bermondsey Church Gardens one evening with a bottle of ale for comfort she was intrigued. The man looked as though he was earning a living by the state of his boots, and his sorrowful look prompted her to approach him. When she enquired casually about his general health and well-being Jack told her his past life history, his current position, and his intention of doing away with himself if things did not look up.

Amy had heard enough. She suggested to him that he might lodge in her house. That evening the yard man went to inspect his prospective room in Abbey Street and gave her one week's rent there and then. As the days passed Amy Cuthbertson became more and more kindly disposed towards her lodger, and one evening she plied him with stout and took the startled inebriate to her bed.

The new arrangement suited Jack Oxford admirably, and Amy too.

As he walked home through the fog along Abbey Street, Jack whistled to himself. The house was warm as he let himself in and he could smell mutton stew cooking.

'I'm in the scullery, deary. Tea's nearly ready,' Amy called out.

Jack ambled into the front room and flopped down in an armchair with a blissful sigh. He just could not believe how lucky he was.

Across the street Arthur Cuthbertson shifted his position in the shop doorway and scowled as he stared over at the house. Some of the people in the neighbourhood were still friendly with Arthur, and from what one of them had told him he had good reason to worry. Amy had found herself a bloke and they appeared to be very happy, he had been informed. Since his new lady friend had walked out on him, Arthur had realised he made a mistake in leaving Amy. He had been intending to go back to her cap in hand, hoping for a reconciliation, but this seemed unlikely now that she had found herself a new man. Well, there was only one thing to do, he decided. Amy's lodger would have to be frightened off if there was to be any chance of getting back with her. He would give them time to have their tea and then he would make an appearance, he told himself, fingering the piece of lead piping which was tucked into his wide leather belt.

After he had finished his meal Jack settled himself beside the fire and rested his feet on the brass fender. He sighed contentedly as he leaned back and closed his eyes, not taking any notice as Amy got up to answer the loud knock.

Her scream brought him upright in his chair, and as the bulky figure of Arthur pushed his way into the room brandishing a length of lead piping in his large fist Jack knew instantly that he was in serious trouble.

'So you're the whoreson who's took 'er from me, are yer?' Arthur growled at him, moving around the table to get at him.

'I ain't done nuffink,' Jack cried, trying to keep the table between him and his assailant.

'If I get 'old o' yer I'll maim yer, yer dirty ole goat!' Arthur yelled.

Amy was trying to hold her estranged husband back, with little success. 'Leave 'im alone, yer cowson!' she screamed. 'Yer pissed orf an' left me fer yer fancy bit an' now yer want me back. Well, I ain't takin' yer back, yer scruffy git. Go on, get out!'

Amy's outburst only made Arthur more incensed and he brought the lead pipe down on the table with a loud crash.

'Keep still, yer dopey bastard!' he roared at Jack. 'Let me get at yer! I'll do fer yer, I swear I will!'

With Amy holding on to Arthur's arm, the terrified yard man saw his chance to escape. He made a sudden dash for the front door and stumbled out into the foggy street. By the time Arthur had freed his arm Jack was halfway along Abbey Street, looking over his shoulder fearfully as he hurried along, his stockinged feet pattering over the wet cobbles.

Jack Oxford's cosy evenings had been terminated by the sudden appearance of Amy's wayward husband, and as he leaned against a gaslamp to catch his breath he pondered over what he should do next. It was no night to be sleeping rough, he thought with a shudder, and it was unlikely he would be able to get a bed at a doss-house now. There was only one thing to do, he decided. It would have to be the Druid Street arches.

Jack hobbled on along Abbey Street and turned into Druid Street. The fog was getting thicker now and he cursed his luck as he slipped into a narrow alley and then shuffled over rotting garbage and rubbish. He could see the glow of a fire ahead and then the huddled figures sitting around it. 'Any chance of a warm?' he asked timorously as he reached the group.

'Why if it ain't ole Jack Oxford,' one of the men said, grinning widely as he saw Jack's stockinged feet. 'Sit yerself down, mate. Wanna drop o' soup? It's bacon bones an' 'tater peelin's an there's a couple o' crusts left.'

Jack sat down on the plank of wood which served as a bench and rubbed his sore and frozen feet as he looked around at the four men. They were all familiar to him beneath their beards and unwashed faces. The man who had welcomed him handed over a tin of watery liquid and a stale crust of bread which Jack accepted gratefully. He had eaten his fill earlier but the cold had penetrated up from his feet. As he sipped the hot, greasy soup and chewed on the bread, he felt a little less sorry for himself.

'What 'appened ter yer boots, mate?' the man asked.

Jack felt a little embarrassed about telling them the full story and shrugged his shoulders. 'They wore out,' he said simply.

The man facing him chuckled through his huge black beard. 'We're all wearing out, friend,' he said, poking a stick into the fire and putting it to his stained clay pipe. 'Trouble is, it's always the wrong way round. We wear out from the ground upwards. I've always said we should start the other way round.'

Jack's host nudged him with his elbow. 'Bernie's a clever old cock. 'E used ter teach the kids at Webb Street ragged school, didn't yer, Bern?'

The bearded man stared into the fire not hearing, his pipe locked between thumb and forefinger. ''Twould be a mite more merciful that way,' he said quietly. 'When the mind goes, the rest doesn't matter. Just think, we could sit here in front of the fire in sublime ignorance. We would neither understand nor care about the circumstances of our plight. We'd all be happy souls, indeed we would.'

'Bernie lost 'is position at the school, didn't yer, Bern?' Jack's friend remarked.

'The great poets understood,' Bernie went on, ignoring the interruptions. 'Milton, Shakespeare and the like. They were all aware.'

Jack yawned. He did not understand what Bernie was saying but he was aware of one thing: he was not going to chance going back to Amy's house to collect his boots, not now that her maniac of a husband had returned. The bacon-bone and potato soup had warmed his insides and the heat of the fire felt pleasant on his aching feet. Maybe he should never have forsaken the doss-houses for Amy's place, he reflected. At least he could have protected his boots with the bedposts. Jack closed his eyes and soon sleep blotted out the circumstances of his plight.

At the Tanners' house William was lounging in his chair and Nellie was sitting facing him, busily darning a sock. 'Yer not goin' in the yard ternight, are yer, luv?' she asked.

William shook his head. 'There's no need,' he said. 'Everyfing's all right.'

Nellie got on with her darning and William closed his eyes. It was a habit he had adopted when he wanted to think. Nellie was always quick to notice when he was worried and by feigning sleep he could mull over his problems without being disturbed.

It was something Geoffrey had said that morning which was worrying him. 'I think the old man should seriously consider buying a couple of motor vans, Will,' he had remarked. 'Most of the carters are getting them. If we fall behind we're going to be left to pick up the work no one else wants, and at a lower price.'

William pondered his own position. He had worked with horses since he was a boy and had spent more than twenty-seven years with Galloway's. He knew nothing of motor transport, and if the horses went so would his job. George might let him stay on, but for what? Would he end up taking over Jack Oxford's job? Then there was the home the family lived in. What would happen if he was put out of work? Galloway would no doubt employ someone to look after the motor vans and might well offer that person their house as an inducement.

William's forehead wrinkled as he thought about his future and he shifted uneasily in the chair. Nellie had been looking at him for a while. She lowered her eyes again to her darning. She knew that when her husband slept, he snored. He was awake and there was something troubling him, she knew. Will was always loath to talk about his worries and had been that way ever since she had known him. How long was it now? she thought suddenly. Almost nineteen years since they had walked down the aisle at Bermondsey Church. Then Will had been a handsome young man with a proud swagger. He was a good man who had provided for her and the children and she had tried to make him happy during their years together.

She winced as she pricked herself with the darning needle, and as she sucked on her finger wished there was a way to soothe her troubled thoughts. Unlike her husband, she was always ready to discuss and share her troubles. There was only one occasion when she had been unable to confide in him, and it had caused her so much pain and anguish ever since. But William would neither have understood nor forgiven her. She would never be able to unburden herself to him and the secret would have to remain locked inside her until the day she died.

The fog cleared by dawn and the morning sky was clear. By seven thirty all the horse carts had left but there was still no sign of Jack Oxford. At eight o'clock Florrie Axford was just about to whiten her front doorstep when she saw the yard man hobbling down Page Street with sacking wrapped around his feet. 'Gawd 'elp us, Jack!' she exclaimed. 'What yer done ter yer boots?'

He scowled at her. 'I lost 'em,' he replied quickly.

'Lost 'em? Did somebody nick 'em in the kip 'ouse?' she enquired.

The sorry-looking man nodded and hobbled on, leaving Florrie wondering who would be hard-up enough to bother taking Oxford's size thirteens.

Jack managed to slip into the yard without being spotted by anyone apart from Horace Gallagher, who was looking out of the office window as he hobbled in. The ageing accountant turned to William Tanner who was sitting at a desk going through the worksheets. 'Jack Oxford's just come in,' he said, a puzzled look on this thin face. 'He's got his feet wrapped up in sacking. I'm sure the man's going barmy.'

William sighed as he got up to investigate. As he left the office, he was hailed by a large woman who was standing at the gate.

'Excuse me, mister, but could you give this to Mr Oxford please?' she asked, handing him a crumpled bag. 'I tried ter catch 'im up but 'e was too far in front.'

William eventually located Jack in the store shed and watched, bemused, while the yard man took out a pair of boots from the paper bag and found a piece of paper rolled up in one of them. Jack's face screwed up as he glanced at the note. ''Ere, Will, can yer tell me what this ses?' he asked. 'I've never bin one fer readin' an' writin'.'

William read the message, struggling to keep a straight face:

Dear Jack,
Sorry things had to work out this way. Also I'm sorry if my Arthur scared you. He's not a violent man really, and I don't think he would have hit you with that piping. I'm taking him back and we are going to try to make a go of it. He said he still loves me. Look after yourself. You're a very nice man.
Love, Amy

William handed the note back. 'So yer lost yer digs then, Jack?'

'Yeah, but it don't matter, Will,' the yard man replied. 'I've got me ole bed back at the doss-'ouse. I went ter see the bloke this mornin', that's why I was late. He said I could 'ave me bed back on one condition.'

'Oh, an' what's that?'

'On condition I always scrape the 'orse shit orf me boots afore I go in,' Jack said, grinning widely.

Chapter Thirteen

Carrie Tanner was feeling nervous as she waited on the street corner for Billy Sullivan. It was a warm Saturday afternoon in July and the first time she had walked out with a boy. It was true she had got to know Billy and had chatted to him on many occasions but this was her first time out alone in his company, she realised. It had come as a pleasant surprise when she stopped to talk to him on her way home from the factory two nights ago and he had asked if she would like to walk out with him. Carrie felt a very grown-up eighteen as she pushed her wide summer bonnet down on to her head and fidgeted with the satin bow on the front of her tight-fitting dress. Her long fair hair was hanging loose down her back and her high-buttoned boots of patent leather shone in the bright sunlight. She felt a little breathless as she saw Billy leave his house and walk quickly towards her. The bodice of her dress felt tight and she remembered how she had needed her mother to help her button it up.

Carrie smiled as she recalled the remarks her mother had made about her choice of dress. 'It's too tight and it shows yer bust off too much,' she said. 'It's cut a bit too low as well. Respectable girls don't show their wares. I think I ought ter put a few tacks in the front.'

189

Carrie had managed to persuade her that the dress was not too revealing and that she could not bear to be wrapped for winter on a fine summer's day. Her mother had relented but had been careful to point out the dangers facing a young girl when she was in the company of a young man such as Billy Sullivan.

''E's a good-lookin' boy, an' 'e's full of 'imself. Yer gotta be careful, Carrie,' she fussed. 'Boys don't 'ave ter face nuffing when they get a gel pregnant. It's us what 'ave ter bear the shame an' disgrace. They jus' brag about it. jus' be careful, an' don't let 'im take no liberties, understand, gel?'

Carrie laughed at her mother's fears. 'We're only goin' ter the park, Mum. Billy said there's an 'orse show there this afternoon an' 'e knows I like ter see the 'orses.'

Nellie had sighed as she watched her daughter leave the house and trip gaily along the cobbled turning. She had grown up so quickly, she thought. Maybe it was for the best that she was now beginning to take an interest in boys. The suffragette movement had been taking up most of her time and she was much too young to get involved in that sort of thing. Carrie had often spoken of those well-dressed women who devoted all their energies to the cause and they sounded a strange lot. There had been much made about it in the papers and at the music halls. Nellie remembered when Will had taken her to the South London Music Hall at the Elephant and Castle a couple of weeks ago and they watched a sketch about the suffragettes. They had been depicted as cigar-smoking women who dressed in monocles and wore their hair short and parted like men. They had eyed younger, pretty girls and made naughty suggestions to them as they put their arms about them. Nellie recalled how disgusted she was and how concerned she had been for her daughter. William had laughed it off when she confided her fears to him about her daughter's involvement with women like that, but she knew he shared her concern.

As Billy walked up to her with a wide smile on his face, Carrie forgot her mother's anxieties. She was feeling good, and the young man looked very smart in his dark grey single-breasted suit, starched collar and wide-knotted tie, she thought. Billy was not wearing a hat and his dark, curly hair was pushed back from his forehead. His deep blue eyes seemed to sparkle as he appraised her.

'Yer look very pretty,' he said as he fell into step beside her.

'Yer look smart yerself,' she replied, feeling her cheeks flush at her audacity.

They crossed Jamaica Road and walked the short distance to Southwark Park with Billy moving dutifully to the outside of the pavement. When they reached the park they saw the gaily decorated horses and carts going through the gates and Carrie gripped Billy's arm excitedly as she saw the two heavy dray-horses from the Courage brewery enter, pulling a shining, red-painted cart. Inside the park the contestants were manoeuvring into position on the wide gravel path and folk were milling around, the women wearing wide, flowered bonnets and many carrying parasols. The men were all dressed in suits and some wore bowler hats. Children laughed loudly as they rolled around in the grass, and a military brass band played lively music.

'They're shire-'orses,' Carrie said, pointing to the brewery drays. 'Those are cobs pullin' that 'ay cart an' that's a Clydesdale. We've got two o' them at the yard.'

Billy laughed at her excitement and took her by the arm as they walked along the edge of the path. Carrie felt his touch and shivered slightly. It was the first time they had made any real contact with each other and she could feel the heat of his hand. Billy led her past the parade and over towards the bandstand where the musicians sweated under their stiff uniforms as they blasted out a military march. Carrie stood amongst the gathering crowd and was aware of Billy standing very close behind her. She could feel his breath on the back of her neck and the pressure of his hand on her arm. She found herself becoming strangely elated and turned her head to face him. His blue eyes were looking deeply into hers and she averted her gaze, trying to look as though she was fascinated by the music. Billy merely smiled and led her away from the bandstand, his eyes fixed on her hot face as they walked slowly towards the flower gardens.

The sky was azure and the sun beat down on the gravel path as they entered the high, trellised area, and soon found a shaded bench seat beneath a deep pink flowering clematis. They sat close together and Billy took her hands in his.

'Yer know yer've got pretty lips,' he remarked, his smile making her feel as though he were mocking her.

She lowered her eyes, and her heart jumped as he slowly leaned forward and kissed her softly. Carrie kept her lips shut tight and her eyes closed until their lips parted, then she looked him firmly in the eye.

'You're very forward, Billy,' she said, two patches of red flooding her cheeks.

He laughed aloud. 'Yer didn't mind, did yer?'

Carrie averted her eyes. 'I dunno,' she said quickly, becoming more embarrassed beneath his searching gaze. 'It's our first time out tergevver.'

Billy leaned back on the bench and slipped his arm along the back rail so that it rested against her slim shoulders. She moved forward and he sat up straight again, taking her hand in his. 'Do I frighten yer, Carrie?' he said.

''Course not,' she replied, looking suitably indignant. 'It's jus' . . . well, a gel's gotta be careful. I wouldn't want yer ter fink I'm too forward.'

His lips moved towards hers again but she moved back and he sighed deeply. 'Look, Carrie,' he said quietly, 'I've known yer fer a long time an' I've always liked yer a lot. There's no 'arm in me kissin' yer. We're not doin' anyfing wrong.'

She looked at him, her eyes searching his open face. 'I know. It's jus' that I like yer too, an' I'm nervous,' she told him. 'Yer make me feel shaky an' sort of funny inside. I can't 'elp it.'

He leaned forward and this time she did not resist. Their lips met in a warm kiss and his arms went around her tensed body. They heard a scraping sound on the flagstones and parted suddenly. A woman had walked into the garden area carrying a young baby in her arms. She sat down on the far seat, cooing to the baby melodiously.

Billy grinned at Carrie. 'Let's go an' watch the parade, shall we?'

The afternoon had become slightly cooler as the hot sun started to dip in the clear sky, and tired children were being led home by their fussing parents. The show horses and carts had already departed and it was becoming quiet. Carrie walked beside Billy and they talked together amiably.

'I wanna get ter be a good boxer, Carrie,' he said with a serious expression. 'I'll even be the British champion one day. I don't wanna spend the rest o' me life stuck in that factory. I want people ter see me in the street an' say, "There goes Billy Sullivan. 'E's the British champion." I want the kids ter run up ter me an' I'll give 'em pennies jus' like Pedlar Palmer does.'

'Who's Pedlar Palmer?' Carrie asked.

'Pedlar Palmer is the champion,' Billy answered quickly. 'When 'e's seen about there's always people followin' 'im. 'E gives the kids sweets and chucks pennies down on the pavement. Everybody knows Pedlar Palmer. They even say 'e's goin' ter America soon ter fight fer the world title. That's what I wanna do, Carrie,' he said with passion, making two fists and holding them out in front of him. 'It's all I ever wanted ter do.'

She was a little embarrassed by his fervour and smiled shyly at him. 'Don't yer wanna get married one day?' she asked. 'Don't yer want a wife an' kids?'

Billy nodded. ''Course I do, Carrie, but I don't wanna be nobody. I don't wanna struggle like me dad 'as to ter fend fer us all. Look around yer. Look at Bacon Street Buildin's an' that fever-ridden slum in Salisbury Street. Look at the faces o' those people. They've all got that same look o' despair. The women are old before their time an' the men are all coughin' up their lungs an' spittin' in the gutter. Look at the people beggin' fer coppers, an' the kids 'angin' around in rags wiv that starved look on their faces. It's not fer me, Carrie,' he said with a will.

She was moved and roused by his outspokenness. She herself had felt those same feelings of disgust and anger growing inside her at the way people around her were forced to exist. She had been angered too by the way in which the suffragette movement was being ridiculed and discounted by her own kind. It seemed to her that unless women got the vote nothing would change. People would still remain in fever-ridden hovels and women would continue to grow old before their time, having to bear the brunt of bringing up large families and struggling to make the money stretch from week to week by taking in washing, scrubbing floors and going without food and clothes themselves. Billy's words had moved her and, companionably, she slipped her arm in his as they walked out of the park gates.

It was evening time and the sun had sunk down behind the rooftops as Carrie walked beside Billy along the river wall. The quiet warehouses were darkened by lengthening shadows and she could smell the river mud and the tang of hops from the brewery. The low river flowed away eastwards. On the foreshore barges were lying beached on the mud. Seagulls wheeled and dived, screeching noisily as they searched for scraps, and the muddy waters eddied and formed small whirlpools on the turning tide. Carrie sighed contentedly as she looked downriver and saw the colours of evening disappear from the sky. It had been very nice walking out with Billy and listening to his dreams. She had been startled by his sudden show of affection but she had enjoyed his kiss. Now, as they trod the cobbled lane that ran between the tall wharves and warehouses, they both lapsed into silence. They were completely alone and their footsteps sounded loudly as they reached the white stone arch which led under Tower Bridge.

It was then that Billy led her into the shadows of a doorway and turned to face her, his body close to hers. Carrie's heart was pounding madly and her breath was coming fast. She let him press his lips on hers in a passionate kiss that seemed to linger forever. She knew she should push him away and hurry from this unfamiliar, dark place but instead she let the kiss go on. She felt his hands moving down her body, slowly at first and then more urgently. Warning bells sounded loudly in her mind and as his groping hands slipped around inside her thighs she tensed and pushed him from her.

'No, Billy! No!' she cried, feeling as though the day had suddenly been spoiled.

He ignored her protestations as his lips sought her neck. His broad chest pressed against her and she felt helpless in his firm hold on her. He was breathing heavily now. 'Let me love yer, Carrie,' he gasped. 'Let me make love ter yer.'

She had become confused and frightened by his excitement and her whole body was shaking. It was wrong, she told herself. She had let him go on for too long and now he was holding her so tightly that it hurt. With a gasp, she finally managed to push him away. He sagged against the wall watching her warily.

Carrie pulled at her dress and reached behind her for her bonnet which was hanging from her neck on its pink ribbon. 'Yer took advantage of me, Billy!' she said angrily. 'Yer tried ter make love ter me.'

He gave a grin as he moved away from the wall and straightened himself. 'I'm sorry, but I couldn't 'elp it. Yer really are very pretty, Carrie,' he said smoothly.

'We'd better get on 'ome,' she replied, feeling that the magic of the day had now gone.

They walked out from the narrow cobbled lane into Dockhead and along to Jamaica Road. They were both quiet, and when Billy glanced at her occasionally she returned his looks with a hardness in her eyes. It had been so nice in the park, she thought regretfully. They had talked freely of their hopes and aspirations, and it had felt so romantic when they sat together in the flower garden. It was her fault, she told herself. She should never have let him kiss her like that. Now he must be feeling cheated and angry inside at not being able to go further. Well, she was angry too. He had led her on and taken advantage of her naivety, and if she had not stopped him . . . He had tried to seduce her on their first time out together without considering her feelings and she was angry at his heedlessness. Mary at the factory had warned her of the way in which young men treated their lady friends. She knew that deep down she had wanted him to go on, to hold her and caress her body, but he had seemed to care only about his own passion and almost forgotten about her. She realised he would be angry now and would not feel like asking her to walk out with him any more. Well, she didn't care, she told herself. One day she would give herself fully to a man, when she was ready to receive love and when it was the right time for her.

As the two walked back into Page Street, Carrie could see her mother standing at the front door. Florrie Axford was sitting in a rickety chair by her door talking to Maisie and Aggie. Billy's mother Sadie was standing on the doorstep of her house, idly watching children playing hopscotch, and another group of women were chatting together on the bend of the turning. Billy had said nothing on the way back to the street and when they reached his house his younger brothers ran up to him. He gave Carrie a shrug of his shoulders and walked off down the turning.

As the summer light faded and darkness settled over the quiet square, Nora Flynn hummed contentedly. The evening meal had been a happy affair with the boys laughing and joking together and Josephine managing to capture her father's interest for a while. Nora was happy that George seemed to be taking more notice of his only daughter now. It was hard for the child to grow up without a real mother, she thought, though she herself had tried to give Josephine love and protect her from certain things. The girl was thirteen now and growing up very pretty. Unlike her older brothers who were dark and favoured their father, Josephine had her mother's fair hair and deep blue eyes. She had her mother's good nature too, and seemed popular with the other young girls who lived in the immediate neighbourhood.

Nora had been careful in her new relationship with the girl's father. She had not wanted it to be known that George was sleeping in her bed but the two young men of the house had realised some time ago and were happy for her, since they had grown to love her almost as much as their own mother. Josephine, on the other hand, was still very much a child and Nora had insisted to George that she must not be made aware of their liaison. Now, as she tidied up the dining room and folded the embroidered tablecloth, Nora could hear George talking to his sons in the front room. She took one more look about her before going upstairs to her embroidery.

In the large front room the heavy curtains had been drawn and the gaslamp turned high. George Galloway sat back in his armchair with a glass of Scotch at his elbow and a lighted cigar in his hand. He was much heavier in build than his two sons, having put on quite a lot of weight over the years, and he had re-grown his moustache which tended to make him look older than his fifty-three years. His face was heavy-jowled and flushed with the whisky and his dark eyes seemed to be half-closed as he eyed his sons. Facing him, Geoffrey sat back in his comfortable chair and idly twirled the contents of his glass as he listened to his father. Next to him sat his younger brother Frank, dressed for his evening out. There was a remarkable likeness between the boys who could have been mistaken for twins. Both had dark, wavy hair, although Frank was the heavier by almost a stone. Their eyes were dark and deep-set, their features clean and fine-cut.

'I'm aware we've gotta be lookin' ter the future,' George said, puffing on his cigar. 'What I don't accept though is that 'orses are finished. Take the army, fer instance. They're gettin' motor lorries but their 'orses are still crucial, although they don't get 'em from me now,' he added ruefully. 'I know that 'Atcher's an' some o' the ovver carters 'ave got motor vans but they're bigger concerns than us. Besides, where're we gonna keep the vans if we get a couple? There's no room in the yard an' the turnin's too narrer. Christ, I'd be 'avin' anuvver demonstration on me 'ands if I brought motor vans in the turnin'.'

Geoffrey prodded the sheaf of papers on his lap. 'That's what I mean about getting another yard,' he said. 'There's a list here of possible sites and they're all going reasonably cheap. In a year or two prices are going to climb, what with all the space needed. Now's the time to buy or lease some land, while there's a slump. We could still run the yard at Page Street for a couple of years, then we could sell out at a nice profit. I agree with you that the yard's too small for our future needs, that's why I'm suggesting we get another site now.'

'Geoffrey's right, Father,' Frank cut in. 'The slump won't last more than a year or two and then there's going to be a rush for business. It seems to me that you can't afford to wait much longer.'

George puffed nervously on his cigar. 'What yer sayin' is that we go over ter motors an' get rid of all the 'orses?'

Geoffrey shook his head. 'Not for a couple of years. We could pick up the longer-distance cartage with two motors and still see out the existing contracts. But if we don't move, we're going to get left behind. That's a stone certainty, the way I see it,' he concluded, leaning back in his chair.

George took the bottle of Scotch from the table at his elbow and replenished his glass. Geoffrey refused the offer of a refill but Frank took the proffered bottle and poured himself a large measure. For a while George was silent as he sipped his drink.

''Ave you two considered the ovver side o' the coin?' he asked suddenly. Their blank stares prompted him to go on. 'Take the firms what's goin' over ter motor transport. They'll be chasin' after the distance work 'cos that's where they're gonna make their money. But motors are no good round the dock lanes an' they're bloody unreliable as well, by all accounts. Yer need ter remember also that yer gotta pay the van drivers more money ter drive the noisy fings. 'Orses are reliable. If yer feed and care for 'em, they'll work till they drop, an' never complain. Take my word fer it, there's gonna be some good contracts comin' up fer 'orse transport durin' the next few years, I wanna be in from the off wiv my bids, an' when some o' the motor firms go out o' business *that'll* be the time ter step in wiv an offer, fer the business and the land. In the meantime we'll carry on the way we've bin goin'. All right?'

His two sons nodded, each knowing that their father had made up his mind and there would be no shifting him. Frank got up and stretched in a leisurely fashion.

'Well, I'd better be off,' he said with a grin. 'I'm joining a party and we're going to a first night. As I said before, Geoff, you're welcome to tag along. Who knows? You might meet some sweet young thing.'

Geoffrey declined the offer with a smile and a shake of his head, 'I've got other plans tonight,' he said casually.

On Sunday morning Page Street was up and about, and at nine o'clock William Tanner went into the stable yard and harnessed one of the Welsh cobs. At nine-thirty a sleepy-eyed Soapy Symonds trudged into the turning to the ribald comments of the women and drove an open cart out of the yard.

Florrie Axford was organising the women and she had something to say to Soapy as he sat up in the seat with the reins slack in his hands. 'Oi! 'Ow we gonna get up there?'

Soapy was recovering slowly from his Saturday night at the Kings Arms. 'Jump up. That's what I 'ad ter do,' he grumbled, miserable at having allowed himself to be talked into driving the women on their outing.

Florrie gave him a vile look and hurried into her house to

get a chair. Soapy sat motionless while Florrie and Nellie Tanner did the roll-call.

'There's only fifteen. Who's missin'?' Florrie asked.

Aggie Temple came hurrying along the turning. 'Sorry I'm late. I couldn't find me bonnet,' she puffed.

Finally the women were all in position, sitting along both sides of the cart on two benches they had borrowed from the church hall. They were all wearing flowered bonnets, with the exception of Sadie Sullivan who had on an emerald green Bo Beep hat. Getting into the cart had been difficult for the revellers as they were all wearing long cotton dresses, but they were in good spirits as the cart moved off along the cobbled turning, watched by the male population who waved and joked with them. Soapy Symonds was feeling slightly better after Florrie had given him a swig from a bottle of ale, and he perked up no end when Aggie told him the women were going to pass the hat round on his behalf if he gave them a comfortable ride.

The journey was interrupted first by a water stop for the horse, and then at the roadside for the women to stretch their legs and pop behind the bushes. Soapy had been given his orders by Florrie: 'Oi, you! No peepin' or I'll complain ter Galloway when we get 'ome.'

At last the happy merry-makers arrived at Epping Forest and Soapy turned the cart on to a side road which led directly into the greenery. He jumped down from his high seat, and after he had assisted the women from the back of the cart, Florrie presented him with a pint of ale which he downed almost in one gulp.

White tablecloths were laid out on the grass and the women sat down to their picnic. There was cheese, brawn and boiled bacon, freshly baked bread and margarine, cockles and shrimps, and jellied pork pies. There was ample liquid refreshment too, and as the food was devoured and bottles of ale and stout were attacked the party got under way. One of the women strummed on a banjo and Aggie did her impression of a clog dance. At the side of the path the horse munched on his oats and occasionally turned his head at the noise. Soapy had retired some way from the main group and opened his third bottle of ale, burping loudly as he swallowed large draughts.

It was later in the day when the first mishap occurred. Maggie Jones and Ida Bromsgrove went off to pick blackberries, and when Maggie fell into the brambles and got herself hopelessly entangled her friend ran back to get help. It took some time to release the unfortunate woman but she was unhurt, although her new dress had been ripped in places. It was not long after that when Aggie Temple slipped during one of her more vigorous dancing routines and sprained her ankle. Help was at hand however, and Nellie tore off strips from her petticoat and bound up Aggie's ankle after first soaking the makeshift bandages in ale.

The day remained fine and warm and the revellers from Page Street wished that it could last forever, but when the sun began to go down the women decided they would have to leave their idyllic surroundings and return to grimy Bermondsey. As they gathered the remains of the food and drink and loaded them on to the cart they realised they were being observed by two elderly women who stood on the path nearby. They were wearing tweeds and smart hats, and each carried a cane hiking stick.

Maisie Dougall was by now feeling merry from the amount of ale she had consumed. She waved over to the women. 'Fancy a swig, luvs?' she said in a slurred voice.

'Good God, I do believe they're gypsies,' the younger of the two whispered to her friend.

'I don't think so, Pearl,' the older woman replied. 'I think they're factory girls from London. Isn't it disgusting the way they're carrying on?'

Pearl sniffed contemptuously as she dabbed at her neatly coiffured hair. 'They've been drinking, Maud. I think it's absolutely nauseating.'

Maisie had walked over to the outraged women. She held out a quart bottle of stout. ''Ere, gels, why don't yer try a drop? Yer can't beat a good drop o' stout,' she said, blinking in the effort to focus her eyes on them.

'Take that nasty bottle away this minute, do you hear me?' the older woman cried.

Maisie looked crestfallen. She turned to Sadie Sullivan who had walked over to see what was going on. 'They don't wanna drink, Sadie.'

Sadie's large face was flushed under her bright green hat and she scowled as she observed the disapproving look on the two hikers' faces. 'Well, if yer don't wanna be sociable, yer better piss orf out of it,' she said quickly, thrusting out her chin.

The two frightened women hurried off without a word and Sadie put her arm around Maisie's shoulders as they walked back to their group. 'Don't worry, gel,' she grinned. 'Them sort ain't used ter seein' a load of ole sloshers like us.'

Meanwhile there had been a serious discussion taking place over the supine figure of Soapy, who was snoring loudly.

'What're we gonna do?' Aggie groaned, stroking her bandaged ankle.

'It's no good, I've tried ter wake 'im but 'e's too pissed,' Florrie said, shaking her head. 'There's only one fing ter do. Give us an 'and, gels.'

After Soapy had been unceremoniously thrown into the back of the cart, Nellie took charge. Having to drive the cart did not worry her. She had often gone out on trips with

William in the past and he had let her take the reins. The horse was fetched from its resting-place under a clump of trees and tethered to the cart, and when all the women had clambered aboard and Aggie had been made comfortable with her damaged leg resting across Soapy, they started for home. A few hours later a tired, happy bunch of wassailers finally drove into Page Street by the bright silver light of a full moon.

1910

1910

Chapter Fourteen

Early in 1910 an outbreak of diphtheria in the nearby Salisbury Street slums spread to Page Street. Two of the smaller Sullivan boys caught the disease, as did Maisie Dougall's younger son. For days the children's parents could do nothing but wait and pray. When the crisis had passed and the three children began to recover everyone hoped that the scourge had left, but it was not to be. Mrs Jones lost her daughter, Mrs Carmody lost a son, and in Bacon Street Buildings four children died. The tragedies left a terrible scar on the hard-up families, and with the menfolk falling out of work and food prices rising there seemed little to instil hope into the drab lives of the Bermondsey folk. Anger and bad feelings were running high, and activists were beginning to make themselves heard in their efforts to get something done about the slum dwellings in the area. Salisbury Street was a major target for the campaigners, as was Bacon Street Buildings. Meetings took place in church halls, school buildings and on street corners, and the local councillors were roundly berated. The suffragettes were actively stepping up their campaign to win the vote for women and were trying ever more fervently to persuade people that their votes would force change and improve the lives of everyone.

Carrie Tanner had called on her friend Sara Knight at her home in Bacon Street Buildings often during the diphtheria outbreak and she had been moved to tears as she saw the funeral processions leaving Bacon Street. Her sadness and anger found release in the women's movement and she was now becoming more and more dedicated to the cause. She attended every march and meeting she could and volunteered to carry one of the heavy banners, along with Mary and her two friends Jessica and Freda. Local newspapers had been quick to realise that the suffragette movement was gaining many dedicated followers amongst working-class girls and they ran stories and interviews. The *South London Press* and the *Kentish Mercury* were regularly reporting events and publicising the marches to their readers, and support for the women's movement grew.

Nevertheless, there were still many people who viewed the movement in a very unfavourable light, and at Wilson's leather factory the management issued a threat. A notice was pinned up beside the time-clock which read: 'As full-time working has been resumed, any future absenteeism due to taking part in suffragette marches will result in instant dismissal'.

'Well, I don't care,' Mary said firmly as she punched in her time-card. 'I fer one ain't gonna bow ter that sort of intimidation. As far as I'm concerned, the movement comes first, so sod 'em all.'

'What we gonna do about Friday's march, Carrie?' a worried Jessica asked her friend.

'I feel the same way as Mary. I'm not gonna be stopped by that notice,' Carrie replied angrily.

'Nor am I,' Freda said firmly. 'If they sack us, we'll jus' 'ave ter go ter Peek Freans or the tin-bashers. They always seem ter be takin' workers on. Ter tell yer the trufe, I don't fancy workin' in a metal factory, what wiv the noise an' that, but I can't afford ter be out o' collar.'

Mary had a sly grin on her wide face as she turned to Carrie. 'I wonder if the local papers'll be interested in that notice?' she remarked.

On Friday morning the management met to discuss the absence of four of their workers and the disappearance of the warning notice.

'It's going to be embarrassing if the newspapers get hold of that notice,' the personnel manager, Mr Wilkins, remarked. 'It's likely to reflect badly on our good name.'

'I wouldn't worry too much about our good name,' the elderly managing director, Mr Gore, cut in. 'We're an old established business with a good employment record. We don't have strikes at our factory because the workers enjoy good working conditions, and better wages than any of our competitors in Bermondsey, I might add. I think many people are getting a little tired of the suffragettes and the disruption their marches cause. As far as this firm is concerned, our position has been made clear. We can't afford to let our girls go off on those ridiculous marches just when it suits them. In any case, we're within our rights.'

'I take it the four young women will be dismissed then?' the works manager queried, glancing at Mr Wilkins.

Mr Gore nodded emphatically. 'Are there any voices against enforcing our ruling?' he asked, looking round the table quickly. The silence gave him the answer he required and he looked at the personnel manager. 'I take it you'll be able to deal with it, Mr Wilkins,' he said brusquely as he got up and walked out of the room.

The rest of the gathering exchanged glances. 'This could cause trouble,' the works manager, Mr Faraday, remarked. 'The old man was talking about our strike-free record. I think we're likely to lose that. There's been some unrest on the shopfloor since that notice went up.'

Mr Wilkins nodded his agreement. 'I warned him about taking too hard a line. We could have just stopped the day's pay. Sacking the girls is going to give us more trouble than we bargained for, mark my words.'

'We could have spoken up and opposed him,' Mr Hopgood, the chief accountant said timidly.

'Well, we didn't, so there's no point harping on it now,' Wilkins said. 'We'll just have to wait and see what happens next.'

Across the river on Tower Hill that bright spring morning the four workers from Wilson's leather factory were collecting their banners for the big march on Parliament, in blissful disregard of their possible fate. Mary was becoming excited. She pointed to a group of women in aprons and white hats. 'Look over there, ' she enthused. 'They're the matchbox gels from Bryant and May's.'

Smartly dressed organisers were hurrying to and fro, distinctive in their armbands showing the letters 'WSPU'. They wore long dark satin dresses with ruffled sleeves tapering at the wrist and all had on wide hats and patent leather boots. In contrast, the factory girls and women from the working areas of London wore long shabby dresses or factory aprons and bonnets.

There was a mood of solidarity and quiet determination as the column finally set off along Eastcheap and into Cannon Street. Carrie carried a poster that showed apronclad women with raised hands. The wording above the picture announced, 'The Women's Social and Political Union', and beneath the picture was the statement, 'Women demand the right to vote. The pledge of citizenship and basis of all liberty'. Carrie walked proudly beside Mary who was sharing a large banner with Freda, and Jessica strode alongside with a smaller banner to herself. As they progressed along the busy thoroughfare the chant went up, 'Votes for Women!' City workers and fish porters stood watching at the roadside and occasionally an obscene comment was directed towards the column. Women looked down from open windows, cheering the marchers and shouting encouragement. Policemen flanked the column, looking totally disinterested, and up ahead traffic came to a standstill as the campaigners crossed into Fleet Street.

Carrie's arms were beginning to ache. She glanced across to Mary. The young woman's plump face was flushed and she was chanting loudly as she strode along. Carrie grinned to herself. What was going to happen if they lost their jobs at the factory? she wondered suddenly. Her mother had warned her of the possible consequences and would no doubt have much to say, although her father would probably shrug his shoulders and leave the chastisement to Nellie.

The procession moved along the Strand, crossed the south side of Trafalgar Square and turned left into Whitehall, where more police were waiting. Freda leaned towards Carrie with a worried look on her pale face. 'I wonder if they'll try an' stop us before we get ter Parliament?' she said.

Mary heard the comment. 'They can't do that. We're allowed ter lobby, long as we don't cause trouble,' she announced, giving the policeman walking beside her a mean glance.

The suffragettes finally arrived at the looming tower of Big Ben and the column halted while two of the organisers spoke with police at the gates of the House of Commons. Carrie could see the two women walking into the courtyard, flanked between two policemen. She rested her banner against her leg. Mary was sweating profusely and both Jessica and Freda looked tired from the long march.

The police seemed to be getting agitated as the traffic was being forced to divert around the marchers and there was some pushing and shoving going on. A group of women were protesting at being herded away from their vantage point outside Parliament, and as a policeman took one of them roughly by the arm and tried to remove her from the gates a scuffle suddenly broke out. Other women started to cry out against what seemed to be an unnecessary use of force and soon policemen surrounded the growing disturbance. Traffic was coming to a standstill in Parliament Square as the orderly lines disintegrated into a swarming, chaotic throng. Policemen's helmets became dislodged as the violence grew worse. The matchbox women were in the thick of the fray with fists flying.

Carrie picked up her banner and tried to follow her friends to the safety of the central grassed square but a policeman grabbed her arm and yanked her towards the pavement where a Black Maria was parked. Suddenly Mary's heavy banner crashed down on his head, and as he stumbled Carrie pulled herself free.

'Quick, run!' screamed Mary, setting off in the direction of Westminster Bridge.

Carrie held her skirts up from her feet as she followed her friend, tearing across the road. When the two reached the foot of the bridge they leaned on the parapet, gasping for breath.

'They was after arrestin' those what was carryin' banners,' Mary said when she had recovered slightly. 'We better not stop 'ere.'

The skirmishes were spilling on to the entrance to the bridge by now and the two women could see some of the organisers being led away by policemen.

'Quick, let's cross over,' Carrie said, pulling on Mary's arm.

They dashed through the congested traffic, and at the entrance to Whitehall spotted Freda and Jessica who both looked distressed. Freda's dress was torn at the front and Jessica was crying. There seemed to be police everywhere. There was an officer standing near the four young women, carrying a battered helmet in his hand. When he spotted Mary, his face screwed up in anger.

'Come 'ere, you!' he shouted gruffly, beckoning her with his finger.

Mary backed away and turned to run but the angry policeman reached out and grabbed her. 'I'm arrestin' you fer assaultin' a police officer,' he growled.

Carrie stood directly in front of him and looked angrily into his flushed face. 'She ain't done nuffink,' she cried.

'Oh, I see. Yer both wanna be arrested, do yer?' he said, taking her arm.

Jessica and Freda had had enough trouble for one day. They backed away and hurried off in the direction of the bridge. People were standing around watching the incident. One young man wearing a cap and red scarf walked up boldly and confronted the officer. 'Why don't yer leave 'em alone?' he said. 'They ain't doin' no 'arm.'

The policeman turned to the man. ''Oppit, or I'll run yer in as well,' he snarled.

Carrie could feel her heart pounding as she struggled in the policeman's strong grip and tried to prise his fingers from her arm with her free hand. She could see more policemen crossing the road in their direction and bit on her bottom lip. With a deft movement she reached up into her hair and pulled out a hat-pin. With a quick thrust she pushed it into the policeman's leg. He bellowed in pain and at the same time Mary kicked him on the shin. The sudden assault had disabled the policeman and the two young women broke free, holding hands as they dashed off across Westminster Bridge as fast as their legs could carry them.

Once over the river, and realising they had not been chased, the two stopped and leaned against a wall to recover.

'That was a smart fing ter do,' Mary laughed. 'Where did yer learn that trick?'

Carrie grinned. 'That's what Florrie Axford would 'ave done,' she replied.

'Florrie Axford?'

'Yeah. They call 'er "'airpin" Axford be'ind 'er back 'cos she stopped a fight once by stickin' 'er 'airpin in this bloke's leg,' Carrie explained.

'I wonder if Jessica an' Freda got away all right?' Mary asked presently.

Carrie nodded. 'I see 'em both runnin' over the bridge. I reckon they'll be 'ome by now.'

Suddenly they heard a shrill whistle. 'Wanna ride?' a voice cried out.

Carrie looked over and saw that a horse cart had pulled up by the kerb. The carman wore a cap and a red scarf. 'That was the fella who sauced that copper,' Carrie whispered to Mary.

The young man was grinning widely as he jumped from the cart and sauntered over to the girls. 'I see yer managed ter dodge 'em,' he remarked. 'Everybody was laughin' over the way yer bolted orf over the bridge. I was stuck in the traffic. I'd jus' jumped down ter stretch me legs when I saw yer get pulled up. Was yer really in the parade?' Carrie nodded and the young man's grin grew even broader. 'Well, I've never met any suffragettes before. I'm goin' ter Dock'ead if it's any good ter yer?'

'That'll suit us fine.' Carrie smiled and pushed Mary up on to the wheel hub and over the rave of the cart, before hoisting her skirt and clambering up after her.

They set off, with the young carman holding the reins

slack and occasionally encouraging the horse by clicking his tongue. Mary and Carrie stood at the front of the cart, holding on to the back of the seat.

'Me dad always does that,' Carrie told him.

'Does what?'

'Makes clickin' noises ter make the 'orse gee up.'

'Is 'e a carman?' the young man asked.

''E used ter be,' she replied. ''E's a yard foreman now.'

'My name's Tommy Allen. What's yours?'

'I'm Carrie Tanner an' this is my friend Mary Caldwell. We work tergevver – well, we did,' Carrie added.

'What d'yer mean?'

'Our firm said they was gonna sack us if we went on the march,' Mary butted in.

'I reckon that's scand'lous,' Tommy remarked. 'I don't know a lot about those suffragette people meself but the way I see it they got a right ter march if they want to, that's what I say.'

Mary was not used to smiling at men but she made an exception in Tommy's case. 'I'm glad yer fink so,' she said.

The young carman jerked on the reins and the horse quickened its pace as the Elephant and Castle junction came into sight. He turned and winked at Carrie. 'I 'ope yer don't mind me sayin', but ain't yer a bit young ter be suffragettes? I thought it was only them posh ole ladies who chained 'emselves ter railin's.'

Carrie smiled 'There's a lot o' young ladies in the movement,' she informed him. 'It's not only posh ladies what get involved. Me an' Mary go on all the marches. We carry banners too, don't we, Mary?'

She nodded her head vigorously and Tommy laughed. 'I saw the state o' that copper's 'elmet,' he said. 'Did yer really clout 'im?'

'Mary did. The copper was tryin' ter nick me an' she bashed 'im wiv 'er banner,' Carrie replied.

The cart rattled over the tram-lines at the Elephant junction and soon they reached the Bricklayers Arms. Tommy had become silent and Carrie studied him. He was about her own age, she guessed, and had a friendly smile and an open face. His dark hair was thick and curled over his ears, and his brown eyes seemed to light up when he smiled. He reminded her of those young gypsy men who worked at the fairgrounds and she smiled to herself. Many stories had been told about gypsies who travelled with the fairs and stole young maidens, hiding them in their gaily painted caravans. It was said that young girls had disappeared from Bermondsey in the past, never to be found.

One such story she had heard concerned a pretty young girl from Bermondsey who visited the fair at Blackheath one day and never returned. Her family were frantic and organised a search. Everyone was told to keep their eyes open for a pretty girl with long fair hair and a small red birthmark in the centre of her forehead. The police were called in and they looked for her amongst the caravan people at the fair, but without success. Every Easter the fair returned and every Easter the girl's parents visited the fair in the hope of finding their child.

After many years had passed the parents, who were now very old, went to the fair as usual and on this occasion decided to consult the fortune-teller. They duly crossed her palm with silver and asked her if it was likely they would ever see their daughter again. The gypsy fortune-teller stared down into her crystal and said they would see her before the day was out.

The couple waited around at the fair until it got dark and then, full of grief, went back to the gypsy woman. 'I can only tell you what I see in the crystal ball,' she said, lifting her head and pulling her headsquare back from her face. The elderly couple broke down in tears, for there, in the middle of her forehead, was a small, red birthmark.

Or so the story went, Carrie remembered, smiling to herself. She had never believed it, but she still felt it would be a good idea not to say anything about the lift she and Mary had got from the young carman with the Romany appearance.

Carrie Tanner and her three co-marchers had gone to work as usual on the Saturday following the march, only to be sent home again with instructions to report to the personnel office first thing on Monday morning. That weekend in the Tanner household there was much discussion of what was likely to happen.

Carrie's brother James had something to say. 'It's the sack. They'll sack yer fer sure,' he remarked. 'Stan's ter reason they're not gonna let yer go off on marches every time yer feel like it, are they?'

'I reckon they'll jus' tell yer off an' leave it at that,' Charlie said quietly. 'After all, they won't 'ave ter pay yer fer the day out. What they worryin' about?'

Carrie shook her head. 'They put up a notice warnin' us not ter go so I don't see they've got any choice now,' she replied.

'Pity yer didn't take any notice o' the warnin',' James said, leaning back in his chair with his thumbs hooked through his braces.

'All right, don't get nasty,' William cut in. 'Carrie's made 'er choice an' she's gotta accept the consequences. It's no good us lot 'arpin' on about 'er gettin' the sack. There's ovver jobs goin', anyway.'

'Like where? The bagwash?' Nellie remarked. 'As far as I'm concerned she shouldn't 'ave gone on the march in the first place. It turned inter a bloody rabble accordin' ter the newspapers. It's a wonder she never got locked up.'

William glanced quickly at Nellie, entreating her with his eyes not to upset their daughter. 'I don't fink they'll sack 'em,' he said encouragingly. 'Lot's o' women are marchin' these days. Most firms understand what's 'appenin' an' don't go in fer sackin' their workers jus' 'cos they take time off. If yer ask me, I fink they'll eventually get the vote. All right it won't be this year, or even next, but it's gotta come one day.'

Danny had been quietly thumbing his way through a comic. He looked up suddenly. 'Billy Sullivan said a lot o' them suffragettes are toffee-nosed ole bats who ain't got nuffink better ter do,' he declared.

'You shut yer noise an' get on wiv yer comic,' Carrie retorted angrily. 'I don't care what Billy Sullivan 'as ter say.'

Nellie and William exchanged glances. They were both aware that Carrie had not walked out with the young Sullivan since that one time when they visited the horse show together, and Nellie had intimated to her husband, 'I fink 'e tried somefing on, Will. Carrie looked a little bit agitated when she got back that evenin'.'

William had been less suspicious. 'I fink she's too wrapped up in that suffragette movement ter be interested in boys,' he remarked. 'It's a shame if that is the case, though. She's a pretty young fing an' I'd 'ave thought the lads would be callin' round by now.'

Nellie had tried to broach the subject with Carrie but had met with little response. Nevertheless, her daughter's reticence only furthered her suspicions that something had happened that afternoon. Carrie was certainly pretty and well developed, Nellie brooded, trying to convince herself that her daughter was sensible enough to know what was right and wrong. Lads like Billy Sullivan could be expected to try it on with a pretty girl, and if they didn't get their own way might well choose not to come calling. Saying no to a young man was difficult sometimes, she thought. Getting pregnant was easy.

Danny's innocent comment had made Carrie feel miserable. It was a long time now since she and Billy had gone to the park together. She had wanted to keep their friendship alive but the young man seemed to have other ideas. True he still talked to her in the street and appeared not to have been unduly upset by her rejecting his advances, but he had not bothered to ask her out again. He seemed to be more and more wrapped up in boxing, and the last time they had spoken he had said he was getting ready to have his first fight for money at the Blackfriars Ring. It had been difficult at first, Carrie recalled. She would have been happy for him to ask her out again, but it was not to be. Maybe girls like her missed their chances by being careful. Would other young men she might meet in the future feel like Billy and lose interest if she did not let them go all the way? Freda had not said no and she soon fell for a baby. Jessica had said she would get thrown out of her home if she became pregnant. What would happen if she got pregnant herself? Would the family be able to live down the disgrace, or would they disown her?

The thoughts tumbling around in Carrie's mind made her feel more troubled and she fidgeted in her chair. Perhaps it wasn't her shyness and refusal to let him take advantage of her that had persuaded Billy not to ask her out again. Maybe it was her involvement in the movement which had put him off. Danny had said that Billy thought of all suffragettes as toffee-nosed. Well, if that was the case then Billy Sullivan was not worth worrying over. One day she would meet a young man who did not mind her going on marches and being dedicated to improving the lot of women. In the meantime she would forget boys and concentrate her efforts on doing what she thought was right, even if it meant losing her job.

*

· On Monday morning Carrie was prepared for the worst as she walked to work. When she reached the factory entrance, she saw Mary talking to Jessica and Freda. They gave her a wry smile and Mary pushed her glasses further up on her nose. 'C'mon then, let's get the bad news.'

An embarrassed-looking Mr Wilkins was fussing with a sheaf of papers as the four young women were ushered into his office. He avoided meeting their eyes as he delivered the news by reading from a prepared document. 'The company has decided that as you chose to ignore the company notice and absented yourselves from work on Friday of last week to take part in a suffragette march, there is no alternative but to terminate your employment forthwith.'

The young women looked at each other and then Mary leaned forward over the desk. 'Sod the lot o' yer then, an' tell that ole goat Gore we 'ope 'e chokes on 'is supper.'

Chapter Fifteen

Fifteen minutes after work was due to begin on Monday morning, the management of Wilson's factory was summoned urgently to the boardroom.

'What do you mean, they won't start work, Wilkins?' the managing director growled. 'Get them back this minute. Time's money, in case it slipped your mind.'

'But they won't budge, sir,' Mr Wilkins said meekly. 'As soon as they heard of the dismissals, they marched out into the street. I tried to talk them into going back but all I got was abuse.'

'Faraday, go and tell them to get back or I'll sack the lot of them,' the managing director said in a loud voice.

The works manager left the office, feeling apprehensive and wishing that the boss would do his own dirty work.

Down in the street the workforce were milling around the entrance, laughing and joking. When they saw Mr Faraday, they became quiet.

'Who's the leader of this protest?' he asked, looking from one to the other.

A tall, thin young woman pushed her way to the front. 'There's no leader, Mr Faraday,' she said. 'We're all agreed on this. If the management don't take our work-mates back, we ain't gonna start work neivver. It's as simple as that.'

'Oh no it's not!' Mr Faraday replied. 'If you lot don't go in immediately, I'm empowered to sack everyone.'

'Well, if that's what yer gotta do yer better do it, 'cos we ain't budgin', so yer can piss orf,' the young woman said firmly.

Mr Faraday turned back into the factory to the jeers of the girls. He was met at the boardroom door by a very angry managing director.

'Why aren't they back, Faraday?' he demanded.

'They won't move unless we reinstate the four who were sacked,' he sighed. 'They actually told me to piss off.'

Mr Gore's face became dark, and with an angry scowl he hurried to the window and peered down into the street. 'It's blackmail. I'm being put over a barrel,' he growled. 'Well, I won't submit. Sack them all, Wilkins.'

'But how are we . . .?'

'Don't argue, man. Sack them, I said.'

His secretary popped her head around the door. 'The *South London Press* and the *Kentish Mercury* have both phoned in, sir. They want to check that we actually put up the notice. Would you like to talk to them?'

'Oh my God!' he wailed. 'Yes, all right, Mrs Jones, I'll speak to them.' He turned back to his management with a heavy sigh. 'Now then, let's look at the situation calmly. We're all unanimous that our decision stands, I take it?'

The rest of the management was shocked to learn that it was now a group decision but refrained from making any comment, except to nod meekly. Only Mr Wilkins hesitated and he was quickly brought into line.

'Come on, Wilkins, what's it to be? Instant dismissal for the whole workforce?'

Once again the browbeaten personnel manager opened his mouth to speak but was shut up immediately.

'Right then, you get down and deliver the ultimatum. Back to work forthwith or the sack, got it?'

Mr Wilkins was afraid that he was going to get it but he nodded and prepared to face the workers once more. He had barely risen from the table when he was stopped in his tracks by the sound of loud voices in the corridor. A protesting Mrs Jones appeared in the doorway to be brushed aside immediately by a large woman wearing a twill dress and a high bonnet with black buttons sewn along one side. Her hair was cut short to her neck and her dark eyes glared like two burning coals. 'My name is Barbara Lennox-Leeds. I'm the secretary of the South London branch of the WSPU and I wish to speak to the managing director,' she said in a loud but cultured voice.

'I'm Harold Gore. What can I do for you?' the managing director said quickly, looking warily at the large woman.

The intruder stood with hands on hips, fixing him with her intimidating stare. 'Am I right in thinking that you have taken it on yourself to dismiss four young women in your employ for taking part in a march on Friday?' she boomed.

'That's right, I did, not that it's any concern of yours,' Gore replied sharply.

'What happens to my members *is* my concern,' the woman rebuked him. 'Mr Gore, I think I should make one thing perfectly clear. The suffragette movement, in which I am proud to serve, is campaigning for women to take their rightful place in society. When that happens, and when women get the vote, they will use their powers to right the wrongs in our society and ensure that never again will they be treated merely as the chattels of men. Never again . . .'

'What is it you want, Mrs Lennox, er, Lees?' Mr Gore cut in.

'The name is Lennox-Leeds. Miss Lennox-Leeds,' she bellowed. 'As I was saying before you rudely interrupted me, never again will women be reduced to suffering in silence as the unpaid servants of men. They will . . .'

'Look, Miss Lennox-Lees, I understand what you're saying, but what exactly is the purpose of your visit?' Mr Gore asked irritably.

'Lennox-Leeds,' she corrected him again. 'The purpose of my visit is to ask you to reconsider your decision to punish my members for taking part in the cause.'

Harold Gore glanced quickly at the wide-eyed and open-mouthed management team and dismissed them with a nod of his head. After they had hurriedly departed, he waved his visitor to a chair.

'Let me make one thing quite clear,' he began. 'I'm running a business – which, I might add, has been going through a bad time during the past twelve months. We have just reverted to full-time operation and I can't afford to let my workers take time off to attend marches, however strongly they feel about things. Discipline has to be maintained and if I don't reinforce my position the company will founder. In short, my dear, the answer is no, I will not reconsider.'

Miss Lennox-Leeds stood up quickly, glaring across the desk at him. 'I'm not your dear,' she bellowed, 'and you will kindly listen to what I have to say. Unless those four young women are reinstated immediately, the WSPU will see to it that steps are taken which will put your company right back into dire circumstances. In short, Mr Gore, your company may very well founder. I hope I've made myself quite clear?'

Harold Gore stood up quickly and matched his unwelcome visitor in a hard stare. 'Are you threatening me?' he demanded.

'No, I am not,' she replied. 'I am stating the obvious. If you cannot or will not act in a sensible and realistic manner then I will inform the press, the local member of Parliament, ward councillors, your competitors, and anyone else who will listen, that your company is openly demonstrating its opposition to the suffragette movement by victimising members of your workforce who support it. Furthermore, we the WSPU will mount daily pickets outside your premises, suitably armed with banners and posters. Now do your worst, and may you live to regret it.'

Harold Gore stood open-mouthed as the large woman turned on her heel and stormed out of his office, then he collapsed into his chair and rested his head in his hands. For a time he sat motionless. Finally he got up with a heavy sigh and called in his secretary. 'Get them back in here will you, Mrs Jones,' he groaned.

One morning in the first week of May, Florrie Axford hurried along Page Street and knocked on Maisie Dougall's front door.

''Ere Maisie, I was jus' goin' up the shop fer me snuff an' ole Bill Bailey stopped me,' she said, puffing from her exertion. 'Did yer know the King's dead?'

Maisie stood staring at Florrie for a few seconds and then her hand came up to her mouth. 'The King's dead?' she repeated.

Florrie nodded. 'I didn't believe Bill Bailey when 'e told me, ter tell yer the trufe. Yer know what a silly ole bleeder 'e is. Anyway, when I got ter the paper shop I see it fer meself. It's on the placards. 'E died o' pneumonia yesterday. The shop's sold out o' papers already.'

Maisie shook her head sadly. 'It jus' shows yer, Florrie. All the best doctors in the world ain't no use when yer number's up. 'E must 'ave 'ad the best ter look after 'im, it stan's ter reason.'

Florrie pinched her chin between her thumb and forefinger.

'I bin finkin'. It might be a good idea ter get the neighbours ter chip in wiv a few coppers.'

'Yer finkin' we should send 'im a wreaf then?' Maisie asked.

'No, yer silly mare. I mean fer the kids,' Florrie replied forcefully, and seeing Maisie's puzzled look she sighed with exasperation. 'A party. That's what I'm talkin' about. We should 'ave a street party fer the kids.'

Maisie shook her head. She had been present at Bridie Phelan's wake and she remembered how shocking it was to see the fiddler playing beside the coffin and the singing mourners gathered there in the room with glasses of whisky in their hands. 'It wouldn't be right, Florrie,' she said reverently. 'I said so at Bridie Phelan's send orf an' I ain't changed me mind. I fink it's wicked ter get pissed at such a time.'

Florrie reached into her coat pocket for her snuff-box. 'What are yer talkin' about, Mais?' she grated, tapping her finger on the silver lid. 'I reckon it's a good idea ter celebrate the coronation wiv a purty fer the kids. We've got plenty o' time ter save up fer it.'

Maisie's face relaxed into a wide grin. 'I see,' she laughed. 'A coronation party. I thought yer was on about a funeral party, like the one they done fer Bridie.'

Florrie had taken a pinch of snuff and was searching for her handkerchief. 'Gawd, Maisie, yer do get yer stays in a tangle sometimes,' she said with a resigned sigh. 'There's bound ter be a coronation, an' we ought ter celebrate. After all, it'll be somefink ter look forward to.'

Maudie Mycroft was hurrying along the turning towards them and Florrie reached out quickly and touched her friend's arm. 'I can't stand 'ere goin' on about the King, Maisie. I'll see yer later.'

As Florrie hurried off, Maisie turned to greet Maudie. 'I

jus' 'eard the news. I fink we ought ter 'ave a party fer the kids, don't you, gel?'

Maudie was about to tell Maisie that Grandfather O'Shea had finally expired and that her husband was off work with shingles, and she wondered how on earth that gave them cause to have a party.

During the summer months of 1910 there was trouble at the Galloway yard. A lucrative contract with a leather firm had been terminated and complaints had been coming in from the rum merchant's about the general conduct of the hired carmen. Trouble came to a head when the managing director of the rum merchant's phoned personally to complain that two of Galloway's carmen had refused to cross a picket line at the docks and that as a consequence bottling was at a standstill.

George Galloway had had enough. When he drove his trap into the yard on Monday morning, his face was dark with anger. 'What's bin goin' on?' he stormed.

William shrugged his shoulders. 'There's a stoppage at the Rum Quay,' he replied. 'It started on Friday mornin' and it's not bin resolved. I've sent Symonds and Morris out but it's likely they'll be turned back.'

George brought his fist down on the desk. 'I've 'ad the top man on ter me about those two bloody troublemakers. 'E told me they've got casual labour workin' on the quay an' there's two loads o' rum casks waitin' fer collection. Why didn't Morris an' Symonds go through the pickets? The police would 'ave seen to it there'd be no trouble loading.'

William shook his head. 'It's not as easy as that, George,' he answered. 'If our carmen 'ad passed those pickets, we'd be in trouble later on. Most o' the ovver cartage firms around 'ere 'ave gone union. None o' them 'ave crossed the picket lines.'

'I'm not interested in what the ovver firms do,' growled George.

William pulled up a chair and sat down facing his employer. 'I know yer've always bin against the unions, George, but yer gotta face the facts. We'd be blacklisted if we pulled a load off the quay while there was a stoppage. It'd mean the loss o' the contract. Surely yer can understand that?'

Galloway's face was set in a hard scowl. 'Those dockers 'ave tried that little trick before an' it didn't work. Don't ferget they get a call-on every mornin' an' the troublemakers are left on the cobbles. I don't fink we've got much ter worry about on that score. What I am worried about is the complaints I've been gettin' about those two dopey gits o' mine. Apparently Soapy's bin gettin' at the rum an' givin' the manager a load o' cheek, an' there've bin complaints about Sharkey. From what I've bin told 'e's bin makin' a nuisance of 'imself wiv one o' the women an' 'er ole man's bin up the firm sayin' 'e's gonna smash Sharkey's face in. On top o' that, both of them are none too careful wiv the loads. There was two casks damaged last week when they was unloaded, an' they've bin late gettin' back. If I'm not careful I'm gonna lose that contract an' I can't afford it, not on top o' that leavver contract I've jus' lost. If fings go on the way they are, I'm gonna be out o' business, Will.'

'All right,' Will said quietly, 'I'll 'ave a word wiv 'em when they get back.'

Galloway shook his head. 'No, I've 'ad enough from those two,' he said firmly. 'As a matter o' fact, I've sent young Geoffrey along ter the rum firm ter see if 'e can square fings up at that end. If Morris an' Symonds turn round outside the dock gates this mornin', I'm gonna sack the pair of 'em, an' that's final.'

'Yer bein' a bit drastic, 'ain't yer?' Will ventured. 'They've both bin wiv yer fer years. Why don't yer let me talk to 'em first?'

Galloway rounded on his foreman. 'What good would that do?' he asked loudly. 'The trouble wiv you, Will, is yer too easy wiv 'em. It was the same when I wanted ter sack Oxford. I've got a business ter run. I can't afford ter let sentiment cloud me finkin'.'

William shrank back slightly in his chair, and sighed. 'That's always bin the difference between us, George,' he said quietly. 'I could never run a business, but I know 'ow ter 'andle the men. I've kept the peace 'ere fer more years than I care ter remember, an' it's not always bin easy. There's a lot o' discontent over yer refusin' ter let the union in an' if yer sack those two carmen it's all gonna blow up in yer face, mark my words.'

Galloway glared at his foreman. 'I don't see I've got any choice. It's them or the contract. Tell me, what would you do in my position?'

'I'd swop the jobs around,' William replied quickly. 'I'd put Lofty Russell an' Ted Derbyshire on the rum contract. Sid Bristow could switch ter the 'ops in place o' Russell, an' let Morris an' Symonds do the fellmongers' contracts in place o' Derbyshire an' Bristow. That leaves the two new carmen fer the bits an' pieces as usual.'

George shook his head vigorously. 'It's too much disruption. I want it left as I've said. If those two drunken gits get sent back, I want 'em sacked. That's it, finished with.'

William stood up and walked to the door, then he turned to face Galloway, his hands thrust into his trouser pockets. 'You're the guv'nor, George. If that's what yer want, so be it. I'd jus' like yer ter remember that Sharkey an' Soapy are ole servants. If yer not careful, yer gonna 'ave a yard full o' casuals. What price yer contracts then?'

The firm's owner smiled briefly. 'When I started up in business I 'ad nuffink but casuals workin' fer me, except Albert Flynn, an' 'e got 'imself killed,' he said quietly. 'I worked long hours ter build up the business an' I 'ad ter make sacrifices. I didn't see much o' me kids when they were little an' that's somefink I've lived ter regret. I couldn't spend much time wiv Martha, Gawd rest 'er soul, an' I regret that too, but that's the price yer pay fer bein' in business. What I'm not prepared ter do is see the firm go down the drain over carmen who can't or won't do their jobs prop'ly, even if I end up wiv a yard full o' casuals again.'

William left the office without replying, and as he crossed the yard saw Geoffrey coming through the gates. The young man's expression was serious. He beckoned to the foreman. 'I've just come from the rum merchant's, Will,' he said. 'There's a full dock strike brewing and they're anxious to get their consignment today. Symonds and Morris are on their way to the docks. I just hope they get loaded. If they don't, we're in trouble.'

William smiled mirthlessly. 'That's jus' what yer farvver told me,' he replied. 'I 'ope they get loaded, fer their sakes. I've bin told ter sack the pair of 'em if they come back empty-'anded.'

Geoffrey winced. 'Did you argue with the old man?'

William raised his eyebrows. 'I tried ter talk 'im out of it but 'e's the guv'nor. 'E wouldn't be shifted. All I know is we'll be in trouble wiv the union if those two are put off, Geoff. It'll mean us bein' blacklisted at the docks. If our carmen get sent away, there's always ovver firms ter pick up the contracts.'

Geoffrey fidgeted with his tie. 'Would you let the men join the union if it was left to you?'

William nodded. 'Most o' the cartage firms around Bermondsey are unionised now. In time any non-union firm is gonna find it difficult ter get contracts. I've tried ter tell yer farvver that we'll be left wiv next ter nuffink unless 'e changes 'is mind, but 'e's determined ter go on as usual. 'E'll never change, unless it's forced on 'im.'

Geoffrey sighed heavily. 'I don't know what to suggest. The old man won't listen to me. I've wanted to bring a couple of lorries in as you know but he won't even consider the idea. I've been after him to get another yard too but he won't budge. I thought Frank would be able to persuade him otherwise but he couldn't make him see the sense in it.'

William had his own reservations about the firm becoming mechanised but he refrained from making any comment, merely shrugging his shoulders instead. It seemed to him that it would only be a matter of time before all horses were replaced by lorries, and he thought with foreboding about his own future. Working with horses had been his life ever since he had started work at fourteen. He had been with Galloway for over twenty-eight years now and it would count for nothing if all the horses went.

'It shouldn't make any difference to you if we do get motor vans in, Will,' Geoffrey said, as if reading his thoughts. 'There'll always be a place here for you. It'll just mean adapting to a new way of working.'

William realised that his anxiety must be obvious and hid his fears behind a smile. 'I'd better get back ter work.'

It was almost noon when Sharkey and Soapy drove their carts into the yard. 'We've bin sent back,' Soapy told the yard foreman. 'We got turned away at the dock gates an' the firm told us ter report back 'ere.'

William scratched his head in agitation. 'Couldn't yer go in the gates?' he asked.

Sharkey looked pained. 'I ain't crossin' no picket lines,' he asserted. 'It's all right fer that guv'nor at the rum firm ter talk. It's us what's gonna get set about.'

Soapy nodded his agreement. 'There was only a couple o' coppers outside the gates an' there was fousands o' dockers. We'd 'ave got slaughtered if we'd tried ter go in.'

William pulled the two carmen to one side. 'I was told ter sack the pair of yer if yer got sent back,' he said solemnly.

'Sack us!' Sharkey gasped, his ruddy face growing even more flushed. 'After all these years? I can't believe it.'

'I can,' Soapy jumped in, fixing William with his bleary eyes. 'Look at 'ow the ole bastard sacked the Blackwell bruvvers over that union business. Well, I ain't takin' it lyin' down. I'm gonna go along ter Tooley Street an' see the union blokes. I'll get it stopped, you see if I don't.'

'What can they do?' Sharkey grumbled. 'It ain't as though we was in the union ourselves.'

'They can make it awkward, that's what they can do,' Soapy answered. 'That's why the likes of 'Atcher an' Morgan let the union in. They 'ad the sense ter see what could 'appen. Trouble wiv Galloway is, 'e can't see no furvver than 'is poxy nose. Well, I 'ope the union does somefink about it. I'm gonna see 'em anyway.'

William held his hands up. 'Look, I'll 'ave anuvver word wiv the ole man,' he said quickly. 'Not that it'll do much good, but at least I'll try. You two wait 'ere.'

George had been talking on the phone. When William walked into the office, he slammed the receiver down on to its hook. 'That was the rum firm on the line,' he growled. 'They wasn't too 'appy, as yer might expect. Did yer tell those two lazy gits they're sacked?'

'That's what I wanted ter see yer about, George,' the foreman said, closing the door behind him. 'The union are not gonna let this trouble go away wivout tryin' ter do somefing about it.'

'Oh, an' what can they do?' George asked.

'If yer'd jus' listen fer a second yer'd realise there's a lot they can do,' William replied, feeling his anger rising. 'Fer a start yer won't get any more dock work. They'll see ter that. Yer won't get contracts from unionised firms neivver, an' yer gonna be left wiv all the work no ovver firm would entertain. All right, yer'd keep the fellmongers' contracts but who'd be 'appy doin' that sort o' work, apart from yer two new carmen? Let's face it, George, who'd cart those stinkin' skins fer you when they could get more money doin' the same job fer Morgan? If yer ask me I reckon yer bein' unreasonable askin' Sharkey and Soapy ter cross picket lines.'

'Oh, yer do, do yer?' George exclaimed sarcastically, his heavy-lidded eyes brightening with anger as he glared at William. 'What should I do? Pat 'em on the back an' tell 'em it was all right? It's a pity yer can't see my side o' fings fer a change. I'd expect yer ter show me a bit o' loyalty after all the years we've known each ovver. Yer paid ter run the yard, not ter be a nursemaid ter those lazy bastards o' mine.'

William felt his fists clenching and he drew in a deep breath in an effort to control his anger. 'I fink that's jus' what Sharkey an' Soapy might 'ave expected from you,' he replied quickly. 'They'd 'ave liked you ter show 'em a bit o' loyalty. As fer me, I run this yard the way I see fit. Yer 'orses are in good condition an' the carts are kept on the road. What's more, I keep the peace as best I can. If yer don't like the way I work, I suggest yer get yerself anuvver yard foreman.'

For a few moments the two glared at each other, then George slumped back in his chair and stroked his chin thoughtfully. 'Sometimes yer puzzle me, Will,' he said with a slight dismissive shake of his head. 'Yer willin' ter put yer job at risk fer a couple o' pissy carmen. It was the same when I was gonna sack Jack Oxford. Sometimes I wonder jus' where yer loyalties lie. All right, s'posin' I reconsider an' let yer change the work round – what would yer fink?'

'What d'yer mean?' William queried.

George leaned forward in his chair. 'Well, would yer fink yer could barter yer job against any future decisions I might make which you don't like? I tell yer now, if that's the case yer'd better fink again. I won't be 'eld ter ransom by you or anybody else. I make the decisions 'ere, jus' remember that. This time, though, I'll let yer 'ave yer way – but jus' fink on what I've said. Now yer'd better go out an' give them dopey pair the good news before I change me mind.'

Chapter Sixteen

Nellie Tanner was sitting having a chat with her friends from the street. 'It's bin a funny ole twelvemonth when yer come ter fink of it,' she remarked. It seemed to her that the year had been fraught with trouble of one sort or another, and she was eager to see the back of it. 'There was that trouble at Carrie's firm an' I felt sure she'd lost 'er job. It was touch an' go fer a while but fank Gawd it all worked out right in the end.'

Florrie Axford eased her lean frame back in the armchair and reached into her apron for her snuff. 'Yeah, it's not bin a very nice year one way an' anuvver. There was King Edward dyin' in May, an' all that short-time in the factories, then there was that comet flyin' over. That was May, wasn't it?'

Maisie Dougall put her hand to her cheek. 'Don't talk ter me about that comet,' she said. 'Maudie Mycroft drove me mad over that. She come inter my place worried out of 'er life, yer know 'ow she gets. Apparently 'er ole man frightened 'er by what 'e said. 'E told 'er that if it went off course and come down on us, that'd be the end o' the world. Mind, though, Maudie's as nervous as a kitten, she takes everyfing fer gospel. She was really upset when she come inter me. She said they was 'avin' prayers about it at the muvvers' meetin'.'

Florrie took a pinch of snuff from her tiny silver box and laid it on the back of her hand. 'That's the way the world's gonna end, accordin' ter the Bible,' she said, putting her hand up to her nostrils and sniffing. 'I remember readin' somewhere in the Old Testament that the end of the world'll come like a thief in the night.'

Nellie took the large iron kettle from the hob and filled the teapot. 'I used ter read the Bible ter me muvver when I was a kid,' she said, slowly stirring the tea-leaves. 'I 'ad ter read a passage from it every night. She was very religious was my muvver. We used ter say grace before every meal an' she wouldn't allow no swearin' in the 'ouse, not from us anyway. She used ter let fly though, when me farvver come in drunk. She was a country lady, yer see, an' they say country people are very religious.'

Aggie Temple had been listening quietly to the conversation. She looked at Nellie. 'Royalty's s'posed ter be very religious,' she remarked. 'King Edward was by all accounts, an' so's the new King George. It ses in the paper they all go ter church every Sunday.'

'That don't make 'em religious,' Florrie cut in. 'They 'ave ter keep up appearances. Look at Sadie Sullivan. Every Sunday yer see 'er walkin' down the turnin' wiv 'er ole man an' the seven boys on their way ter Mass. She does 'er 'Ail Marys – an' then if anybody upsets 'er durin' the week, she'll clout 'em soon as wink.'

'She's quietened down a lot lately though,' Nellie replied. 'I fink that magistrate frightened 'er. 'E said the next time she goes in front of 'im, 'e's gonna send 'er down.'

Maisie nodded. 'Yer don't see 'er boys fightin' in the street the way they used to, do yer? They're all growin' up fast. Look at that Billy Sullivan. What a smart young fella 'e's turned out ter be. 'E's a boxer now, an' doin' very well, by all accounts. Is your Carrie still sweet on 'im, Nellie?' she asked.

Nellie shook her head. 'She only went out wiv 'im once. Nuffink come of it though. Mind you, I can't say as I was sorry. I wouldn't like my Carrie ter marry a boxer.'

When Nellie had filled the cups and passed them round, Aggie stirred her tea thoughtfully. 'It's gonna be anuvver bad year,' she announced suddenly.

The women looked at her and Florrie laughed. 'Don't yer believe it! It's gonna be a lot better than this year, Aggie, jus' wait an' see,' she said with conviction.

Aggie shook her head. 'I always get *Old Moore's Almanac* every year, an' it said in there that next year's gonna be a bad one. It's nearly always right.'

Nellie sat down and brushed the front of her long skirt. ''Ave yer seen that paper they shove frew the door every month? *Lamplight* it's called. It's always sayin' the end o' the world is nigh.'

Maisie shifted position in her chair and folded her arms over her plump figure. 'Bleedin' Job's witness that is,' she said quickly.

'Don't yer mean Job's comforter?' Florrie laughed.

Maisie waved her hand in a dismissive gesture. 'Yer know what I mean. If yer take notice o' fings like that yer'd drive yerself inter an early grave. You take ole Mrs Brody who used ter live in Bacon Street. She was terrified o' them sort o' fings. I remember once when there was an eclipse an' the sun was blacked out. Middle o' the day it was. Anyway, she was convinced that it was the end o' the world. She got right down on 'er 'ands an' knees outside 'er front door an' prayed. Bloody sight it was. There was 'er on 'er knees an' 'er ole man staggerin' up the street, pissed as a pudden. Singin' at the top of 'is voice 'e was. Mind yer, ole Mrs Brody frightened the life out of 'alf the turnin'. Mrs Kelly was cryin' an' ole Granny Perry was standin' by 'er front door wiv 'er shawl over 'er 'ead. All the kids run indoors, scared, an' there was Mrs Brody's ole man tryin' ter lift 'er up. "Get up, yer scatty ole cow," 'e said to 'er. "Who yer callin' a scatty ole cow?" she shouted. Wiv that she jumps up an' clouts 'im. 'E clouted 'er back, an' before yer knew it they was 'avin' a right ole bull an' cow. By that time the sun was out again an' everybody was at their doors watchin'. Gawd, I never laughed so much in all me life.'

When the laughter died down, Florrie raised her hand. ''Ere, talkin' about that, what about my ole man?' she began. 'The first one, I mean. 'E was a violent git. Well, one night 'e come 'ome from work pissed out of 'is mind. 'E used ter work at the brewery an' 'e was never sober, but this particular night 'e could 'ardly stand. 'E comes in an' flops down at the table. "Where's me so-an'-so tea?" 'e shouts out. I was in the scullery tryin' ter keep 'is meal 'ot an' I ses ter meself, "Florrie, yer in fer a pastin' ternight." Tell yer the trufe, I was terrified of 'im. 'E'd bin givin' me a bad time an' I knew I couldn't stand anymore. Anyway, I looks around an' I spots this rat poison I'd put down by the back door. "Right, yer bastard," I ses ter meself. "I'm gonna do fer yer ternight." I sticks a bit o' this rat poison in the meat pudden I'd made an' I gives 'im a sweet smile as I puts it down in front of 'im. 'E was lookin' a bit grey then an' I thought ter meself, Wait till yer eat the pie. All of a sudden 'e grabs at 'is stomach an' doubles up over the table. 'E was groanin' an' floppin' about in agony. Anyway, I got scared an' I run fer ole Doctor Kelly. Ter cut a long story short they rushed 'im away ter Guy's. Peritonitis it was. 'E was dead the next day. Gawd! Wasn't I glad 'e didn't touch that meal. It jus' shows yer 'ow desperate yer can get at times. Yer does fings wivout finkin'.'

The teacups had been refilled and the four friends sat together talking late into the afternoon. They discussed the weather, the coming festive season, children, and leaving the worst topic till last, the recent rent rise.

'Wouldn't yer fink that ole goat Galloway would 'ave waited till after Christmas ter put the rents up?' Florrie commented.

'What does 'e care?' Aggie said. 'The bleedin' roofs are leakin', the front doors don't shut prop'ly, then there's the draughts comin' in them winders. I fink it's scand'lous ter charge ten shillin's a week fer our places.'

Maisie nodded. 'We'll 'ave ter nag 'im inter doin' somefing. Now 'e's put the rents up we've got a right ter complain, not that 'e'll give a sod about it,' she groaned.

Nellie felt a little guilty as she listened to her friends' grievances, and despite herself was slightly relieved when they finally left. The rent increase had not affected her but there was always a nagging doubt at the back of her mind that one day her husband would fall out with George Galloway and they would find themselves out on the street. In that event she would not be able to bring herself to plead on Will's behalf. She had done it once before and the memory still gave her many sleepless nights.

The new year started cold and damp, and throughout most of January mists drifted in from the river and swirled through the riverside backstreets. Cold and heavy, they blended with the thick yellow smoke from the chimneys and the air became choked with sulphur fumes. There seemed little to be optimistic about in the backstreets as news spread that there would be more short-time working and lay-offs. The docks and wharves were unusually quiet, even allowing for the time of year, and river workers hung about on street corners and outside dock gates, hoping for a day's work or even the odd half-day.

At Wilson's leather factory word had spread that short-time working was inevitable, and the factory girls shrugged their shoulders and prepared themselves for the worst. On the last Friday of January a notice was pinned up beside the time clock. It announced that a third of the workforce was to be made redundant. The girls clustered around the clock anxiously scanning the list, and when Carrie saw her name near the bottom she turned away feeling angry and depressed. Jessica's name was there as well as Freda's, but Carrie had not caught sight of Mary's name amongst the thirty or so.

Freda cursed loudly when she spotted her name on the list. 'I knew we'd be on it,' she scowled. 'They've 'ad it in fer us ever since they 'ad ter take us back.'

Carrie scanned the list once more. 'That's funny,' she remarked. 'Mary's not down 'ere. I wonder why?'

Freda snorted. ''Cos they're crafty, that's why. We can't say we've all bin victimised now, can we?' she pointed out.

Jessica had a miserable look on her round face as the three went to their work bench. 'They didn't give us much time, did they?' she moaned. 'Next Monday we'll all be linin' up down the labour exchange. Well, I tell yer now, I'm not gonna work at that tin bashers. I'd sooner go on the game first.'

'Yer wouldn't earn much round 'ere, Jess,' Freda said, laughing. 'It's only tuppence a time down the alley beside the Star Music 'All.'

''Ow d'yer know what they charge?' Carrie asked with a grin on her face.

Freda kept a straight face as they seated themselves around the long wooden bench. 'Yer might laugh,' she began, 'but I knew a young girl who used ter be on the game. She was only about seventeen an' one night I met 'er on the stairs in our buildin's. She was goin' on about all the money she was earnin.' "Four an' tuppence I earned ternight," she said. "Who give yer the odd tuppence, Ellie?" I asked 'er. "All of 'em," she said. I tell yer straight, Jess, bein' on the game ain't an easy life.'

Their early morning high spirits soon disappeared as the shock of impending redundancy struck home, and the young women became despondent as they discussed the likelihood of finding other work.

'There'll be 'undreds down that labour exchange on Monday,' one of the girls moaned. 'This ain't the only firm puttin' people off, I 'eard that Bevin'tons an' Johnson Bruvvers are puttin' their workers off. Gawd knows what we're gonna do.'

'Well, like I said, I ain't gonna work on no poxy tin machine,' Jessica stated. 'One o' the girls I know lost 'er fingers on a tin machine. There's the bloody noise ter contend wiv an' all. They reckon the noise o' those machines makes yer go stone deaf in time. I don't fink the tin bashers pay as much as this firm neivver.'

'Well, if it comes ter the worst I'm gonna let me fella get me pregnant,' another of the girls said. ''E'll 'ave ter marry me then an' I can let 'im keep me.'

'Don't be so sure,' Freda said quickly. 'I got pregnant when I was sixteen an' the farvver didn't keep me. In fact, I nearly ended up in the work'ouse.'

When the lunch-time whistle sounded the young women hurried from their work benches and gathered in the large room which they used for eating their sandwiches in when the weather was cold. Mary Caldwell approached the three friends with an angry look on her round flat face. 'I'm sorry yer gettin' put off,' she said. 'I was surprised they didn't put me on the list but they've done me no favours. Betty's got the sack.'

Carrie felt sorry for the young woman. Mary and Betty had become inseparable during the last few months and their relationship had become the talk of the factory.

'If that's not bad enough, they've put Mrs Loder on my floor,' Mary went on, looking miserable. 'I don't know if I can stand workin' wiv 'er. I'll end up walkin' out, I know I will.'

Carrie understood how Mary felt. Her friend's new workmate was known for her vitriolic tongue and she had openly condemned Mary's relationship with Betty. It seemed to Carrie that the new arrangement had been carefully thought out by the management in the hope that it would force Mary to do what she was threatening. Carrie looked around her as she ate her sandwiches. She had got to know all the girls during the five years or so that she had worked at the factory and it was going to be a wrench leaving on Friday. What was in store for her? she wondered. Would she be forced to work at one of the tin factories or in one of the local food canneries? She knew that whatever factory job she found it would be the same tedious slog, and began to feel more and more depressed.

At Galloway's yard the general slump had been taking effect, and on that cold Monday morning the firm's owner called his foreman into the office to tell him that the two casual carmen would be put off. There was more bad news too. Yet another leather firm which used Galloway's carts had announced that they would not be renewing their cartage contract.

'It's bad but there's nuffink I can do about it, Will. I'll 'ave ter put Lofty Russell an' Darbo off on Friday,' Galloway said, slumping down at his desk. 'I'm after a contract wiv the bacon curers. If I'm lucky, I'll take the two of 'em back, but there's nuffink definite yet.'

William shrugged his shoulders. He had fought the old man over jobs before but he knew that it was useless to try the way things were now. The mention of the new contract made him think, however, and he looked sharply at his boss. 'That's foreign bacon yer talkin' about, ain't it, George?' he said quickly.

Galloway nodded. 'If I get the work, it'll be local wharf collections,' he replied.

William sat down facing him. 'Are yer aware that if yer lucky wiv the contract the carmen'll need union tickets, especially if the bacon's comin' out of Mark Brown's Wharf? Those dockers there are pretty strict about who they load.'

Galloway nodded. 'I'll see to it they'll 'ave tickets,' he said in a low voice.

William was very surprised at his change of heart. George had never entertained the idea of his carmen joining the union before and now he had agreed without a word. Things must be bad, he thought.

'I've already bin on ter Tooley Street an' the union official there said 'e'll look after it,' George added.

William hid his disgust. His employer and the union official had probably been out for a few drinks together and it was more than likely that George had lined the official's pocket, he reasoned.

Galloway was staring at him with a faint smile on his face and William had the feeling he was being mocked. He could not have divined the reason for Galloway's amusement accurately, however, for his boss said, 'By the way, Will, I've got a special job fer yer. I've bought an 'orse at the weekend. It's a Cleveland Bay an' I got it fer me trap. That pony I've got is goin' lame a lot an' I'm gettin' rid of it.'

'Yer not sendin' it ter the knacker's yard, are yer, George?' William asked.

His boss laughed. 'No, I've 'ad good use out o' Rusty an' I'm gonna put 'im out ter pasture. This Cleveland stands fifteen 'ands an' it's a lovely-lookin' 'orse. I got it fer a snip an' I want yer ter get it ready fer the trap.'

William glanced quickly at his employer. 'Yer mean it's not been in one before?'

George grinned. 'It 'as, but it kicked the traces. It's a devil, Will, but it's got a look about it. Yer know what I'm talkin' about. We've both been around 'orses all our lives an' we fink we know 'em, but suddenly one comes on the scene an' it quickens yer breath just ter look at it. This Cleveland's just like that. I was standin' at the sales at the weekend an' this bloke drives up in 'is trap. 'E jumped down an' started layin' inter the 'orse wiv 'is whip. Yer know me, I'm the same as you where 'orses are concerned. I 'ate ter see 'em ill-treated. Anyway, I 'ad a few words wiv the driver an' 'e told me that the nag 'ad almost killed 'im on a couple of occasions. He reckoned there was Arab blood in the 'orse an' it wouldn't take ter the trap. It's bin gelded too.'

William felt his interest growing. 'Clevelands are good carriage 'orses as a rule,' he remarked. 'P'raps the bloke didn't know 'ow ter 'andle the 'orse?'

George shook his head. 'The man I'm talking about 'as got a cartage business in Peckham. 'E's bin round 'orses fer years an' 'e said 'e's never known a Cleveland ter act the way this one does. Well, I looked the 'orse over an' I was taken by it. Like I say, it was one o' those 'orses that come along once in a while. It was beautiful-lookin', lean an' frisky. It 'ad a look in its eye too. I couldn't resist it. I made 'im an offer an' the bloke sold it ter me there an' then. 'E's bringin' it round terday. See what yer can do wiv it, Will. I want it in the trap as soon as possible.'

William nodded. 'I'll get Jack Oxford ter clean that small stable. It's better if it's kept away from the ovver 'orses, at least fer the time bein'.'

It was late afternoon when the Cleveland was driven into the yard and was pulled up beside the office. The driver, an elderly man with a ginger beard, stepped down from the trap and immediately untethered the spare horse from the rear, leading it towards William. 'Can I leave you to change them over?' he asked.

William nodded and stood holding the bridle of the spare horse as he watched the man disappear into the office, then he led the nag to the water trough and let it drink its fill before tethering it to a post. The Cleveland stood still in the shafts of the trap, light glinting red in its eyes as it warily watched William approach. He talked quietly to the horse as he sidled up and took hold of its bridle. 'Steady, boy,' he whispered as he patted the horse's high neck and ran his hand down the withers. The horse remained perfectly still while William slowly unbuckled the harness, and then when it was being led out of the shafts it suddenly kicked out sharply with its back legs. Jack Oxford was watching from across the yard. He jumped back nervously. 'That's a wild 'orse, Will,' he remarked.

The yard foreman grinned as he held on to the bridle tightly and led the horse to water. He kept his grip on the loose bridle rope while the horse drank its fill, then as its head came up William instinctively tightened his hand on the rope. His intuition was correct for as the Cleveland turned from the stone trough it reared up and kicked out at the tethered horse. The yard foreman slid his hand along the taut rope until he had hold of its bridle. With soft words and a gentle tap on the horse's neck, he quietened it down before leading it to the small stable. The spare horse had been agitated by the antics of the Cleveland. It bucked as William untied the rope but it offered no resistance when it was led to the trap.

After William had finished buckling up the harness and

secured the horse to a hitching-rail, he sauntered over to the small stable and went inside. The Cleveland stood munching at the stall and William was able to look the horse over. It was a bay brown with a small white star on its forehead, all of fifteen hands high and a little on the lean side, he thought. It had a large head and a long, firm neck. The animal's hindquarters were powerful and well rounded, and its legs clean-cut and muscular. It was certainly a fine-looking horse, William conceded as he ran his hand over the withers, but it would need careful handling and training before it could be trusted in a trap.

As he stroked his hand down the animal's flank his fingers came upon several very slight indentations, and a close inspection confirmed his suspicions. The horse had been badly ill-treated at some time with a whip or thong. William gently patted the horse's withers and whispered to it as he sidled along the stall and loosened the bridle rope slightly. When he had made certain that there was enough chaff in the stall trough he eased back and took a look at the horse's hindquarters. From the marks below the hocks and around the pasterns he could see that the horse did not take kindly to the shafts and had damaged itself by kicking out. William shook his head sadly as he stood back and studied the animal. He had seen such signs before and he realised he would have to work hard to gain the animal's confidence if any progress was to be made.

As he walked over to the office, William saw the yard man leaning on his broom. 'I don't want anybody ter go in that end stable, Jack,' he said firmly. 'I'll feed an' water that one.'

Jack nodded enthusiastically, feeling quite relieved. He knew about such devil horses and had very good reason to be wary of such creatures. They had said it was the devil who had got into the horse that kicked the side of his head in.

When the visitor had driven out of the yard, Galloway called his foreman into the office. 'Well, what d'yer fink?' he asked, grinning broadly.

'It's a beauty, but it'll take some time before it's ready fer yer trap,' William replied.

''As it bin raced?' George asked.

William nodded. 'It looks that way. There's lash marks down its flanks an' it's bin flogged. I could tell as I led it ter the trough. Yer'll 'ave ter give me at least a couple o' weeks.'

George nodded. 'Take all the time yer want, Will, an' keep it away from the ovver 'orses. If it kicks out at the Clydesdales, it'll get mangled.'

The Tanner family sat around the table that evening listening to Carrie's bad news as they tucked into their mutton stew which Nellie had fortified heavily with pearl barley and carrots. James was leaning his elbows on the table as he scooped up the broth. He shook his head knowingly when he heard the news. 'What did I tell yer? I knew it,' he remarked, reaching for another hunk of bread and dipping it into the gravy.

''Ave yer got any idea where yer gonna try?' Nellie asked her daughter.

Carrie shook her head. 'I s'pose I'll 'ave ter join the rank at the labour exchange,' she said, moving the spoon around her broth and looking dejected.

'Well, don't let it stop yer eatin',' her father urged, trying to get her to smile.

James looked up from his plate. 'Don't let yer new guv'nor know yer in the suffragettes, fer Gawd's sake,' he said quickly.

Carrie gave him a blinding look as she spooned up her food. 'It's nuffink ter be ashamed of,' she replied indignantly. 'If women 'ad the vote, maybe fings would be different.'

Nellie and William exchanged glances and Danny grinned at Charlie. 'Our guv'nor wants anuvver errand boy. P'raps 'e might take on a gel,' he mumbled, only to receive a sharp kick on the shin from his angry sister.

Charlie gave Carrie a sympathetic smile. 'Maybe yer could get a job in a shop or somefink,' he suggested. 'It'd be a change from workin' in a factory. Or maybe yer could work in one o' those suffragette offices. They take people on full time, don't they?'

Carrie shook her head. 'Yer gotta 'ave an education ter work in one o' those offices. They don't take on workin'-class gels. I might be able ter get a job in a shop though,' she added, perking up slightly.

'What about 'Arris's the pawnbroker's?' Danny quipped. 'Yer don't need much education ter 'and out pawn tickets.'

'If yer don't shut up an' eat yer tea, I'll box yer ears,' Nellie shouted across the table.

William tried to keep a straight face as he glanced sternly at his youngest son. Danny had grown into a robust young man and his cheeky expression was never more roguish than when he was ribbing his sister or James. Strangely enough, though, Danny rarely got at Charlie. Maybe it was because Charlie totally ignored his spirited teasing, merely smiling and shrugging his shoulders. James on the other hand was easily provoked. He was now in his nineteenth year and considered himself to be a full-grown adult who was not to be trifled with.

'Do as yer told an' eat yer tea,' James chimed in now, wiping the last of his bread around the edge of the plate.

Carrie had left part of her meal. She sat back in her chair, looking a trifle sorry for herself. Danny had been ready to make another quip but was stopped by his father's attempt at a stern look and finished his food quietly.

'By the way, we've got a new 'orse in the yard,' William

said quickly in an effort to cheer up his daughter. ''E's a real beauty. Yer can come an' take a look soon, Carrie, if yer want to.'

Her face brightened. It was something she had always loved to do when she was younger and it made her feel sad to think how she had slowly grown out of it, although she still loved to hear her father talk about his charges. 'What is it?' she asked him.

'It's a Cleveland gelding,' he replied. 'Galloway bought 'im fer the trap but 'e's bin ill-treated an' 'e needs ter settle down first.'

''Ow can yer tell it's bin ill-treated?' Danny asked.

'Well, usually yer can see whip-marks on the 'orse's flanks an' yer can tell by 'ow it be'aves,' William explained, warming to the subject. 'Sometimes an 'orse will shy an' buck when yer approach it, especially if yer carryin' a lump o' rope or somefink. Jus' fink what you would do if I whipped yer fer talkin' round the table. Every time I picked up the whip yer'd back away, wouldn't yer?'

Danny grinned widely and Nellie got up from her chair to clear away the plates, realising that her husband was likely to go on for some time now he was on the subject of horses. As she carried the plates into the scullery and filled the enamel bowl with hot water from the copper, she could hear William's deep voice and her children's laughter as they sat around the kitchen table. She ought to feel contented at the happy gathering, she knew, but there was something lurking deep down inside her which made her feel strangely apprehensive and worried for the future.

Chapter Seventeen

Carrie was feeling a little nervous as she left her house in Page Street on Friday evening and walked through the thickening fog to Fred Bradley's Dining Rooms in Cotton Lane. As she turned into Bacon Street and passed the old tenement buildings she heard a baby crying and a woman's angry voice. Carrie wondered how her old school friend Sara was getting on and promised herself that she would call on her very soon. It was quiet and eerie in the riverside streets after the hustle and bustle of the day, and as she crossed into Cotton Lane which ran from the end of Bacon Street down to the river Carrie could see the vague forms of giant cranes looming out of the fog.

It was her father who had told her about the vacancy. He had got the information from Sharkey Morris who often used the dining rooms. Nellie had not been too happy at the thought of her daughter serving meals to carmen but had been persuaded not to worry, and Carrie laughed to herself as she recalled what her father had said. 'It's a sight better than slavin' in a factory, especially the tin bashers,' he had enthused. 'Besides, our carmen use Fred's place all the time an' they'll keep an eye on 'er.'

Carrie reached the shuttered shop which was situated on the corner of the turning overlooking the river. She glanced up at the faded name over the boarded-up window before knocking on the side door. The lane was deserted, and she could hear the swish of water lapping against the shore and the soft murmur of the turning tide. There was the sound of a bolt being drawn and then Fred Bradley was standing in the doorway smiling at her. 'Yer Carrie Tanner, I take it?' he said, standing aside to let her enter.

She followed him into the passage and felt the heat of the coke fire as she entered the small back room. Fred bade her sit beside the fire and planted himself on an upright chair facing her. 'I'm sorry yer 'ad ter drag yerself out on a cold night, missy,' he said. 'I'm kept busy fer most o' the day, especially now Ida's left me in the lurch.'

Carrie smiled. 'It's all right. Me dad wanted ter bring me but it's only five minutes from our 'ouse. 'E told me yer wanted somebody ter wait on the customers?'

Fred Bradley took out his pipe and proceeded to fill it from a leather pouch. 'Ida's bin wiv me fer years but 'er 'usband's took chronic sick an' she's gotta see to 'im night an' day,' he explained. 'They wanted ter put 'im in the infirmary but Ida wouldn't 'ear of it. They never 'ad any children an' they're devoted ter each ovver. Terrible shame really. It's consumption, I fink.'

Carrie took the opportunity to study the man while he was preoccupied with his pipe. He was of about average height, bulky and with wide shoulders. Although his dark wavy hair was streaked with grey his complexion was fresh and his jaw square-boned. His eyes were brown and heavy-browed, and tended to widen as he talked. In between he smiled disarmingly to reveal strong even teeth. Carrie judged him to be in his mid-thirties although his mannerisms made him appear older.

'I never married, yer see,' he went on. 'I took the dinin' rooms over from me parents when they got too old ter manage them. They're both dead now an' I've run the place fer over ten years. Ida used ter take the orders and serve up the food as well as pour the tea. I do all the cookin', which takes most o' me time, but I've got a woman who comes in early in the mornin' ter do the veg an' 'elp me make the meat pies. Yer seem a likely lass so can I ask yer 'ow much yer was expectin' in wages?'

Carrie stared down at her button-up boots. 'I was earnin' fifteen shillin's a week at the factory,' she said quietly.

'Well, I'll match that fer the first two weeks, an' if we both suit each ovver I'll make it up ter seventeen an' six,' he told her. 'Of course, yer'll get yer dinner free an' as much tea as yer want. Ida used ter 'ave a bite ter eat durin' the mornin' as well. I fink we can fatten yer up if nuffink else. Well, what d'yer say?'

Carrie smiled. 'When can I start?' she asked, unable to conceal her enthusiasm.

'Monday mornin', eight o'clock,' he replied with a grin. 'Yer should get away around five o'clock or just after. I like ter be all shut up by 'alf-past. I run the dinin' rooms fer carmen an' dockers, an' there's no trade after five.'

Carrie stood up and straightened her coat. 'Fank yer very much, Mr Bradley. I'll be in at eight o'clock,' she said cheerily.

'Call me Fred, everybody does,' he grinned, showing her to the door.

At 22 Tyburn Square Nora Flynn was sitting with George Galloway in his large front room. The fire was banked up with a pine log and the heat made her feel drowsy. Galloway got up from his comfortable chair and filled his whisky glass from the lead-crystal decanter, his heavy features flushed with the spirits he had already drunk that evening. 'Ter tell yer the trufe it's come as a bit of a surprise, Nora,' he remarked. 'I would 'ave preferred the lad ter wait fer a few more years but 'e's made 'is mind up an' she seems ter be a nice young lady.'

Nora nodded. ''E'll be twenty-five this year. 'E's a man now, George. My 'usband was only twenty-one when we got married.'

Galloway sat down heavily and stirred the pine log with a poker. 'It's the crowd 'e mixes wiv that troubles me,' he went on. 'Those music 'all people are all "dearie" an' "darlin'", an' I get a bit awkward in their company. Mind yer, Bella's all right an' she seems ter fink a lot of our Frank.'

Nora stared into the fire. She had met Frank's future wife on a few occasions and had taken an instant dislike to the woman. She was too brassy, Nora felt, and a lazy bitch into the bargain. If young Frank was not careful she would have him running behind her like one of those Pekinese dogs which that sort were fond of dragging around. She was a very attractive woman, it was true, but then all those music hall artists were. Plenty of paint and powder, and a shortage of manners to boot. It was a wonder George had not seen through her. He was usually a good judge of character, she felt. Perhaps he was blinded by the attention Bella paid him. She was inclined to lay it on thick where George was concerned.

'Don't yer fink she's very sweet on the boy, Nora?' he asked.

'I'm sure she is,' Nora replied without much enthusiasm. 'They seem well suited.'

Galloway sipped his whisky as he stared into the flames and Nora picked up her glass of port. They were well suited in a way, she thought. Young Frank was a manipulative sort, able to twist his father around his little finger. Everything he wanted, he got. He had been determined not to enter the family business and instead learn accountancy, and his father had bowed to his wishes. Now he was planning to marry that flash tart, and again he had George's blessing.

It had not been so with young Geoffrey. The lad had wanted to go his own way but had been as good as forced to enter the business. It was the same with his choice of women. George had been critical of the young ladies he had brought home and now Geoffrey was having a relationship with a married woman, unbeknown to his father. It was Frank, not Geoffrey, who had told her. It had slipped out one night when he was the worse for drink. He had become loose-tongued in a euphoric moment during one of Bella's visits, and while Nora was preparing the evening meal had sat with her in the back kitchen and flippantly talked about the liaison that his elder brother was supposedly keeping secret.

'I've found a replacement fer Rusty,' George said suddenly, looking up from the fire. 'The ole boy's gettin' past it an' I'm puttin' 'im out ter grass. P'raps it was an extravagance, what wiv the way the business is goin', but it looked like a bargain at the time an' I couldn't turn down the chance. A man's gotta keep up appearances when 'e's in business. I learned that a long while ago.'

Nora nodded absently, her mind straying to thoughts of Josephine. She had been waiting her chance to tackle George about his daughter and she decided now was as good a time as any.

'It's strange 'ow the family 'ave all grown up suddenly,' she said casually. 'Take Frank, 'e's gettin' married in a few months' time, an' Geoffrey is doin' well in the business. Josephine'll be fourteen next month. There's 'er future ter fink about.'

Galloway slowly revolved the glass of whisky in his hand and looked closely at his housekeeper. The boys had been no trouble, he had always known how to deal with them, but he was aware how different it was with his daughter. She had been brought up by Nora and had never really taken up much of his time. He had always felt a little uncomfortable when talking to the child, and as she grew older it became more so. She reminded him so much of Martha in her ways and mannerisms. She had her mother's eyes, the same complexion and quiet, light voice.

'Yer should give some thought to 'er schoolin', George,' Nora went on. 'The child's bright an' it might be a good idea ter get 'er fixed up at one o' those boardin' schools, or maybe St Olave's Grammar School.'

George stared back into the fire. He had not really considered the matter before and felt at a loss to know which way to proceed. 'Could yer make some enquiries, Nora?' he asked. 'Yer close ter the child. Find out what she wants ter do an' we can talk later.'

Nora sipped her port and felt a warm glow inside. She was satisfied with the way she had seized the most opportune moment. George was like all men, she told herself. Catch them when they were well fed and supped, and leave the rest to intuition.

On Saturday evening the fog had lifted and the night was clear and starry. William Tanner let himself into the yard through the wicket-gate and held the sprung door open while Carrie stepped through behind him. It was not very often that she went with him to the yard now, he thought as she walked along beside him, but when he had told her about the Cleveland gelding she wanted to see the animal for herself. They crossed the dark yard and William took down the paraffin lamp from above the door of the small stable and primed it.

Carrie smelt the familiar stable aroma as she stepped into

the whitewashed interior, and as her father hung the lighted lamp from a centre post she saw the gelding. She had learned how to pick out the finer points of horses and their strengths and weaknesses but when she cast her eyes on the bay she felt almost at a loss for words. ''E's beautiful!' she gasped, going up to the horse and running her hand down his neck.

'Careful,' her father warned her. ''E's nervous.'

Carrie held out the sugar lump she had brought with her and let the animal take it from her palm. Her eyes were wide with wonderment and William smiled. He had never known her to show any fear of horses and the animal seemed to respond. He bent his head and nuzzled her, then blew loudly as though approving. William took his daughter's arm and urged her away from the animal. 'We mustn't worry 'im too much, Carrie. I'm tryin' ter get 'im settled,' William told her.

Carrie stood watching while her father spread straw down in the stall and replenished the food trough. She smiled as the animal turned his head towards her and fixed her with huge baleful eyes. ''Ow could anybody ill-treat such a beautiful 'orse?' she murmured.

William put down the rake and leaned back against the stall-board. 'This animal 'as bin used fer trap-racin',' he replied. 'It's bin lashed wiv a whip. Look, yer can see the scars. It's also bin tied to a post an' beaten, if I'm not mistaken.'

''Ow d'yer know?' she asked him.

William slipped his thumbs into his belt. 'When I first took 'im out o' the trap and led 'im ter the trough 'e thought I was gonna tether 'im ter the post an' 'e bucked. That's prob'ly what used ter 'appen ter the animal.'

'But why?'

'Clevelands were bred fer carriages, Carrie,' he explained. 'They're proud trotters and they keep their 'eads 'igh. They're not meant ter gallop wiv their 'eads 'eld low. Trouble is, some people like ter race 'em in the traps. They bet on the outcome an' they ferget the whip is fer encouragin' the 'orse, not ter punish it. Sometimes they lose money an' then they take their anger out on the animal. They short tether it to a post or ring, an' larrup it wiv a wet rope. They see it as a way o' breakin' the animal's spirit, but no one can do that. 'Orses'll work till they drop an' they'll pull a load ferever, as long as yer water 'em an' feed 'em. They've got me 'ome in the fog at night an' next mornin' they've gone willin'ly inter the sharves. This animal 'as felt the rope an' it's wary o' the trap. I've managed ter 'arness it up an' get it in the sharves, but it needs more time before it's ready ter go out o' the yard.'

'Mr Galloway won't ill-treat it, will 'e, Dad?' Carrie asked, going forward and patting the animal's neck.

'No, I wouldn't fink so,' William replied. 'The ole man's got some funny ways but 'e feels the same way as I do about 'orses. In fact, young Geoffrey wants 'im ter get rid o' the 'orses an' bring in motor vans but the Guv'nor won't 'ear of it.'

Carrie leaned forward over the stall-board and pulled playfully at the gelding's ear. 'What would 'appen ter you if 'e did get rid o' the 'orses, Dad?' she asked.

William shrugged his shoulders. 'I'd be doin' Jack Oxford's job, I should fink.'

Carrie caught the veiled look of concern in his eye. 'Mr Galloway wouldn't sack yer, would 'e, Dad? Yer've worked fer 'im fer years.'

''Course 'e wouldn't,' her father said, taking down the lamp and putting his arm around her shoulders. ''E'll keep the 'orses as long as 'e can. 'E loves 'em as much as I do.'

A keen wind was gusting as they shut the stable doors and crossed the yard. The sound of horses stomping and blowing in their stalls carried down from the main stable and from somewhere on the river came the hoarse, mournful hoot of a tug whistle.

Sharkey Morris was feeling miserable as he sat slumped on his cart and let the horse set its own pace along Tower Bridge Road. His load of animal hides was reeking and the constant squeak of a dry axle made him grimace. People on the pavement turned their noses away as he drove slowly past them, and Sharkey cursed. Hauling skins about was not a patch on the rum contract, he thought ruefully. Rum casks were clean by comparison, and the smell of raw rum always made him feel pleasantly light-headed. These skins stank to high heaven and the stench got in his clothes and on his body and ended up making him feel sick. There were no perks to this job either, he groaned to himself. At the rum arches there was always a drink going – a drink and Phyllis Watts.

Sharkey pulled up to the kerb and jumped down. The axle felt red-hot so he reached under the dicky-seat for the tin of axle grease and set to work.

'What yer doin', mister?'

Sharkey looked up from the wheel and saw two young lads watching him. 'I'm greasin' the wheel, what's it look like I'm doin'?' he growled.

'Why're yer greasin' the wheel?' one young lad asked.

''Cos it's squeakin', I s'pose,' his companion said. 'Is it squeakin', mister?'

'Yeah, it's squeakin',' Sharkey replied grumpily.

'Why's it squeakin'?'

'I dunno why it's squeakin'. Why don't yer piss orf ter school?' the carman said, fixing the two lads with a hard stare.

'We've 'opped the wag. We're gonna go an' play down the wharf,' the first lad told him.

'Well, why don't yer go an' do that then?' Sharkey said quickly, wiping his hands on a piece of filthy-looking rag.

''Cos we're watchin' yer grease that axle.'

'Well, I'm done now so yer can piss orf.'

'That load o' yours don't 'alf stink, mister.'

'Well if yer don't like the smell, what yer 'angin' around 'ere for?'

'Got a tanner?'

'I'll give yer a clip roun' the ear if yer don't piss orf,' Sharkey told them, waving the grease stick in their direction.

The lads looked at each other and realised there was nothing to gain by staying. 'We're goin' down the wharf now,' the first lad said. 'Can yer give us a ride?'

Sharkey made a threatening gesture and the two boys ran off laughing.

The squeaking had stopped now and the sun had come out. The horse plodded on towards the tannery in Long Lane, its head held low. The miserable carman spat a stream of tobacco juice from the side of his mouth. Things couldn't be much worse, he groaned to himself. His wife Margie was constantly moaning about the smell when he walked into the house, Phyllis had said she wouldn't see him anymore until he changed his job, and her husband was threatening to do for him. Over twenty years he'd worked for Galloway and now he was reduced to carting stinking hides. Maybe it would have been better if Galloway had put him off, he thought. At least he wouldn't have ended up smelling like a polecat.

The axle started squeaking again and Sharkey cursed. He could see smoke coming from the wheel-hub now and the wheel itself was beginning to seize up. He could see the factory gates up ahead and gritted his teeth. He knew that he should pull up and douse the wheel with water but that would take time and he was already running late as it was. If he could make the factory yard he would be able to see to the wheel while they were unloading the cart, he reasoned. There were only a few yards more to go when the axle snapped and the cart tipped violently to one side. Sharkey grabbed the rail of the seat and held on tightly as the full weight of the wet hides tore the side out of the cart, spilling the whole load on to the pavement directly outside a public house.

Things had been quiet in the Galloway yard until the phone rang. Barely a few moments later the firm's owner came to the door of the office and bellowed out for his foreman. 'Sharkey's tipped a load o' skins outside the Anchor in Long Lane,' he shouted when William walked into the office. 'The lan'lord's goin' mad. 'E's got skins a foot 'igh outside 'is doors an' nobody can get in or out. I tell yer, Will, if that's down ter negligence, I'm sackin' Sharkey on the spot, an' I won't be swayed this time.'

'What 'appened ter make 'im lose the load?' William asked.

'Sharkey reckons the axle snapped an' the side's tore out o' the cart,' George growled. 'I've got the fellmonger's men movin' the load, an' the wheelwright in Long Lane is seein' ter the cart. I wanna talk ter Sharkey later. If that wheel over'eated, I'll murder 'im.'

At five o'clock a bleary-eyed carman drove his patched-up cart into the yard and walked unsteadily into the office. Galloway was waiting for him with a glowering expression on his face. ''Ow come yer let that wheel smoke?' the owner snarled.

Sharkey shrugged his shoulders. 'I'd almost reached the factory.'

'I've just about 'ad enough of yer, Morris. Yer finished, d'yer 'ear me? Yer can take yer cards,' Galloway shouted at him.

Sharkey smiled calmly. 'Funny yer should say that, Guv'nor. While the men were clearin' the load I went in the Anchor fer a drink ter steady me nerves. Who should be standin' at the counter but Sammy Spanner. Yer don't know Sammy Spanner, do yer?' Galloway's eyebrows knitted. ''E's the union man fer Tommy 'Atcher's. We 'ad a good chat, me an' Sammy. I told 'im about 'ow I got ter cart stinkin' skins around 'cos o' the trouble wiv the rum firm, an' about 'ow yer used ter go on about not 'avin' the union in 'ere at any price. An' yer know what Sammy said?'

'I ain't interested in what Sammy Spanner said,' growled George.

'Oh, ain't yer?' Sharkey grinned. 'Well, yer ought ter be. Anyway, yer ain't sackin' me, 'cos I've jus' put me notice in. I'm gonna work fer Tommy 'Atcher on Monday, so yer can poke yer skins.'

Chapter Eighteen

Carrie had settled into her new job at the dining rooms and soon became very popular with the carmen and river men who frequented the place. They were all pleased to see a pretty face behind the counter and enjoyed bandying friendly remarks and exchanging cheery smiles with her. Fred Bradley was very pleased with the young lady, too, and did not fail to notice that trade was beginning to improve. The customers were hanging around more lately, which usually meant an extra mug of tea and sometimes another round of toast.

She was happy in her new job and the days seemed to fly past. Every morning she served tea and took the food orders, and when trade quietened down in the lull before lunch-time she cleaned the tables, filled the salt and pepper pots and brewed fresh tea. She presented a pleasant picture with her long hair pinned securely to the top of her head and her flowered apron tied snugly at the waist. The younger carmen and river men often made advances and offered to take her on a night out at a music hall. Carrie was careful to put them off without causing offence. For her, life was simple and uncomplicated, and she was enjoying it that way. She had not even gone to any marches for the women's movement lately, although she still remained committed to the cause. Occasionally she was tempted to have a night out with one or other of the young men but always resisted the urge. Her experience with Billy Sullivan had aroused confused feelings within her and now she was determined to wait until the time was ripe and she was sure of a young man. She had seen Sara on a couple of occasions recently. She was now going with a young lad and talking of marrying him. Jessica from the leather factory was getting married soon too, and Mary Caldwell, who had left Wilson's to work for the WSPU in their South London Offices, had given her news of Freda. Despite her bad experience in the past she had become pregnant again but this time she was going to marry the young man. It did not worry Carrie that she was approaching twenty-one and was still single while lots of her friends and acquaintances were talking of marrying and having children. She felt she was in no hurry.

The cold winter days brought more trade and Carrie was kept very busy. One chilly morning Sharkey Morris pulled up outside in his brand new cart. As he put the nosebags on his pair of greys, Carrie saw him from the window. She had always liked the unkempt carman and had not forgotten that it was he who had first mentioned the job at Bradley's Dining Rooms. When he sauntered in, she had a mug of tea ready for him.

'Cor blimey! 'Ow yer doin', young Carrie?' he asked in his usual loud-voiced way.

She pushed back the two pennies he had slapped down on the counter. 'It's much better than the factory,' she smiled. 'What about you? What's Tommy 'Atcher like ter work for?'

Sharkey grinned widely. 'Much better than workin' fer that ole git Galloway,' he replied. 'I feel sorry fer yer farvver 'avin' ter put up wiv 'is bloody moanin'. When yer see 'im, tell 'im there's always the chance of a job on our firm. I've already spoke fer me ole mate Soapy.'

A line was forming and Carrie quickly had to get back on with serving tea and taking orders. When she finally sat down in the back room to eat her dinner at one-thirty, she realised that she had been on her feet attending to customers non-stop since eight o'clock that morning.

Two months later Fred Bradley called his young worker into the back room just as she was leaving at the end of the day and told her that he was making her money up to one guinea a week. Carrie felt gratified. She liked Fred and had settled into the job and was now a firm favourite with the customers. Sharkey Morris had passed the word to his fellow carmen about the coffee shop in Cotton Lane. He told them they served large toasted tea-cakes and bacon sandwiches made with new crusty bread and mugs of strong tea for tuppence. He also warned them that he was keeping an eye on the nice young girl who worked there.

Things at the Galloway yard were quiet during the cold winter months. Soapy Symonds kept himself out of trouble while he waited to get the word from Sharkey, and Sid Bristow, the other long-serving carman, got on with his work and wondered when his turn would come to be sacked. Four other carmen were employed by Galloway on a casual basis, and William Tanner was becoming more than a little depressed and unsure of his future at the yard as he got on with his job of keeping the horses fit and the carts in good repair. He had, however, been successful in gaining the confidence of the gelding. It was now established in the trap and Galloway was stabling the animal at the ostler's behind Tyburn Square.

Carrie missed going with her father to the yard at weekends to feed and tend the animal but Jack Oxford was secretly pleased. He had never taken to the 'bay devil', as he called it, and whenever George Galloway brought the horse into the yard, Jack kept out of its way. The yard man had another reason for feeling pleased that the horse was no longer stabled there. The doss-house he frequented now played host to a group of Irish labourers who were employed on building the new railway, and they often came in at night the worse for drink and sat playing cards until very late. The labourers were paid on Fridays and on these nights Jack often felt driven to forsake his lodging-house for the peace and quiet of the Galloway stables. Getting into the yard was no problem. He had previously loosened one of the long planks in the fence that backed on to the rear alley, and with some manoeuvring found he could squeeze in and out. Jack's favourite place to sleep was the small stable at the far end of the yard. Straw bales were stored there and they provided a comfortable bed. It was also much cleaner than the chaff loft.

One cold Friday evening Jack Oxford sat in the public bar of a pub in Abbey Street, moodily contemplating his pint of porter. His thoughts drifted back to the little place along the street where he had spent a few happy months before the man of the house's unexpected return. The few pints he had already consumed made him feel depressed and he yearned for company and a quiet chat. The public bar was beginning to fill with Irishmen from the railway workings, obviously in a jolly mood. As they became more inebriated their voices rose and they began to sing patriotic songs. A group of elderly gents started up with their own version of a cockney song and Jack decided it was time to leave.

The night mist was thickening as he ambled along Abbey Street and suddenly remembered the time he had dashed along the same route without his boots. The memory of that night led Jack to think about those old friends whose fire he had shared, and he decided it might be nice to pay them a visit. They were always good for a chat, he thought as he turned into Druid Street and made his way under the arches. He soon saw the glow of the brazier and the huddled figures, and as he approached he recognised the bearded figure of Bernie the ex-schoolteacher. Harold was there, too, and Moishie. The other figure was a stranger. It was he who waved for Jack to join them. 'Sit yerself down, friend,' he said in a deep voice. 'We're short of wood ternight but the fire'll last a while yet.'

Jack sat down on an upturned beer crate and held his hands out to the fire. 'I come fer a chat,' he said, looking around at the group.

Bernie stroked his beard. 'Well, you've come to the right place, my friend,' he said. 'Convivial company and cultured conversation can be guaranteed. It's money we're short on.'

Moishie poked at the fire with a stick. 'I wish I 'ad the price of a good bed ternight,' he grumbled. 'When this fire goes out, it's gonna be bloody cold 'ere.'

Bernie chuckled. ' "It was cold, bloody cold, in Elsinore." '

'What's 'e talkin' about?' Moishie asked.

'Search me,' Harold said, taking a swig from a quart bottle of ale.

'*Hamlet*. I saw it once at the Old Vic. Marvellous performance,' Bernie declared. 'Sir Seymour Hicks played Hamlet, or was it John Whitehead?'

'I'd sooner a night at the Star Music 'All meself,' Harold said, taking another swig from the bottle. "I've seen some luvverly shows up there. I remember one night they put on a show called "The Gels from Gottenburg". Smashin' songs. Brought tears ter yer eyes, some of 'em.'

Jack took the bottle from Harold and put it to his lips. The beer he had already drunk and the cold night air were making him feel a little light-headed. He burped loudly.

Harold was studying him closely. 'I thought yer'd be tucked up at the doss-'ouse on a cold night like this,' he remarked as he took the bottle back.

Jack shook his head. 'Fridays are bad nights at the kip-'ouse. I try ter stay away from there then. I've got meself a nice little nook ter kip down in,' he said, touching the side of his nose with his forefinger. 'It's quiet an' there's nobody ter disturb yer.'

'Do they take guests?' Bernie asked, pulling his tattered overcoat collar tighter around his neck.

Jack gazed at the flames. He had shared their fires before, and their refreshments, he conceded. Maybe he could repay the compliment. It would be a friendly thing to do. 'I might be able ter get yer in,' he replied. 'Yer'll 'ave ter be quiet, though. It's private property.'

When the last plank had burned through and the flames died to glowing embers, Harold drained the bottle of ale. 'Shall we go, gents?' he said, burping. 'Anywhere'll be better than this arch wivout a fire ter keep us warm. The wind fair cuts frew 'ere.'

'Lead on, Macduff,' Bernie said, rising from his egg crate and buttoning up his overcoat.

Moishie and Harold got up and Bernie motioned to the stranger.

'C'mon, Charlie. One for all and all for one.'

Jack led the way out from the arch with the motley group following on his heels. Harold was bent over, his overcoat dangling along the ground. At his side was the tall figure of Moishie with a filthy bowler perched on the top of his head and a ragged overcoat reaching down to worn-out boots. Behind them came Bernie who was stroking his large black beard and holding on to a bundle of rags. Next to him was Charlie who looked the scruffiest of the lot. His overcoat was tied with string and his stubbly face was blackened by smoke from the fire. On his head was a grease-stained trilby that was pulled down around his ears, and in his lapel he wore a dead flower.

The group marched along into Abbey Street and out into Jamaica Road, ignoring the stares of passers-by. As he strode along at their head, Jack was feeling good. He had friends and they were going to be treated to a good night's sleep. Maybe he could stand them supper, he thought. After all, they were his friends. Jack delved into his pocket and took out a handful of coppers. There was enough for three large pieces of cod and chips, he estimated.

Alf Rossi was shovelling more fried chips into the container above the fryer when he saw the party stop outside his shop. 'It's that idiot from Galloway's yard, Rosie,' he scowled. "E's got 'is family wiv 'im.'

'I'm not 'avin' that lot in my shop,' Rosie shouted to her husband. 'Tell 'em ter piss orf.'

Alf was spared the unpleasant task for Jack held up his hands signalling his friends to wait, and then swaggered into the shop alone. 'I want three pieces o' cod an' chips,' he announced. 'Nice big pieces if yer don't mind, Alf.'

'Cod's orf,' Alf told him. ''Addock or skate?'

''Addock. Big pieces,' Jack said, counting out his coppers.

'Who's that lot out there?' Alf asked as he wrapped the portions in newspaper. 'Looks like the 'ole family.'

'They're me pals,' Jack replied proudly, taking the packets and laying them in a line on the counter.

Alf and Rosie exchanged glances and Alf raised his eyes to the ceiling as the yard man opened the wrappings slowly and sprinkled the food with salt, pepper, and a liberal amount of spiced vinegar. 'Anyfing else yer want?' he said sarcastically as Jack re-wrapped the fish and chips.

'Got any 'a'penny wallies?'

Rosie put her hand into a large jar and took out two small pickled cucumbers. ''Ere, yer can 'ave these. Now yer better get goin', before that food gets cold,' she said impatiently.

The tattered wayfarers crossed the quiet Jamaica Road in a line and hurried along to Page Street. Jack was holding the bundles of food to his chest and his friends followed on closely, their nostrils twitching at the appetising aroma. It was dark along the turning, with only the gas lamp on the bend spreading a dull light on the pavement below. As the group shambled round the corner by the yard gates and emerged into the faint circle of light, Jack put his finger up to his mouth. 'That's the place,' he whispered. 'We get in round the back.'

Moishie's feet were hurting and he tutted as they trudged along to the end of the road and turned left into Bacon Street, while Bernie pulled on his beard as he relished the thought of the fish and chip supper they would soon be enjoying. Just past the buildings Jack ducked into the alley with the ragged gang shuffling in his wake, and after tripping and staggering over old bits of iron and bundles of rubbish they finally reached the fence at the back of Galloway's yard. ''Ere we are at last,' Jack grinned, handing Bernie the parcels while he grappled with the loose planking. Suddenly a dustbin lid clattered to the ground and they heard a loud caterwauling. A window in the buildings was thrown up and an object clattered down into the alley, then it became quiet once more.

Jack and his friends had soon settled themselves in the cosy stable. They sat in a circle with their backs propped against the straw bales. A paraffin lamp was hanging from the centre post and by its flickering light Jack halved two pieces of the fish and tore up the newspaper into sections. Soon they were all wolfing down their supper. Bernie took out a dirty penknife and wiped it on his sleeve before delicately cutting the cucumbers into small pieces. 'It's times like this when all's right with the world,' he sighed, spearing a piece of cucumber with his knife. 'All good friends together, or as the song goes, "All good pals and jolly fine company".'

Jack sighed contentedly. It was nice to have company, he reflected. They were good friends, and like him all lonely souls. They spent their days wandering the streets, scrounging bits and pieces, and their nights sleeping under the arches or on park benches when the weather was kind. As he stretched out against the straw, drowsy from the beer and hot food, it seemed to Jack that in the end the simple pleasures of life were all that really mattered.

A full moon shone down on the cobbled yard and in the long shadows the hunched figure made no sound as he tiptoed past the cart-shed and reached the office door. In the old days Charlie had earned his living by stealth. He had once bragged that he could walk over broken glass without making a sound, and had lost none of his guile. He had had to wait until his companions were fast asleep but he was not bothered. He had all the time in the world.

Charlie Hawkins had guessed right. The office door was not locked. There was no need for it to be, since the yard was secured by the main gate. Very carefully he let himself into the dark office and looked around. For a few moments he stood there silently until his eyes grew accustomed to the darkness. He could see two roll-top desks, one near the door and one in the far corner. The first produced nothing, but when he gently slid up the slatting of the far desk he saw the silver watch hanging by its chain from a nail. Charlie sat down at the desk and took out the crumpled newspaper bundle from his overcoat pocket.

While he finished off the few chips he had saved and picked

271

at the haddock bone, he studied the watch. That would bring in a few bob, he thought. He screwed up the newspaper and put it down on the desktop while he examined the silver chain. The links felt heavy and in the darkness Charlie's fingers closed around the small medallion. He grinned to himself as he slipped the watch and chain into his overcoat and turned his attention to the small desk drawers. He could find nothing of value, and as he was about to gather up the screwed-up newspaper he heard someone at the front gate. He quickly slid the shutter down over the desk and crept silently to the window. For a few moments it was quiet, then the gate rattled again and the sound of drunken singing carried into the yard. Charlie breathed easier as the staggering footsteps faded away, and when he was satisfied that all was quiet once more he slipped out of the office and hurried back to the small stable.

Carrie had been busy taking orders and serving for most of Monday morning, and when the dining rooms had become quieter she set about cleaning the marble-topped bench tables. There were only two carmen sitting at the end table and one other old man who sat near the door, slowly sipping his tea. Outside the morning mist still hung over the river and laden horse-carts trundled past.

Carrie hummed to herself as she dried off a table-top. Suddenly a young man slid into the bench seat and grinned at her. 'A large tea please luv,' he said cheerily.

Carrie looked at him and raised her eyes in surprise. 'I know yer, don't I?' she said.

The young man ran his hand through his dark wavy hair and his grin widened. 'Do yer?'

Carrie straightened up, feeling suddenly embarrassed before his wide-eyed gaze. 'Wasn't you the one who gave me an' my mate a lift in yer cart?' she asked.

The young man slapped the table with his open hand. 'You're the suffragette gel. The one who 'atpinned the copper,' he laughed. 'Well, I wouldn't 'ave guessed it. Yer look different in yer pinafore, an' yer 'air's done different too. Well, I don't know. Fancy meetin' yer 'ere.'

Carrie smiled as she went to fetch his tea, and while she was filling the large mug he watched her. 'Last time I was in 'ere ole Ida was servin'. What's 'appened ter 'er?' he asked.

Carrie brought over the tea and placed it in front of him. 'Ida's 'usband is ill. She 'ad ter pack the job up,' she said, picking up the coppers.

'So yer've packed up bein' in the suffragettes, 'ave yer?' he remarked, a smile playing on his handsome features.

'No, I 'aven't,' Carrie said firmly, 'I still go on marches when I can. Only at weekends, though.'

'Well, I'll be blowed. Fancy meetin' up wiv yer again,' he said, shaking his head slowly. 'What about yer mate? Is she still a suffragette?'

Carrie nodded. 'Mary's doin' it full-time now. She works in Blackfriars somewhere.'

The young man put down his mug. 'My name's Tommy Allen, in case I didn't tell yer last time,' he said. 'What's yours?'

'Carrie. Carrie Tanner,' she replied.

'That's right, I remember yer tellin' me now,' he grinned.

Carrie noticed that the two carmen sitting at the end table were listening and hurried back behind the counter to busy herself with the tea urn. Occasionally she stole a glance in the young man's direction. He was handsome, she decided. She remembered thinking the first time she met him that his dark wavy hair and brown eyes gave him the look of a gypsy, and smiled to herself as she recalled the story that had passed through her mind then. He seemed friendly, with his easy

273

smile and laughing eyes. He was wearing an open-necked shirt with a red scarf knotted around his thick neck, and she could see that he had strong hands. His wide shoulders were hunched over the table and he appeared to be deep in thought as he sipped his tea.

Customers were now beginning to come in for lunch and she was kept busy taking orders. Suddenly she saw Tommy Allen get up and go to the door. He turned and smiled. 'Keep out o' trouble, Carrie,' he said, laughing, then he was gone.

For the rest of the day she kept thinking of the handsome young man with the gypsy looks. She was interested to know where he came from, and she found herself wondering whether or not he was married. Carrie tried to put him out of her mind but she had been intrigued by his manner. He was different from the other young men she had met and spoken to, although she realised that her experience of men was very limited and she had not really encountered many handsome young lads apart from Billy Sullivan. She felt strangely elated as Tommy constantly returned to her thoughts. He would come into the café again if he was interested in her, she told herself. But was he? He was most probably married or walking out with a girl. She vowed that she would get him talking next time he came in, and find out more about him.

On Monday morning George Galloway drove his trap into the yard. Normally, when he spent the whole of Monday morning going over the books with his accountant and making phone calls, he would get William to unhitch the gelding and put it into the stall or else tether it until he was ready to leave, but on this particular morning as he hurried into the office George told his yard foreman to leave the horse in the shafts. Jack Oxford busied himself with the broom and gave the Cleveland a wide berth. The old man won't be stopping long, he thought.

Suddenly there was a loud roar and Galloway burst out of the office door, his face scarlet. 'Tanner! Come 'ere!' he bawled at the top of his voice.

William was in the upper stable. He hurried down, surprise showing on his face at the sudden outburst. 'What's up?' he asked quietly.

'What's up? I'll show yer what's up. Come in 'ere,' Galloway shouted.

William followed his boss into the office, trying to puzzle out what could have made him so angry.

'Somebody's nicked me watch-an'-chain. An' that's not all. Take a look at this,' he growled.

William walked over to the open desk and saw the haddock bone lying on the greasy strip of newspaper. His first instinct was to burst out laughing but he managed to control himself. 'Who could 'ave nicked yer watch, George?' he asked incredulously, scratching his head.

'The same bastard who 'ad those fish an' chips,' Galloway said pointedly.

'I guessed that much, but who could 'ave took it?' William wondered, frowning.

George stood with hands on hips, shaking his head. 'I took it off when I 'ad a sluice on Friday afternoon, an' I fergot ter put it back on when I left 'ere at five. It couldn't 'ave bin any o' the carmen, they was all finished before I left. There was only you an' that idiot Oxford left.'

'Well, I didn't take it,' William said quickly.

'I'm not sayin' yer did, but I wouldn't mind bettin' Oxford took it. Who else would be stupid enough ter leave fish-an'-chip scrapin's in the desk?'

'Come on, George,' William said, turning on his employer. 'Jack Oxford wouldn't 'ave took yer watch. I know 'e comes in 'ere at times but the man ain't a thief.'

'Well, if it wasn't 'im, who could 'ave took it?' George growled. 'Could somebody 'ave come in the yard after I'd gone? It's not the watch so much, it's losin' the fob piece. Yer know 'ow long I've 'ad that.'

William nodded. The fob had gone the way it came, he thought to himself. 'The only fing I can fink of is that somebody got in 'ere over the weekend,' he offered. 'It might 'ave bin an ole tramp. 'E might 'ave got in frew the back fencin'. I'll go an' 'ave a look see.'

Jack Oxford moved smartly away from where he had been standing near the office door and bent over his broom industriously as the foreman came out into the yard.

Within a few minutes William had returned to the office. 'There was a loose plank by the end stable,' he told Galloway. 'That's 'ow they got in. I'll get it nailed up straight away.'

George puffed angrily and slumped down in his chair, grimacing with exasperation at his sudden loss. The explanation seemed to satisfy him, but William made a mental note to have a word with Jack Oxford as soon as Galloway was out of the way. He had noticed that the plank had been loosened from the inside.

Chapter Nineteen

George Galloway was in a bad mood as he stood in front of the mirror in his bedroom and tried to fix his cravat. He had had to replace his watch-and-chain, and now his new grey suit felt tight around the chest. Nora looked in through the open door and when she saw George puffing, came in.

'Let me fix it,' she said, reaching up on tiptoe.

George sighed. 'We're gonna be late,' he grumbled. 'It'll take at least an hour ter get ter Brixton.'

Nora stepped back from her handiwork. 'There, that looks better,' she said, glancing in the mirror and adjusting her wide bonnet. It seemed right that she was going along with George to see Frank get married, as she had watched him and his brother and sister grow up and had taken care of the three of them. It was the first time she had gone to a wedding since she and her husband walked down the aisle together. 'I should 'ave bought the grey bonnet,' she said. 'This looks more suitable for a funeral.'

George pulled a face. 'Yer look very nice,' he remarked.

'Yer look very smart yerself,' Nora said, appraising him with a smile. 'Grey suits yer. Now c'mon, it's time we left.'

Nora sat straight-backed in the trap as they left the square. It was the first time she had ridden in it and she felt a little apprehensive as the gelding broke into a trot in response to George's flick of the reins. The high wheels rattled over the cobbles and she gave George a quick glance as they turned into Jamaica Road. He looked very distinguished, she thought. His grey Homburg matched his suit and his greying hair was swept back at the sides and plastered down with brilliantine. He had trimmed his full moustache and was wearing cashmere gloves turned back at the wrists. Nora noticed the glances from people they passed and she smiled to herself. Her life was now happy once more, she reflected. She had the independence that she needed and the love of a good man as well. He was considerate, if a little moody at times, but she was not a young woman with her head full of childish romantic notions. George came into her bed on regular occasions and she was happy with their relationship. The one thing that made her feel sad, though, was the way he often ignored young Josephine and seemed to have very little room for her in his life. Josie was growing into a pretty young thing and she needed her father to show an interest in her. He seemed uncomfortable in her company and rather curt at times, but maybe that was understandable and even excusable in a way, Nora allowed. He was a gruff, coarse man who had never really tried to refine himself and it seemed that he harboured no desire to change now.

The journey took over an hour and the wedding guests had already assembled in the church when George and Nora arrived. Heads turned as they walked along the aisle. George's shoes were squeaking loudly. 'I should 'ave stuck some axle-grease on 'em,' he said in a voice loud enough for those nearest him to hear.

Nora winced as the couple in front turned around and

looked blankly at them. 'Keep yer voice down,' she whispered, smiling at him through clenched teeth.

A hush had descended. Suddenly the church organ boomed out the Wedding March. Heads turned as Frank's bride Bella came down the aisle on the arm of her father with four bridesmaids holding her train. Josephine was one of the first pair and Nora nudged George as the procession passed them. 'Doesn't she look lovely?' she whispered.

He was looking at Bella and nodded.

'I was talkin' about Josie,' Nora muttered sharply.

Bella looked relaxed and self-possessed as she walked slowly towards the altar. She was wearing a full-length white dress cut very tight at the bodice to accentuate her large bosom. She wore a full veil crowned with a flowered tiara and her face was heavily made-up. Nora could not help feeling that she looked anything but a demure bride. She was glancing from side to side and smiling in that artificial way, fluttering her eyelids and running her tongue over her full, glossy lips as if she was putting on a show and loving every minute of it. Nora felt a little guilty for her thoughts. Maybe she was being unkind to Bella on her wedding day and maybe the marriage would be a blessed one, but Nora could not help having her doubts.

The wedding reception was held at the Ram, a large public house nearby. The guests sat down to a lavish meal in a large first-floor room and George mumbled under his breath every time the feasting was interrupted by someone getting up to make a speech. Nora nudged him after one effeminate young man rose to his feet and showered praises on Bella and her successful run at the Collins Music Hall. 'P'raps yer should get up an' say a few words?' she suggested.

George shook his head vigorously. 'I'd 'ave ter be pissed before I got up an' said anyfing,' he told her, tucking into his food.

Nora had been studying the various guests closely during the meal and had noticed the young woman sitting near Geoffrey who seemed to have eyes only for him. When the young man got up to read out the telegrams and give the customary toast to the bridesmaids, she sat with her chin resting in her hands, seemingly enraptured. He glanced constantly in her direction and Nora's sharp eyes read the silent messages that flashed between them. The woman looked older than Geoffrey and was dressed modestly. She was attractive with dark hair, and Nora became intrigued. Was that Geoffrey's lady friend, she wondered, the married woman he was seeing?

The wedding feast was over, and as the guests moved into an adjoining room for drinks a team of workers swiftly cleared away the tables. Musicians were gathering on a raised dais at one end of the large room and very soon they struck up with a waltz tune. Frank and Bella took the floor and led off the dancing. George stood watching the swirling figures with a large whisky in his hand and Nora stood at his side, her eyes still studying the group. They were mainly theatrical folk who laughed loudly and made exaggerated gestures. The women seemed to float sooner than walk, she thought, and the men stood in various stagey poses, their thumbs tucked in their waistcoat pockets as they guffawed together with little or no restraint. One or two of them were already becoming drunk and their laughter was getting louder. George looked as if he felt quite out of place and seemed determined to get drunk too, swallowing large draughts of Scotch whisky as if to drown his inhibitions.

More couples were dancing now as the pianist and the string quartet played a medley of popular dance tunes. Nora noticed that Geoffrey was dancing with his lady friend. Their bodies were close together and they were staring into each other's eyes. Bella looked as though she was having a serious conversation with one smart young man, while Frank was surrounded with a group of dandies at the far end of the room. While George wandered off somewhere Nora sat down on a soft window seat and sipped her port. She became aware of a young woman eyeing her up and down. Nora smiled briefly at her, but the woman looked away quickly. It was not long before George returned, strolling over to the window with an elderly man and woman. He was holding a full glass of Scotch and his face was flushed.

'Nora, this is Bella's muvver an' farvver,' he said in a slightly exaggerated voice.

Nora got up and shook hands with them and the woman took her arm and steered her to one side. The man took a sip from his drink and turned to George. 'Young Frank tells me you're in the cartage business,' he said with a pompous jerk of his head.

George took a swig from his glass and pulled a face as he swallowed a mouthful of whisky. 'That's right. What d'you do fer a livin'?' he asked, swaying slightly.

'I'm in banking,' Bella's father said. 'What exactly do you cart around?' he added quickly.

'Rum, skins, 'ops an' foodstuffs mainly,' he replied.

'Skins? Animal skins?'

''S'right. It's not the best sort o' contract,' George told him. 'The trouble wiv 'andlin' skins is the smell. Stink ter 'igh 'eaven they do, but the contract pays well.'

'Frank tells me that you've been thinking about buying some vehicles,' the banker said, raising an eyebrow.

'The boy's bin tryin' ter push me inter gettin' motors but I'm keepin' the nags,' George told him with resolve.

'Really? I would have thought there were good arguments for cartage firms to mechanise,' Bella's father commented. 'I understand there's a lot of freight up for the taking, the way the food firms are expanding. Then there's the dock freight as well.'

George swayed back on his heels and fixed the tall, thin banker with his bleary eyes. 'I've bin lookin' inter this business o' mechanisation,' he began. 'Yer pay out a tidy sum fer a lorry, then yer gotta pump it full o' petrol, an' that's not all. Yer put water in it, an' oil fer the engine. Then ter start it yer gotta crank the bloody fing, an' if yer ain't got yer magneto set prop'ly yer quite likely ter rupture yer bloody self. I've seen drivers tryin' ter start those motors on frosty mornin's. It's bloody nigh impossible.'

The banker raised his hand as he tried to get a word in. 'The latest vehicles are much improved, George,' he said quickly.

Galloway laughed derisively. 'Let me tell yer somefink. My carmen collect their 'orses from the stable first fing in the mornin', an' once they've got 'em in the sharves they're off. While the carman loads an' unloads the van the 'orse 'as the nose bag on, an' when the carman sees a water-trough on 'is route 'e lets the 'orse drink its fill. It's as simple as that. Yer can turn an 'orse-an'-cart round in any backstreet. Try doin' that wiv a lorry. I'll ter yer somefing else an' all. When it turns nasty an' the fog comes down like a blanket yer gotta leave the lorry where it stands. Yer don't 'ave ter wiv 'orses. Yer get yer wheels in the tramlines an' let the 'orse 'ave its 'ead. They can smell their own stable a mile off. Motors are unreliable. 'Orses'll work till they drop. So yer see, pal, I'm not in any 'urry ter mechanise.'

Bella's father had the sudden urge to mingle and George glanced over to Nora, but saw that she was in earnest conversation with Bella's mother. He walked unsteadily into the adjoining room and went up to the improvised bar counter. While his glass was being refilled, he looked around at the other wedding guests. A shapely woman in a fur stole was sitting near the window. When she caught his eye, she got up and came over to him.

'You're Mr Galloway, aren't you?' she said, smiling at him. 'I'm a friend of a friend of Bella's, and frankly I don't know what I'm doing here.'

'Well, I'm enjoyin' a good drink. I s'pose that's a good enough reason as any fer bein' 'ere,' he said, grinning lopsidedly.

The woman put down her empty glass and looked him over. 'I saw you talking to Bella's father a minute ago,' she remarked. 'I think he's a pompous old bastard, if you'll excuse the expression.'

George laughed loudly. 'Yer can say that again! The silly ole sod was on about me gettin' rid o' me 'orse-an'-carts an' goin' in fer motors. I told 'im, though.'

'Good for you,' the woman declared. 'By the way, my name's Rose. Rose Martin. What's your first name?'

'George,' he replied. 'Are yer on yer own, Rose?'

She shook her head. 'I was with a young man when I came in, but I think he's found himself a young lady.'

'Well, 'e ought ter be ashamed of 'imself,' George said with gusto.

'Oh, it's quite all right,' she laughed. 'To be honest Desmond's a bit of a silly billy. Actually, I prefer the company of older men.'

George was intrigued by her candour and studied her while she sipped a fresh drink. She looked to be in her mid-forties, he thought, very attractive and well preserved. Her smile showed off her perfect teeth and her grey eyes seemed to sparkle mockingly. Her hair was fair and cut close to her neck, and she was wearing expensive clothes. Her fur must be worth a pretty penny, he told himself, letting his eyes wander down her body. She was full-bosomed with wide hips, and he noted that she carried herself well.

'Are yer on the stage?' he asked her.

Rose raised her hands in front of her. 'Good God, no! I'm a lady of leisure. I let wealthy men keep me in luxury,' she explained, seemingly amused as he raised his eyebrows.

'Do any of your men friends take yer out fer a ride in a pony an' trap?' Galloway asked her, smiling slyly.

'No, I've never had that pleasure,' she lied.

'Would yer like ter try it?' he asked her.

'It sounds exciting. Are you offering?'

He nodded. 'Why not?'

Rose adjusted her fur stole as she glanced over his shoulder. 'It seems that dear Desmond is looking for me,' she said with a grimace. 'Come and visit me soon, during the afternoon. I've got rooms in Acre Lane. It's the big house next to the church. Two knocks. Can you remember that?'

George nodded and turned away as Desmond came up. He had left Nora to her own devices and thought it was time he rejoined her. The band was playing a slow foxtrot as George went back into the other room and he saw Geoffrey dancing with the same woman who had been monopolising him earlier. They seemed to be absorbed in each other, he thought, and looked as though they knew each other well. George had never seen her before today and frowned as he watched their progress around the dance floor. Geoffrey was a deep young man, and it seemed to George that he had strange tastes in women. He was a good-looking lad and well educated. He could take his pick of desirable young women, and there were certainly some of those in Bermondsey, but the few he had brought home in the past were either quiet and withdrawn or else 'those campaigning women', as George called them. Geoffrey's present partner did not look the quiet and reserved sort, though, he thought. She was attractive and carried herself well, and looked at least as old as the boy if not a few years older.

George's thoughts were interrupted by Nora who came up to him looking a little peevish. 'Who was that brassy woman you was talkin' to at the bar?' she asked. 'She looked as though she was all over yer.'

George grinned. 'She's wiv a young lad-about-town, an' jus' asked me if I was Frank's farvver.'

Nora gave him a cold stare. 'She looked no better than she should be, if you ask me. If she'd stood any closer ter yer she'd 'ave bin in yer pocket,' she complained.

George shrugged his shoulders. 'Who's that woman our Geoff's dancin' wiv, Nora?' he asked, nodding in the direction of the dance floor. 'They seem very good friends.'

She shook her head. 'Jus' somebody 'e's met, I s'pose,' she answered. She had been observing the couple for some time, however, and had come to the conclusion that they were more than just friends. Nora felt suddenly sorry for Geoffrey. He had become very secretive lately and there would be trouble ahead for him if, as she guessed, he and this woman were lovers.

The evening wore on and George seemed to be achieving his aim of getting drunk. He had started to reel about and become more noisy. Nora found him a seat and then she went to speak to Geoffrey. 'Yer farvver's not gonna be able ter drive that trap back,' she told him. ''E's 'ad too much whisky. I couldn't stop 'im. Yer know what 'e's like.'

Geoffrey squeezed her arm reassuringly. 'Don't worry, Nora. I'll drive it back. By the way, I'd like you to meet Mary O'Reilly. Mary and I are friends.'

The young woman reached out her hand. 'So you're Nora. Geoff's told me all about yer,' she said, smiling.

Nora smiled back and looked discerningly at her. Her hair was raven, enhancing the deep blue of her eyes. Her manner was easy and friendly, although there seemed to be a defensiveness about her. It was understandable, Nora conceded. If she was married and she and Geoffrey were having an affair, it would be natural for her to be on her guard. Geoffrey did not seem at all bothered however and slipped his arm around Mary's waist as they stood talking to Nora.

'Are yer enjoyin' yerself, Nora?' Mary asked.

'Ter tell yer the trufe, I feel a bit uneasy in this company,' Nora replied. 'I'm not used ter bein' around so many people.'

Geoffrey laughed. 'Don't tell me that, Nora. I saw you drinking port and chatting away merrily. I'll tell you what, could you keep Mary company for me while I go and see if Father's all right?'

Mary took hold of Geoffrey's arm. 'Before yer go, can yer get us anuvver drink? Nora needs one too by the look of it,' she said, smiling sweetly at him.

When the drinks arrived the two women sat on the soft, velvet-covered window seat and Nora sipped her port, studying the dancers. 'Are you an' Geoff walkin' out tergevver?' she asked suddenly.

Mary smiled and looked down at the drink she held in her hand. ''As Geoff spoken ter yer about me?' she asked.

Nora shook her head. 'No. As a matter o' fact 'e's bin very secretive lately. One time 'e used ter confide in me, but I s'pose it's ter be understood. 'E's a man now an' 'e needs 'is privacy.'

'Geoff's very fond of yer,' Mary said, taking a sip from her glass. ''E's told me 'ow yer looked after them all when 'is muvver died. Don't be too upset about 'im not sayin' much lately. Things are a bit difficult fer both of us. I'm married, an' that makes seein' Geoff a bit awkward.'

Nora looked at Mary with feigned surprise. 'Oh dear,' she said.

Mary studied her drink. 'My 'usband's not one o' those men who knocks 'is wife about or who comes 'ome drunk,' she began. 'In fact, 'e's a very nice man. It's just that we've grown apart the last couple o' years. Maybe if we'd 'ave 'ad kids it would 'ave bin different, but it wasn't ter be. I'm in love wiv Geoff an' I fink 'e loves me. I couldn't 'elp fallin' fer 'im. It jus' 'appened.'

'Does yer 'usband know about Geoff?' Nora asked quickly.

Mary shook her head. ''E doesn't know about us an' I can't bring meself ter tell 'im. Not that I 'aven't tried. I've tried dozens o' times but I jus' can't. Maybe I'm wrong, but it's jus' that I can't 'urt 'im. As I said, 'e's a good man an' a good provider. Christ! It's so difficult.'

Nora lifted her eyes from her drink. 'It must be difficult fer Geoff as well,' she said with feeling. ''Is farvver expects a lot from 'im an' I don't know 'ow 'e'll take it when 'e finds out. 'E's gotta find out some time.'

Mary winced. 'I realise that. I only 'ope 'is farvver doesn't disown 'im when 'e does find out. Geoff works 'ard at the business, from what I can make out. It wouldn't be fair.'

'What is fair?' Nora asked. 'Geoff lost 'is muvver when 'e was at a young age. 'E grew up in a sad 'ouse. Most o' the time 'is farvver was eivver at the yard or sittin' in 'is room wiv a bottle fer company. The boy couldn't 'ave bin blamed if 'e'd 'ave kicked over the traces an' gone off ter sea or somefink. 'E never did though. Mind yer, 'e never ever wanted ter go in the business. 'E only agreed fer 'is farvver's sake. Geoff's a good boy. 'E's got more feelin' than Frank an' I wouldn't like ter see the boy unhappy.'

Mary was about to say something but Geoff was coming

over to them. 'I'm afraid Father's beginning to make a nuisance of himself,' he said raising his eyes to the ceiling. 'He's been telling the women all about horse fever. If that wasn't bad enough, he then started on about animal skins and the danger of anthrax. Frank's new mother-in-law looked like she was going to faint. Anyway, I managed to steer the old man away from them. I left him sitting in a corner with a large whisky. I think I'd better get the trap before he really gets into his stride.'

The night was cold and a bright moon shone down from a starry sky as the party returned to Bermondsey. Iron wheels rattled over the gaslit cobbled streets and Geoffrey held the reins taut as the gelding trotted at a fast pace with its head held high. It had been stabled at an ostler's during the wedding reception and was feeling fresh and frisky. George was slumped in the side seat with his head lying on Nora's shoulder and Mary sat beside Geoffrey, holding tightly on to his arm. Josephine was not with them. She had been invited to stay overnight at Bella's parents', along with the other bridesmaids.

Nora was deep in thought as the trap rattled over the tramlines at the Elephant and Castle and turned into the New Kent Road. Geoff's married woman friend had been forthcoming with her about their relationship and Nora could not help but feel apprehensive for the young people's future. It was not difficult for her to understand why Geoffrey had been so secretive lately. Unlike his brother Frank, he was expected to conform to certain standards. His father had as good as forced him to go into the business and it had caused the young man more than a little unhappiness. He seemed to have come to terms with the idea of one day taking over the firm but now there was another problem looming. Knowing George the way she did, Nora was sure that he would expect his elder son to provide a male heir to carry on the family name. He would no doubt take a very destructive attitude towards Geoffrey's relationship, she fretted, as the trap turned into Jamaica Road.

Chapter Twenty

Fred Bradley was very pleased with the way his custom was growing. In the six months since Carrie had come to work for him he had almost doubled his trade, and knew that a lot of his success was due to her. She had a pleasant personality, a ready smile, and all the regular customers called her by name. Carrie had had some ideas of her own regarding the business, and Fred was now supplying a more varied fare. He had been forced to take on help in the kitchen, and a helper for Carrie too during the rush periods of the day. The café owner had experienced a sudden change of fortune and had begun to see his assistant in a new light. He had been used to working long hours in the kitchen with only an elderly assistant for company, but now there was a pretty young woman working with him, long dormant feelings began to stir. He found himself looking at Carrie and studying her face as she went about her chores. Fred would hardly admit to himself that he was attracted to his young assistant but he knew deep down that she was responsible for his change of outlook. Now he shaved every morning without fail and put on a clean pressed shirt and fresh apron. Customers began to notice the change in him and one or two of the more perceptive among them started to talk.

'I reckon our Fred's set 'is cap on Carrie,' one remarked.

'See the way 'e keeps on lookin' at 'er?' another said. 'I've never seen the bloke lookin' so smart.'

Sharkey Morris had noticed the change in Fred, and feeling in a way responsible for Carrie's well-being he made a point of speaking to the young girl when he got the chance. 'Are yer all right, luv?' he asked her one day with a pointed look of concern. 'What I mean ter say is, nobody's tryin' ter take liberties, are they?'

Fred had been careful not to let Carrie see him watching her and she was oblivious to her employer's growing interest in her. She was a little puzzled at Sharkey's sudden curiosity. 'They're all friendly, an' they don't mind if they 'ave ter wait fer their grub,' she replied.

He grinned at her innocence. 'No, what I mean is, luv, nobody's givin' yer any ole lip or comin' the ole soldier,' he said by way of explanation.

Carrie was still unsure exactly what Sharkey was hinting at and shook her head. 'Everyfing's fine.'

'If yer do get pestered, jus' let yer ole mate Sharkey know an' I'll put 'em ter rights,' he said firmly.

Sharkey Morris would have been more concerned had he known that Carrie had been making some discreet enquiries about a certain young man with a Romany appearance. He had only come into the dining rooms on a few occasions since the first time but always at a busy period, and Carrie had not been able to talk at length to him. Nevertheless, she had learned that he worked for a grain merchant and his job meant he had to shovel hot grain mash from the brewery into his cart and transport it to farms in the outskirts of London. She had been able to tell from Tommy Allen's powerful build and muscular arms that the work was very hard, and the elderly carman who knew him explained to her that it was a job only for fit young men. Carrie found herself hoping Tommy would come into the dining rooms again.

It was one Friday morning that Tommy made one of his rare appearances, and on this particular day he picked a quiet period. Carrie tried to suppress a feeling of excitement as she brought over his tea and took his order for a cheese sandwich.

'I'aven't seen yer fer some time. I thought yer'd changed yer café,' she said, surprised at her boldness.

He smiled. 'I wasn't in the area. I've bin wonderin' 'ow yer bin. 'Ave yer missed me?'

Carrie's cheeks glowed. 'I bin too busy ter notice,' she said quickly.

Tommy sipped his tea while she went for his order. When she returned and put the plate down in front of him, he looked into her eyes. 'I've missed comin' in 'ere, ter tell yer the trufe,' he remarked, biting on the sandwich.

Carrie turned away in embarrassment and he grinned as she got on with stacking the clean mugs. Customers were starting to come in and suddenly Tommy was at the counter.

'I've gotta get goin',' he said. 'Would yer fancy comin' ter see a show at the South London Music 'All on Saturday evenin'?'

Carrie felt her heart leap but stifled her excitement. 'I dunno,' she replied, wishing she had said yes.

Tommy was not to be put off. 'Look, it's a good show. I'll come knockin' if yer like. Tell me where yer live an' I'll call round about six o'clock.'

'Go on, Carrie, tell 'im where yer live,' one of the carmen joked.

'Can't yer see the young man's waitin'?' his friend said, laughing.

Carrie felt her cheeks growing hot. 'Twenty-four Page Street. Next door ter the stable,' she rattled off.

Tommy grinned widely. 'See yer at six,' he said as he walked out of the dining rooms.

The conversation had been overheard by Fred and he felt suddenly angry with himself. He had wanted to ask Carrie out for some time but had not been able to muster enough courage to approach her. Now it looked as though he had left it too late. He had begun to think that Carrie was showing a little interest in him. She had seemed to get over her initial shyness and chat to him a little more whenever there was a quiet spell. She had told him she was very happy in the job and once or twice she had actually commented favourably about his appearance. Maybe he was too old for her anyway, he told himself. She was only twenty-one and he was in his mid-thirties. Why should she be interested in him? She hadn't noticed how much he had smartened himself up, or if she had noticed she hadn't mentioned it to him. Fred carried on with the cooking, feeling depressed.

It had been a few weeks now since the theft of the watch and Jack Oxford was biding his time. He had denied ever bringing anyone back into the yard and when William had confronted him about the planking being loosened from the inside Jack merely shrugged his shoulders and hoped the yard foreman would let the matter rest, but it was not to be.

'As long as I don't know I couldn't care a sod if yer decide ter kip in the yard,' William told him, 'but when fings go missin' I do care. I'm responsible fer the place an' I'm not gonna stan' by an' let yer drop me in the shite. If yer know who nicked that watch, I suggest yer get it back off 'im.'

Jack had thought hard about which one of his friends could have taken the watch. He had known them for some time and had never had reason to suspect that any of them might take advantage of a good turn. Charlie was the only one he did not know prior to that night. He would be the most likely one to have filched the watch, Jack reasoned.

Working on that assumption he had visited the arches on a few occasions, pretending that he was just turning up for a chat, but Charlie was never there. Harold, Moishie and the eccentric Bernie did not seem to be hiding anything, and when Jack asked after Charlie on his last visit he was rewarded with a shrug of the shoulders.

'We ain't seen 'air nor 'ide of 'im since that night we all went ter the stables,' Harold told him. 'Funny bloke 'e was. 'E Jus' showed up 'ere one cold night an' asked if 'e could 'ave a warm by the fire. 'E told us 'e'd bin chucked out by 'is missus a few years ago an' 'e was livin' rough. 'E ain't a Londoner by all accounts. I fink 'e told me 'e come from Manchester, or was it Newcastle? Somewhere like that anyway.'

'Cornwall,' Bernie piped in. 'Charlie come from Bodmin in Cornwall.'

'Oh, well, I knew it was somewhere like that,' Harold said.

Moishie poked at the flaring brazier. 'I never trusted the bloke meself,' he said. 'I woke up one night an' saw 'im rummagin' frew 'Arold's bundle. 'E said 'e was lookin' fer a match ter get the fire goin' agin.'

Jack came away from the arches that night convinced that Charlie was his man and determined that he would find him eventually.

On Friday evening Florrie Axford took her old friends to the Kings Arms for a drink. As they sat chatting amiably in the snug bar, Florrie was in a happy frame of mind. She had 'come into a few bob' as she put it, and her friends were more than a little surprised at her attitude.

'Yer could 'ave knocked me down wiv a feavver,' she was saying. 'I was up ter me eyes in washin' an' this bloke knocks at me door wiv the news. Five guineas 'e give me. Apparently it was a policy in my name an' 'e told me I'd bin payin' it in wiv the insurance. It was only fourpence a week but it'd bin paid in fer years. I couldn't work it out fer a moment, then I suddenly tumbled it. It was from that second 'usband o' mine. The ole goat took 'is policies when 'e walked out on me an' I didn't fink any more of it. From what I can gavver 'e was livin' wiv 'is married sister when 'e pegged it. Choked on a chicken bone by all accounts.'

Maisie shook her head. 'What a way ter go.'

Florrie shrugged her shoulders. 'Least 'e was eatin'. Could 'ave bin worse. 'E could 'ave starved ter death.'

'Don't be wicked, Flo,' Nellie said, stifling a chuckle.

Florrie sipped her milk stout. 'Why should I be upset over 'is passin'? 'E left me in the lurch years ago an' I ain't laid eyes on 'im since. I ain't losin' no sleep over 'im.'

'Still 'e was yer 'usband, fer better or fer worse,' Aggie piped in.

'It was all worse where 'e was concerned,' Florrie retorted. 'I've got more money orf the bleeder since 'e's bin gorn than I ever did when 'e was alive.'

Grace Crossley was leaning on the counter and her wide ruddy face split into a grin. 'Yer wanna be careful talking like that o' the dead, Florrie. Yer ole man might come back an' 'aunt yer,' she said.

'I don't fink so,' Florrie replied, downing the last of her drink. ''E never spent much time in our 'ouse when 'e was livin'. I don't s'pose 'e'd be too anxious ter pay me a visit now 'e's dead.'

Aggie was getting a little frightened by the way the conversation was going. She got up and leaned on the bar counter. 'Give us all the same again, Grace,' she said, fishing in her leather purse. 'Talkin' o' ghosts 'as made me come over all shivery.'

The buxom landlady laughed aloud as she poured the drinks. 'Yer don't believe in them sort o' fings, do yer, Aggie?' she asked in a mocking tone of voice.

The slim woman pulled the fur trim of her coat down over her wrists and leaned forward over the counter. 'My 'Arold reckons 'e see a ghost one night when 'e was lightin' the lamps. It floated across the street large as life,' she whispered. 'My ole man said it frightened the life out of 'im. Come out of one o' the 'ouses in Cotton Lane it did.'

Grace frowned in disbelief. 'It must 'ave bin a bit o' fog swirlin' around,' she replied as she put the drinks down on the counter.

Aggie shook her head vigorously. 'No, it was a clear night, so my 'Arold said. This fing floated over the cobbles and then it jus' evaporated. That wasn't the end of it neivver. A couple o' weeks later 'Arold was lightin' the lamps in the street an' this ole man come up to 'im an' asked 'im if 'e 'ad change of a tanner. 'E said 'e wanted some coppers fer the gas meter an' when 'Arold give 'im the change, the ole man went in the 'ouse where the ghost come out of. Anyway, a couple o' nights later the gas board dug the turnin' up outside the same 'ouse an' my ole man got talkin' ter the night-watchman. 'E told 'im that they was mendin' a gas leak an' they was puttin' new pipes inter the 'ouse at the same time. When my 'Arold told 'im about the bloke askin' 'im fer change fer the gas the watchman laughed at 'im. 'E good as called 'im a liar. Apparently the place 'ad been empty fer years an' the gas 'ad been cut off fer ages.'

Grace pulled a face and hurried away to serve in the public bar, leaving Florrie grinning over the counter.

'I've 'eard 'Arold tell that story a dozen times,' she whispered to Maisie and Nellie. 'Each time it's a different street.'

As the women friends settled down to enjoy fresh drinks in the tiny snug bar, the conversation turned to more mundane topics.

''Ow's your Carrie gettin' on at that dinin' rooms, Nell?' Maisie asked.

'She's doin' fine,' Nellie replied. 'She likes it better than the factory. Mind yer, she's kept on the go most o' the day. Still, the gel's 'appy there, which is more than I can say fer the boys. James is fed up at the sawmills an' 'e's tryin' ter get anuvver job. Young Danny's workin' in the shop now. I'm glad 'e don't 'ave ter run around on the errand bike but 'e don't like it. 'E said 'e'd like ter go on the barges. Trouble is it's 'ard ter get a job on the river. It's all farvvers an' sons. The only one who's 'appy is young Charlie. 'E's doin' well in that office. They've give 'im a rise an' 'e's in charge o' the mail by all accounts.'

Maisie nodded. 'It's nice ter see yer kids get on. My two's doin' well,' she said. 'Ronnie's in a shippin' office an' Albert's workin' in Tooley Street fer a provision merchant's. I'm glad they never went in the factories. That's no life fer kids slavin' away in those places.'

Florrie leaned back in her chair and folded her arms. 'I 'eard Galloway's younger son got married. Sid Bristow's wife told me. She said the girl sings in the music 'alls. 'E's done well fer 'imself.'

'That's all right if they like that life,' Aggie remarked. 'Those music-'all people travel all over the country. I don't s'pose the boy's gonna like 'er gallivantin' all over the place. I wouldn't like it if my ole man was never 'ome.'

'I can't see your ole man singin' on the stage,' Nellie laughed. 'Jus' imagine, 'Arold the singin' lamplighter.'

The friends' conversation was suddenly interrupted by the arrival of Betty Argent and Maudie Mycorft who nodded to the group as they walked up to the counter and ordered their drinks. Maisie noticed that the two looked rather quiet and leaned across the table. 'Yer look a bit upset,' she remarked. 'Everyfing all right?'

Maudie pinched her chin with her thumb and forefinger. 'It's Betty's 'usband,' she said gravely.

'Ain't 'is bronchitis no better?' Maisie asked.

Betty shook her head. 'It ain't that. 'E went back ter work last week an' now 'e's orf sick again.'

'What's the matter wiv 'im this time?' Maisie rejoined.

''E's come out all over in a rash. The doctor told 'im it's the shock comin' out,' Mrs Argent told her.

'What, the shock o' goin' back ter work?' Florrie joked.

Betty pulled a face. ''Im an' 'is gang was layin' track down by Bermondsey Junction on Wednesday night an' they come across this body. It'd bin 'it by a train by all accounts. Terrible mess it was in. My Dougie said it was prob'ly an ole tramp by the look of 'is clothes. 'E said the strangest fing was, although the clothes was in rags there was a watch-an'-chain on the body. Seems strange fer a tramp ter be wearin' a watch-an'-chain.'

Late on Friday evening Jack Oxford left the little pub in Abbey Street and walked slowly towards the lodging-house near the spice wharves in Dockhead. The beds were tuppence dearer than those in Tooley Street but at least he could be assured of a reasonable night's sleep, he told himself. The owner there did not allow gambling and noisy behaviour, and he had already barred Fatty Arbuckle from staying there after the incident of attempted boot-stealing. Jack had enjoyed a quiet few hours at the pub and had eaten a good supper.

Now he was feeling quite content as he made his way past the shadowy, deserted wharves. As he reached the lodging-house he saw a policeman standing outside the entrance and his heart missed a beat. There was no turning back now, he decided, trying to maintain a steady pace. Better to sweat it out.

Inside the lodging-house owner was talking earnestly with two men, and when he saw Jack called him into his office. 'These two gentlemen are from the police. They wanna talk ter all my regular customers,' he said.

The larger of the two detectives motioned towards a chair. 'Sit yerself down,' he said, taking a notepad from his inside pocket.

Jack struggled to keep calm as he settled his lanky frame on the seat. 'What's the trouble?' he asked, feeling his mouth going dry.

'Can we have your name first?' the detective asked, eyeing him closely.

When Jack had told him, the other detective took over. 'Do you lodge here regularly?' he began. 'Do you know any of the tramps who have been using this neighbourhood during the past few months?'

Jack nodded to the first question and shook his head to the second.

'We're trying to establish the identity of a tramp who was killed by a train at Bermondsey Junction,' the officer told him. 'The body was too mangled for us to get a picture done of him but we've got a description to go on. The man was about five foot seven and in his mid-thirties. He was dark-skinned and brown-eyed. His clothes were ragged and he wore a long black overcoat with a rotted flower in the buttonhole. The most unusual thing was that he was wearing a silver watch-and-chain. Have you ever seen anyone who looked like that, Mr Oxford?'

Jack shook his head. 'I've never seen anybody like that,' he said quickly. 'I don't know anyfing about a watch-an'-chain. It's nuffink ter do wiv me.'

The detective brought his face closer to the worried man's. 'Tell me, Mr Oxford, why are you getting so excited over a watch-and-chain? All I said was, the tramp was wearing a watch-and-chain. You seem nervous. Should you be?'

Jack looked around him in an attempt to gather his thoughts. 'I'm tryin' ter fink if I did see a tramp walkin' about round 'ere,' he faltered.

The detective glanced at his colleague. 'Is there anything else you want to ask Mr Oxford?'

'There is one thing puzzling me,' the other officer remarked, and turned to Jack. 'Why did you say it was nothing to do with you when the watch-and-chain was mentioned?'

'I, er, I dunno. I thought yer might fink I give the watch ter the tramp,' Jack stammered.

'No, Mr Oxford. All we want to do is try to identify the victim. Put a name to him, that's all – for the moment.'

Jack lowered his eyes and jumped noticeably as he felt the hand on his shoulder.

'Thank you, Mr Oxford. We're finished with the questions,' the officer said.

After Jack had left the room the senior of the two officers turned to the lodging-house owner. 'What do you know of him?' he said, nodding towards the door.

''E's 'armless enough,' the owner told him. 'Bin comin' 'ere on an' off fer years. 'E was stayin' at a place in Tooley Street until it got a bit too noisy fer 'im an' 'e started comin' back 'ere. Noise upsets 'im, yer see. 'E got kicked in the 'ead by an 'orse an' 'e's bin a bit dopey ever since.'

Jack sat on his bed and tried to stop himself from shaking. Charlie was dead, he told himself, and it was his fault. If only he hadn't chased him when he spotted him in St James's Road.

He should have left him when he ran up on to that railway embankment. The poor sod never stood a chance.

Jack shuddered as he recalled looking down on the mangled body. Miraculously the watch-and-chain was undamaged but he had not been able to bring himself to pick it up. It had caused Charlie to get killed and suddenly it no longer seemed important to return it to Mr Galloway. As he stood there in the cold staring at the watch-and-chain Jack had felt a sudden horrible fear, as if the thing might be alive.

He undressed and climbed into the cold bed, and for the first time in years did not bother to stand the legs of the bed over his boots.

Chapter Twenty-one

Carrie sat in the quietness of her tiny back bedroom and studied herself in the dressing-table mirror. She had scrubbed her face until it was glowing and then brushed out her long fair hair and set it up on top of her head, firmly securing it with pins and a wide tortoise-shell comb. She was wearing her best white linen blouse which buttoned high in the neck with a ruched turn-up collar, and had put on the long black satin skirt that her mother had made for her twenty-first birthday. It was cut tight at the waist and flared slightly from the knee down. Her shoes were of patent leather and canvas, buttoned up at the side and with small heels. Her mother had told her she should be wearing a stay bodice and Carrie had tried one on but could not endure the feeling of being squeezed breathless. She turned sideways and looked over her shoulder at her reflection. Her bosom did protrude. She smiled to herself as she pulled back her shoulders even more.

It had been an irritating time since she announced to her family that a young man was going to call on her. Her mother had questioned her about the lad and offered advice on the dos and don'ts and the pitfalls of letting a young man go too far. James had leaned back in the chair with his thumbs hooked into his braces and embarrassed her with his mocking smile and his comment about the likelihood of her beau having horse dung on his boots when he called. Charlie had had little to say apart from being curious about what the young man looked like, and Danny, who was preoccupied with the local boys' club, had said even less. Her father had looked worried when she told him she was going to the South London Music Hall and warned her that the Elephant and Castle could be a rough place on a Saturday night.

Carrie glanced at the loudly ticking alarm clock on the chair beside the bed and adjusted the collar of her blouse. Tommy would be calling soon. Her stomach turned over as she gathered up her cape and white gloves. At least the boys were out of the house, Carrie thought as she took a last look at herself in the mirror before going out into the parlour.

Her parents looked up as she entered the room and Nellie got up from her chair. 'Twirl round, let's see 'ow that skirt's 'angin',' she said.

William put down his paper and watched them fussing over the hem of the skirt and the tiny strand of cotton that was hanging down. How alike they were, he thought. They were both endowed with well-rounded figures and long fair hair that reminded him of new straw. They both had pale blue eyes and lips that traced a saucy curve, and when Carrie twirled around with her hands held out and her face flushed with excitement William felt a lump rising in his throat. She was a pretty thing, he owned with a bittersweet feeling. She was young and full of vitality, ready to be courted and eager to make her way in life, but how soon would it be before she was bowed beneath the burden of children and prematurely aged by the constant struggle to make ends meet? Nellie had been fortunate in that he had been in regular work over the years. She still had her looks and beauty. Would Carrie fare as well?

The loud knock on the front door roused William from his troubled thoughts and he smiled at his daughter's reaction as she gathered up her cape and gloves and hurried from the room.

The air was mild and the evening sky suffused with a glorious shade of gold as the two young people walked quickly along Page Street. Tommy wore a brown single-breasted suit with the buttons undone to show off his waistcoat and silver chain, and his brown boots were brightly polished. Her wore brass and enamel cufflinks in his turnback shirt-cuffs, and the white, starched collar of his shirt had rounded peaks which smartly set off the wide-knotted grey tie that was secured in place with a small pin. His dark wavy hair was neatly combed into a quiff over one eye and he walked along proudly, rolling his shoulders in a confident manner, his lips curled in a smile as he offered Carrie his arm. She laid her hand lightly on his jacket and looked directly ahead as she spotted Florrie Axford at her front door. People were talking on their doorsteps, and as they cast glances in her direction Carrie felt her face redden. Tommy was looking about him as though enjoying the casual curiosity and smiled at the women as he passed them.

It was after they had left the street and turned into Jamaica Road that he turned to her. 'Yer look very nice,' he said.

Carrie let her eyes glance quickly up and down to appraise him and gave him a big smile in return. 'Yer look very smart too,' she replied demurely.

Tommy's face became serious as he leaned his head towards her slightly. 'If yer smell a funny pong don't worry, it's the moth-balls,' he said with a grave expression. 'My ole mum always puts 'em in me suit when she pawns it.' His face suddenly broke into a wide grin. 'It's all right, I'm only jossin' yer. It's bin weeks since she pawned it.'

Carrie squeezed his arm playfully as she caught the mischievous look in his large dark eyes. He was certainly a handsome young man, she thought, and very sure of himself too. 'Whereabouts d'yer live?' she asked him, trying to start a conversation.

'St James's Road, near John Bull Arch,' he told her. 'Me an' me ole mum live in one o' those 'ouses facin' the shops.'

'What about yer farvver?' Carrie asked.

Tommy shrugged his shoulders. 'I never knew 'im. 'E left years ago. When we was all little. All me bruvs an' sisters are married, there's jus' me at 'ome. I sort o' look after the ole gel. She's gettin' on a bit now.'

''Ave yer always bin a carman?' Carrie asked.

Tommy smiled. 'I started work in a sausage factory in Dock'ead an' I flitted in an' out o' factory work till I was seventeen. By that time I couldn't take anuvver job in a factory so I got a job on the brewery as a cart boy. That's where I learned ter drive a team of 'orses. I've bin a carman ever since. Well, that's my life story, what about you?'

'I worked in a leavver factory until I got put off, then I got the café job,' she replied.

''Ow comes yer got mixed up wiv the suffragettes?' he asked.

'There was a gel who worked at the factory an' she was always goin' on marches an' she was always askin' me ter go wiv 'er. In the end I went on one o' the marches an' it sort o' grew on me. I could see the sense in what the women were campaignin' for an' I wanted ter be a part of it.'

They had reached the tram stop and Tommy leaned against the post. 'I always thought it was those upper-class women who done all the protestin' an' gettin' 'emselves chained ter railin's.'

'Those women usually organise the meetin's, but there's

loads o' workin'-class gels who march,' Carrie informed him.

'You've never chained yerself ter railin's, 'ave yer?' he asked her, smiling broadly.

Carrie shook her head. 'I've bin on meetin's an' marches that got really rough, though.'

Tommy laughed. 'I was at one of 'em, remember?' Then his face became serious. 'Is that right they force-feed suffragettes in prison?' he asked with a frown.

Carrie nodded. 'My mate Mary knew a woman who was force-fed. She said this woman 'ad a steel clamp put in 'er mouth an' then a tube pushed right down inter 'er stomach. All 'er gums were cut, an' when they fed 'er some o' the food went inter 'er lungs. She got pneumonia an' nearly died.'

Tommy looked shocked. 'That's terrible. I reckon women should 'ave the vote anyway. I bet my old mum would vote if she got the chance. She's always goin' on about 'ow unfair fings are fer women. Mind yer, she ain't 'ad much of a life what wiv the ole man pissin' off — sorry, runnin' off — an' 'avin' ter look after all of us kids. That's why I didn't get married when I 'ad the chance.'

The tram was slowing to a halt and Carrie had to wait until they were aboard before she could satisfy her curiosity. 'Yer was sayin' yer 'ad the chance ter get married,' she reminded the young man. 'Was she nice?'

Tommy nodded. 'Yeah, she was nice. We was courtin' fer two years an' she wanted ter get married. It was 'ard at the time. Me muvver was ill an' there was no one but me ter look after 'er. Fings jus' got impossible.'

'Did she leave yer?' Carrie asked, forgetting herself as she became intrigued.

'No, not really. She was seein' anuvver bloke while she was goin' wiv me an' I found out. I caught 'em tergevver one night an' there was a big fight. After it was all over she came back ter me pleadin' ter start again, but I couldn't. Fings would 'ave stayed the same, an' it wasn't fair ter 'er. She went back ter the other bloke an' last I 'eard she'd married 'im an' 'ad a kiddie.'

Carrie felt a sudden wave of pity for the young man. 'Yer must 'ave bin very young,' she remarked.

'I was nineteen at the time we broke up. That was ten years ago this November,' he answered.

They lapsed into silence as the tram carried them towards the Elephant and Castle and Carrie could feel the pressure of Tommy's shoulder against hers and sense the faint smell of the toilet water which he had dabbed on his clean-shaven face. She was relaxed now that they had got over their initial awkwardness. Tommy had spoken of his earlier romance and how it had failed without sounding bitter or sorry for himself, she thought. When he answered her questions he didn't seem to be looking for any pity, although he could not quite conceal the sad look in his eyes. Carrie was feeling mixed emotions. Tommy was a good-looking young man and it was sad that he had loved and lost, but he would surely have no trouble where finding lady friends was concerned. Apart from his good looks, he had charm and a sense of humour. Why had he suggested she go out with him for the evening? Carrie began to wonder. Perhaps he wanted to start a new relationship, or then again maybe he was just feeling lonely. She must be careful, she told herself. It would be easy to fall for someone like Tommy. Her lack of experience would go against her if she found herself in a tricky situation with him, and she could quite easily be overwhelmed by his charm and persuasive behaviour. It had been difficult that time with Billy. Rejecting his advances on that one occasion had obviously cooled him as far as she was concerned.

Carrie realised she was clenching her hands into fists as she sat beside Tommy. She was silly to take the blame, she told herself. Billy Sullivan was now making his name as a professional boxer and his sole ambition was to fight for the championship one day. Their brief time together had meant nothing to him except a chance to prove his manhood. With Tommy it might be different. They had met by chance and become attracted to each other. She was determined to let things progress slowly between them, and quietly resolved that she would not be carried away by his attractiveness and his debonair ways.

The tram squealed to a halt at the Elephant junction and they climbed down and crossed into London Road. Crowds were milling around outside the music hall and Carrie felt excited as Tommy took her arm. She had only ever been to the South London Music Hall on one occasion when her parents took her to see a pantomime, and could remember very little about it. As Tommy led her into the main hall Carrie looked about her and saw the well-dressed couples who stood around waiting to go into the stalls and the more soberly dressed people, some with young children, who milled around by the entrance to the gallery. Tommy led her up to a kiosk and bought her a tube of Nestlé's chocolates and then they climbed the wide staircase to the circle.

When they were seated comfortably Carrie looked up at the high ceiling and gazed at the sputtering gas-jets around the gilded, blue-painted walls. She could smell peppermint and the strong scent of lavender, and sighed with anticipation as the orchestra took their places. Suddenly the conductor raised his baton and loud brassy music filled the auditorium. Carrie sat enthralled as the show began with a dancing troupe. In the darkness she felt Tommy's hand reach out to hers. She kept her eyes fixed on the stage as the artists followed each other in quick succession, aware of his fingers gently caressing the back of her hand. Red-nosed comics followed the tumblers and jugglers, and when the baritone finished singing and the lights came up for the interval Tommy leaned towards her. 'Would yer like an orange?' he said.

Carrie was fearful of marking her new skirt and shook her head.

He grinned and leaned back in his seat. 'It's bin quite a while since I was 'ere last,' he remarked, looking around at the flickering gas-jets and up at the lofty chandelier.

Carrie glanced quickly at him and saw a faraway look in his eyes. This was where he brought his lady friend, she thought. This was where he sat holding her hand in the darkness and whispering words of love in her ear.

Tommy turned towards her, smiling as he raised his eyes to look at her hair and then glanced at the place where her stand-up collar touched the tip of her ear.

'I must 'ave bin still at school when I was 'ere last,' he said. 'I remember sittin' in the gallery wiv me bruvvers an' sisters. Eight of us there was, as well as me muvver an' this smart bloke who said 'e was our uncle. None of us believed 'im, or if any of us did, we know better now. We 'ad a lot of uncles after me farvver left. I don't blame me muvver. She 'ad a tribe of us ter clothe an' feed. Fings wasn't easy.'

Carrie felt she wanted to hug him. He looked so childlike and yet so handsome, and she sighed inwardly as she watched the glint of wry humour flicker in his dark expressive eyes. She wanted to go on talking with him, but the orchestra was coming back and the lights were dimming. She sat quiet in the dark, and as the show resumed felt Tommy's hand reach out for hers once more.

The orchestra struck up with 'Has Anybody Here Seen Kelly' and the star of the show walked out to the front of the stage. He was tall and lean, and when he started to sing his Irish tenor voice carried out to the far corners of the auditorium. He performed his repertoire of popular tunes and received loud applause and cheers from the enraptured audience. When the Irishman finally held up his hands and smiled graciously the audience knew that this was his own song and there was a hush. The orchestra led him into 'Meet Me Tonight In Dreamland', and the singer's silky voice seemed to float out from the stage and linger timelessly in the darkness of the smoke-filled theatre. When he finally reached the end of the song everyone jumped to their feet applauding wildly and Carrie found herself standing beside Tommy, moved with a strange elation by the poignancy of the singing. It was something to remember, she told herself with a thrill of pleasure. A wonderful ending to the show.

After the two young people had left the theatre they soon found a coffee stall at the Elephant and Castle where they stood eating hot meat pies and sipping sweet, scalding tea. Tommy was amused as Carrie tried to keep the soft filling of the pie away from her clothes and held her mug of tea for her while she struggled to retain her dignity.

The night had stayed mild and the sky was filled with stars as they walked slowly along the New Kent Road. Carrie held on to her escort's arm and they chatted happily about the show. Late trams trundled past and hansom cabs sped by, their large wheels spinning over the cobbled roads as the lean ponies trotted along at a lively pace. Piano music and singing voices drifted out from public houses, and as they reached the Bricklayers Arms a drunk staggered out from a bar and reeled dangerously beside the kerb before recovering himself and stumbling back through the door.

Carrie took a tighter grip on Tommy's arm as he led her into the warren of backstreets. She could feel his body next to hers as they wound their way through the gaslit turnings. Sounds came from the houses – babies crying, voices raised in anger, and badly tuned pianos playing popular songs – and slowly faded away into the ominous nighttime silence that surrounded them. Drunks reeled past and clung to the lampposts, mumbling and cursing. Carrie felt relieved when at last they emerged from the maze of narrow streets into the brightly lit Grange Road. She was feeling tired now and her shoes were pinching. They had been walking for quite some time and when they finally reached Jamaica Road and turned into Page Street it cheered her to hear the familiar sound of a tug whistle on the river. She saw the light burning in her parlour window and turned to Tommy as they reached her front door.

'Thanks fer takin' me ter the show, Tommy. It's bin a lovely evenin',' she said, looking up into his eyes.

He smiled, and without replying bent down and kissed her gently on the cheek. 'I'd like ter take yer out again soon, if yer fancy it,' he said quietly.

Carrie nodded. 'I'd like it very much.'

He stood there while she slipped her hand into the letterbox and withdrew the door key. Then, as he was about to walk away, Carrie quickly stretched up and kissed him on the side of his mouth. Tommy grinned in surprise and stood watching as she hurried into her house, then he turned and walked off, whistling loudly.

On Monday morning George Galloway drove his trap into the yard and strode into the office with a look of irritation on his florid face. 'The bloody spring's gone on the trap,' he moaned to Geoffrey. 'Get on ter the coachmaker's right away, can yer? I'll be needing it this afternoon.'

Geoffrey looked up from his desk, reluctant to impart more bad news. 'Symonds is leaving, Father,' he said gently. 'He put in his notice a few minutes ago.'

Galloway sat down at his desk and swivelled the chair around to face his son. 'Did Symonds say why 'e was leavin'?' he asked.

Geoffrey nodded. 'He's got a job with Hatcher. He said it's more money. Oh, and Bristow's wife called in this morning. He's down with bronchitis again.'

Galloway puffed noisily. 'I'll 'ave ter replace Bristow. I can't afford ter keep payin' 'im while 'e's off sick. I'm not runnin' a benevolent society,' he growled.

Geoffrey turned away to use the phone and his father got up and paced the office in agitation. It was bad enough having a broken trap without more problems on top, he groaned to himself. Rose was expecting him to take her for a ride today and he wanted to make a good impression. Her benefactor was out of London on business and he was eager to make the most of his good fortune. Rose had proved to be a very lissom, energetic woman, and she had told him in no uncertain terms that her elderly provider was beginning to flag and she was now looking for a more virile partner. George found her remarks flattering but had no ambition to become sole patron of the woman. She had been set up in a comfortable flat, with a personal allowance to go with it, and he did not intend to make himself responsible for that side of her affairs. Going to visit her during the day while her benefactor was away on business was an ideal arrangement. The old man would not be any the wiser, and nor would Nora.

Geoffrey put down the phone. 'They're sending someone along right away,' he said.

George felt slightly better. He sat down heavily in his chair. 'Did Tanner fix us up wiv casuals?' he asked his son.

Geoffrey nodded. 'We got a couple of decent carmen in but we'll have to get a permanent man to replace Symonds,' he pointed out.

Galloway leaned his elbow on the arm of his chair and stroked his chin thoughtfully. 'I've bin finkin' o' bringin' Jake Mitchell in,' he said almost to himself. 'I 'eard 'e's moved over this side o' the water an' 'e shouldn't be 'ard ter get 'old of.'

Geoffrey's face almost paled with sudden alarm. He had never seen Jake Mitchell, but he remembered when he was younger how the name had loomed in his mind, dark and threatening like a spectre. The sinister image of the man had been invoked many times around the meal table when he and Frank were children and their father was in one of his talkative moods. Even now the mere mention of his name conjured up endless tales of wild exploits over the years and Geoffrey wondered whether his father really was losing his powers of judgement and common sense. Jake Mitchell was a vicious brawler. He had a reputation for getting violently drunk and attacking anyone without reason, and he was known for assaulting policemen. As a young man he had fought in the fairground boxing booths, and he was as strong as an ox. Some years ago he had been sentenced to four years' hard labour after attacking a slightly built man in a public house and almost killing him with his fists. Stories of Jake Mitchell's evil doings still abounded, and Geoffrey ran his fingers through his dark hair in perplexity. 'Surely you're not thinking of letting Mitchell work here, are you, Father?' he said in disbelief. 'After what you've told Frank and me about him. You said yourself the man's an animal.'

George smiled slyly. ''Ave yer 'eard about the Bermon'sey Bashers?' he asked.

Geoffrey shook his head and his father leaned back in his chair and clasped his hands together in his lap.

'When you an' Frank were still at school, there was a group o' local publicans who banded tergevver an' sponsored fighters. They called 'emselves the Bermon'sey Bashers. They each 'ad their own fighter. I can tell yer there was a lot o' money changed 'ands when those fights took place. Twenty-rounders they was, an' I've seen some o' those fighters 'ammered ter pulp. They used ter 'old the fights in the pubs. It was eivver in the back yards or in one o' the large rooms upstairs.'

'What's that got to do with Mitchell?' Geoffrey asked, but the answer was already dawning on him.

'I'm comin' ter that,' George went on. 'The bettin' on those fights got out of 'and. People were layin' their bets on street corners wivout knowin' the form o' the fighters concerned. Word jus' got around that so-an'-so was fightin' a new boy, an' o' course the police got wind of it. They raided the Eagle in Tower Bridge Road one night an' nicked everybody who was there. At least 'alf a dozen publicans lost their licences an' it came to a stop. Well, I've jus' bin told on good authority that it's startin' up again. This time, though, it's gonna be run more tightly. They've even changed their name. Now they're gonna be known as the Bermon'sey Beer Boys. It's got a nice ring to it, don't yer fink?'

'And you're thinking of sponsoring Jake Mitchell?' Geoffrey remarked incredulously.

His father grinned. 'Jake's still more than an 'andful fer anybody the Bermon'sey Beer Boys can put up. 'E's still only in 'is mid-thirties. 'E was only twenty-five or -six when I brought 'im over from Cannin' Town ter fight fer me at the Eagle. I won a packet that night. Funny enough, it was only the followin' week that the police raided the place. Fortunately I wasn't there that time.'

'But won't the local publicans cotton on to your scheme, especially if Mitchell's already fought in the pubs?' Geoffrey asked.

George shook his head. ''E only fought once an' that was

at the Eagle. There's a new publican there now, an' besides, Mitchell fought under the name o' Gypsy Williams, an' that was ten years ago.'

Geoffrey flopped back in his chair. 'So you're going to give him a job as a carman and back him in the ring.' He shook his head slowly. 'Supposing he won't agree to fight – that's if and when you do find him?'

Galloway stretched out his legs and clasped his hands, pressing his thumbs together. 'Jake never could turn down a scrap an' I'll make it well werf 'is while,' he said with a satisfied grin. ''E can also 'andle a pair of 'orses as good as anybody. All I gotta do is find 'im.'

'Who told you Mitchell was living over this side of the water?' Geoffrey asked.

'It was Nora, funny enough,' George told him.

'Nora?'

'That's right,' he replied. 'Nora don't know Jake, o' course, but she does know most o' the people in the turnin', an' that's where she 'eard the story. It turns out that there's a new copper on the beat an' 'e's one o' those who likes ter take 'is coat orf an' sort the trouble out in 'is own way. Well, accordin' ter Nora, this copper come across two jack-the-lads 'angin' around outside a pub an' they was gettin' a bit boisterous. This copper tells 'em ter bugger orf an' one ses, "Yer wouldn't say that if it was Mad Mitch standin' 'ere." Anyway, the copper gets a bit shirty an' 'e ses, "Tell this Mad Mitch that I'm keepin' me eye out fer 'im, an' if I come across 'im 'e'll know all about it." A couple of hours later one o' the blokes comes back an' by that time 'e's well tanked-up. As it 'appens 'e bumps inter the same copper. " 'Ere, yer was lookin' out fer Mad Mitch, wasn't yer?" 'e ses. "That's right," ses the copper. "Well, I'm 'im," the bloke ses. It turns out they 'ave a right set-to, an' apparently the copper give as good as 'e got. Come ter fink of it, p'raps I ought ter offer the copper a job instead,' George added with a chuckle.

Geoffrey did not see the funny side of his father's attitude and grimaced openly. 'Well, I don't like the idea of it, to be perfectly honest,' he said firmly. 'I can see trouble coming from all of this. What happens if Mitchell gets shirty with Will Tanner? Will's the yard foreman and he gives the carmen their orders. He won't take kindly to being undermined by the likes of Jake Mitchell.'

'That'll be no problem,' George replied. 'While 'e's in the yard Mitchell does 'is share o' the work. I'll make sure 'e understands that right from the start. I want 'im ter save 'is energy fer the ring. Anyway, I've already put the word out fer 'im ter contact me. Now do us a favour an' get on that phone again an' chase that bloody coachbuilder up. I've got an important meetin' wiv a prospective customer an' I wanna be on time,' he said, hiding a smile.

Chapter Twenty-two

Carrie Tanner was finding her working week unbearably long. Each day she waited hopefully for Tommy Allen to make an appearance but he did not call into the dining rooms. Each day she tried to put him put of her mind as she waited on the tables and served endless cups of tea and coffee. One or two of the regular customers who had been there when Tommy asked her out made bawdy comments and laughed when she rounded on them. They joked with her about seeing the young man with a couple of young ladies on his arm. Carrie tried hard not to show that she was concerned but she could not help wondering what had happened to Tommy and why he had not bothered to contact her again.

Fred Bradley had been acting rather strange too, she thought. Normally he would chat to her at every opportunity but all week he had been withdrawn and moody. Carrie felt that he must be feeling unwell. It couldn't be the business, she reasoned. They were doing more trade than ever, and now that the new berth was operating at Bermondsey Wall even more dockers were coming in.

It was Sharkey Morris who helped to shed light on Fred's mysterious behaviour when he called into the dining rooms on

Friday morning. There had been the usual amount of banter between the carmen, then one of them said loud enough for Carrie to hear, 'I ain't seen anyfink o' Tommy Allen lately.'

'Nor 'ave I. I reckon 'e's got 'imself locked up,' another said.

'Nah, 'e's frightened ter come in 'ere in case we jib 'im,' a third piped in.

Carrie tried to ignore the chit-chat but found herself getting more and more irritated by their childish comments. Sharkey could see her face becoming darker and he turned to the first carman. 'Who's this Tommy?' he asked.

'Don't yer know 'im?' the carman replied, grinning broadly. 'Tommy Allen's our Carrie's young man, ain't that right, luv?'

Sharkey jerked his eyes towards the back room. 'What's Fred gotta say about that then?' he joked.

'P'raps yer better ask 'im,' the carman said.

''Ere, Fred, yer don't allow Carrie ter walk out wiv scruffy ole carmen, do yer?' Sharkey said, grinning.

Suddenly Fred came out of the back room and leaned over the counter. 'Why don't yer stop yer silly talk?' he said angrily. 'What the gel does in 'er own time is no concern o' mine, an' it shouldn't be none o' yours neivver. Now if yer finished yer grub, why don't yer piss orf an' make room fer somebody else?'

The customers were surprised at Fred's sudden outburst and became subdued. Carrie too was surprised at Fred's behaviour and felt a little embarrassed as she got on with serving the tea. When Sharkey Morris finished his meal, he got up and walked over to her on his way out.

'Take no notice o' the lads, luv,' he said quietly. 'They was only 'avin' a bit o' sport. Fred should know 'em by now. If yer ask me I'd say the bloke's jealous, the way 'e carried on.'

Carrie dismissed the idea with a laugh but as she watched Sharkey leave the shop her brow creased in a puzzled frown. Fred *had* been unusually moody and quiet since that day Tommy asked her out, she thought. Maybe there was something in what Sharkey had said. Fred had been very talkative and he had certainly smartened himself recently. No, it didn't mean anything, she told herself. If he was interested he would have asked her to walk out with him. Fred was a good bit older than her anyway, and he was too set in his ways.

For the rest of the day Carrie busied herself with her chores, glancing up hopefully as customers came into the dining rooms. Later, as she was getting ready to leave, Fred called her into the back room.

'I'm sorry if I frightened yer, shoutin' at those carmen the way I did,' he said quietly. 'I thought they was upsettin' yer.'

'I didn't take any notice, and they didn't mean any 'arm,' she replied, smiling.

Fred nodded. 'Just as long as yer all right. I wouldn't want yer ter get upset an' leave. Business 'as picked up quite a bit since yer've bin workin' 'ere an' I appreciate it. I want yer ter feel free ter come an' talk ter me if anybody does upset yer. I know I'm almost old enough ter be yer farvver, but if ever yer feel the need, don't 'esitate, all right?'

Carrie nodded as she buttoned up her coat. There was something in the way he spoke that reawakened her earlier misgivings. Perhaps he did want to ask her out but felt he was too old for her, she thought, realising that she would have to be careful not to give him the wrong impression by becoming too familiar with him. It would be difficult though. She had grown fond of him in the short time she had been working at the café. Fred was kind and considerate, and she felt comfortable chatting to him. It would upset him if she suddenly shunned him. He was a sensitive man who had always behaved very properly towards her. A girl could do a lot worse than marry a man like Fred, she thought. She would have to think carefully about the way she dealt with the situation. Things were unsure enough between her and Tommy at the moment without any further complications.

Carrie had left the dining rooms and was walking along the narrow turning that led into Bacon Street when suddenly she saw Tommy driving his pair of horses towards her. He waved and pulled up to the kerb, jumping down and hooking a brake chain around the front wheel as she walked up to him. 'I'm sorry I've not bin in ter see yer, Carrie,' he said quickly. 'I've bin off work fer a few days.'

''Ave yer bin ill?' she asked him anxiously.

'No, it's the old lady,' he replied. 'She fell down the stairs last Sunday night.' Carrie winced and drew in her breath sharply. Tommy slowly shook his head. 'I'd jus' gone ter bed when I 'eard the crash. She'd bin at the gin again. I told 'er ter sleep down in the front room but she would insist on goin' up the stairs. I 'ad ter 'ide the bottle before I could get the silly ole mare ter bed, an' as soon as she 'eard my bedroom door go she got up ter look fer it.'

'Is she badly 'urt?' Carrie asked him.

'I dunno yet,' Tommy shrugged, leaning back against the shafts. 'I got the doctor in an' 'e said there was no bones broken, but she started actin' funny the next day. She was ramblin' away an' talkin' a load o' gibberish. I couldn't leave 'er, she'd 'ave set light ter the 'ouse or somefink. Anyway on Wednesday she was no better an' I got the doctor in again. 'E got 'er inter St James's Infirmary. They've got 'er under observation.'

Carrie smiled sympathetically and touched his arm. 'I thought yer didn't want ter see me any more.'

Tommy looked down at his boots for a moment, and when

his eyes came up to meet hers Carrie saw how sad they looked. 'I really enjoyed last Saturday night,' he said quickly. 'I wanted ter ask yer out durin' the week but I couldn't leave me muvver. Besides, I'm in an' out o' the infirmary now. The ole gel's frettin' in there. She always dreaded goin' in that place an' now she reckons she ain't comin' out. Ter tell yer the trufe, Carrie, it drives me roun' the twist goin' in ter see 'er. They're all ole ladies in 'er ward an' I 'ave ter sit wiv 'er fer a while. Trouble is, yer dunno what ter say 'alf the time, an' she keeps ramblin' on. She asked me ter send the ole man in ter see 'er last night. Bloody 'ell, 'e's bin gorn fer years.'

'Would yer like me ter come in wiv yer ternight?' she asked him.

Tommy's face lit up. 'Would yer, Carrie? Would yer really?'

She smiled. ''Course I would. Knock fer me when yer ready an' I'll be waitin'.'

'It's seven till eight visitin' time,' he said, releasing the brake chain. 'I'll be round at ten ter seven.'

Carrie watched as he climbed up on to the cart and jerked on the reins. 'I'll be ready,' she said.

Trouble had been brewing in the Tanner household all week. On Friday evening, as soon as the meal was over, Nellie glanced across at Danny, hunched sulkily in his chair. 'It's no good yer sittin' there lookin' all mean an' 'orrible,' she said sharply. 'I told yer I don't want yer goin' ter that boxin' club. In fact, I've a good mind ter see Billy Sullivan's muvver abaht it. Billy should 'ave more sense.'

'But I like boxin', Mum,' Danny answered, twirling a knife. 'It's nuffink ter do wiv Billy. Yer'll make me look silly if yer see 'is muvver.'

'It is somefink ter do wiv Billy Sullivan,' Nellie said,

gathering up the plates. 'It was 'im who kept on ter yer about boxin', an' it was 'im who took yer ter the club in the first place. I told yer before, I don't want no fighters in this family. All them knocks ter the 'ead can't do yer no good.'

William had his head buried in the evening paper and huffed defensively as Nellie rounded on him.

'Yer sittin' there takin' no notice. Why don't yer tell 'im?' she said sharply.

He folded the paper and laid it down on the table. 'I fink yer makin' too much of it, Nell,' he said quietly. 'It's a good club an' they don't let the kids get 'urt. It's not like professional fightin'.'

'That's 'ow they start though,' she complained. 'That's 'ow Billy Sullivan started, an' now look at 'im. I saw 'im the ovver day – 'is face was all bruised an' 'e 'ad a nasty black eye. Is that 'ow yer wanna see Danny turn out?'

'Billy's gonna fight fer the area title next week,' Danny said loudly. ''E's gonna be the champion soon.'

'See what I mean?' Nellie groaned. 'Mind yer, I blame meself. I should 'ave stopped 'im 'angin' around wiv that Billy. The way it is now 'e finks the sun shines out of 'is arse. Gawd, as if it wasn't bad enough nursin' 'im frew that bronchitis an' pneumonia! Now 'e's gonna be knocked stupid as well.'

James had been listening to the argument. He pushed back his chair and stood up. ''E'll be all right, Muvver. It'll knock some sense into 'im,' he said, winking at Danny.

'That's it, take 'is part,' Nellie stormed. 'Ain't you got anyfink ter say?' she rounded on Charlie.

The quiet lad looked up, surprised at his mother's anger. 'I reckon in the end it's up ter Danny what 'e wants ter do, Mum,' he said. 'If 'e takes up boxin', at least nobody's gonna pick on 'im.'

Nellie picked up the plates and hurried out of the room, sighing loudly. Once she had gone, William turned to his youngest son. 'Look, yer shouldn't keep on about that boxin' club in front of yer muvver,' he said in a low voice. 'Yer know 'ow she feels about it. If yer wanna go, then go, but keep quiet about it. She'll get used ter the idea, but give 'er time.'

Danny's face brightened a little. He turned to Carrie who was folding up the tablecloth. 'Will yer come an' watch me when I 'ave me first fight?' he asked, grinning.

'Only if yer promise ter win,' she said as she hurried out to the scullery.

Nellie was scraping the plates as Carrie entered. She cast an anxious glance at her daughter. 'P'raps I worry too much about that boy but I can't 'elp it,' she fretted, wrapping the leavings up in a piece of newspaper. 'Especially after that illness 'e 'ad. It leaves yer chest weak.'

'I shouldn't worry too much, Mum,' Carrie replied. 'Danny's as strong as an ox.'

Nellie took the kettle from the gas-stove and poured hot water into the enamel bowl. 'I s'pose I shouldn't 'ave jumped at yer farvver the way I did,' she said. ''E's worried enough the way fings are goin' at the yard. What wiv Soapy puttin' 'is notice in, an' Galloway talkin' about gettin' rid of ole Sid Bristow. The way fings are goin' yer farvver could be next.'

Carrie took a wet plate from her mother. 'Galloway wouldn't put Dad off, surely,' she reassured her. 'Dad's savin' 'im a fortune the way 'e cares fer those 'orses. There's the men too. Dad knows 'ow ter 'andle 'em an' they respect 'im. No, I can't see 'im puttin' Dad off.'

Nellie rinsed the last plate and passed it to Carrie. 'Don't yer be so sure,' she said. 'Galloway wouldn't fink twice if it suited 'im. 'E's 'ard, take it from me.'

'But who's gonna look after the animals if Dad goes?' Carrie asked, putting the stack of plates in the cupboard.

'Fings are changin' fast,' her mother replied. 'Young Geoffrey's got ideas of 'is own. 'E wants ter bring in lorries ter do the cartage. A lot o' firms are changin' over now. In a few years' time yer won't see 'alf the 'orses yer see on the road now, mark my words.'

Carrie leaned back against the copper and folded her arms. 'What would 'appen if Dad did get the sack? Would we 'ave ter leave 'ere?'

Nellie shrugged her shoulders. 'I can't see Galloway lettin' us stay.'

'But we could pay rent like the rest o' the tenants,' Carrie said.

'It's not as simple as that, luv. If they did change over ter motors, they'd need somebody ter look after 'em an' 'e'd 'ave the 'ouse. It'd go wiv the job,' Nellie told her.

Carrie blew out her cheeks. 'No wonder Dad's worried. Why can't fings stay the same? Why does everyfing 'ave ter be so complicated?'

Nellie laughed resignedly. 'Life's complicated, Carrie. Nuffink's simple fer long. One fing's certain though – we'll manage some'ow. We always 'ave.'

The evening air was chill and the sky a mass of dark brooding clouds as the young couple walked through the infirmary gates and along the gravel path to the main building. Carrie was holding on to Tommy's arm and they were both silent. She had never been inside the building but the stories she had heard about the place filled her with dread.

'They go there from the work'ouse,' her mother had said. 'They send 'em there when the poor bleeders are too old ter work an' when they start goin' orf their 'eads.'

Carrie gripped Tommy's arm tightly and he smiled encouragingly as they climbed the stone stairs to the second floor. The walls were tiled in brown and cream, and the stone floor scrubbed clean. The nurses they passed were wearing long dark uniforms with white, starched hats that covered their foreheads and hung down their backs triangular fashion. Their clothes rustled and keys hanging from their black canvas belts jangled as they hurried by. Carrie shivered inwardly as they entered the dark ward and walked past the rows of beds along the walls. Hollow eyes followed them as they passed. When they reached the last bed on the left, Tommy leant over the frail figure lying there and kissed her forehead gently.

'I've brought somebody ter see yer, Mum,' he whispered.

Carrie leant forward and smiled at the vacant-eyed old lady. ''Ello, Mrs Allen. 'Ow are yer?' she asked in a low voice.

A long, bony hand slipped out from beneath the bedclothes and gestured feebly.

'Jack? Is that Jack? I got the ticket. I'll get yer suit out on Friday. I'll . . .'

The croaky voice trailed away and the bony hand dropped limply on to the bedclothes.

'She finks it's me farvver,' Tommy whispered as he pulled up a chair for Carrie. 'She's on about the pawn shop again. It was the same last time I come in.'

Carrie looked down at the white-haired old woman. She could see the faint pulse beating in her thin neck. The woman's eyes were closed but they seemed to be moving beneath her dark eyelids. Carrie could not think of anything to say and looked up at Tommy. He was standing over the bed holding his mother's hand. He bent down to stroke her forehead gently with his other hand. 'It's Tommy. It's yer son Tommy, Ma,' he whispered. 'Open yer eyes, Ma.'

The old lady's eyes flickered and closed again. 'Tommy?'

she murmured hoarsely. 'Yer a good boy ter yer ole mum. Tell yer farvver I'll be 'ome soon. Bring me clothes in next time, Jack. I can't stay in 'ere.'

Tommy looked at Carrie and shook his head. 'It's no good, she keeps wanderin',' he said softly.

Carrie looked around the ward. Like the long corridor, the walls were tiled in cream and brown and the highly polished floor smelt of carbolic. Here and there a few wilting flowers stood in glass vases beside the beds, and in the centre of the ward there was a polished wooden table where the ward sister sat writing. Beside her was a large vase containing a spray of bright yellow chrysanthemums. They seemed out of place in the drab, sterile surroundings.

Tommy stood over his mother, whispering to her and squeezing her limp hand for a while, then straightened up and turned to Carrie. 'I fink we should leave now,' he said. 'She doesn't know us.'

Carrie got up and stood at the foot of the bed while Tommy bent over and gently kissed his mother's lined forehead, then took his arm as they walked quickly from the ward and along the gloomy corridor.

They walked in silence until they had crossed the quiet thoroughfare and then Tommy turned to her. 'Would yer like a drink?' he suggested. 'I need one.'

Carrie looked at him rather apprehensively. 'In a pub?' she queried.

He nodded. ''Ave yer never bin in one?'

She shook her head. 'Will they let women in?'

'It's all right. This one does,' he laughed. 'Long as yer wiv somebody.'

Carrie soon found herself sitting in a small public house in Jamaica Road, sipping a ginger beer and gazing wide-eyed around the bar. Most of the customers were men but there were a few women sitting in secluded corners with their escorts. A fire was burning in a large open fireplace, and around the papered walls hung ornaments of pewter and brass alongside dark-coloured pictures of river scenes.

Tommy took a large draught from his pint of ale, afterwards wiping his mouth. 'I shouldn't 'ave let yer come wiv me,' he said quietly. 'It's a depressin' place. It gives me the creeps every time I go in there.'

Carrie tried to comfort him with the ghost of a smile. 'I'm glad I did come wiv yer,' she said. 'The place doesn't seem so frightenin' ter me now. It's jus' so sad ter see all them old people lyin' there.'

Tommy nodded, and then paused for a moment. 'Look, Carrie, I've bin doin' a lot o' finkin' since last Saturday night. I can't expect yer ter walk out wiv me, not the way fings are. I've got me ole lady ter look after an' it wouldn't be fair ter yer. We couldn't go out much an' I can't let meself get serious wiv anybody, not fer the time bein'.'

Carrie looked at him with concern in her large blue eyes. 'Why did yer ask me out in the first place?' she said quickly.

Tommy looked down at his drink. 'I was feelin' a bit lonely, I s'pose,' he replied. 'I wanted somebody ter talk to, an' yer was very nice ter me when I come in the café. Besides, I was curious about yer. Yer a very pretty gel, Carrie, an' anybody would be proud ter walk out wiv yer.'

'Curious? Was that why yer asked me out?' she checked him, a note of anger creeping into her voice. 'Was yer lookin' fer a free an' easy gel who might let yer take advantage of 'er?'

He shook his head vigorously. 'No, 'course not. I could see yer wasn't that sort o' gel the first time I spoke ter yer when yer was strugglin' wiv that copper, an' I've 'ad no reason ter change me mind since. What I'm tryin' ter say is, I couldn't give yer much o' me time. I'm under the cosh, Carrie, an' I ain't gonna expect any gel ter share that wiv me any more. I tried it once an' it didn't work out. I'm sorry, but that's the way it is.'

'I'm not any gel,' Carrie replied with vigour. 'I can understand fings. I know 'ow it is wiv yer mum bein' ill an' yer 'avin' ter care fer 'er. I'm not stupid.'

'That's why I'm sayin' it, Carrie,' he said in a tone of despair. 'I fink yer somefink special an' I ain't gonna expect yer ter wait. There shouldn't be any pretendin'. I wanna court yer but I can't, not the way fings are.'

'We could see each ovver now an' then,' she said. 'We could be good friends wivout puttin' an end to it.'

Tommy looked up at her and his large expressive eyes stared into hers. 'I want us ter be friends, Carrie, but I don't want yer ter expect too much. If yer do yer gonna get 'urt. We both will.'

When they left the pub they walked back through the gaslit streets without speaking, mindful that something had grown between them. It was not long before they reached Tommy's house, and as he opened the door and they stepped into the dark passage she was in his arms, her mouth pressed to his, her body moulded against him as she wrapped her arms around his neck. She could hear her own heartbeats and felt a delicious sensation flowing up from deep inside her as his arms enfolded her tightly and he held her close to him in the darkness. He was kissing her ears and her soft white neck. She shuddered as she let him move his hands down along her body, feeling no inclination to deny herself such a pleasurable experience. She was breathing more quickly when Tommy suddenly eased the pressure of his arms around her willing body, tenderly holding her close to him without moving for a while, to temper their rising desire. She clung to him, feeling his chest rise and fall, calmly and deeply. She was near to giving herself to him completely but she knew deep down it would not be now, not yet. Tommy seemed to understand too, she could tell.

'I'd better get yer 'ome,' he said suddenly, releasing his hold on her and breathing deeply in an effort to quell his lingering passion.

As they walked quickly to Page Street Carrie held his arm tightly, her stomach fluttering with the delicious feeling that had awoken deep inside her. Their friendship would grow from this night on, she felt sure. Whatever happened, whatever fate had in store for them, there would always be a closeness between them.

Chapter Twenty-three

Will Tanner slumped down at Galloway's desk in the yard office and clipped the worksheets on to the bundle. Monday mornings seemed to be more difficult lately, he sighed. In the old days the carmen would have their usual moans about the work rotas and then drive out of the yard without more ado, but Soapy Symonds had left now, Sid Bristow was still off ill, and they were the last of the old crowd. The new men were a different sort altogether, casual carmen hired on a week-to-week basis, most of them unfamiliar with the type of carting they were expected to do. Many of them were footloose drifters, scratching a living where and when it suited them. Few of them could competently handle and load the large hop bales or scotch up the rum barrels so that they stayed in place on the cart. Occasionally one of them mistreated a horse and then William would have to make sure he never came back for a day's work.

George Galloway seemed quite happy with the state of affairs even though it sometimes caused problems with the firms he dealt with. Will had quickly realised the motive behind his employer's thinking. Carmen were only hired when they were needed and now none of them was ever left hanging about the yard as in the old days. The hire rate was less too, and William could only suspect that contracts with their customers were obtained by undercutting all the other cartage firms. Galloway probably lined the pockets of the firms' transport managers and still made a good profit, he guessed.

At nine o'clock that morning Horace Gallagher walked into the office and peered at William through his thick-lensed spectacles.

'George and Geoffrey not in yet?' he queried, easing his long, lean frame into his desk chair.

William shook his head. 'I expect they're on business. They're always in by this time,' he answered.

Horace was already busying himself with a ledger and the yard foreman got up to leave. He had never liked the accountant very much and was wary of discussing his employer with him. Horace had been with Galloway from the very beginning and handled all the firm's financial arrangements.

As William made for the door, Horace looked up from his desk. 'Have you got a minute?' he asked.

William sat down in the chair again and folded his arms. 'Yeah. What's wrong?'

'Nothing,' Horace said quickly. 'I just wanted to ask you something. Have you ever heard of a man called Mitchell? Jake Mitchell?'

William shook his head and Horace leaned forward in his chair. 'Does the name Gypsy Williams mean anything to you?' he asked.

'Wasn't 'e the one George brought over from Cannin' Town ter fight at the Eagle a few years ago?' William remarked, his eyebrows fixing into a frown.

Horace nodded. 'That's right. His real name is Jake Mitchell and I understand he's coming to work here as a carman. I thought you should be warned, although I would ask

334

you not to let on you already know when Galloway tells you,' he added quickly.

William tried to hide his feelings of disquiet. He had never met Mitchell but Galloway had spoken about him often enough and Sharkey Morris had told him of the night he saw Mitchell almost kill his opponent at the Eagle public house before the fight was stopped. What reason did Galloway have for suddenly employing the man, he wondered, and why should Horace break the habit of a lifetime and confide in him? It seemed very strange to William and he stared at Horace, trying to gauge the man's reasons.

'Why should I be warned, Horace?' he asked with a guarded look.

The accountant glanced at the door anxiously before replying. 'As you know, Will, I've worked for this company for a very long time and I thought I'd seen everything there was to be seen. Lately, however, I've started to question some of the things that have happened here. I've been ordered to make Sid Bristow's money up. He's being put off, did you know?'

William nodded.

'The man's worked here for over twenty years, for Christ's sake!'

William was shocked by Horace's sudden show of feeling and wondered what else lay behind his outburst.

'I guessed Bristow was goin' from what Galloway said last week,' he remarked. 'I'm gonna try an' talk 'im out of it, but I don't see what I can do. All the old carmen 'ave eivver left or bin sacked. It seems ter suit the ole man but it's affectin' the business in one way or anuvver. I can't understand 'im lately.'

Horace let slip a short, bitter laugh. 'No, neither can I. Anyway, you asked me why I should warn you about Mitchell. That man is a nasty piece of work and I'm afraid you're going to have a hard time dealing with him. That's why I wanted to put you on your guard. I wouldn't like to see you be forced to leave. Just be careful.'

William nodded. 'Thanks for the warnin', 'Orace. An' don't worry, I won't let on I know.'

Horace turned his attention to the ledger and William walked out into the yard, unable to still his troubled thoughts. There was something strange about Horace's behaviour, he told himself. And what was Galloway's reason for bringing Mitchell in? There had been no boxing matches at the local pubs since the Eagle's landlord lost his licence. Some of the publicans must be planning to start up again, he decided. What other reason could there be for Galloway's move?

William continued to puzzle over the problem while he bandaged a lame horse's fetlock. Just as he was leading the animal into the small stable, Galloway drove into the yard. Geoffrey was with him and there was another man sitting beside them. Galloway hailed William and waved him over.

'I want yer ter meet Jake Mitchell, Will,' he said breezily. 'Jake's gonna start work termorrer. Jake, this is Will Tanner, me yard foreman.'

William studied the man as he shook his hand. He was about his own height, he guessed, but at least a couple of stone heavier. His bullet head sat squarely on broad shoulders and his face was flat and fleshy. William could see by the way Mitchell's nose was twisted that it had been broken several times, and there were white scars over both his eyes. His short coarse hair was greying and spiky, and as his mouth parted in a thin smile he displayed chipped, yellow teeth.

'I'm puttin' Jake on the 'ops contract, Will,' Galloway went on. ''E's done that work before so there'll be no problems. Oh, an' when yer got a minute, I wanna see yer in the office.'

William nodded and glanced quickly at Geoffrey. The young man sat motionless in the trap, looking uncomfortable.

George seemed perfectly at ease. He joked with Mitchell as they got down from the trap and walked into the office.

As Geoffrey stepped down, William discreetly called him aside. 'I don't know 'ow much yer know about Mitchell, Geoff,' he said quietly, 'but if yer ask me I'd say yer farvver's playin' wiv fire employin' the likes of 'im.'

Geoffrey shrugged his shoulders. 'I don't make the decisions, Will,' he replied quickly.

'I fink it's about time yer started then,' William said sharply as he walked away.

He had tethered the lame horse outside the small stable. When he walked back over to it, he saw that it was sweating. He led the animal into the stall. It stood quietly as he rubbed it down vigorously with sacking and handfuls of straw until its coat was dry and shining. As William filled the box with chaff, George walked into the stable.

''Ow is it?' he asked, running his hand down the horse's withers.

'I've rubbed it down an' it's eatin'. It'll be all right in a day or two,' William told him.

Galloway leaned back against the centre post and eyed his foreman closely. 'I take it yer know all about Mitchell?'

'Should I?' William asked curtly.

'Jake Mitchell used ter fight fer me on the pub circuit,' Galloway went on. 'If yer remember, I brought 'im over this side o' the water ter fight at the Eagle a few years ago.'

William nodded. 'I remember, but I'd never met the man. Gypsy Williams 'e was known as then, wasn't 'e?'

Galloway smiled crookedly. 'That's right. 'E's still good, an' 'e can beat anybody round 'ere that I know of.'

William wiped his hands on a piece of sacking and looked quizzically at Galloway. 'What I can't understand is why yer brought Mitchell 'ere. If yer need an extra carman, why not get Lofty Russell back, or even Darbo? At least they were reliable.'

Galloway stood up straight and slipped his hands into his trouser pockets. 'Jake Mitchell's reliable enough, an' besides, 'e ain't in as an extra. 'E'll be takin' Sid Bristow's place,' he said firmly.

William threw down the piece of sacking in disgust. 'Yer tellin' me yer actually gone and sacked Bristow 'cos the man's bin off sick fer a few weeks? Christ Almighty! Bristow's bin wiv yer almost as long as I 'ave.'

Galloway shrugged his shoulders. 'Bristow's gettin' past it, Will. 'E's 'avin' trouble managin' the work an' 'e never puts in a full week nowadays. I got a business ter run, not a bloody friendly society.'

'But yer could give 'im the light van an' let 'im do the runabouts. That's the least yer could do,' William said with passion.

'Look, it's no good yer tryin' ter make me change me mind,' Galloway replied firmly. 'Bristow's goin' an' that's the end of it. Mitchell takes 'is cart over termorrer.'

'But why Mitchell? Wouldn't it 'ave bin better ter get one o' the ovvers back?' William asked.

Galloway shook his head. 'The Bermon'sey Bashers are startin' up again,' he said, smiling. 'I should fink that makes it obvious why I want Mitchell.'

The yard foreman nodded his head slowly. 'So that's it,' he said quietly. 'Well, I 'ope 'e does 'is fair share o' the work round 'ere, George, an' I'll tell yer straight, while I'm the yard foreman 'e'll take orders from me like the rest of 'em.'

Galloway bit on his lip in irritation. He needed Jake Mitchell to fight for him. He was more than a match for anyone the local publicans could put up, and there was quite a pretty penny to be earned betting on the outcome. God knew, he needed the extra money. Rose was becoming more demanding, and she had expensive tastes.

Galloway's silent stare angered the yard foreman and his eyes blazed. 'I mean what I say, George,' he said forcefully.

Galloway raised his hands in a conciliatory gesture. 'All right, Will, all right,' he sighed dismissively. 'That's understood. I've already told Mitchell. Yer'll get no trouble from 'im, an' if yer got any complaints come an' see me an' we'll get it sorted out. That all right?'

William nodded. 'I still fink yer've bin 'ard wiv ole Sid Bristow,' he remarked, looking Galloway in the eye. 'Sid was the last o' yer ole carmen. It don't seem right ter me.'

George walked to the stable door and then turned to face his foreman. 'Look, Will, I don't wanna argue wiv yer. As I said, me mind's made up. Don't you worry though, there'll always be a job 'ere fer you. Why, me an' you was kids tergevver. I ain't likely ter ferget that.'

William watched him cross the yard and sighed deeply as he cut the wires on a hay bale. Talk was cheap where Galloway was concerned, he reminded himself. What if he went down sick? Would Galloway still feel the same then? The horse had started sweating again and William felt troubled as he grabbed another handful of sacking.

Carrie was in a thoughtful mood as she left the dining rooms and walked the short distance home. She had gone with Tommy to the Infirmary on two occasions that week and his mother seemed to be rallying. She was now propped up in bed and had recovered enough to have snatches of conversation with her son. The doctor had said she would be able to go home soon, although there had been some permanent damage and she would never fully recover. Tommy had taken the news quietly. He had not said much, but Carrie was aware that he would be hard put to it to hold down his job as well as care for his mother. One or two of her neighbours had offered to go in and see her during the day but as Tommy had said, she was a difficult woman to deal with and her few friends would soon find it too much to stand.

Carrie thought about their long walks together after they left the Infirmary. They had strolled along the riverside in the cool of the evening and watched the seagulls wheeling over the moored barges. She had taken his hand and they had stolen kisses in the shadows of the lofty wharves, but she had felt that Tommy always seemed to be holding back. He had not invited her to his house again, and when he walked her to her front door he kissed her hurriedly as though all the street were watching him. Carrie believed she understood his reasons and it made her angry with the lot fate had dealt him. She understood that he had loved once before and lost, and now he could not bring himself to open his heart to her and love her the way she wanted to be loved. It seemed to her that Tommy was afraid to take things further, although he must realise that theirs could not remain a simple boy and girl friendship. Carrie felt that she was now ready to experience love completely, and he was the one she wanted to give herself to.

Nellie was laying the table when Carrie walked in. She raised her eyes to the ceiling in a secret sign to her daughter and nodded in the direction of the menfolk who were all sitting around talking together.

'I'm startin' work there on Monday,' James was saying. 'There's no future in the sawmills an' it's about time I 'ad a change.'

'Well, if that's what yer wanna do, Jim,' his father replied. 'Cabinet-makin' is a good trade. Yer can learn French polishin' an' veneerin' as well. I wish now I'd gone in that trade. There's more of a future in furniture than workin' wiv 'orses. In time, it'll be all motors on the roads.'

Jim sat back in his chair and hooked his thumbs through his braces. 'I made me mind up ter get out o' the mills when ole Benny Taylor lost two fingers in that band-saw the ovver week,' he said with conviction. 'Took 'em right off it did. 'E fainted right over the saw, an' if it wasn't fer the foreman grabbin' 'im 'e'd 'ave bin split right down the middle.'

'Do yer 'ave to, Jim?' his mother admonished him. 'We'll be 'avin' tea soon. I don't wanna 'ear fings like that at teatime.'

Jim grinned at his father. 'Bloody shame about poor ole Benny,' he went on. ''E plays the pianer in the pub. Well, 'e did do. 'E won't be able ter do that anymore.'

'I s'pose 'e could always use 'is elbows,' Danny said to bursts of laughter.

Carrie stifled a laugh as she saw the look on her mother's face. 'Jus' fink, Mum, Jim'll be able ter make yer a nice bedroom suite soon,' she joked.

Danny moved round in his chair to face James. 'D'yer fink I could get a job at the cabinetmakers, Jim?' he asked. 'I'm gettin' fed up wiv servin' in that shop. Only women should 'ave ter serve in shops.'

Carrie cuffed him lightly around the head. 'Don't yer be so cheeky. One day women'll be doin' all the jobs men do, jus' you wait an' see,' she told him forcefully.

'What, drive 'orse-an'-carts an' be dustmen an' fings?' Danny said, laughing.

'I drove an 'orse-an'-cart once,' Nellie cut in. 'It's surprisin' what women can do.'

'I'd like ter see 'em go in the boxin' ring,' Danny said derisively.

'They'd take their gloves off an' pull each ovver's 'air out, I should fink,' James said, winking at his younger brother.

'Sadie Sullivan wouldn't,' Nellie remarked. 'She's still a match fer any man.'

'That family's bloody mad,' James declared. 'If they're not thumpin' ovver people, they're knockin' each ovver silly.'

'Not now they don't,' Danny said quickly. 'Billy's the only one who fights now, an' 'e's earnin' money fer doin' it.'

'Well, that's as it may be, but yer can get it out of yer 'ead if yer fink me an' yer farvver are gonna let you be a boxer,' Nellie told him firmly.

William hid a grin as Danny looked appealingly at him. 'There's a fighter started work at the yard. Jake Mitchell 'is name is,' he said, turning to Nellie. ''Ave yer clapped eyes on 'im yet?'

Nellie nodded. 'Ugly-lookin' git. I see 'im drivin' up the turnin' the ovver mornin'. Usin' the whip 'e was. I don't like ter see 'em whippin' those 'orses.'

'If I catch 'im usin' the whip there'll be trouble,' William said quickly. 'Yer'll never get the best out of an 'orse by usin' the whip. 'Orses 'ave gotta be coaxed.'

'What's this bloke doin' workin' fer Galloway if 'e's a fighter?' Danny asked.

''E fights in the pubs, or 'e used to before the police stopped it,' William told him.

'Billy told me all about those pub matches,' Danny said. 'Billy reckons they don't fight under the Marquis o' Queensberry rules, an' some o' the fighters put liniment on the gloves.'

'What's that for, the bumps an' bruises?' Nellie asked innocently.

'Nah, it's ter blind the ovver bloke,' Danny answered amid laughter.

'When's tea gonna be ready?' Charlie said suddenly, looking up from his book.

'Five minutes. I'm waitin' on the greens,' Nellie told him.

William smiled to himself. Charlie was so different from his brothers, he thought with amusement. He seemed able to lose himself in a book despite all that was going on around him. James always had something to say and was ever ready to get into an argument, and Danny was the cheeky one, restless and inclined to sudden changes of mood. Charlie could sit curled up in one corner with a book or the paper for hours. Nothing seemed to worry him and his two brothers had long ago given up trying to bait him.

Nellie was serving up steaming mutton stew and Carrie sliced the bread as the family gathered around the table. William looked at the eager faces of his sons and Nellie's set expression as she evened out the portions of stew. He glanced at Carrie and noticed how grown-up she had become. He sighed contentedly. Things had been uncomfortable in the yard lately, he felt, and his future there looked uncertain, but it was easy to push all that to the back of his mind as he sat down to eat with his family around him.

Nora Flynn was feeling unhappy as she cleared the table after the evening meal. George had been out two evenings that week – to meet with prospective customers he had said, but Nora felt he was lying to her. When George went out in the evenings to meet clients or future customers, he never took the trap. Usually he would go to a local public house and discuss business over drinks. Handling the trap when he was inebriated was something George did not relish and he had told her as much. Now that he had a lively and spirited animal between the shafts he was even more loath to take the vehicle on his business jaunts, but on the last two occasions he had used the trap and returned comparatively sober. Either George was losing his taste for a tipple or he was dealing with teetotal clients. Nora realised that nothing could be more unlikely. This was something or someone else.

Loud laughter came from the front room where Josephine was entertaining some of her school friends. Nora forced a smile as she put away the washed plates and cutlery. Laughter had been in short supply in the house for a long time, and it was very quiet now that Frank had left to get married and Geoffrey always seemed to be out with his married lady friend. Nora closed the dining-room door and climbed the stairs to her room. The summer evening was drawing in and she gazed down at the long shadows spreading across the quiet square. Her feeling of sadness deepened as she sat down in her favourite armchair and stared out at the evening sky. Her life had been dramatically changed since she and George had become lovers. He had reawakened feelings inside her that she had thought were gone forever. She had felt young and lighthearted again, happy and contented, until the last few weeks.

George seemed to have changed since Frank's wedding. His nocturnal visits to her bed had become less frequent and lately they had exchanged a few harsh words. When she had asked him for a little extra money to buy some lace curtains for the front windows he had suddenly grown angry and stormed out of the room. He seemed to be getting very mean lately, and he had never behaved that way towards her before. Something must have changed him, but what?

Not for the first time she wondered whether there was another woman. Perhaps he had met someone at the wedding reception who had taken his fancy, she thought as she tried to picture the occasion in her mind. He had spoken to many people there but he had been drunk and making a nuisance of himself for a great deal of the time, she recalled. There was one woman though. She had been in his company at the bar and had seemed to be hanging on his every word. Then again, she was with a younger man and had left quite early. Perhaps she was being silly. George was no spring chicken and he was working hard at the business. Perhaps it was she who had become possessive and domineering, forcing him to seek pleasure outside the house.

Nora got up and walked over to the mirror. Evening shadows filled the room and darkened the glass as she studied her reflection. Slowly and deliberately she removed her hairpins and let her raven hair fall down around her shoulders. It was how George liked it, she brooded as she raised a stiff brush to the tangled tresses. It had taken her some time but she had won the man's affections and now she was resolved that she would fight to keep him. Tonight she would not lie awake and wait for his key in the door and pray for his footsteps on the stairs. Tonight she would beard the lion in his den.

Chapter Twenty-four

Life in Page Street beyond the yard gates carried on in the usual way as the summer days went past. Canvassers came round and knocked on doors with a petition to the local councillors for action over Bacon Street Buildings. Sadie Sullivan wanted her whole family to sign but was informed that only one signature was allowed from each household. She signed twice, once for herself and once on behalf of a make-believe cousin, who lived a few streets away but was visiting and had just popped out to the shops, the petitioners were solemnly informed. Maggie Jones and Ida Bromsgrove signed with vigour, and Maudie Mycroft peered through her lace curtains to make sure everyone else was signing before she committed herself. 'Yer can't be too careful, Ernest,' she warned her long-suffering husband. 'They could be anarchists.'

Ernest puffed loudly as he tried to read the account of a society scandal. 'That's right, luv,' he answered with a suitable amount of seriousness in his voice. 'Puttin' our names on paper could be tantamount ter treason. Mind yer, if we don't sign the petition it could be seen as somefing else an' we could be murdered in our beds.'

347

Maudie decided that Ernest might have something there and hurried to the door to sign. Dot Argent signed, as did Maisie, Aggie and the redoubtable Florrie Axford. Nellie Tanner put pen to paper and got Jack Oxford and three of the carmen to sign as well.

Billy Sullivan won his latest fight on a knockout and was now a serious contender for the middleweight title. Danny Tanner knocked at Billy's house the next morning and got his idol out of bed for his signature so that he could show it off to all the customers. Everybody knows about Page Street now, and when I become British Heavyweight Champion the street will be famous, he told himself, puffing out his narrow chest.

Once again, sheer pluck and devilment served to enhance Florrie Axford's already formidable reputation in the street. It happened a few days after Jake Mitchell came to work for Galloway's. Florrie was whitening her front doorstep when Mitchell came by, driving his team at a lively pace. She got up off her knees and watched the cart rattle into the main road, a scowl on her thin face.

'They've all bin told ter take it steady till they get out o' the turnin',' she reminded her friend Aggie who was on her way to buy the morning paper.

'Yer right, Flo,' Aggie agreed. 'Nellie Tanner said 'er Will always tells 'em ter mind the kids when they come in an' out o' the street.'

'Well, I'm gonna keep me eye out fer that ugly-looking git,' Florrie vowed. 'I tell yer straight, Aggie, if 'e comes in this street at a gallop ternight I'm gonna go in that yard an' see Galloway 'imself.'

It was nearing five o'clock when Florrie heard the frantic clatter of iron wheels on the cobbles and quickly peered out through her clean lace curtains. Her face darkened as she saw Jake Mitchell sitting forward in his seat, his gnarled hands pulling on the reins to slow the fast-moving pair of greys as they went through the yard gates. 'Right, that's it!' she exclaimed aloud to herself as she buttoned up her coat and pressed her bonnet down on her head.

The noise of the horses cantering into the yard had already alerted William in the upper stable. He hurried down, ready for a confrontation.

'In future don't drive the cart in like that, mister,' he growled. 'I've already told yer the rule 'ere that ses we walk the 'orses down the turnin' 'cos o' the women an' kids.'

Florrie was more vociferous when she reached the yard. 'Oi! You!' she shouted at Mitchell as he was climbing down from the cart. 'Next time yer drive that soddin' cart down the turnin', make sure yer not drivin' like the devil's on yer tail ovverwise yer gonna end up killin' somebody.'

Jake Mitchell scowled at Florrie and turned his back on her, which only served to infuriate her. 'Oi! Are yer dumb as well as bein' bloody stupid then?' she shouted at him.

Mitchell rounded on the woman. 'Piss orf, missus. Why don't yer go 'ome an' nag yer ole man?' he snarled.

Florrie could not contain herself any longer. 'I ain't got no ole man. 'E looked like you, that's why I got rid of 'im,' she screamed, rushing towards him with her fists clenched.

Mitchell backed away, surprised by her fury, but before Florrie could reach him William stepped in front of her and took her by the shoulders. 'All right, luv. Calm down,' he said placatingly. 'I'll sort this out. Yer right ter complain, but let me 'andle it.'

Florrie puffed loudly and pressed her hat down on her head. 'All right, Will, but yer better tell 'im straight, ovverwise I'll be straight in ter see Galloway.'

William watched the irate woman march out of the yard then he turned to Mitchell, his face dark with anger. 'Next time yer drive in like that yer finished 'ere, understand? An' while I'm about it, yer better get one fing straight. As long as yer a carman 'ere yer don't get no special treatment. Yer take orders jus' like the rest of 'em. If yer got any complaints on that score, yer better see Galloway. Right?'

Mitchell matched his foreman's stare. 'I'm not in the 'abit o' takin' that sort o' talk from any woman,' he growled.

'Well, in this case you ain't got no bloody choice,' William told him. 'An' I tell yer what – Florrie Axford's as good as gold till she's upset an' then she'll front yer, big as you are. Yer'll do well ter remember that.'

Mitchell sneered as he turned his back on William to unhitch his horses and the foreman walked away, feeling better for a confrontation that had been overdue.

Carrie took Tommy's arm as they left the Infirmary and walked slowly along the quiet thoroughfare. The doctor had said that his mother was well enough to go home the following day. Tommy was quiet as they walked under the railway arch and then turned into St James's Road, and Carrie understood what he must be thinking. The chance of their relationship flourishing seemed remote and she was feeling desperate. She needed him, wanted him to love her, and she was prepared to settle for the way things were. The alternative was a sterile friendship that would surely not survive as their normal emotional needs were smothered and withered by circumstance.

They were passing his house on the opposite side of the road. Suddenly she leant her body against his a little, indicating with a subtle pressure that they should cross the road. Tommy instinctively responded and they walked over to his front door. No words were spoken as they entered, and in the darkness of the passage she went to him, moulding her body against his and entwining her arms around his neck. Her lips searched for his and with a deep shuddering sigh she pressed her mouth to his. She had boldly seized the initiative, feeling that the time had come. She was ready, a willing partner, urging and guiding his searching hands until he was fully roused. There could be no going back now.

His lips were on her now. She could feel the deliciousness of his mouth wet against her neck, kissing her ears, her closed eyes, and brushing her soft throat. His arm slipped around her waist as he led her slowly into his bedroom and suddenly she was in his arms, poised above the bed. Tommy moved forward and his lips were hard on hers as they fell backwards, down on to the soft covers. Carrie was gasping, urging him on. She felt a short, sharp pain as he groaned above her. She was his now, and moaned as the ecstatic pleasure of his loving flowed through her willing, trembling body.

Horace Gallagher was alone in the office as he turned back the pages of the bound ledger and glanced at the entries. It seemed to him that the whole of his past life was represented there in the bold, sloping handwriting in purple ink. He saw the entry for two hard-bristle yard brooms dated 1905 and a faint smile came to his face. Galloway had made a fuss over that purchase, he recalled. Why two brushes when there was only one yard sweeper? he had argued. Lower down the page Horace noted the sale of one dozen Irish Draughts to the Royal Artillery and had a vision of women lining the street and Nellie Tanner marching up to the hosepipe with a chopper in her hand. It was all there, he thought. Stories hidden behind dates and figures. Another entry caught his eye and Horace rested his chin on his hand. 'Collection and transport of one carcass' the entry read. He had never thought of himself as a horse lover but that docile little Welsh cob had been everyone's favourite animal. He remembered young Carrie Tanner sitting on its back when she was small and how she had sobbed uncontrollably when it died of colitis. Horace turned the pages which marked the passage of the years. There were entries for sale and purchase of horses, carts and animal foodstuffs, and one entry near the front of the book back in 1895 which read simply, 'One small wreath, John Flynn'.

Horace closed the ledger and stood it on the shelf beside the rents and wages ledgers. It was all there, he reflected. More than twenty years of his life spent setting down in ink the progression of George Galloway and Sons, Cartage Contractor and Horse Trader. The ledger would one day be filled to the last line of the last page, he thought with a smile, and wondered who might be sitting there writing in it. Eventually all the books would be gathering dust on dark shelves until some time when they were taken down and pored over out of idle curiosity. The elderly accountant reached forward and pulled a sheet of plain paper towards him and then unscrewed the cap of his fountain pen. For a while he stared down at the blank sheet of paper, and then he leant forward low over the desk and started to write in his flowing style.

At thirty minutes past the hour of four Horace Gallagher closed and locked his desk and stood the sealed envelope against the sloping lid. Then he put on his coat, and following the habit of a lifetime, buttoned it from top to bottom before donning his trilby and taking up his beechwood cane. As he walked out of the yard, Jack Oxford called out goodnight but Horace did not hear him. He walked slowly along the turning and touched the brim of his hat to Florrie Axford as he passed her. At the end of the street Horace stopped and turned to face the darkness towards the yard gates, then set off on his usual walk to London Bridge Station.

Trams clattered past and people were spilling out of the offices in Tooley Street as he walked in the shadow of the high railway arches and reached the steep flight of steps that led to the station forecourt. Horace climbed them slowly with his head held low, ignoring the young men who dashed past him taking the stairs two at a time. There was no hurry, he thought. The trains were frequent at this time of day.

The platform was packed with tired, jaded workers. Horace stood with his back resting against the waiting-room wall, not seeing their blank faces. Another day, another shilling, he thought, smiling to himself.

The station announcer's voice crackled over the loudspeaker and passengers moved forward as the four-fifty-five drew into the station. Elbows were raised and shoulder pressed against shoulder as workers stood abreast, each attempting to be first into the carriages. Horace waited and as the train drew out of the station he started to tap his foot with the tip of his cane. Trains are frequent this time of day, he told himself once more. When the next train announcement came over the loudspeaker he moved forward, and as the four-fifty-nine to Sidcup drew into the station Horace Gallagher threw himself under the wheels.

The afternoon was mild, with feathery clouds wafting across a blue sky, as George Galloway sat back in his trap and let the gelding set a lively pace. He was looking forward to what promised to be a very pleasurable afternoon, and whistled tunelessly to himself as he drove along Brixton Road. Bringing Jake Mitchell back to Bermondsey was a very good idea he told himself, and the sooner the fights got under way the better. The gold pendant resting in his waistcoat pocket had cost a packet, and so had the bangle he had given Rose only last week. She did not like cheap, gawdy jewellery and she had been very pleased with her expensive gift, promising to keep it out of sight whenever her elderly patron was on the scene. She would be pleased with the pendant. Maybe he had been a bit extravagant, but it didn't matter.

Rose had turned out to be quite a catch. He had not been disappointed in her. She was all woman, with a highly developed carnal appetite and a taste for adventure. Their mutually enjoyable afternoons were becoming quite a feature of his life and so far Rose had been very discreet. Her provider was happy to keep her in the fashion she was accustomed to, and seemed none the wiser. He visited her during the evenings, business permitting, and she was left free to pursue her own interests during the day. George grinned to himself as he neared Rose's house in Acre Lane. A woman like her needed much more than her elderly provider could give her, he thought smugly, and it seemed only right that he should be given a little help with the lady.

George pulled the trap up outside the ostler's yard opposite Rose's house and gave the man his usual half a crown to take care of the horse and vehicle, then crossed the road and let himself in through the front door. The arrangement was a good one, he gloated. Each Tuesday and Friday afternoon Rose's patron attended board meetings and there was no possibility of their being disturbed by his unexpected arrival. Rose had given George a key and a time which he strictly adhered to. He smiled to himself as he hurried up to her flat on the first floor and knocked gently on the door. Rose always wore a flimsy nightdress under a wrap when she greeted him, and he was usually rewarded with a big hug as he stepped through the doorway.

This time George was disappointed. The door was opened by a large young man who casually grabbed him by the coat lapels and pulled him roughly over the threshold. George found himself standing in the middle of the room looking down at his tearful mistress. Beside her stood a distinguished-looking gentleman, immaculately dressed in a grey suit and derby hat to match. He wore spats over his black patent shoes and was holding a silver-topped cane. The young man stood to one side, eyeing George malevolently, hands tucked into his coat pockets.

'I don't think I've had the pleasure,' the older man said, smiling sarcastically.

George straightened his coat and glared back. 'What's your game?' he growled, trying to compose himself.

'I might ask the same of you,' the man replied calmly, walking slowly towards George. 'It appears that you have been visiting Miss Martin on various occasions during the past few weeks. Tuesdays and Fridays, to be precise. You arrive at two-thirty in the afternoon and stay until around five o'clock. Later on one occasion.'

George swallowed drily and searched desperately for a way out of his predicament. 'That's right,' he said quickly, his eye catching the piano in the far corner of the room. 'I give 'er pianner lessons every Tuesdays and Fridays.'

The older man's face broke into a cruel smile and he looked down at the distressed figure of Rose. 'That's not what Miss Martin told me before you knocked on the door,' he said with measured relish. 'She told me you were her uncle who had lost his wife and was feeling lonely, and so you came round to have a nice little chat. Now which of these stories should I believe? Surely you're not both lying?'

Rose dabbed at her eyes with a small lace handkerchief and George stared helplessly at his tormentor.

'Norman, will you show our visitor to the piano? Perhaps we could be honoured with a brief demonstration of the gentleman's talents,' the older man said quietly.

The beefy young man took George by the arm and led him over to the piano.

'Are you familiar with Chopin's Nocturne in E-Flat?' the senior man said in a silky voice. 'Opus nine number two. Or maybe you'd like to entertain us with your interpretation of Liszt's Hungarian Fantasy.'

George looked down at the piano keys and then stared back dumbly.

'Perhaps you'd prefer to offer us a short medley of popular tunes,' the man said condescendingly.

George's mind was racing. He had lived by his wits all his life and suddenly he felt as if he was back in the days of his youth, cornered beneath the stinking arches with policemen closing in, their truncheons drawn ready to beat a lone young animal into submission. He could feel the blows again and the laughter as they walked off, leaving him bloody and barely alive.

George smiled thinly as he bent over the keyboard, and delicately tested the keys with his forefinger, his other hand resting on the top of the piano, inches away from a cut-glass vase. 'Pass us the music, will yer?' he said casually, pointing to the table.

For an instant the young man's attention was distracted and George knew that he could not hesitate. In one swipe he grabbed the heavy vase and smashed it with all the force he could muster full into the hoodlum's face. The young man dropped as though pole-axed and George wheeled, a snarl on his face as he closed on the older man.

'Don't you touch me!' he cried, backing away.

George made a grab for him and the man tumbled over Rose's legs and collapsed in a heap, his hands covering his head. George stood for a moment looking at Rose, wondering what he should do.

'Go!' she shouted. 'Just go.'

Beads of sweat were starting on his forehead as he hurried down the stairs and out into the street. He was still sweating profusely as he sat in the trap and let the horse have his head.

It was a quarter to five when Galloway drove his trap into the yard. He did not want to go home and face Nora's searching gaze, and as he sat watching the rising and falling of the gelding's flanks his thoughts were still racing. What would happen to Rose? he wondered. She would no doubt suffer a beating, but she would survive. She would gush tears and swear her loyalty, and maybe the excuse for a man who kept her would forgive her and shower more gifts upon her. He'd survive without Rose too – in fact he'd be better off. With Jake Mitchell coming to fight for him and being a good earner, he wouldn't have to waste his money on that woman. He grinned smugly.

George crossed the yard and walked into the empty office. He sat down at his desk and reached for the whisky bottle, aware of the loud ticking noise from the clock. For a while he sat at his desk and then he swivelled around and stretched out his feet. He glanced up at the clock and noted that it was one minute to five o'clock. It was then that his eyes caught sight of the sealed envelope that was propped against the far desk. George felt a sudden sense of bewilderment and he frowned as he tore open the letter. As he read the few words written in a flowing script he groaned loudly and lifted his misted eyes to the ceiling. He was still staring up as if transfixed when William walked into the office.

'What's wrong?' the yard foreman asked in alarm.

George passed the note over without a word and William slowly read the short message:

Dear George,

When you read this note my life will be over. Loneliness is a cross I could no longer bear. Only my work sustained me through the years. And now that's been taken away from me. Take heart, the books are in order and up to date. Just one last thought: value old friends. Without them life is empty, as I have sadly discovered.

Yours in eternity,

Horace Gallagher

'Oh my Gawd! The silly ole fool,' William breathed. 'Why? Why did 'e do it, George? Surely 'e could 'ave talked about what was troublin' 'im? We might 'ave bin able ter 'elp the poor bleeder.'

George shook his head. 'I doubt it. I doubt if anybody could. 'Orace was a private man. 'E kept 'imself to 'imself.'

William suddenly recalled the day Horace had warned him about Mitchell. He must have been planning to take his own life then, he thought. He slumped down in Horace's desk chair and looked across at his employer's strained face. 'I can't understand what 'e said about bein' lonely. 'E 'ad a wife, didn't 'e, George?' he said in a puzzled voice.

The firm's owner made a pained grimace and nodded slowly. 'Yeah, 'Orace 'ad a wife, that much I do know. She left 'im more than twenty years ago.'

William picked up the note again and after studying it for a few moments he looked up at his boss. 'This bit about "only my work sustained me". Yer wasn't finkin' o' puttin' 'im off, was yer, George?' he asked, frowning.

Galloway shook his head vigorously. ''E was too valuable. 'Orace knew 'e 'ad nuffink ter worry about on that score.'

The two sat staring down at the floor in silence, then

suddenly George got up and walked over to the corner of the room. He took down a ledger from the shelf and opened it on his desk. 'Come 'ere, Will,' he said after a few moments. 'Take a look at this.'

William studied the unfamiliar entries and looked in puzzlement at George. 'What is it? he asked.

'There's yer answer,' the firm's owner said positively. 'Jus' look at those entries. These are the latest ones. See 'ow they run inter the lines on the page? The earlier entries are much neater. 'E could 'ardly see what 'e was doin'. The poor bleeder used ter polish those glasses of 'is all the time. I thought it was just 'is nerves. That's what 'e meant when 'e said that bit about 'is work sustainin' 'im.'

'Yer mean . . .'

'That's right, Will. 'Orace was goin' blind.'

Chapter Twenty-five

The evening was stormy and unseasonably cold, and outside heavy rain was falling from the dark, massed clouds that hung in the sky like a pall. Nora sat alone in the back kitchen, her slippered feet warming in front of the small open fire. The rocking-chair creaked rhythmically as she worked at tucking and tacking hems on a new pair of curtains, and she glanced up at the covered window every time she heard a loud roll of thunder. George had gone to his room soon after tea, saying he had some papers to look through, and Josephine was visiting her school friend in the house across the square. Nora welcomed the evening solitude as she threaded the needle in and out of the fabric. The last few weeks had been a very trying time for her. When she had gone to George's room that fateful night, full of fire and indignation and ready to face her lover down, she had ended up trying to console him over his accountant's sudden death, searching vainly for words of comfort until finally he fell into a drunken sleep.

Horace Gallagher's suicide seemed to have affected George more badly than Nora would have predicted. He was slipping back into his old ways, becoming morose for no reason and spending a lot of time alone, and he was drinking heavily again.

It worried her that he had begun to use the trap for his evening pub meetings now. Often he would return from the yard or a pub with the gelding sweating and flecks of foam spattered along its flanks, having raced it along the cobbled streets and sometimes through traffic, and then Nora found herself fearing for his life. It was a small glimmer of comfort to her that she had stayed with him on that terrible night and tried to share his grief, and he had not shut himself up in his room away from her. He appeared to have forsaken his afternoon trips out lately too, and she guessed that whatever attachment he had formed was now over. Nora knew that she had neither youth nor beauty to offer, but she felt that the love she had shared with George had been genuine, growing slowly from a feeling of needing and being needed. She considered herself to be a practical woman, and tried to make herself believe that the depression afflicting George would pass and she would be able to draw him back to her and stop his dangerous drinking.

She started from her reverie as the front door opened and closed and she heard the sound of footsteps coming along the passage. Geoffrey walked into the room, puffing loudly as he removed his sodden hat and coat and threw them over the back of a chair.

'It's raining cats and dogs out there, Nora,' he said, giving her a smile. 'Any tea in the pot?'

She made to get up but he waved her back. 'I'll get us some,' he said cheerfully, taking the teapot from off the hearth.

They sat facing each other beside the fire, Nora slowly rocking back and forth with the unfinished curtains across her lap and Geoffrey sitting forward in his chair, sipping his tea thoughtfully. Outside the storm was raging unabated. Thunderclaps broke the quietness of the room.

'The old man's asleep by the fire,' Geoffrey said. 'I looked in on him as I came in.'

''E's back on the drink, Geoff,' she said quietly. 'I'm worried about 'im.'

Geoffrey shrugged his shoulders. 'He's upset over Horace. It was a terrible shock to all of us but Father's taken it badly,' he remarked, staring into the fire. 'It's strange really. All the years Horace worked for us and we knew practically nothing about the man. He never socialised with Dad, at least not that I know of. All the time he was in the office, his head was bent over the ledgers. He kept them in tiptop order. He was always on hand with advice about money matters, and I suppose we came to see him as part of the furniture. He wasn't the sort of man you could have a casual conversation with.'

Nora nodded her head sadly. 'Yer farvver showed me the letter 'Orace left be'ind before 'e took it ter the police station. Loneliness is a terrible fing. I know what it's like.'

They were silent for a while, both staring into the fire, then Geoffrey frowned and stretched out his legs.

'The old man was asking me about Mary,' he said suddenly. 'He wanted to know if it was her I was walking out with.'

'I'm surprised George remembers anything o' that weddin', considerin' the state 'e was in,' Nora replied. 'What did yer tell 'im?'

'I told him the girl at the wedding was just someone I'd met and she wasn't the girl I'm seeing,' he said ruefully.

'Why, Geoff? Why not tell 'im the truth? Nothing good can come out of deceivin' yer farvver. 'E's got ter know one day,' Nora warned him.

Geoffrey sighed as he stared into the flickering flames, then he raised his eyes to hers. 'He's never understood me, Nora,' he said sadly. 'He wants me to marry and give him an heir. He's set standards for me and I'm expected to conform. How could I bring Mary home and tell him she's a married woman? He'd shun her and we'd get to arguing. No, I'll just carry on seeing her and leave things the way they are for the present.'

'I've only met 'er the once but she seems a nice young lady,' Nora said, taking up her sewing. 'D'yer fink she'll get a divorce eventually?'

Geoffrey shrugged his shoulders. 'I don't know, Nora. I guess not. We'll go on seeing each other, and when the old man asks me why I don't bring her home I'll do the same as I'm doing now, I'll make excuses.'

Nora shook her head sadly. 'It seems such a shame. Fings could be so different,' she said quietly.

Geoffrey looked up at Nora and suddenly felt sad for her. She was a good woman and he knew of the love she had for his father. It was all too plain in the way she spoke of him and in the way she looked at him. His father was treating her badly by ignoring her and drinking to excess, knowing how she hated it. Nora was right, he thought, things could be so different.

Later that summer a small group of Bermondsey publicans staged their first illegal boxing tournament in the Crown, a seedy public house near Dockhead. The pub was a regular haunt of the Russian and Scandinavian merchant seamen who manned the timber ships that sailed into nearby Surrey Docks, and it attracted a regular crowd of prostitutes who plied their trade inside and outside. The women had a lot of business and guarded their patch well. Strange faces who were seen to be soliciting soon found themselves roughly thrown out of the pub with a warning of what they could expect if they had the temerity to show up in the area again.

The group of publicans who called themselves the Bermondsey Beer Boys saw the Crown as an ideal site for their first meeting. The merchant seamen had money in their pockets and could be relied upon to lay fair-size bets on the fights, with due encouragement and prompting from the prostitutes who had a special arrangement with Fat Donald McBain the landlord. The Crown also had a large back yard with a bolt-hole, a back gate opening on to a riverside alley that led to a warren of backstreets.

The Bermondsey Beer Boys were careful to keep the tournament a secret from the general public. Only their most well-known and trusted customers were invited, along with street bookmakers who paid for the privilege. Each of the publicans had his own fighter and put up the stake money on him as well as making side bets. Certain trusted outsiders were allowed to bring along their own fighters and supporters providing they staked the fighter and were responsible for the behaviour of the camp followers. The Bermondsey Beer Boys insisted that the rules must be enforced, for if the police or the breweries got to hear of what was taking place in the pubs, the landlords concerned would most definitely lose their licences.

The contests were scheduled to go for twenty rounds with a knock-down counting as the end of the round, as in the bare-knuckle fairground fights. The contestants would wear standard-size gloves that were little better than ordinary leather gloves. The padding was minimal, and the facial scars and cauliflower ears on some of the older fighters testified to the damage they caused.

The marquee that had been hastily erected in the back yard of the Crown and lit with Tilley lamps was filling with excited spectators. There was a ring in the middle of the covered area and the floor of the roped arena was strewn with sawdust. People were crowding on to the benches that were placed around the ring, and at the back of the marquee the street bookmakers stood chewing on cigars and passing out betting-slips.

There was a sudden hush as the fighters emerged from the changing-room behind the saloon bar and marched into the marquee. Each had a blanket draped round his shoulders. As Jake Mitchell ducked under the ropes for his contest there was complete silence, but when his opponent got into the ring loud clapping broke out.

George Galloway stood beside Jake, leaning on the ropes and eyeing the other fighter closely. 'Now remember what I said, Jake. 'E comes in like a bull so watch 'is barnet. 'E's young an' full of 'imself so be careful, an' don't let the crowd see yer use yer thumbs. It looks like some of 'em 'ave taken a shine ter the boy.'

'I gathered that much,' Jake growled, banging his clenched fists together and glaring over at his young opponent.

Don McBain ducked under the ropes to perform the ceremonies and Galloway looked around the ring, nodding to acquaintances and nervously chewing on his fat cigar. Mitchell was introduced as 'Battling Jake Mitchell from the East End' amidst a few boos and cat-calls. The young Scottish fighter whom McBain had brought down from the Glasgow Gorbals was presented simply as 'Jock McIver' and the announcement brought forth loud cheers and clapping. Galloway had learned about the Scot from McBain, who had bragged about his man and described his technique when the two of them were drinking together. Galloway felt that the young fighter was ideal fodder for the rougher and more experienced Jake, and had made a few sizeable bets on his man at fair odds.

The marquee was becoming filled with smoke and the noise died down as the crowd waited for battle to begin. An impatient timekeeper sitting at a small table beside the ring rang a handbell to start the fight and the two contestants moved confidently out of their corners.

As Galloway had predicted the young fighter rushed Mitchell, his fists flailing. The older fighter took most of the blows on his arms but one sharp jab caught him on the nose and as he jerked back blood started to trickle down on to his chin. Mitchell was undaunted. He moved into the centre of the ring and stood his ground as the younger man charged in again with his head held low. He could hear the crowd willing the Scot on, and as they clinched moved his left arm under his opponent's head. Mitchell had fought in boxing booths around the country and knew that the boy was little more than a novice, strong and brave perhaps but unprepared for his devious tactics. He brought his hand up sharply and with his thumb prodded the young Scot in the eye, his foul play shielded from the crowd by the man's lowered head.

They parted and moved around in the middle of the ring and Mitchell could see his opponent blinking his right eye as he tried to clear his sight. The tactic had worked and Mitchell felt confident, since his left hook was his best punch and it would be coming from the Scot's blind side. As the young man rushed him again, Jake looped his left fist round. His opponent did not see it until it landed hard on his temple. He staggered slightly and shook his head, holding his hand close to his face as he prepared to come forward again. His raw courage was his undoing. Instead of keeping out of reach until his head had cleared, the Scot charged in again and Mitchell caught him with another looping left hand that sank him to his knees. The crowd were disappointed as the young man was half dragged back to his corner, and Jake Mitchell grinned cheekily to the booing punters.

As the contest went on the young man's spirit and endurance began to wear down against Mitchell's experience and his face was becoming bloody. His eyes were swollen, blood was dripping from his nose and his lips were split. He managed to stay on his feet for the duration of each round until the fifth, when he was caught by a swingeing blow and dropped like a stone. Mitchell felt sure that the young man was finished, but to his astonishment he climbed painfully to his feet and staggered to his corner.

When the Scot came back out he seemed to have gained a second wind, bobbing and weaving his way out of trouble until the bell ended the round. Galloway was becoming worried. He had wagered heavily on his fighter and he could see that Mitchell was tiring. He had never had to go the whole twenty rounds, and it seemed that unless he could despatch his man in the next round or two, youth and stamina would beat him.

The betting was changing now. The odds were lengthening, and with the outcome of the fight still unsure Galloway laid down another bet. It was all or nothing now. He realised that he stood to lose a lot of money unless his fighter pulled something out of the hat. The appointed second was working hard on Mitchell, dousing him with water and whispering words of advice in his ear, and when the timekeeper reached for his bell to start the next round Galloway bit through his unlighted cigar.

The men traded punches in the middle of the ring and Mitchell was gasping for breath. The young Scot tried to keep his opponent on his left side, and the crowd were cheering every blow that he landed. Suddenly they were in a clinch. Mitchell used his thumb again, bringing it up sharply and stabbing his opponent in the left eye. As they broke apart Mitchell knew that he had his man now. The youngster was blinking and moving his head from left to right, trying to focus his eyes. Mitchell gathered his flagging strength and moved in, swinging a flurry of left and right hooks in a desperate frenzy. A hard left swipe caught the Scot on the point of his chin and he went down and rolled over on to his face. Jake had felt the jar right up to his shoulder, and knew instinctively that the young man's fight was over. He was dragged to his corner still unconscious, and when the bell rang to start the twelfth round a towel was thrown into the centre of the ring. There was barely any applause as Mitchell ducked under the ropes and with a blanket draped around his heaving shoulders walked wearily out of the marquee, without glancing back at his defeated opponent.

Throughout the summer of 1913 the suffragette movement continued to attract attention with large marches and gatherings, and more of the women's leaders were arrested and imprisoned. The newspapers carried stories of hunger strikes by the women prisoners, and the accounts of their force-feeding inflamed the passions of their supporters even more. One of their leaders who had suffered the torture, Emily Davison, threw herself in front of the King's horse during the Derby and died a few days later in hospital. When her funeral took place the West End streets were lined with women followers, many of them factory girls from the backstreets of London.

Carrie wanted to join the mourners along the route but decided against it. She was ashamed at letting her allegiance falter and felt it would be hypocritical to attend. Her two ex-workmates from the leather factory went along, Jessica defying her future husband's wishes and Freda holding her young baby in her arms. Mary Caldwell was given the honour of acting as representative for working-class women, and along with the other representatives, she walked beside the cortège, dressed in white and wearing a wide black sash.

Carrie had been growing steadily more depressed as the summer months wore on. Her dreams and hopes for the future seemed to be slowly dying as Tommy was compelled to spend more and more time caring for his ageing mother. There had been occasions when she and Tommy had gone back to his house and she had wanted him to make love to her but he had resisted her importunings. Carrie could see that he was not relaxed and was always waiting for his mother's inevitable call, and felt a mixture of pity and anger towards him. It was wrong for a young man to be burdened so, she thought, but wished he could be more firm and less willing to hurry at his mother's every whim. She was using him, denying him a life of his own, and Carrie found herself arguing constantly with Tommy about what it was doing to their relationship. He invariably became sullen with her and had told her on more than one occasion that his mother would always have to come first. It could go on like this for years, she thought, and things would not improve as long as he allowed himself to be manipulated by the old lady. She was taking advantage of her son's gentle, caring nature and it angered Carrie and made her sad to see the change in him. It had been his happy-go-lucky nature and his considerate attitude towards her which had first endeared him to her. He was so different from Billy Sullivan, who had proved to be self-centred and interested in only one thing, apart from boxing. Tommy had made her feel good and made her laugh a lot, but now he had grown morose and hard to talk to.

It was very hard for the young man, she had to admit. He was being pulled in two different directions. Carrie had agonised about breaking off their relationship, wondering whether it would perhaps be better for everyone concerned if they parted. Even on the rare occasions when they went to bed, Tommy had been nervous and unable to satisfy her. It was as though he was terrified of making her pregnant, and when she became excited and aroused he did not respond in the way she wanted him to and she ended up feeling terribly alone.

Carrie was in low spirits as she walked to work on Monday morning, unable to quell the troubled thoughts tumbling around in her mind. As she neared the dining rooms she could see the horse carts parked outside, the animals munching from their nosebags while the carmen chatted together. A group of dockers were standing outside the shop and one grinned at her as she approached.

'C'mon, Carrie, poor ole Fred's run orf 'is feet in there,' he joked.

Normally she would have been quick with an answer but on this particular morning Carrie ignored the comment and hurried inside. Fred Bradley bade her good morning as she slipped off her coat and put on her clean apron, and his eyes fixed on her enquiringly as she mumbled a reply. Instantly regretting her sullenness she gave him a wan smile and got on with her chores. There was little time to dwell on things as she served endless cups of tea and waited on tables, and for most of the morning Fred was hard put to it in the kitchen to keep up with the orders for bacon sandwiches and toasted teacakes. The regular carmen and dockers joked with Carrie as they came and went, and when Sharkey Morris came in he managed to bring a smile to her face with his account of Soapy Symonds' latest exploit.

'Yer'd never credit it, Carrie,' he began. 'Soapy took this load of 'ops ter the brewery last Friday an' yer know what 'e's like where there's a chance of a drink. Anyway, Soapy gets 'is ticket fer a free pint an' when 'e goes ter the tap room 'e finds out that the bloke what's servin' the beer is an ole mate of 'is. One pint leads ter anuvver an' by the time 'e's finished Soapy's three-parts pissed. From what we can make out 'e must 'ave fell asleep on the way back an' the 'orse decided it'd bring 'im 'ome. Trouble was, the nag took one o' the little turnin's too sharp an' the back wheel caught one o' them iron posts they 'ave on the street corners. Over the top Soapy goes an' lands on 'is 'ead in the kerb. Out like a light 'e was. When this copper comes up, 'e calls a doctor from nearby who must 'ave bin pissed 'imself 'cos 'e said Soapy was dead. Anyway, they cart 'im orf ter the mortuary an' leave 'im on the slab wiv a sheet over 'im while they send fer the pathological bloke. Meanwhile, Soapy comes to an' sits up. 'E told us the first fing 'e remembered was 'earin' an awful scream. It must 'ave bin the mortuary attendant. 'E's pissed orf an' nobody can find 'im. Poor sod must 'ave bin frightened out of 'is wits seein' Soapy sit up under that sheet.'

Carrie could not help bursting out laughing at Sharkey's tale, and for the rest of the day kept herself busy and tried to forget her depression.

It was as she was preparing to leave that Fred called her into the back room.

'I 'ope yer don't fink I'm pryin', Carrie, but yer seemed a bit upset terday,' he said, looking at her closely.

She shrugged her shoulders. She wanted to tell Fred about her emotional problems, he seemed genuinely concerned, but instead she smiled briefly and decided it was too personal. 'It's nuffink, Fred,' she said quickly. 'It's jus' bin one o' them days.'

He nodded and looked down at his feet as he struggled for words. 'If there's anyfink I can do, anyfink at all,' he continued with an earnest tone to his voice.

Carrie shook her head. 'Franks fer yer concern, Fred, but it's nuffink really,' she replied.

'Like I said, I don't wanna pry,' he went on, looking up at her, 'but lately yer've not bin yerself an' I thought there might be somefing wrong. If yer don't wanna talk about it that's all right, but if yer ever feel the need I'm always willin' ter listen. Yer see, Carrie, I fink a lot of yer. I'm not very good wiv words, but what I'm trying' ter say is, if yer ever need a friend, somebody ter confide in, I'm 'ere.'

Carrie saw the strange, distant look in his eyes and felt a sudden shock as she realised. Fred was in love with her! There was no mistaking his expression, nor the feeling in his measured words. She searched his face as if looking for a way out and saw that he was flushing with embarrassment as he averted his gaze.

'I'll remember that, Fred,' she answered softly, giving him a warm smile.

'I've never 'ad much ter do wiv young ladies, it's always bin the business,' he went on haltingly. 'I s'pose I missed out when I was younger, but it don't stop me 'avin' feelin's. I feel a lot fer yer, Carrie, an' if yer ever get ter finkin' likewise I'd be proud ter walk out wiv yer.'

'Yer a nice man, Fred,' she told him. 'I won't ferget what yer said. I like yer a lot, but love ain't the same as likin' somebody.'

'I realise that,' he said, looking down at his feet again. 'P'raps yer could learn ter love me, given time? I won't 'arp on it an' I promise I won't pester yer, but jus' remember, love can grow on somebody. I'd marry yer termorrer if yer'd 'ave me, an' yer'd never regret it. I'd look after yer an' care fer yer.'

She reached out and touched his arm in a spontaneous gesture. 'I know that, Fred. I'll keep it in mind what yer said, I promise.'

He smiled awkwardly as she walked to the door. 'Mind 'ow yer go 'ome,' he called out.

Carrie left the café with her head spinning. Fred was older than her and set in his ways, and it must have taken a great deal of resolve to declare his love for her. She admired him for that. She knew she should feel flattered at the compliment, but it left her with a strange feeling in the pit of her stomach.

*

The long summer days encouraged everyone out, and the women of Page Street stood on their clean doorsteps after their chores were done and enjoyed a good chat together. All the business of the little turning was aired, and heads nodded eagerly as another choice piece of gossip spread from door to door.

'Don't say I told yer but Florrie Axford's took a lodger in,' Maisie Dougall said in little more than a whisper.

Aggie Temple's eyes opened wide at the revelation. 'Good Gawd! After all she said about 'avin' anuvver man in the 'ouse,' she gasped.

'Well, I'm not sayin' there's anything in it, mind,' Maisie replied quickly. 'She's got them two spare rooms upstairs, an' what wiv the rent goin' up as well . . .'

'What's 'e like?' Aggie asked.

''E's a nice-lookin' bloke. About twenty-four or twenty-five, I s'pose,' Maisie went on. ''E's got luvverly curly 'air an' 'e's very smart. I see 'im goin' in yesterday. Smashin' blue pin-stripe suit 'e 'ad on. I could see 'is shoes were polished an' 'e 'ad a collar an' tie on. Bit different from the blokes round 'ere.'

'What about Florrie?'

'What about 'er?'

'Well, did she say anyfing ter yer?' Aggie asked impatiently.

Maisie shook her head. 'Yer know Flo, she don't let 'er right 'and know what 'er left 'and's doin' 'alf the time. Mind yer, she was sayin' somefing about lettin' those upstairs rooms a few weeks ago. I assumed she was talkin' about a married couple. I didn't fink she'd take a young bloke in. It's bound ter start 'em all gossipin', yer know what they're like round 'ere.'

'Don't I!' Aggie replied, pressing her hand against her

pinned-up hair. 'Remember that time my 'Arold was seen 'oldin' that woman round the waist in River Street? They all reckoned 'e was 'avin' it orf wiv 'er. Poor cow fainted right under the streetlamp an' my 'Arold was 'elpin' 'er 'ome. 'E told me 'imself 'e took 'er in an' made 'er a nice cup o' tea. It jus' shows yer what lies people fink up. Jus' 'cos 'e was seen goin' in 'er 'ouse. My 'Arold wouldn't do anyfink like that, after all the years we've bin tergevver.'

Maisie nodded, although the story she had heard of Harold Temple's adventure was a little different from Aggie's version. ''Course 'e wouldn't,' she said. 'Mind yer, it's always a bit awkward when a woman on 'er own takes in a young man as a lodger, especially a nice-lookin' bloke. Tongues will wag.'

'Fing is, Florrie's got a bit of a name wiv the men,' Aggie remarked. 'She's bin married twice, an' there was that bloke at the shop where she works.'

'Oh, an' what was that all about then?' Maisie asked, her curiosity aroused.

'Didn't yer 'ear of it?' Aggie said with surprise. 'It was all round the street. Florrie was s'posed ter be 'avin' it orf wiv Willie Lubeck, the bloke who 'ad the butcher's before ole Greenbaum took it over. Yer remember ole Lubeck. 'E 'ad a cropped 'ead an' a big moustache. Proper German 'e was.'

'Greenbaum's a German too, ain't 'e?' Maisie asked, folding her tubby arms over her clean apron.

'Yeah, 'e's a German Jew by all accounts,' Aggie informed her. 'I like 'is faggots an' pease-pudden better than when the ovver bloke 'ad the shop. Mind yer, ole Lubeck used ter sell some nice 'alf sheep's 'eads. We often used ter 'ave sheep's 'eads on Saturday nights fer our tea.'

Maisie nodded. 'I like them skate's eyeballs. They go down well wiv a dob o' marge. Mind yer, yer gotta be careful yer don't over boil 'em or they go all gristly.'

Maudie Mycroft was walking along the street. When she reached her two neighbours she put down her shopping-bag and pressed a hand against her side. 'Me kidney's bin playin' me up again,' she announced, feeling in need of a little sympathy. 'Always seems ter be worse in the summer. My Ernest said I should go in an' 'ave it done but I'm terrified of 'ospitals.'

'What is it, Maud, stones?' Maisie enquired.

Maudie nodded. 'I've 'ad 'em fer years.'

Aggie pulled a face. 'Nellie Tanner was tellin' me once 'er Will 'elped the vet bloke operate on one o' the 'orses fer a stone. Large as a cannonball it was, and all colours o' the rainbow. She said 'er ole man pickled it. I don't know if she's still got it but it used ter be on 'er mantelshelf. I ain't seen it when I've bin in there though, not lately.'

Maudie turned pale. 'Well, I'd better get orf in,' she said quickly, wondering what colour her stones might be.

The two watched her walk off along the street and Maisie turned to her friend. 'Funny woman she is, Aggie. Frightened of everyfing. D'yer remember when we all come out an' stopped ole Galloway exercisin' them 'orses? She was terrified we was all gonna get locked up.'

Aggie nodded. 'I don't fink she was scared fer 'erself, though. She was more concerned about what the muvvers' meetin' was gonna say, accordin' ter 'er Ernest.'

'She don't still go ter them meetin's, does she?' Maisie asked. 'I thought she packed it in when they caught the vicar wiv 'is 'and in the collection-box.'

'Nah. Maudie's got a crush on the new vicar,' Aggie informed her. 'She reckons the sun shines out of 'is arse.'

'Mind yer, I've seen 'im about,' Maisie said. ''E's not a bad-lookin' bloke, as vicars go. Not my sort though. I like 'em when they look like that new lodger o' Flo's.'

'I wonder if Florrie's lodger comes from round 'ere?' Aggie asked, wanting to get all the facts straight in her mind before she told Mrs Bromsgrove.

'I dunno,' Maisie replied. 'The face is familiar. I fink I've seen 'im wiv that crowd o' jack-the-lads who stand outside the Crown at Dock'ead on Saturday nights. Rough 'ole that is.'

Aggie nodded and looked along the street quickly before turning back to her friend. 'My 'Arold gets ter know fings, 'im lightin' all the lamps round 'ere,' she said in a low voice. ''E reckons they've started 'avin' them there fights at the Crown again.'

Maisie did not show any surprise as she scratched away at her elbow. 'I 'eard the same,' she said. 'Flo told me, though Gawd knows where she got it from. She reckons that Jake Mitchell 'ad a fight there an' 'e nearly killed the ovver bloke.'

'What, that ugly-lookin' carman who works fer Galloway? 'Im wiv the flat nose an' cauliflower ear?' her friend queried.

'That's 'im.'

'Well, if we stand 'ere much longer we're gonna get the name o' gossip-mongers,' Aggie remarked as she straightened her apron.

Maisie chuckled as she stepped back into her passageway. 'Mind 'ow yer go, Aggie, an' if I 'ear any more about you know who, I'll let yer know . . .'

1914

1914

Chapter Twenty-six

On 4th August 1914, the country was plunged into war.

'Once we get our soldiers out there it'll all be over in no time. I give it six months at the outside,' Alec Crossley the landlord of Page Street's little corner pub told his customers.

Harold Temple and Ernest Mycroft were sitting together with Fred Dougall and Daniel Sullivan around a table and they all nodded agreement. William Tanner was leaning against the counter next to Joe Maitland, Florrie Axford's lodger. He looked across at the group.

'I dunno so much,' he said pensively. 'If yer bin readin' the papers, yer'd see it's not that simple. Everybody's arguin' wiv everybody else. Accordin' ter what I've bin readin', all the countries 'ave signed pacts wiv each over an' it's a stone certainty they'll all be drawn inter the fight. I don't fink it's gonna be that easy. This war could go on fer years.'

Alec Crossley chuckled. 'Well, one fing yer can be sure of – there won't be a lack o' volunteers, what wiv all them poor bleeders who's scratchin' fer work. They'll be only too glad ter sign on. At least they'll get a bit o' food in their bellies.'

The landlord of the Kings Arms had prophesied correctly, for within days of the outbreak of war the recruiting offices around London were beleaguered by young men eager to get into the battle before it was all over. Recruiting sergeants were hard put to it to keep order. They smiled with benign tolerance at the volunteers and twiddled their waxed moustaches as they formed the jostling young men into single lines. 'Don't push an' shove, lads. Yer'll all get yer chance ter fight fer King an' Country. That's right, sign 'ere, lad. Well, all right then, jus' put yer mark alongside 'ere. No, I'm sorry, we can't give yer a rifle straight away. There's a medical ter go frew first.'

So it went on. The lines swelled with eager, bold and brash youngsters, and men who were not so young but still keen to get their names on the list. Many stood in line with disablements that would prevent their being allowed to don a uniform, but they stood with their fellows anyway. A man with one eye argued with the recruiting sergeant that he had all he needed to sight a rifle, and another man with a club foot told the sergeant that he could outwalk most of his pals any day. Men afflicted with coughs that wracked their thin bodies lined up with beefy men whose shirtsleeves were rolled up high on their arms. Men with trades, blacksmiths, wheelwrights and engineers, shuffled along behind men with no trade who had spent their adult lives in unskilled factory work or on the roads as labourers. Dockers stood beside clerks and shopworkers, stevedores rubbed shoulders with carmen, everyone laughing and elated now that their humdrum lives were suddenly being transformed.

'We'll be in France afore yer know it.'

'Wait till I tell my ole dutch. She'll be glad ter see the back o' me, that's fer sure.'

'I've got five Gawd-ferbids an' anuvver on the way, an' I ain't seen a day's work fer two months. She'll get a few bob from the army now.'

All day long the lines slowly moved forward and more men

arrived to volunteer. Those who had signed left the noise and excitement to break the news to their loved ones, and many began to question what they had done as they found themselves suddenly alone walking home through the backstreets.

The early days of the war were filled with a strange carnival. Military bands marched through the streets and along the main thoroughfares, and behind them came the volunteers. They were a motley crowd of men. While some were comparatively well dressed, others were in ragged clothing. Men prematurely bowed from years of toil walked alongside proud upright youngsters who threw out their chests and swaggered to the cheers of the folk who lined the pavements. The bands marched along to the recruiting offices with blaring brass and beating drums, and along the way men joined the procession, some pulling against restraining hands and disregarding crying children. Old women dabbed at their eyes as they stood at the roadside, and old men who had seen action in the Boer War and in the North-West Frontier troubles sucked on their clay pipes and shook their heads sadly.

'They're like a load o' bleedin' pied pipers,' one old man remarked, nodding towards the bandsmen.

'It's no 'ardship now, but wait till the music stops an' the shootin' starts, then Gawd 'elp 'em,' another said bitterly.

The early days of the war were an anxious time for Nellie and William Tanner. Their three boys were old enough to enlist and James had announced that he was going to volunteer shortly. Charlie too had indicated that he wanted to join up along with all the other young men at his office, but Danny was not so impatient to put on a uniform. His life was centred around his boxing and he felt that joining up might lose him the chance of fighting in the club championships. Carrie was very worried with the likelihood of her three brothers going off to fight. She loved them all dearly and the thought of their coming to harm caused her many sleepless nights. It seemed to her that life was becoming more and more cruel. She was still walking out with Tommy, but things had not improved during the past year. The old lady was making her usual demands on her son and her drinking had got worse, while the war had made Tommy more sullen than ever, as he knew that he was not in a position to volunteer.

Carrie was feeling worried as she sat talking to her parents one evening when the boys were all out of the house.

'D'yer fink they'll all volunteer, Mum?' she asked. 'They're all so young ter be soldiers.'

Nellie was near to tears as she sat beside the unlit grate with her sewing lying untouched on her lap. 'I don't see as we can stop 'em,' she said sadly. 'Me an' yer farvver 'ave tried ter talk 'em out of it, but all their friends are joinin' up. It's only natural they wanna do the same.'

William sat staring into the grate. 'Danny might not go,' he said, 'at least not yet. As far as the ovver two are concerned, I reckon they'll go soon. Charlie said 'is pals are all signin' on this week an' Jim told me most o' the young blokes at 'is factory 'ave already left. There's nuffink we can do, Carrie, nuffink at all. All we can 'ope for is that it's soon over.'

'D'yer fink it'll last long, luv?' Nellie asked him.

'I don't fink so,' he lied. 'Once the army gets over there, it'll all be sorted out.'

'I've 'eard that women can volunteer as nurses,' Carrie said, looking down at her clasped hands thoughtfully.

'Yer can put that idea out of yer 'ead soon as yer like,' her mother said firmly. 'It's bad enough 'avin' the boys all goin' off, wivout you as well. I'll be in a loony-bin before long wiv all this worry.'

William put a comforting arm around Nellie and she

leaned her head against his shoulder as her tears started to flow. Carrie slipped into the scullery and put the kettle on to boil. She was making the tea when Danny came in.

'Billy Sullivan's volunteered, Carrie!' he said excitedly.

She looked at her brother as he stood in the doorway and sighed sadly. He was still only a boy, she told herself. His short fair hair was dishevelled and fell forward over his forehead. His eyes were enquiring, like those of a young child, and apart from a few hairs around his chin his face was still smooth.

'I 'ope you're not finkin' o' followin' 'is example?' she questioned him anxiously. 'It's bad enough Jimmy an' Charlie wantin' ter go, without you startin' too. Somebody's gotta stop at 'ome, Danny.'

'It all depends,' he said in an offhand manner. 'I might. It all depends what 'appens at the club.'

Carrie sighed irritably. 'Oh, I see. If yer don't get the chance of knockin' somebody's 'ead off, yer'll join up. That's charmin', that is.'

Danny frowned. 'Don't keep on at me, Sis. It's bad enough Mum an' Dad goin' on about me stoppin' at 'ome. Everybody's joinin' up. Why should I miss out on it?'

'D'yer fink it's gonna be all nice an' friendly?' Carrie snapped at him. 'Yer could get killed or badly wounded. Would yer like ter spend the rest o' yer days in a wheelchair or lyin' on yer back paralysed or somefink?'

He mumbled an answer and his saucy face broke into a grin. 'All right, Carrie, I promise yer I'll fink about it,' he said quietly. 'I'll see what me bruvs do before I make me mind up. Jim's gonna go fer sure, but I dunno about Charlie. Yer never know what 'e's gonna do.'

Carrie smiled as she reached out and hugged him to her, and Danny patted her back gently. 'It'll all turn out right in the end, you'll see,' he reassured her.

*

Across the River Thames in Ilford another conversation about the war was taking place. Frank Galloway lounged across the bed and watched Bella as she applied a touch of dampened soot to her long eyelashes.

'It won't last long, will it, darling?' she asked him. 'I couldn't bear it if it dragged on into one of those awful wars.'

'All wars are awful, Bella,' he told her, thinking that she wouldn't have much choice but to bear it. 'There's no pretty war. But no, I don't think it'll go on too long.'

She looked at him in the mirror of her dressing-table and smiled sweetly. 'I do hope so. Look, darling, you really don't mind my going, do you? If you do, just say so and I'll stay in. I'm sure it'll be one of those terribly boring parties with everyone just gushing compliments and saying how much they adore each other. It's so false. I know you don't like these theatrical get-togethers, that's why I asked if Hubert would escort me. He's a silly billy really but at least I can rely on him not to go off and abandon me. I get so nervous when I'm left stranded at those functions.'

Frank bit back a caustic remark and smiled at her. 'You go and enjoy yourself. I've got some work to do anyway,' he told her, but inside he was seething. As far as he could remember he had never told her he didn't like theatrical parties. In fact, he enjoyed the back chat, and the wine and champagne that were always in plentiful supply. And as for Bella being nervous of managing alone – well, he doubted whether she had ever been nervous in her entire life. She loved the compliments that flowed in her direction, and especially the attention Hubert danced on her. Frank felt he could easily find a more suitable way of describing him than 'silly billy'. The young man was madly in love with Bella, and it was only the fact that she treated him as a boy which prevented her husband from punching the silly billy on the nose.

Bella finished applying rouge to her face and studied the impression. 'You've been looking tired lately, darling,' she said in a soothing voice. 'Don't wait up, there's a dear.'

Frank made to kiss her but she backed away. 'Mind my face, Frank. It's taken me ages to get ready.'

The clock beside the bed showed ten minutes past eight and Bella became anxious. Hubert had promised he wouldn't be late. He was so unreliable, she thought, pouting, so unlike dependable Frank. But how much better in bed! Frank was manly, rough with her, and totally selfish. He had no conception of her needs. Hubert was different. He was a sweet boy who acted like a feckless clown but dominated her between the sheets. He was slim, almost girlish, with long thin legs and narrow arms. His hairless body was lithe and reminded her of an uncoiled snake. He was the best lover she had known. If only he had Frank's dependability, she rued. But then, if he did, he wouldn't be Hubert, she thought with a smile, the silly billy she wanted to slip away early with to return to his flat in Bloomsbury.

Bella heard the motor car pull up outside and a light knock on the front door. 'The boy's late as usual,' she said with a sigh. 'He can be so annoying at times. You go to bed early, darling. Promise?'

Frank watched from the window as she stepped into the Daimler, then he walked over to the sideboard and picked up the bottle of brandy. He heard the roar of the car pulling away as he gulped down a large measure of the spirit and sat down dejectedly in a soft armchair. He seemed to be having very little social life lately, and now the war had started most of his colleagues at work had left. Bernard Roseman had become a lieutenant in the London Rifles and Paddy Burns was now up in Scotland doing his training. Then there was Violet Ashley. She had left her desk, and the last he heard was off to France with the field ambulance. Dear Vi – she was as discreet as she was free with her favours. Frank's face creased into a grin as he recalled the time she had told him about her and Bernard Roseman. He was the first Jewish lad she had had. Frank remembered how good it made him feel when Vi told him he was the best lover she had ever known. Paddy was always the worse for drink and he made a song and dance of it, she had said. As for young Arnold Robins, the lad got so flustered when he couldn't untie his shoelace that he jumped into bed with the shoe still on! Vi had quickly put his mind at rest by telling him that she wouldn't discuss him with any of her other lovers. He was the best, she told him, and thus he had the privilege of knowing all about his rivals' prowess in her bed.

Frank raised his glass to Violet Ashley and wished her well, wherever she was. As for him, he would try to stay out of the war as long as he could. Johnson wanted him to stay on, now that the company had been deprived of its most experienced staff. The old man could certainly get him excused if it came to compulsory enlistment. He would just have to wait and see, he thought as he poured himself another stiff drink.

Geoffrey Galloway pushed back the last of the ledgers and pressed his thumb and forefinger to his throbbing temples. He was alone in the office and could hear the muted sound of children playing in the street outside. The war had not touched the business as yet, he thought, but it was still early days. Unlike some of the local cartage concerns, the firm still employed carmen on a casual basis and there were always men looking for work. As for the contracts themselves, Geoffrey envisaged an upsurge in dock work now that there was a large army which had to be supplied and fed. The local food factories would be extending their contracts too and he saw business increasing.

The thumping in his head started to ease and Geoffrey stretched out in his chair and thought about his own position. Lately the old man had pushed more work on to him and he had had to make more day to day decisions, as well as taking care of the ledgers. Will Tanner was a good yard manager, and as far as the men went he took a lot of pressure off Geoffrey, but to sit out the war by working in the business was something he felt he could not face. Time was slipping by and things were developing fast. His long-standing affair with Mary O'Reilly was the one bright thing in his life, but he was determined that even that could not be allowed to influence him. He had to take the decision soon, however upset his father might be. Maybe Frank could take over? He was married now and might be less inclined to volunteer. Geoffrey thought about talking it over with his father but quickly put the idea out of his mind. He knew that he would end up arguing with the old man and be made to feel selfish and inconsiderate. No, he decided, he would volunteer first and face his father's wrath later.

Outside the yard, in the Tanners' house, Nellie was sitting with Florrie and Maisie discussing the war, and her face had a worried look as she sipped her tea.

'My Jim's volunteered and Charlie's gonna foller 'im soon,' she told her friends.

Maisie shook her head and stared down at her cup.

'My two boys are goin',' she said. 'My Fred tried ter talk 'em out of it but they just laughed at 'im. It's a bleedin' worry. There's Sadie Sullivan worried out of 'er life, too. Billy's done it, an' the rest of 'em are all talkin' about goin' as well. Michael an' John are old enough ter go an' she's worried about young Joe. 'E's seventeen now.'

Florrie put down her cup and pulled out her silver snuff-box. 'That lodger o'mine come in drunk last night,' she said, tapping her fingers on the lid. 'Apparently 'e got turned down at the medical. Somefing about 'is ears. Right upset 'e was. I told 'im straight 'e should fink 'imself lucky. I dunno what them men must be finkin' about. They seem bloody keen ter get inter the war.'

Maisie nodded. 'My Fred told me 'e'd go if 'e was younger. I said over my dead body 'e would, an' 'e jus' laughed. "I'd do that an' all," 'e said.'

'Mrs Bromsgrove's ole man volunteered by all accounts,' Florrie told them. ''E got turned down as well.'

'I should fink so too,' Maisie said indignantly. ''E must be all of fifty if 'e's a day. 'E's got that wonky leg as well.'

Nellie reached for the teapot. 'Accordin' ter the papers there's fousands o' youngsters givin' wrong ages. Some are only sixteen, still wet be'ind the ears. Gawd 'elp us, what's it all comin' to?'

Maisie took a refilled cup from Nellie. 'I was readin' in the papers there's fightin' goin' on in France already,' she said. 'Mons, I fink the place was. The news didn't seem too good. It said they was retreatin'. Trouble is, yer never get the trufe. Gawd knows what is really goin' on out there.'

Nellie felt the conversation was getting too depressing and she looked across at Florrie. 'What's that lodger o' yours do for a livin', Flo?' she asked quickly.

''E's still a bit of a mystery ter me. 'E goes out in the mornin' an' I don't see 'im till late in the evenin'. I get 'im 'is tea an' sometimes 'e's orf out again or 'e goes up in 'is room. Whenever I ask 'im what 'is job is, 'e jus' tells me 'e's in buyin' an' sellin'. That's all I ever get out of 'im. Mind yer, I'm not one ter pry, an' if 'e don't wanna tell me that's up to 'im.'

''E's a smart-lookin' bloke,' Maisie said, glancing quickly

at Nellie. 'I'm surprised I 'aven't 'eard the neighbours talkin', Flo. Yer know what they're like.'

'I couldn't give a monkey's,' Florrie replied quickly. 'I'm almost old enough ter be 'is bleedin' granny. Mind yer though, there's many a good tune played on an old fiddle,' she added, laughing.

The women sipped their tea in silence for a while, wrapped up in their thoughts, and then Maisie turned to Nellie Tanner. ''Ere, 'ow's your Carrie gettin' on wiv 'er young man, Nell?' she asked.

'I dunno,' Nellie sighed. 'That gel's worryin' me. Tommy's a nice enough bloke but I can't see anyfing comin' of it. 'Is ole muvver's a piss artist by all accounts, an' the poor sod's run orf 'is feet what wiv lookin' after 'er an' goin' ter work. 'Im an' Carrie don't go out much, an' when they do Carrie seems ter come back 'ere wiv the 'ump.'

'Bleedin' shame,' Maisie remarked. 'Is she still in wiv them there suffragettes?'

Nellie shook her head. 'Not since she's bin workin' at the café. She 'as ter go in on Saturdays, an' then there's this bloke.'

Maisie pursed her lips. 'I was readin' about that force-feedin' they're doin' in the prisons, an' there was somefink in the papers about this new law they've brought out. When the women are nearly starved ter death, they let 'em out ter get better then make 'em go back in again. Seems a bleedin' liberty, if yer ask me.'

'That's down ter that ole goat Asquith,' Florrie told them. ''E brought that law in. It's the Cat an' Mouse Act. They're tryin' ter get it stopped.'

'I should fink so too,' Nellie said forcefully. 'The way they treat those women is disgustin'. Carrie was tellin' me only the ovver night about some' o' the fings that go on. She said 'er friend who she used ter work wiv was arrested an' put in prison. She told Carrie they made 'em strip an' wash in cold water, an' when they won't eat the warders ram rubber tubes right down their gullets. Mus' be awful. That's what worried me about my gel, when she used ter go on those marches. I was worried sick till she got 'ome.'

'D'yer fink women will ever get the vote?' Maisie asked her friends.

Florrie looked at the other two and her eyes narrowed with conviction. 'It'll come as sure as night follers day,' she declared. 'What we gotta fink about is what we do wiv the vote when we get it. We've gotta be a lot more fussy when it comes ter puttin' people in power. If we don't start askin' questions an' tellin' 'em what it is we want instead of 'avin' 'em dictate to us, then we might just as well leave it ter the men, an' they've bin ballsin' it up fer donkeys' years.'

Later, as Nellie stood at her front door watching her two friends walk off along the turning, she heard the distant sound of a brass band. It slowly grew louder as it approached and the sound of a bass drum carried down from the main road. She could see them now, passing the end of the turning, uniformed bandsmen being followed by yet another batch of volunteers. It all seemed so unreal, she thought, almost like a carnival. How long would it be before they returned, if they ever did? How many of them would be crippled and scarred for life?

She closed the door quickly.

Chapter Twenty-seven

The first Yuletide of the war was a quiet one for Bermondsey folk, with many empty places around the tables. Most of the early volunteers were now fighting in France, and news from the front had been bad. The first casualty lists of troops involved in the Mons retreat and the Battle of Ypres were being published in the newspapers, and hospital ships had begun arriving from France and Belgium before Christmas. Stories of carnage in the mud and slime, and the horrors of sickness and frostbite suffered in the winter trenches, had started to temper the recruiting fervour, but young men still enlisted, roused and fired by tales of heroism and the chance to escape the hardships of their everyday lives. Men who had stood outside the dock gates and fought each other over a day's work turned their backs on Bermondsey and set off for France. Young lads in their early teens, sick of life in the factories, lied about their age and joined their elder brothers at the front. Posters were appearing on the streets now, bearing a picture of Lord Kitchener pointing his finger, and above the legend, 'Join Your Country's Army! God save the King' and, 'Your Country needs YOU'. Another message struck home to many who were undecided about joining up, asking the question,

'Be honest with yourself. Be certain that your so-called reason is not a selfish excuse.'

Thousands of young men who had volunteered in the first days of the war had been rejected on medical grounds, many of them underweight and suffering from industrial-related diseases, tuberculosis or chronic bronchitis. They returned to their jobs, often to be branded as cowards by those who did not know why they had been rejected. The white feather was adopted as a mark of cowardice, and sent anonymously through the post to men not in the services. Stories abounded of young men who took their own lives when they received the white feather after being rejected for military service. Many of the men who had not yet volunteered received the symbol of the craven and immediately enlisted.

Frank Galloway received his white feather in the morning post. When he opened the envelope and saw it, he felt the hot blood rushing to his face. It was like a kick to the stomach. It took him a few moments to collect himself. He sat back from his desk and looked around him. Everyone appeared preoccupied with their own affairs and no one had seemed to take an undue interest in him while he was opening his mail. It could be anyone, he thought as he put the letter into his coat pocket. It wouldn't have been sent to him by any of Bella's crowd, he felt sure of that at least. They all seemed to be against the war, and many of them were openly talking about refusing to enlist if it became compulsory. It could be someone from Page Street who had a down on the firm, he thought, or even one of the carmen who might have sent it out of sheer malice. The list of suspects could go on and on and there was no use dwelling on it, Frank decided. He promised himself that he would burn it when he got home as an act of defiance.

Later that day he was summoned to the managing director's office.

'I expect you'll be leaving us soon,' Abe Johnson said, brushing his hand over his clipped moustache.

'The army you mean, sir?'

'What else, Frank, unless it's the navy you've got your sights on?' Abe queried.

'To be honest, I haven't given it much consideration,' Frank replied, eyeing the elderly man who faced him across the huge leather-topped desk. 'I thought we were hard pressed now that Roseman and Burns have gone, as well as Miss Ashley?'

'Nonsense, lad. We'll bring back some of our old servants to fill the breach while you young men are off doing your bit for King and Country. Patriotism, lad. We must all make sacrifices,' Abe asserted, banging his fist down on the desk. 'Young Roseman's regiment is a good one, or maybe you'd prefer the King's Royal Rifles or the Rifle Brigade? They're first-class outfits. You should be able to get a commission in any one of them with your education, laddie. They're both East End regiments too. You come from the East End, don't you?'

'South London, sir,' Frank corrected him.

'Well, that's of no consequence. You go off and volunteer with our blessing. I'm sure we can fill your place for the duration.'

Frank left the inner sanctum feeling even more depressed than when he had entered. Stupid old fool must be losing his reasoning, he thought. The firm had already played its part. The business would end up being run by a lot of doddering old fossils who'd forgotten how to prepare accounts years ago. They'd probably be dying on the job all over the place. Well, he wouldn't be browbeaten into enlisting, he told himself. Abe Johnson could think what he liked.

Frank returned to his desk and sat for a while looking at a pile of papers he had not yet started work on. While he was lost in thought, Ginger Parry sauntered over. Ginger had been with the firm since its beginning and was now nearing retirement age.

'Trouble, Frank?' he asked. 'You look down in the dumps. The old boy hasn't upset you, has he?'

Frank gave him a brief smile. 'Not really. He asked me in to find out what my plans were.'

'About enlisting?'

Frank nodded. 'I thought he'd be only too glad to keep me here, but I thought wrong.'

Ginger grinned. 'I'm afraid you don't know the old man. He's from the old school. Both his sons are serving with the colours. Sandhurst and all that. His elder boy's a major, and if he survives this war he'll most likely be made up to staff officer. I don't think he'd mind too much if you enlisted tomorrow, Frank.'

George Galloway sat with William in the yard office, cradling a glass of whisky in his hand.

'It's gonna put a lot more work on all of us, Will,' he said. 'I'll 'ave ter take over the accounts meself now, until I see what young Frank's intendin' ter do. I'm 'opin' 'e's gonna agree ter take over from Geoff.'

William nodded. 'I s'pose yer expected yer lad ter volunteer, didn't yer, George? All the youngsters seem pretty keen ter get in the fight. My Jim an' Charlie are both goin' soon. I'm tryin' ter talk young Danny out o' goin' but I s'pose 'e'll join 'is bruvvers.'

Galloway took a swig from his glass and pulled a face. 'I s'pose if we were younger we'd be in it. Look at the scrapes we got in as kids. It's all a big adventure ter them, till they get up the front.'

William shrugged his shoulders. 'Well, I 'ope it's all over soon.'

'It'll drag on fer a few years, mark my words,' Galloway replied, emptying his glass. He stared down at his boots for a few moments in silence. 'I should fink we'll be gettin' busy, the way fings are. What about the 'orses? Any lame?'

William shook his head. 'They're all in good condition, except the Clydesdale. He's bin off colour fer a few days an' I'm restin' 'im in the small stable, just in case it's anyfink infectious. I don't fink it's anyfink ter worry about though.'

Galloway poured himself another drink and offered the bottle to his foreman. Normally William would have refused but today he took the bottle and poured himself a stiff draught. 'What about Jake Mitchell?' he asked suddenly. 'Is 'e volunteerin'?'

George laughed. 'Jake enlist? Yer jokin', ain't yer? He gets all the fightin' 'e wants in the ring, or 'e did until the war started. 'E was doin' well too. Four fights 'e 'ad an' they all ended pretty quick. We've run out of opponents, an' now all the young men 'ave joined up it's gonna be even 'arder ter get 'im a match. I was talkin' ter Don McBain the ovver evenin' an' 'e reckons they'll be forced ter pack it in till the war's over. It's a bloody shame really.'

William made no reply. He disliked Mitchell intensely, although he had to admit that the man had given him no reason to apart from the one time when he first came to work at the yard. He did his work well enough, and after the roasting he had received from Florrie Axford his driving had been faultless. It was his surly manner that William did not like, and the mocking look in his eye which barely veiled the violence and ruthlessness lurking just below the surface.

Galloway had settled down with the bottle of Scotch. William made his excuses and walked out into the yard. Jack Oxford was leaning on his broom, a vacant look on his long gaunt face, and beyond the gates William could see Florrie talking with Maisie in the morning sunshine and Sadie whitening her front doorstep. The country was at war and most of the young men had gone to fight in France but around him nothing seemed to have changed. At the end of the turning the knife-grinder was busy, his foot working the treadle as he bent his head over the revolving stone. Trams passed by in Jamaica Road and women came into the turning carrying shopping-baskets. Everything appeared to be calm and normal, he thought, but who could begin to imagine what was happening behind a multitude of closed street doors and drawn curtains now that the casualty lists were being made known?

Carrie left her house that evening and met Tommy at the street corner. He had asked her to go with him to the Star Music Hall and she took his arm as they crossed the main road and walked along towards Abbey Street. It was getting dark as they passed the Catholic church and they could hear the choir practising and the solemn notes of the church organ.

Tommy had been unusually quiet and as they turned into Abbey Street, he broke his silence.

'I've volunteered, Carrie,' he said suddenly.

She stopped and turned to face him. 'Yer've volunteered?! I don't believe it,' she cried.

He nodded and smiled sheepishly. 'I went an' signed on terday.'

'But what about yer muvver?' she asked incredulously.

'Me eldest bruvver's gonna take 'er ter live wiv 'im an' 'is wife,' he replied.

'I don't understand,' Carrie said, her brows knitting together. 'All this time yer've bin lookin' after yer mum 'cos none of yer family would, an' now yer tell me yer bruvver's gonna take 'er?'

Tommy looked down at his shoes. 'I went ter see Bob an' I

told 'im I'd enlisted. I told 'im I'd done my share of carin' fer the ole lady an' if 'e didn't take 'er she'd be left on 'er own an' end up in the work'ouse. We 'ad a few words but 'e finally agreed ter take 'er fer a month or two, an' then 'e's gonna get one o' the ovvers ter do their share.'

'But s'posin' Bob 'ad said no, would yer still have gone an' left 'er on 'er own?' Carrie asked him.

Tommy smiled. 'I volunteered after 'e said 'e'd take 'er. I wouldn't 'ave left the ole gel on 'er own if 'e'd said no.'

Carrie pulled away from him as he attempted to take her arm and walk on. 'But what about us?' she cried angrily. 'Yer could 'ave made some sort of arrangement like this ages ago. Yer know what it's bin doin' ter both of us. Yer couldn't do it fer us, but yer could do it so yer could go away an' fight. I jus' can't understand yer, Tommy.'

He looked into her eyes and saw tears welling up. 'I know yer don't, Carrie,' he began softly, 'an' I can't explain it really. But yer gotta try an' see it from my point o' view. It's bin 'ard copin' wiv the ole lady. I've 'ad ter put 'er in bed when she's bin too drunk ter make it up the stairs. I've 'ad ter pay the neighbours ter do the washin' an' ironin'. I've cooked the meals an' kept the place clean, on top o' goin' ter work, I might say. I managed though an' I never begrudged doin' it, but now the war's started I can't miss out on it. I've got ter be part of it. A woman can never be expected ter understand 'ow a man feels about these fings. It's just somefink inside me that tells me I mus' go, even though I might get killed or badly wounded.'

Carrie shook her head slowly, trying to understand the idiocy of it all. 'D'yer fink it's some sort o' game?' she asked, her voice rising. ''Aven't yer read about what's 'appenin' out in France wiv all them soldiers bein' killed or maimed? Christ Almighty! Yer mad, Tommy. I'll never understand yer. I never will, as long as I live.'

He could find no words to say that would calm her, no words to explain how he felt inside, and stood facing her helplessly as she backed away from him.

'We're finished!' she sobbed. 'I don't wanna see yer again, ever!'

Tommy reached his hands out to her but she turned away and hurried off, her footsteps echoing loudly in the dark street.

At the Galloway house in Tyburn Square Nora Flynn was sitting beside the kitchen fire with the evening edition of the *Star* lying in her lap. She had finished reading the latest news from the front and glanced up quickly as Josephine bounded into the room.

'I was just about ter start on that silver,' she said, yawning and stretching out her feet towards the fire.

'Leave it, Nora, you look tired,' Josephine said, squatting down on her haunches on the hearthrug and holding her hands out to the warmth.

Nora shook her head and eased herself out of the rocking chair. 'Never leave fer termorrer what yer can do terday is what I say,' she intoned with feigned severity, wagging her finger at the young woman. 'I like ter keep meself busy. It stops me finkin'.'

'You're worried about Geoff, aren't you,' Josephine said, getting up and turning her back to the fire.

Nora went over to the dresser and picked up a large silver salver which she loaded with small silver dishes from the cupboard. 'These should 'ave bin done ages ago. They're really stained,' she said.

Josephine watched as Nora spread a cloth over the table and laid out the pieces of silverware. 'You are worried, I can tell,' she said. 'It's the news in the paper. I've already seen it.'

Nora rubbed away furiously at a dish with a piece of cloth

she had wrapped around her forefinger. ''E'll be goin' soon. I wish 'e 'adn't volunteered,' she sighed.

Josephine sat down at the table facing Nora and rested her chin in her cupped hands. 'I've decided to leave school,' she announced, looking at Nora's bent head.

'But yer only seventeen. Yer've got anuvver year ter go yet,' Nora replied, looking up quickly.

Josephine hunched her shoulders. 'A lot of the girls are leaving now the war's on. I've decided to train to be a nurse. They need lots of nurses and it's what I want to do,' she said firmly.

'And what did your farvver say when yer told 'im?' Nora asked, breathing on the dish and rubbing it with the cloth.

'I haven't told him yet, but I don't care what Father thinks, I'm doing it anyway,' Josephine answered defiantly.

Nora studied the young woman for a few moments then dropped her gaze to the dish she was polishing. How quickly she had grown up, and how like her mother she was in looks. She had her father's determination and wilfulness as well, and would not be easily dissuaded. 'But I thought yer've gotta be eighteen before yer can be a nurse,' Nora queried.

'Yes, that's right, but they said I could be a volunteer with the Red Cross,' Josephine replied quickly. 'I can do duty at the railway stations when the wounded soldiers come home on those troop trains. There's lots of things to do, like giving the men drinks and helping them write letters to their family. There's other things I can manage, too. They need volunteers to help with the dressings and things.'

'It doesn't sound very nice fer a young gel your age ter do those sort o' fings,' Nora said, concerned. 'They won't be pretty sights. There's men what's bin blinded an' crippled, an' some o' those wounds'll be terrible ter see. Are yer sure that's what yer wanna do, luv?'

Josephine nodded with conviction. 'I've made up my mind, Nora. It's something worthwhile and I won't be put off.'

Nora smiled and put down the dish. 'No, I don't fink yer will an' I'm proud of yer, but yer must realise, Josie, it won't be an easy fing ter do. Yer'll be seein' terrible sights. I was readin' about these casualties in the paper an' it was makin' my stomach turn.'

'I've read it, Nora, and I know what it'll be like,' the girl replied. 'I've been worried about Geoffrey and I got to thinking, supposing he got wounded. I'd want someone to care for him and make him comfortable. I couldn't just get a job in an office and leave it up to other people to volunteer. I just couldn't.'

'I know, dear,' Nora said kindly. 'Now that's enough o' the war fer the time bein'. Pass me the rest o' that silver, could yer? Gawd, I'll be 'ere all night wiv this lot.'

The kitchen fire burned brightly. Its flames were reflected in the shining silver dishes lined up on the dresser. Heavy curtains were drawn tightly against the darkness outside, and while the rising wind howled and rattled against the windows the copper kettle was warming steadily on the hob. The two women sat comfortably by the hearth. Nora's rocker creaked as it moved back and forth. The older woman looked down at her sewing through glasses perched on the end of her nose, and the younger sat back in her chair, pale blue eyes staring unblinking into the glowing coals. Neither had spoken for some time, each wrapped up in her own private thoughts. The newspaper lay discarded at Nora's feet, the headline banner proclaiming, 'Heavy Casualties at the Marne'.

Nora put down her sewing and took up the tongs to place a large knob of coal on the fire. The shower of sparks roused Josephine from her reverie and she cast her eyes around the shadowy room.

'Did you know my mother very well, Nora?' she said suddenly.

'What made yer ask that, Josie?'

'Oh, I was just thinking.'

Nora pressed her feet down on the floor to stop her chair rocking and folded her arms. 'I knew yer muvver, but not all that well,' she replied slowly. 'I used ter meet 'er sometimes an' we'd stop an' talk like yer do. She was always very pleasant, an' she liked ter talk about the boys an' about yer farvver. She never was one ter talk about 'erself as I remember.'

'Do you think Father and her were happy together, Nora? Really happy, I mean?' Josephine asked.

'Yer a strange gel! The fings that go frew that 'ead o' yours. 'Course they were – at least, I should fink so. I never 'ad reason ter fink ovverwise,' Nora answered.

Josephine stared down at the fire again. 'Are you and Father . . . I mean, do you and Father like each other?' she asked falteringly.

Nora looked at the top of Josephine's lowered head. 'If yer mean, do we be'ave like man an' wife, no. At least not any more.'

'You and Father have been lovers then?'

'Yes.'

'I guessed as much,' Josephine said, looking directly at Nora.

'Does that shock yer?'

Josephine leaned forward and squeezed the housekeeper's arm gently. 'I'm not shocked. Why should I be? I've always looked on you as my mother. You're the only mother I've ever known. It seemed right that you and Father should, you know, sleep together. Why aren't you now?'

Nora sighed deeply and started the chair rocking again.

'Yer farvver's never really got over yer muvver dyin' the way she did. I'm sure 'e blames 'imself fer what 'appened. I just filled a gap in 'is life. I was there when 'e needed comfortin'.'

'But you're still here, Nora. Why must he turn to the bottle for comfort?' Josephine asked, frowning.

Nora looked down at her folded arms. 'I dunno the answer ter that one, Josie. I expect the ache inside of 'im is too much fer the likes o' me ter ease. Whisky does it fer yer farvver. It dulls the pain 'e's feelin' an' finally sends 'im off ter sleep. It'll kill 'im in the end though, I'm sure it will.'

Josephine sighed sadly. 'I don't think Father blames himself for Mother's death – he blames me. Having me killed her, I know that.'

Nora sat upright in her chair. 'Now listen ter me, young lady,' she said quickly, 'yer farvver doesn't blame you at all. Yer mustn't dare fink that. It was 'im what made yer. If there's anybody ter blame it's yer farvver, nobody else, but there just ain't nobody ter blame. Least of all you.'

'But why can't I talk to him, Nora? Why does it always feel like he's pushing me away from him?' Josephine asked, her eyes searching the older woman's for an answer.

''E doesn't mean to, child,' Nora told her kindly. 'Yer farvver lives in a man's world. 'E 'ad two sons before you come along. I don't want yer ter take this wrong, but yer farvver's got no refinement, no finesse. 'E can't relax wiv women, I know. It's not just you. Yer mus' try ter understan' what I'm sayin'. Promise me yer won't dwell on it, Josie.'

The young woman nodded slowly, her eyes fixed on the housekeeper's. 'Do you know, Nora, sometimes I feel that this family is doomed,' she said slowly. 'Sometimes I lie awake nights with a dreadful feeling in my stomach. It's as though there's a curse hanging over us. I can see no future, nothing good, only bad. Why? Why should I feel like I do?'

Nora forced herself to smile reassuringly. 'Listen ter me, yer a young woman who's just findin' 'erself,' she said quietly. ''Avin those sort o' thoughts is not so terrible as yer might fink. It's all part o' growin' up. One day soon yer'll meet a nice young man an' grow ter love 'im. 'E'll love yer back an' make yer feel good inside. 'E'll comfort yer an' protect yer, an' yer'll be able ter laugh at yer fears. Yer'll see.'

Josephine smiled as she bent down to rouse the dying fire. 'I expect you're right, Nora,' she said, feeling suddenly cold in the firelit room.

Chapter Twenty-eight

Early in 1915 James and Charles Tanner prepared to leave for France as privates in the East Surreys. William felt proud as he walked along to the Kings Arms with his two sons, both looking trim and smart in their tight-fitting uniforms, peaked caps and puttees wound up around their calves from highly polished boots. James was now a brawny young man a stone and a half heavier than Charlie, who still had a baby face and red cheeks. Their fair hair had been cropped short and both had the look of young men eager and impatient to be off on a big adventure. The stories filling the newspapers of heavy fighting on the Western Front had not caused either of them to lose any sleep, but as pints of ale were downed in quick succession and the customers joked about the girls they would meet, their father became quieter, struggling with the secret fears that he had to hide from everybody.

Alec Crossley had seen many such family gatherings during the last few months, and wondered how many of those young men would be drinking in his pub once the war was over. Already the toll was growing, and almost every evening someone came with stories of lost relatives or friends. His pub seemed to be full of old men and uniformed boys like the

Tanners or Billy Sullivan who had left for France only a few weeks ago. Alec pulled pints and watched how the smooth-faced soldiers drank them down with bravado, sometimes turning a shade of grey as the unfamiliar drink took effect.

'Yer know, luv, I fink 'alf of 'em would be better orf wiv toffee apples than pints of ale,' he remarked to his wife Grace.

She smiled sadly as she pulled down on the beer-pump. 'I can't 'elp finkin' of young Alfie Finnegan when I see these young soldiers. I remember when Alfie was sittin' outside the pub wiv a glass o' lemonade an' munchin' on an arrowroot biscuit. It seems like only yesterday, an' now the poor bleeder's gorn. I still can't get over it. Six weeks, that's all 'e was out there. Six weeks.'

Nellie Tanner had fought back tears as she watched her two boys march off to the pub with their father. She felt grateful that at least Danny wasn't in uniform. He had managed to get the job he was hoping for, and was now articled to a lighterage firm and excited at working on the barges. At least he wouldn't be going off to war, she thought. She was terribly worried about his brothers, but Charlie caused her particular anguish. He was different from Jim in many ways. He had been sired in fear and anger, had always seemed set apart from the others when he was growing up, and now he was a man. He would show courage and endure hardship just like his brother, Nellie felt sure, but he was different. She had always been able to see it in his grey eyes.

Many local young men were now in uniform. Geoffrey Galloway had been commissioned into the Rifle Brigade and was already in France. Maisie Dougall's two boys, Ronnie and Albert, were also in the Rifle Brigade and were doing their basic training on the Isle of Sheppey. Sadie Sullivan bade her eldest son goodbye as he left for the front and then dared the rest of her brood to follow him.

'It's bad enough Billy goin' orf wivout you lot wantin' ter go wiv 'im,' she told them. 'Jus' let me 'ear one peep out o' you lot about joinin' up an' I'll tan yer 'ides, big as yer are.'

'But, Muvver, we can't let Billy do all the fightin'. 'E's gonna need a bit of 'elp,' John the next eldest told her.

''E's got all the 'elp 'e needs wivout the rest of yer puttin' on a uniform, so let's be done wiv it, or I'll tell yer farvver.'

'Yer not bein' fair, Mum,' Michael cut in. 'John an' me are over eighteen, so's Joe. We're old enough ter fight. If we enlist, yer'll still 'ave Shaun an' the twins ter look after yer.'

'Look after me!' Sadie raged. 'I'm tryin' me bloody best ter look after you lot. 'Ave yer got any idea what it's bloody well like out in France?'

Patrick and Terry were standing behind their mother and mimicked her as she waved her fist at Michael, while Shaun the youngest picked up the broom and started to prod the armchair with it in an aggressive manner.

Sadie sat down heavily in her chair and put a hand to her forehead. 'Yer'll be the undoin' o' me, yer will,' she groaned. 'Can't yer be like ovver muvvers' sons? Do yer 'ave ter drive me right roun' the twist?'

'All the ovver muvvers' sons 'ave volunteered,' Joe moaned.

'Well, you lot ain't gonna do no such fing, d'yer 'ear me?' Sadie screamed.

'My mate at work got a white feavver. Would yer like us ter get a white feavver?' Michael asked his mother.

'I don't care if they send yer the 'ole bloody bird, the answer's still no,' she growled, screwing up her fists.

The three eldest boys recognised the danger signs and they quickly made excuses and left the house together, sauntering dejectedly along the little turning with their hands stuffed deep into their trouser pockets.

'C'mon, I've got enough dosh fer a pint,' John said, his eyes brightening.

As the three young men walked into the Kings Arms, Alec Crossley nudged Grace. 'Old tight, gel, lock up the glasses, it's the fightin' Sullivans,' he said with mock seriousness. 'What yer 'avin', boys?'

John pulled out a handful of coppers and started counting them. 'Gis us a pint o' porter each, Alec,' he said sadly. 'This is gonna be our last pint as civilians. We're signin' on termorrer fer the East Surreys.'

Alec shook his head as he pulled on the pump. 'If this keeps up I won't 'ave enough bleedin' customers ter make up a domino team,' he groaned. ''Ere, lads, 'ave this one on the 'ouse. All the best.'

The Sullivan boys took their drinks to a far table. When they had settled themselves, Michael turned to his brother John. ''Ere, Johnbo, why d'yer tell Alec the three of us were signin' on termorrer?' he asked.

'Well, I 'ad ter do somefink,' John replied, sipping his beer. 'I only 'ad enough money fer two pints.'

Carrie Tanner finished wiping down the last of the tables then walked over to the window of the dining rooms that looked out on to the riverside lane and the river beyond. She could see the belching smoke-stack of a cargo ship as it chugged towards the Pool with its escorting tug whistling noisily, and in the lane itself could see one or two horse-carts parked ready for a call on to the jetty. It had been dreary lately with all the younger men going off to war. She missed their funny sayings and saucy remarks as they came and went, caps askew and red chokers knotted tightly round their necks. Now most of the customers were older men with less to say, except when they cursed the war and wished they were young enough to go instead of being left to do all the work. Fred had told her that he had thought a lot about whether he should volunteer and had decided against it. He had gone so far as to talk with a friend of his who was a recruiting sergeant and he had advised him that he would be exempt anyway because of the nature of his business and he should forget about taking the King's shilling and leave the fighting to the younger men. She sighed to herself as she watched the progress of the cargo ship. She missed her brothers badly, and wondered where Tommy might be right at that minute. He had come into the dining rooms only once since she had told him their romance was over. He had looked uneasy as he ordered his tea and sandwich, and then just as he was leaving had told her he was going into the Queen's Bermondsey Regiment the following week. The café was full of customers at the time and Carrie had found herself coldly wishing him luck and a safe return as he turned away with an embarrassed look on his face and walked out of the door, and now she wished she'd been kinder. But it was too late.

The days seemed long and tedious, with little to smile about. The only light relief was when Sharkey Morris and Soapy Symonds made their appearance. They usually came in together and were full of funny stories, often about their own misfortunes. Both were now in their late fifties and still fairly robust, although Soapy was becoming bad on his legs and always seemed to be limping these days. They had not changed in character since she was very small, Carrie reflected. They were a reminder of those carefree childhood days when she rode on the back of Titch the Welsh cob and her father took her on those lovely country trips to fetch the hay bales. She remembered her friend Sara and the look of wonderment on her face as they drove into the farm and saw the animals and the line of waddling ducks leading their

411

unsteady offspring to the muddy pool. Sara was married now and doing well, the last Carrie heard.

Fred Bradley had been kind and considerate towards her, and since that one time he had opened his heart to her, had kept his distance, for which she was grateful. She had been afraid that he might try to force himself upon her in some way but he had been especially nice, leaving her alone to get on with her work and never harassing her at the end of the day when she cleared up and went home. Carrie knew, though, that he was still waiting patiently for her to have a change of heart, and she felt flattered that Fred wanted her to be his wife. The age difference was not so terrible. Many young girls were marrying older men who could offer them security, men who would be less likely to burden them with lots of children. Fred Bradley would be a good husband, she knew, but she was not in love with him. She sighed deeply.

It was a few minutes to five o'clock in the empty café and Fred's helper Bessie Chandler came out of the kitchen and raised her eyes to the ceiling as she sat down at one of the tables. Carrie smiled knowingly as she carried over two mugs of tea and sat down facing her. It was usual for them to have a quick chat together and catch their breath before they left for home in the evenings. Bessie was a large woman in her forties with a wide round face and fuzzy ginger hair which she always kept hidden under her headscarf. Her face was freckled and her small green eyes stared out from beneath drooping eyelids, making her look perpetually sorry for herself. Bessie had been employed to work mornings only at first but when trade increased Fred had asked her to work full-time. She prepared the raw vegetables and made pastry for the pies, afterwards helping Fred with the orders, but she talked incessantly and he felt that she was slowly driving him mad with her accounts of the doings of all her neighbours in the buildings. Fred seriously thought about getting rid of her, but she was such a good cook and very competent in the kitchen that when her endless talking grew unbearable he simply went out into the yard and puffed deeply on a cigarette as he steeled himself to face her chattering once more. Bessie was childless, and her husband worked nights at the biscuit factory. Fred joked with the carmen that she probably spent so much time gassing to the neighbours, she had no time left for anything else.

Bessie sipped her tea slowly, her doleful eyes staring at Carrie over the mug. ''E's bin in a funny mood lately,' she said in a quiet voice, putting her tea down and nodding in the direction of the kitchen. 'I reckon 'e's gettin' old an' miserable.'

Carrie smiled. 'What's the matter wiv 'im?' she asked, knowing that she was about to find out anyway.

Bessie shook her head slowly. ''E's bin very jumpy lately an' I'm sure 'e just ain't listenin' when yer talk to 'im. If I didn't know 'im better, I'd say 'e 'ad woman trouble. 'E seems miles away.'

Carrie stared down into the tea-leaves as she experienced a familiar sinking in her stomach. Bessie's comment about woman trouble was probably a little nearer the truth than she realised.

'I was only sayin' ter Elsie Dobson the ovver night, 'e's a funny bloke that Fred,' Bessie went on. ''E's never married or got 'imself involved wiv a woman. I mean ter say, 'e ain't a bad-lookin' sort o' fella, as fellas go. 'E'd be a good catch too. 'E mus' be werf a few bob. 'Is family 'ad the business fer years an' 'e prob'ly come inter money when they died.'

'P'raps 'e 'as got a woman tucked away somewhere,' Carrie cut in quickly. 'After all, we don't know what 'e does in 'is spare time.'

Bessie laughed. 'I've known Fred an' 'is family fer years. That's 'ow 'e come ter ask me if I wanted ter work fer 'im. Fred's ole muvver was a funny ole cow. She used ter dote on 'im. Very strict though. I never see Fred wiv a young lady on 'is arm. 'E was always workin' in 'ere from the time 'e left school. Never 'ad annuver job. Mind yer, 'e built this place up. It was a proper gaff when the ole couple run it. Let it go right down the pan they did, 'specially when the old fella was gettin' on in years. I don't s'pose the poor sod 'ad time fer women, what wiv the way 'e 'ad ter work.'

'Was Fred the only child?'

'Yeah. There was annuver child, a gel I fink, but she died as a baby,' Bessie replied. 'I fink 'e should find 'imself a nice young lady. I fink it'd be the makin' of 'im. It ain't right fer anybody ter go frew life on their own. As I was sayin' ter Elsie . . .'

Bessie's ramblings were interrupted as Fred came out of the kitchen. She winked to Carrie as she looked over at him. ''Ave yer covered that pastry 'cos o' the flies?' she asked him.

Fred nodded and gave Carrie a quick glance, raising his eyes to the ceiling in exasperation. 'Yer better be off, it's turned five,' he said.

Bessie got up and slipped on her coat. 'Yeah, I'd better be orf 'ome an' make sure my ole fella's up fer work,' she sighed.

Carrie smiled at Fred as his assistant left the dining rooms and he sat down at the table, sighing loudly. 'Bessie's a diamond but she does go on,' he groaned. 'D' yer know what she was on about terday? She wanted ter know why I never married. She reckoned I should find meself a nice young lady.'

'What did yer say?' Carrie asked as she got up to put on her coat, suddenly feeling nervous.

414

'I told 'er when I meet the right woman, I'll consider gettin' married,' he answered.

'Yer'll meet the right gel one day,' Carrie told him, making for the door.

'I already 'ave,' he said in a low voice.

Carrie walked home feeling wild with herself for making such a stupid remark as she left the café. She had said it on the spur of the moment without thinking, and realised she would have to be more careful in future. Any chance remark like that might make Fred feel that she was prompting or encouraging him, and it would be embarrassing for both of them if he asked her plainly to walk out with him and she declined. He was too nice a man to upset but she knew that if he did offer she would refuse him. She was still aching over her romance with Tommy and could not bring herself to think of starting another relationship.

As Carrie walked past Bacon Street Buildings she found herself thinking again of Sara. Had she found happiness with her young man, she wondered, and hoped she would never have to struggle the way her mother had.

Carrie turned the corner into Page Street and saw the women standing at their front doors, chatting together. She saw Maisie talking to Aggie, and Ida Bromsgrove sweeping outside her front door. Young children were swinging from a rope tied to a lamppost, an old man tottered along supporting his frail body with a stick and mumbling to himself. Another old man stood in a doorway smoking a clay pipe, his eyes fixed on the paving-stones. Despite all the people, she felt how strangely quiet the turning seemed to be. There were no young men standing about to ogle her or smile as she passed them. All the vitality and youthfulness seemed to have been taken out of the street. Carrie thought of those young men: Tommy, Billy Sullivan, the Dougall boys and her own two brothers.

Where were they now? Would she ever see them again? She sighed deeply. The war would not last for long and the young men would soon be home. All of them, she told herself as she reached her front door.

In the dining room at 22 Tyburn Place the curtains had been drawn against the cold night and a fire burned brightly in the open hearth. Five chairs had been placed around the heavy oaken table although only four were occupied. The meal was over and George Galloway sat at the head of the table, thoughtfully rolling an unlighted cigar between his fingers as Nora replenished the coffee cups. Frank sat on his father's right. He was leaning back in his chair, staring down at his cup. Josephine was facing him, and exchanged glances with Nora as the two men pondered. George lit his cigar and blew a cloud of smoke towards the ceiling, a look of expectancy on his face as he waited for Frank's answer. Nora caught Josephine's eye.

'I fink I'd better get cleared away,' she said, getting up and pushing her chair against the table.

Together the two women carried the stack of used crockery out into the kitchen. Josephine gave the housekeeper a knowing smile. 'It looks as though Father's got his way, Nora,' she said quietly. 'Poor Frank looks very upset.'

Nora shook her head slowly. 'There ain't much choice fer 'im, is there? I fink that white feavver business upset 'im too, although 'e tried ter make light of it.'

Josephine's face became serious. 'Why are people so wicked, Nora? My brother's not a coward. Frank's married now and he's got responsibilities. If he was single, he'd be the first to volunteer.'

'I'm sure 'e would,' Nora replied, looking up at the clock on the mantelshelf. 'I'll see ter the dishes. Yer'd better be off or yer'll be late.'

Josephine left for a meeting of Red Cross volunteers at the church hall in Jamaica Road. In the dining room the two men continued their discussion. A blue smoke haze hung over the table as Frank lit another cigarette.

'The trouble is, you never get to find out who's responsible for sending them,' he said, exhaling smoke and nervously tapping his cigarette against the ashtray.

George nodded. 'I wouldn't worry about it. 'Undreds o' people are gettin' 'em. Yer done the right fing, burning it. Don't give it anuvver thought.'

'I was wondering if it was someone at the office,' Frank remarked, looking at his father.

George puffed in exasperation. 'There yer go! Yer ain't gonna stop worryin' about it, are yer? It's why they send 'em, can't yer see? Whoever it was who sent it wanted jus' that. Why not do as I say an' ferget it? Now let's get down ter what we were talkin' about,' he said testily. 'Yer said yer guv'nor was expectin' yer ter volunteer. If yer carry on workin' there, 'e's gonna be a bit awkward wiv yer, ter say the least. Those top-brass military families are all the same. King an' Country, an' all that bloody twaddle! They stand back an' dish out the orders an' it's the poor bloody soldiers who face the bullets. I reckon they should get all that top brass from us an' Germany tergevver an' put the 'ole bloody lot o' the bastards in a field somewhere an' say to 'em, go on then, get on wiv it. The bloody war'd be over in five minutes. They'd all be on the piss tergevver.'

Frank chuckled, then his face changed as he glanced over to the vacant place at the table. 'I wonder how Geoff's getting on,' he said quietly.

George dropped his gaze for a moment and then stared at the lighted end of his cigar. 'The boy'll be all right,' he declared firmly. ''E's a sensible young man, 'e won't take no unnecessary risks. I only wish 'e 'adn't bin so 'asty. Geoff was doin' a good job at the yard an' I was really upset when 'e told me 'e'd volunteered. I miss 'im, an' it's upset Nora too. It was 'er idea ter leave a place at the table fer 'im. She reckons it's lucky. She's a strange woman at times, is Nora.'

Frank was quiet as he stubbed out his cigarette, then looked up at his father. 'All right, I'll put my resignation in first thing in the morning,' he said suddenly. 'They'll need a couple of weeks to get a replacement, unless the old man gets shirty and tells me to go there and then.'

George's wide florid face broke into a grin. 'Jus' tell the ole git yer've volunteered. Tell 'im yer wanna leave right away ter get yer fings in order. I don't s'pose 'e'll be too concerned, from what yer've told me.'

Frank nodded. 'All right, I will. I suppose the sooner I start the better. By the way, Father, have you thought any more about getting lorries to replace some of the horses? It'll be a sensible move, especially now.'

George relit the stub of his cigar and puffed on it thoughtfully. 'Look, you jus' get yerself familiar wiv the runnin' o' the business first,' he told him. 'Once yer've sorted the books out, we'll talk again. There's a lot ter consider. Fer a start, if I get lorries I'll need a mechanic ter keep 'em on the road. That's what the ovver cartage firms 'ave 'ad ter do. What's gonna 'appen ter Will Tanner? Once the 'orses go I'd 'ave ter get rid of 'im. I couldn't afford ter keep 'im an' a mechanic as well. Then there's the 'ouse. I'd 'ave ter give 'im notice ter quit.'

'Couldn't you let him stay and pay a rent?' Frank asked.

George shook his head. 'The mechanic would need a place ter live an' there's no 'ouses vacant, not yet anyway. I'd need the bloke ter be on 'and. It's no good if 'e lives miles away from the yard. We'd need more space too, don't ferget. Yer couldn't garage many lorries in the yard, there's no room ter manoeuvre 'em. It's not like 'avin' 'orse-an'-carts.'

Frank lit another cigarette. 'You should have bought a bigger place when Geoff and I suggested it,' he said reprovingly.

George smiled. 'Yer've only just agreed ter come in the business an' already yer tellin' me 'ow ter run it! Well, maybe that's not a bad fing. I'd like yer ter bring yer own ideas in. I ain't gettin' any younger. You an' Geoff should be able ter make a good go of it, please Gawd. In the meantime, let's 'ave a drink ter celebrate. Now where did Nora 'ide that brandy . . .'

Chapter Twenty-nine

In the early summer a troop train from Southampton arrived at Waterloo carrying a large contingent of troops from the East Surrey Regiment who had seen action in France. The train pulled into the station beside another bearing a bold red cross on all of its carriages. As the troops alighted their noisy gaiety and laughter were suddenly stilled by the sight that met them. A line of stretchers ran the length of the platform, bearing casualties ashen-faced beneath their blankets. Soldiers with bandages over their eyes were being led away in line, each resting his hand on the shoulder of the man in front, and other troops were hobbling along the platform on crutches. Doctors and medical orderlies walked along the long line of stretchers, giving aid and glancing at the medical notes pinned to the top of the blankets. Nurses in Red Cross uniforms bent over the casualties, writing notes and placing lighted cigarettes between the lips of grateful men. Around them the usual station activities went on as if it was a normal day. Porters pushed laden barrows, and steam from the tenders drifted up to the high iron rafters.

James Tanner stepped down from the train and walked along the platform beside his younger brother Charlie, both of them pale and subdued as they gazed down on the faces of their wounded comrades.

'Christ, I need a drink!' James said in a husky voice.

'That's the best fing yer've said all mornin', Tanner,' one of the other troops remarked, putting his arm around James's shoulder.

As they neared the ticket gate, Charlie spotted one of the wounded struggling with something in his hands and he broke away from the group.

'You go on, I'll catch yer up,' he said, walking towards the stretcher.

'We'll be in the 'Ole in the Wall, Charlie,' his brother called out as he passed through the gate with their mates.

Charlie bent over the wounded soldier. ''Ere, let me do that,' he said quietly, taking the cigarette packet from the man.

'Fanks, pal. Bloody fingers are all numb,' the soldier replied.

Charlie opened the packet and lit a cigarette, placing it between the man's lips. 'There yer are. 'Ow's that?' he said kindly.

The soldier exhaled a cloud of cigarette smoke and sighed contentedly. 'Gawd, that's good,' he smiled.

'Where d'yer cop it?' Charlie asked.

'It's me toes,' the soldier told him. 'I lost 'em all wiv frostbite. Still, I'm lucky, I s'pose. That poor sod lost 'is leg.'

Charlie looked at the next stretcher and saw the still form lying beneath the blanket. 'I jus' feel grateful ter be alive,' he said, holding the cigarette to the soldier's lips.

A young Red Cross nurse bent down over the stretcher and read the medical notes pinned to the blanket, then she smiled at the soldier. 'Are you in a lot of pain?' she asked softly.

'Nah, it's all right, luv. I jus' wanna know when they're gonna move us. It's bloody cold layin' 'ere,' he answered.

Charlie took the cigarette from the soldier's mouth and his eyes met those of the nurse.

Suddenly, she smiled. 'Aren't you William Tanner's son?'

Charlie looked puzzled. 'Should I know yer?' he asked.

She laughed. 'I'm Josephine Galloway.'

Charlie stood up. 'Well, I'll be blowed!' he exclaimed. 'I wouldn't 'ave reco'nised yer. Yer look all grown-up.'

Josephine smiled, showing even white teeth. 'If I remember right, you're Charles. Father told me you and your brother James had joined up. Is he with you?' she asked.

Charlie nodded. ''E's wiv the rest o' the lads. They've gone ter the pub. By the way, call me Charlie,' he said, holding out his hand.

''Ere, when you two 'ave finished yer little chat, could I 'ave anuvver puff o' that fag?' the wounded soldier cut in.

Charles bent down over the stretcher. 'Sorry, mate. That's the first chance I've 'ad ter talk ter a pretty face fer a long while.'

Josephine bent down and wrote something on the chart, then she stood up and went to the next stretcher. Intrigued, Charlie followed her.

'The last time I remember seein' yer was when yer bruvver Geoff brought yer in the yard ter see the new 'orses. Yer couldn't 'ave bin no more than nine or ten, an' now look at yer,' he said, shaking his head in disbelief.

'I'm eighteen, going on nineteen,' she replied.

'Well, I'll be . . .' laughed Charlie.

Josephine studied the chart and straightened up. 'How long are you home for?' she asked.

'Seven days. Seven long days,' he said, smiling. 'I promised meself I'd get drunk every one of 'em.'

'It must be dreadful out there,' she said.

Charlie nodded awkwardly, a serious cast suddenly clouding his features. 'It's not very nice. In fact, it's terrible,' he said quietly, and then his face brightened again. 'Look, I know I said I was gonna get drunk every night, but if yer like I could maybe take yer ter the music 'all? It'd be a lot nicer than gettin' boozed, an' we could 'ave a long talk about when we was kids. What d'yer say?'

Josephine smiled at him. He looked so handsome in his uniform and there was something in the way he was gazing at her which made her heart leap.

'I'd like that,' she replied, suddenly noticing the matron coming along the platform. 'When?' she asked quickly.

'Termorrer?'

'Yes, all right. Look, I've got to go now,' she said anxiously. 'I'll be on duty until six o'clock. Meet me at the church hall in Jamaica Road, opposite the Drill Hall. Is that all right, Charles?'

'That's fine, an' it's Charlie,' he reminded her.

The stern-faced matron gave him a brief glance and turned to Josephine. 'Lord and Lady Dunfermline have arrived,' she said in a loud voice. 'I want you to make sure all those blankets are straightened, and none of the soldiers is to smoke. Is that understood?'

Josephine nodded. 'Yes, Matron.'

'Well, see to it.'

Josephine busied herself, stealing a last glance in the direction of the young soldier as he walked across the station concourse.

The overhead clock showed ten minutes past the hour of one as the official party came into the station, attended unctuously by a few of the military top brass and a group of civilians wearing morning suits and top hats.

424

Lord Dunfermline was tall and stooped slightly as he walked unsteadily beside Her Ladyship. She wore a silver fox stole over a long black coat, and a wide-brimmed hat with a large satin bow. They both looked miserable as their entourage fussed and worried, and when Lady Dunfermline asked if there was a powder room the escorts were thrown into a state of panic. A room was finally provided, compliments of the station master, and Lady Helen sat down heavily in a chair.

'I do wish you wouldn't let yourself get talked into this sort of thing, Albert,' she moaned. 'You know how sensitive my stomach is.'

'Sorry, m'dear. Couldn't be avoided. We've got to play our part,' he reminded her. 'It could be worse. The Chalfonts are at a military hospital and Sir Norman Kirkby's doing the St Dunstan's thingy. Nasty one that.'

Lady Helen sighed and rubbed at her ankles. 'Don't take too long, Norman. Just walk quickly and don't stop at every stretcher or we'll be here all day long. I've an appointment at the dressmaker's, and then there's the party tonight. I do like to go looking my best and I can't if I've spent most of the day talking to wounded soldiers. It is annoying. I do wish they'd chosen any other day but Friday.'

'Sorry, old dear, can't be helped,' he said in the comically musical tone that he knew amused her.

Outside the station master's office a haughty-looking man in gold-rimmed spectacles and a bowler hat was trying to calm the agitated young army doctor. 'I'm sure they won't be long. They've had a tiring journey from Hampshire and Lady Dunfermline's got a bit of a headache,' he said in a silky voice.

The doctor gave him a wicked look. 'Those troops have not exactly been enjoying the trip,' he protested. 'They've had a rough crossing, and they've spent nearly three hours on a train in cramped conditions, and now they've been lying on the cold platform for the past hour. Now you go in and tell Lord and Lady What's-their-names that if they're not out in five minutes I'll tell my orderlies to put the stretchers on the motor vehicles and despatch them to the hospitals, is that quite understood?'

'But, but, I – I can't do that,' the official stuttered.

'Please yourself,' the doctor said casually, marching off quickly.

The official chewed on his fingernails in consternation and paced back and forth trying to think of some way to hurry the proceedings along without upsetting the venerable Lord and Lady. His torment was suddenly resolved as Lord Dunfermline emerged from the office looking a trifle distracted with Lady Helen at his side. 'Lead on, Brown,' he said with a sweep of his bony hand, and the official could smell brandy on his breath.

When he reached the first stretcher on the platform Lord Dunfermline stopped and smiled down at the pale-faced young soldier. 'Feeling well, are we then?' he said, walking on without waiting for an answer.

Further along the line he looked down at another casualty, the entourage at his heels bumping into each other as he stopped suddenly. 'Rifle Brigade I see. Good man. Arm is it? Never mind, we'll soon have you on your feet,' he said cheerfully.

The young army doctor gritted his teeth in disgust. 'The man's lost his leg for God's sake,' he almost shouted at the matron.

Lady Dunfermline stood beside her husband mumbling at him to hurry along and finally the dignitary reached the last stretcher in the line. 'How are we?' he asked.

Josephine was adjusting the soldier's bandages and she looked up with surprise. Her patient leaned up on his elbows and puffed loudly. 'Well, I don't know about you, pal, but I don't feel too good,' the soldier said sharply.

'Steady on, private,' an accompanying staff officer said quickly.

'It's corporal, mate,' the soldier replied.

Josephine had moved to the head of the stretcher and she clasped the soldier's arm firmly, trying to restrain him with a slight shake of her head. The officer flushed the colour of his headband and Lord Dunfermline looked taken aback.

'East Surreys I see. First-class regiment, corporal,' he remarked in a casual lilting tone. 'What's the injuries then?'

Lady Dunfermline bit on her bottom lip, dreading what she might hear, and Josephine held her breath as she waited for an outburst, but the corporal was not feeling very expansive.

'Legs,' he replied.

'Sorry to hear that, old chap. How did it occur?'

'Shrapnel.'

The dignitary straightened up and stared down on the wounded corporal. 'Well I'm sure you feel proud and honoured to have done your duty for your King and Country, corporal. We all have our part to play in this war you know,' he said in a loud voice, glancing around at the smiling members of his entourage as they nodded their heads enthusiastically and cleared their throats.

The corporal gritted his teeth as he pulled himself up on to his elbows. 'Right now I'm only proud o' this lot,' he said in an icy tone, his eyes flashing along the line of stretchers. 'They've all bin well an' truly right frew the shit, an' it ain't doin' 'em any good layin' 'ere on this draughty poxy platform so the likes o' you can do yer bit fer the war wiv yer stupid remarks, so if yer finished can we all get goin' ter the 'orspital now?'

Josephine could hardly refrain from laughing aloud and her hand tightened on the corporal's arm. Lord Dunfermline had been rendered speechless and he seemed to have become rigid as he stooped forward looking down at the soldier, his eyes popping and his face crimson. His lady wife was holding her hand to her brow, looking as though she was going to pass out. Murmurings went on around them and the staff officer looked like he could have cheerfully despatched the insolent corporal with a bullet from the revolver clipped to his shiny Sam Browne belt.

'I'm awfully sorry, Lord Dunfermline,' he groaned. 'The man's obviously suffering from shell-shock. I can only apologise sincerely for what he said.'

'It's all right, Willington, no need,' the dignitary replied, backing away from the stretcher and the soldier's burning gaze. 'I think we've finished here. I'll look forward to seeing you at the club this evening.'

As the group walked off the staff officer bent down over the stretcher, his face flushed with anger. 'I'll be wanting your name, rank and number, soldier. You could well be court-martialled for this outrageous behaviour,' he barked.

Josephine's eyes blazed and she stood up to face the officer. 'Do you realise this man is badly wounded? I won't have you talking to him like this,' she declared, her voice charged with emotion. 'I'm going to fetch the doctor.'

The corporal grinned. 'It's all right, luv,' he said cheerfully, and the grin did not leave his face as he looked up arrogantly at the staff officer, 'I won't be court-martialled,' he told him offhandedly. 'When I got this little lot I finished bein' a soldier. I s'pose yer could 'ave a go at gettin' me pension stopped though. Let the bastard starve, eh? Don't worry, pal, I ain't gonna lose no sleep over a few coppers any ole 'ow. Now why don't yer piss orf wiv the rest o' yer menagerie an' let us all get orf this poxy platform.'

The staff officer's expression became apoplectic and he stormed off slapping his thigh with his cane and mumbling to himself about shooting the man where he lay. The corporal sank down on the stretcher, grinning up at Josephine's bright red face as he forgot for a short moment the pain of his shattered legs. Behind him the army doctor sat on an empty wheelbarrow trying to compose himself.

'I've never witnessed anything like that before,' he croaked to the matron, who was trying to keep a straight face herself. 'And did you see the way our little nurse squared up to that pompous git?'

'They won't do anything to the soldier, will they, doctor?' she asked with concern.

The doctor wiped his eyes with the back of his hand. 'Out of the question,' he answered quickly, mimicking the irate officer's clipped tones. 'You heard what that idiot told Lord Dunfermline. The man's shell-shocked. Evidently,' he laughed.

Laughter rang out for the first time in months at the Tanner household as the whole family gathered together in the small parlour. James sat beside his brother Charlie, both still in uniform and looking slightly the worse for drink, and Danny listened eagerly to their account of a certain company sergeant who had apparently filched the men's rum ration and later brought in four German soldiers at bayonet point after taking them by surprise when he fell into their trench in a drunken rage.

Danny laughed with his brothers as they finished the story, not quite knowing whether to believe it, and felt a sudden pang of envy. He had settled himself into a hard life on the river and felt happy in the job, but the nagging thoughts that he was missing out on the war plagued him. Now that his brothers were home and looking fit and well, Danny knew that he could not delay enlisting for much longer. After all, the war might be over soon, he thought.

Nellie fussed over the boys and tried to remain cheerful. She had been aware for some time that Danny would inevitably join his two brothers in uniform and struggled to hide her fears from her husband. William knew too, although he did not show the concern he felt inside. He laughed and joked with his soldier sons, happy that they were back safe and feeling as though his heart would burst with pride. Carrie had hugged her two brothers with tears welling in her eyes as she saw how grown-up and smart they looked in their uniforms. Now she sat between the two of them with her arms around their shoulders as James told yet another tale of army life. They did not talk about the fighting and the dying, and the family did not encourage them to. They were simply glad to be all together, and for a few short days able to forget the war.

Charlie joined in the laughter but his thoughts were elsewhere as he sat in the cosy parlour. He pictured the pretty young nurse and recalled the smile she had given him on the platform that morning, her eyes flashing and pert lips parting invitingly. He remembered those lovely eyes and how they seemed to be perpetually laughing. He wanted to tell his family about Josephine and how grown-up she had looked, but resisted the urge. He knew his mother did not like the Galloways and his father had always kept his distance from them considering himself to be just another employee of George Galloway's even though the two of them had grown up together in the local backstreets. He would wait and see how things turned out before saying anything, he decided. After all, he would soon be back in France.

Along the street Sadie Sullivan and her husband were talking together in their parlour. Sadie was distraught. She sat at the table with her chin cupped in her hands and her broad shoulders hunched. Her face was still wet with tears.

'I knew it all along, Dan,' she groaned. 'I told 'em. I even dared 'em, but they still went an' done it. As if it ain't bad enough our Billy bein' in the war. What we gonna do?'

Daniel scratched his wiry grey hair and looked down at the fire. 'Gawd knows,' he sighed. 'What can we do? They're old enough. It ain't as though they're under age. We can't stop 'em goin'.'

'But surely if yer went down the recruitin' office an' told 'em there's already one Sullivan in the army, they'd scratch their names off the list?'

'They won't take no notice, Sadie,' he replied. 'Yer've only gotta look round yer. There's two o' the Tanners in the army, Maisie Dougall's two boys are in France, an' there's fousands o' people round 'ere who've got more than two sons serving. Yer know we can't do that.'

She sighed and dabbed at her eyes. 'Why didn't they take any notice o' their muvver? They know 'ow I worry over 'em.'

'Don't yer fink I'm worried too?' Daniel said irritably. 'We'll jus' 'ave ter grin an' bear it like all the ovvers do. The boys'll be all right. Anyway, the war might be over soon. I reckon when the Germans find out the Sullivans are on their way, they'll sue fer peace instantly.'

Sadie did not realise that her husband was joking and continued to stare dejectedly down at the white linen tablecloth.

'D'yer fink they'll let the three of 'em stay tergevver?' she asked tearfully.

'I bet they will,' he answered. 'The Queens is a local regiment. There's lots o' bruvvers in the Queens.'

Sadie suddenly sat up straight in her chair and glared at her husband. 'I tell yer somefink, Dan. The twins are eighteen this year, an' if they try ter sign on I'll go down that bloody recruitin' office an' tear the list up meself, an' I don't care if I do get nicked! Four kids in the army out o' one family is more than enough fer anybody.'

'Don't worry, gel. If the twins try ter sign on, I'll come down there wiv yer an' burn the bloody place down.'

Less than a mile away in the gymnasium of the Dockhead Boys' Club a discussion was taking place between the Sullivan boys that would have horrified their already distressed parents.

'Muvver's bound ter be upset but she'll soon get over it,' John remarked.

'I can't wait ter go,' Michael said, rubbing his hands together. 'We're bound ter see Billy out there.'

'D'yer reckon it'll be over before we get there?' Joe asked anxiously.

'Nah, the war's gonna go on fer years yet. Well, a couple at any rate,' John told him. 'Fing is, we've gotta stick tergevver. If they try ter split us up, we'll jus' tell 'em no.'

'Yer can't do that in the army, stupid,' Michael said. 'Yer can get court-martialled and drummed out, or if it's really bad they can shoot yer.'

'Shoot yer?' gasped Shaun, the youngest. 'Well, I ain't goin' in if that's the case.'

'Shut yer trap. Anyway, the war'll be over by the time yer eighteen,' Joe cut in.

The twins, Patrick and Terry, were reclining on a tumbling

mat and listening with interest. 'D'yer fink we'll be in time?' Terry asked his brother.

''Course we will,' Patrick replied. 'Matter o' fact, we could volunteer termorrer. We could tell 'em we're eighteen, an' by the time they find out we'll be in France. Anyway, it's only four months ter go fer our birthdays.'

Shaun slipped down from his perch on the vaulting-horse and faced his brothers. 'If you lot fink I'm gonna let yer all go wivout me, yer got anuvver fink comin'. I'd 'ave ter stop 'ome an' watch Muvver cryin' over all of yerse, an' when yer win all yer medals an' yer show 'em ter people, they'll say: "'Ave you got any medals, Shaun?" an' I'll 'ave ter say, "No, me muvver wouldn't let me go." Well, I tell yer straight, I ain't stoppin' 'ere. No bloody fear. I'm gonna sign on wiv yer. I look eighteen anyway. I do look eighteen, don't I, John?'

'Nah. I'd say yer look about fifteen,' he said, winking at Michael.

Shaun rushed at his elder brother with his fists flailing and his mouth screwed up in temper. Michael grabbed him around the body and the twins jumped up. 'Leave 'im alone,' they shouted, trying to pull Shaun free.

John attempted to calm his younger brothers, and as he stepped in Joe turned on him. 'You started it,' he yelled.

Soon the Sullivan boys were a struggling, fighting ball of arms, legs and heads. Michael came out of the mass with his nose dripping blood. As soon as he put his hand up and realised his injury he dived back in, his arms swinging like a windmill. Their bodies locked in fierce combat, they fell against the vaulting-horse, sending it crashing to the floor. Harold Roberts the club leader rushed over and tried to break up the fight but was sent reeling by someone's fist. It was only when a boxing coach strode across and roughly yanked them apart that the fight was stopped. The boys looked a sorry sight as they were lined up to be read the riot act. Harold Roberts dabbed at his lip as he faced them.

'It was a black day fer this club when you lot joined,' he growled at them. 'Jus' look at yerselves. Yer bruvver Billy wouldn't be very proud of yer if 'e could see yer now. In fact, I fink 'e'd be downright disgusted. I'm sorry, there's nuffink I can do but expel the lot o' yerse. Yer know the rules. Any, fightin' in this club is done in the ring, not outside of it. That's the way it is.'

John Sullivan lowered his head in shame then stepped forward to plead their case. 'I'm sorry, Mr Roberts,' he said in a low voice. 'It was my fault. I started it. If yer gonna expel anybody, it should be me, not this lot.'

'You Sullivans are all the same,' the club leader shouted. 'What was it over?'

'Well, yer see, we're goin' in the army, me, Michael an' Joe,' the eldest brother replied. 'We didn't want Shaun ter go an' we was jossin' 'im.'

'But Shaun's only sixteen.'

'Yeah, but 'e's gonna put 'is age up,' John told him.

'An' what about the twins?'

'They're signin' on as well.'

'Oh my good Gawd!' the club leader exclaimed. 'Seven Sullivan bruvvers in one army. Yer commandin' officer's gonna end up shootin' 'imself! What about yer parents? What did they say when yer told 'em?'

'They don't know about it yet,' Shaun butted in.

'They do about us,' John said, pointing to himself, Michael and Joe.

Harold Roberts looked at the boxing coach and raised his eyes heavenwards. 'Well, I'm prepared ter waive the rules this once,' he sighed, shaking his head, 'seein' as yer all gonna be soldiers. Any more fightin' though an' yer out, is that understood?'

The boys all nodded in silence and a smile began to play around the club leader's lips. 'All I can say is, Gawd 'elp the Germans when you lot get ter the front,' he added. 'Now off 'ome wiv yer, before I change me mind.'

Chapter Thirty

Charlie Tanner leant against the cold iron guard-rail and gazed at Josephine as she stared sadly across the river in full spate. How like Carrie she was in looks, he thought. She had a similar pert nose and shapely lips and her fair hair shone the way Carrie's did. Josephine was shorter and slighter, although her figure was still curvy and womanly. Her eyes were different though. Carrie's were pale blue and wide-set, but Josephine's eyes were an intense blue, almost violet, and oval in shape. Charles studied her round forehead and saw how long her eyelashes were. She was a striking young woman.

There was a deepness to her which he could not fathom, and it had been a new experience being with her during the past few days. They had been wonderful days he would never forget. They had taken long walks in the warm sunshine, down as far as Greenwich and the park. They had climbed the hill and then rested beneath the shade of an old chestnut tree, looking down over the twisting silver band of river and watching the sun dip towards the west, changing the azure sky to fiery hues of red and gold. He had felt relaxed in Josephine's company, listening rapt as she told him about her work and watching that delightful twitch of her nose when she smiled. She was doing it now, he noticed as she smiled briefly at him and then stared back over the river.

It had been a restful week but it was over so soon. The days had flown by so quickly and tomorrow he would be returning to his regiment. He remembered kissing her clumsily that first night when they returned from the music hall, almost missing her lips in his hurry, and she had shyly kissed him on the cheek before walking quickly into the square. He had been taken by her beauty from that first evening when he met her outside the church hall. She had been nervous as she stepped out beside him, he recalled, keeping her distance and laughing too quickly at his jokes. It had all been so innocent and easygoing, but now there was a deep longing for her inside him and he sensed she felt it too.

Josephine was training during the evenings for her nursing certificate. Every night he met her at the church hall when she finished and escorted her home, saying goodbye to her in the quiet church gardens near her square. He held her gently, kissing her warm lips and letting her rest her head against his chest. It was her first experience of being alone with a young man and she had not been ashamed to tell him. He was very inexperienced, too, although he tried to hide it from her. But Josephine would have seen through it by now, he thought. She had laughed at his nervousness and fixed him with those beautiful, mocking eyes, as though daring him, willing him, to grow bold and impetuous. Now, as he watched her staring out over the river, strands of her tied-back hair loosening and blowing in the slight breeze, he became frightened. The war was drawing him away again and he would have to leave her.

Josephine turned to face him, framed by the distant towers and walkway of Tower Bridge. 'It's getting late,' she said softly.

He nodded and sighed deeply as he turned to look

downstream. 'It's bin a wonderful week,' he replied. 'I was jus' finkin' 'ow quick it's gone.'

'You will be careful, Charlie,' she urged him. 'I want you to come back soon.'

'Will yer write ter me?' he asked her.

'Every day, as soon as you let me know where you are,' she replied, smiling.

He moved away from the rail and realised that the riverside path was deserted. She had noticed it too and suddenly she was in his arms, her lips pressing against his, arms about his neck as her fingers moved through his short cropped hair. His arms were wrapped around her slim waist and shoulders and he squeezed her, feeling her warmth as she cuddled up against him. 'I fink I'm fallin' in love wiv yer, Josie,' he said in a voice he hardly recognised.

'I already have with you,' she replied in a breathless whisper.

They walked slowly back to Tyburn Square through the quiet summer evening, hardly speaking, dwelling on their imminent parting and trying hard not to think about the dangers ahead. They walked close together, and as Josephine held his arm tightly Charlie treasured the feeling of her beautiful slim body close to his.

They reached the square and stood for a few moments, holding each other close and dreading the moment when they would say goodbye. Suddenly Josephine stiffened and broke away from his embrace. They both heard it, the sound of trotting hooves on the hard cobbles, and quickly hid themselves beneath the overhanging branches of a large tree. The trap came into view and they saw George Galloway slumped down in the side seat, holding on to the reins as the gelding steered the conveyance into the square. He had not seen them but Josephine seemed uneasy.

'I'd better go now,' she said quickly.

They kissed briefly and she looked into his sad eyes. 'Come back soon, Charlie,' she told him. 'I'll pray for you every night.'

He smiled and watched her back away from him, waiting until she had reached her house and hurried up the steps. He saw her wave to him and then she was gone.

Charlie walked home slowly, his mind full of the young woman with whom he had shared his wonderful week. They had been discreet and secretive about the time they were spending together which seemed to make it more romantic. He had not told his family about Josephine and she had kept their meetings secret too. He had agreed with her that it might be better that way, at least for the time being. Their families were linked through the business and it was possible that there could be problems. Josephine had told him that her father could be difficult at times and she did not feel close enough to him to speak openly about herself and her friends. Charlie shared her fears. He too found it difficult to feel that his family completely understood him, although their home was a happy one. They would all have to know in time, he realised, but until the war ended and he was home for good, the romance would remain a secret.

The early summer of 1916 saw the exodus of thousands of young men from Bermondsey, bound for the battlefields of France. Every day Red Cross trains brought more casualties from the seaports and fresh recruits took their place in France to join the forces massing for the Somme offensive. German Zeppelins flew over London and the newspapers carried stories of civilians being killed and injured. In early June Lord Kitchener, the man who stared down from countless war posters, was drowned when his ship struck a mine off the

Orkneys. The war was becoming real for those at home now, and as more young men left for the front, more families waited and worried.

The three elder Sullivan boys had enlisted and Sadie sought comfort from her good friends in Page Street. 'I still can't believe it,' she said tearfully. 'Four of 'em in uniform, an' now the twins are talkin' about goin'. Gawd 'elp us, what am I gonna do?'

'There's nuffink yer can do, Sadie,' Florrie told her. 'They're all grown-up now. Yer can't keep wipin' their noses an' molly-coddlin' 'em. All yer can do is pray.'

Maisie nodded. 'My two wouldn't listen ter me or their farvver. They couldn't wait ter go. It's upset my Fred. 'E don't say much but 'e idolises them boys. 'E was only sayin' last night, if 'e was younger '*e'd* go. I didn't 'alf coat 'im. "Ain't I got enough worry wivout you goin' on about joinin' up?" I said to 'im. It's enough ter put yer in an' early grave.'

Nellie passed round the tea. 'When I see my two walkin' off up the turnin', I could 'ave bawled me eyes out,' she told her friends. 'It's funny, but I don't worry so much about James. 'E's always seemed ter be the strong one. It's young Charlie I worry over. 'E's so quiet. D'yer know, that week they were 'ome on leave Jimmy got drunk every night. 'E come in lookin' like 'e was gonna fall inter the fireplace, but young Charlie 'ardly touched a drop. 'E was out wiv a young lady friend, by all accounts.'

''E never brought 'er 'ome ter meet yer, then?' Florrie remarked.

'Not 'im,' Nellie replied. ''E's a proper dark 'orse is Charlie. I couldn't get much out of 'im at all. Apparently 'e met 'er on the station when 'e got off the train. She's a Red Cross nurse. That's all 'e'd say. I fink 'e liked 'er. 'E was out wiv 'er every night.'

Florrie sipped her tea noisily. 'Joe Maitland's upset,' she said presently. 'There was a letter waitin' fer 'im an' when 'e opened it 'is face went the colour o' chalk. It was one o' those white feavvers. Poor sod was really upset. Trouble is, 'e looks fit as anything. Yer wouldn't fink there's anyfing wrong wiv 'im ter look at 'im, would yer?'

'Who'd be wicked enough ter send them fings frew the post?' Maisie asked.

Florrie put down her teacup and reached into her apron pocket. 'There's plenty o' wicked gits about, Mais,' she replied, tapping on her snuff-box with two fingers. 'I dunno about the sign o' cowardice – *they're* the bleedin' cowards, those who send 'em. They never put their names ter the letters.'

Nellie refilled the teacups and made herself comfortable in her chair again, stirring her tea thoughtfully. 'I know yer won't let this go any furvver,' she said, looking up at her friends, 'but Frank Galloway got one o' those white feavvers. The ole man 'imself told my Will.'

Florrie shook her head slowly. 'I dunno where it's all gonna end, what wiv one fing an' anuvver.'

'Is 'e workin' in the yard regular, Nell?' Maisie asked. 'I've seen 'im go in there a lot this last year.'

'Yeah, 'e's took young Geoffrey's place,' Nellie replied. 'I liked Geoff. 'E was a quiet fella, an' very polite. Frank's different. There's somefing about 'im I don't like. I can't exactly put me finger on it but there's somefing there. Mind yer, I ain't 'ad much ter do wiv 'im, 'cept pass the time o' day. Funny 'ow yer take a dislike ter some people.'

Florrie nodded. 'I know what yer mean, Nell. I took an instant dislike ter that Jake Mitchell first time I clapped eyes on 'im. Right box o' tricks 'e is. 'Ow does your Will get on wiv 'im?'

Nellie shrugged her shoulders. 'Will don't say much but 'e's bin quiet an' moody ever since that Mitchell started work fer the firm. I reckon 'e's worried in case Galloway forces 'im out an' puts Mitchell in 'is place, that's my opinion.'

'But your ole man's bin wiv the firm fer donkeys' years,' Maisie cut in. 'Surely they wouldn't do that?'

'Don't yer be so sure,' Nellie said quickly. 'Galloway's got Jake Mitchell in fer a reason an' they're thick as thieves. Will was tellin' me they're gonna start that fightin' up again at the pubs. They stopped it when the war started, yer know. I s'pose George Galloway's finkin' of 'ow much 'e's gonna earn on the bloke. There's a lot o' bettin' goes on at those fights.'

'It's a wonder the police don't stop it,' Maisie remarked. 'They did before, so yer was tellin' me.'

Nellie smiled cynically. 'Those publicans are prob'ly linin' the 'ead coppers' pockets, if yer ask me.'

Florrie took another pinch of snuff and blew loudly into her handkerchief, eyes watering. 'Joe Maitland was tellin' me the ovver night that there's 'undreds o' pounds changes 'ands at those fights. 'E used ter go an' watch 'em at one time. Nasty turnouts they are, accordin' ter Joe.'

Maisie got up and stretched. 'Well, I better be off,' she announced with a yawn. 'I got some washin' in the copper.'

Florrie nodded. 'I've got a load ter wring out. I seem ter be washin' an' ironin' all bloody day since I took Joe in. Still, never mind, it's nice ter see a man around the place again,' she said, grinning slyly.

Carrie had resigned herself to the dull, monotonous routine at the café. The days seemed to drag by, the next one just like the last. The same old faces came in every day, and when it became quiet Bessie Chandler sat down at a table and went on endlessly about her friend Elsie Dobson and the man in the next flat who played his accordion at all hours of the day and night and would never be quiet, no matter what her husband threatened to do to him. Fred Bradley tried to stay cheerful but the constant and inane chatter from his indomitable helper usually put an end to that, and more than once Carrie found him out in the back yard, drawing deeply on a cigarette and muttering under his breath.

Soapy Symonds and Sharkey Morris sometimes put in an appearance, and they helped to put a smile back on Carrie's face with their comical tales. It was Soapy who revealed the secret life of Bessie Chandler one afternoon when he saw her coming out of the kitchen to run an errand for Fred. The café was quiet at the time and Soapy beckoned Carrie over.

'I didn't know Bessie Bubbles worked 'ere,' he said in surprise.

'Bessie who?' Carrie laughed.

'Bessie Bubbles,' Soapy said, grinning. 'Cor blimey, everybody round our way knows Bessie. It was the talk o' the street a few years ago. Yer remember me tellin' yer, don't yer, Sharkey?'

The long lean carman nodded dolefully, winking at Carrie as he raised his eyes to the ceiling. 'Yeah, I remember,' he said without enthusiasm.

Soapy leaned forward on the table and clasped his hands together. 'Yer see it was like this,' he began. 'Bessie's ole man works nights at Peek Frean's. Worked there fer years 'e 'as. Every night after 'e'd gone ter work, Bessie used ter go out o' the 'ouse carryin' a shoppin'-bag. Same time every night it was an' it was late when she got back. People started ter talk an' everybody reckoned she'd got 'erself a fancy man. Anyway, one night a few o' the lads went up town fer a night out an' one of 'em suggests they 'ave a walk roun' Soho jus' ter see the sights. Well, ter cut a long story short the lads are lookin' in a shop winder when this ole brass comes up an' asks 'em if they want a good time. They turns round an' who should it be standin' there but Bessie. She's all dressed ter the nines an' she's got this bubbly blonde wig on. The lads said she did look a sight. Now Bessie's reco'nised 'em, yer see, an' she don't know what ter do. She pleads wiv 'em not ter let on back in the buildin's an' one o' the lads, Mickey Tomlinson it was actually, comes up wiv a suggestion. Bessie wasn't too 'appy about it, but there was nuffink else she could do. They all ended up 'avin' a good time an' poor ole Bessie didn't get paid.'

Carrie tried to keep a straight face. 'Yer said it was the talk o' the street. Did they let on after all?'

Soapy chuckled. 'Nah, it wasn't them. What 'appened was, unbeknownst ter Bessie, 'er ole man was 'avin' it orf wiv this woman at work. Bin goin' on fer years by all accounts. Anyway, Bessie's ole man buys 'is fancy piece a new dress an' 'e brings it 'ome in a bag an' 'ides it under the bed. That night before Bessie gets 'ome from work, 'er ole man takes the bag from under the bed an' leaves 'er a note sayin' 'e's gotta go in early on overtime. Now when Bessie comes ter go out she finds 'er make-up an' wig is missin' an' there's a nice new dress in its place. 'Er ole man 'id the dress in the same place, an' in the 'urry 'e picked up the wrong bag. A couple of hours later in 'e walks wiv a nice shiner an' lookin' all sorry for 'imself. Apparently 'is lady friend didn't go a lot on the present 'e bought 'er. 'Im an' Bessie 'ad a right bull-an'-cow but they soon made up. There was nuffink else they could do, after all. They was both in the wrong. Bessie showed 'im 'ow she looked in 'er wig an' 'er ole man seemed ter fink it suited 'er. 'Im an' 'er ended up goin' out fer a drink. She was wearin' the dress 'e bought fer 'is lady friend an' 'ad the wig an' make-up on as well. She did look eighteen-carat. Mind yer, she didn't wear it fer long, not after all the kids in the street kept on callin' 'er Bessie Bubbles.'

Carrie was laughing aloud and Sharkey had a smile on his face as Bessie came walking into the shop, and they tried not to look too guilty. When she had disappeared into the kitchen Carrie leaned forward across the table. ''Ow did yer come ter know all what went on?' she asked curiously.

Soapy grinned. 'Elsie Dobson told my ole dutch. Elsie gets ter know everyfink. She's Bessie's next-door neighbour.'

'Yeah, I've 'eard Bessie mention 'er once or twice,' Carrie said, grinning back at him.

Trade had picked up at the Galloway yard during the early summer and more casual carmen had been employed. William Tanner was hard put to it to keep the horses and carts on the road and there were always lame animals to take care of. Jack Oxford made himself as inconspicuous as possible but even he found it difficult to take his afternoon nap now without someone calling for him. There was more chaff-cutting to do and more harnesses to clean and polish. The yard had to be swept clean of dung at least twice every day and the stables needed frequent mucking out. Sometimes Galloway left the trap standing in the yard and Jack made sure that he gave the gelding a wide berth. The cart-horses did not trouble him but the trap horse was different. It reminded him too much of the wild stallion that had almost trampled him to death all those years ago. The gelding had a fiery nature, and sometimes as it was driven into the yard in the morning Jack was sure that it looked at him with an evil glint in its devil eyes, just to let him know that it was going to get him.

Life had changed very little for Jack over the years. He still slept in the lodging-house, although the owner was taking in more strangers than usual now and some of them were young men who looked to Jack as if they were on the run. The police often called and many times he had been woken from a deep sleep by a torch flashing in his face. He had wondered whether he could sleep in the stables during the summer months, like he had before on occasions, until the trouble over the watch-and-chain. With all the extra carts and bales of hay stacked in the yard it seemed to him that he could easily loosen a fence plank without its being discovered. It would mean being extra careful, though, that no one saw him and no one came back with him. It was his good deed that led to his being found out the last time, he remembered. William had been good about it that time but the old man's other son was different to young Geoffrey. He would not think twice about sacking him if he was found out. He would have to decide soon, though, if things got much worse at the lodging-house.

Jack walked over to the harness shed and sat down on an upturned beer crate. It was mid-afternoon and soon the carts would be coming in. He might be able to get the yard swept before he left if they were not too late, he thought to himself. Then he could get on with those pieces of harness first thing next morning. Jack leaned back against the wall of the shed and waited. He liked things to be clear in his mind and once he had made a decision he felt happier. It had been miserable lately, he reflected. Frank Galloway was always grumpy and Jake Mitchell was forever taking the rise out of him. He was a nasty bloke and it wouldn't do to upset him. Even William Tanner seemed to be gloomy lately. Everything was dreary now. The war seemed to have made everyone miserable, and since Soapy and Sharkey had left no one laughed any more.

Jack stretched out his legs and closed his eyes. It was all quiet and there was nothing he could do for the time being, he reasoned, unless he started on cleaning the harness. No, he couldn't do that now. He had already said he was going to start on that in the morning. Maybe he should take a short nap. He would hear the carts coming in and he would feel a bit more fresh and ready to get the yard swept.

It was late afternoon when Jake Mitchell drove into the yard behind another cart and jumped down from his seat holding his aching back. 'Where's that bloody idiot Oxford?' he moaned at the carman who was just about to unclip the harness-chains from the shafts. The carman looked at him blankly and Jake stormed off towards the small shed at the end of the yard. As he strode into the dark interior, he stumbled over the yard man's outstretched legs and fell against a wooden bench.

Jack woke up with a start. 'Wassa matter?' he mumbled, still not properly awake.

'Wassa matter? I told yer ter fix that seat fer me last night,' Jake growled. 'Yer never done it. I've got a poxy backache over that seat. It wouldn't 'ave took yer five minutes.'

Jack stood up. 'I didn't 'ave time, Jake. Mr Galloway told me ter sweep the yard up before I went 'ome,' he said quickly.

Jake Mitchell leaned forward until his face was inches from the yard man's. 'Yer got time ter doss in 'ere though, yer lazy long bastard,' he snarled.

Jack's gaunt face took on a pained look. 'There's no need ter start callin' people names. I told yer I didn't 'ave time,' he said placatingly.

Jake's large hand shot out and gathered up a handful of the yard man's coat lapels. 'Why yer saucy ole git,' he growled. 'I've a good mind ter put one right on your chops.'

'I ain't scared o' yer,' Jack croaked. 'I ain't gonna let yer bully me.'

Mitchell suddenly let go of Jack's coat lapels, raised his arm and swung it down in a long swipe, the back of his hand catching Jack a sharp blow across his cheek. The yard man stumbled sideways and fell on all fours by the door. He blinked a few times then painfully staggered to his feet.

'I ain't frightened o' yer,' he said with spirit, moving around just out of Jake Mitchell's reach.

'Yer will be when I'm finished wiv yer,' Mitchell snarled, grabbing Jack and drawing his hand back for another swipe.

The unfortunate yard man closed his eyes and clenched his teeth as he waited for the blow, but it never landed. There was a sudden scuffle and his coat lapels were released. Jack opened his eyes and saw William Tanner standing between him and his tormentor.

'What the bloody 'ell's goin' on?' the foreman asked in a loud voice, looking from one to the other.

'I ain't takin' no lip from 'im,' Mitchell sneered.

'I wasn't givin' 'im any lip,' Jack said ruefully, rubbing his cheek.

'Right, that's it,' the foreman shouted. 'Get in the office. Sharp!'

Jake stood his ground, glowering at William. 'What about 'im?' he asked.

William stepped a pace closer to the red-faced carman. 'I'm talkin' ter you, not 'im,' he said menacingly. 'Now get in the office or I'll sack yer meself an' we'll see what the guv'nor's gonna do about that.' He turned to the yard man. 'You an' all.'

Frank Galloway was checkin' over a ledger, with his father peering over his shoulder. They looked up in surprise as the three men walked into the office.

'I've jus' stopped 'im settin' about Jack Oxford,' the foreman announced, jerking his thumb in Mitchell's direction. 'Yer better get this sorted out. I'm not puttin' up wiv fightin' in the yard.'

449

George puffed loudly. 'Look, Will, we're tryin' ter sort these books out, can't yer deal wiv it yerself?'

William's face was white with anger as he stood in the middle of the office. 'If it was left ter me I'd sack Mitchell 'ere an' now,' he said loudly.

George sat down at his desk and swivelled his chair around to face the men. 'Right, you first, Mitchell. What's bin goin' on?' he asked wearily.

When the two men had finished giving their differing versions and William had told how he came across Mitchell attacking the yard man, George leaned his heavy bulk forward in his chair and stared down at his feet for a few moments. 'Right, Will, leave this ter me,' he sighed. Then he turned to the yard man. 'Yer better get orf 'ome, Oxford,' he said. 'You too, Will. I'll talk ter yer in the mornin'.'

Once the two had left, George rounded on his carman. 'What did I tell yer about causin' trouble?' he shouted. 'Yer shouldn't 'ave slapped the stupid git. Yer puttin' me in a very awkward position. I told yer ter bide yer time, Jake. The fight circuit's startin' up any time now an' yer'll 'ave plenty o' chance ter paste someone's face in. It ain't the time ter cause any trouble 'ere.'

'Sorry, Guv', I wasn't finkin',' Jake mumbled, staring down at the floor.

'So yer should be,' George said, slightly mollified by Mitchell's show of remorse. 'Now piss orf 'ome, an' first fing termorrer yer'll apologise ter Will Tanner an' that idiot Oxford, understand?'

'But, Guv'. . .'

'No buts. Yer'll do as yer told,' Galloway shouted at him. 'Wait till yer got the foreman's job before yer start queryin' what I say.'

Frank had been silent during the whole of the episode, but

as soon as Mitchell had left the office he turned to his father. 'I don't think you should have said that to Mitchell about the foreman's job,' he said with a frown. 'You could give him a few ideas and cause a lot of trouble between him and Tanner.'

George grinned as he reached for the bottle of Scotch. 'I know what I'm doin', Frank,' he said confidently. 'That foreman o' mine is gettin' ter be a pain in the arse lately. I know 'e don't like Mitchell an' it's obvious ter me the feelin's mutual. It's a case o' playin' one against the ovver.'

'Well, I'd tread carefully if I were you,' Frank remarked. 'Tanner's got quite a temper. You said yourself the man knows horses, and if you pushed him too far and he had to leave we'd be hard pressed to find someone as reliable as him.'

'Mitchell knows 'orses too,' George replied. ''E's capable o' lookin' after the minor ailments an' 'e can always call the vet in if 'e don't know what ter do – that's all Tanner does. An' as far as the men go, I don't fink Jake would 'ave much trouble on that score.'

Frank studied his fingernails thoughtfully. 'Will Tanner's been with you a long time, Father,' he said, frowning. 'Wouldn't you regret losing him?'

George gulped a mouthful of whisky. 'Look, Frank, I've got a business ter run,' he said, glaring at his son. 'Will Tanner knows that. I get a bit fed up wiv the man comin' in 'ere tryin' ter mess around wiv my affairs. 'E don't seem ter know 'is place sometimes, an' 'e takes a bit too much fer granted. All the time 'e's worked fer me 'e's 'ad no rent ter pay an' I don't give 'im bad wages. It's about time 'e knew what goes around 'ere an' what don't. Anyway, 'e wouldn't 'ave much trouble gettin' anuvver job wiv 'is knowledge of 'orses.'

Frank watched as his father poured another Scotch. It was just an angry outburst, he told himself, but hearing him speak so ruthlessly about an old friend made Frank feel a little afraid. The old man seemed to have become even more obsessed with money lately, to the exclusion of everything else. The value of friendship, and the mutual respect that grew between people after long acquaintance, apparently meant nothing to him. It had been Geoffrey's main worry that having sown the seeds, their father would one day reap a bitter harvest.

Chapter Thirty-one

Carrie held her summer dress above her ankles as she stepped down from the tram at Greenwich. The late August Saturday afternoon was warm and sunny, with just the hint of a breeze, and the sky was cloudless. She crossed the busy street and walked through the tall iron gates into Greenwich Park, eager to meet Freda and Jessica after such a long time. A group of children screamed and laughed loudly as they played together beneath a leafy tree and in front of her a woman was pushing a perambulator along the gravel path which led up to the observatory. Carrie could see the copper dome glistening up ahead of her through the branches of tall trees which lined the path. In the distance she could hear the muffled sounds of a brass band playing. It was the bandstand where the three of them had arranged to meet and Carrie hummed a tune as she climbed the rise briskly in the warm sunlight.

It had been such a surprise meeting Jessica a week ago in Jamaica Road. She had been on her way from the market to catch a tram home to Deptford. They had not really had a chance to talk properly but Jessica had suggested that the three old friends should get together, and Carrie immediately welcomed her idea. Both Freda and Jessica were married with children now and it would be interesting to see how much they had changed, she thought. It would be nice, too, just to talk about little, everyday things and try to forget the war and all its tragedies and heartbreak.

Carrie was hot and breathless when she reached the level. Ahead of her she could see the bandstand and people standing around or sitting on the grass, listening to the Royal Artillery band. The scarlet and blue uniforms of the bandsmen contrasted brightly with the pale cotton dresses of the older women, who stood around beneath parasols, and the sober suits of their menfolk. Most of the younger women were alone or walking in pairs, but there were a few who were being escorted, and one or two on the arm of soldiers. Carrie's eyes searched the green and suddenly caught sight of her two friends, sitting together on the grass. When they spotted her they got up on to their knees and waved excitedly. Carrie hurried over and kissed the two of them on the cheek before she sank down beside them on the grass, puffing after her tiring walk.

The band was playing 'Roses of Picardy' and the rich sounds carried out over the wide expanse of green as the three friends sat together. Carrie could not help noticing the difference between her two old workmates. Jessica was wearing a smart dress adorned with buttons and bows, and her mousy hair was well groomed and neatly pulled up into a bun on top of her head. Her face still had a chubby look and her ample neck was bulging under her high lace collar. Freda seemed poorly dressed by comparison. Her long grey skirt looked worn and her frilly white blouse hung loose on her thin frame. Freda had never been robust but Carrie was shocked to see how gaunt she had become. Her cheeks were hollow and her large eyes seemed unusually bright and staring. She looked ill, Carrie thought.

''Ere, I almost fergot,' Jessica was saying, 'guess who I

saw the ovver day? Mary Caldwell. She's doin' war-work in some factory, makin' shells fer the guns, so she told me. I was surprised she left that job wiv the suffragettes. She said they've closed the office till the war's over.'

Freda held her handkerchief up as she coughed and wiped her watering eyes. 'I 'eard they've agreed ter call off the protests an' do war-work, providin' women get the vote,' she said, when she had recovered her breath.

'Are yer all right, Freda?' Carrie asked with concern. 'Yer don't look well.'

Her friend nodded. 'It's jus' me chest. The doctor said it's bronchitis. Trouble is, I'm pregnant again. He told me I shouldn't 'ave any more kids but what can I do? I can't lock 'im out o' the bedroom. Knowin' my bloke, 'e'd break the door down if I tried that.'

Jessica tutted. 'My Gerald's not like that,' she said quickly. ''E's very good really. In fact, 'e's mindin' the two little ones so I could come out this afternoon.'

'I could see my ole man doin' that,' Freda snorted. ''E's good at makin' babies but 'e don't like lookin' after 'em. Me mum's lookin' after mine. She reckoned it'd do me good ter get out fer a bit.'

Carrie suddenly felt as though a cloud had obscured the bright sun. Marriage had changed Freda for the worse, and she felt very sorry for her. All her old bounce and liveliness seemed to be missing, instead she looked crushed. Carrie sighed inwardly as she reclined on the cool grass. Was that what she herself could expect from marriage? she wondered with a sinking feeling.

Jessica was staring at her. 'Ain't yer got a young man, Carrie?' she asked suddenly.

She shook her head. 'I was walkin' out wiv a young man but we parted. 'E's in the army now.'

'My Gerald wanted ter join the army but 'e said 'e couldn't bear ter leave me an' the children,' Jessica remarked. 'We're worried now they've made it compulsory for married men too. 'E'll 'ave to go now anyway.'

'Our Jimmy an' Charlie are both in the army,' Carrie told them. 'And Danny said 'e's goin' soon, an' four o' the Sullivan boys 'ave joined up too. All the young men 'ave gone from our street. It seems so quiet now.'

Freda was racked with another spasm of coughing and leaned back, exhausted. 'I'm gonna get rid o' this one,' she said after a while.

Carrie and Jessica stared at her, visibly shocked. Freda had spoken so casually.

'Anuvver kid would finish me,' she went on. 'I know I'm takin' a chance but this woman's s'posed ter be pretty good. I jus' 'ope it don't turn out like the last time. That ole bag I went ter see nearly killed me.'

Carrie could see the despair and veiled fear in Freda's eyes and looked away, glancing around at the well-dressed women and gazing over towards the bandstand. The musicians were striking up with 'A Bird in a Gilded Cage' and as the brazen melody sounded out across the grass people around them began to sing the sad words. Carrie had been looking forward to a pleasant afternoon with her friends. Now she was beginning to feel desolate.

Suddenly she sat up straight. 'C'mon, let's go an' get a nice cup o' tea an' a fluffy cake,' she said, smiling. 'My treat.'

The café was busy but the young women soon found a shaded table out on the terrace and made themselves comfortable. As they sipped their tea they watched the horse-drawn carriages grind past along the gravel drive, and Freda seemed to cheer up. She giggled as she took a bite from her cream cake and the filling squirted out on to her chin. Jessica sat upright, trying to look demure as she bit into her own cake, but she ended up looking messier than Freda as the cream spread around her mouth. For a moment then Carrie felt that they could have been back at the leather factory. They were all laughing again, just like they used to at their factory bench or when they went on those tiring and often frightening marches. She thought of the times they had carried the heavy banners and tried to look very confident and bold, although inside they were all nervous and fearful of what might happen to them. She thought of Mary Caldwell and the determined look on her round face as she chanted the slogans and cheeked the police and hecklers. Carrie felt the smile on her face growing wider and wider, and as she bit her own cake the cream squirted up on to her nose.

Jessica laughed as she watched. 'Penny fer yer thoughts,' she said, chuckling.

Carrie smiled. 'I was jus' finkin' about when we used ter go on them marches, I was terrified.'

'So was we all,' Jessica admitted.

'I used ter admire those posh women who got 'emselves locked up. They didn't seem worried at all,' Freda remarked. 'I used ter like that one who was always on about women goin' on sex strikes. Yer remember 'er, the woman wiv that short 'air. Margaret, I fink 'er name was.'

'That's right,' Jessica cut in. 'That was the woman Mary fell in love wiv. She used ter swoon over 'er, didn't she?'

'She was the one who was tellin' us about those fings ter stop yer gettin' pregnant,' Carrie reminded them.

'Yeah, that's right. Contraceptives, she called 'em. She said men put 'em on their fings when they go wiv women,' Freda recalled. 'I remember 'er sayin' yer could buy 'em. I wish my ole man would. Mind yer, I don't s'pose 'e'd wear one anyway.'

'That's what that Margaret was sayin',' Carrie went on. 'She said a lot o' men fink it does 'em 'arm an' they won't wear 'em.'

'That Margaret 'ad a lot o' good ideas,' Jessica remarked. 'I remember 'er goin' on about what the government should be doin'. She said they should be settin' up special clinics jus' fer women an' then we'd be able ter find out 'ow ter stop gettin' pregnant.'

'I can't see that ever 'appenin',' Freda said. 'Not till we get the vote anyway. The only way we can stop gettin' pregnant now is not ter let the men 'ave their conjugals. That way we wouldn't get pregnant but there'd be fousands o' women walkin' about wiv black eyes.'

'I fink I'll stay single,' Carrie said, laughing.

'That won't stop yer gettin' pregnant,' Freda replied. 'I can vouch fer that. The only way is ter give up men altergevver an' do what Mary does – 'ave a woman fer a lover.'

The friends finally left the café and strolled through the rose gardens, walking in a slow circle and arriving back to where the path led down towards the gates. They gazed down at the afternoon sunlight reflecting on the quiet river below them, beyond the classical white walls of the Royal Naval School. The air was fresh and Carrie breathed deeply as she stood with her two workmates on the brow of the hill. How different it was from the suffocating closeness of the little backstreets with their dilapidated houses and tenement blocks. They set off slowly, walking down the hill towards the faint sound of the early evening traffic, and Freda began coughing again.

In late summer Page Street's first war casualty was back home after being disabled in the Somme offensive. Billy Sullivan sat at his front door in the warm afternoon sunshine, his shoulders hunched from the shrapnel wound in his chest and his breathing laboured. Danny Tanner sat with him, saddened to see his idol looking so unwell, and doing his best to cheer him up.

'Yer'll soon be fit as a fiddle, Billy,' he said encouragingly. 'Pedlar Palmer'll 'ave ter watch out then. You'll beat 'im easy.'

'I've 'ad me last fight, Danny ole son,' Billy replied, grimacing. 'Yer need all yer wind in the ring. I can't even get up the stairs wivout puffin'.'

'Yer'll get better, don't worry,' Danny said quickly, trying to reassure him. 'The war won't last ferever an' then yer'll be back in that ring knockin' 'em all out. I can be yer second if yer like. We'll make a good team, you an' me.'

Billy smiled cynically. 'I wish now I 'adn't bin so bloody keen ter get in the war,' he muttered. 'It seemed like it was a big adventure we was goin' on. I remember when I signed on – the band was playin' an' all the blokes were laughin' an' jokin', sayin' what they was gonna do when they got out there. Everybody was clappin' an' cheerin' us, an' givin' us fags. It was the same all the way ter the recruitin' office. They're not laughin' now, none of them. There's no bands playin' an' nobody's rushin' ter join up. They've all got more bloody sense.'

Danny looked into his friend's faded blue eyes. 'Well, yer out of it now, Billy. Yer'll get fit again soon an' back in that ring, jus' wait an' see,' he coaxed.

Billy shook his head sadly. 'I'm never gonna put a pair o' gloves on again,' he said, his voice faltering. 'It's up ter you now, mate. Jus' remember what I told yer: keep those fists up an' stay light on yer feet. Do as the trainer tells yer an' train 'ard. Who knows? One day we might 'ave a national champion in Page Street after all.'

Danny's face became serious. 'Yer'll always be the

champion as far as I'm concerned, Billy,' he said staunchly. 'As fer me, boxin's gonna 'ave ter wait till the war's over. I signed on terday.'

The autumn days were growing shorter, with chill winds heralding a cold winter as more troop trains rolled in to Waterloo Station, full of veterans from the long campaign. Many young men having experienced the horrors of trench warfare in winter-time were filled with dread at the possibility of another spell at the front in bitter weather. One young soldier who became too terrified to return was Percy Jones from Page Street. When his short leave was over he did not catch his allotted train. Instead he walked into the Kings Arms and got drunk. That night he slept like a baby. The next morning he got up and strolled down to the quayside and watched the ships being unloaded and the barges being brought upriver. Percy tried to forget the mud and blood of the battlefields and the comrades he had lost. As he gazed at the river, he remembered how carefree and happy his childhood had been. He sat for hours at the dockside, recalling the times he and his friends had climbed down into the barges in search of coconut husks. Then he took a long stroll to London Bridge and over the river to Billingsgate. Percy smiled as he walked the greasy wet cobbles and saw the last of the fish vans leaving. As a lad he had strolled through that market much earlier in the day, and often taken home haddock or mackerel or sometimes a large plaice, depending on what was available and how close to it the market policeman was. Next morning he would get up early and stroll through the market while it was busy, he promised himself.

That evening Percy Jones put on his threadbare suit, clumsily knotted his red silk scarf around his neck and pulled on his highly polished boots, giggling as he realised that he had them on the wrong feet. Maggie Jones was near to tears as she confronted her son, but he did not seem to understand why.

'If yer don't intend ter go back orf leave, why don't yer go an' stay wiv yer sister down in Surrey?' she suggested to him anxiously. 'They'll be comin' fer yer soon, Perce, an' they'll frogmarch yer out o' the street. They done it ter Mrs Wallis's boy. Gawd, I wish yer farvver was still alive. 'E'd know what ter do.'

Percy shrugged his shoulders as he walked out of the house. He wondered what his mother might mean and suddenly felt lonely and lost, a young lad whose friends had all gone away. Why would they come for him? he thought as he entered the Kings Arms and ordered a pint of ale.

The public bar was filled with smoke and an accordionist was standing beside the piano playing 'Bill Bailey, Won't You Please Come Home?' People were singing loudly and Alec Crossley was busy pulling pints.

Grace Crossley had spotted Percy Jones sitting alone and she nudged her husband. ''Ere, Alec, I've bin watchin' that Percy. I wonder if 'e's all right? 'E looks sort o' funny,' she remarked.

'What d'yer mean, funny?' he asked her. ''E looks all right ter me.'

Grace scratched her head thoughtfully. 'I'm sure 'e was due back on Thursday,' she recalled, 'at least that's what 'is muvver told me.'

'P'raps 'e's got an extension,' Alec suggested.

'I dunno,' Grace said. 'Maybe 'e's deserted. Mind yer, I wouldn't blame 'im if 'e 'as. Poor sod looks shell-shocked ter me.'

''Ow d'yer know what shell-shock looks like?' Alec laughed.

'I see Mrs Goodall's boy, an' that young Johnnie Ogden from Bacon Street. They was both shell-shocked,' Grace replied indignantly. 'Mrs Goodall told me 'erself. She told me about Johnnie Ogden too. Percy's got that same funny look on 'is face.'

'Percy's always 'ad a funny look on 'is face,' Alec chuckled. 'I fink it runs in the family. Maggie Jones always seems ter be vacant when yer see 'er in the street.'

The pub door suddenly opened and Fred Dougall came in. He stood looking around the bar for a few moments, and when he spotted the young man hurried over to him.

'The army's bangin' on yer door, Percy,' he whispered. 'There's a couple o' coppers wiv 'em an' there's a Black Maria outside yer 'ouse as well.'

'Fanks, Fred. I'll go out in a minute,' he said calmly.

Alec and Grace Crossley were gazing out through the windows and people were gathering in the street as Percy pulled his cap down over the top of his ears and strolled out of the Kings Arms. He shuffled calmly up to a military policeman sitting at the wheel of a car and gave him his special cross-eyed stare as he climbed in next to him. Percy had been doing that stare for years to make his friends laugh. He made one of his eyes turn so far inward that the pupil almost disappeared. The military policeman rounded on him angrily. 'Oi! Get out this motor, yer stupid git,' he growled.

Percy looked appealingly at the soldier. 'Gis a ride, mister,' he said.

'If yer don't get out o' this motor, I'll knock yer bloody 'ead orf yer shoulders,' the soldier snarled, leaning towards him threateningly.

'I only wanted a ride,' Percy moaned, climbing out of the vehicle.

Mrs Jones was standing at her front door, having suffered

the indignity of seeing her whole house being searched. As she spotted her son standing beside the army car, she nearly fainted on her doorstep.

'We'll be back,' a policeman told her as he strode out of her house. 'If yer son does show up, tell 'im ter give 'imself up straight away. The longer 'e overstays 'is leave, the worse it's gonna be fer 'im when we do catch 'im.'

Percy stepped back to let the other military policeman get into the vehicle, giving him one of his best stares and saluting eagerly. When they had left he grinned widely at his mother and walked calmly back into the pub.

On a chill Sunday morning in September as the church bells were calling people to worship, Nora Flynn put on her hat and coat and smiled to herself. She always looked forward to the morning service at St James's Church and particularly enjoyed the sermons given by the new minister. He was a fiery orator and the sound of his deep, cultured voice resounding throughout the lofty stone building filled her with a sense of calm. It was there too that she met her old friends and chatted with them after the service as they walked together through the well-tended gardens.

Nora Flynn did not attend that morning service, however, for as she came down the stairs there was a loud knocking on the front door and she was confronted by an elderly army officer who brought the tragic news that Lieutenant Geoffrey Galloway had been killed on the Somme.

Chapter Thirty-two

Throughout the cold winter months the curtains at number 22 Tyburn Square remained drawn. The draughty house had become almost like a mausoleum, with guarded voices speaking in whispers and footsteps sounding strangely loud in the silent rooms. Nora tried her best to comfort George in his grief and was saddened to see how the tragedy aged him. He had lost his upright posture and stooped as he trudged around, a shadow of his former self. Since the fateful Sunday in September, his eyes had grown more heavy-lidded and bleary with the amount of whisky he was drinking, and his hair had become totally grey. The running of the business had been left to Frank. The only time George left the house was late at night when he drove his trap through the gaslit streets down to the river, where he would sit watching the tide turn and the mists roll in.

When she had recovered from the first shock of Geoffrey's death Nora realised she had a painful duty to perform. Mary O'Reilly would have to be told. Nora's eyes filled with tears as she went to the sideboard drawer and took out the slip of paper from inside her family bible. She remembered Geoffrey joking with her when he gave her his lady-friend's address for safekeeping in case anything should happen to him. 'Put it in your bible, Nora,' he had said laughing. 'Father won't find it there, that's for sure.'

Geoffrey had told her that his lady-friend's husband was always out of the house during the day, so on Tuesday morning Nora boarded a tram to Rotherhithe and then walked through the little backstreets to Mary O'Reilly's home near the river. It was a three-storey house at the end of a narrow lane and Nora bit on her lip with dread as she climbed the four steps and knocked timidly on the front door.

As soon as Mary opened the door she recognised Nora and her mouth sagged opened. 'Oh no! Not Geoff?' she gasped.

Nora nodded slowly, reaching out her hand to clasp the young woman's arm. 'I'm so sorry. I had to come,' she said softly. 'I felt I 'ad ter tell yer. They told us last Sunday mornin'.'

Mary closed her eyes tightly and swayed backwards, and as Nora took her by the arms she rested her head against the housekeeper's shoulder. 'I was dreadin' this,' she sobbed. 'I knew it was gonna 'appen some day.'

Nora helped the young woman into her cluttered parlour and made her sit down in an armchair. Mary was shaking with shock and she leant against the edge of the chair, clutching a handkerchief tightly in her shaking hands.

Nora had noticed Mary's condition. She put a hand on her shoulder. 'Is it Geoffrey's?' she asked, knowing the answer already.

Mary nodded. 'I wrote an' told 'im. I've got 'is last letter in the drawer. Geoff was gonna tell 'is father about us an' the baby as soon as 'e got 'ome. Now 'e'll never see 'is child,' she sobbed.

Nora made the distraught young woman a cup of strong tea, and when she saw that Mary had composed herself sufficiently she asked her, 'Does yer 'usband know it's not 'is?'

Mary laughed bitterly. 'We've not slept tergevver fer months. I couldn't put off tellin' 'im an' as soon as I did 'e walked out. I couldn't blame 'im, Nora,' she sobbed. ''E was a good man despite everyfing, but 'e's got 'is pride. I expected 'im ter give me a good 'idin', or at least tell me what a slut I was, but 'e didn't. 'E didn't say anyfing. 'E jus' left wivout a word. Oh Gawd! I jus' want ter die.'

Nora bent down and gripped Mary's hands in hers. 'Now listen ter me,' she said firmly. 'Yer got a duty ter look after yerself fer the baby's sake. Young Geoffrey would 'ave bin so proud, 'specially if it's a boy. Yer gotta go an' see Geoff's farvver soon as the baby's born. 'E'll be able ter provide fer both o' yer.'

Mary looked up at her visitor, her eyes red with crying. 'I won't take charity. I'll manage some'ow,' she said forcefully.

Nora patted the young woman's hand. 'Yer must tell George Galloway,' she urged her. 'Wait till the time's ripe an' go an' see 'im, Mary. Yer'll need all the 'elp yer can get. Bring Geoff's letter wiv yer, the ole man'll 'ave ter believe yer then.'

As Nora left the drab house in the lane by the river she felt the cold biting into her bones. She hoped the young woman would see sense and go to Galloway, but there had been something in her eyes that told Nora otherwise.

Josephine had borne the tragic news with courage, and the following Monday evening attended her nursing training at the church hall as usual. She had tried to talk with her father and find some common comfort with him but found it impossible. Geoffrey's death seemed to have widened the barrier between them and Josephine was left to grieve alone. She was determined to be strong and threw herself into her work, but each day as she gazed down at the sick and maimed soldiers on the endless rows of stretchers she thought of Geoffrey, and found herself mumbling frantic prayers that Charlie Tanner would return safely.

The death in action of Geoffrey Galloway had saddened everyone who knew him. William Tanner was particularly upset. He had always found Geoff to be a friendly and easy-going young man with a serious side to his nature. He had managed the firm well and at times gone against his own father when he deemed it right. William felt that this was something Frank Galloway would not be inclined to do. The younger brother was less approachable than Geoffrey had been. He was more like his father and seemed to have the same ruthless streak.

The young man's death had come at a time when there was already a tense atmosphere in the yard. Jake Mitchell had grudgingly apologised for his assault on Jack Oxford but still displayed a sullen, mocking attitude. William could not help dwelling on the frosty meeting he had had with George the morning following the attack on the yard man. Galloway had spelt out in no uncertain terms the reasons why he was not prepared to get rid of Mitchell and there had been a thinly veiled threat in the owner's words. William knew for certain now that if it ever came to a choice between him and Mitchell, he would be the one to go. In that eventuality Jack Oxford would be sacked too, William was sure, and he felt sorry for the tall, clumsy yard man. Jack did his work well enough and asked only that he be left alone to get on with it. He too had worked in the yard for many years, although William was well aware that this did not seem to count for much where Galloway was concerned. There was also a distinct likelihood that things would begin to change for the worse now that he had lost his elder son. William felt that the loss of Geoffrey would make Galloway even more ruthless than ever.

During the quiet days of late December, after the Christmas festivities, Fred Bradley suddenly summoned up the courage to invite his young employee out for the evening. Carrie was wiping down the tables after the last customers had left, and Fred sauntered over looking a little awkward.

'Look, Carrie, would yer like to come to the music 'all on Friday night?' he said suddenly. 'The Christmas revue's still on at the Camberwell Palace, and it's supposed ter be really good.'

Carrie looked at him in surprise. 'This Friday?' she asked, too taken aback to say anything else.

Fred nodded, his face flushing slightly. 'Well, after all, everyone else has been enjoyin' 'emselves over the 'oliday. The break'd do yer good,' he said, smiling nervously. 'As long as yer can put up wiv an old geezer like me escortin' yer while all the young lads are away . . .'

Carrie was touched by Fred's disarming remark, and the wide-eyed look of anticipation on his face made her chuckle. 'All right, Fred,' she replied. 'Thank you, that'd be very nice.'

'We can go in the first 'ouse,' he went on, 'an' I'll see yer back to yer front door, don't worry.'

As the time of the outing approached, Carrie began to feel apprehensive. She remembered the times she had gone to the music hall with Tommy and she was worried in case Fred tried to become too familiar with her. But it turned out to be a lovely evening.

Fred looked smart in his tight-fitting suit, starched collar and sleeked-back dark hair, and he held his head proudly erect as he escorted Carrie along the Jamaica Road to the tram stop.

The show was very entertaining, and Carrie was tickled by Fred's noisy laugh. During the interval he bought her a packet of Nestlé's chocolates wrapped in gold paper, which they shared, enjoying the sweet taste. When the lights dimmed for the second half of the show, Fred sat forward eagerly in his seat, looking directly in front of him as though afraid he might miss something, and Carrie was touched by his boyish enthusiasm.

When the performance was over and the audience crowded into the street, Carrie held on to Fred's arm tightly and screwed up her face against the cold as they waited at the tram stop.

As good as his word, Fred saw her back to her home in Page Street, and as they walked they chatted together like old friends. At the front door Carrie thanked him for the evening and he made a slight, comical bow, smiling awkwardly. Then he turned away and walked off through the gaslight, whistling loudly as though to hide his embarrassment.

A week later, at the beginning of January 1917, Carrie heard from one of the carmen who called in the café that Tommy Allen was home from the war. She was unable to glean much information from the customer except that Tommy was wounded and had got his discharge. The news threw Carrie into a state of confusion, wondering whether she should go to see him. She could still remember clearly all the anger and remorse she had experienced at the end of their affair, and yet despite all that had happened between them she was still very fond of Tommy.

When she finished work that Saturday morning Carrie walked through the railway arches into St James's Road and knocked on Tommy's front door. She stood there waiting in the cold air for what seemed an eternity. Finally she heard noises in the passage and the door opened. Tommy seemed taken aback to see her but quickly invited her in and led the way into the tiny parlour. He was leaning on a walking stick and his left foot was heavily bandaged and encased in a boot that had been cut away at the instep.

'One o' the customers told me yer was 'ome,' she said, sitting herself down beside the lighted kitchen range.

Tommy smiled awkwardly. 'News travels fast. I only got back a few days ago. I've been fer convalescence in Wales.'

Carrie watched as he eased himself back in his chair and stretched out his bandaged foot towards the fire. 'What 'appened?' she asked.

'Frostbite,' he answered simply. He saw her enquiring look. 'I lost me toes.'

She winced visibly. 'I'm so sorry. Are yer in a lot o' pain?'

He shook his head. 'There's not much pain now. The only problem is, I can't walk prop'ly. I'll be able ter do wivout this stick in time but I've gotta get used ter 'obblin' about.'

Carrie felt uncomfortable under his gaze and glanced towards the fire. Tommy pulled himself up straight in the chair. 'I'm sorry, I should 'ave asked yer if yer wanted a cup o' tea,' he said quickly.

'I'll get it,' she said, getting to her feet, but Tommy stood up and reached for the teapot.

'I'll do it. I'm not exactly useless,' he remarked with a note of irritation in his voice.

Carrie watched him as he poured the tea and could see that he had lost weight. He looked pale and drawn, and there were dark shadows around his eyes. His short-cropped dark hair showed signs of premature greying. ''Ow's yer mum?' she asked, trying to ease the tension.

'She's all right. She's still wiv me bruvver,' he answered, handing her the tea. 'I'll be 'avin' 'er back, soon as I can.'

She sipped in silence, her eyes straying down to his

bandaged foot. She grew more uncomfortable, realising she could not think of anything to say.

Tommy suddenly brightened. 'I'm not complainin'. I was one o' the lucky ones,' he told her, smiling. 'I was on a night patrol, the last in the line, an' I slipped in a shell-'ole. It was freezin' cold an' I couldn't call out. I jus' sat there until the patrol come back. By that time I couldn't feel me feet an' that's 'ow I got frostbite. As I say, though, I was one o' the lucky ones. The next day I was carted off ter the forward 'ospital an' at the same time me mates went over the top. It was sheer murder, so I was told. I could 'ave bin wiv 'em if I 'adn't fell in that shell-'ole.'

Carrie looked down into her empty cup. 'My bruvvers are all in France. Danny, the youngest, 'as only jus' gone over there,' she said quietly.

'They'll be all right,' Tommy said cheerfully. 'It'll be over soon. There was talk about an armistice when I was in the 'ospital.'

'I 'ope yer right,' she said with feeling. 'We're all worried sick. Me mum didn't want Danny ter go, 'im bein' the youngest, but 'e wouldn't listen.'

'None of us would,' Tommy replied, easing his position in the chair. 'Anyway, let's change the subject. What about you?'

'I'm well, an' I'm still workin' in the café,' she told him. 'It seems strange now, though. Most o' the customers are older men. There's only a few young ones come in. It's the same in our street. All the young men 'ave gone in the army.'

Tommy looked into the fire. 'I bumped into Jean,' he said suddenly, his eyes coming up to meet hers. 'Yer remember me tellin' yer about Jean? She was the young lady I used ter go out wiv. Apparently she's split up wiv 'er bloke an' we've been out a few times. She wants us ter get tergevver again.'

'Will yer?' Carrie asked him.

'I dunno,' he answered, prodding at a torn piece of linoleum with his walking stick. 'It all went wrong before an' now I'm takin' me muvver back as well.'

'Does Jean know?' Carrie asked.

'I told 'er, but she still wants us ter try an' make a go of it,' Tommy replied.

Carrie's eyes searched his for an indication. 'Do yer really want to?'

He nodded slowly. 'I've bin finkin' over all that's 'appened an' I realised I didn't give 'er a fair chance. It was the same wiv me an' you, Carrie. We were doomed right from the start. I've decided ter try again wiv Jean, an' this time I won't let the ole lady come between us. One fing's fer sure, though, I'll never ferget our time tergevver. We did 'ave some good times, didn't we?'

Carrie nodded, a strange feeling of sadness and relief welling up inside her. Tommy had been her first love, but she knew that he was right. Their romance had been doomed to failure. She had come to accept their parting and realised that he had too. Although she was sad at the thought of what might have been, it was some relief to know that Tommy had a prospect of happiness.

'I wish yer all the best, Tommy,' she said, getting up from her chair.

'That goes fer me too, Carrie,' he said, taking her arm and planting a soft kiss on her cheek. 'I 'ope we can stay good friends.'

Carrie walked back through the railway arches deep in thought. The war had cruelly changed Tommy just as it had Billy Sullivan. How many more young men would be maimed or killed before it was over? she wondered, trying not to think about her three absent brothers. A train passed overhead and the rumble sent a flock of pigeons into the air. A chill wind stung her face and Carrie shivered as she crossed Jamaica Road.

Since his brother's death Frank had been hard put to it at the yard. His father had lost interest in the business and very rarely shown his face in Page Street. It was only after many arguments and much pleading that Frank managed to persuade the old man to become involved in the firm again. At first George called into the yard once or twice a week, but as time went by he began to turn up more regularly, and it was obvious to everyone how he had changed. He was an embittered man, and he made life uncomfortable for those around him. Jack Oxford was always an easy target for the firm owner's anger and he kept himself out of sight whenever possible.

On Saturday morning George Galloway drove his trap into the yard and jumped down, looking agitated. "'E's bin droppin' 'is 'ead. I fink it's the knee joint,' he said to William.

The foreman bent down and lifted the gelding's foreleg, gently running his thumb and forefinger down from the knee to the fetlock. 'It's a thoroughpin,' he pronounced, lowering the horse's leg.

'A what?'

'An inflamed tendon sheath. Look, yer can feel it.' William showed him.

'What yer gonna do, poultice it?' Galloway asked.

William nodded. 'I'll put the 'orse in the small stable an' put a linseed poultice on. It'll need a couple o' days' rest.'

Galloway nodded and walked away, mumbling under his breath.

Frank looked up as his father came into the office. 'There's a message from Don McBain,' he told him. 'He said it's on for next week.'

George allowed himself a brief smile. 'Well, that's a bit o' good news. Don's bringin' anuvver punch-bag down from Glasgow,' he said, lowering himself heavily into his chair. 'I'm sure Jake'll be pleased. 'E's bin waitin' fer this one.'

Frank shook his head slowly. 'You ought to be careful, Father. One of these days someone's going to put Mitchell down on the floor and you'll lose a packet.'

'I know what I'm doin',' George said quickly. 'I can judge a fighter, an' if the opposition looked too good I wouldn't lay a bet. Besides, McBain pays 'is boys ter climb inter the ring. I pay Jake Mitchell on results. That way there's an incentive. Not that Jake needs any goadin'. 'E's got a vicious nature, an' when 'e pulls those gloves on 'e wants a lot o' stoppin'. Jake jus' loves ter fight.'

Frank shrugged his shoulders and got on with the books. He was feeling worried and not in the least inclined to hear about Jake Mitchell's prowess. Bella had told him she was pregnant, and she was none too happy about it either. Frank had already been rowing with her over her socialising, the endless round of parties she had been attending with that nancy boy Hubert. Not that there was reason to suspect him of any impropriety, Frank thought to himself with a smile. Even Bella admitted that Hubert preferred men to women. Frank knew that the young man had many contacts in the theatrical profession, and being seen in Hubert's company was helping to further Bella's career, but he felt angry that she never asked him to attend the parties as well. He seemed to be totally ignored. Well, her little forays would soon be over, he told himself. Even Bella would blanch at the thought of attending one of those parties in an interesting condition.

There was another problem causing Frank considerable anguish and dismay. He had been receiving a spate of anonymous letters and the most recent one was torturing him. Enclosed was the usual white feather, but the contents of the letter itself had grown darker and even more hateful. It was printed in crude capitals and badly composed but the message was clear enough. Frank was accused of getting rich from the war, exploiting the poor workers under him while being an abject coward, hiding away while his elder brother did his fighting for him and laid down his life on the battlefield. Frank knew that he should have burnt all the letters as he had the first one but found himself carefully keeping every one hidden in his desk drawer at home, aware that he might never find out who had written them.

That Saturday evening was quiet in the Tanner household. William dozed in front of an open fire and Nellie sat quietly working on her embroidery. Carrie was curled up in an easy chair, reading a short story in the *Star*, her eyes occasionally flitting to the drawn curtains as the wind rattled the window-panes. After a while she folded up the newspaper and dropped it on the floor beside her. How different from when the boys were at home, she thought. Usually there was a fight for the paper and the fireside chair, or an argument over cards or a game of dominoes. Usually James and Danny would be doing the arguing, with Charlie burying his head in a book and refusing to get involved. They were all involved now, Carrie sighed.

As though reading her mind, Nellie looked up from her sewing. 'Wasn't the newspaper bad terday?' she said in a worried voice. 'It was full o' the war. There don't seem no end to it.'

William stirred. He sat up, scratching his head. 'I ought ter see if the geldin's all right,' he said wearily.

'Yer changed the poultice this afternoon,' Nellie said without looking up from her sewing. 'Surely it'll keep till the mornin'?'

'I s'pose yer right,' he nodded. 'I'll change it first fing termorrer.'

'Was it Galloway's fault the 'orse fell lame?' Carrie asked.

William shrugged his shoulders. 'It's 'ard ter say,' he replied. 'What 'e is or what 'e ain't, George don't ill-treat 'is 'orses. But 'e might 'ave run it a bit 'ard, 'specially if 'e'd bin at the booze.'

'It's a beautiful 'orse,' Carrie remarked. 'It'll be all right, won't it, Dad?'

'It's an inflamed tendon. It'll be fine in a few days.'

Nellie got up and stretched. 'I'll put the kettle on an' see 'ow that currant pudden is,' she said. 'It's bin boilin' fer over two hours.'

Suddenly there was a loud rat-tat on the front door and Nellie exchanged anxious glances with Carrie as William went to see who it was. Immediately, he rushed back with a serious look on his face. He grabbed his coat from behind the door and snatched the yard keys from the mantelshelf.

'It's 'Arold Temple. 'E reckons there's smoke comin' from the stable,' he shouted as he dashed from the room.

Carrie and her mother jumped up and put on their coats, following him out into the street. William quickly unlocked the wicket-gate, and as he was about to step through into the yard the end stable burst into flames.

'Quick!' he shouted to Harold. 'Run up the pub an' tell 'em ter phone the fire brigade!'

William stumbled through the gate and dashed across the yard, aware that the gelding was tethered in the flaring stable. He could hear its terrified neighing as he drew close and he felt the heat of the flames on his face. There must be a way of getting in there somehow, he thought frantically. In desperation he grabbed a saddle blanket draped over the hitching-rail and threw it in the horse trough to soak it, intending to shroud himself and dash through the flames, but then the side of the stable was suddenly kicked out and the singed animal darted out into the yard, bucking and rearing. William just managed to throw the blanket over the animal's back as it reared up and sent him sprawling. The stable was now burning fiercely and the heat of the flames was making it difficult for him to breathe. He could hear the women screaming as the horse reared up above him, about to trample him. He tried to dodge the hooves and Carrie was suddenly beside him, grabbing at the gelding's trailing bridle-rope. William rolled out of the way and Carrie struggled to reach the bridle as she pulled back on the rope. The gelding was backing into the far corner of the yard, away from the flames, and Carrie was being pulled forward despite leaning her whole weight back. William staggered to his feet, fearing for his daughter's safety, but she was slowly managing to urge the terrified animal towards the gate. It was still rearing up, frightened by the crackling flames, as he ran to the gate and slipped the main bolts.

'Take 'im up the street, Carrie,' he shouted as he threw open the heavy gates.

Once he saw that she was in no danger from the horse, he dashed back into the yard and grabbed a bucket. As fast as he could he scooped water from the horse trough and tried to contain the fire, but soon realised it was no use. The stable contained bales of hay which were burning fiercely. Smoke was billowing up to the main stable and he could hear the animals there neighing and crashing their hooves as they tried to get out of their stalls.

'Quick!' he screamed at Nellie as she stood by the gate. 'Get me somefink ter cover the 'orses' 'eads wiv. Towels, coats, anyfing.'

Smoke was now seeping into the upper stable and William dashed up the slope carrying his coat. There were a dozen horses stamping and crashing their heavy hooves against the stall-boards. With great difficulty he managed to untie the far horse, throwing his coat over its head as he ran with it down the ramp. Nellie grabbed the bridle-rope from him and quickly led the frightened animal out into the street as William dashed back up the ramp. By the time he had rescued seven of the horses the stable was filling with smoke. Flames were licking at the dry weatherboards and he realised that he might not be able to save all the horses before the whole place went up in smoke. He had to save the Clydesdales, he thought, grabbing a blanket that Nellie held up for him and dashing back up the ramp. The two animals worked together in the shafts and one might follow the other down.

He managed to free the first of the massive beasts. Once it had the blanket over its head, it allowed itself to be led towards the ramp. It was a desperate gamble, William knew. He was taking a change that the animal would not bolt while he was freeing the other Clydesdale. If it ran down the ramp it would either stumble and break its neck or else career into the onlookers in the turning and probably kill someone.

William finally managed to untether the second Clydesdale. It reared up, massive hooves crashing down on the stone floor. There was nothing to cover its head with and the yard manager said a silent prayer as he grabbed the first horse and led it down the ramp, whistling loudly at the other animal. The second horse reared up again and stared wildly for a few moments, then it trotted forward and followed its partner down to the bottom of the ramp. When they were beyond the gates the horses became quiet and allowed themselves to be led away up the street.

William felt near to exhaustion after his efforts and Nellie was screaming for him to wait until the fire brigade arrived but he knew he must try to save the last three horses. They had broken loose in the upper stable and were likely to cause themselves injury or worse if he did not get to them quickly. As he staggered up the steep ramp, gasping for breath and with his heart pounding, Carrie ran into the yard. She had helped tether the horses together at the end of the street and they were being calmed by Florrie and some of the local menfolk. Nellie cried out to her as she dashed past but she ignored her mother's entreaty. Suddenly she was grabbed by Florrie's lodger Joe Maitland, who forcibly dragged her screaming back to Nellie.

"Old 'er!' he shouted. 'I'll give yer ole man an 'and.'

When Joe Maitland reached the upper stable he could barely see William who was dodging about, trying to stay clear of the horses' flying hooves. Joe made his way over to him, and together they managed to grab one of the terrified animals. There was no time to cover its head. Joe brought the horse rearing and kicking down the slope, holding on to the tether as tightly as he could. Once out in the street the animal quietened down, and Joe ran back up to the smoke-filled stable as he heard the fire bell coming. The yard foreman had his back against the far wall, holding on to a tether and trying desperately to shorten the rope. Joe slid along the side of the stalls narrowly avoiding being struck by the kicking hooves and the two men pulled the last but one of the horses to the exit. The animal had kicked and reared until it was exhausted, and blew hard as they led it down the ramp.

Firemen were dashing from the tender and the first hose had already been connected to a stand-pipe as the two men ran back to save the last horse. They could hear the water being played on the fire and against the walls of the main stable as they reached the top of the ramp. The terrified horse was lying on its side with its foreleg trapped in a splintered stall-board, unable to get up. The two men found it difficult to breathe in the dense smoke as they worked to free the animal. Desperately they tried to prise the planking away but it resisted all their flagging efforts.

'It's no good!' William shouted. 'We need somefink ter lever it wiv!'

Joe dashed back down the ramp and soon returned with a fireman who set to work with his axe.

'Is its leg broken?' Joe shouted to William.

The foreman shook his head. 'I don't fink so. We'll soon find out.'

Finally the animal was freed and it struggled to its feet. The fireman led the limping horse down to the yard, followed by the two staggering rescuers who had their arms around each other's shoulders to hold themselves up. Folk were clapping and cheering as the men stumbled out through the gates and collapsed on the pavement.

The blaze had been contained and the main stable saved. Firemen were dousing the weather-boards and black smoke was rising into the air from the ruins of the end stable as Nellie brought out mugs of tea for the two exhausted men.

'It's Joe, ain't it?' William asked, holding out his hand.

'Yeah, that's right,' the young man answered, his white teeth gleaming in his blackened face.

'Well, I couldn't 'ave saved all them 'orses on me own, Joe. I'm much obliged,' William said gratefully. 'It took guts ter do what yer did.'

The two rescuers were finishing their tea when the fire officer walked out of the yard with a serious look on his smoke-streaked face.

'Is the owner here?' he asked William.

'Somebody's gone fer 'im,' Nellie cut in.

'I'm the yard foreman,' William said, standing up.

The officer took him by the arm and led him to one side.

'Keep this to yourself,' he said in a low voice, 'we think there's a body in the stable. We can't be sure yet but I've sent for the police.'

Chapter Thirty-three

The smell of charred timbers hung over the little backstreet on Sunday morning. Inside the Galloway yard office, Inspector John Stanley leaned back in his chair as he addressed the group.

'We've established that it was a body and at the moment we're waiting on the pathologist's report. If it points to foul play, Scotland Yard will have to be called in. That's the usual procedure,' he said matter-of-factly.

George Galloway was busy pouring drinks from a bottle of Scotch. He looked up quickly. 'What about identification?'

The inspector gave his subordinate a quick glance before answering. 'I took a good look at the remains and I would say that the body was charred beyond recognition. The pathologists might be able to come up with something but I'm not too hopeful.'

Detective Sergeant Crawford nodded his agreement. 'It's always a problem with fire victims,' he added. 'Unless there's something noncombustible on the body that would give us a clue to the identity.'

'Have you established how the fire was started?' Frank asked the inspector.

The policeman nodded. 'According to the fire people, there was a paraffin lamp in the centre of the stable. They seem to think that's what started the fire. It's quite possible the victim lit it and then knocked it over accidentally.'

'How did he get in?' Frank asked.

'We found a loose board at the rear of the yard,' the detective cut in.

'I thought you fixed all them boards,' George said, glaring at William.

'I did,' the foreman replied sharply.

'Well, I must say, we wouldn't have discovered it if we hadn't tried from the outside,' the detective said in support of William.

Frank looked intently at the police officer. 'You don't really think that the victim was murdered, do you?'

'As I say, we've got to wait for the report.'

George handed out the drinks. The inspector took his glass and stared thoughtfully at it before swallowing the whisky at a gulp. 'Have you chaps any reason to suspect who the victim might be?' he asked.

George looked at his son Frank and then over at William who was sitting in one corner. 'What about Jack Oxford?' he suggested. 'Could 'e 'ave been kippin' down in the yard, Will?'

William nodded. 'P'raps, George. 'E might 'ave discovered the loose board and got in that way,' he said, trying to hide his sudden sickening misgiving.

'This Jack Oxford, was he an employee of yours?' the inspector enquired.

''E still is,' George answered. 'Oxford's employed as a yard man. 'E does all the odd jobs an' keeps the yard clean.'

'Well, we can soon eliminate Mr Oxford from our

enquiries,' the detective said brightly. 'Can we have his address?'

George stroked his chin. 'The man sleeps in a lodgin'-'ouse, as far as I know. D'yer know which one, Will?'

The foreman shook his head. ''E moves about a lot. Last time I 'eard 'e was kippin' in Tooley Street.'

The detective sergeant was pinching his lower lip. Suddenly he looked up at the inspector. 'Oxford . . . that name rings a bell,' he said. 'I remember interviewing a Mr Oxford when we called at the lodging-houses over that railway death a few years back.'

'You'd better follow that up, Sergeant,' the inspector said quickly, then turned to George Galloway. 'Incidentally, is Mr Oxford a tall man, and is he in the habit of wearing a watch-and-chain at work?'

''E's over six foot I should say, although 'e's got a stoop,' George replied. 'But 'e don't wear a watch-an'-chain, at least I've never seen 'im wearin' one. I don't fink the silly ole sod can tell the time.'

William gave his employer a hard look and turned to the inspector. 'Was there a watch-an'-chain on the body?' he asked.

'If there was it would have melted with the heat,' the inspector answered, fishing into his pocket. 'We found this in the yard though,' he added, taking out an envelope and turning it out on the desk beside George.

The firm owner suddenly sat up straight in the chair, his eyes bulging. 'That's my watch-an'-chain! I'd know it anywhere. It was stolen from this office a few years ago. That ole bastard did take it after all,' he growled, turning to William.

'Yer don't know fer sure,' the foreman said quickly.

'It all points to it,' George said emphatically. 'That was

485

Jack Oxford's body yer found an' 'e was wearin' my bloody watch.'

The inspector sighed. 'As I said, Mr Galloway, the victim couldn't have been wearing it. It would have melted. That watch was found beneath a charred timber. As you can see the glass is broken and the hands are damaged but it hasn't actually been in the flames. As a matter of fact it was still attached to a nail in the timber by the chain. In other words, we suspect that the victim took it off and hung it on the nail before getting his head down for the night, and from what you've told us, Mr Tanner, the horse must have kicked out that piece of timber in its fright. You said the side of the stable crashed out into the yard, didn't you?'

William nodded and turned to George. 'I still don't fink that body is Jack Oxford's, an' I don't fink 'e took yer watch in the first place,' he said firmly.

'Tell me, did you report the theft of that watch, Mr Galloway?'

George shook his head. 'I didn't bovver. I thought it might turn up again.'

'Well, it certainly did,' the inspector said with a smile.

George stared down at the damaged timepiece and the little fob medallion. He could see it clearly: the old toff lying on the ground in that alley off the Old Kent Road and the two of them rifling through his pockets. William was gazing down at the watch too. The medallion had brought its original owner bad luck, and it had certainly not been lucky for the man who was wearing it in the yard last night.

'Crawford, will you pop back to Dockhead and check up on Mr Oxford?' the inspector asked. 'I'll wait here for you. I need to go over a few things with these gentlemen.'

The detective scooped up the watch-and-chain and placed

it back in the envelope. 'I'd like to check this out,' he said, slipping the envelope into his coat pocket.

William left the office to check on the horses. The upper stable still smelt of smoke although it had been cleaned and fresh straw had been laid in the stalls. The animals seemed a little jumpy to William and he talked quietly to them and patted their manes reassuringly as he walked in and out of the stalls. The horse which had been trapped by its foreleg looked none the worse. William had bandaged its cuts and bruises, and all the horses had been brushed and curry-combed. The gelding was stabled along with the rest. It munched away at its hay unconcernedly as the foreman gently stroked its singed mane. He had been so lucky, he told himself again. Carrie's quick thinking had most probably saved his life. Joe Maitland too had been a hero. He was obviously used to handling horses.

William frowned as he thought of Jack Oxford, wondering whether it really was his body in the stable. He had to admit to himself that it was quite likely. Jack was still in the habit of sneaking into the yard, although he rarely slept there in winter. Of course he had not been about to tell the police that, not in front of Galloway. He had known about the loose plank for a while now. This time it had been less obvious. He had discovered it quite by chance one day when he was replacing another plank that had been damaged by the wheel of a cart and the one next to it sprang out. William had seen that all the nails had been removed and only one shorter nail secured it. It would be easy for someone to give it a sharp kick from the outside and spring the plank from its fastening. Jack had never caused any problems by sleeping in the yard since the trouble over the theft, and was always careful not to be found out. The watch-and-chain was the real mystery. How could it have shown up after all this time? William wondered. It was inconceivable that Jack would wear it in the yard, even if he did take it originally. There must be another answer. Perhaps the police might be able to sort it out, he thought.

One hour later William was summoned back into the office. He noticed that the detective sergeant looked pleased with himself.

'Well, I've some news,' the subordinate said, looking at the inspector for permission to proceed. 'Jack Oxford was staying at the lodging-house in Tooley Street. I spoke to the owner over the phone and he told me that Oxford has been lodging there regularly for the past year or so. Last night he didn't book in. It seems he had a row the previous night with a man known as Fatty Arbuckle. The lodging-house owner told me he threw this Arbuckle character out on his ear as a troublemaker. Mr Oxford might have lodged somewhere else last night or he might have decided to sleep in the stable. I've also got a preliminary report from the pathologist. There's no indication of foul play. They've ascertained however that the victim was around six feet tall, possibly six two. So at the moment it seems quite likely that the body is that of Jack Oxford, although we can't be certain. We can be certain of one thing, though. That watch-and-chain was found on a body we scraped off the railway lines at South Bermondsey. Records show that the man was a tramp and his body was never formally identified, thus the watch-and-chain were not claimed. I don't know if you're aware, but all items not claimed after a certain length of time are sold and the proceeds go to the police widows' and orphans' fund. This watch was sold to a pawnbroker in Tower Bridge Road. Our station sergeant remembered it by the unusual fob-piece. He went through the records and came up with the information. One of us will be seeing the pawnbroker first thing tomorrow and he may have some record of who bought it, although it's unlikely.'

George slumped back in his chair, contemplating his whisky-filled glass. 'Jack Oxford could 'ave nicked the watch an' sold it ter the tramp,' he remarked.

William was beginning to feel irritated by Galloway's insistence that Jack was the thief. 'That watch was nicked by the tramp 'imself,' he asserted. 'If Oxford 'ad taken it in the first place 'e wouldn't 'ave bought it back from the pawnbroker, surely? Anyway, 'e might be simple-minded but 'e's not a thief.'

George looked hard at the yard foreman. 'Yer've got to admit it's possible Oxford jus' decided ter do 'imself a favour. 'E must o' known it was werf a few bob.'

William stood up quickly, his face flushing with anger. 'Yer make me sick,' he said in a loud voice. 'The poor ole sod might be dead an' already yer blackin' 'is name. 'Ow long as 'e worked fer yer? An' 'ow many times 'ave yer 'ad anyfing nicked from the office? Yer always on about loyalty. I reckon yer should staιt finkin' about yer loyalty ter yer workers.'

George was about to respond as William stormed from the office but he checked himself. 'Never mind,' he said to the assembled company. 'Will's still a bit shook up from last night. 'E'll calm down.'

The inspector nodded. 'From what the fire people told us your foreman did a marvellous job saving those horses. There was another man too, Mr Maitland who lodges in the street. Apparently he helped too.'

George nodded and got up to see the policeman out. 'Remind me ter see Will Tanner about that, Frank,' he said quietly. 'I fink the man deserves a reward.'

On Monday morning William Tanner opened up the yard at seven sharp and soon the carmen started to arrive. Horses were brought down from the upper stable and put in the carts, and sacks of chaff collected from the loft. Normally it was Jack Oxford who brought down the sacks but this morning the men did the chore without complaint. Word had got round the neighbourhood about the body found in the stable fire and the morning papers carried the full story. William had been constantly glancing along the street, hoping that he would see the familiar figure of Jack Oxford strolling along in his usual shuffling manner, but after ten minutes past seven he knew that the yard man would not show up. Jack was never late. By seven-thirty William sadly admitted to himself that it must have been the simpleton who had perished in the fire after all.

The morning paper said that the police were anxious to trace Jack Oxford and the carmen were all convinced that he had indeed been the victim.

'Poor bleeder. 'E never 'armed a fly. Fancy 'im goin' like that,' one said.

'Fancy sleepin' in the stable. Surely 'e could 'ave found a kip-'ouse or somefink,' another piped in.

'P'raps the police was after 'im. It said in the paper they wanted ter trace 'im,' the third remarked.

One elderly carman took his clay pipe from his mouth and spat a jet of tobacco juice in the direction of the yard cat who had only just returned after the fire. 'I reckon Oxford done away wiv 'imself,' he began. ''E was always a bit funny, ever since 'e got that kick on the 'ead. Mind yer though, if I was gonna do away wiv meself I wouldn't choose fire, nor poison. Gassin' yerself's best. I remember an ole boy down our turnin'. 'E done away wiv 'imself. Took rat poison 'e did. Terrible ter see 'im it was. Rollin' aroun' the floor an' kickin' 'is legs up in the air. It took 'im ages ter die. Then there was that ole Mrs Copperstone. She tried ter do away wiv 'erself. Drunk a tin o' metal polish she did. They 'ad ter pump 'er out.'

'Are yer gonna stand 'ere chewin' the fat all day, or are yer gonna get out on the road? Jus' let me know,' William said sarcastically.

The elderly carman aimed another jet of tobacco juice at the cat as he climbed up into his seat, hitting it on the head. 'Did Jack 'ave anybody, Will?' he asked. 'I expect the boys would wanna put a few coppers in the 'at.'

The foreman shook his head. 'As far as I know, Jack was on 'is own. 'E never mentioned 'avin' anybody ter me.'

'Bloody shame,' the carman said as he jerked on the reins.

William watched him drive out of the gate followed by the others, and when the last cart had left he picked up the broom and swept the yard. Inside he was still seething over George's remarks about Jack Oxford, especially as they had been made in the presence of the police.

When he finished tidying the yard William went over to the store shed. This was Jack's domain, he thought sadly as he looked around at the little bits and pieces. How many times had he caught him snoozing in the corner? There was the stained tea-can and the faded picture of Queen Victoria as a young woman hanging behind the door. Polishing rags, dubbin and a tin of metal polish were all strewn on the workbench and beside them there was a bridle that Jack had been mending, with a large needle still embedded in the leather. William sat down on the upturned crate and took the *Daily Mirror* out of his pocket. He had read the story twice already but he opened the paper again and looked down at the paragraph.

BODY FOUND IN BERMONDSEY FIRE

Firemen tackling a blaze at the Galloway cartage firm in Page Street, Bermondsey late on Saturday evening discovered a charred body in the fire. Police say that no formal identification was possible as yet but they are anxious to trace the whereabouts of Jack Oxford, an employee of the firm. Oxford went missing from his lodgings in Tooley Street on Saturday evening and police would like anyone with information on the missing man to contact them at Dockhead Police Station, Bermondsey.

William folded the newspaper and put it into his coat pocket. For a while he sat back with his head resting against the wooden slatting. It still seemed unreal that Jack was gone. He tried to understand why he should have gone to the stable in mid-winter. He could have found a different lodging-house, after all. There did not seem to be any sense to the whole affair, and the more he thought about the tragedy the more puzzled he became. With a sad shake of his head he stood up and made his way out of the yard for his breakfast.

Nellie was looking thoughtful as she scooped two rashers of streaky bacon and a fried egg on to his plate. 'D'yer know, I still can't believe that was Jack Oxford in the fire,' she said with a frown. 'Jack never wore a watch. An' ain't it strange that it was the one Galloway 'ad pinched?'

William nodded slowly as he dipped his bread into the soft egg. 'I'd back me life on Jack not takin' that watch, Nell, but s'posin', jus' s'posin', 'e did take it. It could 'ave preyed on 'is mind an' suddenly 'e sees it in the pawnbroker's. 'E could 'ave bought it, an' when 'e went ter the yard ter put it back, 'e some'ow started the fire.'

Nell shook her head vigorously. 'Yer fergettin' one fing, Will. Yer told me yerself Jack's scared o' that geldin'. There's no way 'e would 'ave slept in that stable while that 'orse was in there.'

William did not look convinced by his wife's argument as

492

he chewed on the bacon. 'Well, as a matter o' fact I thought about that meself, Nell,' he replied. 'But 'e might 'ave got drunk an' staggered back, fergettin' about the geldin' bein' in there. 'E could 'ave dropped the lamp in fright an' set the 'ole bloody place alight.'

Nellie pondered on it as she refilled his teacup. 'But in that case, surely Jack would 'ave run out o' the stable before the fire got goin'?' she said finally.

'P'raps 'e tried to. P'raps 'e fell over an' cracked 'is 'ead,' Will countered. 'Anyfing could 'ave 'appened. I don't s'pose we'll ever know.'

'It's a terrible fing ter 'appen but it's worse when it's somebody yer know,' Nellie said sadly.

William pushed his empty plate away and got out his cigarette tin. 'I know what yer mean,' he sighed. 'I was prayin' fer 'im ter come walkin' along the turnin', an' as the time went on I began ter realise it really was Jack's body they found after all. We've known 'im a few years, Nell. The poor ole sod wouldn't 'arm a fly, an' when yer come ter fink of it 'e didn't 'ave much of a life. That's why I got so mad at Galloway an' that miserable-lookin' boy of 'is. They don't seem ter 'ave an ounce o' pity between the two of 'em. All George seemed ter be worried about was that bloody watch of 'is.'

Nellie sat down at the table and rested her chin in her hands. 'Yer wanna be careful, Will,' she warned him. 'They might try an' put the blame on you fer Jack Oxford gettin' in an' startin' that fire. They won't fink about the way yer risked yer life ter save them 'orses. From what I can see of it they only need an excuse ter get yer out, so be careful what yer say.'

William looked serious as he carefully rolled the cigarette between his fingers and ran his tongue along the gummed edge of the paper. 'I keep finkin' about the way Carrie calmed that geldin' down,' he said quietly. 'If it wasn't fer 'er I'd 'ave got trampled fer sure. She's certainly got a way wiv 'orses. Ter be honest I don't fink anybody else could 'ave managed that 'orse.'

'She takes after 'er farvver,' Nellie remarked, giving him a smile. 'Mind yer, Will, that Joe Maitland was bloody good the way 'e 'elped yer. I've never spoken to 'im until yesterday. 'E seems a nice sort o' fella.'

William blew a cloud of cigarette smoke towards the grimy ceiling. He watched idly as Nellie cleared away the breakfast things, then his eyes slowly travelled about the room. He noticed how the varnish was wearing off the back of the door, and how faded and dirty the flowered wallpaper looked. He had promised Nellie he was going to replace it last summer. He glanced at the sideboard, with the framed photos of the children when they were small, and one of him and Nellie standing together outside the railway station the day they went on the trip to Southend. He gazed at the iron ornaments of torch-carrying maidens and the old clock that needed a shake every time it was wound. He smiled to himself as he noticed the illuminated address Carrie had brought back from one of her suffragette marches which Nellie had placed behind an ornament. He glanced down at the open fire and the brass fender, the copper-plated coal-scuttle that Nellie polished vigorously once every week and the coconut mat which covered the worn linoleum. He noticed the sooty black circles around the gaslights on the chimney-breast and how cluttered and untidy the recess shelves each side of the fireplace were. Most of the bits and pieces belonged to the boys and Nellie had insisted that the things stay where they were while the lads were away. The whole room looked shabby and overcrowded, William thought. The whole house was ramshackle and badly in need of renovation but it was the family home, the house he and Nellie had lived in since they were first married.

On Monday morning Maudie Mycroft swept the house, changed her lace curtains and then whitened her front doorstep. It was still early and she decided to get the copper going. Mondays was always a very busy day for Maudie. She liked to have the house cleaned by midday and there was time for her to do her hair and change into her best bits for the mothers' meeting at the church. Maudie got down on her hands and knees on the stone floor of the scullery and raked out the ashes from under the copper, then she put in sticks of wood and pieces of torn-up newspaper. Satisfied that all was ready she threw in a piece of rag soaked in paraffin and set it alight. Next she inspected the mousetraps by the door and saw that the bits of cheese were still there. Setting the traps was a job she did not relish, especially when the mothers' meeting usually began with the hymn, 'All things bright and beautiful, all creatures great and small', and she would find herself thinking about the mice as she was singing it with feeling. Those creatures had to be kept down, Maudie told herself as she walked back into her front parlour. Ernest was frightened of the mousetraps. He had laid them himself at one time all over the house, until he trod on one in the bedroom and ended up with a blackened big toenail. Now he left it to her and she confined the traps to the back door. Ernest had wanted her to get a good mouser but Maudie could not stand cats. They smelt the place out, she thought. Florrie's place always smelt of cats and snuff. She liked her house spic and span when Ernest got in at night, not smelling of cat's piss.

The copper was heating up nicely and Maudie took off the lid and threw in her weekly wash. When she got back from the meeting there would be time to run it through the wringer while the scrag of mutton was cooking, she told herself. Monday was always mutton day and Tuesday she would get a nice piece of fresh plaice or a half sheep's head. Wednesday was going to be a problem though. If Ernest managed to get a full day's work at the docks she could get faggots and pease pudden, otherwise it would have to be a slice of brawn and a few potatoes. It was no use worrying about the rest of the week, she sighed. It all depended how Ernest's work went. At least the house would be nice and tidy for him to come in to.

At twelve noon Maudie made herself a cup of tea and decided to do without bread and cheese. There was barely enough for Ernest's sandwiches and in any case there were always biscuits with a cup of tea at the meeting, she reminded herself. The copper was nice and hot now and Maudie shovelled up some small pieces of coal and threw them in. There was just time to do that bit of sewing before getting herself ready, she thought as she checked that the curtains were hanging right. She should have cleaned those windows, she realised, but they had only been done on Saturday and the neighbours might think she was getting house-proud. Being aware of what the neighbours might be thinking was something Maudie attached great importance to. She had heard Florrie going on about Aggie's fetish for cleanliness and did not like to think that the same was being said about her.

Maudie was a worrier, and when there was nothing to worry about she invented something. Childless and in her early fifties, Maudie had got religion. Next to Ernest and her tidy home, the church had become the most important thing in her life. Maudie worried about what the other women would think of the black raffia hat that Ernest had bought her as she put it on and secured it with a large hat pin, and she was still worrying as she hurried along the little turning. The day was cold and the wind stung her face as she crossed Jamaica Road and took the short cut to Dockhead Church.

Reverend Mercer was standing by the door greeting all the ladies. She gave him a warm smile as he nodded a greeting to her. When the venerable gentleman smiled back, Maudie felt all fluttery. She was sure Reverend Mercer reserved his best smile for her and worried in case any of the other ladies had noticed.

Maudie took her place and solemn organ notes filled the hall as the short service began. As usual the first hymn was 'All things bright and beautiful' and Maudie began to worry about the mousetraps. She heard Reverend Mercer's musical voice leading the congregation and soon it made her feel better, although his choice of 'The feeding of the five thousand' for the sermon made her empty stomach rumble and she worried in case anybody heard it. It seemed an extraordinarily long time before they settled down to their usual tea and biscuits and Maudie got into her customary state in case there were not enough biscuits to go round. All was well, however, and she munched thankfully on a custard cream while the lady sitting next to her went on about her wayward husband.

'I wouldn't mind if I was a bad wife,' she was saying. 'I worked my fingers to the bone, and what was my fanks? My 'usband ran off wiv this flighty piece an' I was left ter struggle on. Mind yer, 'e came back. Once 'e found out I'd bin left the 'ouse an' I was takin' in lodgers, 'e came back like a shot. Must 'ave thought I was well off, I s'pose.'

Maudie nodded, worrying that the Reverend might overhear them. 'My Ernest is a very good man, fank the Lord,' she managed quickly before the woman started off again.

'Yer should be grateful,' the woman told her. 'I've not 'ad

the best of 'usbands. I was glad ter see the back of mine, in actual fact.'

Maudie was beginning to get confused. 'I thought yer said 'e came back?'

'Oh, 'e did, fer a few weeks, then 'e ups an' goes again,' the woman said casually. ''E wouldn't allow me ter take in lodgers an' I 'ad ter get rid of 'em. Mind yer, I took 'em in again after 'e buggered orf, but I wonder if I've done the right fing sometimes. I've got this bloke stayin' wiv me an' 'e's bin actin' very strange.'

'In what way?' Maudie asked, her curiosity aroused.

'Well,' the woman began, looking around to make sure she wasn't being overheard, 'this lodger o' mine left fer work this mornin' as usual an' ten minutes later 'e was back. White as a sheet 'e was. I asked 'im if 'e was ill but 'e jus' shook 'is 'ead an' went straight up to 'is room. Somefink mus' be worryin' 'im, I ses ter meself, 'e's bin pacin' that room all mornin'. I went up ter see if 'e wanted anyfing before I came out but 'e jus' gave me a stare. The way 'e jus' stared really frightened me, I can tell yer.'

Maudie shivered in sympathy. 'Yer gotta be so careful, the fings yer read about these days.'

'I never read the papers,' the woman said. 'They're too depressin', what wiv all that war stuff.'

Maudie nodded. 'There was somebody burnt ter death in our turnin' on Saturday night. It was in this mornin's papers. As a matter o' fact they fink . . .'

Reverend Mercer's loud voice interrupted the conversation. 'Right then, ladies, let us form ourselves into groups for the discussion,' he called out. 'Oh, Mrs Mycroft, could I ask you to join our new ladies' group? You'll be able to get them started.'

Maudie felt very pleased that Reverend Mercer should

single her out and gave him a big smile as she hurried over to join the group.

The other woman was cross at not hearing the rest of Maudie's story and promised herself she would break a habit and buy a paper as soon as she left the meeting.

Chapter Thirty-four

Detective Sergeant Crawford was not feeling too optimistic as he hurried along Tower Bridge Road on Monday morning. He had had reason to call on Beckford's the pawnbrokers a few times in the past and had never made much progress. In fact he was sure that Benjamin Beckford was a fence. The man had a shifty nature and always seemed to be in a hurry to get the interview over. From what he had been told by his contacts, Detective Sergeant Crawford gathered that Beckford was not the most popular businessman in Bermondsey. He haggled over the few coppers he paid out on the pledges and was quick to put the unredeemed items in the window, unlike most of the other pawnbrokers in the area, who gave their customers a few weeks' grace before marking their possessions up for sale.

Crawford strode purposefully past the market stalls that were being set up along the kerb. As he reached the pawnbroker's shop, he saw a small huddle of people standing outside with bundles, waiting to be admitted through the side door. They looked cold and forlorn, hopeful of a few coppers for a threadbare suit or a pair of bedsheets, and he sighed sadly to himself as he went into the shop and produced his warrant card. The bespectacled young assistant stared at it for a few moments as though unsure what to do, then he disappeared into the back of the shop and returned with the owner.

Benjamin Beckford looked irritated as he waved for the police officer to follow him. When he had made himself comfortable at his desk he looked up disdainfully. 'Mondays are always busy. What can I do for you?' he asked quickly.

Detective Sergeant Crawford stared down at the plump, rosy-faced pawnbroker and noted the smart grey suit he was wearing and the expensive-looking rings on his podgy fingers. He smiled inwardly. He had been stationed in the East End and Hoxton before moving to Bermondsey and never had he seen a struggling pawnbroker. They seemed to thrive on poverty and deprivation, he thought to himself, and wondered how the fleshy-faced character before him felt as he undid the bundles and haggled over pennies with the hard-up folk waiting outside. Crawford produced a crumpled receipt from his coat pocket and put it down on the desk.

'I need some information about the person who purchased that item, a silver watch-and-chain, and gold medallion,' he said. 'As you can see from that receipt, it was one of a batch of items you bought from the station.'

The pawnbroker waved Crawford into a chair as he studied the crumpled slip of paper, his hand stroking his smooth chin. 'I can't keep a record of all I buy and sell, officer,' he said officiously. 'But I do seem to remember this item. It was an unusual medallion. Might I ask why you need the information?'

'That watch-and-chain was found on a fire victim and we need positive identification,' Crawford replied.

Beckford pushed back his chair. 'You'd better have a word with my assistant. He might be able to help you,' he said getting up. 'I'll mind the shop while you talk to him.'

The young man nodded as he looked down at the receipt.

'Yes, I do remember that item,' he said, looking over his spectacles. 'The medallion was a copy-piece. Not very well done. It was the strange carving which attracted my attention.'

'Can you remember who bought it?' Crawford asked.

'Yes. He was a poorly dressed man but well spoken,' the assistant replied. 'He seemed very interested in the medallion. As a matter of fact, we got into quite a discussion over it. Very interesting.'

'Did you get his name?' Crawford asked.

'No.'

'Can you tell me any more about this man?' the detective encouraged him.

The assistant scratched his head and looked thoughtful. 'I've seen him in the market quite a lot. As a matter of fact, he usually talks to the chap on the fruit stall outside. He'd most probably know his name.'

Sergeant Crawford made to leave. 'Well thanks for your help,' he said to the assistant. 'By the way, you said that the medallion was a copy-piece?'

'Yes, the design was taken from an ancient Nordic monument. It's Runic.'

'I beg your pardon?'

The young man smiled indulgently. 'Runes are line carvings and they're from the alphabet used particularly by the Scandinavians and Anglo-Saxons. They're modified by using the Greek and Roman letters to suit the carving.'

'Is that so?' Crawford said, none the wiser.

'Runes are often seen on ancient monuments, and the style of the inscription on that medallion was Runic,' the young man went on. 'Ancient architecture is a hobby of mine and the design seemed familiar so I looked it up. Apparently it refers to Loki, who was an evil god of fire in Scandinavian mythology. As a matter of fact, the chap who bought the watch-and-chain said he thought the medallion had something to do with the Freemasons, but I don't know if that's so.'

'Well, I'm grateful for the lesson,' Crawford smiled, holding out his hand.

The market was busy now. Benjamin Beckford watched from the window as Sergeant Crawford chatted intently to the fruiterer. When the police officer finally walked off, Beckford turned to his young assistant. 'Tell Riley's courier he can come down now,' he said out of the corner of his mouth. 'And tell him to use the back door, just in case.'

Carrie was kept busy all morning at the dining rooms. The bitter cold weather meant that more mugs of tea than usual were sold and more bacon sandwiches served up, brown and crispy, to the huddled carmen and dockers as they crowded in. Bessie went on endlessly all morning as she helped Fred in the kitchen and the harassed café owner could almost hear himself screaming at the woman to shut up for just five minutes. He gritted his teeth and did his best to ignore the unending saga of the buildings where Bessie lived, trying to concentrate his mind on what he was intending to do that evening.

He had spent much time during the weekend deep in thought and had come to the conclusion that he was a fool. In fact, he had been a fool for the best part of his adult life. His parents had expected him to work in the café. His own aspirations, such as they were, had never been considered. He had never been in the way of meeting young ladies, and on the very rare occasions when there was a chance for him to do so, his mother had been quick to make things difficult for him. He had been a fool for not standing up for his rights and asserting himself, but that was all in the past. Now he had the chance to court and win a beautiful young woman, and what was he doing but being his usual self and allowing the chance slowly to pass him by? Well, it was about time he did something about it, he reproved himself, before he became a doddery old bachelor with only regrets to keep him company on long winter nights. Maybe Carrie would spurn his advances, he thought as doubt gnawed at his insides. Well, he would never know unless he had the courage to try.

The afternoon wore on, and when the café became quiet it was Carrie's turn to suffer the eternal wagging of Bessie's unflagging tongue. She had heard about the woman on the first landing who had threatened the man on the second landing with a chopper, and the man had responded by throwing a bucket of dirty water over her and was then attacked himself by the woman's husband, or was it the husband who attacked his wife? Carrie was totally confused about the goings-on in Bessie's building, and was glad when Fred let Bessie go home early. He remarked that she must be tired after such a busy day, catching Carrie's look of gratitude and raising his eyes to the ceiling. It seemed quiet in the café after her departure and as Carrie wiped down the tables the last of the carmen left.

Fred quickly turned the 'Open' sign round and slipped the bolts. 'I'll let yer out the side door, Carrie,' he said. 'If I don't close now, we'll be open till midnight.'

When she had finished wiping the tables, Fred had a cup of tea waiting for her in the kitchen.

'Sit down a minute an' drink that,' he told her, taking off his messy apron and sitting down himself at the freshly scrubbed table. 'I wanted ter talk ter yer fer a few minutes, if yer can spare the time.'

Carrie eyed him over the steaming tea and saw that he was looking slightly nervous. 'Fanks. I need ter recover from Bessie's goin' on,' she joked.

Fred had his hands clasped and Carrie noticed how he was twirling his thumbs.

'What is it, Fred?' she asked encouragingly.

'I've bin doin' a lot o' finkin' over the weekend, Carrie,' he began. 'I know yer bin ter see Tommy Allen since 'e's bin 'ome, 'cos Bessie told me, an' I know you an' 'im split up before 'e joined up. I don't know if yer both plannin' on gettin' tergevver again, so I'll come out wiv it plain an' simple. Will yer marry me?'

Carrie was startled by Fred's outspokenness and for a few moments could only stare at him. 'I don't know what ter say,' she faltered.

Fred looked into her blue eyes and wanted to take her in his arms there and then. 'Are you an' Tommy gettin' tergevver?' he asked uneasily.

She shook her head. 'It was over before he went in the army, Fred,' she told him. 'I wanted ter see 'im but only ter find out 'ow 'e was. Tommy's goin' back wiv 'is first lady friend.'

Fred nodded. 'Well, I'm askin' yer ter be me wife,' he said candidly. 'I don't expect yer ter make up yer mind straight away. Take all the time yer want, but remember I love yer. I fink I've loved yer from the first time I set eyes on yer.'

Carrie felt a lump rising in her throat and she gulped hard. 'I like yer a lot, Fred, but as I said once before, likin's different ter love.'

'It's a good start,' he said, smiling. 'Likin' can turn ter love. Yer could grow ter love me in time, Carrie. Yer'd never regret it, I promise yer.'

She felt not at all threatened by Fred's proposal, and was touched by the look in his large dark eyes. She reached out and laid her hand on his. 'I'm really flattered,' she said quietly.

'But I can't give yer an answer jus' yet, Fred. There's the war, an' I'm worried sick over me bruvvers. Besides, I've jus' come ter accept that I won't be marryin' Tommy, an' now I've bin caught off balance.'

Fred's open face became very serious as he slipped his hand over hers. 'Take all the time yer need, Carrie. Jus' remember what I said. It's taken me a long time ter come out an' say I love yer, but it's true, I swear it.'

Carrie left the café feeling bewildered. She had been trying to restore some sense to her life and suddenly it had been turned upside down. It had surprised her when Fred first opened his heart to her, but this time he had made it very plain. He had actually said that he loved her and wanted her to love him in return. It was out of the question, she told herself, they were only friends. He was ten years older than her, and they had only walked out once together. They'd enjoyed themselves at the music hall, but it wasn't how she had imagined love and marriage to be in her daydreams. She had always felt that it would be so exciting when she was courted, with her beau taking her in his arms and proposing to her in the moonlight. Then there would be the engagement, with both families meeting each other and making plans. She had held on to her dreams, even though her romance with Tommy had left her feeling unhappy and dispirited. In reality it had been so very different, with no moonlight and no arms about her. Instead she had faced him across a table and he had proposed to her over a cup of tea!

Carrie was lost in thought as she walked along the dark street. It was quiet, with the yard gates locked and all the front doors shut against the cold. The corner gaslamp had been lit and its glow shone on the Tanners' front door as she let herself in. Her mother was laying the table and Carrie noticed that she had a curious, puzzled look about her face.

'Where's Dad?' she asked as she flopped down beside the burning fire and kicked off her shoes.

'Gawd knows what's goin' on,' Nellie replied, rubbing the side of her face. 'A woman knocked 'ere about an hour ago with a note fer yer farvver. I told 'er 'e was in the yard but she wouldn't go in there. She said it was urgent an' could I give 'im the note soon as 'e got in.'

'What did the note say?' Carrie asked.

Nellie shrugged her shoulders. 'I dunno, it was in a sealed envelope. Anyway, when yer farvver read it 'e went straight out. All 'e said was fer me ter put 'is tea in the oven.'

'Dad's not got a fancy piece, as 'e?' Carrie said, smiling. 'What did the woman look like?'

Nellie chuckled at the thought. 'She was a big woman. In 'er fifties and well dressed. I'm sure I saw her go in the yard once. If it wasn't 'er, it certainly looked like 'er.'

'I wonder if it's got anyfing ter do wiv that fire?' Carrie asked.

'Gawd knows,' Nellie answered. 'We'll jus' 'ave ter wait till yer farvver gets back. 'E could 'ave told me before 'e went out, 'e knows 'ow I worry.'

'P'raps that's why 'e didn't tell yer, Mum. It might be somefink serious,' Carrie remarked.

'Maybe yer right. Anyway I'd better dish the tea up, I can't keep it all in the oven,' Nellie moaned.

When the clock struck the hour of seven, she put down her embroidery and sighed loudly. 'Where's that farvver o' yours got to?' she complained. 'Look at the bleedin' time. That chop'll be baked up. Jus' wait till 'e gets in 'ere, I won't 'alf give 'im a piece o' my mind.'

Suddenly Carrie cocked her head to one side. 'That sounds like 'is footsteps now,' she said.

They heard the front door open and close and both stared

at William as he walked into the room and collapsed into his fireside chair.

'Where yer bin, fer Gawd's sake?' Nellie said irritably. 'I didn't know what ter fink.'

William gave his wife and daughter an exhausted grin. 'Yer never gonna believe this,' he said breathlessly. 'I couldn't believe it meself.'

'What is it?' Nellie almost shouted in her impatience.

'Jack Oxford's alive an' well,' he said, reaching down to take off his boots.

'Oh my Gawd!' Nellie gasped.

''Ave yer seen 'im?' Carrie asked excitedly.

William leaned back in his chair and sighed deeply. 'It's a long story.'

'Well, go on then,' Nellie urged him.

'The note that woman gave yer said ter go ter this 'ouse in Abbey Street about Jack Oxford,' he begun with an amused smile. 'Anyway, when I got there this woman said that Jack 'ad only jus' started lodgin' wiv 'er the previous night an' now 'e was upstairs in 'is room an' wouldn't come out. Accordin' ter 'er, Jack left fer work this mornin' an' ten minutes later 'e was back. She thought 'e was took bad at first but when she 'eard 'im pacin' the floor she got worried. She told me she'd 'eard about the fire from one o' the ladies at the muvvers' meetin' an' on the way 'ome she went an' bought a paper. Anyway, she went up an' 'ad a talk wiv 'im. Jack told 'er somebody stopped 'im on the way ter work an' told 'im the police were lookin' fer 'im about a fire. It must 'ave frightened the life out of 'im. Jack told 'er ter fetch me but not ter talk ter anybody else in the yard. I tell yer, Nell, when I saw Jack's face I could 'ave cried. As yer know 'e can't read an' 'e asked me ter read out what was in the paper. 'Is landlady 'ad already read it out twice but 'e wanted ter 'ear it again.'

Nellie and Carrie were sitting forward in their chairs, listening intently. 'Did Jack know who it was in the fire?' Nellie cut in. 'Did yer tell 'im about the watch they found? It wasn't in the paper, was it?'

'I'm comin' ter that,' William replied. 'Jack said that after 'e 'ad that row in the doss-'ouse wiv Arbuckle, 'e walked out. 'E said it was freezin' cold an' 'e decided ter kip under the arches in Druid Street. Apparently 'e knew some o' the tramps who stayed there. One of 'em, Bernie I fink Jack said 'is name was, used ter be a teacher at Webb Street ragged school an' Jack said 'e was wearin' that same watch-an'-chain that the police found in the fire. This Bernie said 'e'd bought it from the pawnbroker's in Tower Bridge Road 'cos 'e took a fancy ter the medallion on the chain. It was somefink ter do wiv the Freemasons accordin' ter what 'e told Jack. 'E said it was a special symbol.'

''Ow did Jack know it was the same one?' Nellie asked.

'Well, one night Jack brought some o' the tramps back ter kip down in the stables an' that was the night the watch-an'-chain got nicked out the office,' William went on. 'Jack knew which one o' the tramps took it. It wasn't one o' the usual crowd, an' 'e tried ter find 'im an' get the watch back. One evenin' Jack spotted this tramp an' 'e chased 'im. The tramp run up on the railway lines an' got killed by a train. Jack said 'e saw 'im layin' there all mangled up but the watch-an'-chain was still fixed on the tramp's waistcoat. It wasn't even marked. Jack said 'e couldn't bring 'imself ter take it off the body, but 'e'd know that watch-an'-chain anywhere after that night.'

'So it was the school teacher, this Bernie fella, who died in the fire?' Carrie guessed. 'What made 'im leave the arches that night an' come down 'ere ter the stable?'

'Well, that's anuvver story,' William said, taking out his cigarette tin. 'Yer remember that carman Sammy Jackson.'

'The one who beat Jack up over Mrs Jones's daughter?' Nellie asked.

'That's right,' William replied. 'Well, Jackson's down on 'is luck an' sleepin' rough. 'Im an' a few of 'is mates stumbled on the Druid Street tramps an' tried ter take over their fire. Course, when Jackson spotted poor ole Jack, 'e started gettin' nasty. They were all eyein' Bernie's watch-an'-chain too. After all, it must 'ave stood out. It ain't the usual fing yer see on tramps, is it? Anyway, Jack an' this Bernie left the arches in an 'urry. Jack said 'e was perished wiv the cold an' the only place 'e could fink ter kip down was the stable.'

'So Jack Oxford slept in the stable that night as well?' Nellie butted in with a puzzled frown.

'Yeah, 'e did,' William went on. 'But like yer said, Jack was scared o' that geldin' an' 'e took Bernie up in the chaff loft. Jack said that Bernie wasn't too 'appy about sleepin' there. 'E said it was cold an' draughty an' decided ter kip down in the small stable where 'e'd slept the last time.'

'Poor fella,' Carrie said sadly. 'If 'e'd 'ave done like Jack suggested, 'e wouldn't 'ave died.'

'Well, 'e started the fire some'ow,' Nellie said. 'If 'e'd 'ave slept in the chaff loft wiv Jack the two of 'em might 'ave gorn, an' all the 'orses as well.'

William glanced from one to the other with a serious look on his tired face. 'Bernie didn't start the fire,' he told them. ''E was murdered.'

'Not Jack!' Nellie gasped.

'It was Sammy Jackson who killed Bernie, an' Jack saw 'im do it,' William said darkly.

'Sammy Jackson!' the two women exclaimed in unison.

William nodded. 'Jackson must 'ave followed the pair of 'em back ter the stable. Jack told me that a little while after Bernie 'ad gone back down to the yard 'e 'eard a noise. 'E looked out o' the loft just in time ter see Sammy Jackson aim a lighted paraffin lamp into the small stable. Jack said 'e shouted out an' Jackson dashed back out o' the yard. 'E said Bernie never stood a chance. The stable was filled wiv smoke an' flames in seconds, an' Bernie was drunk anyway, accordin' ter Jack. 'E said 'e tried ter save 'im but the flames beat 'im back, an' when 'e 'eard the wicket-gate bein' unlocked 'e dashed out frew the back fence.'

'My good Gawd!' Nellie muttered. 'What'll 'appen now?'

'Well, Jack's job's gorn, that's fer certain,' William said with conviction. 'I'm not gonna be able ter do anyfing ter 'elp 'im this time. As fer Sammy Jackson, the police'll pick 'im up soon. I left Jack at the police station makin' a statement.'

'What a terrible fing fer that Sammy Jackson ter do,' Carrie said with a shiver.

''E must 'ave blamed Jack Oxford fer gettin' 'im the sack an' 'e saw 'is chance o' gettin' even,' William remarked. 'If it wasn't fer the geldin' bein' in that stable, 'e would 'ave.'

'It was strange that watch-an'-chain bein' found the way it was,' Nellie reflected. 'It was a wonder the poor bleeder wasn't wearin' it.'

William nodded his head slowly. 'I s'pose 'e would 'ave been if 'e'd 'ave bin under the arches, but as 'e was on' is own 'e prob'ly thought it was all right ter 'ang it up on the post. Who knows?'

He lit his cigarette and blew a cloud of smoke towards the ceiling. 'I s'pose the coppers'll give it back ter Galloway when this is all over,' he sighed. 'If I was 'im I'd take the watch, chain an' that bloody medallion an' chuck the lot in the Thames. It's brought nuffink but bad luck to everybody who's worn the bloody fing.'

*

512

On Tuesday morning Jack Oxford walked out of the Galloway yard for the last time, clutching his week's pay. Will Tanner watched sadly as the tall, stooping figure ambled along the turning and disappeared from view. He had tried to plead on Jack's behalf but George Galloway had ranted and raved, saying that the yard man was lucky to be getting any wages at all considering the money it was costing the firm to replace the stable. He was furious about the gelding too. It was nervous and jumpy because of the fire and unsuitable to be used in the trap. William had asked for time to work with it but the yard owner was adamant. 'It's goin' ter the auctions. The bloody animal's too dangerous now ter take out on the roads. That idiot Oxford's got a lot ter answer for,' he growled.

Had George Galloway seen his ex-yard man's face as he walked along the street that Tuesday morning he would have been even more angry. Jack was actually smiling to himself. The policemen had been very nice to him, he thought. They had thanked him for his help and said that they would have another chat with him when they caught Sammy Jackson. Jack was happy to be back in such nice lodgings and Amy Cuthbertson was looking into the possibility of getting him a job at a tannery in Long Lane. Amy knew the foreman there and the man had promised to speak on his behalf. It was so fortunate that he had bumped into her in Abbey Street on Sunday morning, he thought to himself. She told him her husband had left her for good and she was now taking in lodgers once more. Jack had jumped at the chance, and as he ambled out of Page Street for the last time with a huge grin on his face he felt that things were beginning to look up for him at last.

Chapter Thirty-five

As 1917 wore on the newspapers reported new, larger battles in France. Casualty lists grew, and like Ypres and the Somme before them, Messines, Cambrai and Passchendaele were becoming household names. During early summer the tragedy of war reached into yet another Bermondsey backstreet, when at the battle of Messines in June Private James Tanner of the East Surreys Regiment fell in action. Corporal Charles Tanner was wounded in the same offensive and one of the stretcher-bearers who helped carry him back from the line was his younger brother Danny.

The summer of that year was a wretched time for the mourning Tanner family. Nellie became almost a recluse, hardly ever venturing out of the house after hearing the terrible news, and her friends in the street could do little to ease her pain. William went to the yard every morning, his grief bottled up inside him, and in the evening sat with his distraught wife in the silent, cheerless house that had once echoed with laughter and noise. Carrie too had to suffer her grief privately. Every day she put on a brave face and forced a smile as the carmen and dock workers came into the dining rooms. It was only when she was alone in her bedroom at night, clutching a photo of her eldest brother to her breast, that she let go, trying to ease the grinding, remorseless pain of her loss as she sobbed into the pillow.

Carrie felt grateful for Fred Bradley's support during that terrible time. He was very kind and understanding, and seemed to know instinctively when she needed to chat and be consoled and when he should remain discreetly in the background. Bessie was large-hearted too, although the well-meaning woman often upset Carrie by her open displays of sympathy and tears. There were times too when Bessie tried to cheer the young woman up with her tales of the buildings and only succeeded in making her more depressed and tearful than ever, and Fred would think desperately of ways to shut his kitchen-hand up.

The only grain of comfort for the Tanner family during that long hot summer was receiving letters from the two boys in France. Danny wrote home often and Charlie sent an occasional letter from a hospital some way behind the lines. He made light of the fact that he was suffering from a bullet-wound in the chest and told them that he hoped to be sent home before the year was out. Little mention was made of their brother's death since that first poignant, joint letter in which the surviving boys described visiting James's grave, saying that they felt he was happy to be resting beside his fallen comrades.

The huge toll of young life mounted, and during that hot summer John and Michael Sullivan were both killed in action, and Maisie Dougall's son Ronald also fell. A terrible quietness seemed to descend over the little turning and folk held their heads low and talked in hushed voices as they stood on their doorsteps, in respect for the street's fallen sons. Mrs Jones walked proud. Her son Percy had finally returned to the front and in July she read in the newspaper that he had won the Military Medal at Messines.

The grieving Sadie Sullivan and her husband Daniel took on the War Office when their remaining sons got their call-up papers. Sadie argued angrily that the loss of two sons was price enough for any mother to pay. She finally won the day, and the twins, Pat and Terry, and the youngest boy, Shaun, were not required to go into the army. Every family in Page Street had signed Sadie's petition and Florrie put into words on the bottom the thoughts of everyone: that in the three years of war so far Page Street had already given up the lives of four of its young men, two more had been wounded in battle, and another had won the Military Medal.

The war was changing everyone's life. Since his son's death George Galloway had become morose and almost unapproachable. He barked out his orders and changed his mind regularly without reason. Nothing seemed to satisfy him. The carmen stayed clear of him and even his own son began to dread going into the office each morning. Nora Flynn did her best to bring a little light into the Galloway house but only rarely was she able to get George out of his room and away from the ever-present bottle of whisky. Her hopes had been raised when Frank told her that his wife Bella was pregnant; she had thought that the news might help rally her employer. George did brighten up for a short time, and it was evident how much he still cherished the idea of a grandson to carry the family name, but his depression soon returned and the bottle once again became his constant companion.

Josephine Galloway spent as little time as possible at the gloomy house in Tyburn Square. During the day she was busy working for the Red Cross, and now that her training was over for the time being she visited her friends most evenings or sat with Nora in the back kitchen before going to her room and writing long letters to Charlie Tanner. Her days with the Red Cross had taught her many things. She had witnessed the suffering and tragedy of war at first hand and had been privy to much forbearance and courage, and, occasionally, instances of utter stupidity. Returning casualties had on occasion been aided, tended and nursed by dedicated medical workers, and then left on cold platforms to be visited by ageing dignitaries who found it difficult to string two sensible words together.

In November bitter fighting was taking place at the Ypres salient and Cambrai, and by the end of the month Red Cross trains were rolling into Waterloo with terrible regularity. After four days of tending the returning wounded, Josephine felt exhausted as she sat chatting with the rest of the medical team one Friday morning while they waited for the first train of the day to pull into the station.

'Well, as far as I'm concerned they can do what they like,' the young doctor said defiantly. 'As soon as we get the word from transport, the stretchers will be moved off the platform.'

'But the colonel said the party will be arriving soon. Hadn't we better hold a few of the less serious back?' his colleague asked anxiously.

'Look, Gerry, I'm taking responsibility for this and I'm saying no,' the doctor declared in a challenging voice.

'All right, on your own head be it, Alan,' his colleague said, holding his hands up in resignation. 'I just hope the colonel won't be too put out. Those politicians can be an awkward bunch of sods.'

'My instructions are quite clear,' Alan replied. 'Render emergency medical attention then forward all wounded personnel to transport forthwith for conveyance to military hospitals as designated. There's nothing in the orders that states we delay transportation until all bloody visiting parasites and leeches are fully sated and glorified to the detriment of aforementioned personnel. I've had just about enough of it.'

Josephine chuckled. She had been listening intently and felt she could hug the young doctor. He had already incurred the wrath of the powers that be and she knew that he was bravely walking a very thin line.

'They're detestable,' she said with passion. 'The way they walk along looking down their noses, as if just coming here makes them feel dirty.'

The young doctor suddenly grabbed her by the shoulders and planted a kiss on her cheeks. 'Josie, you've just given me a great idea!' he exclaimed, his eyes sparkling.

Ten minutes before the train was due to arrive, the party of dignitaries marched into the station with the usual fuss and bother. The station master was waiting together with the young doctor and an elderly staff officer, all looking very serious.

'I think we're all ready,' a flustered-looking young man at the head of the official party said as he approached them.

The station master held up his hand. 'I'm sorry, but there's a little bit of a hitch,' he said apologetically.

'A hitch?' the official queried haughtily.

'The doctor will explain,' the station master replied.

'I've just got word from Southampton,' he began, looking suitably stern. 'I'm afraid there's a suspected typhoid case amongst the casualties. Apparently the man was wrongly diagnosed as having trench fever. The error was discovered too late to stop the casualty travelling. We'll need to get the man away from the station as soon as possible, but of course I don't want to stop your party from talking to the men. I can only advise extreme caution.'

The group looked taken aback and one or two were already backing away. The young official turned to the chief dignitary. 'Sir?'

'Well, I, er, – I think we should let the doctor get the men away quickly, as he suggests. What do you say, Parish?'

'Jolly good idea,' his aide said in a relieved voice.

As the party hurriedly left the concourse, the station master turned to the young doctor, smiling broadly. 'I'll make sure your part of the station is cleared of civilians,' he told him. 'We don't want them exposed to any risk, do we, doctor? Besides, it'll help you get the men away quicker. Good luck.'

The young doctor turned to the staff officer for his nod of approval but the elderly colonel was already hurrying away.

At twelve noon the Red Cross train steamed into the terminus and the platform was suddenly crowded with casualties, hobbling on crutches or being carried on stretchers. Several with bandages over their eyes were forming a line and slowly being led away. Nurses in Red Cross uniform and white-coated doctors moved amongst the men, and slowly order began to be imposed upon the confusion. Tea was handed out by volunteers and some of the helpless casualties dictated letters that were hastily scribbled down by helpers. Some of the soldiers were laughing and joking, but others looked blank-faced and shocked. Some were mumbling to themselves, ignorant of the noise around them as they suffered in their own solitary nightmare. One stretchered casualty lifted his head and looked around anxiously as he was carried from the station. Suddenly he grinned and tried to raise himself on his elbows as a young nurse hurried towards him. Josephine smiled with relief as she bent over the soldier and kissed him, then she took his hand in hers and walked beside the stretcher to the waiting ambulance.

Early in December Inspector Stanley and his assistant called at Galloway's yard.

'We've picked up Sammy Jackson,' he said, easing his bulk into a chair. 'We found him sleeping rough under the arches.'

'Did 'e admit ter startin' the fire?' George Galloway asked.

The Inspector shook his head slowly. 'He admitted to starting the fire, but I don't think there's much chance of him going to the gallows. He was ranting and raving when I interviewed him. He was going on about doing the work of the Lord. Unless I'm very much mistaken Sammy Jackson will spend the rest of his life in a loony bin. By the way, the sergeant has managed to track down the victim's next of kin,' he added, nodding to his assistant to take up the story.

'Bernard Dewsbury's sister is the only surviving relative,' the sergeant began. 'They weren't very close. Apparently he was lodging with her until he was thrown out of the teaching profession for abusing one of the children. For a while he worked as a labourer on the roads and moved about the country quite a bit. He returned to London last year but his sister refused to take him back. Until his death, Dewsbury was sleeping under the arches in Druid Street.'

'Pity 'e didn't stay there instead o' takin' notice o' that idiot Oxford,' George remarked.

'I don't suppose he'll be missed much,' Frank Galloway commented.

The Inspector shrugged his shoulders. 'From what we could gather from the headmaster of the school, Dewsbury got on well with the rest of the staff and was a very good teacher until he suddenly started going downhill. It seems he got involved with some religious group, according to his sister, and from then on started acting strangely. Anyway, the matter will have to rest there for the time being. I expect Jackson's trial will take place early in the new year and the whole sorry mess will get a good airing. By the way, Mr Galloway, we'll need to hold on to the watch-and-chain until the trial's over. I don't see any reason why you shouldn't have it back afterwards,' he concluded.

The sergeant left immediately afterwards and the Inspector

stood at the gate chatting with George Galloway. Presently he gave the yard's owner a quizzical look.

'I understand you've got a good man in Jake Mitchell?' he queried, smiling as he saw the surprised expression on George's face. 'It's all right, Don McBain's a friend of mine. I was just wondering what Mitchell's prospects were against Don's latest boy? From what he tells me this young fighter's been doing well up in the north-east.'

Galloway smiled slyly. 'If I was a bettin' man, I'd put me money on Jake Mitchell,' he told him. 'From what I've 'eard, McBain's lad is a rough 'andful but 'e's got a glass jaw. I don't fink 'e'll trouble my man.'

The Inspector took out a large, white five-pound note from his wallet and handed it to Galloway. 'Put that on your man for me, will you?' he said with a wink. 'I'll call round after the fight.'

Nora Flynn leaned back in her comfortable armchair and closed her eyes. The newspaper she had been reading lay on the floor beside her and her glasses rested in her lap. The accounts of the battles raging in France had made depressing reading and she tried to think of happier things as she let the heat of the fire permeate her aching body. She had been very busy that day going through the house, turning out drawers and clearing out the odd corners. She had polished the silver, scrubbed the kitchen and stairs, changed the front room curtains and generally tried to brighten up the drab, miserable house. When she was finished Nora had felt no better for all the hard work. There was no one to praise her efforts or remark on how nice the place looked except Josephine, and she was hardly ever at home these days.

It saddened Nora that George spent so little time in her company, preferring to go to his room after the evening meal and sit alone with his thoughts, and the inevitable bottle of whisky. For months now he had almost ignored her, treating her merely as a paid housekeeper and forgoing the intimate chats they had once had together. It seemed ages since he had shared her bed, and Nora was beginning to face the hard truth that George Galloway had used her the way he used everyone. She had been available to him when he needed a woman, and that was the beginning and ending of it. She had been silly and foolish to expect more. She was a middle-aged widow, plain and staid, with little physical allure to ignite a man's passion. Why had she allowed herself to be used? she wondered almost desperately. Did she really want to build a new life for herself before it was too late, or was it just loneliness?

A light tap on the door made Nora start. She sat up in her chair as Josephine looked in. 'Come in, luv, I was jus' takin' a well-earned rest,' she said stretching.

Josephine sat down in the chair facing her and spread her hands towards the fire. 'I saw Charlie Tanner at the station today, Nora,' she said, smiling. 'He was on the first train.'

'Is 'e badly 'urt?' the housekeeper asked anxiously.

'It's a chest wound but he's all right. He's been taken to Woolwich. I'll be able to visit him soon.'

'Have you told your father yet?' Nora asked, her eyes searching the young woman's face.

Josephine shook her head. 'I know I've got to tell him, Nora, but I keep putting it off. I made up my mind that I'd do it tonight but I'm frightened of what he might say.'

'Look, Josie, yer goin' on fer twenty-one,' Nora said firmly. 'Yer've a right ter pick a young man an' go courtin', the same as anybody else. Yer farvver's got the right ter know when yer find that young man, so tell 'im, but let 'im see that yer know what yer doin'. 'E'll be pleased for yer, I'm sure.'

'Do you really think so?' Josephine asked, concern showing in her deep blue eyes.

Nora smiled at her. 'Go an' see 'im now,' she urged. 'Get it over wiv, an' don't ferget what I said. Let 'im see that yer know what yer doin'.'

Josephine stood up and walked to the door. 'Wish me luck,' she smiled, holding up her crossed fingers as she left the room.

Chapter Thirty-six

As soon as the Tanners returned home from the Woolwich Military Hospital, William rounded angrily on his wife.

'I fink yer should 'ave at least waited till the boy was on 'is feet before sayin' what yer did,' he shouted.

'I'm sorry if it upset 'im but 'e's got ter know 'ow I feel about it,' Nellie shouted back. 'Nuffing good's gonna come out of 'im an' that gel o' Galloway's gettin' tergevver. Christ! There's plenty of ovver gels round 'ere wivout 'im gettin' mixed up wiv 'er.'

'Look, Nellie, we've got no right to interfere,' William countered. 'Charlie's entitled ter make 'is own choice. From what 'e was sayin', yer could see 'e finks a lot of 'er.'

'I don't care,' Nellie said, tears welling up in her eyes. 'I don't want a son o' mine marryin' inter the Galloway family. George Galloway's a bad man an' 'e's put 'is mark on 'is children. That bad streak runs in 'em an' I won't 'ave Charlie marryin' inter that lot.'

'But that's silly talk,' William retorted. 'Yer condemnin' the gel wivout knowin' 'er. S'posin' Galloway told 'is daughter ter keep away from our Charlie? Yer'd be up in arms then, wouldn't yer?'

525

'No, I wouldn't. 'E'd be doin' Charlie a favour,' Nellie said, her voice breaking with emotion.

Carrie had been listening quietly and felt moved to say something. 'She seems a nice enough gel, Mum.'

Nellie turned on her daughter. 'That's right, side wiv yer farvver,' she complained angrily. 'Yer 'ardly know the gel, anyway. I'm tellin' yer, she's a Galloway, an' that's enough fer me. It's bad enough yer farvver 'as to work fer the man wivout Charlie marryin' inter the family.'

William shook his head slowly as he slumped down in his chair. 'I reckon yer upsettin' yerself fer nuffink,' he said in exasperation. 'The lad said 'e likes 'er an' they'll be walkin' out tergevver when 'e gets 'ome. 'E ain't said anyfing about gettin' married. Besides, why all the sudden fuss about me workin' fer Galloway? It's honest work an' I bring in regular wages. That's more than can be said fer a lot o' poor bastards round 'ere.'

'Yer know I've never bin 'appy wiv yer workin' fer 'im,' Nellie replied quickly. 'I've seen yer slave fer 'im fer years, workin' nights an' weekends wiv those sick 'orses. An' what's yer fanks bin? Sod all, that's what. Yer said yerself George Galloway's got no feelin' fer 'is workers. Jus' 'cos you an' 'im ran the streets tergevver once don't mean yer can expect any favours. When it suits him yer'll be put off, an' when that day comes we'll all be out on the street.'

William looked appealingly at his daughter as Nellie hurried from the room. 'What's got inter yer muvver ter make 'er carry on like that?' he wondered aloud.

Carrie sighed and stared down into the fire. 'I s'pose it was the shock o' seein' Charlie lyin' there. 'E did look queer, didn't 'e?' she said quietly.

'I dunno what ter fink,' William sighed. 'It's not like yer muvver ter get upset the way she did. She knows we can't do anyfink if Charlie an' that Galloway gel get tergevver. It's up ter them what they do. I'm jus' wonderin' 'ow George Galloway's gonna react when 'e finds out, if 'e don't know already.'

Charlie Tanner's hopes of being home for Christmas had been dashed when his wound became infected. While he was lying in a haze of pain, he received a visit from Josephine. Now, as he sat propped up in bed against a mound of pillows, he could recall her sitting beside him, holding her cool hand to his forehead. A nurse was putting the finishing touches to a gaily decorated Christmas tree that stood in the centre of the ward and the young soldier watched idly, occasionally lifting his eyes to the high window and watching the dancing snowflakes as they fell against the frosty panes. It was Christmas Eve. Charlie felt warm and comfortable now that the pain had left him and looked forward to seeing Josephine once more. He let his tired eyelids shut out the activity around him, and as he hovered between sleeping and waking he was aware of light footsteps and the scent of lavender as soft lips brushed his forehead. Josephine sat down beside him, and he held her hand in his as she asked him how he was feeling and poured him a drink from the bedside container. She seemed cheerful, he thought, but her striking eyes looked sad, almost melancholic, and he was moved to ask her, 'Is there anyfing wrong, Josie?'

She shook her head but her eyes gave her away. He pressed her soft hand. 'Yer would tell me if there was somefink wrong, wouldn't yer?' he entreated her.

Josephine stared down at the clean white counterpane for a few moments. When she looked up and met his gaze, he knew he had been right.

'It's my father,' she said in a low voice. 'I told him about us and he's forbidden me to see you.'

Charlie looked deep into her troubled eyes. 'Why, Josie?' he asked.

'He said I'm too young to be thinking of courting and he wants me to go to college as soon as the war's over,' she replied.

'Was that all?' he asked. 'Did yer farvver not mention me?'

'That was all he said,' Josephine told him.

Charles shook his head. 'Josie, I'm not a child. I can imagine the rest of it. 'E said yer should marry somebody wiv prospects, somebody who 'ad money an' was able ter provide fer yer. Am I right?'

She nodded, her eyes avoiding his.

'Would yer be surprised if I told yer me own family don't like the idea neivver?' he asked her. 'I told 'em about us last time they came in ter see me. Farvver was all right, but me muvver was shocked, ter say the least. I couldn't understand 'er attitude.'

'I didn't realise how much dislike there was between the two families,' she sighed. 'Why should there be, Charlie? What's happened between them?'

Charlie shrugged his shoulders. 'I wish I knew. My ole man's worked fer yer farvver fer donkeys' years. I jus' can't understand it as far as my folk are concerned. As fer yer farvver, at least there's a proper reason, much as I don't like it. The point is, what d'yer intend ter do about it, Josie?'

Josephine looked at him, her deep blue eyes burning with determination. 'I want us to stay together, Charlie,' she replied in a very quiet voice. 'I want us to be lovers. I want you to hold me and never let me go.'

He smiled and stroked her hand. 'That's the way I feel too,' he said, his eyes staring back into hers. 'There could never be anybody but you. I thought of nuffink else all that time I was in the trenches. I carried a picture of yer in me mind an' it 'elped ter keep me from goin' mad.'

Josephine's eyes brimmed with tears and she gazed at Charlie's hand on hers. 'Every day when I saw the troop trains pull into the station I said a prayer that you'd be kept safe,' she said. 'When I saw you lying on that stretcher I felt I was going to die. I knew then that I wanted to spend the rest of my life with you. I couldn't live without you, Charlie,' she whispered.

The ward sister was ringing a handbell and looking very stern. Josephine got up and leaned over him, her lips meeting his in a soft, tender kiss.

'As soon as you're back from convalescence I want us to go away somewhere, Charlie,' she said. 'I want us to spend a couple of weeks together, just the two of us. Will you promise?'

He kissed her open lips for answer, and she walked away, turning at the door to wave to him.

Father and son sat facing each other across the highly polished table at number 22 Tyburn Square. Spread out in front of them were the company ledgers and sheaves of paper containing columns of figures. To one side was a whisky decanter which was slowly being depleted. George Galloway toyed with a full glass of Scotch as he pored over the last of the figures Frank had presented him with. The older man's florid face had a set expression and his heavy-lidded eyes did not blink as he scanned the columns. Frank leaned back in his chair and sipped his third drink, feeling irritated by his father's reluctance to make the final decision. How much longer was the silly old fool going to take? he wondered. It was all straightforward and simple to understand. There was the initial outlay, which would be offset by the substantial bank loan he had negotiated, the first year's trading projection and the evidence of the ledgers too. It was all in front of him.

George took a swig from his glass. 'Are yer sure these figures are right?' he asked, looking up at Frank.

The younger man nodded. 'It's time we got moving, Father. We're going to be left at the post if we don't start moving pretty quickly,' he said testily.

'So we sell off 'alf the 'orses, an' buy the four Leyland lorries to start with?' George queried.

'That's right. We can accommodate the lorries in the yard once the carts have gone and we'll start looking for larger premises in the area,' Frank reiterated. 'If I place the order now the lorries will be delivered in January. If all goes well we can increase the fleet at the end of next year.'

George nodded slowly and reached for the decanter. 'I'll give Will Tanner 'is notice as soon as we get the confirmation of delivery,' he said, his face muscles tightening. 'I want 'im out o' the yard as soon as possible. That business wiv young Josie is the last straw as far as I'm concerned.'

Frank stared at his refilled glass thoughtfully. His father had been adamant that Josephine must stop seeing Charlie Tanner and there was no moving him. The girl had gone to her room in tears after the confrontation and his words of comfort had done little to help. Why should his father take such a hard line with Josephine? he wondered. She was old enough to make her own mind up and his attitude was only going to harden her resolve. Something must have happened in the past between the families to make his father so desperate to stop her seeing the Tanner boy. Maybe nothing had, though. It was quite likely the old boy was just being cantankerous, he allowed. He had certainly become terribly moody and short-tempered since Geoffrey's death. Even the birth of Caroline had not cheered him to any great extent. If Bella had presented him with a grandson instead of a granddaughter perhaps he might have shown a little more enthusiasm. He was keen to have a male heir to carry on his name, but it was just one of those things.

It was fortunate he hadn't been present when Bella came out of the hospital, Frank thought. She had made it clear then that she wasn't intending to have any more children and that she was anxious to get back into the theatre as soon as possible. It had been so pleasant during the later months of her pregnancy as well. Bella had become resigned to her condition and had finally stopped worrying about her figure. Nancy boy Hubert stayed away for some time and Frank had been hoping he had seen the last of him, but it was not to be. Hubert was back on the scene now, large as life and as obnoxious as ever.

'Are yer goin' in fer a large family?' George asked suddenly, as though reading his thoughts.

'I expect we will,' Frank said, grateful that Bella could not hear the conversation.

'An only child gets spoilt, 'specially if it's a gel,' the old man commented 'Yer wanna 'ave a few boys. It shouldn't be no trouble fer Bella, she's wide in the girth.'

Frank nodded, thinking that the old man was getting her mixed up with one of his horses. 'She'll be wanting to get back to the stage as soon as she can,' he told his father.

'I wouldn't be in too much of an 'urry ter let 'er get back if I was you, Frank,' George said sternly. 'She'll 'ave ovver responsibilities now. Yer muvver never left you an' young Geoff. She was a good woman.'

Frank nodded sadly and clenched his hands under the table. It was always the same when his father had too much drink inside him. He pushed back his chair. 'I'd better be off if I'm going to get the last train,' he said quickly.

George did not look up as his son bade him goodnight. The whisky was beginning to depress him and his mind was already dwelling on an unpleasant matter.

531

*

Christmas came and went. There was little festivity in the Tanner household. Nellie had been very quiet and moody. As she sat in the parlour her eyes would constantly stray to the photograph of James, which she had shrouded with a piece of black velvet, and the Christmas card which Danny had sent from his rest camp. William had gone to the Kings Arms on Christmas morning to sit with Daniel Sullivan and Fred Dougall, their thoughts far removed from Yuletide revelry. The piano player sipped his beer and played in subdued fashion, while around the bar eyes glanced furtively in the direction of the three sad men. Alec and Grace Crossley served up pints and chatted quietly with their customers, aware of the silent grief prevailing in the little bar. There was no bawdy laughter, and unlike other Christmas mornings no one stood beside the piano and sang in a strident voice.

Carrie felt it had been the most miserable Christmas she had ever known and was glad to get to work once more. She had been hoping that Charlie would be home in time for Christmas but he had been too ill, and with her vivacious younger brother away as well the house had seemed deathly quiet. Her mother's strange behaviour had been puzzling her, and as she served teas and took the orders for food on her first morning back Carrie was lost in thought. She continually served up the wrong food and forgot to relay orders to Fred, receiving more than a few frosty looks from the impatient customers. Fred had not failed to notice how distracted she was, and when the café emptied took her quietly to one side.

'Yer seem miles away, Carrie. Is everyfing all right?' he asked her gently.

She nodded and forced a smile. 'It's jus' bin a miserable Christmas,' she said. 'I'll be all right termorrer.'

*

William was busy in the newly built small stable, replacing a bandage on one of the Clydesdales. The massive horse had kicked out while in the shafts the previous day and had damaged a back tendon, causing the yard foreman an awkward problem. The two Clydesdales pulled a heavy dray which hauled rum kegs from the London Dock to Tooley Street, and they always worked as a team. He had to choose whether to pair the other horse with one of the Welsh cobs or else send it out with a single-horse cart. William had decided that it might be wiser to give it a rest from heavy hauling until its partner had recovered and so the Clydesdale was harnessed into the small van.

All day long the massive horse trudged around unfamiliar streets, driven by a carman who was more used to the sprightly cob and who became increasingly impatient with the heavy horse's constant plod. Neither the whip nor the carman's blasphemous tongue intimidated the animal which trudged on in its usual way, missing its partner and the smell of rum as the dray was loaded on the quay. The small cart it was tethered to now was hired daily to transport treated leather from a Long Lane tannery to various leather workers, and the massive horse was hardly aware of the two-ton load it was pulling. The impatient carman did not appreciate that the Clydesdale was built for power and not speed. Normally he would hurry around his regular deliveries, picking up a few coppers in tips on the way, and then spend a spare hour in a local coffee shop before returning to the yard. With the Clydesdale there was no spare time left at the end of the day, and it was almost five o'clock by the time he drove the van into Jamaica Road.

There was one more stop the carman always made before driving into the yard and that was to buy a paper from Solly Green and exchange a few words with the grizzled ex-boxer who always stood at the top end of Page Street. The carman normally slung the reins across the back of the Welsh cob, and it would not set off until it felt him stepping on to the shafts as he climbed into the dicky-seat. He had never used the wheel-chain with the cob, and did not think to anchor the wheel on this occasion. The Clydesdale was not used to waiting with slack reins and it leaned forward to test the resistance from the chain. The carman realised his mistake too late. The horse had smelt the stable and it set off, eager to dip its nose into the water trough and settle down in fresh straw.

William had finished parking the carts and as he crossed the yard he suddenly saw the Clydesdale clopping down the turning with its reins trailing on the cobbles and the carman running behind, trying to catch it up. The yard foreman's first thought was to grab hold of the reins and slow the animal in case anyone got in its way. He raced from the yard and reached the beast just as the carman grabbed at the reins, making the horse veer towards the kerb. The nearside shaft caught William full in the chest and he was thrown violently on to the pavement. The carman quickly managed to stop the cart and rushed over to the gasping foreman.

'I'm sorry, Will. It took off on its own,' he said fearfully as he bent over him.

Florrie Axford had heard the commotion and was outside in a flash. 'Don't touch 'im!' she shouted at the frightened carman. 'I fink 'e's broke 'is ribs.'

William was ashen-faced as he staggered to his feet, holding his chest. 'I'm all right,' he gasped, racked with a knife-like pain as he breathed. ''Elp me indoors, Flo.'

The carman was sent to fetch Doctor Kelly. Meanwhile Nellie and Florrie eased the injured foreman into a chair and removed his shirt with difficulty. The elderly doctor soon arrived and looked stern as he gently prodded and pushed.

'You're a lucky man, Tanner,' he announced as he finally

stood up straight. 'You've got a couple of cracked ribs. It could have been much worse. I'll put a tight strapping on. It'll ease the pain, but you'll need to lie up for a couple of weeks.'

That evening Frank Galloway looked in on his way home and seemed sympathetic as he chatted with William. 'Don't worry, we'll get Mitchell to take over for a couple of weeks. You just take it easy,' he said as he left.

The fire had burned low and the ticking of the clock sounded loudly in the quiet room. William had been helped up to bed earlier and was sleeping fitfully, propped up with pillows. Carrie had finished the ironing, cleared out the copper grate and laid it ready for the morning before going off to bed herself, leaving her mother sitting beside the dying fire. Nellie frowned and chewed her lip as she stared at the glowing embers. It seemed strange seeing Galloway in the house, she thought. In all the years her husband had worked at the yard, this was only the second occasion a Galloway had graced the house with his presence. The first time had been many years ago now and it was the memory of that visit which filled Nellie with loathing for George Galloway. Fate had decreed that the lives of the two families would be interwoven from the very beginning, and now the threatened union between Charlie and the Galloway girl felt like a cord tightening around her neck to choke the life out of her. She could never allow it to happen, whatever the cost.

At eleven o'clock the following morning George Galloway made his second visit to the Tanner household. He looked tense in his heavy worsted overcoat with the astrakhan collar pulled up close around his ears. His face was flushed, and he leaned on a cane walking-stick as he removed his trilby and ran a hand over his grey sleeked-back hair. He refused the offer of a seat and stood beside the table instead, looking down at William as he reclined in an armchair.

''Ow's the ribs?' he asked, frowning.

'Painful,' William replied, knowing instinctively that the time had come.

'I'm sorry ter 'ave ter tell yer, Will, but I've got ter put yer off,' Galloway said. 'We're finally gettin' the lorries, an' the 'orses'll 'ave ter go. I'm givin' yer two weeks' wages an' a little bonus.' He put a sealed envelope down on the table.

Nellie looked at her husband and saw the blank expression on his pale face, then she stared up at Galloway, her eyes hardening. 'Couldn't yer wait till Will was on 'is feet before tellin' 'im?' she said cuttingly.

Galloway returned her hard stare. 'I would 'ave done, Nell, but I need the 'ouse. I've got a motor mechanic startin' in two weeks' time an' 'e'll need a place ter live.'

William looked up dejectedly at the bulky figure which seemed to fill the tiny room. 'Yer not givin' us much time,' he said.

Nellie was shocked by her husband's quiet manner and felt cold anger rising in her own stomach. 'Is that all yer've got ter say, Will?' she complained. 'Yer've bin a good servant fer more than firty years an' now yer bein' chucked out o' yer job an' yer ouse, an' all yer can say is, "Yer not givin' us much time." Christ, I can't believe yer can be so calm!'

William looked appealingly at his wife. 'We knew it was gonna come,' he told her. 'What d'yer expect me ter do, beg fer me job?'

Nellie turned her back on her husband and glared at Galloway. 'Two weeks. Two weeks ter clear orf after 'e's done a lifetime's work fer yer,' she said bitterly. 'Years of lookin' after those 'orses an' keepin' yer business goin', an' that's all the time 'e gets. Yer a cruel, unfeelin' man, Galloway. Yer jus' use people. Yer taint everyfing yer come near. I'll be glad ter be done wiv yer, by Christ, an' I'm glad my Will won't 'ave ter

536

be at yer beck an' call any longer. Yer not welcome 'ere, so I'd
be obliged if yer left.'

Galloway walked to the door and turned suddenly. 'It'll be
fer the best,' he said, a dark glitter in his eye. 'I wish yer good
luck, Will.'

Nellie turned away as Galloway walked out, and closed the
front door behind him. She flopped down in the chair facing
her husband and lowered her head, covering her falling tears
with her hands.

'It's not fair,' she groaned. 'Yer should 'ave told 'im, Will.
It's jus' not fair.'

'Life's not fair, Nell,' he said quietly. 'I've always done me
best an' I couldn't do more. I wasn't goin' ter plead fer me job,
it'd make no difference anyway. 'E's always bin 'ard. I dunno,
p'raps it's the life 'e's 'ad. There's jus' no compassion in the
man.'

'But yer 'ad no start in life yerself,' she reminded him. 'Yer
was a waif the same as 'e was. At least yer didn't turn out like
'im, fank Gawd.'

Her body shook as she sobbed bitterly. She knelt down by
her husband's chair and dropped her head into his lap.
'What'll we do now, Will? Where can we go?' she sobbed.

He winced as the pain started up again in his chest. 'Don't
worry, gel. We'll get a place,' he said softly. 'I'll go an' see 'em
at the estate office in Jamaica Road in a day or two. They'll
'ave somefink fer us, I'm certain.'

'What's Carrie gonna say?' Nellie asked, looking up at him.
'An' what about the boys? Charlie's gonna be 'ome soon, an'
young Danny, please Gawd. This is the only place they've ever
known.'

William did not answer. He stroked his wife's head as he
looked around the tiny room, feeling as though the floor had
fallen away from him. It wouldn't be easy to get a job at his

age, he realised, and there wouldn't be many empty houses like the one they were living in at the moment. The alternative was too bad to think about. He sighed deeply as he stroked Nellie's long fair hair, unaware of the secret anguish she was suffering.

Chapter Thirty-seven

Ten days later William Tanner walked slowly back along Page Street, his chest still heavily strapped and his head hanging down. He had tried all the local estate offices and the only choice he had been given was a two-bedroomed flat in Bacon Street Buildings. It would have to do for the time being, he told himself. Nellie and Carrie were not going to be very pleased but the only alternative was the workhouse and that was unthinkable. It might not be too bad once the women put some curtains up and cleaned the place. Nellie knew a few of the people who lived in the buildings and it was only around the corner from Page Street. It could be worse, he thought.

Nellie was standing at the door, and as he approached her knew by the look on his face that her worst fears had been realised. Her eyes met his and his answering nod needed no clarification. She could see how dejected and tired he was and her heart went out to him.

'Sit yerself down, Will. I'll get yer a nice cuppa,' she said consolingly. 'It won't be so bad. It'll do us fer a while, anyway. We'll get somewhere better before long, you'll see.'

She had just poured the tea when there was a loud knock.

She heard a deep chuckle as William opened the door and then Sharkey Morris walked into the room.

''Ello, gel. 'Ow the bloody 'ell are yer?' he asked, his thin, mournful face breaking into a wide grin.

Nellie poured him a cup of tea as he made himself comfortable. The irrepressible carman looked enquiringly from one to the other. 'I 'eard the news from one o' Galloway's carmen,' he told them. 'What a bloody dirty trick! I 'ope the 'oreson chokes on 'is dinner ternight. After all those years yer bin wiv 'im. I'm glad I got out when I did.'

William smiled and stretched out his legs in front of the fire. 'It's nice o' yer ter call round,' he said.

'I was passin' by an' thought I'd drop in. I've gotta pick up a load o' corned beef from Chambers Wharf so I left the cart at the top o' the turnin',' Sharkey explained. He paused for a moment. 'I was very sorry ter 'ear about Jimmy. I understand young Charlie's on the mend though,' he added quickly, seeing the sad look on both their faces. 'I expect Danny'll be 'ome soon as well, please Gawd. Anyway, the reason I called round was, I thought yer might like a bit of 'elp wiv yer removals. I can use the cart, long as I let ole Sammy Sparrer know.'

'Well, that's very nice of yer, Sharkey,' Nellie said, patting his shoulder fondly. 'We're movin' inter Bacon Street Buildin's on Friday.'

William noticed the carman's faint grimace and smiled briefly. 'Yeah well, there was nuffink else goin'. It was eivver the buildin's or the work'ouse,' he said, sipping his tea.

'I'll be round about four o'clock then, all bein' well,' Sharkey informed them. 'I'll get ole Soapy ter give me an 'and. 'E won't mind.'

''Ow is 'e?' William asked. 'Still makin' a nuisance of 'imself, I s'pose.'

Sharkey put down his cup and took out his cigarette tin.

''Ere, I gotta tell yer. Soapy's got 'isself in trouble again,' he said, grinning. 'It all started the ovver week when Scatty Jim told the blokes 'e was gonna get married.'

'Who's Scatty Jim?' Nellie asked with a chuckle.

''E's one o' the carmen,' Sharkey replied. ''E's mad as a March 'are. Anyway, when Scatty told the blokes 'e was gonna get spliced, our Soapy decided ter get a collection up. So when all the carmen got their wages on the Friday, Soapy's standin' outside the office shakin' this bag. All 'e's got in there is nuts an' bolts an' a few washers. "C'mon, lads, chip in fer Jimbo," 'e's callin' out. Anyway, all the carmen make a show o' puttin' a few bob in, an' Scatty's standin' back rubbin' 'is 'ands tergevver. Yer can imagine what it looked like. The bag's gettin' 'eavier an' Soapy keeps winkin' at Scatty. "There'll be a nice few bob 'ere when I'm finished, Jimbo," 'e tells 'im. One o' the carmen pretended ter put a ten-shillin' note in the bag an' Scatty's eyes nearly popped out of 'is 'ead. Now on top of all this palaver, Soapy managed ter got 'old of an accordion case. There was no accordion inside it but as far as Scatty was concerned it was kosher. Well, Soapy cleaned up the case an' tied a bit o' ribbon round it an' over the top o' the lid, an' all week it was on show in the office. Now Scatty's waitin' fer the collection, yer see, but Soapy tells 'im that before 'e can 'ave it an' the accordion 'e's gotta bring 'is marriage lines in ter show the blokes on Monday mornin'. None o' the carmen believe 'e's really gettin' married an' they wanna prolong the poor sod's agony.

'Now ter cut a long story short, come Monday mornin' Scatty walks into the yard wiv a bloody great suitcase. 'E told the blokes that 'is young lady's muvver who 'e was lodgin' wiv chucked 'im out after 'er daughter give 'im the elbow. Poor sod looked really upset. The blokes was all laughin' an' one put an axe frew the "accordion" in front o' Scatty, an' ter crown it all Soapy was shakin' the bag an' tellin' everybody ter line up and get their money back.'

Nellie was holding her hand up to her mouth as she listened, her face changing expression as the story unfolded. 'Ah, fancy 'avin' the poor bloke on like that. Yer should be ashamed o' yerselves,' she said with mock seriousness.

Sharkey finally finished rolling his cigarette. 'That wasn't the end o' the story,' he went on with a big grin. 'When Scatty got back ter the yard that evenin' 'e picked up' is suitcase from the office an' walked out o' the place wiv a face as long as a kite. All the blokes were clappin' 'im an' givin' 'im a right ribbin', an' ter crown it all Soapy follers 'im ter the tram-stop an' stands there tryin' ter cheer 'im up. Well, when the tram pulls up there's no more room, an' as it pulls away from the stop Soapy chucks the poor bleeder's suitcase on. Scatty goes chasin' after it, 'ollerin' an' 'ootin' – it was so bleedin' funny. Anyway, when it pulls up an' the conductor jumps down ter change the points, Scatty climbs aboard ter get 'is case and now the conductor finks 'e's tryin' ter pinch it an' grabs 'im. Somebody fetched a copper an' they run the poor sod in. Mind yer, 'e finally convinced 'em it was 'is case an' they let 'im go.

'By this time Scatty's just about 'ad enough. Anyway, next mornin' 'e come ter work wiv a chopper under 'is coat an' soon as 'e claps eyes on Soapy 'e goes fer 'im, swearin' 'e's gonna put the chopper in 'is bonce. The blokes managed ter calm 'im down but every time Scatty sets eyes on Soapy 'e leers at 'im an' points to 'is 'ead. Soapy's scared out of 'is life. 'E's convinced 'e's gonna get choppered when 'e's not lookin'.'

The house was filled with laughter and Nellie wiped her eyes on the edge of her pinafore. 'Well, all I can say is, if Soapy does get choppered, 'e thoroughly deserves it,' she gasped.

Sharkey got up and dusted tobacco from his coat. 'Well, I'd better be orf,' he announced. 'I'll see the pair o' yer Friday, an' if Soapy's still breavin' I'll bring 'im along as well. So if yer see a chopper stickin' out of 'is bonce, take no notice.'

When the word got around the little turning that the Tanners were leaving, Nellie's old friends gathered together in Florrie Axford's parlour.

'Now we all know Nellie's bein' kicked out,' Florrie said, tapping on her snuff-box. 'I fink us ladies should try an' do somefink ter show Nellie we're still 'er friends.'

'Nellie knows that already,' Maisie cut in. 'She's known us long enough.'

'Well, I fink this is a time when we need ter prove it,' Florrie told her. 'I reckon we should put our 'eads tergevver an' try ter fink o' somefink really nice.'

'We should go in the yard an' cut Galloway's froat,' Sadie suggested.

Aggie was stirring her tea thoughtfully. 'Why don't we club tergevver an' get 'er a little present?' she said suddenly.

'I'm not tryin' ter be funny, Aggie, but I don't fink we've got more than a few coppers between the lot of us,' Florrie said, placing a pinch of snuff on the back of her hand. 'All we're gonna get 'er wiv that is somefing orf Cheap Jack's stall. No, we've gotta fink o' somefing really nice.'

'I've got a nice pair o' green curtains I bin keepin'. She could 'ave them,' Maudie said.

'An' I've got a lace tablecloth in me chest o drawers,' Maggie Jones added.

Florrie sneezed loudly and dabbed at her watering eyes. 'Nellie wouldn't be 'appy takin' our bits an' pieces,' she remarked. 'C'mon, gels, we can do better than that. Let's get our finkin' caps on.'

'I know somefing we could do, somefink very nice,' Ida Bromsgrove said suddenly.

All the women stared at her and Florrie got out her snuff-box once more as Ida paused for effect. 'Well, go on then, Ida, put us out of our misery,' she said impatiently.

Ida looked around at the assembled women. 'Why don't we go ter Bacon Street Buildin's an' give Nellie's flat a good doin' out before she gets there?'

'What a good idea!' Florrie exclaimed. 'We could give the floorboards a good scrubbin'.'

'An' we could clean 'er winders an' put a bit o' net up,' Aggie said quickly.

'We could wash the paintwork down wiv Manger's soap an' run a taper roun' the skirtin',' Maisie added.

'We could clean the closet wiv some o' that carbolic acid. It brings them stained piss'oles up a treat,' Maggie remarked.

'Right then,' Florrie said loudly. 'Are we all agreed?' Voices were raised in unison and she held up her hands. 'Now we gotta plan this prop'ly. We know the Tanners are movin' on Friday afternoon. What we gotta do is get in that flat first fing Friday mornin'. One of us will 'ave ter collect the key.'

'Will they give it ter one of us?' Maisie asked.

'S'posin' Nellie goes round 'erself in the mornin'?' Aggie suggested.

The women all ended up looking enquiringly at Florrie who pulled on her chin thoughtfully for a few moments.

'Look, I'll 'andle that side of it,' she told them finally. 'You lot be outside the buildin's at nine sharp, all right? An' don't ferget ter bring the cleanin' stuff. I'll make us anuvver cup o' tea while yer decide who's bringin' what.'

Carrie left the house on Friday morning feeling very sad. Her few personal belongings had been parcelled up and left alongside those of her brothers. The bundle did not amount to very much, though one letter had evoked such emotion that Carrie tucked it into her handbag and carried it to work with her. It was a childish note from Sara Knight which had been passed from desk to desk, via the Gordon brothers who had both managed to get to school that morning. The thank-you letter said how much Sara had enjoyed the day at the farm and the lovely trip on top of the hay cart. It also said that Carrie would be her best friend for ever and ever. How much had happened since those happy, carefree days, Carrie thought, remembering the trips with her father, the smell of fresh straw and the noises in the dark upper stable as she went with her father to see the animals. She clenched her fists tightly as she walked along to the dining rooms, and thought about the vow she had taken as she looked around the house for the last time. One day she would pay George Galloway back for the way he had treated her father. And one day she would have enough money to look after both her parents and take them away from the squalor of Bacon Street Buildings.

On Friday morning Florrie Axford got up very early, and as soon as she returned from her cleaning job knocked at Nellie Tanner's front door.

'Is there anyfink yer want me ter do, Nell? I could 'elp yer wiv the packin' if yer like?'

Nellie shook her head. 'Fanks fer the offer, Flo, but it's near enough all done. I'm jus' waitin' fer the van ter call.'

'When yer collectin' the key?' Florrie asked as casually as she could.

'There's no rush. Sharkey won't be 'ere till this afternoon. Will said 'e's gonna call in the office after dinner.'

'Well, I'll let yer get on then,' Florrie said.

The Page Street women's deputy made her second call of

the morning and was angered by the young man who stood facing her over the counter.

'I'm terribly sorry, Mrs Axley, but . . .'

'Axford,' she corrected him.

'Well, I'm sorry Mrs Axford but I can't give the key to anyone but the person who signed the tenancy forms,' the young man informed her, looking awkward. 'It's the rules, you see.'

'Sod yer rules,' Florrie said in a strident tone. 'I live in Page Street an' I'm sodded if I'm gonna walk all the way back there ter tell Mrs Tanner that yer won't let me 'ave the key. Like I said, she's got 'er ole man down wiv the flu an' she can't get up 'ere' erself. She said yer was a very nice young man an' yer'd be only too glad ter let me 'ave the key. I'm beginnin' ter fink she made a mistake. Yer not very nice at all. Yer don't care that 'er' 'usband's very poorly an' she don't know which way ter turn. Movin's a very nasty business, 'specially when yer movin' inter a poxy 'ole like Bacon Street Buildin's. Still, if yer won't budge, I'll jus' 'ave ter speak ter yer manager. I'm sure 'e'll be a little more understandin'. Will yer go an' get 'im, if yer please?'

The young man scratched his head, feeling very embarrassed. It was only his first week at the office. He recalled the advice the manager had given him: be helpful and don't be afraid to use your own initiative. Well, the manager was out of the office and he had been left in charge. Mrs Axford seemed a genuine enough lady, even if her tongue was rather sharp. He would have to make a decision.

'All right, Mrs Axley . . .'

'Axford.'

'All right, Mrs Axford, I'll give you the key, but you must promise me you'll give it to Mrs Tanner immediately,' the young man said firmly.

'Cross me 'eart an' 'ope ter die,' Florrie said with mock reverence.

The young man passed over the key with a flourish and Florrie smiled at him.

'I fink yer a very nice man after all,' she said graciously, 'an' I shall tell the manager so, soon's I see 'im.'

There was one more little lie to tell, Florrie thought as she walked quickly back to Page Street. The church clock showed five minutes to nine when she walked in the turning and knocked at Nellie's front door once more.

'Sorry ter trouble yer, luv, but the man from the estate office knocked at my door by mistake an' I told 'im I'd pass the message on,' she said. ''E said ter tell yer not to worry about callin' in the office fer the key, as 'e's gotta go ter the buildin's ter do some inspectin' an' 'e'll leave it wiv the porter. All right, luv?'

'Well, that's a journey saved, Flo,' Nellie replied. 'Got time ter a cuppa?'

Normally Florrie would have accepted but she had visions of women marching up and down Bacon Street with brooms and mops over their shoulders. 'No fanks, Nell,' she said quickly. 'I've gotta get over uncle's right away before 'e 'as a chance ter put that ring o' mine in the winder. The bleedin' pledge was up yesterday, an' yer know what ole Beckford's like. 'Is arse is always makin' buttons.'

Florrie hurried along the street and turned left at the end. The gloomy building loomed up large and forbidding against the tidy little houses. Her friends were gathered together with folded arms outside the first block.

'Right then, up we go,' Florrie said, leading the way up a long flight of rickety wooden stairs. The walls were shedding plaster and there was a large sooty mark around the bare gas jet. The first narrow landing led along from the head of the stairs to another similar flight. On the second landing Florrie stopped to catch her breath. 'C'mon, gels, one more flight,' she said encouragingly to her friends as they followed, puffing with exertion.

There were four flats on the landing and Florrie went to the door directly at the head of the stairs and inserted the key.

'Good Gawd! Look at the state of it,' Sadie exclaimed as she went inside. 'We're gonna 'ave our work cut out 'ere.'

'It looks like it's bin used as a bleedin' stable,' Aggie remarked.

'It smells like a bleedin' stable,' Maisie cut in.

'Open that bloody winder, fer Gawd's sake,' Florrie commanded.

The two bedrooms proved to be even more filthy, and when Florrie looked into the tiny scullery which led directly from the front room, she shook her head sadly.

'I thought our places were bad enough but compared ter this they're bleedin' palaces,' she murmured.

Beneath the scullery window there was a small sink and a copper. Facing the sink was an iron gas-stove which was caked in grease, and beyond the stove a door leading to the toilet.

'D'yer realise yer could sit on the pan an' cook a meal at the same time,' Maggie remarked. 'I reckin it's bloody disgustin'.'

'Well, c'mon then, let's get started,' Florrie said bravely, filling a galvanised pail and putting it on the gas-stove to heat up.

The women set to work. Maisie cleaned the windows, Maggie cleared out the hearth and blackleaded the grate, and Sadie started scrubbing the bare floorboards. Florrie rolled up her sleeves and tackled the filthy gas-stove, while Maudie pottered about with a wet cloth around the woodwork.

Ida Bromsgrove realised that her bright idea had given

everyone a mammoth task as she got down on her knees and helped Sadie with the scrubbing. 'D'yer remember the time we all went on that outin' an' Nellie brought us all 'ome after ole Soapy Symonds got pissed?' she said with a chuckle.

Sadie leant back on her heels and ran her hands across her forehead. 'Do I! Remember those pair o' toffee-nosed ole cows I nearly set about, Ida?' she laughed.

Ida jerked her thumb in the direction of Aggie who was busy with a toilet-brush. 'Remember when we all lifted 'er in the cart an' she was frightened we was gonna drop 'er? What a day that was,' she said, grinning.

Suddenly there was a loud banging on the front door. Maudie looked worried as she hurried over to open it and was confronted by a large, middle-aged man with a walrus moustache.

'What you lot doin' in 'ere?' he demanded.

'We're doin' a bit o' cleanin' fer Nellie,' Maudie said meekly.

'Oh, is that so?' the man said haughtily. 'Well, I'm Mr Pudsey the porter an' I'm in charge o' this 'ere buildin'.'

'Please ter meet yer, Mr Pudsey, I'm sure,' Maudie replied.

The porter hooked his hands through his braces and glared around at the women. 'Yer'll 'ave ter leave,' he said in a loud voice. 'Yer should 'ave come an' seen me before yer decided to stroll into the flat.'

Sadie got up and made for the door with a malevolent look in her eye but Florrie beat her to it.

'I'm Florrie Axford an' I'm in charge o' this lot, so anyfing yer got ter say yer can say ter me,' she told him firmly.

'Yer'll 'ave ter leave is what I'm sayin',' the porter said, eyeing her warily.

'Oh, that's what yer sayin', is it?' Sadie growled over Florrie's shoulder. 'Well, yer can piss off orf out of it. We're cleanin' up this pigsty an' that's that.'

The porter knew all about the Sullivans and he stepped back a pace. 'I've got me job ter do, missus,' he said in a less commanding voice.

'Yeah? An' we've got our job ter do, so why don't yer leave us ter get on wiv it?' Sadie berated him.

Florrie had often found herself acting as the leader not least because of her guile and cunning, and on this particular Friday morning she was not found lacking. 'All right, Sadie, jus' get on wiv yer scrubbin',' she said quietly. 'Me an' the buildin's manager are goin' ter 'ave a little chat.'

Albert Pudsey had been called a few names in his time by the tenants of Bacon Street Buildings but never a 'manager'. He brushed his hand across his bushy moustache as Florrie slipped out on to the landing and pulled the door half closed behind her.

'I've often seen yer pass me winder an' I never knew yer was the manager o' these buildin's, Mr Pudsey,' she remarked. 'I was only sayin' ter Mrs Dougall the ovver day, "Maisie," I ses, "who's that big fella walkin' up the street?" An' Maisie ses ter me, "Yer know, Flo, I fink 'e's a copper, one o' them plainclothes coppers." 'Ave yer ever bin in the police, Mr Pudsey?'

The porter shook his head. 'Nah. I used ter be on the roads, before I got this job,' he said, throwing out his chest.

'A commercial traveller?'

'Nah, I used ter dig 'em up,' he told her.

'What, the roads?' she asked innocently.

The porter was not sure whether the woman was making fun of him or whether she was just tuppence short of a shilling. He backed away. 'Look, I've got me rounds ter do,' he said. 'Don't ferget ter make sure that door's shut when yer leave.'

Florrie gave him a big smile. 'All right, Mr Pudsey. Jus'

leave it ter Auntie Flo. Oh, by the way, the manager at the office said you'd 'ave ter see Mrs Tanner in, so I'd better drop the key through yer letterbox. She should be 'ere about five o'clock.'

Later that morning the porter watched the band of weary women marching away and shook his head slowly. 'It's gettin' bloody worse round 'ere,' he muttered.

The following Monday morning Carrie arrived at Fred Bradley's and took her place behind the counter. All day the usual comings and goings went on, and as she served the teas and coffees, took the food orders and tidied the tables, Carrie's mind was racing. She had decided what she was going to do now and there could be no turning back. It was a decision born of desperation but her inner feelings told her that it was the right one, the only one. She would have to be bold and straightforward. There must be no misunderstanding.

She felt a churning in her stomach as she walked resolutely into the back kitchen after Bessie Chandler had left, and sat down at the freshly scrubbed table.

Fred was hanging up the pots and pans and looked at her in surprise. 'I expected yer ter be makin' buttons ter get away, Carrie,' he said, smiling. 'Yer look as though yer don't fancy the prospect o' goin' 'ome ter Bacon Street Buildin's.'

Carrie stared down at her fingernails and took a very deep breath. 'There's somefing I wanna ask yer, Fred,' she said, her eyes coming up to meet his.

He sat down facing her, concern on his face. 'Yer not gonna ask me ter let yer leave, are yer?' he said quickly.

She looked down at her hands and then fixed him with her eyes again. 'Yer told me some time ago that yer wanted ter marry me. D'yer still feel the same way?' she asked quietly.

Fred dropped his gaze momentarily. 'There's no need ter ask, Carrie,' he replied. 'I could never change the way I feel about yer.'

'Well then, I will marry yer, Fred,' she said, her voice quavering.

He stood up, his eyes open wide and his mouth hanging open. 'Christ! I don't know what ter say,' he gasped, holding his hands out to her.

Carrie stood up and walked around the table and the next instant she was in his arms. She closed her eyes tightly as he kissed her cheek.

She had spent the whole day thinking about her decision and was convinced she was doing the right thing. For a long time now Fred had been more than just an employer. He had become a very good friend. She was almost twenty-seven and at that age most of the girls she knew were already married with children. She had no one special in her life since Tommy, and her mother was always asking her when she was going to find a steady lad. Carrie was aware that it would be difficult to find another man as good as Fred. The dining rooms could soon be improved, and with a little thought and a lot of hard work there was no reason why she should not be able to earn enough money to take care of her parents. She had vowed not to let them spend the rest of their lives in that rotting tenement block. Fred was stroking her back tenderly as she nestled in his arms and she said a silent prayer.

'Yer've made me very 'appy,' he said, releasing her and looking into her blue eyes. 'I jus' can't believe it!'

Carrie took his hands in hers. 'I've bin doin' a lot o' finkin' an' I realised I couldn't keep yer waitin' too long,' she said. 'I like yer very much, Fred, an' I can learn ter love yer, I know I can.'

'I'll make a good 'usband an' I'll take care o' yer, Carrie,' he said with feeling. 'One day yer'll know that yer love me. We both will. Now what about a nice cup o' tea ter celebrate?'

She laughed warmly. 'Yer a lovely man, Fred Bradley,' she said.

Chapter Thirty-eight

One evening early in February Charlie Tanner walked into block A of Bacon Street Buildings and slowly climbed the stairs. The crumbling, insanitary tenement was not unfamiliar to the young veteran. He had played in and out of the blocks when he was a lad and many times had felt the boot of an angry porter on his backside. The place looked smaller now, and even more dilapidated The walls had become more cracked, the gas-jet had lost its mantle and glass shade, and paint was peeling from the front doors.

Charlie was completely out of breath by the time he reached the third floor and knocked on the door of number 9. When Carrie threw her arms around him, he grinned sheepishly. 'So this is where we're livin' now, is it?'

She took him by the arm. 'Look who's 'ere, Ma,' she called out.

Nellie came hurrying out from the scullery, her face flushed with the heat. She embraced Charlie, smiling, and stood back, still holding on to his arms.

'Yer've lost weight, son,' she said, looking him up and down. 'Sit yerself down by the fire an' I'll get yer a nice cuppa. Dinner won't be long.'

'Where's Dad?' he asked.

''E's gone off ter work,' Nellie told him, and saw his puzzled look. 'Yer farvver's workin' as a nightwatchman fer the borough council. It's only fer the time bein'. There's nothing else about at this time o' year, he lined up fer hours at the labour exchange. 'E'll get somefink better soon, I 'ope. Trouble is, 'is age. 'E's sixty next birthday.'

Nellie went back into the scullery and Carrie sat down in the chair facing her brother. 'Are yer prop'ly better, Charlie?' she asked.

He nodded. 'Just a bit breathless at times, but the doctor tells me it'll pass.'

'Tell yer bruvver the good news, Carrie,' her mother called out.

'I'm gettin' married in April,' she said, smiling.

'Who's the lucky man?' Charlie asked with a look of surprise.

'It's Fred Bradley.'

''E's a bit older than you. Yer not worried?' he asked her.

'Fred's a good man. I'm gonna be 'appy wiv 'im, Charlie,' she said, pulling her legs up under her.

'Well, that's all that counts, Sis,' he said, smiling.

Carrie gazed at him as he looked slowly around the room. He had lost weight and his face had grown thinner. He looked much older, she thought.

'This isn't a bit like our old 'ouse, is it?' he remarked.

'Florrie Axford an' some o' the women cleaned it all out fer us,' Carrie told him. 'Mum was really surprised. It was very nice of 'em, wasn't it? The people round 'ere 'ave bin really good. Yer remember Sharkey an' Soapy who used ter work at the yard? Well, they borrowed a cart ter move us. They got the bedroom furniture out frew the upstairs winder an' Soapy smashed one o' the panes o' glass. Mum was a bit worried but 'e said if Galloway ses anyfink about it, tell 'im the removal men done it an' 'e'll 'ave ter claim orf o' them.'

Nellie came into the room carrying a large pot and started to serve up the mutton stew. 'I've bin keepin' this 'ot. I 'ad ter do it earlier 'cos o' yer farvver,' she said, holding her head back from the steam. When he had wiped his plate clean with a piece of bread, Charlie leant back in his chair and rubbed his stomach. 'I've bin missin' yer cookin', Ma,' he grinned. 'It's a lot better than the muck we got in France.'

Nellie smiled at him and then her eyes strayed over to the shrouded photograph of James on the wall and the photos lining the mantelshelf. 'I wonder 'ow young Danny is?' she said anxiously. 'It's bin a long time since we've 'eard from 'im.'

''E'll be all right. The war won't last much longer,' Charlie replied encouragingly. 'I should fink Danny'll be in a rest camp by now. 'E's done 'is time in the line.'

The two women started to clear the table while Charlie made himself comfortable by the fire. He had been thinking about telling his family that he had spent a few days with Josephine in Ramsgate after leaving the hospital but had decided against it. Now that his father had lost his job and the family had had to leave the old house, they would naturally be bitter towards the Galloways. It made Charlie sad to think about his father and how he must feel ending up as a night-watchman. He was skilful and experienced with horses, but men like him were a dying breed now. In a few years' time the roads would be full of lorries.

Charlie could hear the clatter of crockery coming from the scullery and the women's voices chattering, and he thought about Carrie's forthcoming marriage to Fred Bradley. She had often talked about him and said what a decent man he was, but she had also said he was a bit set in his ways and old-fashioned. What had made her suddenly agree to marry him? he wondered. Maybe she wanted to put herself in a position where she would be able to take care of their parents. It was just the sort of thing Carrie would do. Well, Fred Bradley had better take good care of her, he told himself, or he would have her two brothers to answer to.

Nellie and Carrie joined Charlie around the fire and began chatting about everything that had been happening. They talked of the fire at the yard and the body that was found in the ashes, and Nellie spoke about the trial of Sammy Jackson which had taken place the previous week.

'Accordin' ter what yer farvver 'eard, the police didn't fink Sammy Jackson would go ter trial,' she explained. 'They reckoned 'e'd be unfit ter plead but the doctor who examined 'im said 'e was sane as the next man. It was in all the papers. It seemed strange reading about yer own street an' people yer know. Anyway 'e got sentenced ter death. Apparently there's an appeal but yer farvver reckons 'e'll 'ang. Mus' be terrible standin' there an' seein' the judge put on that black cap.'

'P'raps Sammy Jackson played it straight instead of actin' mad,' Charlie said. 'Maybe 'e knew the alternative was ter spend the rest of 'is life in a lunatic asylum.'

Nellie nodded. 'Well, the papers said it was a deliberate attempt ter kill Jack Oxford. We all thought it was 'im in that fire. I'll never ferget the look on yer dad's face when 'e come back an' told us Jack was alive an' well. 'E always 'ad a soft spot fer ole Jack. Mind yer, 'e's doin' well now, by all accounts. I was talkin' wiv 'is lan'lady an' she said Jack's got a cushy job at the tannery. 'E's smartened 'imself up too. 'E wears a nice suit an' 'e goes out wiv 'er ter the pub an' the music 'alls. I reckon the next fing we'll 'ear is that 'er an' Jack's got spliced.'

'Galloway done Jack a favour givin' 'im the sack, but 'e didn't do Dad any favours, did 'e?' Carrie said bitterly. 'After savin' all 'is 'orses too.'

'Yer can bet yer life 'e blamed yer farvver fer the fire. The way Galloway sees it yer farvver should 'ave made sure nobody could get in the yard,' Nellie remarked.

'I was terrified when I see Dad pullin' them 'orses out,' Carrie recalled with a shudder.

'So was I when I see yer strugglin' wiv that geldin'. I thought the pair of yer was gonna get trampled under its 'ooves,' Nellie said, shaking her head.

'Yer was sayin' that lodger o' Florrie's 'elped Dad ter get the 'orses out,' Charlie said.

'Yeah, Joe Maitland,' Nellie replied. 'Florrie told me George Galloway gave 'er a letter fer 'im an' there was a five-pound note in it. Florrie said that when she gave 'im it 'e made 'er take the money an' 'e chucked the letter on the fire. She said she couldn't understand why 'e done it. Florrie told me 'e's a bit of a mystery, 'E's got no time fer Galloway an' 'e was really angry when 'e got that letter. P'raps 'e's got good reason ter be the way 'e is.'

'Is 'e from round 'ere?' asked Charlie.

'No, I don't fink so. Florrie reckons 'e comes from over the water,' Nellie told him. ''E's 'ad a few letters wiv a Stepney postmark an' a few from Poplar. She can't get much out of 'im, but yer know 'ow shrewd Florrie is. One day she'll get ter the bottom of it.'

'What does 'e do fer a livin'?'

'There again, it's a mystery,' Nellie said. 'Florrie said 'e goes out in the mornin' an' don't come in till six or seven. She reckons 'e's got a business o' some sort. Always got a few bob in 'is pocket 'e 'as, an' now an' again 'e treats 'er on top of 'is lodgin' money. Very nice bloke by all accounts.'

Charlie spread out his legs and yawned. 'I'm ready fer an early night,' he sighed.

'Yer'd better use the over bedroom,' Nellie told him. 'Yer'll 'ave ter share the bed wiv Danny when 'e comes 'ome. Carrie can use the chair-bed in this room. It ain't very nice but we can't do nuffing else wiv only two bedrooms.'

'Well, I'll be goin' back when this is 'ealed,' Charlie said, rubbing his chest.

'Yer mean they ain't gonna discharge yer?' his mother asked in a shocked voice.

'Yer need ter be a little bit worse off than me ter get a discharge,' he laughed. 'It's all right though, I won't be goin' back ter France. They told me I'm gonna be made up ter sergeant an' be posted ter one o' the trainin' camps. It'll suit me till the war's over.'

Nellie felt guilty for her feeling of relief at the news. She had been expecting Charlie to be discharged and then take up with Galloway's daughter. At least now he wouldn't be able to see the girl. Maybe it would all come to nothing and the girl would find another young man, she prayed.

Nora Flynn was deep in thought as she prepared the table for the evening meal. Since Josephine had the confrontation with her father she had become withdrawn and unhappy. She was rarely in the house now, and the evening meal had become a quiet and strained affair. George ate his food in silence, and Nora would sit opposite him, trying to make conversation and draw him out of his moodiness, but it always proved impossible. She had come to realise that she was just wasting her time. The large gloomy house was becoming like a mausoleum now that Josephine's infectious laughter could no longer be heard and Nora had the urge to throw open all the windows and all the doors and tear down the musty drapes.

The place needed sunlight, young spirits, laughter and noise, but there was just her and George now, an ageing man, bitter and cynical, and his middle-aged housekeeper. Why should I stay with him? she asked herself. There was nothing to keep her here apart from Josephine, and it seemed very likely that she would soon leave.

The evening meal passed as usual with George hardly speaking. As Nora pushed back her plate she looked hard at him across the table. This had gone on long enough, she decided. She had to try to make him see the unhappiness he was causing his daughter, and her too. He would have to listen to her, and if he refused then she would leave the house and let him fend fer himself.

George had become aware of her looking at him and leaned back in his chair and stared back. 'What's wrong?' he asked testily.

'I was just finkin' 'ow quiet the 'ouse is wivo[...] remarked, looking down at her teacup.

'Well, if she's decided she don't like our company, there's not a lot we can do about it, is there?' he said sarcastically.

'If yer 'adn't bin so 'ard on the gel she'd be sittin' 'ere wiv us now,' Nora rebuked him.

George sighed irritably as he rolled a cigar between his thick fingers. 'Look, Nora, this is a family matter,' he said sharply. 'If I choose to criticise the young men my daughter associates wiv, I'll do so. It's fer 'er benefit. If I didn't care about 'er welfare I'd let 'er walk out wiv any ole Tom, Dick or 'Arry. It's not fer you ter say what I should or shouldn't do.'

Nora pursed her lips in anger and took a deep breath. 'Now you jus' listen ter me fer a minute,' she began in a cool voice. 'Yer asked me ter be yer 'ousekeeper when Martha died, an' ever since I've looked after yer children, especially Josie. I fink I've a right ter let yer know 'ow I feel about the way yer treatin' the gel. If I was an outsider I'd say yer was right, but I'm not an outsider, George. Yer've taken me inter the family an' I've played me part. I've kept a good clean 'ouse. Yer food's always bin on the table ready an' I've bin there when the children needed me. I was there too when yer needed comfortin', but it seems ter me yer've used me the way yer use everybody. Well, I'm gonna tell yer this, George – yer've got no compassion or feelin' in yer soul. Yer an 'ard, inconsiderate man, especially where yer daughter's concerned. Yer jus' can't see the un'appiness yer've brought that child. She's a lovely gel, an' yer destroyin' 'er. Don't try ter run 'er life fer 'er. Let 'er make 'er own choice in young men. After all, she's a grown woman now, not a kid.'

Galloway had sat in silence while Nora berated him, his face set firm and his dark, moody eyes never leaving her face. As she stopped for breath, he leaned forward over the table. 'Listen ter me, woman,' he said in a low husky voice. 'Yer say I'm inconsiderate where Josie's concerned. Well, I'll tell yer this – I love that child even though I 'aven't always shown it. It's there inside me,' he said, tapping his chest. 'There's plenty o' young men around 'ere wivout 'er takin' up wiv the Tanner lad. I'm not gonna let 'er ruin 'er life an' I've ferbidden 'er ter see 'im. On that score I won't be swayed, whatever yer say.'

'I can't understand what yer've got against the lad,' Nora persisted, shaking her head. ''Is farvver's worked fer yer fer years. Josie's in love wiv the lad, she's told me often enough.'

'Love?' George said, his face flushing as he clenched his fists on the table. He seemed to pause for a moment, then he stared hard at Nora and grimaced. 'All right, yer won't be satisfied until yer know the trufe, so I'm gonna tell yer. P'raps then yer'll understand.'

The light from the glowing coals flickered on the high

ceiling and around the walls and lit up the old framed prints as George Galloway spoke slowly and deliberately. His housekeeper sat silently throughout, and when he finally slumped back in his chair Nora stood up and left the room without saying a word.

During the bitter cold winter of 1918 there was little news from the Western Front, and at the beginning of February the morning newspapers were able to report on the front page that Sammy Jackson's sentence had been commuted to life imprisonment. In the early spring, however, large headlines told of a new German offensive on the Western Front and once again the Red Cross trains were returning thousands of casualties. In March, Corporal Charles Tanner was passed fully fit and posted to a training unit on the Isle of Sheppey with the rank of sergeant. Private Danny Tanner was one of the few survivors of his regiment, which had borne the brunt of the new offensive, and along with the others he was sent to a rest camp behind the lines.

Back in Bermondsey the delayed delivery of the first of Galloway's lorries took place in March and people watched from their front doors as the vehicles chugged noisily down Page Street and drove into the yard. Another lorry arrived at the Galloway yard the same day and left carrying the two massive Clydesdales. George Galloway watched the loading of the animals with an impassive face, and then he walked back into the office to look at the plans of the proposed new site which Frank had spread out on the desk. The street folk watched the comings and goings with sadness. The horses clopping out of the yard each morning and returning in the evening with their heads held low had been a way of life for the little community; now they would have to get used to the sound of noisy engines and the noxious smell of petrol fumes.

Florrie Axford had been among the most vociferous in the past, protesting about the dangerous way in which some of the carmen drove their carts along the turning. Now she shook her head as she stood at her front door, chatting to Maisie and Aggie. 'I dunno what next,' she groaned. 'They should never allow lorries down 'ere. The turnin's too narrer. Somebody's gonna get killed wiv one o' them lorries, mark my words.'

'Gawd knows what Will Tanner will make of it,' Maisie remarked. 'I reckon 'e'll be glad 'e's done wiv it all.'

Aggie was pinching her chin between thumb and forefinger. 'I dunno so much,' she said. 'I saw Nell down the market the ovver day. She looked really miserable. She's got one o' them back flats an' 'er bedroom is right over the dustbins. She said the stink's makin' 'er feel really ill. She was worried about 'er 'usband as well. She said since Will's bin doin' that nightwatchman's job, 'e's a changed man. She said 'e's got so moody.'

'Well, I reckon it's a bloody shame the way that ole bastard Galloway treated 'im,' Florrie declared. ''E won't get anuvver bloke like Will Tanner.'

'It seems strange not seein' Nell standin' at her door,' Aggie said.

'What's the new people like?' Maisie asked.

Florrie pulled a face as she took out her snuff-box. 'I ain't seen 'im, but she looks a miserable cow. She was cleanin' 'er winders the ovver day an' when she sees me she turned 'er 'ead. Sod yer then, I thought ter meself.'

Aggie looked along the turning and shook her head sadly. 'We'll never be able ter keep our winders clean now, not with all that smoke 'angin' about,' she said.

Florrie smiled. 'Never mind, Aggie. 'Ere, cheer yerself up. 'Ave a pinch o' snuff.'

*

On a balmy Saturday morning early in April a pleasure boat left Greenwich Pier bound for Southend. Aboard were Red Cross nurses and doctors taking a well-earned break. As the craft steamed out on the tide, one of the doctors was playing a piano accordion. The pleasure boat chugged downriver while Josephine sat quietly re-reading the letter she had received from Charlie just two days before. She felt out of place among the noise and merriment, and when a young doctor pulled her up to dance she had to force a smile. The music sounded tuneless to her and her dancing partner's cheerful asides grated on her troubled mind and seemed meaningless. Above the clamour of merrymaking she could hear her father's voice, and all she could think of as she looked over the young man's shoulder were the boldly written words of Charlie's letter.

The music ceased while the revellers took refreshments and Josephine climbed the steep rungs to the upper deck. It was quieter here, she thought as she looked out at the widening estuary and the distant banks. She had to think clearly. Charlie had asked her to marry him and now she had to make a clear, final decision before she let herself touch her first drink. There would be time enough later to blot out the anguish and heartache that seemed to be tearing her apart.

For a while she stared out across the river, feeling the strong breeze on her face and listening to the steady chugging of the engines below. She watched the screaming seagulls as they hovered and swooped above her and dived towards the swirling rushing waters of the river. It was all an obscene, swirling madness, she said to herself as she leaned against the guard-rail. Once more she took the letter out and read it, then she folded it carefully and returned it to her handbag before she went down to join the revellers.

*

George Galloway sat alone in his front room, a glass of Scotch whisky at his elbow and a large sheet of paper spread out on the floor beside him. The plan depicted a group of adjoining riverside properties headed 'Felstead Estates', and as George studied it he fingered the medallion hanging from his watch chain. Frank had been optimistic about the purchase, he recalled. There were two old houses which had become derelict and a small yard leased by an engineering firm which was heavily in debt to the bank. The corner property, a working men's café, would be the only one to worry about, Frank had said. The lease was running out very soon and it was vital that the freehold was obtained beforehand. Planning permission would be no problem, he had been assured. New local transport concerns were being encouraged by the borough council to cope with the rising demands of trade, and a few palms had been greased as well. Felstead Estates were keen to sell the land, Frank had told him. They were in the process of raising money from their less profitable sites to finance a deal to buy property in the West End. The whole riverside site could easily be razed to the ground and replaced with a garage for a dozen lorries and yard storage space. Frank had been quick to point out that two sides of the site abutted on warehouses which would mean only two sides to fence and secure. It looked very promising, George thought as he sipped his drink.

The rat-tat on the front door roused him from his thoughts and he heard Nora's footsteps on the stairs as she hurried down to answer the knock. Her face was pale and anxious as she led the two police officers into the room. They took off their helmets as George got up unsteadily from his chair.

'Mr George Galloway?' one of the policemen asked.

'What's wrong?' he asked, feeling dizzy as he straightened up.

'I'm afraid we've got some bad news, sir. It concerns your daughter.'

'What's 'appened?' he blurted out.

'I'm very sorry to have to tell you that your daughter Josephine was lost overboard from the "Greenwich Belle",' the officer said in a low voice.

George collapsed into his chair, his head in his hands and his whole body convulsed with sobs. Nora stood aghast with her hand up to her face and stared white-faced at the policeman. ''Ow? Where?' she croaked.

'The last time she was seen was about eight o'clock this evening,' the officer replied. 'We've taken statements from the passengers and those who knew her said she'd been drinking heavily. It would appear that she fell from the upper deck. That's where she was seen last. According to the skipper the boat would have been approaching Galleons Reach on the return journey at about that time. The river police are searching the whole stretch of water but they've informed us that it might be some time before they recover the body. There are quite a few locks and dock entrances leading off Galleons Reach you see. I'm very sorry.'

Nora showed the two police officers out, her body suddenly becoming ice cold. Poor Josephine, she thought over and over again. And the poor lad.

She walked back to the door of the front room and stood there for a few moments without saying anything, then she turned and climbed the stairs to her room.

Chapter Thirty-nine

On the last Saturday morning in April Carrie Tanner was married to Fred Bradley in St James's Church, Bermondsey. She wore a full-length white satin dress, and the three young bridesmaids who walked behind her were dressed in a beautiful coral pink. Jessica's two children were full of smiles in their dresses and beamed at the camera but Freda's three-year-old daughter needed a lot of coaxing to pose, finally giving the photographer a gap-toothed grin that made everyone smile. William Tanner gave his daughter away. He was looking smart in his grey pin-striped suit and starched collar with a wide-knotted silver tie. Nellie shed a few tears as she watched him proudly escort Carrie down the aisle and noticed how grey his hair had become. He seemed to have lost the sharp bearing she had so admired. Although he still walked upright, his shoulders drooped. Charlie had been given a weekend pass to attend the wedding and he sat at the back of the church looking wan and hollow-eyed.

All the neighbours were there. Florrie had put on her best hat and coat and before she left had slipped her ever-present silver snuff-box into her pocket. Perhaps she might be able to take a pinch to steady her nerves, she thought. Weddings always made her feel nervous, although it was many years since she had attended one. Maisie was there too, resplendent in a pink coat and wide white hat. She sat with Florrie and constantly dabbed at her eyes with a handkerchief. Aggie sat in the pew behind, along with Maggie Jones, Ida Bromsgrove and Grace Crossley from the Kings Arms.

Sadie sat at the back of the church, feeling decidedly out of place in a Church of England establishment. With her was Maudie who was used to singing hymns. Her voice made Sadie wince as it lifted above everyone else's.

At the giving and taking of the vows, Sadie nudged Maudie. 'Don't 'e look old ter 'er?' she remarked.

Maudie never liked to chatter in church. 'Umm,' she said in a soft voice.

'She looks lovely though,' Sadie went on.

'Umm.'

'Yer Catholic services are much longer than this, yer know.'

'Umm.'

'The vicar's stutterin' a bit. I reckon 'e's bin at the communion wine,' Sadie continued.

'Umm.'

Sadie looked at Maudie's erect head. 'Is that all yer can say, "Umm"?' she complained in a loud voice, just as the vicar paused for the handing over of the ring. Everyone looked round.

Maudie turned a bright red, and as soon as the newly-weds went out to the vestry for the signing she turned to Sadie. 'Yer shouldn't talk durin' the service,' she hissed. 'I didn't know where ter put me face.'

Sadie mumbled under her breath and amused herself by studying the people on the opposite side of the aisle.

The reception was held in the adjoining church hall and

although Carrie mingled with the guests and accepted their good wishes with a smile, her happy day was marred by seeing her brother Charlie looking so sad and forlorn. She was worried too about her youngest brother Danny who was still out in France, and felt very sad that James was not there to joke and gently tease her as he probably would have done. Fred's constant attention helped ease her heavy-heartedness, and when it was time to leave the guests and catch the train for their week's honeymoon at Margate, Carrie hugged Charlie tightly.

William Tanner watched his daughter and her new husband leave the hall with mixed feelings. She was no longer the little girl he used to take with him to the stables and on those trips to the farm. She had grown into a beautiful woman and now she was married to an older man. Carrie had looked radiantly happy, but William sensed that his daughter had grabbed at marriage. Her decision had been sudden. There had been no courtship and no mention of Fred Bradley as a possible suitor. Her decision to marry him had come just after her father had lost his job at the yard and been forced to give up their family home. Would she have made the same decision if he were still working for Galloway? he wondered. Nellie had thought so. She had said that Carrie was being sensible in marrying a steady man who could provide for her and who would be less likely to weigh her down with a large family. Nellie had dismissed the age gap as being of little importance, and was quick to point out that there was a ten-year difference between their own ages. Perhaps she was right, thought William.

The women were gathering together in small groups and the men were beginning to congregate around the beer table. Not wanting to get involved in small talk, William strolled out of the hall and leaned against a stone column while he rolled a cigarette. As he searched his pockets for his matches he heard a rattle and turned to see Joe Maitland grinning at him and holding out his box of Swan Vestas. William smiled as he lit his cigarette and stepped down into the garden with Florrie's lodger falling into step beside him.

'I don't know many o' the blokes so I decided ter get a bit of air while they're all bunnyin',' Joe said, kicking at a stone. 'Florrie asked me ter come ter the weddin'. She said it was a chance ter get ter know some o' me neighbours.'

'Don't yer come from round 'ere?' William asked.

Joe shook his head. 'I was born in Stepney, as a matter o' fact. I've always lived there, up until I decided it was time ter push off. Fings change, an' so do people. Bermondsey seemed as good a place as any ter put down me suitcase. I'm quite 'appy bein' this side o' the water, although it's a mite different from Stepney.'

William caught a certain bitterness in the young man's voice and glanced at him. 'Did yer get in a bit o' trouble?' he said, and then quickly held up his hand. 'Sorry, I didn't mean ter pry.'

'It's a long story,' Joe told him.

'It usually is,' William laughed.

They strolled along the path in silence for a while, then suddenly Joe looked intently at the older man. 'What's yer feelin's towards Galloway?'

William shrugged his shoulders. 'If yer want me honest opinion, I've got no feelin's at all fer the man. Not after gettin' the push,' he replied.

Joe stuck his hands deep into his pockets. As they reached the wide iron gates, he turned to face William. ''Ave yer ever bin ter those fights they 'old at the local pubs?' he asked.

William shook his head. 'No. I don't care ter watch two blokes bashin' each ovver's brains out jus' so a few people can get rich bettin' on the outcome.'

Joe's face creased in a brief, appreciative smile. 'Florrie reckons yer a bloke ter be trusted, so I'm gonna put me cards on the table,' he said, looking William in the eye. 'But yer'll 'ave ter understan', Will, that what I'm gonna tell yer is between us alone. I've not even let on ter Florrie what I'm doin' this side o' the water, but I will in good time, 'cos I might need a few friends. As I said, it's a long story so I might as well start at the beginnin'.

'I come from a river family. Me ole man an' 'is farvver before 'im were lightermen. Patrick, me older bruvver, follered the tradition, but as fer me they decided I should get an education an' break the mould. It's an 'ard an' dangerous life bein' a lighterman as yer'll appreciate. Anyway, schoolin' an' me didn't get on all that well an' I left early ter work in Poplar Market. I used ter 'elp out on the stalls an' when I was eighteen I 'ad one o' me own. I used ter sell fruit an' veg an' I made a go of it. Then I got in wiv a dodgy crowd an' from then on it was shady deals an' lookin' over me shoulder all the time.

'I didn't take after me bruvver Patrick, 'e was as straight as a die. 'E was a big strappin' man who could 'andle 'imself in a fight. 'E used ter go ter the fairs an' 'ang around the boxin' booths. Patrick couldn't resist a challenge an' I've seen 'im give a good account of 'imself more than once. 'E won quite a few bob too. One or two o' the pubs in Stepney started these boxin' tournaments, jus' like yer've got over this side o' the water. 'Course, bruvver Patrick 'ad ter get involved an' 'e 'ad a few fights, winnin' 'em all wiv no trouble, I 'ave ter say.'

'Did 'e 'ave a manager?' William cut in.

'Only the ole man,' Joe replied. 'I used ter go along an' 'elp out but they didn't like me bein' there. I s'pose they was worried in case I got the bug. Anyway, Patrick built up quite a reputation. "The Battlin' Lighterman" 'e was known as. Then George Galloway came on the scene.'

'Galloway?' William said in surprise.

'Yeah, Galloway,' Joe said bitterly. ''E used ter travel all over the place ter see a fight, an' before long 'e was promotin' 'is own fighter.'

'Jake Mitchell,' William said quickly.

Joe nodded. 'Or Gypsy Williams, as 'e used ter be known. Mitchell was in 'is prime then an' 'e was matched wiv Patrick. There was a lot o' money staked on the outcome an' me bruvver was odds-on ter win. Anyway, while Patrick was gettin' ready ter go on an' me an' the ole man were fussin' around 'im, we was paid a visit by a couple o' villainous-lookin' blokes. They didn't waste no time tellin' us that eivver Patrick lost or else we'd be sorted out. The bribe money was put inter me farvver's 'and an' then they left. There was no way on earth that me bruvver was gonna chuck that fight an' that night 'e 'ad the best scrap of 'is life. It was the last one 'e ever 'ad.

''E dropped Jake Mitchell in the third round, an' then before I knew what was 'appenin' a crowd o' me farvver's pals grabbed me from the ringside an' bustled me out o' the pub. Me farvver knew there'd be trouble an' 'e wanted ter make sure I got 'ome in one piece. The villains was mob-'anded an' they caught up wiv Patrick an' me farvver as they was climbin' out o' the winder at the back o' the pub. Me farvver was done up bad an' 'e never worked again. As fer Patrick, 'e tried ter fight 'em off but they laid 'im out wiv an iron bar. It was the only way they was gonna stop 'im. 'E was taken ter 'ospital in a coma an' never recovered. A week later 'e was dead.'

William shook his head sadly. 'Was Galloway involved?' he asked.

Joe shrugged his shoulders. 'I dunno, but 'e 'ad a good few friends in Stepney,' he replied. 'One fing I do know – 'e tried ter blind Patrick. There was somefink on Mitchell's gloves an' me bruvver was fightin' out o' one eye after the first round. Exactly a year after that fight me farvver died, I swear it was from a broken 'eart. 'E idolised Patrick.'

'What about yer muvver?' asked William.

'I never knew 'er. She died when I was very young,' Joe told him. 'What I'll never get over is the fact that I wasn't there ter 'elp Pat an' the ole man. What I did do though was ter go round an' sort out the publican. 'E swore 'e didn't 'ave anyfing ter do wiv it but I wasn't listenin'. I was done fer grievous bodily 'arm an' I got four years 'ard labour. When I got out o' the nick, I got tergevver wiv a few o' me farvver's ole pals an' one or two o' Patrick's best mates an' eventually we got the names o' four out o' the five villains be'ind me bruvver's killin'. Two of 'em are doin' long stretches, one died o' syphilis before they get 'old of 'im an' anovver one ended up in the river, compliments o' Patrick's mates. The fifth one was never named. We're still tryin' ter identify 'im. Me an' the rest o' the lads managed ter get the tournaments stopped, though. Names, locations and times was forwarded ter the police. It was then that I decided ter take a look at Galloway.'

'So yer fink 'e might be the last one yer lookin' for?' William asked.

'I'm not sure, but that's what I 'ope ter find out,' Joe replied. 'Galloway didn't show 'is face in Stepney after me bruvver was killed. I tried ter find out where 'e'd disappeared to but all the leads came ter nuffink. At that time I 'ad a stall in Roman Road an' I was buildin' up a nice business. Anyway, one day out o' the blue I suddenly got word that Jake Mitchell was fightin' in Bermondsey an' I guessed that was where Galloway was. It didn't take me long ter find 'im. I knocked on a door in Page Street lookin' fer lodgin's an' the woman there sent me ter Florrie's 'ouse.'

'Didn't Galloway reco'nise yer when yer moved in the street?' William asked. ''E must 'ave seen yer about.'

'It's almost eight years ago since Patrick climbed in that ring wiv Jake Mitchell,' Joe answered. 'I was jus' somebody who stood in Patrick's corner as far as 'e was concerned. I'd never 'ad anyfink ter do wiv Galloway in any case.'

''E'd remember the name though, wouldn't 'e?' William said. ''E would 'ave read about yer gettin' put in prison, or at least somebody would 'ave told 'im.'

Joe smiled. 'I thought about that when I knocked on Florrie's door so I told 'er me name was Maitland. In fact it's Murphy. Our family come from Ireland originally.'

They had strolled slowly back to the hall and when they reached the entrance steps William turned to face the young man. 'I've got no reason ter like Galloway,' he said, frowning, 'but I've known 'im since we were kids tergevver. 'E's a lot o' fings, but I don't fink 'e'd get involved in murder.'

'Well, we've got four names an' I'm not gonna rest till we get the fifth,' Joe replied. 'What's more, I'm gonna get those tournaments stopped. I owe it ter me bruvver Pat. If in the process I find out Galloway was be'ind me bruvver's killin', so much the better.'

They had climbed the few steps and William turned at the entrance to the hall. 'I was told yer go ter the fights,' he said with a wry smile. 'So that's the reason why.'

Joe nodded. 'I've got enough evidence tergevver, an' if it was a straightforward matter I'd 'ave turned it all over by now,' he said bitterly.

'What's the problem?' William asked.

The young man looked at him and smiled cynically. 'If I walked inter the Dock'ead nick an' gave them the evidence, the next mornin' yer'd be readin' about me. I'd be fished out o' the river or found in some alley wiv me throat cut. One o' the

576

top coppers at Dock'ead nick is takin' a cut. 'E wouldn't be too 'appy ter fink I was spoilin' 'is little earner, would 'e? What I've gotta do is bide me time until I can get 'im dead ter rights, then I'll turn the lot over ter Scotland Yard an' let them deal wiv it. Now yer can understand why I don't want this ter go any furvver. If the wrong person got wind o' me little game, I'd be done for.'

William gave him a reassuring smile. 'Yer got no need ter worry on that score, Joe,' he replied. 'There's one fing puzzlin' me, though. Why did yer 'elp me save those 'orses from the fire? I would 'ave thought yer'd be 'appy ter see the 'ole business burn down.'

Joe laughed. 'In the first place I was scared yer daughter was gonna get 'urt. After she pulled that wild 'orse away from yer she tried to go back. I 'ad ter stop 'er. She's a brave young woman is Carrie. The ovver fing is, nobody'd suspect I'm out ter get Galloway seein' me 'elp yer save the 'orses, would they? In fact Galloway sent me a letter o' fanks wiv a fiver in it. I burnt the letter an' gave Florrie the money. There was no way I'd take anyfink off 'im.'

William laughed and put his arm round Joe's shoulder. 'D'yer know somefink?' he said. 'I'm beginnin' ter feel a little sorry fer George Galloway. Now what about a drink? I could do wiv one.'

The Saturday evening train was chugging through the Kent countryside as Carrie sat close to Fred, idly watching the wisps of steam from the engine drift away and disappear over the green fields. The wedding had gone off very well, she thought. The bridesmaids had been really sweet and well behaved. It was nice to see Jessica and Freda once more but it was a pity her old school friend Sara had not been there. Carrie had written to her last-known address but there had been no reply. Carrie guessed she must have moved. She was sorry too that Mary Caldwell could not come. She was doing war-work in a munitions factory in the north of England but had sent her best wishes.

The newly-weds were alone in the carriage except for an old lady who was nodding off to sleep. Fred shyly slipped his arm around his bride. It had been a mad dash back to his house, where Carrie changed into a flower-patterned summer dress and a long cotton coat of powder blue. Her blonde hair was still nicely in place on top of her head and Fred looked admiringly at her as she snuggled back in her seat. He felt all dressed-up in his blue serge suit and collar-and-tie, with his highly polished shoes and sleeked-back greying hair. Carrie had been intrigued by the blue shadow which showed around his square chin even though he had taken care to strop the razor before shaving that morning. She felt it made him look strong and protective. She had dusted the confetti from his hair and suit and removed the carnation from his buttonhole before they left his house. Now they were on their way to Margate and Carrie sighed contentedly as she gazed out of the window. Already she had made plans to brighten up the café and encourage Fred to expand the business, but now she was looking forward to a whole week in which to get to know her new husband. She had to put aside all her secret fears and make certain that the marriage would be a happy union. Carrie leant her head back against the seat and closed her eyes. She was starting out on a new adventure, she thought excitedly, but any casual observer would just think they were a married couple taking a trip to the seaside.

The old lady in the carriage was feigning sleep. She had watched as the young couple boarded the train at London Bridge Station and had noticed how the young man held the lady's arm as he assisted her into the carriage. The pretty young thing had blushed as he squeezed her hand in his and she noticed how the young woman kept glancing at the ring on her finger. They were newly-weds for sure, the old lady told herself. It was all so obvious. Maybe she should offer the couple her good wishes for the future, but that might embarrass them. Lots of couples were not too happy to let the whole world know that they were going away to make love together. That was the way she had felt all those many years ago. Perhaps it would be better if she pretended to sleep. It would allow the couple to whisper sweet nothings in each other's ear and the young man to slip his arm around the young lady. They certainly wouldn't do it while they were being watched, the old lady felt.

The train chugged on, passing open fields and tiny hamlets, and Fred glanced quickly at their fellow traveller before stealing a kiss. The old lady saw the kiss through slitted eyes. She was right, she told herself, they were newly-weds. Wasn't it clever of her to spot all the little signs? Well, it would be an hour yet before the train arrived at Margate. Perhaps she should take a short nap. Yes it was clever of her, she told herself, having completely forgotten that it was the pieces of confetti in the man's hair which had first revealed to her their secret.

Chapter Forty

Frank Galloway poured himself a large whisky and soda and then walked back into his bedroom. He had heard Caroline crying but the nurse had reassured him that it was only a bad dream or a tummy pain and his daughter was now sleeping soundly. Why did Bella have to go out so much in the evening? he wondered resentfully. After all, she had landed the part in the new show and should be home with him and their daughter. Once the show opened, he would see very little of her. There were to be two performances nightly as well as the matinee, which would leave Bella exhausted. Sunday would be her day of recovery as it had been the last time she was in a show, and then she had only a small part. Now that she had landed the female supporting role, Bella would be expecting him to run around the flat at her every whim, like a trained poodle. Well, he was no one's lackey. That was nancy boy Hubert's job. The detestable young oaf had put in his dreaded appearance once more and now seemed to be almost living in the flat. He knew where the Scotch was kept and certainly drank his share. What was it Bella called him? A popinjay? Frank knew a few more colourful ways of describing the obnoxious idiot and felt like trying them out on him next time he called at the house.

Rain was lashing against the window-panes and thunder rolled in the distance as Frank got out of bed, glanced at the alarm clock and walked over to the drawn curtains. It was only nine o'clock. They would be hours yet. As he looked out at the rain beating down on the empty street, he bit anxiously on his lip. It was a sneaky thing to do, pretending he had the shivers and saying he was going to take a sleeping pill, but he had to find out just what kind of game Hubert was really playing. Normally Bella would expect him to look out of the window as the cab pulled up and she usually made a big thing of shouting a goodnight to Hubert as she left him. Would things be different tonight when she thought Frank was sedated? he wondered. Maybe he would catch her kissing the nancy boy goodnight or blowing him a passionate kiss as she ran up the steps to the front door. At least it would prove that Hubert was not the effeminate little toe-rag Bella made him out to be. Well, if Frank did spot any untoward goings-on, Hubert would be sorry the next time he showed his spotty little face in the flat, he vowed.

He swallowed his drink and walked back into the lounge to refill his glass.

The young nurse looked up in surprise. 'I thought you were asleep,' she said demurely as he made for the drinks cabinet. 'I don't wish to interfere, Mr Galloway, but it's rather dangerous to mix sleeping pills and spirits.'

Frank smiled at her. 'It's all right, I didn't take the pill. Those things are inclined to make me sluggish next day.'

The nurse went back to her magazine and Frank eyed her as he filled his glass. She wasn't a bad-looker, he thought. Rather plump on the hips, but her eyes were a nice shade of blue behind those ugly spectacles. Maybe she was a tigress beneath that professional demeanour, stringing along several young men and dominating them. Or maybe she preferred the older man. Someone like himself who was worldly and discreet. Well if he tried his luck Bella couldn't blame him. She gave him little enough of her time these days or nights.

'Could I offer you a drink?' he asked.

The young lady shook her head vigorously. 'I never touch strong drink when I'm on duty,' she replied. 'The agency would be horrified.'

'But they'd never know,' Frank said slyly.

'No, thank you, Mr Galloway.'

Frank nodded and walked back into the bedroom. I'm sure Bella hand-picked that one, he thought.

Silly fool, the nurse was thinking in the other room. Anyone who allowed his wife to have an affair right under his nose deserved all he got, and he wasn't getting anything from her. It was so obvious that something was going on between the other two, she thought. Surely he could see it? Perhaps he was condoning it. She had heard about those strange people who got their enjoyment by listening to their promiscuous partner's graphic accounts of their experiences. The nurse shook her head and went back to her magazine.

At ten minutes after midnight Frank heard the motor cab draw up outside and quickly went to the window. Bella seems to be taking a long time getting out, he thought as he peered through the curtains. Ah, there she is now, and there's Hubert. My God, he's kissing her on the lips! Frank screwed up his fists with rage as he saw the effeminate young man waving to Bella from the cab as it drew away. Hubert was going to have trouble with his lips very soon, and the rest of his face, Frank promised himself as he lay down in bed and pretended to be fast asleep.

Carrie and Fred returned from Margate on Sunday evening, and early on Monday morning the café opened its doors once more to the usual clientele of dockers and carmen. Bessie was as garrulous as ever as she helped in the kitchen but Fred did not seem to mind this morning. Carrie served the tea and coffee as usual and took food orders, telling herself that the first alteration would be to get a large printed menu put up behind the counter instead of that silly little sheet of paper that was pinned to the wall. The whole place could do with a coat of paint as well, and the end storeroom wall could be knocked down to make room for a few more tables, she thought. She would have to talk to Fred about the lease too. He had told her some time ago that it was running out and it would be a good idea to try to purchase the freehold.

There was no time to dwell on the changes needed as the café began to fill up with hurrying workers who tempered their impatience with bawdy humour.

'Find out what Fred's doin' wiv my bacon sandwich, will yer, Carrie?' one of them asked her. 'I've bin waitin' ten minutes. I s'pose 'e's 'avin' a doze back there, tryin' ter catch up on all that sleep 'e's bin missin'.'

'Come out an' show yerself, Fred,' a carman called to him. 'Let's see if Carrie's put a twinkle in yer eye.'

The teasing went on throughout the morning, and Fred smiled in embarrassment as he worked in the kitchen while Carrie laughed and joked with the men. There was no sense in taking offence, she thought. They were honest, hardworking men just having a bit of fun. They meant no harm, and if she was going to help her husband build up the business she could not afford to be too prim and proper.

The first day back at work seemed to pass very quickly but Carrie was grateful when she finally slipped the bolts and pulled down the blinds. She felt then that she really was in her own little place with her husband at last. Fred had already decorated the dingy flat above the shop and had turned the cluttered-up store-room into a cosy sitting-room. The upper room at the front looked out on a good view of the river in both directions and Fred had converted it into a bedroom, installing a large double bed and a satin walnut bedroom-suite. The downstairs room at the back of the shop was kept as a parlour, and that evening after tidying up the shop and wiping off the tables Fred and Carrie sat down together there, sipping their tea and unwinding. Fred had an evening paper spread out over his lap, and as Carrie glanced at him over her cup she noticed how that lock of dark, greying hair was hanging over his forehead again. It made him look younger than his years, she thought. He was staring down at the newspaper and as he read she noticed how he occasionally moved his lips, as though concentrating over a particular word or sentence. He had told her he was not a good scholar and that reading did not come easy, but Carrie knew that he ran his business very well and was certainly no fool.

As she gazed at him she thought about the honeymoon and their first night together. He had been touchingly shy and seemed to caress her body as though handling a delicate piece of china. He had not fulfilled her on their first night but she had been happy to lie close to him and let him feel how responsive she was to his nervous caresses. It was on the second night that their marriage was consummated and she had felt a warm glow inside her as she finally fell asleep in his arms. It would be a good, loving marriage, she thought. Fred had a wonderful nature. He was kind, considerate and loving, and his easy laugh made her feel happy and contented.

A knock on the side door made him look up quickly. 'I wonder who that can be?' he said as he got up from his chair, frowning.

When Fred showed the young woman into the room, Carrie

jumped out of her chair excitedly. 'Sara!' she gasped, holding out her arms.

The two women hugged each other warmly and then Sara looked at Fred with a smile on her face. 'We were ole school friends,' she said, and turned towards Carrie. 'I 'ope 'e's takin' good care of yer,' she joked.

The two young women chatted happily together while Fred was brewing fresh tea. 'I got yer letter when me an' Norman got back from Scotland,' Sara said. 'I was so sorry ter miss yer weddin', but never mind, I'm 'ere at last.'

Carrie looked closely at Sara, hardly believing it was the same girl. Her face was rosy and plump, and she was smartly dressed. Her dark hair had been cut short to her neck and neatly waved, and her fawn dress and silver-buckled shoes looked expensive. Carrie recalled how her friend used to come to school in a ragged coat, a tattered dress and worn-out shoes.

''Ow's yer family?' she asked.

'All married,' Sara laughed. 'The two boys are in the army an' me youngest sister married a grocer. They've got a nice 'ouse in Bromley an' mum an' dad live wiv 'em.'

'Yer look like yer done well fer yerself,' Carrie said with a smile.

Sara grinned. 'My Norman's a partner in an estate agent's. We're very 'appy, I'm glad ter say.'

'Any children?' Carrie asked.

Sara's face became serious for a moment. 'I can't 'ave any,' she said quietly.

Fred brought in the tea and then discreetly left the two young women to chat alone with each other.

'Fred seems a nice man. I'm sure yer'll be very 'appy,' Sara said, smiling.

'Did yer know me dad lost 'is job?' Carrie asked her.

Sara nodded and her face became serious. 'Yeah, I bumped

inter Jessica a few weeks ago an' she told me,' she said. 'It must 'ave bin terrible comin' on top of everyfing else. When I 'eard yer'd moved inter Bacon Street Buildin's I could 'ave cried. Of all the bloody places! It's about time they pulled those 'ovels down.' She made a face, and then looked intently at her friend. 'Carrie, about the future? Are you an' Fred plannin' on stayin' 'ere?' she asked.

Carrie gave her friend a quizzical look. 'Yeah, of course.'

Sara crossed her legs and straightened her skirt. 'The reason I asked is,' she went on, 'my Norman's firm does a lot o' business wiv the firm that actually manages this ground fer the owners. Norman's got a few acquaintances in the ovver firm, naturally, an' one of 'em told 'im they've bin ordered ter put the land up fer sale. Apparently the owners are raisin' money fer a big deal. It's all very complicated but I think yer ought ter know that George Galloway 'as put in an offer fer all the available land. 'E wants it fer a new yard.'

Carrie's face hardened at the mention of Galloway and she clenched her fists on her lap in anger. 'Yer mean we wouldn't be able ter renew the lease?' she muttered.

Sara shook her head. 'What would 'appen is, the Galloway firm would take vacant possession an' then 'e'd pull this place down an' the next two old 'ouses which are empty anyway. 'E'd get the engineerin' yard as well. The engineers are not renewin' their lease. Norman told me they've gone skint.'

Fred had come back into the room. He sat down with a worried look on his face. 'The lease is due this month,' he said. 'I didn't think there'd be any problem in renewin' it.'

'It's a pity yer didn't buy the free'old,' Sara remarked.

'I've tried before, but it was never on the market,' Fred told her. 'I never knew it was goin' up fer sale now.'

'Well, it's only bin made official this mornin' but Galloway must 'ave bin given the nod 'cos 'is bid came in terday,' Sara replied, glancing at Carrie. 'I wouldn't 'ave known anyfink about it, 'cos Norman don't usually talk ter me about 'is work, but I'd showed 'im yer letter, yer see, an' when 'e saw the address 'e mentioned about the land goin' up fer sale. Norman was surprised 'ow quickly Galloway's bid come in. I s'pose the ole goat's bin buyin' drinks 'ere an' there ter get the information.'

'Can 'e do that, pull the places down fer a transport yard?' Fred queried.

'As a matter o' fact I asked my Norman the same question an' 'e said the borough council is 'appy for firms ter build up their business,' Sara replied. 'It's all down ter more rates, I s'pose. In any case, money speaks all languages. Galloway's prob'ly put a few bob in somebody's pocket.'

Fred slumped back in his chair, feeling suddenly sick. 'This Galloway geezer's startin' ter mess fings up already,' he groaned.

'Well, 'e ain't gonna mess fings up any bloody more,' Carrie said quickly, her face flushed with anger. 'George Galloway kicked me farvver out an' 'e's not gonna do it ter us, if I can 'elp it. Can we afford ter buy the place, Fred?'

Sara held her hand up before he could answer. 'Look, I've already 'ad a long chat wiv Norman,' she said. 'I told 'im about us bein' ole friends, an' about the way yer farvver's bin treated by Galloway an' 'ow 'e chucked yer out o' the 'ouse. By the time I was finished Norman was on your side, an' 'e told me that if I wanted ter be of any 'elp I should call round ter see yer as soon as yer got back from yer 'oneymoon. I knew from your letter yer'd be back terday. I never ferget a kindness, Carrie, an' I'll always remember 'ow kind yer was ter me when we were at school tergevver. I also remember that time yer mum an' ole Florrie Axford looked after my mum when she was poorly, so don't you worry. If yer can see yer way clear ter buyin' the free'old, pop roun' ter our place termorrèr. Norman said it shouldn't be too 'ard persuadin' the ovver people ter 'old on ter Galloway's bid, an' 'e'll leave a few details wiv me ternight about what yer should do. If yer get in quick, yer'll beat the 'oreson at 'is own game,' she said, grinning.

The teacups were replenished and the three sat chatting together for some considerable time. When Sara finally took her leave, Carrie hugged her at the front door. 'Fanks fer comin', Sara, an' fanks fer everyfing,' she said affectionately.

'There's nuffink ter fank me for, yet,' Sara replied. 'You an' Fred talk it over, an' if yer can manage ter find the money come roun' an' see me termorrer. Norman'll be able ter sort it all out fer yer, or else 'e'll 'ave me ter deal wiv.'

Nora Flynn sat by the window of her upstairs flat in Rotherhithe and stared out at the early May sky. The sun had dipped down beyond the chimney-stacks and the evening shades of red were now fading and changing to a darker hue. She sighed sadly as she recalled that fateful Thursday morning just over a month ago. Josephine had slipped into the house after her father had left and when she opened the letter from Charlie her face had lit up. 'He has asked me to marry him, Nora!' she said excitedly. 'Fancy that, proposal by letter. Don't you think that's romantic?'

Nora recalled how she had tried to forewarn Josephine by telling her that she needed to talk to her father before she made up her mind to say yes to her young man, but Josephine had placed her hands on her hips in indignation and jutted out her chin assertively. 'I can't talk to him. I never could,' she had said loudly. 'I'm going to marry Charlie and that's the end of it, Nora. I'll tell Father tonight and if he tries to stop me marrying, I'll leave this house and never come back.'

Her words had been prophetic. In the growing darkness of her room, Nora brushed away a tear. She could still hear that terrible, heart-rending cry as Josephine dashed from the house on that Thursday evening; still see her running out of Tyburn Square, sobbing and distraught. It was the last week Nora spent in the house. Early on Monday she packed her battered old suitcase and left. She did not see George Galloway that morning, nor did she want to. The curt note she left on the kitchen table had to suffice. She had left that gloomy house forever, and at last she would be able to sleep easy and enjoy the few good memories of her years in Tyburn Square.

May flowers in the local church gardens and a warm sun shone down on the dingy Bermondsey backstreets as Florrie Axford stood with her arms folded at her front door. Lorries were now trundling along the turning where once there had been only horse-carts, and she could see Billy Sullivan sitting outside his house with his arms folded and his head resting against the brickwork. Those bloody fumes can't be too good for his chest, she thought. Aggie was cleaning her step as usual, the third time this week, Florrie noted, and Maisie was coming in her direction carrying a laden shopping-bag. Must ask how Fred is, she reminded herself, and as she watched Aggie gathering up her cleaning rags made a mental note to ask her about Harold. He had been off sick with a bad back. She had to keep abreast of what was going on in the street and lately the gossip seemed to have dried up.

Florrie took a pinch of snuff and wiped her watering eyes on the corner of her pinafore. ''Ello, luv. 'Ow's yer ole man's shingles?' she asked as Maisie put down her shopping and pressed her hand against her side.

''E's got right grumpy bein' stuck in the 'ouse all day long,' Maisie told her. 'Mind yer, Doctor Kelly said 'e can go back

ter work next week, fank Gawd. We've 'ad no money comin'
in fer two weeks. I've 'ad ter take Fred's suit over uncle's. Still,
'e's not likely ter need it yet awhile.'

Florrie continued her enquiries. ''Ave yer 'eard 'ow
Aggie's ole man is?' she asked. ''E's bin orf work this week.'

''E's a bit better, so she told me,' Maisie replied. ''Ere, by
the way, did yer 'ear about ole Jack Oxford? 'E's courtin'!'

'Not Jack Oxford?!'

'Well, I wouldn't 'ave believed it eivver,' Maisie said,
pressing a hand to her side again. 'Maudie told me. It's 'is
lan'lady 'e's courtin'. 'Er ole man's left 'er an' Jack's got 'is
feet in front o' the fire.'

''Ow did Maudie find out?' Florrie asked.

'She 'eard about it at the muvvers' meetin',' Maisie replied.
'Jack's lady friend goes there. Apparently she's goin' in fer a
divorce an' then 'er an' Jack's gonna tie the knot.'

'They won't be able ter get married in a church, that's fer
sure,' Florrie remarked quickly. 'Still, it's prob'ly just as well.
Imagine ole Jack sittin' in the pew waitin' fer 'is bride ter
come marchin' down the aisle. 'E'd be snorin' 'is 'ead orf, an'
then when the vicar ses that bit about do yer take this woman
ter be yer lawful wedded wife, 'e'll most prob'ly say, "If yer
like"! I fink we'll 'ave ter go ter that weddin', Maisie, even if
it is a register office. It's about time me an' you 'ad a good
laugh.'

Maisie smiled. 'Young Carrie's weddin' was a nice turn
out, wasn't it, Flo?' she remarked. 'Mind yer, 'e's a bit older
than 'er. Still, it's 'er choice.'

Florrie nodded. 'Funny 'ow quick it all 'appened,' she said,
a thoughtful look on her face. 'P'raps she married 'im fer
security. 'E must 'ave a few bob.'

'Yer don't fink they 'ad ter do it, do yer?' Maisie asked in
a whisper.

Florrie shook her head vigorously. 'Not Carrie. She's too sensible ter go an' get 'erself inter trouble, though I s'pose it could 'appen. They say it's always the nice gels what get pregnant.'

Maisie nodded in agreement. 'Didn't Nellie's Charlie look ill?' she said. 'Mind yer, the weddin' was so soon after 'is young lady got drowned. Charlie didn't stop long after Carrie left. 'E 'ad ter go straight back ter the army camp, so Nellie told me. I tell yer what I did notice, Flo. 'E sat all on 'is own in the church. Normally families sit tergevver.'

'P'raps they fell out over 'is young lady,' Florrie suggested. 'After all she was Galloway's daughter. Nellie can't stan' that ole goat at no price, 'specially after 'im sackin' Will the way 'e did.'

'It's such a terrible shame, none the less,' Maisie remarked. ''E's a nice boy is Charlie. 'E's very quiet, not like poor James an' the younger one, Danny. Nellie was tellin' me 'er Danny's the worst one o' the lot. She reckons it's since 'e got in wiv that there Billy Sullivan. Mad on boxin' 'e is. Nellie said 'e's done boxin' since 'e's bin in the army, an' yet when 'e was a kid 'e was such a puny little sod.'

Florrie removed the snuff-box from her apron and tapped her fingers on the lid. 'I noticed 'ow big 'e'd got when 'e was 'ome on leave that time,' she said, taking a pinch. 'Sadie told me it was the only time 'er Billy bucked up, when Danny Tanner was on leave.'

'Yeah, they're right mates them two,' Maisie replied, looking over at the young man sitting outside his house. 'That's anuvver poor sod the war's ruined. Sadie said 'er Billy won't go out an' look fer a job. She said 'e jus' sits mopin' aroun' the 'ouse all day long. It's 'cos 'e can't do that boxin' anymore, that's the reason why.'

Florrie wiped her eyes on her apron and looked up and

down the street before leaning towards Maisie. 'Did yer know Ida's ole man's back on the turps again?' she whispered.

Maisie looked suitably shocked. 'Gawd 'elp 'er. I remember last time. 'E didn't 'alf give 'er a pastin'. Terrible black eye she 'ad.'

'Ida was tellin' me it was since 'e got that job at the tannery. Pissed nearly every night 'e is. 'E brought a goat 'ome the ovver night.'

'A goat?'

''S'right. 'E won it in a pub raffle,' Florrie went on. 'I know it's wicked but I 'ad ter laugh when she told me. She said 'er ole man come staggerin' down the turnin' wiv this bloody goat on a lump o' rope. It was as pissed as 'e was. All the men 'ad bin givin' it beer ter drink while it was tied up outside the pub. Anyway, when 'er ole man brought it 'ome she 'ad a right bull-an'-cow wiv 'im over where 'e was gonna keep it. It fell against the dresser an' smashed all 'er best china, then it shit all over the yard. Ida was furious when she was tellin' me. She said 'er ole man wanted it fer the milk, but it turned out ter be a billy-goat. She made 'im get rid of it. She said it was eivver that goat or 'er. 'Course yer know 'ow aggravatin' 'e can be when 'e's 'ad a drink. Know what 'e done?'

'No.'

''E 'ad the cheek ter toss a coin up,' Florrie continued. ''E told 'er she'd won so 'e'd get rid o' the goat. 'E took it up the butcher's shop.'

'Well, if that 'ad bin me I'd 'ave opened the 'oreson,' Maisie said angrily.

'I s'pose Ida's frightened of 'im. After all, 'e can get very nasty in drink,' Florrie replied. 'She's 'ad 'er share o' black eyes ter contend wiv.'

'Well, I'd 'ave waited till the ole git went ter sleep, I'm afraid,' Maisie persisted.

Across the street Ida Bromsgrove peered through her lace curtains. I wonder who those two are gossiping about? she thought. I wish I had time to stand at the street door gassing all day. She clicked her tongue and went out into the scullery to see how the currant dumplings were doing.

Chapter Forty-one

Frank Galloway stood in the office doorway and watched as his father walked slowly along Page Street, leaning heavily on his silver-topped walking stick. The June morning was bright with early sunlight as the hulking figure trudged towards the yard. Frank had noticed how downcast the old man had become during the past few months. His hair was completely grey now and his heavy shoulders sagged. Gone were the jaunty step and upright stance he had once had. He looked older than his sixty-one years although he had lost none of his scowling arrogance. Frank felt he had become even less approachable. He had seen how the carmen kept out of the old man's way as much as possible, and Jim Baines the mechanic seemed to have adopted a surly attitude after a few clashes with the firm's owner over the state of the vehicles. Jake Mitchell appeared to be the only employee who was not affected by his employer's black moods and he went about his work with the usual indifference.

Despite feeling a little sorry for his father, Frank despised him for bringing so much upon himself. He had hounded Josephine out of the house with his obstinacy and hard-heartedness and now he was suffering under the terrible burden of guilt over her tragic accident. The inquest had given the verdict as accidental death due to drowning, but they both knew that Josephine was heart-broken when she left the house for the last time and must have been in a terrible state when she took that trip. It was so unlike his sister to drink more than one glass of port or sherry, but on that occasion she had been seen severely intoxicated. She would never have fallen overboard had she been sober. The shameful burden of guilt had aged his father and now he lived alone in that sombre house in Tyburn Square. An elderly woman had taken Nora's place as housekeeper. She came each morning to clean and prepare his evening meal, and would leave as soon as the table was cleared. Frank knew that his father was missing Nora's company, although he would not admit it. She had been much more than a good servant; she had brought a little sunshine into the house.

George Galloway walked into the yard and glared at the mechanic who was bent over the raised bonnet of the big Leyland lorry. 'Is that gonna be fixed terday?' he called out.

Jim Baines straightened up and turned to face him, a large spanner in his greasy hand. 'It's the cylinder gasket. It'll be ready by ternight,' he answered offhandedly.

George entered the office and slumped down at his desk. 'That's the second time this week we've 'ad a lorry off the road,' he growled. 'They're a sight less reliable than the 'orses. It's the bloody cylinder gasket now.'

Frank ignored his father's ill temper and nodded towards the roll of papers on his desk. 'I've got some new sites for you to look at,' he said resignedly. 'There's one here that looks pretty good.'

George got up and leaned over his son's shoulder. 'Is this the Abbey Street site?' he asked.

Frank nodded. 'It's a ninety-nine-year leasehold and it's

bigger than that riverside site we went for,' he replied.

The mention of the riverside property brought Josephine sadly to mind and a change came over George's florid face. He had been poring over the plans that evening when the policemen called. Frank had put in the bid for him but he had neglected his affairs for weeks and done nothing further. By the time he returned to the matter of the crucial corner property, the working men's café had already been sold.

'Right then, you make enquiries. I'll leave it up ter you,' George said with a resigned sigh as he slumped down into his leather chair.

Frank glanced quickly at his father before rolling up the plans. His attitude was very different from what it had been in the past, he thought. The old man seemed a pathetic shadow of his former self as he stared down at the papers on his desk. All his enthusiasm and drive had deserted him, and he seemed to have no sense of purpose any more. He had not even asked after Bella or Caroline lately, not that the apparent lack of concern for his family troubled Frank unduly. After his recent matrimonial differences with his wife he did not feel inclined even to mention her name. She had taken him for a complete fool. Nevertheless, the memory of the confrontation he had with her and Hubert brought a wicked smile to Frank's lips.

It had been hard to contain himself and pretend he was still ignorant of what was going on after what he had witnessed from his bedroom window that night, but Frank had restrained himself until the following evening when Hubert called to take Bella to a charity ball. The young man had looked crestfallen when he saw that the Scotch was missing from its usual place on the sideboard and shuffled his feet uneasily as he faced the man he had made a cuckold.

'I'm afraid there's none there,' he called out over his shoulder when Bella told him to help himself.

Frank smiled evilly. 'You've been helping yourself to my wife for the past year. You can hardly expect me to keep you in Scotch as well, Hubert, now can you?' he said without warning.

'I say, now look here old boy,' Hubert said quickly, his face reddening painfully.

'I'm not your old boy, you spotty-looking little rat,' Frank snarled, reaching forward and taking hold of the white scarf draped around Hubert's narrow shoulders.

'Bella!' the young man shouted in panic as Frank glared at him vengefully.

She hurried from the bedroom, a large powder puff in her hand, and gasped: 'Frank, what are you doing? Put Hubert down this minute! Do you hear me?'

Hubert's face was turning blue as he tried to release Frank's grip on his silk scarf. Frank hit him hard with the back of his hand and sent him sprawling across the room. Bella screamed loudly and jumped on to her irate husband's back, pulling his hair.

'You brutal pig!' she raved. 'Look what you've done to Hubert's face!'

The young man staggered to his feet and dabbed at his bloody lips with the scarf. 'He's quite mad! He should be locked up,' he moaned as he backed towards the door.

Frank had managed to dislodge Bella from his back. He gripped her by the shoulders and shook her violently. 'You're not going anywhere tonight, do you hear?' he shouted at her. He turned to face Hubert. 'Get out of here,' he snarled, 'before I change that face permanently!'

Frank realised that he was clenching his fists and snarling to himself as he recalled the confrontation, and sagged back in his chair. His face relaxed and he smiled to himself. He had forced himself on Bella that night and had been surprised at her lack of resistance. In fact, she had seemed to become rather responsive after an initial show of temper. At least she would know better than to bring any other young gad-about-town back to the flat in future. As for waiting on her hand and foot, well, that was a thing of the past.

When Hubert beat a hasty retreat and Bella collapsed sobbing loudly on to the divan, only to be dragged unceremoniously to her feet and thrown into the bedroom, Frank did not know that the demure young nurse from the agency had been listening at the door of Caroline's room. As the house became quiet again the nurse smiled to herself and tiptoed over to the crib. Maybe she had been a little premature in her assessment of the man, she thought. He had certainly ended that little affair, and the mistress of the house appeared to be in for a hard time this evening. Masterful men were so exciting, she thought to herself, taking off her glasses and touching her hot cheek.

The summer of 1918 was one of heavy fighting in France and Belgium, and the newspapers were full of casualty lists and battle maps. A full German offensive was met with stubborn resistance, and foreign place names were on everyone's lips. Marne, Amiens, Picardy and Arras were theatres of bitter fighting, and in early August the German offensive was broken. At home people were hopeful of a speedy end to the war, and in Page Street life went on as usual. Lorries rumbled continually down the little turning. Florrie Axford shook her head sadly as she stood with folded arms at her street door. Aggie Temple cleaned her doorstep every other morning now but Maisie Dougall decided that it wasn't worth the effort. 'What's the good, Aggie?' she tried to convince her. 'Soon as it's clean the poxy lorries splash mud all over it. Give us those 'orse-an'-carts any day. The noise o' them there lorries is a bloody disgrace.'

Maggie Jones was above all the nagging and moaning. Her son had been decorated by the King on his visit to France and she walked proudly to the market with her head in the air. Sadie Sullivan went to the Catholic church in Dockhead every morning and said a prayer in remembrance of John and Michael, and a prayer for Joe's safety, and a special prayer for Billy that he might, 'get orf 'is backside an' find 'imself some bleedin' work'.

Maisie Dougall was not disposed to church-going but she also said a prayer every night by the side of her bed. Her surviving son Albert was recovering from frostbite in a field hospital.

In nearby Bacon Street Nellie Tanner worried over her youngest son Danny, although she felt relieved that Charlie was not at the front. She worried too over William, who seemed to be more morose and withdrawn than ever. His job at the council depot meant that he was still working nights and weekends, and he had become a pale shadow of himself. Only Carrie was able to make him laugh with her accounts of the customers who frequently called in at the café and Nellie knew how much her husband looked forward to her regular visits. She had to admit that her daughter seemed happy and contented; she had never seen her looking so radiant. Married life seemed to suit her and Nellie was impatiently waiting for news of a baby, but had refrained from broaching the subject with Carrie. She tried to discuss it with William, however, but he sighed irritably as he sat listening to her.

'She should be finkin' o' startin' a family before it's too late. After all, 'er Fred ain't exactly a young man, is 'e?' Nellie remarked. 'If they leave it too long the fella's gonna be too old ter play wiv the child. Besides, it don't do ter 'ave yer first one when yer turned firty. Fings can go wrong. Look at that woman in Page Street who 'ad that imbecile child. She 'ad ter push it everywhere in the pram till it was seven. Then she 'ad ter get it put in one o' them children's 'omes, poor little bleeder.'

'Christ! What yer goin' on about, Nell?' William sighed. 'That woman was nearly forty, an' she wasn't all that bright 'erself. She used ter 'ave fits, an' look at 'er ole man. 'E wasn't all there neivver. Carrie's doin' all right fer 'erself, an' if she wants ter wait a year or two, good luck ter the gel.'

Nellie was not to be put off. 'P'raps they can't 'ave any kids,' she suggested anxiously. 'Sometimes men o' Fred's age can't manage it, 'specially if they marry late in life. Ida was tellin' me only the ovver mornin' about 'er cousin Gerry. Forty-five 'e was whe 'e got married, an' . . .'

'Will yer give it a rest, woman?' William growled, rounding on her. 'I'm ten years older than you an' we 'ad no trouble makin' babies, an' they all turned out all right. Let the gel be, fer Gawd's sake.'

Nellie watched sullenly as her husband took down his coat from the back of the door and strode heavily out of the room. She sighed regretfully. Life had changed drastically for her since William had lost his job at the stables. Making herself look nice for him was not the joy it had once been. It was only very rarely that Will showed feelings of love for her now, and it wasn't anywhere near as pleasurable as it used to be. He seemed to have lost interest in everything these days, Nellie rued, and that old goat Galloway was to blame. Once he had almost destroyed her family life; now he was totally to blame for the miserable existence she and her husband had been reduced to. Well, at least Carrie had managed to get one up on him, she told herself, and with that small consolation Nellie set about washing up the breakfast things in the dingy tenement flat.

*

Throughout the long, hot summer the Bradleys' café in Cotton Lane was always full of carmen and river men. Carrie had insisted that the dining rooms should be smartened up, and after the premises closed each evening the renovation work began. For two whole weeks Carrie and Fred spent long evenings scraping at the grimy paintwork and rubbing down the wooden benches. Each night they went to bed exhausted but happy with the progress they were making, and slowly the results of their labours began to show. The ceiling was given two coats of whitewash, and varnish was applied to the benches. All the woodwork was painted pale blue and behind the counter a large menu was displayed, something of which Carrie was very proud. She had painstakingly painted the sign in black paint on a large whitewashed board and Fred had nailed it up above the tea urn. At the back of the café a new seating area was set out in what had once been the store-room and a few of the managers from local firms started to use this for their morning coffee. The outside of the café had been re-painted too and above the large windows Fred had painted the word 'Bradley's' in large gold letters. Carrie had decided early on that there should be a greater variety of food, and soon kippers and bloaters were added to the menu. All the hard work had eventually paid off, and Bessie soon found less and less time to chat about her friend Elsie Dobson as the café filled every morning.

The busy days hurried by, and as autumn approached the general feeling was that an end to the long war could not be far off. There had been a new offensive against the Kaiser's army and the newspapers were full of the battles at Meuse-Argonne, Flanders and Cambrai, where British, American, French and Belgian troops were advancing. Carrie was becoming more fearful for Danny who was back in action and experienced a sick feeling in the pit of her stomach every time she thumbed through the ever-increasing casualty lists.

During that summer and autumn Carrie gradually became accustomed to life as a married woman. Most nights Fred was exhausted and too tired to give her the attention she desired, and on the rare occasions when he did manage to love her it was soon over, leaving Carrie with little sense of fulfillment. Her disappointment was tempered by her husband's kindness and concern for her. She loved to feel his arm around her shoulders as they shut the shop each evening, and the brief kisses he stole in quiet moments during the day. Carrie knew that her sudden decision to become Fred's wife had been influenced in no small degree by what had happened to her family, but she had carefully considered everything and was determined to make the union a happy one, come what may.

Joe Maitland sat facing his landlady with a serious look on his handsome face.

'Look, Florrie, I know what yer sayin', but it's not as easy as all that,' he said. 'Fer a start, I can't just expect the Yard blokes ter believe me wivout givin' 'em the proof they need. Don't ferget I've done time as well. Ter them I'm a lag. They wouldn't believe me in front of one o' their own, 'im bein' an inspector an' all.'

Florrie leaned back in her chair and toyed with an empty teacup, pursing her thin lips. 'Well, what the bleedin' 'ell are yer gonna do?' she said finally. 'Yer could be goin' on like this ferever, an' yer need ter remember what'll 'appen if somebody finds out what yer really doin' at those fights. After all, anybody could walk in there from over the water who reco'nises yer, an' then it's goodbye Joe.'

The lodger allowed himself a brief smile. 'I've jus' got ter be patient fer a while longer,' he said quietly. 'I'm accepted as one o' the regulars now an' I put meself about while I'm there. All the bookies know me an' sooner or later somebody's gonna let somefing slip. I'll find out who that last toe-rag is. I'll get ter the bottom of it all, in the end.'

'Well, don't go takin' no chances, son,' Florrie warned him. 'If ever yer do find out who it was, let the coppers 'andle it. Yer only one on yer own. Yer wouldn't stand a chance wiv that lot o' no-good 'ore-sons.'

Joe's eyes narrowed. 'When I find out fer sure, I won't trouble the coppers, Flo. That's somefink I'm gonna take care of meself,' he said firmly. 'They can 'ave the proof about the goin's-on there an' the crooked copper, if I ever do get any, but that bastard who was involved in me bruvver's death is gonna answer ter me, I swear it.'

Florrie stood up with a sigh and gathered together the empty teacups. 'Well, I'm glad yer told me everyfing, son,' she said. 'I was beginnin' ter wonder about yer comin's an' goin's. I 'ad a feelin' there was somefing goin' on. Don't worry though, I won't breave a word about what yer up to. Yer can trust yer ole Florrie ter keep 'er trap shut. Now what about a fresh cuppa?'

At eleven o'clock on the eleventh day of the eleventh month of 1918 the war finally came to an end. Along the river tug-whistles sounded, their high-pitched notes almost drowned by the booming fog-horns of the large berthed ships. Maroons were fired from the Tower of London, and paper-boys ran excitedly through the streets with special editions. Fireworks were let off and terrified horses shied, setting the carmen struggling desperately with the reins. Factories and tanneries in Bermondsey shut down for the day, and when Florrie Axford looked through her fresh lace curtains and saw Maisie

Dougall talking excitedly to the neighbours she was quick to put on her coat and hurry out to the group lest she miss any of the latest news.

'My ole man told me. Come back down the street 'specially, 'e did,' Maisie was going on. ''E said 'e bumped inter Alec Crossley on 'is way ter work an' Alec told 'im the pubs are gonna stay open all day. Well, as long as the beer lasts out anyway.'

Aggie Temple chuckled as she turned to Sadie Sullivan. 'I fink I'll tong me 'air an' get me best coat out the wardrobe,' she said. 'I might even get me ole man ter take us up the Kings Arms before 'e gets legless.'

Sadie puckered her lips. 'There's special Mass at Dock'ead terday. Me an' my Daniel are goin' there first. 'E can get pissed afterwards,' she declared.

Ida Bromsgrove had also seen her neighbours gathering and she knocked on Maggie Jones's door. 'Come on, Mag, there's a meetin' down the street,' she told her.

The two women joined the group, quickly followed by Maudie Mycroft who was getting ready for the women's meeting. 'Good Gawd!' was all she could say when she heard the news.

Florrie began to frown. 'Well, this is one time I'm not gettin' wedged in that snug bar,' she growled. 'I fink us women should all march inter the public bar. If they don't like it – well, sod the bleedin' lot of 'em. Our money's as good as theirs.'

Maudie pulled on her bottom lip. 'S'posin they turned us out? I'd feel such a fool,' she said in a worried voice.

'Let 'em try,' Sadie said, showing Maudie her clenched fists. 'If any o' the men try ter chuck me out, I'll smash 'em one.'

'All the dockers'll be in there, an' the carmen from the yard,' Maudie said fearfully.

Maggie nodded. 'It won't 'alf be packed in there. I bet we won't get a seat.'

'Well, I'm not standin' in that poxy snug bar like a sardine in a tin,' Florrie asserted. 'We're all gonna walk in that public bar an' if the men don't offer us a seat we'll all stand at the counter, an' when they see they can't get served they'll soon change their tune.'

'Good fer you, Flo,' Sadie shouted. 'Now come on, gels, let's get ourselves ready. C'mon, Aggie, I'll tong your 'air an' then yer can do mine.'

Early that evening the women of Page Street marched into the public bar of the Kings Arms and were immediately offered seats. Drinks were sent to their tables and the publican did not offer any objections. The sight of Sadie Sullivan and Florrie Axford leading the women into the establishment, with the large figure of Ida Bromsgrove following close behind, was too daunting even for the likes of the landlord.

Chapter Forty-two

During the bitter cold November and through into December the soldiers' homecoming was celebrated, with Union Jacks hanging from upstairs windows and bunting tied across the narrow Bermondsey backstreets. In Page Street the flags were flying and folk stood at their front doors as the young men arrived back home from the mud and carnage of the Western Front. Maisie's son Albert was the first to arrive, looking pale and thin but in good spirits as he strolled proudly down the street in his khaki uniform with its shining buttons, wearing puttees over his highly polished boots. One week later Joe Sullivan came home to a tearful reunion with his mother. His father stood back, smiling broadly and brushing a tear from his eye as he waited for his wife to release their son from a huge bear-hug. Billy stood beside his father and waited to greet his younger brother, smiling broadly and holding himself erect even though his chest was hurting. One week later the Jones boy sauntered into the street wearing his MM ribbon and chewing arrogantly on a plug of tobacco.

In early December Danny Tanner arrived home to a flag-bedecked Bacon Street and an emotional reunion with his parents. Nellie stood back and eyed him up and down critically.

'Yer look pale. Yer need a good dinner inside yer, son,' she said, fighting back her tears of joy.

William pumped his son's hand and immediately noticed the power in his grasp. 'Yer look well, boy. Yer put on a bit o' weight too,' he remarked.

Danny shrugged his broad shoulders and grinned, his blue eyes twinkling in his wide face as he picked up his kitbag. 'I bin doin' some boxin', Pop. I was the regimental champion,' he said proudly.

Nellie shook her head and sighed deeply. 'I'll never understand you men. Didn't yer see enough blood wivout knockin' yer mates silly?' she moaned.

Danny glanced quickly at his father and then beckoned to a strong-looking lad who was watching the homecoming. ''Ere, son, carry me kitbag upstairs fer me, will yer?' he asked, handing the lad a silver threepenny piece.

'Ain't yer comin' in?' Nellie said with a disappointed look on her face.

'Later, Ma. I wanna see Billy Sullivan first,' he replied, backing away up the street.

Danny was stopped in his tracks by a loud shriek as Carrie came running into the turning. He staggered back a pace as she threw herself into his arms.

'I knew yer'd be all right. I jus' knew yer'd come 'ome in one piece,' she gasped, kissing him.

Danny was grinning as he finally broke away. He gave the lad by his kitbag an exaggerated glare. 'Well, go on then, carry it up,' he growled.

Carrie slipped her arm through his and smiled lovingly at him. 'C' mon in an' I'll tell yer all the news,' she said excitedly.

'Look, sis, I wanna slip round an' see Billy first,' he said.

Carrie took a tighter grip on his arm. 'Billy can wait a bit longer. First yer gonna eat,' she laughed, pulling him close to her. 'Fred give me some sardines fer yer. I told 'im 'ow much yer like sardines.'

Danny knew it was useless to protest any more and he allowed himself to be led up the dusty wooden stairs to the family home.

The Kings Arms was packed with customers on Friday evening and in the public bar the Tanner family was gathered to celebrate Danny's homecoming. Carrie sat with her mother in one corner and they chatted happily their eyes occasionally straying towards their menfolk who were standing at the counter. Fred and William were listening to Danny's account of his experiences in France but their attention was being distracted by a noisy conversation going on beside them. The large figure with a bloated and battered face was leaning on the counter his massive fists clenched on either side of his half-empty glass of ale.

He suddenly turned his head sideways, his eyes boring into his companion's. 'That was the fifth inside the distance. None of 'em last very long,' he sneered. 'Not against me they don't.'

'Got anyfink lined up?' the carman asked respectfully.

His harsh laugh boomed out. 'Yer better ask Galloway. I don't make the matches or pick me opponents, I only knock 'em out.'

Danny was becoming irritated by the man's loud boasting. 'Who's that loud-mouthed git?' he asked, the muscles in his jaw tightening.

His father's face became stern. 'That's Jake Mitchell,' he told him. ''E's always in 'ere braggin' about the fights 'e's 'ad. Take no notice.'

Danny became quiet as he sipped his drink. While he was away Carrie had been writing to him about everything that was happening at home and she had explained how Jake Mitchell had taken over their father's job. Danny's blood had boiled when he learned of his father's treatment at the hands of George Galloway and now he could feel his anger slowly rising again as he listened to the ring-scarred brute at the counter. His handsome face became set hard. Slowly he moved so that he was standing against the counter with his back to Jake Mitchell.

'Does 'e 'ave ter shout? We don't all wanna 'ear 'is business,' Danny said loudly.

William shook his head and pulled a face but his son ignored the warning. 'Does 'e fink everybody's deaf in 'ere?' he went on goading.

Mitchell was bellowing with laughter, unaware of what Danny was saying, and the young man became impatient. He turned to Mitchell's companion and whispered something in his ear. The carman's face took on a frightened look and he stared at the young Tanner with wide eyes.

'What's 'e say?' Mitchell asked quickly, seeing the carman's reaction.

'Nuffink, Jake.'

'I asked yer what 'e said,' the large man growled menacingly.

Danny turned to face Mitchell. 'I told 'im ter tell yer ter keep yer voice down. We can't 'ear what we're talkin' about,' he said, putting his glass down on the counter.

The frightened carman backed away from the counter as he saw Mitchell's eyes start to bulge, and William quickly stepped in front of his son. ''E's just back from the front,' he said quietly, trying to defuse the situation.

'So this is yer boy, is it?' Mitchell sneered. 'Got a lot ter say fer 'imself, ain't 'e? Well, if I was you I'd tell 'im not ter get too lippy, 'e might come unstruck.'

Before William could reply, Danny took him by the shoulders and gently eased him to one side. 'So you're the famous Jake Mitchell, are yer?' he said quietly. 'I've 'eard a lot about you. Bin knockin' 'em all out, so yer told everybody. Well, maybe now the war's over you'll get a better class o' fighter up against yer.'

Mitchell moved forward menacingly. 'Yer not includin' yerself on that list, are yer, sonny?' he sneered.

Danny grinned calmly. 'Yer past it, Mitchell. Yer wouldn't go the distance wiv me.'

Carrie and her mother had jumped up from their seats and as they tried to pull Danny away Alec Crossley leapt smartly over the counter and placed himself in front of Jake Mitchell. 'The war's over, pal, an' I'm not gonna be a party ter any more 'ostilities. Now drink up an' let's 'ave no more of it. That goes fer you too, Danny. Understood?'

Mitchell's eyes were bulging. 'Me an' you, sonny, first opportunity. An' we'll 'ave our own little side bet on the outcome,' he sneered.

Danny nodded. 'Suits me fine. Sooner the better,' he said, turning his back.

'You'll be 'earin' when, Tanner,' Galloway's foreman shouted over as the publican hustled him to the door.

When Mitchell had left Nellie rounded on her son. 'I'm not 'avin' it!' she raved. 'I told yer, I won't allow a boy o' mine ter be a fighter. Christ Almighty! Ain't yer 'ad enough o' fightin'? Do somefink, Will. Tell 'im.'

William shrugged his shoulders. ''E's a bit too big fer me ter chastise. Did yer see the way 'e put me ter one side?' he grinned.

Nellie gave him a withering look and flounced back to her

seat, while Carrie smiled slyly at her younger brother. 'Yer'd better get inter trainin',' she said quietly.

Florrie Axford was sitting in her parlour with her friends. Nellie had joined the company but looked pale and ill. She clasped her hands nervously as Florrie banged her fist down on the table.

'We done it before at the Kings Arms an' we'll do it again at the Crown,' she declared. 'If we all go there tergevver, they daren't stop us goin' in. We'll tell 'em we want ter place bets an' we're gonna cheer our boy on.'

'I couldn't go,' Maudie said, shuddering. 'First drop o' blood spilled an' I'd be ill, I know I would.'

'Well, nobody's makin' yer. Jus' give us yer bet money an' we'll put it on fer yer,' Sadie scowled at her.

'I couldn't bet on men killin' each over,' Maudie went on.

'Don't be so melodramatic,' Florrie said sharply. 'Danny ain't gonna kill 'im. 'E's only gonna knock that ugly great git right out, ain't 'e, Nell?'

Nell looked very worried. 'I wish 'e'd never got 'imself inter this,' she sighed weakly. ''E knows 'ow I feel about fightin'.'

Sadie waved her anxieties away with a sweep of her large arm. 'Don't worry, Nell,' she blustered. 'My Billy's 'elpin' 'im wiv 'is trainin' an' 'e knows all about such fings. Matter o' fact it's a pleasure ter see Billy takin' an interest in somefing at last. 'E's bin a different lad since your Danny come back 'ome. It was nice ter see the pair of 'em this mornin', goin' out runnin' in the park. Mind yer, my Billy come back lookin' like a train 'ad 'it 'im an' 'e was wheezin' like a concertina. Poor sod's chest ain't too good.'

Florrie held her hand up for silence then leaned forward over the table. 'Now listen, gels, me an' Sadie 'ave bin puttin' our 'eads tergevver an' this is what we're gonna do . . .'

*

Carrie Tanner shivered against the cold wind as she stood beside her brother on the platform at Waterloo Station. All around them soldiers in full kit were hugging their loved ones and sweeping young children up into their arms before climbing aboard the military train to Southampton. Charlie turned anxiously to his sister.

'Now listen, Carrie,' he said as he looked at her intently, 'I want yer ter be 'appy. Try an' keep an eye on Mum an' Dad, won't yer?'

She sighed heavily. 'Gawd, I wish yer 'adn't signed on, Charlie,' she said sadly. 'I won't be seein' yer fer ages an' ages, an' I'm gonna miss yer terribly.'

He smiled at her and softly kissed her cheek. 'It's fer the best, Carrie,' he said quietly. 'I wouldn't 'ave 'ad any 'appiness if I'd stayed in Bermon'sey. It 'olds too many memories, too many ghosts. Anyway, India sounds like an excitin' place,' he added quickly. 'Who knows? I might get the chance ter ride an elephant or be the guard of honour in some prince's 'arem!'

His lightheartedness was lost on Carrie who bit back tears as the guard appeared on the platform, holding his flag.

'Now you take care, bruv,' she cried as she hugged him tightly. 'Write ter me as soon as yer can.'

He climbed aboard the train quickly and stowed his kitbag in the luggage rack before leaning back out of the carriage window.

'Be 'appy, Carrie, an' don't worry about Danny. 'E's gonna win,' he shouted above the din as the train started to move. 'I love yer, sis.'

Carrie stood in the pale January sunlight and waved until the train was out of sight, then she turned slowly and walked out of the station, blinking back her tears. Charlie had looked cheerful, but the deep sadness in his eyes had cut into her like a sharp knife. She could still see the look on her mother's face as she said goodbye to him that morning. Nellie had embraced him gently and then stood there gazing at him with a faraway look in her eyes. It felt to Carrie almost as if something inside her mother died.

She pulled her coat around her against the cold as she stood at the tram stop, and a feeling of dread began to grow inside her. Her mother had been looking ill lately, and Charlie's departure seemed to have shaken her badly. She had already been worried out of her life over Danny's coming fight with Jake Mitchell. Carrie knew instinctively that her mother needed her, and decided to go straight home. Fred would be able to take care of the café for a while, she was sure.

By the time Carrie stepped down from the tram in Jamaica Road and reached the dilapidated buildings in Bacon Street it was nearing midday. She climbed the dusty wooden stairs and knocked on the front door of her parents' flat. As she stood waiting she could smell the stench rising up from the communal dustbins below. It seemed a long time before anyone answered, and when her mother finally opened the door Carrie could see dark circles around her puffed eyes.

'Are yer all right, Mum?' she asked with concern as she walked into the flat.

Nellie did not answer. She slumped down into a chair beside the table and buried her head in her arms, sobbing bitterly.

'I couldn't tell 'im, Carrie,' she moaned. 'I dunno what I should've done, but I couldn't tell 'im.'

Carrie bent down and slipped her arm around her mother's shoulders. 'What is it, Mum?' she said gently. 'What couldn't yer tell 'im?'

For a while Nellie said nothing, and then after what seemed

like an eternity she took Carrie by both hands and pulled her down into a chair beside her. Nellie's eyes looked tortured.

'I was just a young woman, not much older than you are now, Carrie,' she began in a broken voice. 'James was a baby at the time an' there was fousands o' men round 'ere out o' work. Yer farvver was gettin' a load of 'ay from the farm when George Galloway called roun' ter see me one mornin'. 'E told me 'e might 'ave ter put yer farvver off 'cos o' the slump. Galloway said 'e wanted me ter know before 'and so I could look fer anuvver place ter live. Oh, 'e was very sorry an' full of apologies an' 'e said 'e'd give us a reference ter 'elp us get a place. 'E told me not ter let on fer the time bein' in case fings changed, but it looked very likely if there was no more contracts comin' in the yard.'

'What are yer tellin' me, Mum?' Carrie asked, suddenly feeling sick as the awful truth began to dawn on her.

Nellie tugged at the handkerchief in her hands as she went on: 'I was so terrified we'd get put out on the street I pleaded wiv Galloway not ter let yer farvver go. I broke down and cried, an' 'e put 'is arm aroun' me. Yer gotta understand 'ow desperate I was, child. It was as though I was turned ter stone. I couldn't feel anyfing, an' I didn't try ter stop 'im when 'e got familiar. That mornin' George Galloway got me pregnant. Charlie is George Galloway's son.'

Carrie looked at the floor, feeling sick. She could think of nothing to say. She felt her mother's pleading gaze on her.

'Don't 'ate me, Carrie,' Nellie said, bursting into tears. 'Don't 'ate me.'

Carrie's eyes misted and she hugged her mother tightly. 'I don't 'ate yer, Mum,' she said gently. 'It ain't your fault.'

Nellie sobbed loudly. 'Charlie told me 'e'd asked Josephine ter marry 'im,' she spluttered. 'The poor child must 'ave found out when she asked 'er farvver fer 'is permission. It come out at the inquest that she was very drunk. She must've done 'erself in.'

'Yer mustn't blame yerself, Mum,' Carrie implored her. 'We'll never know what really 'appened ter Josephine. An' if anyone's ter blame,' she added fiercely, 'it's that evil stinking bastard Galloway, not you.'

Nellie dabbed at her eyes. 'I've carried this cross all these years fer yer farvver's sake,' she sobbed. ''E's a lovely man an' I could never bring meself ter tell 'im.'

'Ain't Galloway ever shown any remorse fer what 'e done?' Carrie asked angrily.

Nellie nodded. ''E offered me money but I refused. We've always 'ad ter scrape an' scheme ter live, an' yer farvver would 'ave found out if I suddenly 'ad extra money ter play wiv. Besides, I'd 'ave felt like a common whore takin' Galloway's money. Yer farvver mus' never know,' she pleaded. 'Promise me, Carrie. It'd kill 'im, the way 'e is.'

Carrie felt herself breaking into sobs as she hugged her mother and kissed her forehead. 'Don't worry, Mum,' she said as tears ran down her cheeks. 'I won't tell Dad.'

Chapter Forty-three

On the last Saturday evening in January the Page Street women together with Nellie and Carrie all marched up to the Crown public house at Dockhead.

Sadie grabbed the arm of an elderly man who was going in the pub and said, 'Oi, you, tell the guv'nor 'e's wanted outside.'

The startled man nodded and hurried into the bar. Soon Don McBain came out and faced the determined women. 'Sorry, ladies, it's fer men only,' he smiled. 'Get yer men ter place yer bets fer yer.'

Florrie put her hands on her hips and glared at the publican. 'It's 'er boy who's fightin',' she told him, nodding her head towards Nellie. 'We're gonna cheer 'im on so yer'd better let us in.'

McBain shook his head. 'Sorry, gels, I can't,' he replied, turning on his heel.

Sadie grabbed him by the arm. 'Now listen 'ere, you,' she growled. 'We know the brewery don't know about these fights yer put on, an' nor do the coppers, but they soon will if yer don't let us in. We might even tell the local papers as well. I should fink they'd be interested, wouldn't you, Flo?'

Florrie nodded her head vigorously. 'That's fer sure.'

McBain sighed in resignation. 'All right, go through the back door,' he said wearily, 'but no screamin' an' 'ollerin', an' keep yer traps shut, all right?'

Meanwhile in the bar Soapy Symonds and Sharkey Morris were standing close to a few of the bookies' runners and chatting noisily.

''Ow the bloody 'ell is the boy expected ter do any good when 'e's only got one good eye?' Soapy puffed. 'It ain't as though 'e's up against any ole fighter. That Jake Mitchell's an experienced bloke, an' jus' look at 'is record. Nah, I can't see the boy lastin' two rounds wiv 'im.'

'Wassa matter wiv 'is eye then?' Sharkey asked in a loud voice.

'Well, accordin' ter Florrie the boy got gassed in France,' Soapy replied, sipping his beer and glancing quickly around the bar. ''E was blinded fer a time, by all accounts. 'Is left eye's ruined. Mustard gas ruins yer eyes, yer know. Florrie said Danny's muvver told 'er about 'im bein' 'alf blind. Yer know what a nosy ole cow Florrie is. She gets ter 'ear about everyfing.'

'Well, I'm glad yer told me,' Sharkey said, banging down his empty glass on the table. 'I fink I'll save me money.'

'Anuvver fing, that gas affects yer chest,' Soapy went on. 'Florrie reckons the boy should never be in the ring, what wiv 'is coughin' an' wheezin'.'

Florrie's plan to raise the stakes in their favour had been executed to perfection. Now all that remained was for the bets to be placed.

The women filed into the large marquee and took their places on the wooden benches. Nellie felt her heart beating faster and bit on her bottom lip as she gazed at the roped arena. She could picture Danny lying there, cut and battered, with anxious people bending over him. She squeezed her daughter's hand in hers. 'Can yer see yer farvver?'

Carrie looked around and pointed. 'There 'e is, Mum. 'E's sittin' next ter Joe Maitland.'

Nellie tried to stay calm as the master of ceremonies ducked under the ropes. She glanced across at the anxious face of her husband and he waved over to her reassuringly.

Florrie meanwhile had been placing the bets and she was looking very smug as she rejoined her friends. 'Five ter one we got. That ugly git Mitchell is odds-on,' she grinned.

'What's odds-on mean?' Ida asked.

'It means it ain't werf wastin' yer stakes,' Florrie replied, still grinning widely.

Danny Tanner was announced to the spectators and as he strode behind Billy Sullivan towards the ring the Page Street women cheered loudly, ignoring the cat-calls and cries of derision from Mitchell's supporters. Danny ducked under the ropes and stood quietly banging his fists together beneath the overcoat which was draped over his shoulders. Jake Mitchell's entry was greeted with loud cheers from his cohort of fans. When he slipped off his wrap and walked into the centre of the ring to get his instructions from the referee, Nellie winced and turned to Carrie.

'Jus' look at the difference in size,' she groaned. 'That Mitchell looks twice as big as Danny.'

Carrie squeezed her mother's arm. 'Danny can look after 'imself, Ma,' she said, trying to sound confident. 'Besides Billy's bin 'elpin 'im. 'E'll be all right, yer'll see.'

There was a sudden hush as the two contestants walked back to their respective corners, but as soon as the bell sounded a roar went up. Jake Mitchell moved towards Danny menacingly and started circling him slowly. His right fist shot out and caught Danny's brow.

'Oi, mind 'is eye!' Mrs Bromsgrove shouted out, but her voice was drowned by the roar of the crowd.

Another right shot out and this time it caught Danny high on his head. Immediately Mitchell charged in, sensing he had his man reeling, but a straight left jab full in his face stopped him dead. Danny was moving around now, his body ducking and weaving and his feet shuffling lightly across the canvas-covered floor. Mitchell growled and charged in again, hoping to grab his opponent and use his head on Danny's left eye, but as he came on he was rocked by a fusillade of blows. Billy Sullivan was screaming out for Danny to keep moving and the Page Street women were shouting at the tops of their voices. 'Do 'im, Danny! Knock the ugly git out!' Sadie screamed.

Carrie had felt no anxiety as she waited for the fight to begin, only a numbness. She had felt numb inside ever since that terrible day when she discovered her mother's awful secret. Now as Danny punched his fist into Mitchell's face, she jerked her shoulders forward as if she were there beside him, urging him on. She felt a cold hatred towards Galloway's champion, as though he were Galloway himself. She did not hear the other voices around her as she rose to her feet with hatred in her eyes, screaming hoarsely, 'Kill 'im, Danny! Kill 'im!'

Danny was pummelling Mitchell relentlessly with a series of heavy lefts and rights, and only the bell saved the heavier man. He staggered back to his corner and the crowd were quiet. Only the women were laughing and joking with each other.

For the next four rounds Mitchell took a terrible beating. Danny was lighter and fitter and he stayed out of reach of Mitchell's swinging punches, dancing in to hammer lefts and rights into the carman's bloodied face. The bell sounded for the end of the fifth round and by now most people in the marquee knew that the fight could not go on for much longer. Mitchell knew his strength was failing, and glanced over to where his sponsor was sitting. George Galloway sat impassively beside his son with his hands clasped over the silver knob of his walking-stick and did not meet his fighter's eye.

Mitchell lasted another two rounds, his face cut and streaked with blood. By now everyone had stopped cheering. Nellie was ashen-faced. She alone had sat silent for the whole fight. She could no longer watch, preferring to gaze at the floor instead. Carrie had slumped back down beside her. Her own hatred had made her feel dirty, and every time Danny landed further blows on his opponent she winced.

Near the end of the eighth round Danny struck Mitchell with a wicked right-hand punch high on the head and the carman sagged down on the canvas. With a last supreme effort he rose on shaking legs but a barrage of heavy blows floored him again. This time he was counted out by the referee and dragged back to his stool.

Carrie felt physically sick at the sight of Mitchell's face. She looked over to where William was sitting just in time to see him leaving. She had felt her compassion growing for the beaten fighter, but as she glanced over at Galloway's bowed figure a smile came to her lips.

Danny left the ring to loud acclaim, and when Mitchell finally stood up from his stool and was assisted out of the ring the applause was almost as loud. Everyone present had been moved by the man's courage in holding on for eight rounds against a much fitter and younger opponent. Even the Page Street women were generous to the man they had been ready to hate and stood up to clap him as he walked unsteadily from the marquee. George Galloway had turned his back on Mitchell and was talking to his son with a guarded expression on his florid face. Frank looked at him as if surprised and slowly shook his head as they walked slowly out of the marquee.

In a small room at the back of the pub Mitchell sat alone, plasters over one eye and across the bridge of his nose. Suddenly the door opened and George Galloway walked in.

''Ow d'yer feel, Jake?' he asked, leaning heavily on his cane.

'I've felt better,' Mitchell replied, trying to grin through his swollen lips.

Galloway walked slowly across to a bare wooden table and leaned against it. 'Yer met yer match ternight,' he said without a trace of pity. 'I warned yer, didn't I? I told yer the booze would catch up wiv yer, but yer chose to ignore me. I told yer one day some young striplin' would give yer a good pastin'. I'm only sorry it turned out ter be Tanner.'

Jake Mitchell winced as he felt the lump on his cheekbone. 'I'm sorry, Guv', if it cost yer ternight but yer gotta admit yer've done well in the past. I jus' wasn't meself,' he said quickly.

Galloway smiled and looked down at his black patent boots. 'Oh, I didn't lose. My money was on the Tanner boy,' he said with emphasis.

Mitchell looked up quickly, his bruised features rigid with shock. 'Yer mean yer backed the ovver bloke?' he asked hoarsely.

'That's right, I did,' Galloway replied. 'There was a bit o' rumourmongerin' goin' on an' it looked like somebody was out ter skin the bookies. I've lived round 'ere fer long enough. I know these people. There was a lot o' confidence in the boy, so I placed me money accordingly. I got a good price on Tanner.'

Mitchell looked hard at his employer. 'Yer knew that an'

yer didn't fink ter warn me?' he snarled. 'Yer let me go in against the boy wivout a word o' warnin'? What sort of a bloke are yer?'

'I'm a businessman,' Galloway replied pointedly. 'I back winners, not losers. It's why I'm where I am terday.'

The beaten fighter slumped back in his chair. 'All right, so I lost ternight. There'll be ovver times,' he said in a low voice.

'Not wiv me there won't,' Galloway said quickly. 'All the young bucks'll be linin' up ter fight yer now, Jake. Take my tip, get yerself a steady job an' ferget the booths an' the pub circuits, or yer quite likely ter end up sellin' papers like 'im up at Dock'ead.'

'Yer mean yer sackin' me?' Mitchell said in a shocked voice.

George Galloway straightened and flicked at an imaginary object with his cane. 'That's right. There's two weeks' wages in there,' he said, throwing an envelope on the table. 'There's yer cut o' the purse money in there as well. Do yerself a favour, Jake, an' jack the fightin' in, before yer get 'urt bad.'

Mitchell watched dumbfounded as Galloway turned on his heels and walked out of the room. Slowly he stood up, holding his aching ribs as he reached out for the envelope. He was still counting the money when Billy Sullivan put his head round the door.

'My bloke wants ter 'ave a word wiv yer, if it's all right,' he said.

Mitchell nodded as he pocketed the envelope. 'Tell 'im ter come in.'

Danny Tanner walked in, followed by his father, and immediately held out his hand. 'No grudges?' he asked.

Mitchell smiled as he gripped the young man's palm. 'No grudges. Yer a good fighter. I reckon yer'll go a long way,' he said, sitting down heavily. 'If yer take my advice, though, yer'll get out while yer in one piece, before the likes o' Galloway gets their 'ooks inter yer.'

Will Tanner stepped forward and held out his hand. 'I gotta say yer got a lot o' guts, Jake,' he said. 'Most would 'ave stayed on the floor but you didn't.'

The battered fighter shook his hand and smiled painfully. 'Fanks, mate. By the way, I'm lookin' fer work as from Monday mornin'. If yer 'ear of anyfing, I'd be grateful fer a nod.'

'Yer mean Galloway sacked yer, jus' 'cos yer lost?' William asked him in a shocked voice.

Mitchell nodded. 'It seems 'e only backs winners.'

William leant against the wall and looked intently at Mitchell. 'Tell me straight, Jake. What's yer feelin's terwards Galloway now?' he asked quietly.

Mitchell spat, 'As far as I'm concerned, 'e can rot in 'ell.'

'Will yer do me a favour before yer go 'ome? Will yer 'ave a word wiv a pal o' mine?' asked William.

Mitchell nodded. 'Why not?'

The Tanners left the room and William walked quickly over to Joe Maitland who was waiting in the yard. ''E said 'e'll see yer. Good luck, Joe.'

Florrie Axford was sitting in her parlour with a mug of tea at her elbow. Joe Maitland sat facing her, his face impassive as she questioned him.

'Well, tell me 'ow yer come ter get the proof yer needed then,' she coaxed.

He grinned finally. 'As a matter o' fact, Jake Mitchell come up trumps,' he said. ''E told me 'e was in the yard office when that crooked 'oreson of a copper put bets on wiv Galloway. What's more, 'e said 'e's actually seen the inspector at a couple o' the fights. Best of all, Mitchell's willin' ter make a statement.'

'Christ! 'E's takin' a chance, ain't 'e?' Florrie said.

'Not really,' Joe replied. 'I've sent everyfing ter Scotland Yard. Once it's out in the open, they'll give 'im protection. Anyway, Mitchell's leavin' Bermon'sey. 'E's goin' back over the water. 'E'll be safe enough in Stepney.'

'What about you, Joe? Are yer goin' back over the water ter live now yer've sorted fings out?' Florrie asked.

The young man leaned back in his chair, a sly smile on his face. 'Why should I? I like it in Bermon'sey,' he said. 'Besides, if I did leave yer might fink I 'ad somefink ter do wiv what 'appened ter the publican o' the Crown. I wouldn't want yer ter fink that, Flo.'

'I wouldn't fink anyfink o' the sort,' she said with a contrived show of disdain. 'The papers said 'e fell down the cellar steps an' died of a broken neck. Even 'is own wife said 'e'd bin drinkin' 'eavily that evenin'. Who am I ter say different.'

'Quite right too,' Joe replied, the smile still lingering on his face. 'After all, there's no reason fer anybody ter fink that somebody 'ad a score ter settle wiv 'im 'cos o' somefing that 'appened a long time ago, now is there? Nope, I fink I like it in Bermon'sey. I fink I'll move me buyin' an' sellin' over this side o' the water, an' the first fing I'm gonna do is get ole Will Tanner ter work wiv me. The poor bloke needs a decent job. Now put yer coat on an' I'll take yer up the Kings Arms fer a pint. I feel like celebratin'.'

Florrie took his arm as they walked up the street. 'If yer not careful yer'll 'ave the neighbours talkin' about us,' she grinned.

'Let 'em,' Joe laughed. 'If anybody asks what me an' you are doin' out tergevver, I'll tell 'em we're drinkin' a toast ter Jake Mitchell. After all, 'e did come up trumps.'

Florrie gave her lodger a crafty look. 'Yeah, I reckon 'e did,' she said.

*

Carrie Tanner crossed the busy Jamaica Road laden with shopping as she walked from the market through the thickening February fog. She wanted to see her parents before she returned to the café, and the urge to walk down the little cobbled backstreet where she had spent so much of her young life overcame her tiredness. As she turned into Page Street she saw the large weather-beaten sign over the Galloway yard looming out above the spluttering gas-lamp on the corner. It seemed to exude a vague sense of menace. The muted sound of a fog-horn carried into the turning and from somewhere nearby Carrie could hear a baby crying.

She changed the shopping-bag to her other hand and drew her coat tighter around her against the penetrating cold. The house where she was born and where she had grown up looked drab and cheerless now, with the last of the paint peeling from the front door and the windows heavily draped and showing no light. Carrie could almost hear the former laughter of bright sunlit days in the turning. In her imagination she could picture poor James walking along the road with his thumbs hooked through his braces and his cap askew, Charlie sitting unconcernedly before a banked-up coke fire with his head bowed over a book, or Danny fidgeting at the table and forever going on about Billy Sullivan's boxing skills. Well, her young brother had developed skills of his own now, Carrie thought, and smiled to herself as she passed the yard and walked towards Bacon Street.

After the trials and tribulations of January, she felt sure that it would be a good year from now on. Trade at the café was booming, and Fred was a kind and devoted husband. Danny was back working on the river, and she sensed a new closeness growing between her parents now. Her mother did not look so ill anymore, and seemed to have made peace with herself after carrying her secret burden alone for much too long. Her father seemed happier than he had been for a long time, now that he had started working for Joe Maitland.

Before she reached Bacon Street Carrie stopped and glanced back along the little turning. She could see the fog swirling in the light of the gas lamp and suddenly recalled the times she had peeped through the drawn curtains as a frightened child and taken comfort from the soft, warm glow of the streetlight. She smiled to herself as she remembered the times she had ridden back atop a laden hay-cart and heard her father encouraging the tired horse with the click of his tongue as it pulled the load into the cobbled turning and drew into the shadowed yard.

Carrie unconsciously brushed her hand across her flat stomach as she thought about the new life that was just beginning to form inside her, and she sighed contentedly. Fred would be so happy when she found the right time to tell him.

Yes, it would be a good year, Carrie told herself as she walked through the gaslight in Page Street.

Waggoner's Way

Harry Bowling

Waggoner's Way is a small backstreet on the southern boundary of Bermondsey, home to a close-knit community of predominantly railway folk and their families. The Brennens and the Kellys are among those who live there. They've been friends for years; Joe Brennen and Tom Kelly both work on the railway and their wives, Ada and Mary, spend much of their time trying to unravel their children's tangled love lives. The war has taken its toll, but now that it's over, the future looks bright. But how will this hard-up, hard-working community fare in the rapidly changing East End?

Waggoner's Way is a poignant portrayal of a tight-knit community finding its place in an East End changing beyond all recognition.

Warm praise for Harry Bowling's novels:

'What makes Harry's novels work is their warmth and authenticity. Their spirit comes from the author himself and his abiding memories of family life as it was once lived in the slums of south-east London' *Today*

'The king of Cockney sagas packs a close-knit community good-heartedness into East End epics' *Daily Mail*

978 0 7553 4035 4

headline

Tuppence to Tooley Street

Harry Bowling

As he lay in the mud on the beach at Dunkirk, Danny Sutton didn't think he would ever see his home in London's docklands again. But he was one of the lucky ones.

Returning home, he is reassured to find that things are just the same: the smell of the wharves and warehouses in Tooley Street; the usual hubbub in Dawson Street, where aproned figures stand in doorways discussing the war, the men are all down The Globe, and children play tin-can copper in the gutters. And at number 26 Danny's family crowd round to welcome their beloved son home.

But, scarred in mind as well as body, Danny is to realise that things have changed – for good. Unable to do heavy work because of his injuries – and women have taken over the light jobs – he struggles to adjust to a very different way of life. And, worst of all, his childhood sweetheart, Kathy, didn't wait for him . . .

Tuppence to Tooley Street is a moving depiction of a man struggling to regain his place in life – an experience shared by so many of those who survive the horror of war.

Warm praise for Harry Bowling's novels:

'What makes Harry's novels work is their warmth and authenticity. Their spirit comes from the author himself and his abiding memories of family life as it was once lived in the slums of south-east London' *Today*

'The king of Cockney sagas packs a close-knit community good-heartedness into East End epics' *Daily Mail*

978 0 7553 4036 1

headline

As Time Goes By

Harry Bowling

Carter Lane is an ordinary backstreet in Bermondsey and, for Dolly and Mick Flynn, it is home. They've raised their family with not much money but lots of love. When World War Two breaks out they know that nothing will be quite the same again.

As the Blitz takes its toll and the close-knit community in Carter Lane endures the sorrows and partings which they had dreaded above all else, they find comfort in one another and solace in the knowledge that their wounds will eventually heal – as time goes by.

As Time Goes By is a vivid portrayal of an East End community struggling to survive the horror of the Blitz. Heartbreaking and compelling, this is the story of a community in its darkest and yet finest hour, a community which has all but disappeared.

Warm praise for Harry Bowling's novels:

'What makes Harry's novels work is their warmth and authenticity. Their spirit comes from the author himself and his abiding memories of family life as it was once lived in the slums of south-east London' *Today*

'The king of Cockney sagas packs close-knit community good-heartedness into East End epics' *Daily Mail*

978 0 7553 4030 9

__headline__

That Summer in Eagle Street

Harry Bowling

Linda Weston has always lived in Eagle Street, a back-water off the Tower Bridge Road market. Life in the street isn't easy: money is tight, the house is overcrowded and everyone knows your business – whether you like it or not. But it's a solid, tight-knit community that laughs, cries and fights together – and helps one another out in difficult times.

Linda fell in love with Charlie Bradley just before the outbreak of World War Two and now the war is over, they hope to build a bright new future together. But Linda and Charlie are to find themselves caught in the middle of two rival gangs fighting for a stranglehold over south-east London. The consequences could be devastating.

Poignant, nostalgic and funny, *That Summer in Eagle Street* is a vivid and atmospheric portrayal of a south-east London that has all but vanished.

Warm praise for Harry Bowling's novels:

'What makes Harry's novels work is their warmth and authenticity. Their spirit comes from the author himself and his abiding memories of family life as it was once lived in the slums of south-east London' *Today*

'The king of Cockney sagas packs a close-knit community good-heartedness into East End epics' *Daily Mail*

978 0 7553 4031 6

headline

The Glory and the Shame

Harry Bowling

On the night of Saturday 10th May 1941, amidst the horror of the devastation caused by enemy bombers, Joe Carey and Charlie Duggan risked their lives to save people trapped in an air-raid shelter. Despite their efforts, six men and women died.

It's now 1947 and the inhabitants of Totterdown Street are trying to rebuild their lives. The post-war years are proving to be difficult and, already faced with a violent factory strike, the close-knit inhabitants of the street must also cope with news which not only exposes the glory of the past but the shame as well.

The Glory and the Shame is a vivid portrayal of a hard-working community struggling to rebuild their lives in the post-war era. Heartwarming and compelling, this is the story of the East End in its finest and yet darkest hour, a community in which most, but not all, behaved heroically.

Warm praise for Harry Bowling's novels:

'What makes Harry's novels work is their warmth and authenticity. Their spirit comes from the author himself and his abiding memories of family life as it was once lived in the slums of south-east London' *Today*

'The king of Cockney sagas packs a close-knit community good-heartedness into East End epics' *Daily Mail*

978 0 7553 4032 3

headline

Paragon Place

Harry Bowling

Paragon Place, an ordinary square of two-up, two-down houses in Bermondsey, has pretty well survived the Blitz. But the war has taken its toll on a hard-working and tight-knit community – even the old sycamore tree in the middle of the square has been scarred by shrapnel.

Despite going through the very worst of times – the never-ending fight against poverty, rationing and bombs – the residents of Paragon Place have been drawn even closer together by laughter and tears in the face of despair. And now that the war is finally over, they can look forward to a brighter future.

Paragon Place is a powerful and compelling portrayal of the East End during its finest hour, and a way of life that has vanished forever.

Warm praise for Harry Bowling's novels:

'What makes Harry's novels work is their warmth and authenticity. Their spirit comes from the author himself and his abiding memories of family life as it was once lived in the slums of south-east London' *Today*

'The king of Cockney sagas packs a close-knit community good-heartedness into East End epics' *Daily Mail*

978 0 7553 4033 0

headline

Now you can buy any of these other bestselling
books by **Harry Bowling** from your bookshop
or *direct from the publisher*.

FREE P&P AND UK DELIVERY
(Overseas and Ireland £3.50 per book)

As Time Goes By	£6.99
That Summer in Eagle Street	£6.99
The Glory and the Shame	£6.99
Paragon Place	£6.99
Tuppence to Tooley Street	£6.99
Waggoner's Way	£6.99

TO ORDER SIMPLY CALL THIS NUMBER

01235 400 414

or visit our website: www.headline.co.uk

Prices and availability subject to change without notice.